# Of Wrath and Storms

By Karen C.P. McDermott

*For my husband Patrick. Sorry, honey. There are still no dragons in my "Penthouse Forum with dragons."*

*I love you lots, though. So there's that.*

# Pronunciation Guide

**People**

Cyra = SEE-ruh

Bressen = BREH-sen

Samhail = SAM-heyl

Aidan = ĀY-den

Jasper = JAS-per

Maziren = MAZ-ur-in

Axenus = AX-en-uhs

Jaylan = JĀY-lin

Brix = BRIKS

Eddin = ED-in

Pryn = PRIN

Raina = RAY-nuh

Ursan = UR-sen

Jerram = JAIR-em

Glenora = Gle-NOR-ah

Phaedrus = FAY-druhs

Aramis = AIR-ah-mis

Sandrian = SAN-dree-an

Morland = MOHR-land

Clarice = Cla-REECE

Magdalene = MAG-dah-leen

Praya = PRAY-uh

Diora = Dee-OR-uh

**Places**

Fernweh = FURN-way

Thasia = THAY-zhuh

Callanus = KAL-an-uhs

Hiraeth = HĬ-rayth

Solandis = Sō-LAN-dus

Polaris = Puh-LAH-rus

Gendris = JEN-dris

Derridan = DAIR-ĭ-den

Seatherny = SEE-thur-nee

Rowe = RŌ, Rown = RŌN

Carkinos = KAR-kĭn-ōs

**Other**

Angelus = AN-jell-us

Perimortal = PEHR-ĭ-mohr-tl

Demoni =Deh-MAH-nee

**Triumvirate** (Trī-UM-ver-et): A group of three people who share power. In the book, Thasia is ruled by a group of three lords and/or ladies, each of whom also oversees one of the country's three territories.

*True Historical Note*: The "First Triumvirate" in ancient Rome included Julius Caesar, Pompey, and Crassus in 60 BC. The "Second Triumvirate" was an alliance between Antony, Lepidus, and Octavian in 43 BC.

**Content Advisory**

This book includes mature (18+) themes and potentially upsetting situations that include graphic violence, death, attempted rape (non-graphic), situations of human trafficking and sexual slavery (non-graphic), a recounting of the accidental death of an infant, mention of a miscarriage, danger to mother and child during labor, and multiple explicit depictions of sex, including some slightly non-traditional sexual practices and proclivities.*

* For details see https://karencpmcdermott.com/of-wrath-and-storms


**Recap of *The Last Triumvirate* (Book 1)**

If you need a reminder of what happened in book 1 of the series, please visit https://karencpmcdermott.com/tlt1-summary for a brief summary of the major action and plot points.

# Map of Thasia and Surrounding Countries

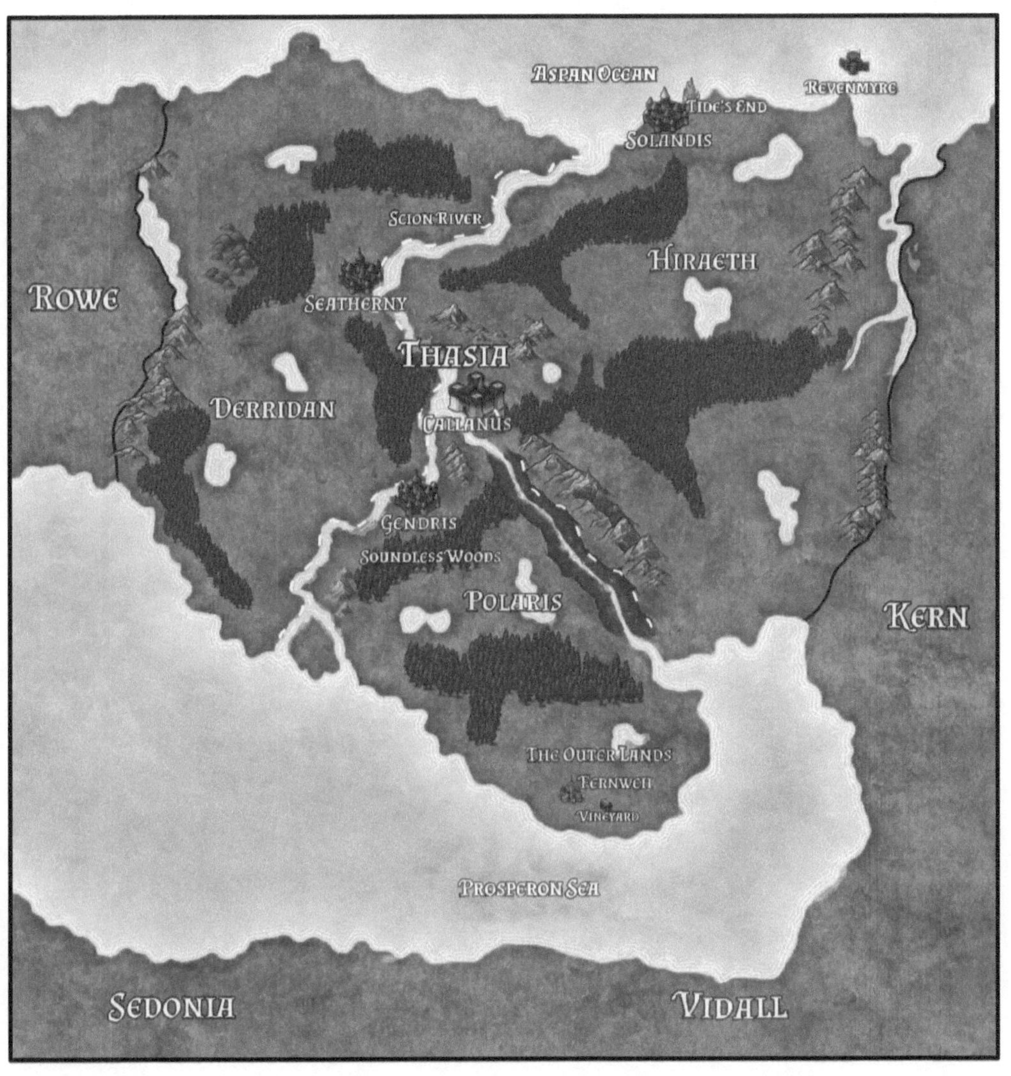

# Prologue

The assassin held her breath as long as she could before exhaling slowly, then sucking in another deep lung-full of air through her mouth. Twelve other girls, many almost a decade younger than her, stood packed into the windowless back of the wagon as it jostled along the streets.

There was a bucket for relieving themselves, but the rocking of the wagon had caused it to tip, and its contents now sloshed against their feet. The assassin hadn't seen any of the girls in the wagon actually use the bucket, which meant it had been there a while. She hoped they were close to their destination, or she might soon give in to the urge to vomit the way at least two of the girls had.

Her plan had seemed simple enough. Shift her appearance to look like a waif in her mid-teens with dirty-blonde hair and large timid eyes, then simply get into the wagon. The men would take her straight to her target.

One of the men loading the girls had seemed confused for a moment when she stepped up, realizing there was one more of them than he'd anticipated, but he'd only shrugged. After all, having one extra was better than being one short.

The assassin was planning to kill all these men anyway, but after this wretched ride, she'd do it painfully. Slowly.

Well, slower. She did have somewhere else to be.

In truth, she would've killed these men for free if she'd known this was going on, but she'd only learned of them when they'd accidentally taken a nobleman's daughter a week ago after the girl had snuck out of her parents' house dressed as a servant. The girl had likely been meeting friends or a lover, and the men had snatched her up in a back alley.

One of the nobleman's servants who'd followed the girl saw the whole thing and ran back to the house to raise the alarm. The city guard was called in, but the girl had disappeared by then, and her father eventually sought other means to get her back.

Find The Raptor of Avril, someone had told him, and so he had.

The assassin had contacts in most major cities on the Arystrian continent who kept an ear out on her behalf, and she paid them well for sending work her way. One of her contacts in Gendris had heard about the kidnapping and learned the nobleman was willing to pay just about anything to get his daughter back.

The wagon lurched to a halt, and two men flung open the doors. Fresh air rushed in, and the assassin inhaled deeply as the girls piled out.

They were ushered into the back of a building, and the assassin glanced up long enough to assess her surroundings. She'd managed not to vomit in the stagnant, putrid air of the wagon, but she nearly did now as she took in the scene before her in the warehouse they entered.

Cages lined the walls, each with four or five girls packed inside, from those barely in their teens to women in their early twenties like her. There were easily thirty or so girls, not counting the twelve she'd come in with.

"Line up!" one of the men shouted, and the girls stumbled into a row.

The assassin took her place among them with her head tucked down against her chest. She listened to the scuff of boots as one of the men paced before her, and she tried not to wrinkle her nose at the stench of sour sweat that poured off him. A quick glance revealed a man more well-dressed than the others who was flanked by two new lackeys.

"Welcome, ladies," the well-dressed man said.

The assassin shifted her head slightly to look from side-to-side. She needed to be sure she wasn't missing any other men who might be hiding in the corners of the room, but there seemed to be only the five.

There was a pause as the scuffing of shoes stopped.

"Is there something you're looking for, my dear?" the well-dressed man asked. His voice dripped with mock concern as he stepped closer to her, and she caught the flash of metal from a ring of keys on his belt.

"Are you looking for a way out?" he went on. "Or someone to help you? Because you'll find neither of those things here."

The assassin lifted her head to meet his gaze, and the man scowled at her impertinence. She saw his hand coming and pulled her head back just in time so only the breeze from his intended slap wafted across her face.

He looked shocked for a moment at having failed to hit her.

"You little bitch," he snarled. "Who do you think you are?"

She smiled at him. "Most know me as The Raptor."

"The what?" he asked, brows pinching.

"The Raptor," she repeated. "It's fine if you don't know me, but it seems your man does."

The well-dressed man turned to see that the face of one of his underlings had indeed drained of color.

"You know this girl?" the well-dressed man asked him. "Who is she?"

The second man swallowed before whispering one word: "Assassin."

The man's head snapped back to her, and he started in shock.

Her face was no longer that of the waif, but that of a young woman with hazel green eyes shaded by long lashes. Coppery hair replaced the dirty blonde strands that had framed her face seconds ago, a face no less beautiful for the cold sneer it now wore.

The man's shock was probably less about her shift in appearance and more about the feel of her dagger sliding into his gut, though.

His mouth worked, opening and closing, but no sound came out until he suddenly coughed, and blood dribbled over his bottom lip.

The girls in line all cried out and backed away as the man slumped to the floor, his wet choking sounds still audible above their screams.

The dagger slipped free of his body as he fell, and the assassin lifted the hem of her skirt to pull a second blade from her other thigh sheath.

By the time the man's body hit the ground, she was once again the waif. Few people ever saw that other face, and those who did usually didn't live long. Tonight, this man would be the only one to see it.

"Kill her!" one of the other men yelled as his wide eyes fixed on his boss's body lying in an ever-widening pool of blood.

Two of the men drew daggers of their own and stepped toward the assassin, but she disappeared right before their eyes, and they stopped short. A moment later, one of them gurgled horribly as she slid her dagger across his throat from behind, and blood spilled down his chest. The second man was too stunned by her sudden reappearance to avoid her other dagger as she quickly plunged it into his heart.

Both men fell together, and the assassin turned toward the last two men as the shrieks of the girls rose higher around her. Those she'd come in with began to run while those in the cages around the room screamed and rattled the bars in their desperate attempts to break free.

The assassin turned her attention toward the man who'd recognized her. Neither he nor his companion had moved.

"You can port," the man said. "You're a gods' damned perimortal!"

"Was he in charge of this operation?" she asked, ignoring his outburst. She pointed her dagger at the well-dressed man on the floor.

"Fuck you, bitch!" the other man spat out.

She sighed and ported behind him. He anticipated the move and turned quickly to face her, but not fast enough. One of her daggers pierced his side and the other slid into the artery at his neck. Blood filled his mouth and poured over his lips, and she shoved him over before he could cough it on her.

"I'll ask once more," she said to the final man. "Was he in charge?"

The man nodded.

"Are there any others in your operation?"

He shook his head.

She narrowed her gaze. "Are you sure?"

His head wobbled to indicate 'more-or-less.' "It…it was just us here in Gendris," he clarified, "but there are networks in other cities."

Her stomach dropped. She'd been afraid of that. Unfortunately, she didn't have time now to deal with an operation that large. She had somewhere else she needed to be by the end of the week.

But she could issue a warning at least.

The assassin appeared next to the man and pressed her dagger to his cheek. He yelled out as the blade sliced his skin, but he didn't move.

"Hold still," she said as she cut a line down his face. Two more cuts left a bleeding red "R" on his cheek.

"That's to remind you I'm watching," she told him. "Let the others know I'm coming for them. They can either let all the girls they've taken go and close up shop, or I'll close them up permanently. Understand?"

The man nodded as his body shook.

"Get on your hands and knees," she told him.

The man lowered himself warily to the floor and did as she said.

She squatted next to him. In a flash, she dropped her larger blades and drew two more smaller daggers from the sheaths in her boots. She plunged them into the man's hands to pin them to the wooden floor.

He screamed and tried to pull back, but the reflexive attempt to yank his hands away only made him scream louder.

"You can leave once we're gone if you can find a way to unpin your hands," she told him as he whimpered.

She stood, walked to the body of the leader, took the keys from his belt, and unlocked the cages. The twelve girls she'd been brought in with had long since scattered, and those in the cages now cowered in corners.

"Go. You're free," she told them, but most didn't move until she'd passed by, leaving the doors open for them.

It wasn't until the last cage that she saw the girl she sought, the one who matched the description of the nobleman's daughter.

"Arianna," she asked, and the girl's face snapped up. "Your father sent me to bring you home."

The girl burst into tears as the assassin helped her up and led her out of the building. The wagon they'd come in was still waiting outside. None of the girls had thought to commandeer it, and the assassin helped Arianna up onto the driver's bench with her before snapping the reins.

More girls were still out there, kidnapped and sold into slavery, but at least the assassin could return this girl to her family. She'd celebrate that small victory at least before she left for Solandis tomorrow.

Her next job was simple enough on the surface. Embed herself in the household of Lord Bressen of Hiraeth and play spy until her employer, Sandrian, the former King of Rowe, needed her to do more.

She wasn't sure where Sandrian had found the huge sum of money she'd requested up front, but he hadn't even blinked when he'd thrown the sack of coins down on the table in front of her at their meeting.

She knew the job wasn't nearly as easy as it seemed.

For one, Lord Bressen was a mind wraith with a fearsome reputation. People called him the Nemesis Incarnate, and rumor had it he could kill a person with a single thought. He was also the overseer of Revenmyer prison, a place where its inmates were haunted by their most feared and depraved memories. Sandrian's face still bore a hollowness months after he'd escaped the place, which made the assassin wonder what he'd seen.

She wasn't necessarily worried about Lord Bressen's mind reading. As a masque, a kind of shapeshifter, the assassin could not only morph her features and voice into those of someone else, she could disguise her mind to an extent. The ability wasn't a mind shield exactly, but rather a way to cloak who she really was if anyone tried to read her thoughts, a superficial veil that kept her true self hidden from any run-of-the-mill mind wraith.

The only trouble was that Lord Bressen wasn't just any ordinary mind wraith, but supposedly the most powerful one currently in existence. She'd never tested her mind masking against someone of his capabilities, so it remained to be seen if she could fool him.

In truth, the lord was the kind of cruel bastard she delighted in killing, yet it wasn't Lord Bressen that Sandrian was most interested in. It was his fiancé, Cyra of Fernweh, the first known syphon in four hundred years.

Sandrian didn't want the woman dead, though. Not yet anyway. The assassin's job was to observe the lord and lady and report on their activities. She had no idea why, and it wasn't her job to ask. She'd been paid up front to spy on them, and she'd do it, no questions asked.

Tonight, she'd return Arianna to her father with the hope that the girl's ordeal hadn't been as bad as she suspected, then tomorrow, she'd head north to Solandis to seek a position in Lord Bressen's household. The lord and his fiancé were returning there from the capital city of Callanus for their wedding in a few weeks, and she'd learned they were hiring new staff in preparation. She planned to be among the new hires, even if it meant…eliminating the competition.

# Chapter 1

*Cyra*

I fidgeted again in one of the Triumvirate seats on the dais, uncrossing and then recrossing my legs for the third time in under a minute. The chairs were large enough to seat a person twice my size, and they had cushions designed for long hours of sitting while their occupants received messengers or petitioners at the Citadel, so comfort wasn't the problem.

The problem was that I didn't belong in one.

The three Triumvirate chairs usually sat in a semi-circle here in the Great Chamber, but they'd been moved so only two of them now stood next to each other in the center. Bressen, Lord of the Hiraeth territory in Thasia and my fiancé, sat carelessly in his own chair with one leg crossed over the other. Unlike me, he'd barely moved since we sat down.

"You can sit on my lap if you don't like the chair," Bressen purred.

His tone was teasing, but the look in his eyes told me he wanted to reach over and pull me onto his lap.

I bit my lip and fought down the urge to let him.

I didn't usually see Bressen during the day since he had work to do, so being near him now made my fingers ache to thread through his night-black hair or run along the barely-there stubble on his chiseled jawline to the irresistible dimple in his chin. He was easily the most beautiful man I'd ever seen, and just being near him did things to my body that made it hard for me to concentrate.

"Are you sure it's appropriate for me to sit here?" I asked, trying to ignore how the muscles between my thighs tightened at his words.

Bressen's bright turquoise eyes sparkled as they shifted to me. His posture and expression all exuded that practiced look of boredom I remembered so well from my first meeting with him in this very chamber.

Back when I'd still been terrified of him.

"Who's going to tell you not to sit there?" he asked, flashing the charmingly arrogant smile that never failed to make my insides flutter. "I'm the only Triumvirate lord left, and I say you can sit there."

I winced at his words and shifted in the chair again. I felt like a child in it. Tall and muscular as Bressen was, the chairs were even big for him. The only person who might fit comfortably in them was Samhail, who was nearly seven feet tall in his human form. Even in his larger gargoyle form, the chairs might almost accommodate the warrior, wings and all.

More daunting than the size of my chair, though, were the responsibilities and expectations that came with it. I wasn't yet used to being a titled lady or the consort to Thasia's most powerful ruler.

Well, Thasia's *only* ruler at the moment since Ursan and Jerram had been killed two months ago. I also wasn't officially a titled lady or Bressen's consort until he and I married in a few weeks, but close enough.

"I know I have permission," I said, "but is it *right* for me to sit here?"

Bressen sat up straighter. "There's no right or wrong anymore," he said. "Thasia has never been without two Triumvirate rulers before, and we're a country that's used to having more than one person in charge."

I nodded in understanding. Two bodies weren't three, but they were better than one, especially for a country that zealously believed three to be a sacred number. Thasia's triumvirate system wasn't perfect, but it provided a degree of checks and balances that kept any one ruler from holding too much power. Not that I was in a position to check Bressen's power, even if I wanted to. He wasn't just Thasia's most powerful ruler. He was one of the most powerful perimortals to ever live.

I was powerful too, perhaps even more so than Bressen in some ways, but having power didn't mean I knew how to use it yet. I'd only recently learned I was a syphon, and I was still getting used to the vast array of abilities I now had at my fingertips.

At least the people of Thasia wouldn't have to wait much longer to officially refill one of the country's Triumvirate seats.

As if reading my thoughts – which he might have been – Bressen said, "It will be good to have Aidan join the Triumvirate. It's been exhausting managing all three territories, especially with the attacks recently."

I reached over to put a hand on Bressen's, and he smiled at me. He'd come to bed late every night this week after heading to one town or another around Thasia after they'd been attacked by armed men who'd rampaged through the streets killing and wounding whoever they could.

The attacks never lasted long, and there didn't seem to be any reason for them other than to cause devastation. As best we could tell, the attacks were simply bouts of lawlessness brought on by the recent upheaval as some groups took advantage of the lack of leadership to create chaos.

"Do you know anything about the trials Aidan won to earn his place as Lord of the Derridan territory?" I asked.

"I know a bit," Bressen said. "Samhail sent me regular updates."

"Do you know what Lord Aidan's powers are?"

Bressen gave me a sly smile. "Are you wondering if he'll have anything new for you to add to your collection?"

I glared at him. "Of course not. I'm just curious."

I really was just curious, but now that Bressen mentioned it, it was true that whatever power Lord Aidan had would likely become mine as well. As a syphon, I could harness the power of any perimortal I came in contact with to make it my own.

Bressen was about to answer my question when the doors of the Great Chamber opened, and Gilbert, the Captain of the Guard, strode in.

"Lord Aidan will be here in a minute, my lord," Gilbert said.

"My lord and lady," Bressen corrected him.

Gilbert seemed confused for a moment but then looked quickly to me. "Apologies, my lady. Lord Aidan is on his way here now."

I nodded my thanks, and Gilbert bowed before hurrying out.

"It's not necessary to make him acknowledge me," I told Bressen. "I'm sure he still sees me as that dirty, bedraggled girl who flew in by gargoyle a few months ago."

"All the more reason he should recognize your new status," he said. "Not only are you my lady, you're the woman who saved him from having to serve Jerram and Glenora. He should be on his knees thanking you."

I gave Bressen a weak smile. I still had nightmares about what had happened two months ago when Glenora had killed her lord husband and staged a coup with Jerram, the lord of Derridan at the time, to eliminate Bressen and overthrow the Triumvirate.

Normally Bressen and I might have met Lord Aidan and his retinue out in the courtyard of the Citadel, but the weather had taken a turn this week, and heavy snow was currently falling. Bressen had thus opted to have Lord Aidan presented to us here in the Great Chamber instead.

I'd argued for a more informal meeting, but Bressen had insisted on this audience, and I knew it was his way of feeling out the new lord. Derridan had a right to choose their own ruler, but Bressen had to work with that person, and I knew he wanted someone who was capable of holding their own, especially in the face of Bressen's own prodigious powers and fearsome reputation. He didn't want a fellow ruler who'd be afraid to challenge him or the ruler of Polaris once the latter was selected.

Bressen already struck terror in most people because of his powers, but he also cultivated an aura of mystery and unapproachability. It was a defense to keep people from getting too close to him, both physically and emotionally, and one that had failed miserably where I was concerned.

The doors opened again, and Bressen sat up straighter, although he still wore his expression of arrogant boredom.

"My lord and lady," Gilbert said, including me this time, "May I present Lord Aidan of Derridan."

Gilbert swept out of the way so seven people could enter. One man walked ahead in the center of the group, while an older man followed just behind him to his left, and a small woman flanked him to his right. Four guards with spears brought up the rear.

Lord Aidan was attractive, with short reddish-brown hair, tawny skin, and an oval face that softened what were otherwise sharp features. His body was lightly muscled, leaner than Bressen's, but still the physique of a man who could clearly wield a sword. His posture was regal without being rigid, and he walked with sure strides toward the dais.

The man just behind Aidan – his husband, I assumed – looked to be older than him by at least fifteen years or so. He was fit and muscular, more so than Aidan himself, but the slight lines in his face and the touch of gray in the dark brown hair at his temples showed his age. Aidan and the man both wore fine black pants, fitted doublets of royal blue with gold embroidery, and short swords sheathed at their waists.

*How much older is Aidan's husband?* I asked Bressen into his mind.

Bressen's powers were mental abilities that included mind reading, glamoured illusions, and the power to compel, and since I was a syphon, his powers were also mine. I didn't wield them nearly as well as Bressen did, but we communicated easily mind to mind.

I was a bit surprised by the age difference between Aidan and his partner. Perimortals aged much slower than regular mortals, so it was difficult to tell how old they were. That Aidan's husband actually looked older than him suggested there were hundreds of years between them.

*Aidan is actually older than his husband by almost two hundred years,* Bressen replied back, his voice as clear in my head as if he'd spoken. *His husband is mortal.*

I jerked my head to Bressen, but then quickly looked back at the approaching group, trying to disguise the movement as a stretch of my neck. It wouldn't do to let the new Lord of Derridan know we were having a mental conversation about him.

*How long have they been together?* I asked when I'd regained control.

*Seventeen or eighteen years,* Bressen said.

My head reeled at the idea that Lord Aidan, a perimortal like Bressen and myself, had chosen a mortal partner, knowing that he'd far outlive the man. I'd been devastated when I was old enough to realize my two mortal brothers would age and die long before me, before I'd even look older than my twenties by mortal standards. I couldn't imagine choosing a partner I'd be destined to lose so soon. The thought of watching Bressen grow old and die while I stayed young for centuries made me shudder.

The group stopped before us, and my gaze caught Aidan's. I smiled at him, but his face remained neutral, if not wary.

*It's a bit strange to no longer be the most feared person in the room,* Bressen said lightly into my head, and I glanced at him.

His halo glamour was up so that an undulating aura of darkness surrounded him. I knew from experience that any attempt to focus on the halo only made it dissipate. Rather, it seemed to hover in the periphery of one's vision, discouraging a person from looking at Bressen for too long.

*What, no wings?* I asked him teasingly.

Bressen was an angelus and could manifest giant feathered wings at will, usually black ones. That he'd put up his halo glamour now but not released his wings seemed almost reserved for him, given that I knew he was trying to make an impression on the new lord and his court.

I caught the barest shrug of Bressen's shoulders and a curl of his lips.

*The wings seemed excessive,* he said into my mind, and I rolled my eyes.

"Lord Bressen, Lady Cyra," Aidan said, giving us each a bow.

If he was bothered by Bressen's glamour, he didn't show it.

"It's an honor," Aidan went on. "This is my husband Jasper." He extended a hand toward the man, who stepped forward to bow, and Bressen and I nodded in greeting. "And this," he said, indicating the woman, "is my Captain of the Guard, Maziren."

I'd been so preoccupied with Jasper that I'd barely considered the woman on the other side of Aidan. She had black hair braided into a crown around her head, amber eyes, and carob-colored skin. The most striking thing about her was how small she was, though. Likely under five feet tall and slight, she must either have prodigious magical powers or unparalleled skill with a sword to have risen to the rank of Captain of the Guard. Childishly, I wanted to see her stand next to Samhail's giant body.

Maziren wore pants and a tunic with metal plates attached right to the fabric, and she held a helmet with a faceguard under her arm. A short sword was within easy reach at her hip, and she eyed me as though she might draw it if I even looked at Aidan for too long.

I hadn't understood Bressen's comment about being the most feared person in the room, but I did now. These people actually feared me.

The thought ricocheted in my head, and I suppressed a smile as my chest twitched in a silent laugh. It was ludicrous for anyone to be afraid of me. I had access to an array of powers, but I had yet to master them.

I was tempted to see if Aidan, Jasper, and Maziren had mind shields up, but my mental powers were still clumsy sometimes. Bressen was teaching me to use them, but I had a ways to go before I could do so effectively. I'd ask Bressen later if Aidan and his retinue had mind shields up, since I was sure he'd checked. As a mortal, Jasper would likely have trouble creating one, since a predisposition to magic was usually necessary to maintain a shield, but it wasn't unheard of for mortals to do it.

"Lord Aidan, Lord Consort Jasper, Captain Maziren," Bressen said, acknowledging each of them in that silky voice he used when he wanted to charm someone. It was all the smoother for his Hiraethian accent, which elongated his "A"s into sighs and ignored "R"s at the ends of words. "Lady Cyra and I welcome you to Callanus and to the Citadel. Lord Aidan, we look forward to having you join the Triumvirate."

Aidan and Maziren exchanged glances.

"I wasn't aware Lady Cyra was part of the Triumvirate," Aidan said.

Bressen smiled. "She isn't."

Aidan and Maziren exchanged another glance.

"With all due respect, then," Aidan went on, "may I ask why she's sitting in a Triumvirate seat?"

*I told you so*, I said into Bressen's mind.

"She's merely keeping it warm for you," he told Aidan, ignoring me. "It was getting lonely up here by myself these past two months."

Aidan's chin went up a notch. Jerram hadn't had any living relatives, so there'd been no obvious heir. The trials in Derridan to select the new lord of the territory had taken weeks to plan and then another three weeks to put on. During that time, their Triumvirate seat had sat empty. Bressen's comment was thus a complaint about the time Derridan had taken to decide their new ruler, but Aidan recovered quickly.

"Do you know when Polaris will select their new lord or lady?" Aidan asked. A reminder that Derridan wasn't the only territory dragging its feet.

Bressen gave an exaggerated sigh. "Your guess is as good as mine. I only hope your addition to the Triumvirate will urge them to make haste in their decision."

I highly doubted that. Polaris was currently controlled by a supposedly interim High Council of generals and advisors who'd been loyal to the late Lord Ursan. The feeling I'd gotten when Bressen and I visited their capital city of Gendris recently was that the council had no immediate plans to give up power. The group became less temporary each passing day as they found one excuse after another to delay the selection of a new ruler.

Raina, my best friend and my former lady's maid, actually had a blood claim to the seat of Polaris, since Ursan had been her father. She was both illegitimate and half mortal, though, and the council used that as an excuse to draw out their time in power. Whenever questions arose about filling the territory's Triumvirate seat, the council simply insisted they were still working on a way to make Raina's claim official.

Raina's illegitimacy was a hurdle, but it was secondary to her being only half perimortal, and a former servant at that. If she was officially made the Lady of Polaris at some point, she'd not only be the first woman to claim a Triumvirate seat in more than three hundred years, but she'd be the first half-mortal to claim one ever.

A loud clang cut the silence and echoed off the walls in the chamber, making me jump. One of Aidan's guards had dropped his spear, and he bent quickly to pick it up, his face looking a bit pale. He mumbled a hurried apology and immediately stood back at attention.

Maziren's hand had flown to her sword at the sound, but she eased back into position after seeing there was no danger.

By contrast, Aidan seemed completely unphased by his guard's lapse.

"The Triumvirate ceremony is tomorrow morning?" he asked.

"Yes, at ten o'clock," Bressen said. "There will be a ball in the evening to celebrate. Tonight, Cyra and I would love to have you join us for dinner at seven. Until then I'm sure you'd like to get settled. The staff in your wing have been working hard to get everything ready for you."

"Thank you. We look forward to dinner tonight," Aidan said. Then he added, "Will Samhail be joining us?"

I felt a tug in my heart at hearing Samhail's name so unexpectedly. The warrior worked for the Triumvirate occasionally when they had a job important enough for them to warrant paying him the huge sum of money he could demand for his services, but he wasn't a permanent member of their staff. In fact, I hadn't seen him in two months since the coup.

Despite a rocky start, Samhail had quickly become my friend – and more – shortly after I met him. He'd spent the last months in Derridan helping Bressen keep the territory in line while they chose a new ruler. Since Aidan had taken control several days ago, though, Samhail was no longer needed. I'd expected him to come back here when he was done, but he hadn't, and I wondered where he was now.

Aidan's question about Samhail was a calculated one, I realized. It was an acknowledgement of the close friendship Bressen and Samhail shared, but Bressen's face showed only the hint of a smile as he answered Aidan.

"Samhail won't be joining us. He isn't in residence right now."

"How unfortunate," Aidan said, his disappointment at least partially genuine. "I wanted to thank him for everything he did to keep Derridan stable while the trials were going on. When do you expect him back?"

"I don't expect him," Bressen said. "That is, he hasn't told me when, or if, he plans to return. I actually don't see him much when there's nothing urgent for him to do."

Aidan looked mildly surprised. "Really? I was told you and Samhail were good friends." He paused before adding, "I've also heard Samhail and Lady Cyra are close."

Aidan's gaze swung to me, and I failed to hide my surprise in time.

Bressen didn't move, but I sensed the change in him and wondered if the crimson flare that lit his eyes when he was angry had flashed just then.

I straightened in my seat and notched my chin up as I looked at Aidan. I had to give him credit. Bressen had gone out of his way to keep Aidan off-balance, yet the new lord was beating Bressen at his own game.

I didn't think it was a secret that Samhail and I were close, but Aidan's comment implied he knew more than he should. He must be trying to read our reactions to see if there was anything to whatever he'd heard.

"You heard correctly, Lord Aidan," I said, forcing calmness into my voice. "Samhail is indeed a good friend to both Lord Bressen and me, but we're not his keepers. I suppose we'll all learn where he's been when he decides to show himself again."

"Indeed," Aidan said, inclining his head.

Bressen relaxed, but there was a clip to his voice when he said, "We've kept you long enough, Lord Aidan. Gilbert can show you to your wing."

As if the room had been listening, the doors swung open so Gilbert and the Citadel guards could lead the way for Aidan to leave.

Aidan didn't bat an eye at the obvious dismissal.

"Until later, Lord Bressen." He nodded to me. "Lady Cyra."

Aidan turned and strode from the chamber, followed by his people. I'd meant to watch both Jasper and Maziren more, but Aidan had kept my attention. It was a quality that would make him an effective lord.

Bressen and I turned to each other as soon as the doors closed again. He'd already taken down his halo glamour, and he looked thoughtful.

"I like him. He's savvy," Bressen said of Aidan.

"He's certainly well-informed," I grumbled.

He shrugged. "Servants can often be bought. I was surprised he remarked on your friendship with Samhail, but not that he knew of it."

"Do you think he knows..." I trailed off, but he caught my meaning.

"I think that night together is one of the few secrets we've kept within these walls. Not that anyone knowing about it would really be an issue. Such dalliances are expected on the Harmilan," Bressen said.

The Harmilan was a holiday that celebrated joining, and most of Callanus observed it by either getting married or just having lots of sex. I'd in fact spent my first Harmilan with both Bressen and Samhail. We'd never discussed whether it would be a one-time affair or if it might happen again, but it was a moot point as long as Samhail stayed away.

"Do you know where Samhail is now?" I asked, willing myself not to linger on memories of that night…of taking Bressen and Samhail into my mouth, of having them thrust between my legs. The feel of their hands threading in my hair, gripping my hips, covering my breasts…

I shook my head clear of such thoughts.

"I don't," Bressen said. "I've kept him busy for a while, so he may need a break from me." His lips turned up in a half-grin. "You may find this hard to believe, but not everyone finds me as enthralling as you do."

I raised a brow at him. "What makes you think I find you enthralling?"

"I can see it in the way you look at me," he said, his eyes turning stormy. "I can tell right now that you want me."

I rolled my eyes. "Your arrogance knows no bounds."

"That's one of the things you love about me."

I huffed a laugh and stood up. "Can we get out of these chairs now?"

Bressen shot forward and grabbed me by the waist to haul me down onto his lap. I shrieked in surprise, then giggled as he pulled me up against him. He ran his fingers down my jaw then tipped my chin up so his lips could find mine for a long kiss, and I went limp against him.

"Did any of them have mind shields?" I asked when he broke the kiss.

"Aidan and Maziren did. Jasper didn't, which isn't surprising given that he's mortal, but he kept his mind impressively blank the entire time. I imagine he's been trained to do that if he spends significant time around perimortals. In fact, all of Aidan's guards except one were fairly adept at keeping their minds clear."

"And the one?" I asked.

"Was having impure thoughts about you that I quickly disabused him of," Bressen said with an edge to his voice.

"The guard who dropped his spear," I said as realization dawned.

"I might have made him think his manhood suddenly fell off," he said.

I gave him an admonitory look. "You didn't."

Bressen shrugged. "I wanted to do worse. He got away easy."

"You're a wicked man."

"And that's another reason you love me," he said as his hand slid up to close over my breast. I arched against his touch with a moan.

"Do you have work to do before dinner?" I asked, my voice raspy.

"Nothing urgent. Was there something you wanted to do?"

"I can think of a few things," I said as I let my head fall back against his shoulder. He ran his teeth lightly down my throat, making gooseflesh rise on my arms. He started to pull up my dress, but I grabbed his wrist.

"I'm not doing anything in these chairs," I said sternly.

Bressen sighed and stood up from his seat, lifting me with him in his arms. "Fine. Where do you want me to fuck you? The dining room table? The garden outside Aidan's wing?"

"Our bedroom?" I suggested, laughing.

"How boring. Find somewhere more interesting," he said as he walked with me toward the doors. He lowered his voice conspiratorially. "I, for one, have always wanted to have sex on the altar at the Priory."

I opened my mouth to protest, but then angled my head as I realized I wasn't fully opposed to it.

"You like that idea!" Bressen said in surprise. "You wicked, irreverent woman! Open a portal to the Priory and let's go."

"Not now, but I won't take that off the table for the future."

Bressen's eyes smoldered as he looked at me. "Nemesis take me, Cyra, tell me where you want me to take you now. Anywhere but the bedroom."

I bit my lip. "I have an idea," I said, letting an image form in my mind.

"The wine cellar," Bressen breathed. "Gods above, I love you."

"Show me."

The look that crossed Bressen's face was nearly feral as he quickened his pace toward the cellar, and I knew that even now servants in the area were remembering urgent business they had elsewhere.

# Chapter 2

My cheeks were still flushed with pleasure when Bressen and I approached the dining room at ten minutes past seven that evening. I was trying desperately to forget what his hands, mouth, and other parts of him had done to me only a little while ago, and I was failing miserably.

In hindsight, choosing the wine cellar for our lovemaking, a place so close to where we'd be dining with Aidan was not the best idea.

*You're blushing like a virgin*, Bressen said into my mind as we passed the threshold. *And gods above, stop thinking about the wine cellar or I'm going to have to change into a looser pair of pants to make it through dinner.*

I blushed even more to realize Bressen had seen what I was thinking. I didn't usually use a mind shield with him, and he didn't read my thoughts as a habit, but we'd found that my mind sometimes called to his.

*I'm trying*, I replied. *Stop looking and smelling so good.*

Bressen let a low growl rumble up his throat. We'd only known each other a few months, but we were deep into the phase of our relationship where we could barely keep our hands off each other for more than a few minutes at a time. Dinner tonight would be…challenging.

I'd had two other lovers before Bressen, and that stage of desperately wanting each other had lasted a week to just under a month with them respectively, but with Bressen, our passion for each other showed no sign of slowing down. If anything, the need for each other that burned all day, every day, was only getting worse. I needed to find some way to control myself around him.

We needn't have bothered keeping our conversation in our heads, in any case. The dining room was empty when we entered except for three guards stationed around the room.

"So much for our plan to arrive fashionably late," Bressen said. "Either Aidan had trouble finding the dining room, or he was intent on arriving fashionably later."

"If I were a betting man," Aidan said from behind us, "I'd put my money on the latter."

Bressen and I turned to see Aidan and Jasper standing arm-in-arm in the doorway. Maziren was just behind them, still dressed in her armor and looking like she was ready to do battle rather than have dinner.

"Well met, Lord Aidan," Bressen said. "I must say, I'm enjoying this little chess match we seem to be having."

Aidan's mouth quirked up in the hint of a smile. "I'm surprised you didn't wear your glamour to dinner, Lord Bressen."

Bressen smirked back at him. "There's a fine line between gamesmanship and just being a prick."

There was a pause before Aidan and Bressen both grinned broadly and reached out to shake hands, any lingering tension from our meeting in the Great Chamber now forgotten. Jasper and I smiled as well, leaving only Maziren immune to the sudden lightening of the mood.

Aidan turned to me and nodded politely. "My lady."

Instinctively, I reached out to shake his hand as Bressen had, wanting to be part of their newfound comradery. After Jerram and Ursan, Aidan seemed like a welcome change, and I was eager to get to know him.

But as I lifted my hand to him, several things happened very fast.

Maziren moved immediately to intercept me, and her own hand closed like iron around my wrist before I got anywhere close to Aidan. I cried out, partially in pain, but more in surprise.

The second the sound left my lips, a blast of pure power reverberated through the room, making my ears pop and my heart skip a beat.

Maziren jerked back, and a scream tore from her. She instantly let go of my wrist to fall back against the doorway and clutch at her head with both hands. Aidan and Jasper stepped toward her, concern on their faces, but Bressen grabbed my arm to pull me behind him.

The three guards drew their swords but held their positions as Bressen put up a hand to stay them. They would've been able to do little anyway given that four of the five other people in the room were perimortals of considerable power.

It happened in seconds, and then all was quiet again as we looked between ourselves while Maziren clutched at her head, breathing hard.

"I'm sorry," I whispered. "I forgot. I-"

Bressen squeezed my arm in a subtle appeal to stop talking, and I fell silent. He turned to look coldly at Maziren.

"That was only a taste of the pain I can make you feel if you ever lay a hand on Cyra again," Bressen said to her, his voice low and calm.

I inhaled sharply, understanding what he'd done. It had likely only been a graze of his power, one sharp blade of it dragging down Maziren's mind shield, but I knew from experience that it was more than enough.

A mind wraith of Bressen's power could get into anyone's mind. He could probe and caress another's shield before slipping through it like smoke slides beneath a door, but he could also attack their shield as well, splintering it to pieces as if his power were an axe. And he'd just swung that axe at Maziren.

I'd asked him once to show me what it felt like when he broke into someone's mind, and he'd adamantly refused. It took me days to convince him to do it, and even then he'd been hesitant. I'd learned why when he finally gave in to my persistent entreaties and attacked my shield.

I'd recoiled in agony as sharp pain shot through my skull and halfway down my body. He'd been at my side in an instant, gathering me close and soothing me as I gasped for breath at the mere memory of the pain.

"She cannot…touch…Lord Aidan," Maziren gasped, as she pushed herself up off the doorframe.

Her hand rested on the hilt of her sword as she looked unrepentantly at Bressen, and I noticed now she was wearing leather gloves. Apparently it was known that I syphoned my powers by touching other perimortals.

"I'm sorry," I said again, trying to defuse the tension. "It's my fault-"

Bressen squeezed my arm again, and I cut myself off.

"Fine, but do not touch Cyra again," Bressen said to her, "or Lord Aidan will need a new captain of his guard."

"Bressen, no," I whispered to him.

We'd only just met Lord Aidan, and things had been going so well until a moment ago. Threatening to kill his captain wasn't the best way to ensure a good working relationship with the newest Triumvirate lord.

When Bressen continued to glare at Maziren, I stepped in front of him and put a hand on his cheek. He lowered his eyes to mine reluctantly, and the tension eased from his body as my thumb caressed his skin.

*I'm fine*, I said into his mind. *She startled me more than anything.*

*I felt your pain*, he answered back.

*She's unexpectedly strong,* I admitted, only realizing now that my wrist was throbbing. *But there was no harm done. We don't want to start things out badly with Aidan and his court.*

Bressen nodded, and I let my fingers run down his face and over his lips before turning back to Aidan. The lord was looking at us with interest. He likely knew we'd been having a conversation in our minds.

"I meant no harm," I said to Aidan as I straightened. "I'm still getting used to…how people feel around me."

Aidan nodded. "I understand, Lady Cyra. My apologies if Maziren hurt you. She was only doing her job. We may all need to talk about some…boundaries and expectations." He looked at Bressen.

A muscle ticked in Bressen's jaw, but he nodded and inclined his head toward the table. "Shall we discuss it over dinner?"

"After you, Lord Bressen," Aidan said. "We're not sure if there are assigned seats or not, so we'll follow your lead."

Bressen's body relaxed even more, and his voice was easier when he answered. "It's not assigned seating so much as it's habitual seating."

We moved toward the twelve-place table in the center of the room. Three giant crystal chandeliers glittered with candles above it, but the room also had a magical ambient light for which I'd never found a source.

Under the last triumvirate, there'd been seats at both heads of the table, but Bressen had removed them so everyone now sat on the sides. By right, he could sit at the head of the table as the senior Triumvirate lord, but he didn't believe that meals were a place for hierarchy.

He took the seat closest to the end, where Ursan had previously sat, and I took my place next to him. Aidan followed our lead and took the seat across from Bressen. Jasper sat down across from me, and Maziren eased down moodily next to Jasper as her eyes shot daggers at me.

As if on cue, servants emerged from the kitchen with bowls of soup and bottles of wine for our first course.

"I've heard much about the wine your family's vineyard produces," Aidan said to me as he held his glass up for a servant to fill. "I hope we're drinking something of yours tonight?"

The servant held out the bottle for me to see. "We are," I said. "This is one of our white wines. It goes nicely with the fish stew they're serving."

Aidan took a sip and his brows raised in appreciation. "Excellent," he said. "Jasper is quite the snob about wine, but I daresay he'll enjoy this."

Jasper looked dubious but took a sip of his wine. His expression told me he did indeed like it but was trying his best not to reveal how much. His only response was a nod of his head.

"I think we can dispense with titles if you agree," Bressen said to Aidan. "We can stand on ceremony if you want, but the previous lords and I just used our given names among each other. I prefer to save my breath for whispering endearments into my fiancé's ear."

My stomach flipped at the memory of Bressen's warm breath close to my ear a couple hours ago in the wine cellar. It hadn't been endearments he'd been whispering then, and my face flushed as I recalled the filthy things that had tumbled from his lips as he'd fucked me over a barrel.

I gave Bressen a sidelong glance and found the bastard grinning.

Aidan seemed oblivious to my sudden fever as he gave Jasper a soft look. "Agreed," he said. Then he looked at me.

"Please, call me Cyra," I confirmed, answering his unspoken question.

"Are you settling in well?" Bressen asked as he sipped his own wine.

"We are," Aidan said. "It will take some time to make it feel like our home away from home, but we'll do our best. Jasper is the one with an eye for design, so I'll defer to his sense of décor."

"I can recommend some shops in the city if you'd like," I said to Jasper. "Bressen is letting me add a few of my own touches to his wing, so I've been doing some shopping myself."

"I'd appreciate that very much," Jasper said with a warm smile.

It was the first time he'd spoken, and his voice was deeper and more velvety than I'd expected. I was instantly under his spell.

"Do you have any questions?" Bressen asked Aidan as we all began to eat our soup. "You and I will meet tomorrow after the ceremony at the Priory, but can I answer anything before then?"

"What I'm most curious to know," Aidan said nonchalantly, "is whether it was you or Cyra who made my guard fear his dick was about to fall off earlier today in the Great Chamber."

Bressen's spoon paused halfway to his mouth, and I had to lower the glass of wine I'd been about to sip from to keep from spitting it across the table. I turned to look at Bressen, but he didn't return my glance as a smile curled his lips.

"Another point to you, Aidan," he said. "I take it the guard was a trap to see if we'd read your minds? It was me, by the way."

"How far ahead am I on points now?" Aidan asked with a gleam of humor in his eye.

"Very far," Bressen assured him. "I need to up my game."

Across the table from me, Jasper rolled his eyes. "Protector save us all from competitive men." He turned to me. "I take it your fiancé is as unable to resist a challenge as Aidan is?"

I remembered the times I'd inadvertently challenged Bressen in the early days of our relationship and how he'd delighted in rising to them. It wouldn't be quite the same with Aidan, but I knew this good-natured rivalry between the two lords was likely just getting started.

"This will only get worse before it gets better," I confirmed.

The lord consort gave an exaggerated sigh.

"To answer your question," Aidan said to Bressen, pointedly ignoring his husband, "yes, the guard was planned. He was told to think something that would provoke a reaction from you."

"It certainly did," Bressen grumbled.

Aidan turned to me. "My apologies, Cyra," he said sincerely. "It wasn't my intention for my guard to fantasize about you. I suppose I should've been more specific in my instructions. I assume the man might have fared worse if it had been you who'd caught him?"

I recognized the question for what it was, Aidan's attempt to get a sense of my own inclinations and limitations when it came to my powers.

I sat back and considered the question for a moment, and a grin spread across my face as the answer came to me. Everyone on the opposite side of the table suddenly looked nervous.

When I'd first come to the Citadel there'd been little for me to do, so I'd taken to walking along the battlements. The guards there had refused to talk to me, so I'd made my own fun one day by telling one of them how I pleasured myself at night. The erection I gave the poor man had likely made him very uncomfortable for a while after I'd moved on. I wanted to say that was a singular incident, but I knew I would've treated Aidan's guard to a similar experience if I'd caught him thinking about me.

"That depends on how you look at it," I said to Aidan with a hint of wickedness. "I probably would have helped the man lean into his fantasy a bit. Made it more…intense for him."

Aidan was doing his best to keep his expression blank, but I saw the effort it took him to not let his jaw fall open. Maziren had no such reservations about the state of her jaw as she stared openly at me, and Jasper simply cleared his throat before taking a sip of wine to hide his smile. When I glanced at Bressen, his eyebrows were raised, and his expression told me we were most certainly going to talk about this later. I just gave him an innocent look.

"And a point to Cyra for rendering my husband speechless," Jasper said as his eyes danced with amusement. "That's hard to do."

I inclined my head to Jasper in silent thanks, and he winked at me. I turned my attention to Aidan, who still hadn't figured out what to say.

"I understand you had to complete a series of trials to win your seat as Lord of Derridan," I said, sparing him from a response. "I'd love to hear all about it if you're willing to share."

Aidan blinked, then recovered himself. "I thought Samhail would've filled you in on the details of the trials," he said, glancing at Bressen.

Another probing comment.

Bressen shrugged. "Samhail doesn't have much of a penchant for storytelling. He sent me messages about the trials and how everyone fared, but they were usually short on details. Please do favor us with some tales."

Aidan glanced at Jasper, who nodded to encourage him.

"Very well," Aidan said. "As you probably know, there were several trials, each designed to test our intelligence, wisdom, cunning, physical prowess, magic, or any combination of those things. The first trial consisted of a series of five puzzles or tasks of increasing difficulty we had to solve. The two candidates to finish last were eliminated."

"Based on what we've learned of you so far," I said to him, "I assume you won easily?"

"Actually," Aidan said, "I was nearly eliminated in the first round."

"How is that possible?" I asked, genuinely surprised.

"Bad luck really. I…have difficulty seeing certain colors, and the first task involved a puzzle where I needed to be able to distinguish color."

My eyes widened. "What happened? How did you solve it?"

I'd heard of such a condition before, but I'd never met anyone who experienced it.

"It took me far longer than it should have," Aidan said. "I'm used to how I see color, but I still had to translate in my mind what I was seeing to what I should've been seeing. That took some time, so when I finally solved the puzzle, I was already well behind everyone else. Luckily, I'm very good at puzzles, so I soon caught up."

"How did you know how the others were doing?" I asked.

"There were walled lanes built in the arena," he said. "I could see the tops of my opponents' heads, but I couldn't see how they were solving their puzzles. Once you finished a puzzle, your assigned judge would verify you'd completed it correctly, and you could go on to the next one. Only the last puzzle had no judge. You simply had to hope you completed it correctly, at which point you walked through a door at the end of the lane to signal you were done. The challenge stopped once the first person walked through their door."

"Who walked through the door first?" I asked.

Aidan smiled. "I did."

"You solved it first?"

Aidan inclined his head in a gesture that said it wasn't that simple.

"Not exactly. I did manage to catch up, but I was still the second-to-last contestant to reach the final puzzle, so if I didn't do well on it, I was in danger of being eliminated."

"Imagine how I felt watching this from the stands," Jasper chimed in. "The banner I'd been waving was shredded to pieces by the end."

"So how did you solve the puzzle?" I asked Aidan.

"I didn't solve it," Aidan said. "I simply realized and accepted that the puzzle was unsolvable. It had no solution."

I raised my brows in question. "I don't understand."

"The trial was as much a test of wisdom as it was intelligence," Aidan explained. "The final puzzle wasn't designed to be solved. It was designed to see which one of us would realize it was unsolvable and have enough confidence to walk through the door.”

I blinked, and Bressen made a sound that indicated he was impressed.

“You were the first to realize it was unsolvable?” I asked.

“I’m not sure I was the first to realize it,” Aidan said, “but I was the first to accept it and walk through the door. I spoke to some of my opponents after the trial, and at least two others also came to the same conclusion I did, but they doubted themselves. They distrusted what reason told them, so they kept trying long after they knew, somewhere deep down, that continuing to work on it was an exercise in futility.”

“You would’ve been eliminated if you hadn’t walked through,” I said.

Aidan nodded. “In one way, being behind probably saved me. I knew I’d be eliminated if someone else walked through the door first, so that knowledge helped me let go. Part of me desperately wanted to stand there and work on the puzzle. Like my opponents, I felt the thread of doubt that told me there was in fact a solution I just wasn’t seeing, but a leader needs to be decisive. They can’t let their doubts hold them back and keep them from acting. Once I realized that’s what the last puzzle was really testing – the willingness to act – going through the door was easier.”

“My heart nearly stopped when I saw him move to the door,” Jasper said, shaking his head. “It was hard to see the puzzles themselves, but I didn’t get the sense he’d solved it. I thought he was giving up.”

Aidan shook his head and tsked lightly. “So little faith in me.”

“What happened when you walked through the door?” I asked.

“The judge on the other side asked me if I’d solved the puzzle,” Aidan said. “I told her the puzzle had no solution. She paused for five of the most heart-stopping seconds of my life before she declared me the winner. I think I fell to my knees at some point thereafter.”

I let out a long breath, but my next thought was cut off by the appearance of Gilbert at the door to the dining room. The captain of the guard seemed flushed and out of breath, as though he’d just run here.

“What is it?” Bressen asked, recognizing something was wrong.

“My lords,” Gilbert said, “we received word that the town of Bronwyn in Derridan is under attack.”

“What?” Bressen and Aidan said together, rising from their seats.

“Another band of armed men?” Bressen asked.

"Yes, my lord," Gilbert said. "They came out of the forest nearby."

Bressen nodded and started for the door.

"Where are you going?" Aidan asked.

"To the armory," Bressen said. "Do any of you need weapons?"

"I do," I said, rising from my chair.

Bressen's eyes met mine. He opened his mouth then closed it. I knew he'd been about to argue with me about going but thought better of it. I hurried to his side, and we looked back at Aidan, Jasper, and Maziren.

None of them had moved.

"Are you coming?" Bressen asked them.

Aidan looked at him in confusion. "Bronwyn is at least two days ride from here. We'd never make it in time to help."

Bressen's expression turned sheepish. "Ah, right," he said. "Did I forget to mention that Cyra can create portals?"

Aidan's face darkened, and I knew he must be thinking about the day and a half they'd spent travelling in the cold and snow from Seatherny when I could simply have created a portal to get them here in an instant. In truth, I'd never thought to ask Bressen if he needed me to create a portal for Aidan and his retinue, and I felt guilty for not thinking of it sooner. I suspected Bressen would have declined my offer anyway.

"Yes," Aidan said, clearly annoyed. "That did slip your mind."

"We can discuss his faulty memory later," I said, giving Bressen a disapproving look. "Right now, we need to get to Bronwyn to help."

Aidan nodded and started to follow us. Jasper and Maziren rose as well, and Bressen led the way toward the armory.

Five minutes later, we were all armed, and I opened a portal to Bronwyn. Screams from the village on the other side immediately met our ears while thick smoke from burning buildings assailed our noses as it wafted through the portal. Aidan, Jasper, and Maziren immediately rushed through, but Bressen stopped me before I could follow.

"I'm going," I told him stubbornly.

"I know, but there are rules," he said. "Don't take unnecessary risks, stay where I can see you, and, above all, fight ruthlessly. Don't wound if you can kill. Can you do that?"

I looked at him, suddenly uncertain now. I'd never killed anyone before, and my inclination in the past had always been to wound or incapacitate. I looked over Bressen's shoulder to what lay on the other side of the portal – the bodies on the ground, the smoke filling the air, the screams of pain – and my expression hardened.

"I can," I insisted.

He sighed, and I knew he'd been hoping for a reason to make me stay.

"Then go," he said as he bent down and kissed me. "And be careful. I'll be extremely angry if you get yourself hurt or killed."

I nodded and stepped around him through the portal and into sheer chaos.

# Chapter 3

I coughed as smoke burned my eyes and lungs the moment I stepped through the portal. We'd emerged onto the main street of a town that looked to be around the size of Fernweh. Several buildings were engulfed in flames, and screams cut the air as people ran through the streets.

I could conjure water, but my powers were too underdeveloped to help with flames that large. I'd never used them for anything grander than making tea and watering grape vines.

The one thing I could do was give myself some breathing room. Wind pushed out around me to disburse the smoke long enough for me to inhale a few deep breaths of clean air.

"Are you alright?" Bressen asked, coming up behind me.

I nodded and closed the portal behind him to keep anyone from slipping through it.

"Stay close to me," he said as he surveyed the street.

"Can't you just render everyone unconscious?" I asked.

He shook his head. "Not in a situation like this. Not without knowing where everyone is and what they're doing. I tried that before and…it didn't end well."

I frowned, but I didn't have time to consider what that meant as I tried to take in what was going on. People fought in the streets, but it was almost impossible to tell who was an enemy and who was a resident of Bronwyn. To one side, two men clashed with short swords, but neither wore anything to indicate which side they were on. To my right, a man with a pitchfork held a man with a knife at bay, and I reasoned the man with the pitchfork was the villager, but I wasn't certain.

"How do we tell which ones are enemies?" I asked Bressen.

"Read their minds," he said as he rushed toward the pair with swords.

I blinked. Of course. Most people here were likely mortal, so Bressen and I could easily read their minds. It was a testament to just how unpracticed I was with my powers that it hadn't occurred to me to do so.

I ran toward the man with the pitchfork and his opponent. I reached out to both of them with my mind, and as I suspected, the man with the pitchfork was a villager.

When I was close enough, I aimed a forcefield at the man with the knife. He was blasted backward and went sliding across the ground. I ran forward with my sword, remembering my promise to Bressen that I wouldn't hesitate to kill. I pulled the blade back, ready to thrust it through the man, but the expression of fear on his face made me pause. The tension in my arm eased as I looked at him, but as soon as he saw my reluctance, his expression changed. His face hardened, and he lunged toward me from the ground with his knife.

Luckily the villager didn't have the same qualms I did. He emerged from behind me and rammed his pitchfork into the man's chest, shoving him backward and stopping the knife inches from my stomach.

I spun around to look at my savior, my heart still in my throat as I tried to remember how to breathe.

"Thank you," I said shakily as he used a foot to dislodge the other man from his pitchfork.

"Who are you?" he asked, wariness still in his expression.

"I'm Cyra, uh, Lady Cyra. I'm with Lord Aidan and Lord Bressen. We're here to help."

The man's eyes widened larger than I'd have thought possible.

"The…the Triumvirate lords are here?" he asked incredulously. "The Nemesis Incarnate is here?"

His expression changed from wariness to outright fear, and he touched three fingers to his lips, which I knew to be a sign of prayer.

"He's here to help," I insisted. "Do you know who these men are?"

He shook his head. "They just came out of the woods and started killing people and setting buildings ablaze. There was no warning."

"Get people somewhere safe," I said. "We'll handle the invaders."

The man looked at the body on the ground and then at me.

"My lady," he said carefully. "You…" He trailed off, but I saw into his mind and knew what his concern was.

"I won't hesitate again," I assured him.

He looked reluctant to leave, especially as he eyed the dress I hadn't had time to change out of, but he nodded and rushed off to help others.

I looked around and located Aidan, Jasper, and Maziren. Jasper was engaged in a sword fight with one man while Maziren was quickly taking care of a group of five men who apparently thought her small size made her an easy target. They couldn't have been more wrong.

Maziren was as fast as Samhail as she took on all five at once, cutting them down before most had time to lift their swords. One man grabbed her from behind, but Maziren easily threw him off. Then she curled her hand into a fist and landed a punch to his face I was certain must have broken his jaw. He went flying with a cry of agony and lay on the ground whimpering. Another man rushed her, but she grabbed his collar with one hand and sent him flying over her head to land several feet away.

I blinked at her strength, and now more than ever I wanted to see her spar with Samhail. She might actually be stronger than him.

Instinctively, my eyes sought Aidan next, curious about his power. He'd just run his sword through a man and was withdrawing it when three men rushed at him from behind.

"Aidan! Behind you!" I screamed as I ran toward them.

Aidan whirled and raised his sword just in time to block the arcing blow from one attacker. He reached out to let his fingers graze the man's blade, and the sword instantly turned to sand that fell to the ground in a pile at his feet.

The attacker's eyes widened in shock as Aidan moved his hand to the man's shirt next, which turned into a kaleidoscope of butterflies that took flight in all directions. As the man stood in shock, Aidan ran him through with his own sword.

One of the other men had also pulled up in surprise, and his hesitation was Aidan's opening to dispatch him before engaging the last attacker.

Transfiguration. Aidan's power was transfiguration.

Bressen was right. I *did* want that for my collection.

"Cyra!" Jasper's shout from somewhere nearby brought me back, and I whirled to see a man with a sword rushing toward me. I just barely had enough time to raise my own sword to block his blow, but the force of his swing sent me sprawling back on the ground. He was above me a second later, his sword poised to slash down on me.

I threw my blade up to block him again, but the man was large, and I knew the force of his swing would likely bring my own sword down on top of me. My mind went blank as I tried to hold my weapon as tightly as I could, and I only prayed I had enough strength to keep his blow from killing me. I saw the shift in the muscles of his arms as his sword began its downswing, and I tightened my own, waiting for the blow to land.

It never came.

The man crumpled to a heap in front of me as his body went limp and collapsed like a rag doll. I scurried back away from him on the ground and looked around, certain Bressen must be somewhere nearby.

He was running toward me, and his eyes glowed a bright fiery red, the expression on his face one of thunderous rage. I assumed that rage was for the man he'd just rendered unconscious, but as he neared, my mind connected with his, and I realized he was also angry at *me*.

I managed to rise just as he reached me, and he dropped his sword to grasp my face roughly in his hands. My own hands flew up to clasp his wrists as the intensity of his reaction shuddered through me.

"Cyra!" he said, anger and relief warring in his voice. "Nemesis take you! What in the three hells were you thinking?"

"I…" I tried to speak, but I was overwhelmed by the flood of emotions pouring off him. I had to disconnect my mind from his and throw up my mental shield so I could think straight.

"Forget your sword!" Bressen yelled at me, his hands tightening around my face. "Use your powers!"

My powers. I'd completely forgotten about them in the heat of the attack. I could have used the forcefields I'd syphoned from Samhail to repel the man, or I could've done as Bressen did and rendered him unconscious. My mind powers weren't as acute as Bressen's, but I'd put two guards to sleep once when I'd been locked in my room by Jerram.

"Gods above, Cyra," Bressen said, pulling me into a crushing hug. "You promised to be brutal. Why didn't you use your powers?"

"I…I forgot," I said as Bressen held me against him. His usual smell of musk and hot cinnamon was muted by the acrid reek of smoke.

"You forgot?" Bressen said incredulously. "Fucking hells, Cyra! I would've killed everyone in this village without another thought if that man had struck you down!"

My breath caught in my throat at his words. My powers told me when someone spoke an untruth, but I saw that Bressen believed what he'd said. Everyone here, including Aidan, Jasper, and Maziren, would have suffered his wrath if something had happened to me. Paralyzing guilt followed that realization, and I sagged against him.

"I'm sorry," I whispered.

The tension left Bressen's body, and he rested his forehead on mine.

"It's my fault. You weren't prepared for this," he said. "You haven't been trained to use your powers, and we need to remedy that."

My heart swelled at the idea that Bressen might call Samhail back to finish the training he'd started with me.

"Is she alright?" Jasper asked from next to us. "Cyra, are you hurt?"

Bressen's arms loosened around me so I could pull back from him.

"I'm fine. A momentary lapse of memory," I said. "I seem to have forgotten I have powers."

Jasper looked taken aback, but a commotion down the street caught our attention before he could reply. Screams rose above the din of fighting, and the three of us turned to see a group of about ten men rushing into one of the buildings that wasn't yet burning.

"Three hells," Bressen said as he picked up his sword. "I better go see what the fuck is happening there." He stopped after a step and looked back at me, though.

A new wave of guilt hit me as I realized he was afraid to leave me unguarded, that I was more just in the way at this point than anything.

"Go," Jasper told Bressen. "I'll keep her with me."

Bressen hesitated only a moment more before nodding his thanks and running toward where the men had disappeared into the building.

I looked apologetically at Jasper, but he just nodded.

"Stay close to me," he said.

I'd just started to nod back when a woman's scream sounded from inside one of the buildings behind me, and I whirled to look. A second scream helped me zero in on which building it came from, and I ran toward it without any further thought of staying near Jasper.

"Cyra! Stop!" Jasper's voice followed me into the building, but I didn't wait for him as I barreled inside, following the sound of shrieks and sobs.

The building appeared to be a general store, and a group of seven men stood inside with two women. Two men to my left held one woman by her waist as she sobbed and struggled to free herself. Four others held another woman down on the ground while she screamed and struggled as the last man knelt to position himself between her legs.

Something in me snapped as I saw what they were about to do, and rage burned up in my chest. I held out a hand to call my summoning power, and the man on his knees was yanked backward away from the woman. My follow-up forcefield sent the other four men sprawling backward away from her before I turned my attention once again to the first man. I closed in on him, oblivious to the six other threats in the room, and I reached out to connect with his mind. I felt the supremacy and power he'd experienced as he'd knelt in front of the woman ready to rape her, and my vision went red as a word formed in my mind.

A command.

*Die.*

I didn't know if this was how Bressen did it when he killed someone with his mind, but I didn't care. I wanted this man to die.

The man screamed and grabbed his head. Blood dripped from his nose as he writhed on the ground, but he remained regrettably alive.

I stepped forward, ready to try again, but burly arms wrapped around my shoulders, and I was lifted off my feet and thrown to the ground. I rolled over to find a huge man standing over me, rank with dirt and sweat.

"Bitch!" he spat. "You just volunteered to get fucked next."

The words were no sooner out of his mouth than his eyes widened, and he jolted forward as the tip of a sword punched through his chest. I rolled out of the way just in time as his body crumpled down next to me.

Jasper stood there, his sword dripping with the man's blood, but we could do no more than exchange a look of shared understanding as the other men rushed him. The two women ran for the door, trying to stay clear of Jasper's blade as he swung at his attackers.

One of the men screamed as the blade cut him across the chest, but Jasper didn't have time to swing again before the rest were on him. They pushed him to the floor and began to kick him.

"No!" I shouted as the men overwhelmed him.

*Sleep!* I tried to send the command into their minds, but they only paused before renewing their assault on Jasper.

Fine, I'd do it individually. I reached into their minds one by one and sent the command for them to sleep. One after another the men around him fell to the floor.

When there was silence, Jasper and I looked at each other.

"Thank you, Lady Cyra," he said, true relief in his voice.

"Cyra," I corrected him, and he inclined his head.

Jasper got back to his feet, stepped over two of the unconscious bodies, and held his hand out to help me up. I reached up to take it but pulled it back again as the incident at dinner surfaced in my mind. I glanced around quickly, half expecting Maziren to come out of nowhere and grab my wrist. Jasper understood my hesitation and seized my hand to pull me to my feet.

"Mortal, remember? I have no powers for you to syphon," he said.

"Of course," I said, smiling weakly.

"Cyra!"

I heard Bressen's call from outside first, then his call into my mind a second later. I felt his power searching for me, and I answered.

*I'm here*, I said. *We're coming out now.*

Jasper and I went back out onto the main street where Bressen, Aidan, and Maziren were standing, all holding swords wet with blood. My own sword was still on the ground where I'd dropped it near the man Bressen had rendered unconscious.

"The rest of the attackers are retreating back into the woods," Aidan said as Jasper and I joined them.

I turned toward the forest where several men were running into the darkness. A moment later they fell to the ground, and I knew Bressen had knocked them out.

"Are we taking all these men back to the Citadel?" I asked.

"We are," Bressen said. "These attacks are getting bolder and more frequent. We need to figure out what's going on."

"Did you learn anything from the men who attacked me and Ursan?" I asked, thinking back to the time the late Lord of Polaris had taken me riding, and we'd been attacked by nearly forty men. It was the first time

I'd seen Ursan shift into animal form, and the first time I'd realized how dangerous he could be.

Bressen hesitated before answering. "Not enough."

I narrowed my eyes at him. There was something he didn't want to say, but I wasn't sure if it was me or Aidan he was trying to hide it from.

"A portal into the Citadel dungeons if you would, my love," Bressen said to me, placing a hand at the small of my back.

I nodded and drew the circle in the air to call the portal. It flared open, and I got my first glimpse into the cold, dark dungeons of the Citadel.

Ironically, I'd been sure I'd be thrown into those dungeons when I was first summoned to Callanus months ago, but I'd never actually seen them until now. I'd been given a lavish guest chamber instead, where I'd stayed until I'd moved into Bressen's own quarters weeks later.

I stepped back from the portal as the men who'd tried to flee picked themselves up and marched back under Bressen's power. I looked to where the huge man that attacked me had fallen and waited for him to rise. I furrowed my brow when he remained motionless next to my sword.

"Bressen, why isn't that man getting up?" I asked hesitantly.

Bressen met my eyes with an expression of resignation, and my stomach hollowed out.

Maziren offered her own scornful explanation in case I hadn't understood Bressen's look. "Lady Cyra, that man is very dead."

"But I thought you only…" My voice trailed off as the look on Bressen's face turned to one of resolve.

"I wasn't taking any chances," he said.

I looked back to the body on the ground. I'd never actually seen Bressen kill someone with his mind. Normally he preferred not to kill if he could help it, but that rule didn't apply to this man. The man had posed an imminent threat to me, and he'd paid for it with his life.

Bressen slipped a possessive arm around my waist and dragged me against him. He brushed his lips against my temple. "I have no mercy for anyone who threatens you," he said against my ear, and I closed my eyes.

That Bressen could and would kill so easily for me was at once frightening, sobering, and…exhilarating.

# Chapter 4

I'd watched people die by the sword before. Samhail had cut down nearly twenty men a day after I'd met him, but there was something different about what Bressen could do, how quickly and cleanly he could take someone's life with little effort. One moment the man had been alive and the next he was dead, too fast to even realize the Nemesis had taken him, courtesy of the Nemesis Incarnate.

I wanted to be horrified by that thought, but I wasn't. I'd tried myself just moments ago to do the same thing. I hadn't succeeded, but I'd wanted to. For the first time in my life, I'd wanted to kill.

"Can you get Aramis here?" Bressen asked me. "There are wounded."

His words brought me back from my dark thoughts, and I nodded before turning to open a portal.

Aramis appeared on the other side of the glowing blue circle at his dining table. He looked up when the portal appeared.

"I'm sorry to disturb your dinner, Aramis, but there was an attack," I said through the portal. "Can you help?"

Aramis and I were getting to know each other better each day, but I still couldn't bring myself to call him "Father" yet.

Aramis rose immediately and stepped through the portal.

"Where do we start?" he asked as he looked around.

"This way," Bressen said, motioning down the way I'd seen him go before. "There was a melee back here."

Aramis and I followed Bressen down the street and into the building he'd gone into before.

"Gods above," I murmured as we entered and took in the scene.

Bodies lay everywhere. Men sat moaning in pools of blood, their shirts and pants soaked crimson. Some were slashed across the body, while others bled from deep cuts on their arms or legs. One man had a brutal gash across his face that seemed to have taken a chunk of his nose off.

"Who do we treat first?" I asked, overwhelmed by the job before us.

Aramis had been trying to teach me to use my healing powers, but I was only a novice. I could heal cuts, burns, and broken bones well enough, but I wasn't sure my powers were up to what I saw now.

Aramis held out his hands and let his power explore the room so it could tell him who the most grievously wounded were. I followed his lead and let my own power fan out to triage the injured. I felt its tug at the same time Aramis did, and we moved toward a man who lay unmoving on the floor with a deep wound across his chest. Aramis immediately knelt to work on him, but he stopped me when I tried to kneel too.

"I can handle this one," he told me. He pointed to another man leaning up against a wall with his hand pressed to a shoulder wound. "Help him. Remember to do your assessment first to be sure you know what's wrong, then start healing from the inside out."

I nodded and headed toward the second man with Bressen right behind me. I knew he wouldn't leave my side.

"I'm Cyra," I told the man as I knelt down next to him. "I'm here to help you. Do you live in this village?"

He nodded, and I hovered my hands over his body as I let my magic examine him. The shoulder wound was his worst injury, but luckily the cut hadn't hit bone, and I set to work trying to knit the flesh back together from within. The man's eyes glazed over a bit as I worked, and I knew Bressen was easing his pain.

It took me a couple minutes to fully heal the man, and then I rose to let my power find the next injured person. It pulled me to the right, and I hurried around a body on the ground toward a man several feet away.

I nearly slipped as my foot slid on a wet patch I hadn't seen on the other side of the body, but Bressen caught me before I went down.

"What is that?" I asked as I eyed the puddle I'd stepped in. At first glance it appeared to be a pool of blood, but it wasn't the right color. The viscous liquid that stuck to my shoe was dark blue and thicker than blood.

Bressen bent down and dabbed the tip of a finger into the liquid. He lifted his hand and smelled it but shook his head.

"I have no idea," he said. "It's nothing I've ever seen before."

My attention was drawn to the man near me by his moan of pain, and I moved toward him, the blue puddle forgotten for the moment.

I knelt down beside him, and his eyes found mine, flaring slightly as he focused on my face.

"Demons," he rasped out.

I furrowed my brows. "What?"

"Demons," he repeated. "Two of them. Like dark blue shadows with no real faces. Just…glowing yellow eyes."

Bressen and I exchanged an uneasy look before he glanced back at the puddle I'd slipped in.

"The men attacked first," the injured man continued, "but then the two demons showed up. They tried to…"

He winced in pain, and I was jolted back to my task as I remembered he was injured.

"Relax now," I said. "I'm a healer, and I'm here to help you."

"I should read his mind to see what he saw," Bressen said.

"Not yet," I told him. "Let me heal him first."

I hovered my hands over the man's body, searching for his wounds, but I jerked back as his hand clamped over one of my wrists.

"You're perimortal," he said, anger replacing the pain in his voice.

"Yes, I'm a healer," I said, trying to pull away.

He thrust me away from him, and Bressen's fury stirred behind me.

"Keep your gods' damned perimortal hands off me," the man spat.

I just stared at him. I knew perimortals were often hated and feared, especially in smaller towns and villages like my own home of Fernweh, but the notion that this man would refuse to let me heal him because I was perimortal stunned me.

"You're hurt. Let me help you," I tried to reason with him.

"Don't you fucking touch me!" he growled.

I was about to ask Bressen to hold his mind while I treated him anyway when someone knelt down beside me. I turned to see an older woman with almond-shaped eyes and graying black hair.

"I'll help him," she said to me, her tone apologetic. "Radnus would apparently rather cut off his own nose to spite his face than accept the generous help being offered him."

She threw the man an admonishing look, but he only glared at me.

"I'm sorry for him," the woman said.

"Who are you?" I asked.

"I'm Nan, the town healer," she said, then added, "A mortal healer."

I watched the woman as she pulled a bag toward her and opened it to reveal the kinds of instruments I'd seen our own healer in Fernweh use. I'd gotten so used to seeing Aramis heal people by magic that I'd forgotten the majority of healers were mortal and had to do things the hard way.

"I'll take care of him," the woman said when I continued to stare at her. "I don't think any of the other wounded will give you trouble."

I nodded finally and stood to look around the room for my next patient, but a commotion outside the building drew my attention. A man was shouting. I couldn't hear what he was saying, but I could clearly hear the desperation in his voice.

Aidan entered a moment later with a man who appeared frantic.

"He needs a healer right away," Aidan said to Aramis.

"Please!" the man screamed as tears streaked down his face. "My wife is pregnant. She was injured in the attack, and I think she's in labor."

Aramis rose instantly, the man he'd been working on only half healed. "Take me to her," he ordered, and the other man turned to lead the way.

"Aramis!" I called to him, but he didn't seem to hear me.

I hurried over to check on the man he'd left. Aramis had staunched the worst of the bleeding and begun to repair the man's leg, but there was still much that needed to be done, and I set to work where he'd left off. I was nearly finished when Aramis's panicked voice sounded in my mind.

*Cyra! I need your help!*

Aramis didn't have mind powers, but Bressen had taught me how to create a dormant link to the minds of others so they could contact me if needed. The power didn't extend very far, but Aramis, Raina, and my brothers, Jaylan and Brix, could all now send me a brief message if they were within a few miles and wanted to speak with me. I could then open a channel to their minds to read their thoughts. I'd wanted to create a link with Samhail as well, but I hadn't seen him again since learning how.

Fear gripped me at Aramis's words, but I forced myself to wait the last few seconds for my magic to finish closing the gash across the man's leg before I rose. He'd have a scar, but it was the best I could do.

"Aramis needs me," I told Bressen. "I'll have to come back after."

Bressen nodded and followed me as I emerged from the building and let my mind reach out to find Aramis. I sensed his presence down a side street and hurried toward him with Bressen close on my heels.

My magic led me to a house midway down the street, and I entered without knocking to head for the bedroom.

Dread hit me like a blast of cold air as soon as I entered, but it wasn't coming from the husband that had sought us out. That man stood frozen in a corner of the room. Rather, the dread was coming from Aramis himself, and I saw why a moment later.

The woman on the bed was deathly pale and barely moving. Sweat drenched her face while blood soaked the front of her skirt and the covers between her legs where Aramis knelt, his hands over her swollen belly.

"What do you need me to do?" I asked as I hurried to the bed.

"We need to remove the child now," he said. "I can't stop the labor."

I nodded, but terror was now beating a drum in my chest as well. I'd helped Aramis deliver a baby once a couple weeks ago, but it had been a normal birth. This was anything but, and I felt alarmingly unprepared.

"I need a sharp knife," Aramis told the husband. "Hurry!"

The man blanched but ran for the kitchen and was back a few seconds later with a large carving knife.

"I'm going to make a cut from here to here," Aramis told me, indicating two points under the woman's rounded belly. "When I get the baby out, I'll give it to you. Get it breathing and check for any issues."

"Yes," I confirmed, barely getting the word past the knot in my throat. "Lord Bressen-"

"I'll take care of her pain," Bressen cut in before Aramis could ask.

Aramis nodded and leaned in to make his cut. My eyes darted to the husband as Aramis's knife sliced through his wife, but his eyes were as vacant as hers, and I knew Bressen must be holding his mind as well.

Aramis finished his cut and reached in to pull the baby out. My breath caught at how tiny it was. The mother couldn't be that far from her delivery time, but I guessed she must have had at least a few weeks to a month before she would've been ready to give birth.

Aramis cut the cord and handed the baby to me, and I laid it carefully on the bed. I used a corner of the sheet to wipe the mucus from its mouth and face, and then rubbed my hand over the baby's torso gently to encourage it to breathe. On the bed, Aramis had his hands splayed over the woman's pelvis as he tried to close the cut he'd made.

"Will she live?" I asked him.

"I'm not sure," Aramis said, and I heard the tremor in his voice. "She's lost a lot of blood, and there's other damage as well."

I nodded and continued to massage the infant, but seconds passed, and the baby had yet to take its first breath. A quiver started in my stomach and worked its way up into my chest as I massaged harder, silently begging the child to breathe.

"Please," I whispered to the baby, but it…*he* remained unmoving.

I looked desperately at Bressen, and his eyes flared as he saw the panic in my face. I stopped massaging and laid my hands over the baby to let my magic search for the issue. Almost immediately the answer came back.

"Aramis! The baby's heart isn't beating! What do I do?" I cried to him.

"Just a minute," Aramis said, his attention still focused on the mother.

I looked down at the infant's tiny, limp body, and terror scorched my insides. I didn't know how to fix an issue with someone's heart, let alone a baby this small. My hands shook as I tried to decide what to do, but I was terrified of making things worse. The baby was so, so small.

"Aramis! You need to help the baby! Please!"

Aramis didn't answer, his attention still fixed on the woman as his hands lay over her abdomen, trying to heal her.

"Aramis!" I cried out again, trying to get his attention.

But his gaze was locked on the woman, and I knew in that moment that he wasn't seeing the woman herself but my mother. My mother had died giving birth to me when Aramis was away helping someone else, and it was the biggest regret of his life that he hadn't been there to save her. Now he was trying to make up for that, to save this woman, possibly at the cost of her child.

I had to find a way to get through to Aramis or this baby was going to die in my arms, and both me and the mother would be shattered.

"Father!" I shouted.

Aramis's head snapped up, and he looked at me as if waking from a daze. I'd only ever called him "father" once when we met, and the word had been foreign on my tongue then. It still seemed strange now, but it at least had the desired effect.

"The baby's heart isn't beating," I told Aramis. "You need to do something. Let me help the mother."

Aramis's eyes darted to the woman, and I saw the indecision on his face before he finally nodded and switched places with me.

A quick assessment of the mother told me Aramis had already repaired most of her injuries. He'd nearly closed the cut he'd made to remove the child, but I still felt the distress in her body. She wasn't out of the woods yet, and I concentrated on letting my magic find and heal her injuries. I had to at least keep her alive while Aramis worked on the baby, or he'd blame himself for her death as he did for my mother's.

The cry of an infant split the air next to me, loud and piercing in the silence of the room, but it was the most beautiful sound I'd ever heard. I nearly collapsed on top of the woman in relief, but I managed to stay upright and continue my work on her injuries.

"Thank the Protector!" I sobbed as tears trickled down my cheeks.

"How's the mother?" Aramis asked as he swaddled the baby.

"Weak but still alive," I said. "I finished closing the cut, but I'm not sure if there's anything else wrong with her."

"Take the babe," he said, and we switched places once again as he laid his hands over the mother, searching for lingering issues.

A minute or so later, he sighed and leaned back.

"She should live," he said, his voice warily optimistic. "You can release her mind, Lord Bressen. She'll want to hold her baby."

The woman blinked as Bressen released both her and her husband's minds, and she took in a gasping breath.

"My baby?" she asked, panic sharpening her voice.

"Here," I said, bringing the baby toward her. "He's safe. It's a boy."

A sob broke from her as I laid the child in her arms, and her husband moved into the space I vacated. He wrapped his arms around both his wife and child as all three family members cried against each other.

"Thank you," the man murmured. "Thank you."

A gentle hand landed on my shoulder, and I turned to see Aramis.

"Well done, Cyra," he said, giving me a bracing smile.

I nodded my thanks, but I couldn't speak.

Bressen turned me toward him, and I buried my face in his shoulder. Now that the danger had passed, emotion overwhelmed me, and I began to sob as he enveloped me in his arms, his head resting atop mine.

I didn't know how long I cried, but he eventually scooped me up and brought me outside to give the couple and their child some privacy.

"It's time to get you back to the Citadel," he said softly as he carried me toward the main street.

"I can't," I said. "I have to help Aramis with the rest of the wounded."

"You're exhausted. I can feel it. You're not going to be able to help anyone this way."

I frowned up at him, prepared to argue, but he stopped me.

"Please, Cyra. Go back. Aramis and the other healer have things in hand. You helped save two men as well as that woman and her child. You've done enough for tonight."

I inhaled, ready to say something, but I pushed the breath out in a sigh instead. I was drained, and whether I wanted to admit it or not, I wasn't as good a healer as Aramis. Even less so tired and weakened as I was. I didn't want to risk injuring someone if I wasn't at my best.

"Fine," I said as Bressen put me gently back on my feet. "Is anyone else going back?" I didn't want to be the only one.

"I could use a portal back," Jasper said, coming up next to us.

Jasper met Bressen's eyes, and the consort bobbed a small nod. The prickle at the back of my neck told me Bressen had likely made a request of him, which annoyed me. I didn't want to be anyone's burden.

I opened a portal back to the dining room of the Citadel and stepped through it after Jasper. I could have sworn it was relief I saw on Bressen's face when I closed the portal behind me again, leaving him in Bronwyn.

Jasper sat back down at the table, apparently prepared to pick up our dinner where we'd left off, but I was no longer hungry. I couldn't imagine going on as if nothing had just happened.

"Cyra, aren't you going to eat?" Jasper asked.

I shook my head. "I've lost my appetite. Please, enjoy the rest of your meal. I need to lie down."

"You should eat," he insisted.

"Did Bressen tell you to make me eat?" I asked, and his guilty look was answer enough.

He stood again and came over to search my face. "Would you like me to walk you up to your quarters?" he asked. His tone was gentle.

"It's kind of you to offer, but I'll be fine."

He was silent, and I knew he was trying to decide if he should insist.

"If you need anything, send someone to get me," I told him before he could, then I turned to head toward the chambers I shared with Bressen.

Back in our bedroom, I slumped into one of the chairs by the fire.

So much had gone wrong tonight. I'd promised Bressen I'd be brutal, but I didn't know how to be. A few months ago, I'd had a small amount of elemental magic that I'd used only for utilitarian purposes. The myriad powers I now possessed were foreign to me, and using them to fight didn't come naturally. Worse, my inexperience had been dangerous to those around me. Bressen and Jasper had needed to take their focus off fighting to keep an eye on me.

Since coming to Callanus, I'd been thrown headlong into a world of unfamiliar dangers, and I wasn't adapting as quickly as I needed to. I also had yet to find my new place in this world.

Bressen had promised me a vineyard when I'd accepted his marriage proposal, but our purchase had hit a snag and we'd started to look for other properties while still trying to keep negotiations alive with the first owner. Meanwhile, that meant I was a winemaker who no longer made wine. I could heal, but I wasn't a healer. I could fight a little, but I was certainly no warrior. I'd soon be Bressen's wife and the Lady of Hiraeth, but those were titles, not callings.

I was a syphon, supposedly one of the most dangerous perimortals in the world, but I'd nearly been killed tonight because I'd forgotten I had magic at all. The Creator had given me a gift, but I had yet to learn what I was meant to do with it, to know why I'd been blessed.

Or perhaps…why I'd been cursed.

# Chapter 5

Hours later I again opened a portal to Bronwyn so Bressen, Aidan, Maziren, and Aramis could return. Then I opened one for Aramis to return home and one more into Aidan's wing of the Citadel so he and Maziren didn't have to trek back through the fortress.

At least I was good at portals. I could get important people where they needed to be.

Much like a horse.

I felt Bressen behind me as I closed the last portal. He didn't touch me, but his presence was always palpable. He might as well have been pressed up against my back the way my spine tingled.

"We both smell like smoke, and I'm covered in blood," he said close to my ear. "We should take a bath."

I trembled a bit at the brush of his breath across my skin and at the suggestion. I hadn't had the energy to bathe or even change clothes earlier.

I followed him toward the bathing chamber where the magic of the Citadel had already ensured a large tub of hot water was waiting for us.

Bressen began to undress me first. I remained quiet but lifted my arms as he pulled my dress over my head.

"What's wrong?" he asked, noticing my somber mood.

"Nothing," I said, trying and failing for an air of breeziness. The smile I tugged onto my face barely lifted the corners of my mouth.

Bressen knelt on one knee in front of me to hook his fingers over my undergarment and pull it down my legs. I put a hand on his shoulder for balance and stepped out of it.

Bressen didn't rise yet. Instead, he pressed his lips to my stomach and kissed a trail up between my breasts before closing his mouth over one pert nipple. I gasped and leaned into him as he sucked on it, running his tongue in circles over it. My fingers threaded through his hair of their own accord seeking purchase.

"What's wrong?" he asked again, his tongue still flicking the nipple.

"Nothing," I breathed, this time more convincingly.

Bressen released my nipple to move to the next one, but I caught his face in my hands. "You need to get up or the bath will get cold," I said.

He rose to his feet. "Fine, but we'll continue this later."

I nodded and began to unbutton the ornate dinner jacket he wore that was now soaked in blood. I'd been splattered with blood as well, and the front of my dress was stained from being pressed against Bressen, but I was nowhere near as covered in it as him. I didn't want to know how many men Bressen had killed that his jacket looked the way it did. For that matter, I didn't want to know why he'd decided to kill so many men when he could easily have rendered them unconscious.

I didn't ask the question, but I had a different one for him instead.

"Back in Bronwyn you said you didn't want to put everyone to sleep," I ventured as I peeled off his shirt. "You said you tried that before and it didn't end well. What happened?"

Bressen stiffened, and he was quiet for a long moment. My hands stilled where they worked at the fastenings of his pants.

"During the war, a small force of Sandrian's attacked a town in Hiraeth," he said finally. "I took only a few soldiers with me to help fight them, figuring it would be easy enough for me to just put everyone to sleep when I arrived and sort everything out later, which is what I did."

He was quiet again for so long that I had to prompt him. "And what happened?"

"Four of the townspeople died because of me," he said. "One man fell into a fire and was burned to death. Two other people hit their heads when they fell and died of fractured skulls and blood loss."

He swallowed. "The last…was a baby. The mother was holding him when she fell. The baby was caught under her and smothered to death."

My hand flew to my mouth. "Oh gods."

Bressen's voice was gritty like sand when he spoke again. "You…you can't imagine what it was like to stand in front of that mother and admit what I'd done, admit that I was responsible for the death of her child."

I didn't want to ask, but I couldn't seem to stop myself.

"What did she say to you?"

Bressen shook his head. "She didn't say anything. She launched herself at me. I'll never forget the sound of her scream or the feel of her fingernails as she clawed at my face."

I clamped my hand against my mouth again.

"My men tried to pull her off me, but I told them to let her go. I tried to keep my eyes out of her reach, but otherwise I let her hit and scratch me until she crumpled at my feet." He exhaled deeply. "I swear I still hear her sobbing sometimes when I first wake."

His eyes were unfocused, as if seeing everything in his mind. I could have connected to his thoughts to see what he was seeing, but I wouldn't have been able to bear it.

"After that, I never used my powers unless I knew exactly who I was putting unconscious and what they were doing," he said quietly, his eyes finally focusing back on me.

"I'm so sorry," I whispered. "I shouldn't have asked."

Bressen shook his head and pulled me to him so my cheek rested against his bare chest. He was normally warm, but tonight his skin seemed cold, and it was sticky where blood had seeped through his clothes.

He leaned down to kiss the top of my head.

"It was a difficult lesson, but one I'll never forget," he said. "I only wish it hadn't cost four lives or a mother her child for me to learn it."

I nestled my head further against his chest despite the chill of his skin, and his arms tightened around me for just a heartbeat.

"We really should bathe before it goes cold," he said, easing back.

My hands went to his pants again to work at the fastenings while he toed off his boots. A moment later he was finally naked, and he stepped into the bath while I took a moment to admire the perfect swells of his ass. He eased himself down and submerged his head under the water, then leaned back against the large tub to look at me. The water turned pink from the blood on him, but the Citadel's magic quickly filtered it, so the water was clear again as I stepped in. Bressen helped me settle between his legs, and I dunked my own head before leaning back against his chest while my coffee-colored hair floated around me.

Bressen took a bottle off the table next to the tub, poured some perfumed soap from it onto a sponge, and began to wash me.

"You tried to kill someone with your mind tonight," he said quietly.

My eyes widened a little. "How did you know that?"

"I sensed your anger and felt your mind cloud. I heard you order him to die as if I'd been standing there with you. I think maybe your mind subconsciously reached out to mine, either for help, or because you wanted me to stop you."

He pressed me forward so he could run the sponge over my back.

"Did you stop me?" I asked. "Is that why it didn't work?"

"It didn't work because you don't have the power or the will to kill someone that way," he said.

My voice hardened. "I wanted him to die. I definitely had the will."

"Wanting someone to die and having the will to make it happen are two different things."

"There were seven of them trying to rape two women," I said.

Bressen loosed a deep breath. "I understand, but I don't want you to do that again."

"Why not?" I asked. "You told me to be brutal. You made me promise to kill rather than wound. Why is killing someone with my mind so different than running them through with a sword?"

Bressen ran the sponge over one of my arms.

"It's very different," he said, his voice growing sharp. "If you're going to kill someone, it should be messy. If you take a life, you should have to look the person in the eye and feel their blood on your hands. It's too easy to forget someone's humanity when you kill from afar, and the easier it becomes to forget someone's humanity, the easier it becomes to lose your own. Willing someone to die is too easy, too neat and clean. Killing should never be easy, but it becomes so when you don't have to see someone's blood, when you don't have to wash it off yourself afterward."

Bressen held up the sponge in front of me and squeezed it. Water that was pink with blood ran into the tub and swirled with the other water there before it was filtered away.

"But archers-" I started to say.

"Archers are very removed from their kills," he said, cutting me off. "They're a necessary evil, especially in wartime where indifference toward human life is practically an art form, but that doesn't make them an ideal."

I swallowed as I considered his words.

"I don't want you to do that again," he repeated quietly next to my ear, "no matter how much of a hypocrite it makes me to say so. Promise me you won't."

I remained quiet, weighing whether or not it was a promise I could keep. I understood why he didn't want me to do it, and, yes, he was a hypocrite for even asking, but I wanted to be sure I couldn't imagine a situation arising where I might need to break that promise. I was loath to give up my option to kill with my mind in case I ever really needed it.

The realization that I probably wouldn't ever be powerful enough to make it work anyway finally prompted me to say, "I promise."

I felt the tension leave Bressen's body.

"Thank you," he said as he kissed my temple.

He took the bottle of soap off the table again, squeezed some into my hair, and began to wash it. I almost moaned at the feel of his fingers working through the strands and massaging my scalp.

"Mmm, jasmine and almond," he said, inhaling deeply.

I smiled. "This was the soap that gave me away that time I was eavesdropping on you, Ursan, and Jerram."

Bressen chuckled. "No, I lied when I told you I smelled you. I sensed your mind, as you originally suspected."

I made an indignant noise, but he pulled me closer.

"I'm not really the one who needs this bath the most," I said.

"You can wash me later. Running the sponge over you is relaxing me."

Well, when he put it that way, how could I refuse?

"It looks like Aidan's power is transfiguration," I said, "and Maziren's is strength."

"And they don't want you to have either," he said, annoyed.

"I could live without the strength, but you were right. I do want transfiguration. That looks like fun."

"We may have to find someone else for you to syphon that power from. I don't think Aidan plans to give it up willingly anytime soon."

"He has to sleep sometime," I joked, and Bressen chuckled again.

He pressed on my shoulders gently to urge me under the water. I obliged, and he ran his hands through my hair to rinse it. I surfaced again as the water filtered itself to remove the soap.

"Can I make a confession?" I asked.

"By all means. I love a good confession," Bressen said as he handed me the sponge so I could finally wash him.

"I want to see Samhail and Maziren fight each other."

Bressen burst out laughing. "Thank the gods," he said. "I was afraid I was the only one."

"Who do you think would win? Assuming Samhail didn't use his gargoyle form, of course."

"All things considered, my money is still on Samhail. According to him, though, he and Maziren were fairly evenly matched when they sparred in Derridan, so it might be close."

I spun around, making the water slosh against the edge of the tub.

"They fought each other already?" I asked, disappointed I'd missed it.

"Samhail said he sparred with the guards and even some of the contestants while he was in Derridan for the trials," Bressen said. "I don't think Aidan ever took him up on his offer to practice, but I remember now that he said Maziren was the first to ask him about training together. He said he underestimated her the first time they fought, as I'm sure everyone does. He sounded impressed."

I frowned at Bressen. "Why didn't you tell me any of this earlier?"

He looked surprised. "I'm sorry. I didn't realize it would interest you. I didn't usually talk to Samhail for long when he updated me, and it didn't seem like anything worthy of note at the time."

Bressen shifted us so I was no longer between his legs but straddling his thighs as I faced him. I reached over and squirted some musky soap from another bottle onto the sponge he'd given me. There was none of the hot cinnamon aroma I usually smelled on him, and I wondered where that part of his scent came from.

I ran the sponge over Bressen's chest and arms. He was bloodier than I'd been, and the sponge was soon stained pink. I rinsed it out and let the magic filter away the blood, then went to work again. My hands dipped below the water to run over his taut stomach muscles and up his powerful thighs, but I skirted around the appendage between his legs.

He pushed out a breath when I ran the sponge up slowly inside his thigh but stopped just short of his groin. His hips lifted just a bit as if seeking my touch, and I smiled.

"You keep missing a spot," he breathed.

"Is it a dirty spot?" I asked innocently.

His voice turned husky. "A very dirty spot. A filthy, filthy spot."

I ran the sponge up the shaft of his cock as the thumb of my other hand rubbed over his tip. He was so hard already, and he groaned low in his throat as his head tipped back against the rim of the tub.

"You have no idea what your touch does to me, Cyra," he rasped.

"I need to wash your back."

Bressen lifted his head, and there was a wicked grin on his face as he pulled me against him so his erection was pressed between us.

"Wash whatever you can reach," he whispered against my lips.

I re-soaped the sponge and pressed my breasts against him so I could reach around and run the sponge over his back. His head dipped into the crook of my shoulder, and he nipped and kissed his way up my neck. My nipples pebbled into hard buds against his chest, and he rocked me over him so his length slid between the petals of my center. In answer, I leaned forward and ran my teeth along his own neck causing him to groan.

"I need to be inside you now," he panted against my ear.

"I'm not done washing your back yet," I said coyly.

"Fuck my back," he growled, and before I could muster any further excuses, he lifted my hips until I could feel his cock poised at my entrance.

Water spurted up between us as he slammed me down onto him, and I gasped at the feeling of suddenly being filled. I wrapped an arm around his shoulder, the sponge still clutched tightly in my hand, while the other hand found his steely bicep to curl around it.

"Move with me," he ordered, and I obeyed, rolling my hips as he thrust up into me.

"Oh gods!" I cried out as pleasure surged in my core.

I dug my fingers into the muscle of his arm as we ground against each other. His breath was hot on my ear as my own warmed his cheek, and he reached down between us to find the bud at my apex and rub two fingers against it. I moaned and jerked against him as bliss skittered over my skin.

"Come for me, Cyra. I want to feel you tighten around me."

His hand threaded through my hair and drew me to him. His mouth crashed into mine, teeth scraping together as our tongues entwined.

"Come with me," I pleaded as we parted for air.

Water churned and splashed around us as though a miniature tempest roiled in the bathtub, and I reveled at the way our bodies slid against each other. I was nearing a precipice, and I threw my head back on a moan. Bressen nipped again at the throat I exposed to him, which only caused me to dig my nails into him harder.

My climax ripped through me as I cried out and pressed myself onto Bressen as far as I could. He roared his own release against my shoulder seconds later as he pinned me to him and erupted inside me. I clenched my thighs together around his hips as we rode out the storm of ecstasy.

I continued to rock against him, letting the water lap gently at us as we savored the last shuddering aftershocks of bliss. Bressen's hand trailed gently over my spine as my hand stroked the nape of his neck. The water settled around us, and I took his face in my hands to kiss him deeply.

"We should get out of the water," I said. "My fingers are pruning."

Bressen chuckled and held my hips to keep me steady as I lifted myself off him. We stepped out of the tub, and he wrapped me in one of the towels he'd left on a chair before grabbing his own.

I felt Bressen's seed drip out of me as I dried myself off, and I pressed my thighs together. I had no desire to get pregnant, but I loved the idea that some part of him remained inside me even after he'd withdrawn.

It was difficult for perimortals to conceive to begin with, but both of us also drank tea with turrow berries every morning as a contraceptive, just in case. I was twenty-two years old to Bressen's one hundred and seventeen, and I'd only met him a few months ago. Our relationship had progressed dramatically fast, but neither of us was ready for a child.

"You mentioned something about training me to use my powers," I said to Bressen as I slipped on the thin silk nightgown I wore to bed.

Bressen donned a loose pair of pants that hung low on his hips and showed off the defined V of muscles there. I'd been determined to learn the names of all the muscles that made up his incredible body, and his obliques were my favorite. Of course, every other muscle he had was in a close tie for second place.

"There's someone I can ask to help," he said as he led me to the bed. "He owes me a favor, and this is important enough to call it in."

"Samhail can't train me?"

"Samhail is a warrior. There's no one better than him to teach you hand-to-hand combat or how to use a sword, but it's your magic that needs training, and that's not Samhail's area of expertise."

I tried to mask my disappointment, but Bressen sensed it.

"I miss him too," he said gently, turning me to face him. "I was getting used to having him around before the coup, but he'll turn up again."

Bressen kissed me and pulled back the covers for me to get into bed, but my stomach growled before I could move.

He frowned at me. "Did you eat when you got back?"

"…Yes."

His frown deepened. "I may not have your truth-seeing abilities, but I know when you're lying," he admonished.

"I didn't feel like eating when we got back," I admitted. "Besides, you haven't eaten either."

"Then we should both have something before bed."

"Agreed," I said as I turned and opened a portal.

We both ducked through it into the kitchen, and a few minutes later we were back in our bedchamber with plates of cold meat, cheeses, bread, and a few sweets we'd pillaged.

"I'm sorry about tonight," I said as we sat cross-legged on the bed.

Bressen paused with a piece of meat halfway to his mouth. "What are you sorry about?"

"I was useless at Bronwyn. Worse than useless. I was a liability. I shouldn't have come."

"You have nothing to apologize for," he said. "You have a lot of power, but I forget you haven't been trained to use it. That's on me, but we'll remedy that shortly." He popped the meat into his mouth.

"Who's this person you know that can train me?" I asked.

He smiled. "I think you'll like him. He's unlike anyone you'll have met before, but I want you to form your own first impression of him."

I narrowed my eyes. "Should I be worried? Is he the Samhail of magical training?"

I'd learned quickly that Samhail was a bit of a taskmaster in training, as my frequent bruises could attest to when he was here.

He chuckled. "Not at all. You might find working with him a nice change of pace, but I have every confidence he can teach you to use your powers in a way that will make the fear people already feel toward you completely justified."

Bressen turned to the platter of sweets we'd brought up, oblivious to the look of shock and horror on my face at his words.

I wanted to learn to use my powers, but justifying people's fear of me was further than I wanted to go. Instilling a healthy wariness in them maybe, but I had no intention of becoming the new Nemesis Incarnate. I was happy to leave that role to Bressen.

# Chapter 6

As we stood outside the ballroom the next night ready to celebrate Aidan's ascendancy to the Triumvirate, I marveled at how much had changed since my first ball at the Citadel. I'd been a frightened girl back then, a prisoner of the Triumvirate in all but name. Now I entered as Lady of Hiraeth, consort to the most powerful Triumvirate lord Thasia had seen in centuries.

Not that I cared about those titles. I was entering as the woman Bressen loved, and that meant far more to me than anything else.

The herald announced us, and a cheer went up from the crowd within as we entered to thunderous applause.

*Do you think they're all still afraid that being near you will cause their brains to leak out of their heads?* I asked into Bressen's mind when I saw more than a few wary looks in the crowd, despite our warm reception.

Samhail had told me at the last ball that people considered it a status symbol to be near Bressen and not have this happen.

*No, they're probably more worried you'll suck all the power out of them and leave dried husks in your wake,* he answered back lightly.

My head jerked toward him, and he gave me a sidelong smile that I couldn't bring myself to return.

*Give them time,* Bressen said. *They'll learn to love you as I do.*

*I hope not,* I answered back. *I get so very little sleep as it is.*

Bressen nearly choked as he tried to hold in his laugh, but his gaze smoldered when he glanced at me.

*I hope you rested earlier because you won't get any sleep tonight either,* he promised.

I sent a sigh heavy with mock weariness into his mind and said, *If such is my burden, so be it.*

Bressen chuckled out loud, causing more than one person to glance at him curiously.

We crossed the room to take our places at a table on the dais while the herald introduced Aidan as the new Triumvirate lord for the Derridan territory. The room once again erupted in applause, and I couldn't help my jealousy at the genuine excitement and affection on everyone's faces.

Aidan and Jasper entered triumphantly and went straight to the dance floor to start the first dance of the evening. The music struck up, and I was immediately mesmerized by their skill as they swept into motion. Jasper was leading, and while I wasn't an expert, it seemed obvious there was something special about his synthesis with the music. His movements not only flowed with it, but almost seemed to enhance it.

"They're wonderful dancers," I said, a bit awed.

"They are," Bressen said, but something in his tone told me his competitiveness with Aidan was once again flaring.

"Please don't drag me into your rivalry with Aidan," I said.

I didn't know how to dance, but Bressen could plant the steps in my mind, as he'd done the first time we danced, and I was wary of his desire to show up Aidan and Jasper.

"The thought crossed my mind," Bressen admitted, "but I promise to behave myself."

The music wound down, and Aidan and Jasper took their bows before we exchanged places with them on the dance floor. Bressen placed his hand on my back near my shoulder blade, and I felt my mind fill with the steps of the dance. The music started, and he swept us into motion.

True to his word, Bressen didn't overdo it, although I did sense him add a couple flourishes here and there.

"You couldn't help yourself, could you," I teased as we returned to the dais.

Bressen gave me an unapologetic wink and held a space up between his thumb and forefinger to indicate he'd only embellished a little.

I rolled my eyes.

"You're excellent dancers," Jasper said when Bressen and I returned.

"Thank you," Bressen said before I could explain how I'd only been along for the ride. "You are as well."

The music started up again, and we watched as other couples took to the floor. There was no formal plan for the evening, and our spot at the table on the dais was only to give us somewhere to retreat to if we needed to get away from the swarm of people crowding the ballroom. We'd already had dinner earlier with a few dozen of Thasia's nobles.

"I see Raina," I said to Bressen, catching sight of my friend across the room. "I'm going to go say hello."

He nodded but hooked a hand around my neck to bring my lips to his first. His kiss, always full of promise, never failed to send warmth spreading through my body, and I rose on unsteady legs to go meet Raina.

My friend, and potential heir apparent to the Triumvirate seat of Polaris, was standing with several of the High Council members when I approached. The members all inclined their heads toward me and greeted me by title, smiling respectfully if not genuinely.

Only one of the members present was perimortal, Lord Marcus of Karch, and he hovered a step or two back from the group as I approached. I tried to remember what his power was but couldn't, and I was tempted to reach out and shake each member's hand effusively, just to see if he'd recoil from my touch. I decided on a more subtly aggressive strategy.

"Raina, we miss you up on the dais," I said as I hugged her warmly. "I hope the council can get your induction as Lady of Polaris sorted out soon so we can have one of these balls in your honor next."

My eyes met those of each council member in turn, and I hoped the smile I gave them held a good balance of optimism and threat. The members returned my grin with tight, nervous smiles of their own.

If people wanted to fear me, fine. I'd put that fear to good use.

"The council is, of course, doing their due diligence," Raina said diplomatically, her own smile telling me she knew what I was doing.

"I'm sure your ladyship is aware of how complicated the situation is," a tall man with deep brown skin and graying hair said to me.

Lord Varun of Turlan. He'd been one of Ursan's generals in his younger years and had later taken a place as chancellor to Ursan when he retired from combat. He was also the only High Council member who didn't seem to fear me or Bressen.

"While Lady Raina does have a blood claim to the seat of Polaris," Varun went on, "she isn't the only one. As you know, Lady Glenora's child has a potentially stronger claim."

"Lady Glenora's as-yet unborn child, you mean?" I asked. "The one she still carries in Revenmyer where she's currently imprisoned for murder and sedition? Is that the child you mean?"

Varun wasn't cowed in the least.

"The child is innocent of its mother's crimes," he said, "and if it turns out to be Lord Ursan's, then it is the legitimate heir to Polaris's seat."

"And if it turns out to be Jerram's, then it's the bastard of two traitors and should have no claim whatsoever," I shot back.

I regretted the words as soon as they were out of my mouth. Varun was right. The child was innocent and didn't deserve to be held responsible for its parents' crimes, whoever those parents might be. If the babe survived Revenmyer, I'd personally ensure it was raised in a loving home, but waiting around for the child to reach maturity – if it was Ursan's – wasn't an option.

Varun opened his mouth, but I spoke before he could.

"My apologies, Lord Varun," I said. "I understand that none of this is the child's fault and that if it is Ursan's, supporting Raina's claim now could cause significant issues in the future. However, you know as well as I do that Thasia is especially vulnerable right now. We can't afford to be without a full Triumvirate, should our enemies decide to take advantage. As admirable a job as the High Council has done so far in the wake of the coup and Lord Ursan's death, it's not a long-term solution. It will be a decade at least before Glenora's child is able to rule – whoever its father may be – and you know we can't wait that long to fill Polaris's seat. Raina may be illegitimate by birth, but she is Lord Ursan's daughter, and her claim to the Triumvirate seat is valid. More importantly, she's old enough and more than capable enough to assume that seat."

Raina's hand went to the center of her chest unconsciously to rest over the birthmark between her breasts. For reasons I never knew, Ursan had always borne a white heart-shaped mark on his chest whenever he transformed into an animal, and the black bears he'd used to spy on the other territories bore them as well. Likewise, Raina also carried the heart-shaped mark on her chest that forever branded her as Ursan's.

I wondered if Glenora's unborn child even now bore such a mark.

"Believe me, Lady Cyra," Varun said, "the council is very aware of all this, and we're doing our best to find a solution that will cause the least amount of strife, both now and in the future."

I clenched my teeth together and felt a muscle tick in my jaw as I forced a smile onto my face.

"Of course, Lord Varun. As Raina said, I'm sure the council is doing their due diligence. I only hope they find a solution before our enemies come knocking."

Varun made to speak again, but this time a councilwoman whose name escaped me cut him off.

"That's enough talk of politics tonight, I think," she said. "We should leave the two of you to visit."

She looked from me to Raina, and then turned to leave. Following her lead, the other council members drifted away as well.

"Thank the gods they're gone," Raina said rolling her eyes when the last member had dissolved into the crowd. "I really appreciate having a friend who scares the shit out of everyone," she said, winking at me.

The smile I attempted failed.

"What's wrong?" Raina asked at my tight expression.

"Nothing. It's just not as exciting to actually be the friend who scares the shit out of everyone as you might think."

Raina gave me a sympathetic look. "I'm sorry. I didn't mean-"

I waved her apology away. "It's fine. I should be used to it by now. Half the people in Fernweh were afraid of me even before I knew I was a syphon. I just hoped things would be different here."

Raina took my hand. "It's easier to fear you from afar than to get to know you and realize how gentle and kind you are."

My smile this time was genuine as I hugged her. "Thank you. I miss seeing you every day."

"You miss having someone do your hair and get you dressed in the morning," she teased.

I laughed. "That too, but mostly I miss playing cards with you at night or talking about…well, everything."

Raina raised a brow. "Not everything. If we'd talked about everything, I would've known sooner that you were fucking the Nemesis Incarnate."

"You're one to talk," I laughed. "I don't exactly recall you telling me one day over cards, 'By the way, Cyra, my father is one of the Triumvirate lords who's afraid you're going to destroy them. Oh, and I'm also a shapeshifter who can turn into a peregrine falcon.'"

"Fine," Raina said, holding up a hand in surrender. "Let's just agree we both left a few things out of our discussions."

"Agreed," I said but immediately felt a pang of guilt at the secret I was still keeping from her. I had yet to tell her about the night I'd spent with both Bressen and Samhail.

"I take it the council keeps a close eye on you?" I asked Raina, changing the subject.

"They rarely leave my side when I'm out of the palace," she grumbled. "They chaperone me like I'm some wayward teenager who's going to give my virginity to the next man who looks at me."

I gave her a wry look. "What virginity?"

Raina only grinned at me and waggled her eyebrows.

"Have you heard from Damian?" I asked.

She shook her head, then scanned the room as if looking for the guard in question.

"It's too difficult with him here in Callanus and me in Gendris," she said when she didn't find him. "I think it also scared him to learn I was Ursan's daughter. There's nothing between us anymore."

Half of my discussions with Raina when I first came to the Citadel had been about her frustrations at not being able to get Damian, a guard in Bressen's service, to move their relationship to a more physical level. Raina had finally taken matters into her own hands on the Harmilan, but it seemed she and Damian weren't meant to be.

"I'm so sorry to hear that," I said genuinely.

Raina shrugged. "I have my pick of the guards in Gendris."

My eyes widened. "Raina!"

She gave me a conspiratorial grin just before her gaze shifted to something over my shoulder. I turned to find Jasper standing behind me.

"Jasper," I said in surprise, stepping back to let him join me and Raina. "How are you this evening?"

"I'm very well," he said with a bow of his head. He reached for my hand, but I instinctively pulled it back before remembering once more that he was mortal and had no powers. Humor danced in his eyes as I extended my hand again, and he brushed a kiss across my knuckles.

"Lady Raina," Jasper said as he kissed her hand as well. "Are you enjoying the evening?"

"I am," she said, giving him a warm smile. "Please, call me Raina."

"Of course, Raina," he said with another dip of his head. "I do hope you'll be joining our little Triumvirate group soon?"

Raina rolled her eyes and shook her head. "Not likely. As I told Cyra, the High Council is enjoying its time in the sun and showing no signs of being ready to cede their power. Even if they do eventually hand over the reins, there's still no guarantee it will be to me."

"How very unwise of them not to see your potential," Jasper said.

"Thank you," Raina said. "In their defense, I'm only half perimortal, and I spent the last few years of my life as a lady's maid. I'm hardly qualified to be a Lady of the Triumvirate."

"Nonsense," I said. "I saw firsthand just how much of the inner workings of the Citadel you were privy to as my lady's maid. I'm sure you already know half of what you need to, and you're more than smart enough to figure out the rest."

The High Council also had Raina attending lessons in everything from etiquette to diplomacy, just in case they did indeed need her to take a Triumvirate seat one day. As a former member of the Citadel staff, Raina had already been trained in some etiquette and how to speak more formally, but I was also serious about her being smart and observant.

"Cyra is my biggest advocate," Raina said to Jasper, "but she forgets I was afraid of my own shadow for much of the time when she first met me. I only just recently found my voice, and it will take me some time yet to learn exactly when and how to use it most effectively."

"I have no doubt you will," Jasper said.

"Thank you," Raina said, "but I'm sure you didn't come over here to bolster my ego. To what do we owe the pleasure of your company?"

"Well, I should apologize in advance for that," Jasper said. "I had an ulterior motive for coming over. I need to borrow Cyra for a bit."

"Me?" I asked in surprise.

Raina raised a brow. "I'm intrigued. Do tell."

Jasper extended his hand out for mine again. "Would you honor me with a dance, Cyra?"

Shock bloomed on my face, even as panic bubbled in my stomach.

"Oh, I don't think that's a good idea," I said. "I'm flattered you'd ask, but I have two left feet when it comes to dancing."

"You're too modest. What I saw earlier belies that," Jasper said.

I smiled wryly at him. "You forget who my fiancé is. Or rather, you forget what his power is."

Jasper paused before understanding dawned on his face, followed by surprise. "You mean Bressen-"

"Puts the steps in my head when we dance," I finished for him. "I'm afraid I'm only as good as he's able to make me."

Jasper nodded with appreciation. "I have to admit, I was impressed with Bressen's dancing before, but I'm even more impressed to know he was dancing for two."

"I've always thought of it more as me as the puppet, and he just controls my strings," I said.

"Regardless, you sell yourself short," Jasper said, "and I'd like the chance to prove it to you. Trust me when I tell you Aidan had three left feet when I met him. I swear he grew the extra one only when we danced and solely for the purpose of stepping on my feet."

I laughed. "I find that hard to believe."

"Aidan is a much better dancer now, but it's because I taught him to be," Jasper said. He leaned in and lowered his voice conspiratorially. "The footwork I taught him helped him win his combat trial in Derridan."

It was my turn to look approving. "That's fascinating. I doubt you'll be able to teach me much between now and the end of the night, though."

He just grinned. "You'd be surprised what I can teach you in such a short time, and now I'm determined for you to let me try. I have a feeling Bressen's…uh, assistance may have primed you for learning to dance, and I'm not too humble to admit I'm an excellent lead."

I sighed. Jasper's resolve was difficult to refuse, and the only way he'd see how hopeless I was as a dancer was by experiencing it himself, so I finally nodded and took his hand.

"Raina, do you mind?" I asked, but she only waved her hand.

"Go. I can't wait to see this," she said.

I only gave her a dubious look as Jasper led me away.

"We'll do something relatively simple this first time," he said as he stopped at the edge of the floor near the orchestra.

I laughed. "First time? I don't think you'll want to dance with me more than once after this."

As the music for the last song wound down, Jasper left me on the side to speak with the orchestra's conductor. He whispered something in her ear, and I saw her nod and say something back. Then Jasper returned to take my hand and lead me out onto the floor.

The crowd hushed as Jasper and I took our places, and my eyes sought Bressen. He stood with Aidan on one side of the room, an eyebrow quirked up at me. His expression showed surprise and something else I couldn't quite read. I gave him a look that said I didn't expect this to go well, but he just smiled. Next to him, Aidan looked far less pleased.

"Let me guide you," Jasper said as we took our places. "I'm going to lead you just as Bressen does, but instead of directing you in your mind, I'll talk you through the steps and lead you with my touch. Try to feel what you need to know based on the pressure from my hands."

"You'll be fine," he added when my face must have shown my panic.

The music started, and Jasper took one of my hands in his own while the other pressed firmly between my shoulder blades. I noticed immediately that he held me where Bressen did, higher up on my back as opposed to at my waist where others I'd danced with held me.

"We'll move on my count," Jasper said. "Just focus on me."

I was terrified, but I nodded, and Jasper gave my hand a reassuring squeeze. His voice was low as he quickly explained the pattern of the beat to me, and then there was no more time to prepare. Jasper nodded a count to me, and we were moving.

I managed to forget everything else and focus on Jasper's voice as he gave me simple directions, letting me know just before we changed course what to expect. To my surprise, I followed him without too much trouble.

"Three steps back then slide to your right," he said, just loud enough for me to hear it above the music, and amazingly, my body did as he said. His hands guided me gently, pushing and pulling me where I needed to go only a fraction of a second before my body had to react. He'd been right. The combination of his words and touch worked much like

Bressen's mental prompts. Our dance wasn't as smooth as when I danced with Bressen, but I'd gotten the hang of it by the end.

"Time for our big finish," Jasper said as the end of the song neared.

"Big finish?" I asked in alarm.

"Trust me. I'll spin you, then end with a small dip."

"That sounds complicated," I argued.

"Not at all. Here we go, and spin…"

Jasper pulled my hand toward him and over my head so I spun into him. As I did, he caught my waist, and the hand that held mine moved to the center of my back.

"Bend your right knee," Jasper whispered as he urged me backward into the dip, and I sank gracefully into it, cradled in his arms as my other leg slid out straight.

The music ended, and we were met with applause that was more enthusiastic than I expected. Jasper pulled me back to my feet and brought my hand to his lips for another kiss.

"Thank you for the dance," he said. "I appreciate your indulgence in what I'll admit was some friendly competition with your fiancé."

"I thought Aidan was the competitive one."

"Normally he is, but dancing is the one thing that brings out my need to show off a bit. My apologies for that."

An idea occurred to me then, and a sly smile crossed my lips as Jasper led me off the floor toward Aidan and Bressen.

"I have a favor to ask if you'd like to make it up to me," I said.

Jasper's brows lifted. "I'm intrigued. More importantly, I can't refuse a favor to a lady. What can I do for you?"

I told him what I wanted. He nodded enthusiastically when I was done and readily agreed to my request just as we reached Bressen and Aidan.

"My apologies for borrowing your fiancé," Jasper said, placing my hand in Bressen's. "I'd have made my intentions known earlier, but I find its always easier to ask for forgiveness than permission."

"This was perhaps the exception to that rule," Aidan muttered to him.

"Not at all," Bressen said pulling me gently against him so my back pressed against his chest. "I was thoroughly entertained, and I commend your skills as a lead, Jasper. No need for either forgiveness or permission."

Bressen's arm was around my waist, his hand resting on my hip, in a way I knew meant he was claiming me. My heart missed a beat as he ran his thumb lazily against me, the subtle gesture promising all the other ways he'd reinforce his claim when we were alone later tonight.

I didn't think Bressen was jealous of Jasper, but I had a feeling the Lord Consort's success in our dance had stirred something competitive in Bressen that would manifest later in ways I'd enjoy.

"Nevertheless, my husband shouldn't have imposed on you, Cyra," Aidan said. "I'm not sure what he was thinking."

I had the feeling his concern was less for me and more for Jasper.

"I was thinking I wanted to dance and that it might be nice to ask either Bressen or Cyra as a way to solidify our new partnership with them," Jasper said lightly to his husband. "I didn't think Bressen would let me lead, so I asked Cyra."

"He's right," Bressen said with amusement, cutting off Aidan's retort. "I wouldn't have let him lead. He made the right call in asking Cyra."

Aidan flashed Jasper a look that suggested there was more to his annoyance, and it occurred to me Jasper felt bad that neither Aidan nor Maziren would touch me, and dancing with me was his way of protesting their behavior. I suspected they'd had an earlier conversation on the subject, and I suddenly appreciated Jasper's invitation to dance that much more. I gave him a grateful smile, and he winked back at me.

My spirits were still high hours later as Bressen and I returned to our room. We'd danced again several times that evening, but each dance seemed to notch up the competition between Bressen, Aidan, and Jasper, and I'd finally told Bressen it was time to go. He'd been reluctant at first until I'd clarified that we just needed to go to bed…not to sleep.

"I didn't have time to tell you earlier, but your new trainer will be here tomorrow," Bressen said as he opened the door to our rooms.

Excitement swelled inside me. I was eager to add some kind of activity back into my daily routine, and I hoped whoever Bressen found was as good as Samhail, although no one could ever really replace him.

"I'll let you know when he's ready to see you, and you'll meet him in the Great Chamber sometime in the morning," Bressen went on.

He followed me into the room with his hand on my waist, but as soon as the door clicked shut he pulled me back, and I found myself pressed between it and his body. He grabbed my wrists and pinned them above my head with one hand, and then his mouth was on mine, devouring me while his free hand explored my body. I groaned and arched into him. I struggled at his constraint, aching to touch him, but he held me fast.

"Seeing you dance with Jasper tonight drove me a little mad," he rasped into my ear. "It took all my strength not to drag you up here and fuck you the moment he handed you back."

I'd suspected as much at the time, but hearing him say the words sent a thrill through me as wetness pooled between my thighs.

"You're not jealous of Jasper, are you?" I asked.

"No, not in the way you mean, in any case," he said.

"Jasper said he felt competitive with you about dancing."

He chuckled. "I feel the same way apparently." His free hand pulled the skirt of my dress up then hooked on the waist of my undergarment and yanked it down. I shimmied my legs to help it the rest of the way as Bressen's lips traced a searing path down my neck.

"Should we get to the bed?" I asked.

"We're not going to make it to the bed," Bressen said as he worked at the fastenings of his pants.

He managed to free his erection, and his hand finally released mine so he could grab me under my ass and lift me onto him. I moaned as he slid me onto his hard length, and I wrapped myself around him as he thrust into me, the unyielding door at my back pressing him into me to the hilt. He drove into me hard, and little cries of bliss punctuated each breath I took as he fucked me, his lips and tongue still roving over my neck.

The tension built at my core as Bressen slammed into me, and I welcomed each punishing drive as my legs tightened around him.

And this was indeed a punishment of sorts, although a playful and welcome one. Bressen had told Jasper he didn't need to ask permission or forgiveness, but the same didn't apply to me. I hadn't asked for either, and now Bressen was administering his 'punishment' for my indiscretion.

It was a game we'd started when he began teaching me to use my mind powers. Sex had become both a reward for my successes, but also a punishment for my failures. The nature of the sex was determined by the outcome of my efforts. Rough sex was – ostensibly – a punishment.

That either outcome ended in sex wasn't something we concerned ourselves with in the least. Nor did Bressen question that I seemed to fail almost as often as I succeeded.

My inner muscles clenched around him as I exploded with my release, and shivers danced over my skin. He groaned into my shoulder a few thrusts later and collapsed against me, pinning me to the door. I kept myself wrapped tightly around him to keep from sliding down his body.

Bressen pulled away from the door and anchored an arm around me, but instead of taking me to the bed as I expected, he sank down onto his knees, so I was now sitting on his thighs.

"Are you alright?" I asked as I cupped his cheek. Strands of night-black hair clung to the edges of his face, and I wiped them back.

"Nemesis damn me, I love you," he rasped, pulling me closer.

I wasn't sure what prompted his surge of emotion, but I only tightened my embrace and whispered into his ear. "I love you, too."

"Sometimes I don't believe you're really mine," he said.

"I am, and you're mine."

He rested his forehead against my own and nodded.

Without warning, Bressen got to his feet, his cock still sheathed inside me. He was so strong. I always marveled at how he could lift and carry me with such little effort. He walked to the bed, and it wasn't until we reached it that he finally lifted me off him and set me down.

We finished undressing before climbing in together, and he curled himself around me. It was only a minute or so before I felt his even breathing, and I sent a light wind to blow out the lamps in the room. I reveled in the feel of him against me and the words of love he'd seemed so compelled to say tonight.

I understood his need to say them. I was often awed by the events that had led us to find each other, and I too needed to remind myself occasionally it was all real. Bressen was mine, I was his, and we were only just starting what I hoped would be a long and wonderful life together.

# Chapter 7

Despite Bressen's insistence that Samhail wasn't an appropriate trainer to help me learn my powers, I still half hoped to see him standing in the Great Chamber the next morning when I entered fifteen minutes after getting Bressen's message. He'd told me through our mental link that the trainer was here and asked me to meet them. The chamber was empty when I arrived, though.

I was about to send Bressen a message when I sensed another consciousness in the room and whirled around. The smile of greeting I expected to give Samhail froze on my face as I spotted the figure leaning against the wall in the shadow of one of the doors. The man was large, but not enough to be Samhail, and my last hopes of seeing my friend scattered like fallen leaves on an autumn wind.

"Are you my new trainer?" I asked.

The man didn't answer, and I stepped closer.

"Who are you?" I asked.

This time his head came up, and he pushed off the wall to walk toward me. I was ready to act as I reached out into his mind to determine who he was, but not surprisingly, he had a shield up.

My eyes flared as he stepped forward, his tall, muscular body bespeaking an obvious warrior's physique. His deep garnet hair was shaved on one side of his head above his ear, but it fell past his shoulders on the other, and his bright cerulean eyes were striking against it.

What drew my attention most, though, was the iridescent blue-green sheen of his skin when it caught the light. I could only see the skin on his face and hands, but I swore it shimmered when he moved.

"Lady Cyra, I presume," the man said, and there was a natural sensuousness to his voice that made me raise an eyebrow at him.

"You presume correctly. Now, for the final time, who are you?"

"Cyra, this is Axenus," Bressen said from the doorway, drawing my eyes to him. "You'll have to excuse his dramatics."

Axenus smiled and stepped forward, reaching out a hand to take mine.

I pulled away and looked at Bressen, sending my question into his mind.

"He knows you're a syphon," Bressen answered me out loud, "and he understands what will happen if you touch him."

I looked back at Axenus, and his eyes seemed to flash. He held out his hand to me again, and I shook it.

"It's a pleasure to meet you, my lady," Axenus said in that same sultry purr, and I glanced at Bressen to see what he made of the tone. He seemed unperturbed by it.

"It's nice to meet you," I said. "I'm told you'll be training me to use my powers?"

"I'm looking forward to being of service."

I saw now up close that Axenus's skin did indeed have an iridescent luster. I wanted to ask what he was, but it seemed rude to do so.

Either sensing my question, or simply because he knew I'd want to know, Bressen satisfied my curiosity.

"Axenus is a merman," he said as he came over and slipped an arm around my waist. "His home is the northeastern Aspan Ocean off of Hiraeth, but he agreed to come to Callanus to begin your training here before we go back to Solandis in a couple weeks."

My eyes widened a bit. I'd heard rumors of the existence of merpeople, but I'd never seen one before. The outer lands of Polaris where I'd lived bordered the Prosperon Sea, but merpeople were said to prefer larger, deeper bodies of water like oceans.

A man in Fernweh who'd once worked as a fisherman claimed to have seen a mermaid out in the Prosperon, but there'd been a healthy bit of skepticism to his claim, largely because of his fondness for ale.

In any case, it was said that merpeople rarely came up on land at all, even less so to stay for more than an hour or two, and I frowned as my gaze instinctively went to Axenus's muscular legs. His knowing chuckle drew my eyes back up to his face.

"I can shift form to walk on land for up to two or three days before I need to return to the water," he said, and I realized as he spoke that the tone I'd heard in his voice had less of a sensual quality and more of a liquid one. His voice flowed over words the way water flowed over stones.

"Are you a syphon as well?" I asked Axenus, a little confused as to how he was going to train me to use my powers.

"No, my lady. My power is to manipulate water."

"I asked Axenus to help you because he's a natural teacher," Bressen explained, "and because he's studied and understands the nature of magic on a fundamental level. He doesn't need to have the same powers as you in order to instruct you. You and I will continue to work on your mind powers together when we can, but Axenus will work with you on everything else."

There was a wicked gleam in Bressen's eyes that I understood well enough, given that our mind training sessions almost always ended with us having sex. We seemed to have set a precedent with the first lesson Bresson ever gave me early on in our relationship. He'd been trying to get me to put up a mind shield and decided to 'motivate' me by bending me over his desk and administering an erotic torment while I struggled to concentrate. He'd withheld my climax – and his own – until I managed to put up my mind shield.

Axenus shot me a curious look as I failed to hide the blush that rose on my cheeks at the memory, and I had to look away from him.

"You should probably let us get started then," I said to Bressen, eager to get him out of here before my body reacted with more than just a blush. Indeed, the hand he held lightly on my hip seemed to burn through the fabric of my pants.

Bressen raised a brow at the dismissal but then leaned in and kissed my temple, letting his lips and breath caress me in a promise.

I tried to hold back my shiver of pleasure but couldn't contain it, and I felt him smile against my skin.

"I'll leave you in Axenus's capable care," he said before slowly pulling his arm from around my waist.

He nodded to the merman. "Axe."

"My lord," Axenus said, nodding back.

And with that, Bressen strode from the room as the doors to the Great Chamber swung shut behind him.

"Thank you for doing this," I said to Axenus. "I'm grateful."

"Not at all, my lady. I'm always happy to assist the Lord of Hiraeth and his intended."

"Please, call me Cyra."

"Of course, Cyra," he said with a bob of his head. "First I need to know what powers you can access. What have you syphoned so far?"

I thought a moment. It had been a while since I'd taken stock of my powers.

"I've always had elemental abilities," I said, "and I syphoned Bressen's mind powers, of course. My father is a healer, and my mother was a dream walker, although I don't actually know what that means. I can create forcefields and portals, and I can summon. I have truth seer abilities as well as negation powers. I likely have Lord Ursan's shapeshifting and animal control powers, but I've never tried to use them."

I went down my mental checklist again. "Those are the powers I know about anyway. It's possible I picked up others I'm not aware of."

"How many of Bressen's mind abilities can you use?"

I noted he dropped the "Lord" from Bressen's name, and I resolved to ask one of them later how they knew each other.

"I can read minds, and Bressen has been teaching me to break down mind shields. I can control others to a degree if they don't have a shield."

Axenus cocked his head. "Is that everything?"

I paused, assuming he was waiting for me to address Bressen's most infamous power.

"Bressen doesn't think I have the ability or the disposition to kill someone as he can, if that's what you're asking."

"Do you want to be able to kill someone with your mind?" he asked.

I thought again. "I want…options."

He nodded. "So you're the child of a healer and a dream walker?"

"My father is a gifted healer. I'm merely a competent one. I can heal cuts and mend bones, and I pulled poison from Bressen's body during the attempted coup. As far as dream walking, I don't know much about what that entails. I only know…" I trailed off, not sure I wanted to tell Axenus about my one and only experience dream walking.

"You only know what?" he prompted.

"I…I've only done it once, and not on purpose."

He looked at me for several seconds. "Bressen," he said. A statement, not a question.

"Yes, Bressen and I met in a dream about a week before I was summoned to the Citadel."

His brows shot up. "You hadn't met Bressen yet when you appeared in his dream?"

"No, not that I'm aware of. Except for the first few months after I was born, I've lived my entire life in the outer lands of Polaris, and I don't think Bressen has ever been out there."

Axenus nodded slowly.

"What do you know about dream walking?" I asked him.

He shrugged. "On its most basic level, it's just as you discovered, the ability to enter someone else's dreams. I've never heard of someone being able to do it with a person they didn't know, but I'll confess my knowledge of mind magics is not as strong as my knowledge of physical ones."

"It seems like an odd power to me. I'm not sure I see the use of it."

"No?" he asked, quirking a brow at me again.

I shrugged. "What use is it?"

"In some ways, dream walking is very much akin to Bressen's mind powers," he said. "If you learned to control your walking, you could enter a person's mind when they were asleep and learn their deepest desires or their worst fears. You could also influence a person's dreams by giving them nightmares or planting ideas in their head. If you so chose, you could haunt their dreams so they were afraid to sleep, and they'd go mad."

My jaw had gone slack by the time he finished. "I couldn't. I…"

"No, I don't think you could," he agreed, watching me closely. "You have the ability, but I can see already you don't have the inclination to do something like that. Not yet anyway."

He motioned for me to move further into the room, and we made our way to the center.

"Show me your elemental powers," Axenus said, stopping a good fifteen feet from me and crossing his arms over his chest.

I blinked at the sudden shift in subject, but I summoned some flames to my hands and held them out for him to see.

"More," he said.

I willed the fire to flare higher in my hands.

"More," he said again.

I tried again, but the flames wouldn't go any higher, and I let them die. "That's as high as I've ever been able to get them to go."

"Water," he said.

It seemed more like an order than a request, but I held my hands apart in front of my chest and summoned some water. I'd practiced this a bit recently and was now able to do more with the element than just shoot it from my hands. I coaxed the water into a large sphere that hovered between my palms and looked at Axenus.

"Shape it into something else," he said. "A fish. Make it swim."

I eyed him for a moment, then shrugged and tried to will the water into the form he requested. I managed to shape it into something that writhed and flopped in the air, but Axenus's wry look of amusement told me it wasn't quite the gracefully swimming fish he'd wanted to see.

"Fill this chamber with water," he said as I dispelled my 'fish.'

I blinked at him. "What?"

"Fill the chamber with water. Water is my power as well, remember," he added when I looked at him in alarm. "I won't let anything get out of control, but I want to see you try and flood this place."

That was a tall order, but I took a deep breath and concentrated on summoning as much water as I could. It was several seconds before anything happened, but then water welled up from the floor as if seeping through the stone. There was only a little at first, but soon more and more gushed in, and Axenus and I were standing in half an inch of water that was slowly rising. Axenus surveyed the liquid slowly creeping up from the floor, and I wondered how high he'd let it get before he stopped me.

"Not bad," he said finally when I'd filled the room about two inches. "Slow, but still a decent amount of water. Now send it back."

I hesitated. Once I called some water, it usually ended up in a bucket, a bowl, or splashed in someone's face, but I concentrated on returning the water to where it'd come from, and the level began to go down. It was a couple minutes before it fully receded, and several seconds more before I was able to pull the last of the moisture from my boots and Axenus's so they were once again dry.

Axenus nodded approvingly. "Very good. I was afraid I'd have to dry our boots myself, but you seem to have decent control of your water abilities. What about earth?"

"I haven't done anything with earth since…since I killed the bear," I said, hoping Bressen had already told him this story so I didn't have to relive it. Thankfully Axenus seemed to know what I was talking about.

"Summon a handful of earth," he said.

I held out my hand and willed it to fill with earth, but it remained resolutely empty. I tried again, but I was secretly relieved when it failed a second time. A strange, irrational fear had been coiling inside me as I waited for the dirt to appear, and its refusal to manifest loosened that coil.

"I can't," I said finally.

I waited for Axenus to insist I try again, but he only nodded. "Air," he said instead.

I knew by now Axenus wanted me to show him my strongest effort, so I let gusts of wind gather and swirl and build around me before I suddenly directed them straight at him. A look of surprise crossed his face as the winds slammed into him, and he staggered backward, only barely keeping his feet. I dropped the winds and waited to see his reaction, ready to apologize if he seemed angry.

He wasn't upset, though. Rather, he seemed impressed.

"Air is clearly your element," he said. "There's still room for improvement, but of the four, it's the one where you seem to have the most power, the most control, and the least inhibition."

I smiled, strangely proud to hear him say so.

"Now show me a forcefield," he said.

I looked around the room, wondering what might sustain the least damage if I hit it with one of my forcefields, but Axenus saw the direction of my thoughts and shook his head. "No, hit *me* with your forcefield."

"I…don't want to hurt you," I said.

He smiled. "It's amusing that you think you can. Now hit me."

I narrowed my eyes. I wasn't sure if he was challenging me or just patronizing me, but either way it raised my hackles. Fine. If he wanted a forcefield, he'd get a forcefield.

I threw both hands out toward him and put everything I had into the forcefield that reverberated out from me in a wave of blurred energy. The wave pulsed toward Axenus, but just before it hit him, a wall of water rose up in front of him to block the forcefield's path. There was a crack like thunder as the forcefield hit his water, and the wall rippled violently as it absorbed the energy of the field. For several long seconds, Axenus and I looked at each other through the water before it once again receded into nothingness.

"Another strength," Axenus said. "You syphoned that ability from Samhail, I assume?"

I blinked in surprise. "I…yes. You know Samhail?"

He sighed. "Oh, I know him," he said. "One more test now."

I raised a brow, not sure what to make of Axenus's reaction to the mention of Samhail, but before I could question him, he held up a hand in front of him, and a ball of water materialized to hover above his palm.

"Negate my power," he said.

I stiffened. The only time I'd ever used this ability was when I'd turned Jerram's own negation power back on him so I could free Bressen from his control. Bressen admitted to me several days after the attempted coup that feeling his power die had been one of the most terrifying experiences of his life, and I promised him I'd never use that power on him.

"Are you sure?" I asked.

Axenus just gave me a look that told me he was waiting for me to get on with it. I sighed heavily and concentrated on snuffing his power.

Nothing happened.

I tried again, but the ball of water still hovered above Axenus's hand, shimmering as it rotated slightly. I was about to tell him I couldn't do it when I remembered how close Jerram had stayed to Bressen when he'd negated his powers. Perhaps there was a threshold to this particular power, and I was simply too far away for it to work.

I took a step closer to Axenus and tried again, but the ball of water remained. Another step, but still the ball rotated in his palm. I took a third step, then a fourth before Axenus suddenly gasped and the ball let loose, splashing his hand and the floor.

He looked a little pale as he said, "That's enough."

I quelled the negation powers, and Axenus inhaled sharply.

"I have to admit, that was more disconcerting than I expected it to be," he said as he took a few more deep breaths.

"I'm sorry," I said, but he waved me off.

"I asked you to do it. You have nothing to apologize for."

"So will you be able to train me?"

Axenus nodded and crossed his arms over his chest again. "Yes, but our focus may be a little different than you're expecting."

I looked at him questioningly, and he went on.

"Despite your late start, you have a significant array of powers already. In fact, some of the first powers you syphoned aside from your elemental ones were from extremely powerful perimortals, like Bressen and Samhail. Some of your abilities are stronger than others, but your real issue, the one keeping you from being as powerful as you could be, isn't physical. It's mental."

I frowned at him, not understanding. The mental powers I'd gotten from Bressen were some of my strongest, and the easiest for me to wield.

"From what I've observed thus far," Axenus went on, "your powers are limited mainly by your inhibitions and your imagination. You've put a damper on them because you don't want to hurt anyone. It surprised me when your wind almost knocked me over because that was the first time you used your power in any kind of offensive way. You don't normally attack. From what Bressen said, you use your powers mainly for defense."

"I have no reason to attack anyone."

"Not until recently," he said, "but you've also internalized the idea that your powers are only for defense or other utilitarian purposes, and that's hampered your development of them. If your powers are a wagon, you've been riding them with the brake on. It's time to release that brake and push the wagon down a hill."

My eyes widened. "That sounds…dangerous."

"No more dangerous than letting you remain unprepared. You're no longer a winemaker. You're a known syphon and the Lady of Hiraeth. The future Lady of Hiraeth," he amended when I opened my mouth to correct him. "When you first entered this chamber, you asked me twice who I was before you finally insisted on the third time that I answer you. You can no longer afford the luxury of letting someone ignore your demands. Bressen would've asked me once before attempting to slash my mind open if I didn't answer. Samhail would have had both his swords at my throat for ignoring him."

Yes, he definitely knew Samhail.

"Bressen and Samhail are warriors," I pointed out. "They were trained to react that way."

"Exactly," he said, "and we need to train you to react that way as well."

I went still. I had a healthy respect for Bressen and Samhail's ability and willingness to kill when they needed to. It had saved my life on multiple occasions, but I wasn't sure I'd ever get to the point where I could take a life with the ease they seemed to do it. I'd tried to kill the man in Bronwyn, but my anger had been in control then. I couldn't imagine being able to do it without that rage driving me.

Axenus seemed to read my hesitation because his face softened.

"I understand this will be a big transition for you and one you may not want to make, but it's one you need to make if you're going to survive. You can no longer rely on a defensive approach. You must be willing to attack, even if you're not sure the threat is real. Do you understand?"

I nodded. I didn't like it, but I understood it.

"Now that you know what we'll be doing together, do you still want me to train you?"

The question surprised me. "I have a choice?"

"There's always a choice," Axenus said. "Yours is to learn how to attack or to continue to leave yourself vulnerable to being hurt, or worse."

I felt relief as I considered that I could just continue on as before and use my powers defensively. It would put me at more risk, but perhaps I could take that chance. I wanted to learn to use my powers better, but I wasn't sure I could accept the stipulation that came with that training, that I'd need to harden myself and learn to kill. I'd almost decided to decline Axenus's offer of training when he spoke again.

"If you won't accept my help for your own benefit, do it for Bressen's."

I frowned. "What do you mean?"

"I've known Bressen for a while," he said, "and I've never seen him like this. It was obvious from the conversation I had with him earlier that he's devoted to you. I don't know what happened that he decided to call me in, but I know if he hasn't already put himself in harm's way to keep you safe, he'll most certainly do so in the future. If you decide not to train, then you only make it more necessary for him to put himself at risk, and I have a feeling that's the last thing you want."

I glared at him. "That's not fair."

"Maybe not, but it's the truth."

I clenched my jaw, but he was right. "Alright. Teach me to think like a warrior then."

"Good. Just so you're aware, I'm going to tell Bressen everything I just told you about your strengths and weaknesses. He wants regular updates on your progress. If you object to that, you'll have to take it up with him. My debt is to him, so he's the one I report to."

I cocked my head at his mention of a debt. Bressen had called it a favor, but Axenus's description of it as a debt made it sound more serious.

"That's fine," I said, "so long as you tell me everything you tell him. If you have concerns about my progress, I want to hear about them directly from you. Bressen shouldn't know anything about my development unless you've already told me first. You can tell him that, or I will, but that's how this is going to work, or it won't work at all."

"I'll agree to that, and I'm certain Bressen will too. It's a fair demand and one that, if you don't mind me saying so, is the first truly authoritative thing you've said so far."

I narrowed my eyes at him, but he went on before I could respond.

"We'll meet here every morning at nine o'clock. As I understand it, you're used to training at that time."

I nodded, but my throat constricted. Nine o'clock had been my training time with Samhail, and it felt wrong to give it to someone else.

"I also have an assignment for you," Axenus said. "When you get here tomorrow, I want you to attack me."

My mouth fell open. "What?"

"Use whatever magic you want, but I want you to attack, no hesitation, no warning. You have until then to come to terms with this training and plan your attack, but your transition to an offensive mentality starts tomorrow. You have healing powers," he reminded me. "There's little you can do to me that you yourself can't heal."

I pursed my lips. Axenus must owe Bressen a large debt if he was willing to risk his own harm to help train me like this.

"Any magic I want?" I asked.

"Any magic but your negation powers," he amended.

I sighed inwardly as he closed the loophole I'd hoped to exploit.

"To be clear," Axenus said, "I'll defend myself from your attack, but if you break through my defenses, I'll owe you a reward."

"And if I don't?" I asked.

"Then I'll choose your punishment. A reasonable punishment," he added quickly when my eyes narrowed, "but an incentive for you to try your hardest to land an attack."

I nodded. "Fine. I agree."

Axenus smiled. "Good. Then tomorrow we'll see just how much of a killer instinct you really have."

# Chapter 8

At three minutes to nine the next morning, I stood outside the Great Chamber still trying to decide how to attack Axenus. The doors, which normally swung open of their own accord, remained shut, as if they knew I wasn't yet ready to enter the chamber. I'd spent most of the previous day considering my options, but by bedtime I still hadn't made a decision. I'd fallen asleep only to wake a few hours later and start worrying again.

My furiously working mind must have woken Bressen, because he'd turned over and pulled me against him.

"Why are you awake?" he'd murmured into my ear, and I'd told him about my assignment and my dilemma.

"You know you're only proving his point, right?" he'd said. "You don't usually have twenty-four hours to decide how to attack someone."

"You're not helping."

He'd only nuzzled his face further into my hair. "This is something you need to decide for yourself, but I can help you take your mind off the decision if you want."

"Oh?" I'd asked, intrigued.

He'd turned me on my back then before his head disappeared below the covers, and for the next several minutes, I had indeed forgotten all about my problem as I writhed on the bed under his tongue's ministrations.

Unfortunately, I was still as stumped the next morning, although perhaps not quite as tense as before.

It might've helped if Axenus had told me what his idea of a reward and punishment would be. My magic always worked better under pressure, and a sufficiently dire punishment might have motivated me.

The best I'd managed to do was discard a few options. Fire was out, both because that power had never worked well for me and because Axenus's water powers would too easily defeat my feeble flames.

Likewise, I'd eliminated any use of water. Anything I could do with water, Axenus could likely do ten times better.

My two best options were my wind or my forcefields. I'd caught Axenus off guard with my wind yesterday, but he'd probably be expecting it today. As for my forcefields, he'd already shown me his water shield could take care of those easily enough. Beyond that, I didn't have much left in my arsenal.

My healing powers and truth seeing abilities were useful, but they weren't offensive powers. Axenus suggested my dream walking could be used as a weapon, but I didn't know how to do it on purpose yet. Controlling animals or shifting as Ursan did were also as-yet untested powers that I didn't want to meddle with until I had Axenus's guidance.

I exhaled heavily outside the doors of the Great Chamber. I had maybe a minute left before Axenus expected me.

Bressen was right. This exercise only proved just how unwilling and unprepared I was to use my magic to fight. His advice at breakfast had been to use the power I felt most comfortable with, but that was probably the mind powers I'd syphoned from him.

My head snapped up. My mind powers. Axenus had forbidden me from using my negation ability, but he hadn't taken mind powers off the table. I rested my hand lightly on the door and felt inside the chamber for the merman's consciousness. I found it at the far end of the room, but he had his mind shield up.

That was only a small problem, though. Bressen had not only taught me how to strengthen my own shield over the last month, he'd also helped me practice breaking through the mind shields of others, namely his.

Bressen could put up varying levels of mind shields, so we'd started small, but I'd managed to break into his mind almost a dozen times now with him making the shield a little stronger each time. Given that Bressen had the most prodigious mind powers of any perimortal alive, it was quite a feat that I'd accomplished that much. I hadn't yet attempted to break into Bressen's mind with his shield at full strength, since there were significant risks to both him and me if we ever attempted it.

He'd helped me work on my stealth techniques as well. It wasn't necessarily difficult to hammer through another person's mind shield if I just needed to get past their defenses, but it was another thing entirely if I wanted to slip past their barrier without them realizing it. After Bressen taught me the basics of stealing past a shield, it became a game to see if I could break into his mind without him realizing it.

I'd ambushed him several times while he was working or exercising, and even once while he'd been bathing. At other times, I tried to break through his shield while we were doing things like eating meals, talking, or even having sex.

I found it especially difficult to break past his shield when we were talking. I tended to lose my train of thought, and it became all too obvious what I was doing.

As for trying to concentrate while he was moving inside me or his head was between my legs…well, I was especially bad at focusing then. Not that I was motivated to try very hard at those times.

My reward if I succeeded in breaking past Bressen's shield was that I got to implant a command in his head to prove I'd gotten through. He was powerful enough to eventually override any commands I gave him, but he'd agreed not to do so as long as my demand was reasonable.

My most successful attempt had been recently when I'd slipped past his shield one morning while he was getting dressed. He was just putting on his shirt when I broke through, and he'd suddenly dropped to the floor to do the hundred pushups I'd ordered. I strolled into the room and took a triumphant seat on his back while he pressed up and down, all the while promising his revenge.

In answer, I'd simply stretched out so I was laying on top of him, my back to his, and told him to let me know when he was ready for breakfast.

Breakfast had been delayed because the second Bressen finished his hundred pushups, he'd bucked me onto the floor, rolled over on top of me, hiked up my skirt, and buried himself inside me. I certainly hadn't objected. I'd even been impressed he wasn't the least bit winded as he drove into me, and we'd climaxed together, pushing each other higher through our mental connection the way birds ride the wind of those in flight with them.

All this was to say, I'd practiced breaking past a mind shield often enough that it was my best shot against Axenus.

I sent soft tendrils of my power out across the Great Chamber toward the merman through the doors. When they reached him, my mind caressed his shield like a warm breeze.

Bressen had taught me that the first touch needed to be the most delicate, subtle enough that the consciousness either didn't notice it or treated it like background noise, unworthy of attention. Only after that initial brush could I push further, increasing the pressure on the shield so my incursion was gradual enough as to be imperceptible, as constant and unnoticeable as the feeling of wearing clothes.

My abilities had come a long way in the last few months, and a touch like the one I brushed against Axenus's shield now was faint enough that not even Bressen would've noticed it at first. Still, I went slowly, not pressing any harder until I was certain Axenus's mind had accepted my presence in it as nothing more than a whisp of air. I pressed a bit harder and exhaled slowly as his mind remained relaxed. Just a little further…

I shrieked as gallons upon gallons of icy water suddenly crashed down onto my head. I sputtered as it trickled down my back, sending chills through me, and my clothes clung to my body, cold and heavy. I blinked the water from my eyes as I looked at the puddle in which I now stood, then turned the handle to open one of the doors into the chamber.

I could've dried myself before going in, but I decided to let Axenus enjoy his victory. After all, seeing the triumph on his face would only motivate me to try harder next time.

I wasn't disappointed. Axenus sat at the far end in Bressen's chair with his leg thrown over one of the arms, and his expression went from amused to absolutely delighted when I walked in soaking wet.

I crossed the chamber, my boots squishing loudly as I trailed water along the floor to where Axenus sat. Before he could speak, I raised my hand and loosed a forcefield at him. He grunted as it hit him in the chest and the heavy Triumvirate chair skidded backward with him in it.

Axenus coughed as the blow knocked the wind out of him, and he took his leg down. He stood and approached me while I dried myself off by pulling the water out of my hair and clothes.

He grinned at me. "I knew the kitten had claws in there somewhere," he said. His voice was a purr, and I resisted the urge to hit him with another forcefield.

"You sensed me trying to break past your mind shield?" I asked.

"It was an impressive attempt," he said. "I only realized you were there because it was just after nine o'clock and you were late. It occurred to me to check my mind shield, and that's when I noticed you."

"So if I'd started earlier I might have gotten away with it?"

He shrugged a shoulder to indicate it was possible.

"And the ice-cold water was my punishment?"

"Yes."

My shoulders slumped. "So I failed my first test."

"The only test was to see if you'd attack, and you did. Twice."

"That's all you wanted?" I asked. "To see if I'd actually attack you?"

"I also wanted to see what power you'd use. I had a feeling it would tell me something about you, and it did."

I crossed my arms. "And what did it tell you?"

"I assumed you'd use your wind or your forcefields to attack. They're two of your most obvious weapons. It didn't really occur to me you'd use your mind powers, although it should have."

"Why?"

"Aside from the fact you're close to Bressen and naturally favor his powers, mind powers are a stealthier weapon. You likely chose them because they allow you to attack without seeming like you're attacking."

I narrowed my eyes at him, not sure if that was a criticism or not.

"I also learned that you're much more willing to strike out when you feel provoked," Axenus went on. "When attacked, you default to defense, but when you're irritated, you finally show some aggression."

"So what does that mean?"

He grinned. "It means I'll have to start provoking you more."

"That may get dangerous for you," I warned.

He only grinned wider. "I guess we'll find out. Now let's get started. I put some large glass vessels to the side of the room. Please bring them over to the table."

Axenus pointed to where four large vessels of about three gallons each stood against the wall and then to a table that was set up close to the center of the room.

I took a step to go get the vessels, but he put out an arm to stop me.

"Magic is like any other muscle in the body," he said, "It gets stronger with use. You have summoning powers, so I expect you to use them."

I nodded and summoned each of the wide-mouthed vessels, placing them one at a time on the table. They all had stoppers, and one had a candle in a holder sitting inside it. I looked at Axenus expectantly when they were all moved.

"Next time, summon more than one at a time," Axenus said. "You need to start pushing yourself."

I nodded my understanding.

"You also need to start thinking more creatively, more…ruthlessly," he went on. "Wind is the most tangible way to think of your air power, and wind can be a weapon itself, but there are other ways to use air as a weapon. For instance, you might kill an opponent by removing the air from their lungs, or alternately, by filling their lungs so full they explode. Likewise, you could also kill them by filling their lungs with water or earth so they suffocate to death."

My eyes widened. All of those would be horrible ways to die.

"That's barbarous," I said.

"That's survival," Axenus said. "I'm not suggesting you torture someone for fun, but if you're alone and don't have any weapons, then you need…options."

I frowned at him for throwing my own words from yesterday back at me, but I nodded.

"Today we'll imagine these vessels are someone's lungs, and you'll practice filling and emptying them," he said. "We'll start with air, since that seems to be your strongest element."

Axenus went over to the vessel with the candle in it and pulled the stopper off the top. "Light the candle, please."

I started to step forward, but he held up a hand to stop me. "We're also going to work on your ability to project your magic. Light the candle from there."

"How?" I asked.

"When you call your flames, you concentrate on drawing the heat to your hands, right? To light that candle, you need to concentrate the heat onto the wick."

I clenched my hands at my sides and tried to do as Axenus said. At first the wick only smoked faintly, but after several seconds, a flame caught, and the candle sparked to life.

"Very good," he said. "You've got the idea. Now you'll work on snuffing the candle. It's the same principle as getting rid of the water, except you'll remove the air from the vessel. You just need to do it before the fire uses up all the air first."

I nodded, and Axenus put the stopper on the vessel to seal it. I focused on removing the air, but I couldn't get my power to latch onto it.

At least a minute or two passed before Axenus lifted the stopper of the jar to let the air back into the vessel, and the candle flared up again.

"What am I doing wrong?" I asked him.

"I suspect you're having trouble harnessing the air because you can't see or feel it as you can the other elements," he suggested. "You need to see the air as an entity in itself, regardless of its intangibility. You need to make the air real for you without having to see or feel it as wind. You already know how to do this with your mind powers. The mind is just as intangible as the air."

I looked at the vessel and suddenly understood. If the vessel was a head, then the air inside was the mind, and I knew how to access that. Bressen had taught me to imagine mind shields as walls or doors, but the shield was just a figment, a way to conceive of a force of resistance that wasn't solid. I was too aware of the candle and vessel, their palpability, but I understood now that the vessel contained something besides the candle, something just as real as water.

"Put the stopper back in," I said, and Axenus complied.

It took me only about ten seconds this time before the flame of the candle went dead, leaving nothing but a whisp of smoke twirling up from the wick like a gauzy ribbon.

"Excellent," Axenus said. "Now refill the air and light the candle."

I smiled, proud of myself at accomplishing this task, and I extended my hand to refill the vessel. I'd only been working at it a few seconds when a strained cracking sound pricked my ears. I realized my mistake a moment too late as the glass vessel suddenly exploded.

I screamed and threw up my arms to cover my face as I waited for the sting of glass to pierce my skin, but nothing hit me. I lowered my hands to see the shattered vessel trapped in a large sphere of swirling water that eddied the glass around within it.

Axenus had manifested water just in time to catch the shards of glass as they shot outward, and he now seemed to be slowly removing the water to shrink the sphere and pull the glass back in toward the table. I watched in awe until all the water was gone, and the glass from the splintered vessel clinked into a pile on the table.

"Thank you," I said to him. "It looks like I was overzealous."

"Why did you throw up your hands instead of using your magic to stop the glass?" Axenus asked.

"I...I didn't think about it."

"It should be reflexive for you to use your powers," he said, "but you've spent your life trying to hide them, so it's not instinctual to use your magic when you're in danger. We need to change that."

"I understand," I said.

"Let's move on to water," Axenus said. "Fill the second vessel."

After air, water was easy, and I filled, then emptied the second vessel in seconds.

"Nicely done," Axenus said. "You have good control of your water power. You might be naturally inclined toward the element, or perhaps syphoning my power gave you some added control. Maybe both."

"Should I fill the next vessel with earth?" I asked.

"We're not done with water yet. Now I want you to fill my lungs."

I stepped back in shock. "What?"

He only looked at me, refusing to repeat himself, and I shook my head frantically. "No. Absolutely not."

"Cyra," he said, but I cut him off.

"Please don't make me try that." I pointed to the shattered glass vessel lying on the table. "You saw what I just did to the vessel when I overinflated it with air. I won't risk exploding your lungs with water."

Axenus stepped closer. I looked away from him, but he just stood there until I finally raised my eyes to his.

"Cyra, you won't hurt me. I can stop you if things get out of control."

"What if you can't?" I whispered.

He smiled. "If I can't stop someone as unpracticed as you, then I deserve whatever I get."

I frowned at him. "Are you trying to provoke me? Because that seems like the opposite of what you want to do right now."

He chuckled. "Fair point, but you still have to do this."

I looked at him pleadingly, but he just crossed his arms over his chest.

I sighed. "You're sure I'm not going to hurt you?"

"I can breathe both water and air," Axenus assured me. "And if I feel you filling my lungs too much, trust me, I'll stop you."

I bit my lip, but Axenus reached out and took one of my hands to place it in the center of his chest.

"Feel the air in my lungs when I breathe in," he said, then inhaled deeply. "Try to gauge how much there is. Between your elemental powers and your healing magic, you should be able to do that easily."

He inhaled again, and I closed my eyes, trying to make my powers sense the air in his lungs. I thought I could feel it, but I wasn't certain. Definitely not as certain as I wanted to be to attempt something like this.

Axenus exhaled. "Do you have a sense of the capacity?"

"I think so."

"Good. Now fill my lungs with water."

I swallowed hard. I needed to do this as slowly as possible. I focused, feeling myself walk a tightrope of control, but I kept my eyes fixed on Axenus's face as I looked for any sign of panic while I began to fill his lungs. His face remained calm, though.

A few seconds later I sensed he was reaching his capacity, and indeed, he held his hand up a moment later. I stopped instantly and searched his face, but he seemed fine. He made a gesture I understood to mean he wanted me to remove the water now, and I slowly pulled it back. Axenus inhaled when the water was gone, and I pushed out my own breath, letting my body sag as my hand fell from his chest.

"Are you alright?" I asked him.

"Perfectly done," he said. "If you're trying to drown an enemy, you'll want to fill their lungs much faster, but for our purposes, that was fine."

"Can I ask a question?" I asked, remembering something that had happened months ago.

"Of course."

"I was taking a bath a while back and put my head underwater. I was under for several minutes, but my lungs weren't burning for air at any point. My lady's maid finally pulled me up. She thought I was drowning."

He angled his head in interest. "You were breathing underwater?"

"I don't know. I was just holding my breath, but I felt like I could've stayed under all day."

He put a hand to his chin to think. "It's possible you were replenishing the air in your lungs without realizing it."

"I can do that?" I asked.

"We'd have to test it out to know for sure, but that's the most logical explanation. If you can, it would mean you could stay underwater indefinitely without coming up for air."

"Can we try it?"

"I'll ask Bressen about using the tub in your chambers sometime. If he's on board, we'll try it in a couple days. I have some other things we should work on first."

I nodded, excited to try out this potential new ability. I loved the ocean, and the idea of exploring underwater for long periods excited me.

For the rest of the lesson, Axenus had me work on fire and earth with the last two vessels. I was able to light a large fire in one of the vessels and keep it burning by constantly adding air to the closed vessel, but no matter how hard I tried, I couldn't fill the final vessel with earth. After almost twenty minutes of trying, I'd failed to call even a single grain of dirt.

"You clearly have some sort of mental block when it comes to earth," Axenus said when he called for me to stop. "I'll give some thought to how to get you over this hurdle."

"What if I don't want to get over it?" I asked quietly.

He looked at me intently before answering. "If you don't want to get over it, then you won't. I know your earth power is connected to a traumatic event, but why would you limit yourself in that way?"

I didn't answer, and he didn't press me.

"Tomorrow, you'll attack me again," he said. "Both your mind and negation powers are off limits, and this time, I want you to draw blood."

My eyes snapped up to meet his. "You want me to what?"

"Not a lot. Just a nick is fine, but I want you to make me bleed."

I shook my head in disbelief. "Exactly what kind of debt do you owe Bressen that you're willing to accept bodily harm for this job?" I asked.

"That's between me and Bressen."

"I'm sorry. I don't mean to pry," I said. "I just don't understand why you agreed to do this."

"You mean aside from the chance to work with the first known syphon in four hundred years?" he said with a small smile.

I shrugged one shoulder, conceding the point.

"I also don't mind a little pain if it means you're better prepared to take care of yourself," he said seriously.

"And will my punishment be more cold water if I fail to draw blood?"

He grinned. "We'll see."

He took a step closer so I had to look up at him. "Maybe a cold bath will help you draw blood on your second try after you inevitably fail on your first."

I glared at him. He was trying to provoke me, and it was working.

"No weapons either," he said. "You're not allowed to bring anything."

"Am I allowed to punch you?" I asked in annoyance.

He grinned wider. "You can try."

I jabbed him in the stomach with my fist. He grunted, but he didn't double over as I'd hoped. I'd probably bruised my knuckles on his hard muscles more than I'd actually hurt him.

"Sorry, I meant to ask if I could punch you *right now*," I clarified, giving him my own grin.

Axenus made a noise that was half cough, half laugh.

"I like working with you, Cyra," he said. "I never know what to expect from you. Hopefully you still want to work with me after I dole out your punishment tomorrow."

"Do I get an extra reward if you require a healer?" I replied silkily.

He huffed a laugh. "It sounds like you're sufficiently provoked."

"I guess you'll find out," I said as I turned on my heel to leave.

His chuckles followed me out of the Great Chamber, but he wouldn't be laughing tomorrow. I knew exactly how I'd make him bleed.

# Chapter 9

I slipped into the Great Chamber just after lunch to practice the power I'd need for my lesson with Axenus tomorrow. The merman had left the Citadel to take a swim in the Scion River that flowed through the city, so I hoped to have a good hour to myself where I wouldn't have to worry about him finding me and learning what I planned to do.

I strode toward the dais at the other end of the room and examined the three large Triumvirate seats. I needed to test the range and limitations of my powers, and I held up a hand, ready to begin.

"Cyra?" The voice from the side of the room made me jump.

My hand flew to my chest, and I turned to find Aidan standing near the wall where he must have been examining one of the tapestries. Apparently I'd been too focused on my mission to sense him.

"Aidan," I said, trying to bring my hammering heart back under control. "I didn't realize anyone was in here. My apologies."

"Not at all," he said coming toward me. "I was just looking around. Were those chairs about to feel your wrath?"

"My wrath?" I asked. I realized a second later he thought I'd planned to incinerate the chairs or otherwise destroy one of them. "Oh no. I was hoping to practice one of my less destructive powers on them."

I doubted Aidan would tell Axenus what I was up to, but I wasn't taking any chances.

"Practice?" Aidan asked. He'd stopped a good twelve feet from me, well out of my reach.

I remembered that Bressen hadn't told Aidan why Axenus was here. He'd introduced the merman the other night at dinner, but he'd simply told everyone Axenus was here to help him out with something. I wasn't sure if the vagueness was for my own benefit or Axenus's.

"We can all use a little practice now and then, no?" I said weakly.

Aidan gestured to the table at the center of the room. "Is all this for practice as well?"

I glanced at the three glass vessels on the table and the pile of glass that had once been a vessel and tried to decide how to answer. Aidan assumed I was a powerful syphon, but nothing was farther from the truth.

"The merman, Axenus, was it? That's why he's here. To help you train your powers?" Aidan went on.

I wasn't surprised he'd figured it out. Jasper had seen how inept I was at using my magic in Bronwyn and had undoubtedly told Aidan.

"I'm sorry for not being the frighteningly powerful syphon you were expecting," I said. "Bressen is still the one you should be wary of."

Aidan looked at me a moment. "Respectfully, I disagree," he said.

I frowned. "I promise you, I'm not more powerful than Bressen."

"I'm not talking about power," Aidan said. "You suggested people should be more *wary* of Bressen than you, and that's different."

"How so?"

Aidan shrugged and stepped a little closer to me.

"Bressen is a known entity," he said. "I know what his powers are, and I generally know what motivates him to use them. I won't deny he's extraordinarily dangerous, and I hope to the gods he never has reason to use his powers on me, but that doesn't necessarily make me wary of him."

"So you're more wary of me because I'm…an unknown entity?"

"Something like that," he said. "It sounds like you haven't quite gotten the hang of your powers yet, but that doesn't make you any less dangerous. Very little is known about syphons and their powers. I assume you gather them by touching your vic-…your source, but I have no idea if that's true. For all I know, you've already syphoned my power and standing this far from you is a moot point."

He was fishing for information again. I should've just smiled and refused to satisfy his curiosity. It's what Bressen would've done, but Bressen was a ruler, and he knew how to play politics. That wasn't me.

It also didn't slip my notice that Aidan had almost called my sources 'victims' before he'd caught himself. That in itself told me how he viewed my powers, and it didn't sit well with me. I didn't want my powers to be seen as a kind of theft that left a victim behind. Maybe a little honesty would make Aidan less wary of me.

"I'm not entirely sure how I acquire the powers of others, but so far touching them does seem to be the most expedient way," I said. "The need to touch my sources may only be temporary. Some information we found suggests I'll be able to syphon powers without needing to touch anyone once my gift is more developed."

Aidan nodded as he considered my words. "So it's possible you've syphoned powers you don't even know of yet then, if you've touched other people that you didn't know were perimortal?"

"It's possible."

"Just how many powers are you aware of?" he asked.

I smiled at him, deciding this was the one time I'd take a page from Bressen's book. "A woman has to keep some secrets to herself," I said.

If Aidan was disappointed, he didn't show it.

"Of course," he said. "But perhaps now you see why I'm more wary of you than of Bressen."

I nodded to acknowledge his point.

"Will you indulge me in one more question?" he asked.

"I'll answer if I can," I said.

"Is it true that you turned a bear to earth?"

I nodded. "It's what brought me to the attention of the Triumvirate. Why do you ask?"

"Curiosity more than anything. It sounds like transfiguration, but it can't be. A basic law of transfiguration is that you can't turn an inanimate object into something sentient and living, or vice versa."

"I've been told as much," I said. Then something struck me as I remembered watching Aidan use his transfiguration powers in Bronwyn. "Wait, you changed a man's shirt into butterflies when we were fighting the other day. Doesn't that defy the laws of transfiguration?"

Aidan grinned. "That's a little trick I taught myself. My transfiguration powers are very advanced, and I learned how to create the illusion of life without actually creating life itself."

I furrowed my brows.

"Let me show you," he said.

Aidan looked around before heading to the table. He touched the pile of glass there, and a second later it burst into a kaleidoscope of orange and black butterflies that scattered in every direction. I watched them flutter around the room for a moment before turning back to him.

"I don't understand," I said.

"Just give it another second or two."

The words were barely out of Aidan's mouth when something fluttered to the floor in front of me. I looked down to see one of the butterflies at my feet, only it wasn't a butterfly. It appeared to be no more than orange and black paper in the shape of a butterfly. I reached down to pick it up and turned the paper over in my hands, then looked up again in time to see paper butterflies floating down all around me.

"The butterflies aren't actually alive," Aidan said. "They're made of inanimate material, but my power allows me to animate them for a short time. They're particularly effective for distraction purposes."

"That's extraordinary," I said, still holding the paper butterfly in my hand. Now I really did want to syphon Aidan's transfiguration powers.

"The only drawback is that it's much harder to transfigure something back into its original form once pieces of it have flown off in every direction," he said wryly.

"I can help with that."

I summoned the scraps of paper into my palm where I crushed them into a ball and stepped forward to drop them onto the table. Aidan tensed as I approached, but I was careful not to touch him, and he relaxed when I stepped back. Then he touched the paper to turn it into glass again.

"Samhail gave you his summoning powers," Aidan observed.

"He didn't really have a choice. I met Samhail weeks before I learned I was a syphon. By then I'd already syphoned his powers, those of the three lords, Lady Glenora's, and some from a few priests and priestesses of the Priory."

I'd thrown the statement out indifferently, but the look of horror on Aidan's face told me he saw what I'd done as something more serious.

"I'm sorry. I didn't mean to be dismissive," I said. "I see the idea of me taking your power upsets you. I'm just not sure why."

Aidan raised a brow.

"Bressen and Samhail never seemed to mind that I syphoned their powers, so I never considered it an issue," I tried to explain.

"For some perimortals it may not be," Aidan said. "Elementals are common enough you can practically trip over them walking down the street, so I don't suppose they're bothered by seeing others with the same power. For perimortals like me who have rarer gifts, it's more disconcerting to have someone come along and steal our power."

"I don't steal anyone's power," I said defensively. "Despite what the word 'syphon' suggests, I don't actually take anyone's powers away from them. I merely replicate them."

Aidan inclined his head. "Perhaps it's ridiculous or even selfish of me to feel possessive of my power, but for now I'm not ready to let you have it. I hope you understand."

I inclined my head back. "Fair enough. I promise I won't purposely try to syphon your transfiguration ability, but I can't promise I won't accidentally syphon it. I'm still learning exactly how all this works."

"I understand."

"I just hope you recognize the sacrifice I'm making," I said teasingly. "Your power looks like a lot of fun, and I have to admit I want it."

Aidan smiled wryly. "Transfiguration *is* a lot of fun. Who knows, maybe someday I'll be ready to share it with you."

"That's good enough for me. Shall we shake on it?" I asked him, holding out a hand.

Aidan cocked a brow at me, and I shrugged. "It was worth a try."

"You're not what I expected, Cyra," he said, eyeing me as if he was trying to see through a glamour I'd put up. "I'm not sure I buy this sweet and innocent air you put on, but I'll at least admit you're not the ambitious, power-hungry woman I was expecting."

I blinked at him. "Thank you?"

"Or perhaps that's all part of the web you weave to lure in perimortals so you can feed on their powers," he said in a tone I couldn't read.

I was no longer sure if he was joking or not. His voice had taken on a hard edge, and I stepped back from him without thinking. Aidan's eyes bore into me for another few seconds before his expression eased, and the hint of a smile returned to his lips.

"I'll let you get back to training," he said. "I've bothered you enough."

I was about to tell him it was no bother, but he turned on his heel and strode from the chamber, leaving me to stare after him.

"I suppose I understand his point," Bressen said when I told him about my conversation with Aidan as we readied for dinner that evening in our bedroom. "I'm not sure how I'd feel about you taking my power if you were someone else."

"Like who?"

"Like someone I wasn't marrying."

"What does that have to do with anything? And I don't take powers, I replicate them," I insisted.

Bressen smiled indulgently at me. "Very well. I'm not sure how I'd feel about you *replicating* my power if you were someone I didn't know and trust."

"I still don't understand," I said. "Morland had the same power as you. Would it have made a difference if he'd syphoned that power from you versus it being his own?"

Bressen considered this. "Yes," he said after a moment. "If Morland syphoned his power from me, I would've felt more responsible for anything he did with it."

"Why?" I pressed. "Regardless of whether he got his power from you or from the gods, what Morland did with that power was his choice."

"Logically, yes, but I'd still feel responsible if Morland only had it because of me, if I'd provided him with a unique means to hurt people."

I sighed in exasperation. "Should the swordsmith feel responsible for every death caused by his blades, even if they're swung by someone else?"

Bressen shrugged. "Perhaps he should. After all, the main purpose of a sword is to take a life. Every swordsmith plies his trade knowing what his creations will be used for. At the very least, he enables death."

"Is Revenmyer full of swordsmiths then?"

Bressen inclined his head to concede the point. "No, you're right. We don't punish people for creating the tools that others use to kill. At least not in this plane of existence anyway, but I also can't speak to the will of the Nemesis. That punishment may very well come later."

"So if I killed someone using your power, you'd feel responsible?" I pressed him.

"I think we established you can't kill someone with my power, but if you could, then, yes. I might feel responsible. It's low on my list of sins, though. When I face the Nemesis, anything you do with my power will hardly compare to the things I've done all on my own."

I blanched, both at the thought of Bressen's eventual death, but also at how he'd be judged when he faced his final reckoning. He was a good man, but he had blood on his hands, and that weighed heavily on him.

"Fine, I give up," I said, crossing my arms. The debate had strayed into an area I didn't want to consider, and I was ready to be done with it.

Bressen smiled and pulled me against him, pinning my arms between us. He brushed his lips up my neck, and I moaned softly as gooseflesh pimpled on my skin.

"As long as you're surrendering…," he said, letting the thought hang there as he grazed his teeth against my throat. I let out a long breath, and he began to walk me backward toward the bed.

"It's almost time for dinner," I protested halfheartedly.

"Yes, and I intend to whet my appetite before we go downstairs."

My legs hit the bed, and Bressen pushed me down onto it before pulling off his shirt. He'd just unfastened his trousers when a knock sounded at the door.

"Go away!" Bressen snarled without taking his eyes from me.

Gilbert's apologetic voice answered from outside. "My lord…and lady, Phaedrus from the Priory is requesting an audience with you. He says he's found something you need to hear."

Bressen exhaled deeply and pulled me up off the bed before laying his forehead against mine. "We'll continue this later."

"Of course, my lord," I whispered, as a growl rumbled in his throat.

"Show Phaedrus into my study," Bressen called to Gilbert, and the captain sounded his acknowledgment.

Bressen pulled me against him again, and I felt the hard length of his erection press against my stomach.

"If the Nemesis ever does consign me to the third hell," he said, "it'll be for killing the next person who keeps me from getting between your beautiful thighs."

# Chapter 10

It was a few minutes before Bressen and I joined Phaedrus in the study. Rather than make the priest wait while Bressen got his erection under control, I'd dropped to my knees and taken him into my mouth.

He'd sworn filthily as I looked up at him while pushing him deep into my throat. His hands had threaded through my hair, and he'd thrust gently as I brought him to a release in half the time it would have taken him to wait out the easing of his ardor.

When we finally entered the study, Phaedrus stood near the meeting table clutching a large book that looked as if it had seen better days.

The priest himself was tall with bright blue eyes that stood out starkly against his deep brown skin. He was bald, although I suspected it was because he shaved his head, not because he'd lost his hair. He looked to be in his early forties, which – for a perimortal – suggested he was several centuries older than me or Bressen. He was the one from whom I'd syphoned my ability to call portals.

"Lord Bressen, Lady Cyra, I apologize for the intrusion, but thank you for seeing me on such short notice," Phaedrus said as Bressen and I sat down at the table.

"I hope this is important," Bressen said. "We were just getting ready for dinner." He glanced wickedly at me. "Unfortunately, Lady Cyra was the only one who got to put anything in her mouth."

I flushed with heat and glared at Bressen.

"I believe it is, my lord," Phaedrus said, either oblivious to Bressen's innuendo or pretending ignorance very convincingly.

Phaedrus laid the book gingerly on the table in front of us. It was covered in what might have been leather, but which looked only like a tattered mess wrapped around pages that seemed so brittle I didn't know how they hadn't already disintegrated. Phaedrus pulled a pair of gloves from his pocket and put them on before delicately opening the book.

"What's this about, Phaedrus?" Bressen asked as the priest flipped through the pages with a wary tenderness that suggested he did in fact expect them to fall apart at any moment.

"My apologies," Phaedrus said as he kept his eyes on the book. He spoke in low, shallow breaths, as if he was afraid the movement of too much air might hurt it. "As you know, I study ancient texts, and this is one of the oldest books on the Trinity ever found. This is the book recently discovered in the temple half buried under a landslide in Saltfell, and thanks to your influence," he inclined his head to Bressen, "it was brought to the Priory to add to our collection."

Bressen nodded, but there was a *get on with it* look in his eye.

"The text is written in a particularly ancient dialect of Arystrian, and I'm one of the few people on the continent who can translate it," Phaedrus went on.

"It looks like it's about to fall apart," I said, instinctively mirroring Phaedrus's low voice and shallow breaths.

"It will if it isn't handled carefully," Phaedrus said. "Luckily the ancients used powerful magic to help preserve these texts, and where their magic ends, those who found the text added their own. When it arrived at the Priory, we added yet more protections, but the book is still extremely delicate. The only thing holding it together at this point is several layers of magic."

"Very old book. Got it," Bressen said impatiently. Then, dropping all pretense he added, "Phaedrus, do you have any idea what I was about to do to Lady Cyra before you arrived?"

"Bressen!" I squeaked, throwing him an admonishing look.

While I couldn't see it on his smooth dark skin, I was sure Phaedrus was blushing profusely as he looked between me and Bressen.

"My lord," Phaedrus said apologetically, "I promise this will be worth the…interruption."

*Doubtful*, Bressen said into my mind, and I shushed him back.

"Please, go on, Phaedrus," I urged him, and he nodded his thanks.

"Not to belabor the point," Phaedrus said, "but this is one of the oldest books currently in existence on the Trinity. It predates anything else we currently have at the Priory, and there are only one or two other texts like it anywhere else on the continent. It's nothing short of a miracle the book has survived to this point."

I nodded to let Phaedrus know we understood the importance of the text, although Bressen continued to look unimpressed.

"I was studying a section this afternoon," Phaedrus went on, his attention now on me, "and I discovered several things I believe may be important. For instance, this section here." He pointed to a paragraph that looked incomprehensible. "This references the 'Hands of the Trinity.'"

"Hands?" I asked.

"Not literal hands," Phaedrus clarified, flexing his own. "The term 'hand' here is used to indicate someone like an advisor, emissary, or proxy who acts on a ruler's behalf. In this case, the hands act for the Trinity."

"Hands, plural?" I asked, "As in, more than one?"

"Three in fact," Phaedrus said.

"Is it a reference to the Triumvirate?" I asked. "The Triumvirate lords are supposed to be the Trinity's emissaries in the mortal realm, right?"

"Yes and no," Phaedrus said. "Thasia's Triumvirate is certainly based on this idea, that there are three people appointed to act in the name of the Trinity in the human realm, but Thasia has one of the last triumvirates on the Arystrian continent. As you may know, most of our neighbors have long since moved to a monarchic system that imbues all power within one king or queen. Bader is the only other country besides Thasia that still maintains this system of rule. Back when this text was written, though, there were no countries as we know them now. There was only a loose collection of territories, and the continent as a whole was ruled by what we might recognize today as a triumvirate."

"I fail to see why this was such an urgent discovery," Bressen said.

"I'm sorry, my lord. I'm getting to that," Phaedrus assured him. "The first thing that struck me was this word." He pointed to a symbol that wasn't familiar to me. "The word is a feminine pronoun, essentially 'she.'"

I flashed a smug smile. "The early triumvirates were female?"

Bressen hadn't moved, but I could tell by the look in his eyes that Phaedrus had finally started to pique his interest.

"Does this refer to a specific triumvirate, such as a particular group of women, or do you get the sense from the text that the Hands of the Trinity were always female?" I asked.

"I'd want someone else who knows this dialect to check my

translation," Phaedrus said, "but I'm leaning heavily toward the latter. As near as I can tell, the early continent was ruled by a triarchy of women who were designated as the Hands of the Gods, authorized by the Trinity to act on their behalf in the mortal realm. There are other texts that support the idea the continent was once ruled by a triumvirate, hence the reason Thasia and Bader use that system, but to my knowledge, this is the first text that suggests the continental triumvirate was female. Moreover, if I read this correctly, it also specifies these women were hand-chosen by the gods...so to speak."

"Well, this certainly is an interesting find," I said, leaning back in my chair and smirking at Bressen. "Maybe we need to do some reorganizing. We don't want to anger the Trinity by not honoring their original vision for a female Triumvirate."

Bressen's lips curled into an answering smile. "I'm more than happy to abdicate my seat and let you take over, my love. My steward can walk you through the paperwork that needs to be done by the end of the week."

Bressen made to get up from his chair, but Phaedrus cleared his throat, and Bressen eased back down with a deep exhale of impatience.

"I assume there's more?" he asked the priest.

Phaedrus nodded. "Everything I've told you to this point was interesting enough, but it wasn't what made me bring this to you."

"Go on," I said, leaning forward with curiosity.

"The text notes that the Hands of the Gods are extremely powerful perimortals, but what caught my attention is how they're described. The text states the hands were imbued with the power to...draw on whatever abilities they needed in order to enact the wills of the gods. If they didn't have what they needed to fulfill a certain duty, they had the power to seek out and collect that ability."

Bressen bolted upright in his chair. Phaedrus had his attention now.

Phaedrus pointed to another symbol in the text that looked like nothing more than random lines and curves to me.

"This here," the priest said, letting his finger hover over the page. "I've never seen this word before, but I found some possible equivalents when I compared it to similar words from later texts. Based on that comparison, and gleaning what I can from the context, I'd translate this word to mean…'syphon.'"

My breath came out in a whoosh of air just as Bressen shot to his feet. Phaedrus took a step back at the sudden movement, but Bressen's look was one of concern, not anger.

"How certain are you about that translation?" Bressen asked urgently.

"Again, I'd want someone else to independently translate the word to see if they come to the same conclusion I did," Phaedrus said, "but I'd say with a high degree of probability it means syphon or is at least a synonym for it."

"So to be sure I understand you correctly," Bressen said as his eyes locked unblinkingly with the priest's, "the entire continent used to be ruled by a triumvirate of females who acted on behalf of the Trinity, and those females were all syphons."

"That's my conclusion, yes," Phaedrus said as he held Bressen's gaze.

Bressen turned away quickly and began to pace behind the table, his muscled arms crossed over his chest, chin propped in one hand.

"This can't mean what I think it means," I said, my eyes meeting Phaedrus's. "It can't mean I'm…"

"That you're one of the Hands of the Trinity?" Phaedrus supplied when I trailed off. "Yes, my lady. If my translation is correct, that's exactly what it means."

I sat back heavily in my chair. "That's not possible," I said numbly.

My head was a maelstrom of thoughts and questions, none of which I could focus on right now.

"It means far more than that," Bressen said. He stopped pacing and leaned on the back of the chair he'd vacated.

I furrowed my brows. "Like what?"

Bressen looked at Phaedrus to see if he'd supply the answer.

"There are three Hands of the Gods," Phaedrus said carefully. "The implication is that there are three syphons currently living."

"I thought I'm the first known syphon in hundreds of years," I said.

"The key word is 'known,'" Bressen said. "Just because we don't know of any others, that doesn't mean there aren't any. They may be in hiding."

"What if the other two are just dead?" I asked.

"I'd have to do some more checking, but I assume that when one syphon dies, another is born," Phaedrus offered. "If syphons are the Hands of the Gods, and there are supposed to be three, it stands to reason the Trinity would create a new one to replace any they lost."

I blinked at him. "But that would mean I was born to replace a syphon who died twenty-two years ago."

"Yes," Phaedrus said seriously.

I shook my head. "No, that can't be possible."

"Cyra," Bressen said gently, "we know syphons are extremely rare, almost unheard of. We have to ask ourselves, then, why a syphon was suddenly born twenty-two years ago."

"Maybe they just wanted a spare," I said stubbornly. "It's not like I would've been able to act as Hand when I was born."

"But if that's the case, then there are more than three living syphons. That seems even less likely," Bressen said. He turned to Phaedrus. "Is there anything else you read that might answer some of these questions?"

"To be honest, my lord," Phaedrus said apologetically, "I haven't finished translating this section yet. As soon as I uncovered the part about the syphon, I brought it to you."

Bressen nodded. "How long will it take you to translate the rest?"

"It's hard to say. This took me a couple weeks, but that was because I had to do some additional cross-checking to translate the word 'syphon.' If I don't run into any other strange words, it could be less time. On the other hand, if I run into too many words I don't know, it could be more."

"Can you do your translating here?" Bressen asked.

Phaedrus looked confused. "You want me to bring the book back and forth to the Citadel?"

"I want you to leave the book here," Bressen clarified. "This is highly sensitive information, and I want to restrict who has access to it."

"I'm the only one in the Priory – the only one in all of Thasia, I think – that can translate this text," Phaedrus said. "Access to it, or at least the information in it, is limited by default."

Bressen nodded, but he didn't look satisfied.

"I can leave it in the vault at the Priory," Phaedrus suggested. "Only a small number of us have access to that. It would be better for me to do my work there since I'll likely need other texts in the Priory's library."

Bressen nodded again. "Fine. But I want this book locked down, and you'll come directly to me and Cyra the moment you learn anything else of consequence."

"Should we tell Aidan about this?" I asked.

Bressen shook his head. "Not yet. This information mainly concerns you. It has no direct bearing on Triumvirate affairs in Thasia. There's no reason to bring Aidan in on this other than as a courtesy, and I'm not inclined to be courteous until we know more about what this means. This stays between the three of us for now." He turned his gaze on Phaedrus. "Do not mention what you found to anyone, or you'll be the first person to learn what it feels like to have your brain melt out of your head."

"Bressen!" I admonished him.

Bressen respected Phaedrus, and his threat of violence shocked me.

Phaedrus's eyes never left Bressen's, however, as he said, "You can trust me, my lord."

It wasn't fear in the priest's voice, but conviction, and I felt a surge of gratitude toward him. Only when Bressen nodded did Phaedrus look at me, and the determination in his face took my breath away. I knew without reading his mind that he'd protect this secret with all his power.

Several minutes later, after Bressen had given Phaedrus some final instructions and exacted the man's promise to provide regular updates, Phaedrus summoned a portal back to the Priory. Bressen still looked reluctant to let him leave with the book, but ultimately the fact that no one else could read it convinced Bressen to let the tome out of his sight.

When the portal had closed after Phaedrus, Bressen went to the cabinet behind his desk to pull out a bottle of wine. He held it up to me in offering, but I waved it away. I was having trouble wrapping my head around what we'd learned, and wine wasn't going to help me think.

Bressen poured himself a glass of the deep ruby liquid and took a healthy sip before coming over to fall heavily into one of the cushy chairs by the fireplace as I took up his earlier pacing.

"Cyra." Bressen's gentle tone a few seconds later made me pause long enough to look at him. "What's going through that beautiful head of yours?" he asked.

"I don't want it," I said.

"Don't want what?"

"This!" I made a frantic gesture as if to indicate everything. "I'm not cut out to be a ruler, let alone a Hand of the Gods. I don't know how any of this happened."

"I suppose that's something we'll learn together. I'm sure Phaedrus will find more answers soon."

I shook my head and resumed pacing until I could no longer ignore the feel of Bressen's eyes on me. I looked at him again. He had one leg crossed over the other as usual, and he held the glass of wine lazily in one hand as his bright turquoise eyes tracked me like a predator.

"Why are you looking at me like that?" I asked.

"Just taking a moment to be in awe of you," he said, sipping his wine.

I quirked a brow at him. "In awe of me? Why?"

"I'm marrying a woman who was chosen by the gods themselves," he said, admiration mingling with lust in his voice.

I rolled my eyes. "My situation isn't all that different from yours."

"On the contrary, our situations are very different," he insisted.

"You're a Triumvirate lord. You were chosen by the gods too," I said.

He shook his head. "No, I wasn't."

Bressen put his glass down on a side table, uncrossed his legs, and held his hand out to me. I took it and let him pull me down onto his lap, then nestled up against his chest as he wrapped his arms around me.

"Cyra," he said, "being a Lord of the Triumvirate doesn't mean I was chosen by the gods. That's what we tell people, but Thasia's triumvirate is a human invention. I have no actual godly authority. Jerram certainly didn't, nor did Ursan, nor does Aidan. We were all chosen in one way or another by human means. Aidan literally won his seat through a competition, and like many of the Triumvirate before me, I inherited mine. There was no divine intervention involved."

Bressen's hand traced lightly down my arm, and I lifted my head from his chest. He brushed his lips down my neck, and desire blossomed in my core, floating out over my body like dandelion seeds on the wind.

"The gods created you as a syphon," he went on. "They gave you specific gifts that allow you to serve them. You were divinely made for a particular purpose."

I tensed as I considered his words. I'd been a winemaker a few months ago, and that gave me purpose. I'd never had aspirations any grander than that. While Bressen tried to involve me in the ruling of Hiraeth and Thasia, it wasn't work I found especially engaging, so the idea that I'd been created to help the gods rule not only the country, but the entire continent, was unappealing. Bressen might marvel at my divine purpose, but I saw it as something imposed upon me.

"Does that bother you?" I asked him.

"Does what bother me?" Bressen asked as his lips trailed lower. He grazed his teeth along my collarbone where the claw marks of the bear I'd killed were still faintly visible, and I arched into him. My skin tingled under his touch, and Bressen pulled one of my legs up to hang over the arm of the chair as he began to gather my dress up toward my waist.

"Does…does it bother you that I'm…" I trailed off, both because I wasn't sure exactly how to phrase my question, and because the feel of Bressen's hand creeping toward the apex of my thighs was making it hard to form both thoughts and words.

"Does it bother me that you're more powerful than me?" he finished.

I raised my head in surprise. "I'm not more powerful than you."

"Yes, you are," he said against my throat as his lips and teeth played along the sensitive skin there. "I have almost a century's more practice with my power than you do, but you are infinitely more powerful."

I would've argued with him, but his hand pushed my undergarment aside to reach the sensitive bundle of nerves between my thighs just then, and his fingers slid over the bud, causing me to gasp and arch up on his lap. Bressen used the opportunity to deepen his mouth's exploration of the skin on my neck and chest.

"And to answer your question," he said between kisses, "it doesn't bother me at all."

"It doesn't…bother you that I'm…chosen by the gods?" I asked in rasping breaths as his fingers glided lazily through the wetness of my slit, teasing me until I was panting.

I gasped as he slipped a long finger inside me, and my body nearly launched itself off him, but his arm tightened to hold me in place. I grabbed the front of his shirt to steady myself. Every nerve in my body was alive as he stroked me, and I undulated my hips against him.

"The only power I want," he whispered, "is the power to make you scream with pleasure."

"Yes," I said, not entirely aware what I was agreeing to.

Bressen slipped a second finger inside me, and they moved more urgently now as his thumb ran circles over my clit. My hips rocked up to meet his hand, and a near-feverish heat flushed my skin as I writhed on his lap. He was merciless as he drove me toward the edge of my sanity.

"Say my name," Bressen breathed against my neck. He pulled me up in the chair, and his teeth scraped against my breast through the fabric of my bodice, making my nipples pebble.

"Bressen." His name came out on a whimper as my hand gripped his shirt tighter. My body was draped across him and the chair, and my hips bucked up to ride his fingers.

"Come for me," he said, and I moaned as his breath teased my skin.

The sweet strain between my legs was nearly unbearable, but I could feel my release coming now as Bressen's mouth on my breast added extra sensation to the already overwhelming tumult gripping my body. His fingers pumped into me, and my hand moved from his shirt to thread through his hair as I held his head in place over my breast. He bit gently on the nipple through the dress, and I went crashing over the edge.

"Oh gods! Bressen!" I cried out as pleasure surged through me.

Bressen bit harder on my breast and pressed his fingers deep inside me once more as I exploded with my release. It came in a torrent for what seemed like minutes until I finally shuddered against him and went slack in his arms. His head lay against my chest as I took in deep gasping breaths, and I felt his erection against my ass. We'd be late to dinner.

"Good girl," Bressen murmured into my ear. "When the gods can do that for you, then maybe I'll worry."

I released a breathy laugh. "Such irreverence. Do you say your prayers with that wicked mouth?"

Bressen growled and lifted me into his arms as he stood up from the chair. "There are far better uses for my mouth than praying, and there's only one being I want to worship right now. How about we skip dinner and raid the kitchen again later."

I could only nod my assent as I lay limply against him. He carried me back to our room and laid me on the bed before undressing himself. I bit my lip as I watched, studying how every muscle in his body moved. Gods above, he was magnificent, and by some miracle, he was mine.

My body was still liquid when Bressen climbed over me and pulled off my clothes, but I opened my legs and moaned as he sheathed himself slowly into my wet heat. He made love to me then, leisurely and sensually, and I did indeed feel worshipped as he used his mouth, his hands, and every other part of him in his devotions. After he'd shattered me apart twice more and pulled me against him to rest, I felt not just like a Hand of the Gods, but like a goddess.

# Chapter 11

Bressen and I never did leave the bed that night to raid the kitchen, and I regretted that by morning. I also felt bad that not showing up to dinner meant Axenus was left alone with Aidan, Jasper, and Maziren. He'd only met them two days ago, and I wasn't sure if he was comfortable enough around them yet to share a meal alone. Bressen assured me he'd sent the merman a message to let him know we wouldn't be down, but while I relished the idea of drawing Axenus's blood today, he was still our guest, and I didn't want him to feel neglected by us.

Axenus was at breakfast when we arrived, and I gave him an apologetic look. He didn't seem perturbed, so I went to the sideboard to make my plate as usual.

"Is that all you're having for breakfast this morning?" I asked Axenus when I sat down. "I suggest something a little heartier. You're going to need your strength today."

Axenus glanced at the fruit, cheese, and smoked salmon on his plate.

"I had a big dinner. I should be fine," he said.

The hint of a smile at the corner of his mouth told me he knew exactly why Bressen and I hadn't made it down to dinner last night, and I flushed straight down to my toes. As if on cue, my stomach grumbled loudly, and I quickly shoved a bite of eggs into my mouth while Axenus chuckled.

"Did I miss something?" Bressen asked as he sat down next to me.

Axenus answered before I could. "Cyra was just attempting some psychological warfare, but her words burn even weaker than her fire."

My mouth fell open, and Axenus had the gall to actually wink at me.

If that's the way he wanted it, then we could certainly play it that way.

"I definitely missed something," Bressen said, looking a bit surprised.

"Just some competitive incivility," Axenus said. "Cyra has to learn that her magic needs to keep the promises her mouth makes."

It was convenient that I hadn't yet picked my jaw up off the table from his last words because it would have fallen right back down after that. It was a few seconds more before I remembered how to inhale and close my mouth.

Okay, I'd give Axenus credit. I'd shot first, but he had a quiver full of arrows and bullseye aim. I wouldn't underestimate him again.

"And Axenus should remember," I said when I found my tongue, "that I'm playing by his rules as a courtesy." I let my negation powers lick at him for just an instant, but it made him wince nonetheless.

"I'll remember that," he said, a hint of concession in his voice.

"Good. Then I look forward to making you bleed after breakfast."

Bressen's head snapped to me as I took a bite of my bacon.

"What?" he asked.

"Cyra's task today is to make me bleed," Axenus explained.

Bressen raised a brow.

"I bet his blood is as red as his hair," I said to Bressen. "I'll let you know for sure later."

Axenus chuckled and tucked back into his food.

I looked up to see Maziren in the doorway of the dining room eyeing the three of us, and I wondered how much she'd heard.

"Good morning," I said brightly to her.

She must have decided she didn't want to know anything more about our conversation because she returned my greeting with a mumbled one of her own and went straight to the sideboard to fix herself a plate.

Bressen and I returned to eating as well, and the four of us sat in silence while Axenus and I continued to exchange gently menacing glances at each other. Axenus finished first and brought his dishes over to put them in the bin near the kitchen.

"I'll see you in a little while, Cyra," he said as he walked to the door. He stopped at the threshold. "There's still a little time for you to practice whatever power you plan to use this morning. Maybe Maziren will let you syphon hers to help."

Maziren's head snapped up, and she gave Axenus a look that said there wasn't a chance in the three hells that was going to happen.

Axenus grinned. "I guess not. Oh well. I hope you're ready then."

"I suggest you worry less about me and more about protecting yourself," I called after him as he left.

His chuckle drifted down the hall, and I ground my teeth a bit.

"The two of you seem to be getting along…well?" Bressen ventured.

"He enjoys provoking me far too much," I told him, "but I find him tolerable."

He raised an amused brow at me.

"Where did you meet Axenus anyway?" I asked, taking another bite of my eggs. I looked up again when Bressen was slow to answer. His expression was serious, and he glanced at Maziren, who was ignoring us.

"I met him outside of Thasia at the start of the war while I was on a diplomatic mission for my father," he said finally.

I considered his words a moment. "A diplomatic mission? Were you trying to get the merpeople to join the war?"

"No, Axenus was away from home at the time I met him. We ran into each other by accident, and I helped him out with a little problem he had."

"And that's why he owes you a debt?"

"It's really more of a favor," Bressen corrected.

"Axenus calls it a debt," I said, looking him square in the eye.

"Axenus is overstating things. It wasn't that big a deal," Bressen said, but the rosy glow that bloomed on his skin from my truth seer abilities said otherwise.

"You remember I can see when you're lying, right?" I told him.

Bressen sighed and glanced again at Maziren, who was still resolutely focused on the sausages piled on her plate.

*Axenus and I met under unfortunate circumstances,* Bressen said, switching the conversation to our mental connection. *Ones I don't think he wants known, so please don't ask me to elaborate. If he considers what he owes me a debt, then that's his business. I consider it a favor between friends.*

Maziren's eyes flicked up quickly when she didn't hear Bressen answer, and I surmised she'd been listening to our conversation after all.

I gave Bressen a quick nod to tell him I understood and then got up to bring my plate to the dish bin.

*It's one hell of a favor given how much I'm going to make him bleed in a little while,* I said into Bressen's mind.

He smiled. *Just make sure you heal him as well. I'm not sure who else I'd get to train you if you hurt him too badly.*

I leaned over and brushed my lips over his in a gentle kiss. When I pulled back, his eyes were bright with promise, and I bit my lip. As I straightened, I caught Maziren watching us, but she looked away quickly.

*Until tonight, my love,* Bressen said.

*Until tonight,* I agreed, then turned to get ready to face Axenus.

Ten minutes later, the doors of the Great Chamber opened before me, and I strode in to find Axenus standing in the middle of the room. I'd expected him to be lounging in one of the chairs again, but it didn't matter. This was actually better. I took a quick furtive glance to the side of the chamber to be sure what I needed was still there, and it was.

I saw with some satisfaction that Axenus was instantly on guard as I approached. I wasn't the same uncertain woman who'd hid outside the doors of the Great Chamber yesterday trying to decide how to attack, or even *if* to attack. There was confidence in my step, and Axenus reacted to it accordingly. It was a heady feeling.

I stopped about fifteen feet from him and took a moment to look him up and down in a display of dominance that I hoped would further throw him off guard.

Axenus arched a brow at me as if to ask what I was waiting for.

"You look different today," he said. "Maybe all that talk at breakfast wasn't just talk after all."

"I feel different today," I said as I stretched my hands out toward him.

His muscles went taut, but he didn't look down at my hands. His eyes were locked on mine as if he was trying to read in them what I intended to do. A smile curled onto my lips, and his eyes widened a fraction before his body twitched to move, but it was too late.

Axenus grunted as the huge Triumvirate chair hit him from behind. Shock showed in his face as the chair knocked his legs out from under him so he fell back into it as it flew toward me from where I'd summoned it. The chair hit the floor and skidded to a halt right in front of me. I leaned forward, resting one hand on the arm of the chair so I could bring my face in close to his.

His eyes were still locked on mine, no longer shocked, but... impressed? Appreciative?

He flinched, and his eyes fell to his hand where drops of blood beaded up from a thin red line. He looked back at me, and I held up the piece of glass from the broken vessel I'd summoned along with the chair.

A grin spread across his face, and he gave me a nod. "Well done."

I looked down and dabbed my finger into the blood along the cut before bringing it to my lips and licking it off my finger.

Axenus's eyes flared.

"It's customary in some places to drink the blood of one's enemy, is it not?" I asked innocently.

He gave me a wry grin. "Is that what I am? An enemy?"

I leaned back again to stand up straight. "Isn't that what you want me to see you as? At least for the purposes of these exercises?"

He canted his head to the side to indicate I had a point and started to stand up. I moved back to give him room to rise, but I didn't go far, so he was still trapped between me and the chair.

Well, trapped was a stretch. Axenus was as tall and solid as Bressen, so he could get around me if he wanted, but that was my intention, to make him be the one to have to move if he wanted to. Of course, now that he was standing, it meant I had to look up at him.

"I'll admit that I didn't see any of that coming," Axenus said. "I left the broken glass there on purpose because I wanted to see if you'd use it, but I expected a much more direct attack."

I shook my head. "You know how to stop flying glass. That wasn't going to work," I said. "I had to keep your mind on something else while I summoned a piece of it."

"You're starting to think more creatively. That's very good. I'm actually surprised you were able to summon the chair. Those are heavy."

"I may have snuck in here yesterday to do a little practicing," I admitted. "I expected you to be in the chair when I summoned it, like you were yesterday, so it was actually easier to move than I anticipated. This worked out better in any case."

Axenus smiled and stepped out from between me and the chair. "Now let's see if you can put it back where it was," he said.

I raised a hand so I could use a forcefield to push the chair back to where it had been, but before I could do so, a small rectangle of paper puffed into existence right before my face. It was a message leaf, a type of magical paper used to send messages instantly, and I plucked the paper out of the air as it floated toward the floor.

I saw Jaylan's name first, but there was something off about it. My older brother's handwriting was usually neat and tidy, but this seemed unsteady, as if his hand had been shaking when he'd written it.

I read the short message on the paper, and the world suddenly tilted to the side as all the air left my lungs. The chamber was spinning, and I couldn't breathe, couldn't think as the words on the leaf sunk in.

"Cyra? What is it?" Axenus asked in alarm.

I heard his voice, but it was muffled and far away.

*Gone?* I thought. *It…couldn't be gone.*

The paper slipped from my hand to finish its descent to the floor, and I lurched forward, looking for something to hold onto as my legs seemed no longer willing to hold me up.

"Cyra!" I felt Axenus's arm around me, holding me up, as his other hand grabbed my elbow.

I needed air. I closed my eyes and tried to draw the air to me, but it wouldn't come. I couldn't fill my lungs no matter how hard I gasped.

"Cyra…Cyra stop!" Axenus's voice was full of warning, but I could barely hear him above the thudding of my heart in my ears.

Pressure built all around me. Air pressed on my body, but I couldn't get it into my lungs. Protector help me, I couldn't breathe.

"Cyra!" Axenus's shout cut through the fog of my mind before pain bit into my face and side, and I felt myself forced to the ground.

I blinked and looked up to see Axenus hovering over me. We were on the floor where he'd thrown me down, and a wall of eddying water stood shimmering next to us.

"You're bleeding," I said flatly as I noticed a gash across his cheek.

I felt the pain in my own face then, and I reached up to touch it. My hand met with something hard and jagged, and I realized there were shards of glass sticking in my cheek and chin. I wrapped my fingers around a large piece to pull it out and felt blood trickle down my face.

"Cyra, no!" Axenus pulled my hand away from my face. "We need to get a healer to remove the glass."

There was still a pressure in my chest, and I couldn't fully breathe. For a moment, I was back on the vineyard months ago with a pile of dirt pressing me down, suffocating me. It felt the same now, only worse.

I started to get up, and Axenus rose with me, pulling me to my feet.

I was vaguely aware of the pain in my side, and I looked at my arm to see that there were shards of glass embedded there and in my side as well. I looked through the wall of water and could barely see that the three other glass vessels on the table were gone, shattered in my attempt to fill my lungs. Axenus had managed to put up a wall, but it had only caught half the glass. I looked at his arm and saw he was bleeding from small cuts of glass as well, and there was a large chunk embedded in his bicep.

"I'm sorry," I said, but the words were perfunctory, said only because somewhere in a corner of my mind I knew I was supposed to say them.

Axenus glanced to where I was looking at his arm, but he shook his head. "It will heal. Cyra, what happened? What did the message leaf say?"

We both looked to the floor where the leaf lay face-down.

"I have to go," I said.

"Go where?" he asked.

I turned away from him and traced a circle in the air before me. A glowing blue outline flared where I'd traced, and I spread my hands out to widen the portal I'd just opened. It flickered a little, as if it was barely holding on. I wouldn't be able to keep it open long.

Axenus looked through the portal and his eyes widened.

"Cyra, let me get Bressen," he said urgently. "Let me get Bressen before you do anything."

He tried to step in front of me, but I sent a forcefield into him without even thinking, and he grunted loudly as he was thrown back onto the floor. I turned toward the portal and walked through it, my foot stepping on the piece of paper that bore Jaylan's unsteady handwriting and the message that had broken something deep inside me.

*They burned the vineyard. It's gone. — Jaylan*

# Chapter 12

Smoke stung my eyes and bit into my lungs as I emerged from the portal onto what had once been our family's vineyard. The fire had burned out, but smoke hung thick in the air, heavy and dense like an ocean fog. Its acrid smell assailed my nose as I closed the portal behind me, cutting off Axenus's shout and his attempt to reach me.

The vines were all but gone, burned to blackened skeletons while trellis wires hung limply from charred, crumbling posts. My brothers and I never kept the vines or rows tidy. There wasn't time for such maintenance, so the long, dried grass and dead leaves had been left for the winter, and they'd provided perfect kindling for the flames as they'd ripped across the fields.

The house was still standing, although one side was heavily scorched. Its presence almost allowed me to breathe again until I saw that the fermentation barn was burned to the ground. A few wooden posts still stood partially upright, showing the outline of where the barn had once been, but the roof had collapsed in on itself and the whole pile had simply burned and burned. Rivulets of wine now flowed out of the structure from when the barrels inside had ruptured, leaving veins of ruby-colored mud on the ground.

Next to it, the horse barn was charred and partially collapsed as well, and my heart constricted as I sent up a desperate prayer to the Protector that the horses had made it out alive. Even if they'd survived the fire itself, they may still have died from the smoke that now clogged the air.

I coughed violently as I tried to inhale only to find nothing breathable around me. I should have brought a cloth with me to hold over my mouth, but I hadn't been thinking, still couldn't think.

I held out my hands and a swift wind swept across the vineyard, pushing the toxic air toward the town of Fernweh off in the distance. The people there had done this, and I wanted the smoke to fill their lungs and make it hard for them to breathe as it was now hard for me.

I was vaguely aware of how cold I felt, both inside and out. It was the middle of winter, and I'd come straight from the Citadel without my cloak, but I didn't care that the frigid air stabbed at my skin. It was nothing compared to how cold I felt inside.

I survey the devastation slowly, remembering the times my brothers and I had played hide-and-seek among the vines, or the times we'd raced from one end of a field to another, each of us in our own row like lanes. As the oldest, Jaylan usually won those races when we were little, but when Brix's legs got longer, he'd started to win his share. Speed was never my forte, so I usually came in last, but it never mattered to me as long as I was with Jaylan and Brix. It was always the three of us together.

The first night after our parents had died of the Great Flu, my brothers had found me in the vineyard, sitting between two rows of vines huddled around a small fire I'd built.

I'd missed my parents so much that I'd actually seen an apparition of my mother standing between two rows of vines that night as I looked out over the vineyard. She'd turned and started to walk away, but I'd followed her deep into the vineyard, trying to speak to her until she finally disappeared. I thought I'd heard her tell me she loved me as the vision dissolved, and I spent several minutes begging her to come back.

Finally, I'd just sat down between the vines, built a fire, and waited to see if she returned. That's how Jaylan and Brix had found me nearly an hour later after searching frantically for me. I hadn't told them about the apparition. Instead, I'd just told Jaylan I'd come out there to feel close to our parents again, since the vineyard was such a huge part of who they'd been and who we were as a family.

Instead of coaxing me back to the house, Jaylan had returned to get blankets, pillows, and food, and we'd all slept right there under the moon and stars among the vines as we shared memories of our parents. We'd huddled together in a pile, and Jaylan had held Brix and I as we cried ourselves to sleep that night.

We cried ourselves to sleep many nights after as well, but only that first night among the vines felt healing as we let our tears salt the earth.

I fell forward onto my knees as I remembered all this, and a long, low wail came from somewhere deep inside me. I buried my face in my hands as my tears began to pour from my already watering eyes. I tried to draw in breath, but even though the air had started to clear, I still couldn't take in enough that I didn't feel like I was drowning. There was a weight on my chest that kept me from being able to inhale, a weight far heavier and more painful than the dirt that had held me down here a couple months ago. It was a stone on my chest that threatened to crush me altogether.

Something banged in the distance, like a door slamming, and I heard my name on the wind.

I couldn't move, couldn't do anything but curl further into myself as my hands clenched the ash-covered earth, and I flinched a moment later as an arm came around me. Then Jaylan's soft voice was in my ear, and I looked up into his face.

One of his eyes was nearly swollen shut from where he'd obviously been punched, and the other was red from crying or the smoke or both. There was a cut across his other cheek, and he seemed to move gingerly.

"Cyra," Jaylan started to say, but I cut him off as my rage flared at the sight of his bruised face.

"Who did this?" I asked, and he recoiled at the menace in my voice.

"Come into the house," Jaylan urged. "You need to get out of this air and the cold. Why aren't you wearing a cloak?"

I rose to my feet as he helped me up, but I didn't follow him as he tried to pull me back toward the house. I realized I'd somehow created a small bubble of air around us that repelled the smoke.

"Who did this?" I repeated, my voice calm with deadly fury.

Jaylan took a step back from me and shook his head, refusing to tell me. He must have seen the promise of vengeance in my eyes.

I didn't need him to tell me, though. He was mortal and couldn't put up a mind shield. I read the answer in his mind clearly enough.

"Eddin," I said, and he jolted.

I probed deeper, finding Jaylan's memories and watching through his eyes as the mob from the town led by Eddin, a former paramour, approached the vineyard with torches. I didn't care that I was invading his thoughts, that I was violating his mind. I needed to know who to punish.

No, not to punish. To hurt. I could admit that I wanted to hurt someone for this, hurt them as they'd never been hurt before.

Bressen had told me once how he'd wanted to hurt the men who'd attacked me and Raina on the wharf in Callanus. He told me he'd wanted to spend days taking them apart piece by piece, and I understood that craving now. Ultimately, Bressen had tasked Samhail with punishing the men instead, afraid of what he himself might do to them if he gave in to his darkest inclinations.

I wasn't as reasonable. I'd indulge my darkness. I'd revel in it and wear it like armor if it meant I didn't have to feel the thousand needles that now stabbed my heart. I wouldn't just give in to vengeance, I'd become it. People might call Bressen the Nemesis Incarnate, but today that title would be mine.

"Are the horses alive?" I asked Jaylan. I barely recognized my voice.

He blanched and shook his head. I shut my eyes tightly as the tears flowed down my face. The need to cause pain had taken over, and I felt nothing but that frozen, empty void inside myself that could only be filled by the screams of those who'd done this.

"I need to go into town," I said.

"Cyra, no!" Jaylan yelled. "Please don't."

He tried to step toward me, but I moved back out of his reach.

"Cyra!"

Another voice drew my attention, and I looked toward the house to see Brix and someone else hurrying toward me. I recognized the other person a moment later as Rodrick, the cooper who made our wine barrels.

My mouth tumbled open in shock at the sight of Brix. His whole face was bruised, swollen, and crisscrossed by cuts and scrapes. His arm hung in a sling, and a twinge of my healing magic told me his shoulder had been dislocated. He'd clearly fought like the three hells to stop the mob and had paid the price for it.

Red rage filled my vision at the sight of Brix's injuries, but Rodrick's words snapped me back.

"Cyra, are you bleeding?" Rodrick asked.

I remembered the glass then still sticking in my face and side. The sharp pain from the cuts was still there, but it was so indistinguishable from the other pain radiating through my body that I didn't notice it.

Jaylan gasped as he took in the side of my face that had been turned away from him when he first approached.

I reached up to feel around and picked a few more pieces of glass from my cheek and chin. Blood smeared my fingers as Jaylan and Rodrick cried out for me to stop, but I just reached up again to pick another shard of glass from my arm and toss it on the ground.

"I need to go into town," I repeated flatly.

"Cyra, there's nothing you can do. What's done is done," Jaylan said.

I looked at Rodrick and saw the fear in his eyes at the sight of me. I'd always thought Rodrick might be the one person in Fernweh who wouldn't turn on me if he knew what I was. His presence suggested he hadn't been part of the mob that burned the vineyard, but he looked as though he wanted to run from me.

"Did you help them burn it?" I asked him.

He jolted at being addressed, but he shook his head.

"Are you afraid of me?" I asked.

Rodrick went pale, and I had my answer. I turned away from him.

"I need to see Eddin," I said.

"Don't you think you've done enough?" Brix spoke up, and I went still at the fury in his voice.

I turned to my younger brother and saw he was angry. At me.

"What have I done?" I asked, narrowing my eyes.

Brix stared me down for several seconds. "It's not what you've done. It's what you are. They did this because they're afraid of you."

"Brix!" Jaylan admonished.

"I've never given them reason to fear me," I said coldly to Brix, "but if they want one, they can have it."

"Cyra, no!" Jaylan grabbed my good arm, but I shook him off.

"Stay out of it, Cyra," Brix said, rage still biting his voice. "We don't want or need your help."

It was as though he'd slapped me. I just stared at the brother I'd always been so close to growing up, my partner in crime. I took in the hate and fury that now filled his eyes, all directed at me, and something broke inside me. The pain of it almost doubled me over. My hand flew to my chest as if to grab at the thing squeezing my heart, but Brix remained unapologetic.

It was an effort not to throw my hand out and blast him with a forcefield, to send him flying backward across the yard, to hurt him as I was now hurting.

I turned away to draw a circle in the air, and a portal flared open.

Jaylan and Brix had seen me call portals before, but Rodrick gasped and stepped back as blue light flared weakly, and the town of Fernweh appeared inside the flickering circle.

Magic fed off magic, but Fernweh had little power to draw from, and the portal I called was unstable at best. I opened it wider and stepped through, heedless of any potential danger. When I turned to close it, Jaylan was stepping through as well.

"Go back," I ordered him.

I ignored the cries and shouts of surprise that surrounded us where we stood on the main street in the middle of Fernweh. Jaylan ignored them as well, his eyes locked with mine, his expression resolute.

"No," he said. "If you're going to do this, you'll do it in front of me."

I looked at him, trying to decide whether to push him back through the portal with a forcefield, but then I shrugged.

"Fine. Is anyone else coming?"

I looked back into the portal at Brix and Rodrick. Brix was still staring daggers at me, but he stepped through as well. I looked to Rodrick, but he stepped back, shaking his head in terror.

I closed the portal on him, leaving him at the vineyard, and I turned to face the crowd gathering around us. I'd brought us right out in front of Eddin's tavern, but he was nowhere to be seen.

Time to let him know I was here.

"Eddin!" I yelled as I sent a huge forcefield straight at the tavern.

The building shook as power erupted from my hands in pulsing waves. A sharp noise split the air as the windows blew in and glass tinkled to the ground. Screams of panic and shouts of rage rose up around me.

"Cyra, stop!" Jaylan yelled behind me, but I only turned to the crowd.

"Who else was involved?" I called out to them. "Who of you laid hands on my brothers? How many of you held a torch to our vineyard?"

"It's not your vineyard anymore!" Brix hissed at me.

I rounded on him and pinned him with a look of fury. He staggered back as his eyes flared wide in shock.

"Nemesis take me," he breathed as he pressed three fingers to his lips in prayer, a gesture I'd never seen him make.

"Witch!" someone yelled, and I turned to see who'd spoken.

I was used to being around people who could put up mind shields in Callanus, but none of the people of Fernweh had ever needed one. As mortals, it would have been more difficult for them to create one anyway, and I marveled for a moment at how open their minds were, how easily I could invade each one of them and make them all do anything I wanted.

I could even kill them, I realized. Bressen didn't think I had the disposition to kill someone with my mind, but in this moment, with the smell and taste of that smoke still in the air and the specter of destruction haunting me, I knew I could kill them all.

I refrained, but not because I'd promised Bressen I wouldn't use my mind to kill anyone. No, I refrained because their deaths would be too quick and clean that way. I wanted them to die slowly. I wanted them to see their deaths bearing down on them like a stampede and not be able to move out of the way.

I smiled at the man who'd yelled that I was a witch. I knew him by sight, but I didn't know his name. I searched his mind for it.

"Jack, is it?" I asked the man, and he stiffened to hear me address him. "There seems to be a misconception that I'm a witch. I promise you I'm not." I paused. "I'm actually much, much worse."

"Cyra, please," Jaylan whispered.

"You were there weren't you, Jack," I said to him, ignoring Jaylan. "I bet you were one of the first to take a torch to our vines."

Jack shook his head, but the red glow on his skin told me the truth. I captured his mind then and froze him in place, and he looked terrified as he realized he could no longer move.

Gods above, the dominance I felt at taking control of him so easily was nearly as good as a climax. The thrill ignited my blood, and I almost gasped in pleasure.

"You fucking bitch!"

I turned toward the tavern to see Eddin had finally emerged and was surveying the damage I'd done to his windows.

I smiled, feeling a strange relief at the sight of him.

"Eddin, so good to see you again," I drawled. "It's been a while. The last time I was here you had a sword to your throat and urine dripping down your leg.”

Eddin went bright red and started toward me. Behind him, his barmaid Pryn came out of the tavern, tucking her shirt back into her skirt.

“Oh!” I exclaimed in surprise, understanding immediately what I’d interrupted. “And how long has that been going on?”

Eddin looked at Pryn and swore under his breath.

“I told you to stay inside!” he yelled at her.

“Oh no, she’s better off out here,” I said. “It’s not safe inside.”

I held out a hand and flames roared up behind Pryn inside the building. She screamed and ran down off the tavern’s porch.

“What the fuck are you doing?” Eddin screamed as he watched his tavern start to burn.

“My questions first,” I said. “How long…Never mind. I’ll find out for myself.”

I looked into Eddin and Pryn’s minds and saw what I wanted to know.

I laughed mirthlessly.

“So that’s why you wouldn’t tell anyone we were together,” I said to Eddin. “You were fucking both me and her at the same time.”

Pryn looked at Eddin as if this was news to her.

There was an explosion in the tavern as the fire reached the alcohol in the storeroom, and the crowd took a collective step back.

“Stop it!” Eddin screamed. “Put the fire out!”

“Did you ever think about putting the flames out when you set fire to our vineyard?” I asked him.

“Fuck you!” Eddin roared. “We should’ve torched that whole damn place a long time ago! You and your gods’ damned family don’t belong here! Filthy perimortals!” He spat onto the ground.

There was another explosion, and Eddin launched himself toward me. I let him get within a foot of me before my mind gripped his, and he froze in place. His eyes widened in fright as I held a hand up to his chest and sent a forcefield into him. My magic sensed one of his ribs crack as he flew backward and went skidding across the ground.

There were murmurs and shrieks from the crowd as they began to stir. They’d been captivated until now, caught between their instinct to flee and their desire to see the spectacle playing out before them, but the tide had turned. They were starting to rally against me, and I relished it. Let them try and attack me. I wanted an excuse to make them pay.

"Witch!" someone else shouted, and the crowd rumbled its assent.

I sighed. "I'm a perimortal, not a witch, and what you all don't seem to understand is that you made the biggest mistake of your miserable lives when you hurt my brothers and destroyed our vineyard. Before today, you might never have seen me again. I bore you no ill-will, and I never would've hurt any of you, but that changed when you attacked my family."

"We don't want your kind here!" someone yelled.

"And you wouldn't have my kind here if you'd left well enough alone!" I spat back. "My brothers are mortal like you. Had you left them in peace, you would've been fine."

"And what do you think you're going to do to us?" a large man I knew as Brune asked, stepping forward.

My mind reached out to search his and found a memory of him attacking Brix. Rage surged through me as I saw his meaty fist knock Brix's head to the side with a brutal punch before he twisted Brix's arm upward at an odd angle. My brother's shoulder popped out of joint, and he screamed in agony as Brune laughed.

"I'm glad you asked, Brune, because you can demonstrate for me," I said to him, a promise of pain in every word.

He lunged as if to grab me, but he froze a second later as I took control of his mind. It was so easy I almost laughed, and I wondered if this is what it was like for Bressen. Gods above, the elation I felt overpowered the pain, and I stepped closer to Brune so my face was inches from his.

"I have powers you can't even imagine," I told him softly, "and one of those powers is that I can make you do anything I want. Like make you walk into that building." I nodded my head toward the burning tavern.

At my words, Eddin rose from the ground, and he, Brune, and Jack all turned to walk toward the tavern.

I'd seen Bressen do this before, march men off toward their reckoning. It had been disturbing the first time I'd watched it, but seeing it now from the other side, it seemed nothing short of…beautiful.

Several people screamed, and the crowd began to jostle each other as they watched Brune, Jack, and Eddin walk purposely toward the tavern that was now fully engulfed in flames. The three men couldn't speak, but they were all making awful guttural noises in the backs of their throats that I imagined must be attempts at screams.

I didn't care. I'd seen in Brune's mind that he was one of the people who'd lit the fermentation barn on fire after he'd beaten Brix, and I was eager to let him taste those flames for himself.

Jaylan and Brix were both yelling at me to stop, but I could barely hear them above the voice in my head shrieking for vengeance. Out of the corner of my eye, I saw my brothers charge toward me, but I sent them sprawling backward with a small forcefield as I calmly watched the three men head toward the glow of the fire.

Eddin, Brune, and Jack were nearly to the porch of the tavern, and I felt their panic as the heat pouring from the building singed their skin.

I drank in their fear and pain, letting it intoxicate me like fine wine. The fire was my wrath, and they would burn.

There was a loud hissing noise as tons of water suddenly spilled from the tavern to quench the flames. It gushed from the broken windows and streamed under the door as it flooded the road and washed right up to my feet where I stood across the street from the once-burning building.

I felt Bressen before I saw him. His power enveloped the area, hanging in the air thicker than the smoke. It crackled through me as I turned to see him step out of a portal after Axenus with Phaedrus on his heels, and I fought back the shiver that threatened to crawl up my spine.

A strange mix of anger and relief washed over me at the sight of him. My silver eyes met his turquoise ones, and for a moment I couldn't move at the look I saw in them. It was part concern, part disappointment, and I almost didn't get my mental shield up in time as his power slammed against my mind a second later.

Bressen's eyes flashed in surprise as he walked toward me. I held his gaze, my chin ticking up a notch in defiance, even though every fiber of my being was urging me to cower back from the power radiating off him.

His halo glamour undulated around him with an other-worldly darkness, and the simple force of him settled over the crowd like a shroud.

I'd seen his glamour before and felt his power, but I couldn't stop my shiver as he stood there, drawn up to his full height, his mere presence demanding attention. It had been a long time since I'd felt wary of him, but that twisting in my chest was in fact fear.

Something constricted my throat. Part of me just wanted to run to Bressen and throw myself into his arms, but the other part wasn't finished tearing this town to the ground.

"Cyra, that's enough," Bressen said, his voice exuding calm authority.

"Stay out of this," I told him, but the words were choked.

"You know I can't do that," he said softly.

He stepped a little closer to me, and I was shocked to realize he was keeping his distance. Axenus must have told him my negation powers had a short range, and he was carefully staying out of my reach.

I blinked. The dreaded Lord Bressen of Hiraeth was wary of me.

This was the first time the two of us had squared off against each other, and I failed to strangle the laugh that rose up my throat as I realized we were both afraid of what the other could do.

Bressen furrowed his brows at my laugh, but he just turned his attention to the crowd.

"Anyone who took a torch to the vineyard stays," he said. "Everyone else, go home."

"And who the fuck are you?" an older woman asked, seemingly indifferent to the power drifting off Bressen like morning mist on a lake.

Bressen just smiled at her and addressed the crowd again.

"My apologies. I assumed you all knew who I was, given that you seem to tell quite a few stories about me down here. I'm Lord Bressen of Hiraeth, although I believe you prefer to call me the Nemesis Incarnate."

A chorus of gasps filled the air before people backed away with screams or prayers to the Protector. A few turned and ran, but some only got a few steps before they stopped dead, apparently immobilized by Bressen after he'd seen their culpability for the vineyard in their minds.

He turned his attention back to me and held out a hand.

"Cyra, it's time to go home," he said.

I shook my head. "No. They expected a monster, so they'll get one."

I turned to Eddin, who'd moved away from the tavern when Bressen's arrival had distracted me enough to sever my control over him. I held out a hand toward him, and Eddin stiffened in terror.

"Cyra, don't," Bressen warned me. "Don't make me stop you."

I knew what he meant. He'd break down my mind shield if he had to, but I didn't care. I'd managed to numb my pain for a while when I'd set the tavern on fire, but it had returned threefold when Bressen arrived. His presence had pulled me back from the brink of the chasm I'd been about to step over, but now that I'd regained some sense of myself, I could once again feel the anguish slashing my insides like a blade.

If Bressen tried to break into my mind, it would be excruciating, but I wanted the pain. I deserved it. Brix had been right. It was my fault that our home, the vineyard where we'd all lived and worked for decades, was gone. The anguish overwhelmed me, and I turned back to Eddin.

Eddin's eyes went wide as I cut off the air from his lungs, and his hands flew to his throat. He clawed at it as if that would open it again.

A wave of water hit me from behind a second later and knocked me to the ground. Eddin gasped for air as he got a momentary reprieve, and I glared up at Axenus, who stood ready to hit me again if necessary. I didn't give him time to. Still on my knees, I threw out my hands, one toward Eddin and one toward Axenus, and they both gasped as their air was cut off.

"Cyra! Stop!"

Bressen's cry seemed far away, and I ignored him as I continued to suffocate the two men. Eddin's eyes were wide with horror, but Axenus met my gaze, his eyes pleading, but not panicked.

I screamed then as Bressen tore into my mind shield, and my vision blurred as every nerve in my body seized in pain. If the furtive techniques Bressen had been teaching me to get past mind shields were like gingerly picking the lock on a door, then what he did now was like kicking the door down. Or burning it down. Or chopping it down with an axe and then burning the splinters.

My spine snapped back in an almost unnatural arch as the pain in my mind tore through me, worse than I'd expected, worse even than the guilt and rage and killing hatred that had been my companions since I'd first received Jaylan's message.

I knew I was screaming. I could feel my throat straining, but I couldn't hear anything beyond the high-pitched whine in my head that threatened to shatter my ears.

Then there was silence.

It hadn't taken Bressen long to tear down my mind shield. I knew it wouldn't. My mind powers had developed by leaps and bounds over the last few weeks, but Bressen's powers still far outstripped my own by every measure. I was no match for him. He'd broken through my shield within seconds, and then the pain was gone.

I knew I was laying on the ground, and a sense of calm settled over me. That was Bressen's doing. I'd seen him calm Raina the same way after she and I had been attacked on the wharf in Callanus. Raina was nearly hysterical when Bressen and Samhail found us, and he'd had to put her into a trance to get her back to the Citadel. I imagined I was in such a trance now.

Bressen's face appeared above me, and I felt him pull me into his arms, but I couldn't move. I tried to speak, but my mouth wouldn't move either. Bressen and I had never needed spoken words to communicate, though, and my mind called out to his now. He answered immediately.

*I'm sorry*, he said. *I couldn't let you kill anyone.*

*I think I wanted you to stop me*, I said.

*I could've hurt you.*

*I didn't care if you did.*

I felt his own pain at my words, but I wouldn't take them back.

*I'm going to put you to sleep now*, he said. *We'll talk more about this when you've had time to rest.*

*Bressen...*

*Yes?*

*I would have killed him. I would have killed them all.*

A pause. *I know.*

And then the world went dark.

# Chapter 13



I tried to take hope in the steady rise and fall of Cyra's chest as I lay in bed next to her. The rhythm of her breathing hadn't changed in three days, nor had she even moved, which I knew because I'd barely left this bed in that time.

I nuzzled my face into her hair, and the smell of smoke mingled with her usual scent of jasmine and almond. I'd tried to clean her up with a sponge as best I could when we got her back here to the Citadel, but I hadn't given her a full bath, so she still bore evidence of her ordeal in Fernweh. The smell of smoke angered me every time I got a good whiff of it, but there was nothing more I could do now, so I tried to ignore the churning in my gut at the scent.

I'd taken the sleep compulsion off Cyra after the first day, but she hadn't woken, and my dread grew with each passing hour that she remained unconscious. Thankfully Axenus had been able to make sure she stayed hydrated, but that was the least of my worries.

My biggest worry was whether she'd ever wake up again, a thought that made my body go cold as ice every time I considered it, so I'd let myself consider it as little as possible.

My next biggest worry was whether or not she'd still be herself when …or if she ever woke.

My mind powers were, to put it mildly, potent, and while most of my abilities left little if any lasting damage, the same couldn't be said of when I had to break into someone's mind by force. Violence was always dangerous.

I'd tried my best to slip into Cyra's mind unnoticed when we'd found her in Fernweh, to use a less dangerous way to get past her shield, but I'd taught her well. I hadn't been able to find a way in. There was no hole to exploit, no crack to slide through. She'd created a solid shield to keep me out, and it had done its job. At least until I'd had to break it down.

I'd begged her to stop what she was doing, but even through her mind shield I could feel the hurt and rage coming off her. It had frightened me because for the first time since I'd met her, she'd seemed beyond my reach. I'd never not been able to connect with her mind.

I'd told Axenus beforehand to use any and every power he had to try and stop her, anything to keep me from having to act myself, but she'd surprised both me and him by taking his air. I'd been left with no choice but to break through her shield. Or so I'd told myself.

I'd made myself feel some of her pain when I'd ripped into her mind. I owed her that much. While her shield had been strong enough that I couldn't slip through undetected, it was no match for the force of my mind when I threw my full power at it. No mind shield ever was.

When Samhail was in residence at the Citadel, he and I would train every afternoon, and part of our training involved me trying to break past the mind shield he put up. Sometimes I'd try to get through by stealth, and sometimes I'd try to get through by force. Samhail liked to get the practice defending against both, but what he didn't know was that I only ever used a small fraction of my power against him.

In truth, I could break into Samhail's mind easily whenever I wanted, but I'd never tell him that. It had destroyed something in Samhail when Morland had taken over his mind during the war, and the only thing that seemed to give him any peace now was the idea of having a nearly impenetrable mind shield. To be sure, his shield was formidable and would keep anyone else out. Just not me.

Samhail needed to believe he could keep me out, though, and so I let him think during our trainings that he could. About half the time at least.

All this was to say that Cyra didn't stand a chance when I could no longer delay and had to break past her mind shield. But I was paying for it now as the woman who'd become the air I breathed hadn't opened her eyes in three days.

I brought a hand up and grazed it gently down her cheek, but she didn't move. I'd tried to wake her multiple times by now, but nothing had worked. I'd left our bed only to relieve myself and to take brief meetings with Aidan, who was still acclimating to his new role as a Triumvirate Lord. There was a lot Aidan needed to know, and I should've been spending most of my days with him to get him oriented. As it was, I often asked him to meet in our bedroom – strange as that seemed – so I could keep an eye on Cyra. He'd been accommodating thus far.

Occasionally Aramis or Jaylan stayed with her so that Aidan and I could meet in my study instead, but I usually cut those meetings short, unwilling to leave Cyra out of my sight for more than an hour or so. If she woke, I needed to be there to be sure I hadn't done any irreparable damage to her, to be sure that…that I hadn't shattered her mind, which was easily a possibility.

I pulled Cyra closer. Her head was tucked against my chest so I could feel her warm breath on my skin, and I sent another silent prayer up to the Protector.

*Please*, I prayed. *Please let her be alright when she wakes up. Please just …let her wake up.*

I was supposed to meet Aidan soon, and I hadn't eaten yet. The tray with my lunch sat untouched on the game table. I'd have to uncurl myself from around Cyra in a few minutes, and the thought left my stomach even more hollow than my lack of food.

Cyra shifted slightly then, and my entire body was suddenly alive. It was the first time she'd moved on her own in days.

Her head lifted off my chest, and I looked down at her, not daring to hope she was finally awake.

My heart nearly stopped when my eyes met her bright silver ones, and I had to resist the urge to crush her to me.

"Thank the Trinity you're awake," I breathed as I rested my forehead against hers for a few seconds.

"How long have I been unconscious?" she asked, her voice hoarse, either from disuse or smoke inhalation or both.

I sighed in relief and brushed a lock of hair behind her ear.

"Three days," I said, and my own voice seemed graveled. "I took the sleep compulsion off you after the first day, but you didn't wake up. I've been going out of my mind ever since."

I sent a mental message to Aramis to tell him Cyra was awake, and I heard him answer in his own mind that he was on his way.

"Who did you call?" she asked.

She'd always been able to sense when I sent messages to others, and it was a good sign that she could still feel it. Yet I couldn't shake the feeling that something felt off between us.

"Aramis. I want him to examine you again. He also wants to see you."

"What happened after you put me down in Fernweh?" she asked.

I winced. "I put you out," I corrected softly, "not down."

"What happened after you put me out?"

"Axenus took you to Aramis so he could heal you both."

She touched her cheek and felt the smooth skin where broken glass had once cut her. I rested my hand over hers, but she pulled it out from under mine, and I tried not to let my body stiffen.

"Gods above," she whispered as she met my gaze, her expression pained. "Axenus must hate me."

"He doesn't," I murmured before kissing her forehead. "We went to the vineyard first before we found you in town. He saw what happened, and he understands. We both do."

She swallowed hard. "What else happened?"

"I found everyone who was part of the mob. They're all in prison in Gendris, although they'd be in Revenmyer if I had my way."

She frowned at me. "Whose decision was it to leave them in Gendris?"

"The High Council's," I said as I let my hand caress her back. "I…had to smooth over some ruffled feathers. In order to get to you before you did anything drastic, I entered Polaris before I had the council's permission. I wasn't really in my jurisdiction when I took half of Fernweh into custody."

She closed her eyes as the gravity of what I'd done, of the bounds I'd overstepped, hit her.

The High Council had been livid when I'd met with them after the fact to explain why I hadn't waited for permission to enter Polaris to retrieve Cyra. That I'd only just barely gotten there in time to stop her from killing three men ultimately convinced the council that my immediate action was excusable, but I knew their forbearance came with a cost. One day soon they'd call in their favor, and I'd have very little leeway to reject any request they made.

"Why am I not under arrest?" Cyra asked, and I grimaced.

That was the other thing I was sure I'd pay dearly for eventually.

"Technically, you're under house arrest here," I said. "Raina has some sway with the High Council, and she convinced them to consider the extenuating circumstances."

A look of devastation crossed Cyra's face, although I wasn't sure exactly what had caused it. It was possibly the idea of being under house arrest, but my guess was that it was more a sense of guilt over the position she'd put Raina in. Her friend now owed the High Council a favor as well, and Raina probably wouldn't like what she'd have to do to repay it. At least the council members still had a healthy fear of me. They'd exercise restraint where I was concerned. Not so with Raina.

"I'm so sorry," she said, and I pulled her closer as I stroked her hair.

"I'm just relieved we got to you before you could do anything you'd regret," I said.

She shook her head. "I don't think I would have regretted any of it."

I went still as I considered her words. She was hurting and wanted to lash out, and that was a feeling I understood well enough, but…

I just kissed the top of her head and wrinkled my nose as the smell of smoke wafted up again. Now that she was awake, I needed to wash away any remembrance of what had happened in Fernweh. Naïve as it was to think so, I couldn't help believing that if Cyra herself was clean, then her mind and soul would be as well. The last thing I wanted was for her to become as jaded as I was.

"We washed you as best we could while you were asleep," I said, "but we didn't give you a full bath. You can bathe when Aramis is done."

"What about Jaylan and Brix?" she asked.

"They're here at the Citadel until we can make other arrangements. It wasn't safe for them to stay on the vineyard. Between the smoke and the townspeople, I convinced them to stay here a while."

"Brix hates me," she said, her voice breaking.

I clenched my jaw. I'd found Cyra's younger brother to be a gregarious and endlessly curious young man when I first met him a couple months ago, but his insistence on blaming Cyra for what had happened to the vineyard was starting to grate on me. I'd been trying to be patient with him since he'd arrived at the Citadel, mindful of his loss, but his refusal to come check on Cyra these last few days had rankled me, and my patience was wearing thin with him.

"Brix is hurt and angry right now and needs someone to blame," I said as evenly as I could. "It's not fair, but you're the safest and easiest target. Give him time."

There was a knock at the door, and Aramis slipped into the room when I called out a command to enter.

I sighed. "I suppose it's time for me to get up now."

I leaned in and kissed Cyra gently on the lips before throwing the covers off and sliding out of bed. I wanted nothing more than to stay there and make love to her until she forgot all her pain and anger, but I'd been neglecting my responsibilities for three days. Now that she was awake and her mind seemed unharmed, I could no longer put off everything I had to do.

I headed to the closet to get dressed so I could meet with Aidan.

## Cyra

Aramis sat down in the spot Bressen had vacated.

"How are you feeling?" he asked, and the gentleness in his tone told me what he was really asking.

"Numb," I said.

"Not surprising. Lay back so I can see how you're healing."

I obeyed, turning over so I was flat on my back. Aramis held his hands over me for several seconds, then lowered them.

"Everything seems fine," he said. "I was able to remove the glass from you, and it doesn't seem to have left any scarring."

"Is Axenus alright?"

"He's fine. You took the brunt of the glass. You're just fortunate none of it hit your eyes. That would have been harder to heal."

His own silver eyes, mirrors of my own, met my gaze.

Bressen emerged from the closet fully dressed in his usual impeccable black ensemble and came over to the bed again. He looked at Aramis who answered his unspoken question.

"Physically she's fine. I'm not sensing any issues."

Bressen turned to me, and his face softened. "I need to go catch up on some work now that you've decided to stop scaring the three hells out of me. I'll be back in a few hours. Call if you need me."

He sat back down on the bed to give me a lingering kiss before he rose again to head out the door, taking a tray of food with him.

"He's as devoted to you as I was to your mother," Aramis said wistfully when Bressen was gone.

His mention of my mother reminded me of something I'd been meaning to ask him.

"Can you tell me about my mother's dream walking?" I asked. "How often did she do it? What did she use it for?"

"It was a service she provided," Aramis explained. "Her patrons were people who frequently had nightmares or those whose worries and conflicts plagued them when they slept. Your mother would follow them into their dreams to observe and then try to interpret what might be the issue. Most people aren't aware when a dream walker is with them, but your mother was powerful enough to approach people within their dreams and talk to them. She was sort of a mental healer in a way."

"Dream walking was her job?" I asked. "Did she…need to know someone before she could walk into their dreams?"

Aramis furrowed his brows. "Usually. There's only one time I know of that she walked into the dream of someone she didn't know."

"And when was that?"

He smiled. "When she walked into mine a week before we met."

I gasped and Aramis looked alarmed.

"What's wrong?" he asked.

I shook my head slowly. "Nothing's wrong. It's just that…I walked into Bressen's dream a week before I met him."

Aramis blinked, his mouth working to find words that escaped him.

"He and I had the same dream the morning I was attacked by the bear," I explained. "We were both walking around his house in Solandis looking for something in the dream, and we saw each other just before Brix woke me up to pick grapes. I didn't realize it was Bressen I saw until later, but he knew it was me when he first saw me in the Citadel."

Aramis was quiet as he took this all in.

"What does it mean?" I asked when he still hadn't spoken.

"I always took it as a sign that your mother and I were meant to be together. Maybe that's what it means for you and Bressen as well," he said.

The tightness in my chest eased a little, and I realized I'd been hoping he'd say that. For some reason, it was important to me to think Bressen and I were meant for each other.

"Axenus told me dream walking could be a powerful weapon," I went on. "He suggested I could use it to learn people's deepest fears and desires, and that the information could be used to control others."

Aramis looked at me sternly. "And you want to know if your mother ever abused her power like that?"

I winced. I hadn't talked to Bressen about any of this, but my hunch was that he wouldn't consider using my power that way to be an abuse. As a ruler who relied on having information and leveraging it to do what he needed to do, Bressen would likely see my dream walking as a valuable tool, but it didn't surprise me that Aramis viewed it differently.

I waved a hand. "Forget I asked. I know she wouldn't have used her power that way."

"And neither should you," Aramis said. "Has Lord Bressen asked-"

"No," I cut him off. "He hasn't asked anything of the kind."

*Yet*, I added in my mind.

When we'd first learned I was a syphon, Bressen had warned me that if anyone ever found a way to control me, they could use me as their own personal weapon. He himself certainly had sway over me, although I didn't think of it as control. Nevertheless, I would do just about anything Bressen asked if I thought it was important to him. He could very well use me as a weapon if he wanted to, although I didn't think he ever would.

Aramis eyed me but nodded.

"I suppose I should get out of bed and take a bath," I said, eager to change the subject.

Aramis stepped back and handed me my robe. I'd need to call one of the Citadel's maids to help me bathe since I felt a bit wobbly when I stood up. I hadn't replaced Raina yet, and I probably wouldn't until we returned to Solandis in a week or so.

"Let Jaylan know when you're out of your bath," Aramis said. "He'll want to see you."

My spirits rose, then immediately fell. "What about Brix?"

Aramis gave me a sympathetic look. "I think the boy may need a little more time to come to terms with what happened."

I tried to ignore the pit in my stomach as Aramis hugged me and then left me to bathe. It was still strange to think of him as my father, despite the evidence that literally stared back at me whenever I looked into his silvery eyes. He'd never fully replace the father in Fernweh who'd raised me as his own, but there was room in my heart for both men.

I summoned a maid and took my bath quickly, both eager and anxious to see Jaylan. I sent him a mental message inviting him up to our sitting room when I was dressed again.

Jaylan knocked several minutes later, and I opened the door, still half hoping Brix might be with him. He wasn't, and I shoved down my disappointment.

"Don't ever do that again," Jaylan said as he entered.

I frowned. "Do what?"

"Just start talking in my head. It's disconcerting."

I flushed. "I'm sorry. I'm just too used to talking to Bressen that way."

Jaylan grunted but then pulled me into a hug. "How are you doing?"

"All healed. How are you?" I asked as I pulled back to look at him. His bruises and cuts were gone, likely thanks to Aramis.

I motioned him toward the couches and chairs of the sitting room.

"The same," he said as he followed me.

The look that passed between us acknowledged that while we were both healed physically, the mental and emotional wounds were still there.

"I assume it's not safe for you to go back to Fernweh for a while because of me," I said.

Jaylan pushed out a deep breath. "I'm not sure it will ever be safe to go back to Fernweh. Not that it was all that safe for us there before…"

He trailed off, but I finished for him.

"Before I tried to murder half the town?"

Jaylan gave me a weak smile as I dropped heavily onto the sofa. He took an armchair next to me.

"Will Brix ever forgive me?" I asked.

"There's nothing to forgive you for. You didn't burn the vineyard. That's entirely on Eddin and everyone who helped him."

"And everything that happened after that?"

Jaylan paused, then said, "You only did what Brix and I both wanted to do. The difference is that you can get away with it now."

I flinched at the last part. I didn't want to be in prison, but it also didn't sit right with me that my position put me above the law. If I wasn't the soon-to-be Lady of Hiraeth, I might be in Revenmyer right now.

"I can't believe everyone in Fernweh hates me so much," I said.

There'd been people in that crowd I'd been friendly with at one time.

"I think they felt a little betrayed and anxious that they didn't know you were perimortal all this time," Jaylan mused. "They fear magic, and you were living right under their noses. It didn't take much for Eddin to spark a fire under them, and we both know why he did that."

I knew very well why. I'd broken off my relationship with Eddin just before Samhail arrived in Fernweh to bring me to Callanus. Even worse, after Eddin had threatened to make trouble for me, Samhail had paid him a visit and made him wet himself by putting a sword to Eddin's neck. In short, I wasn't one of Eddin's favorite people, so I wasn't surprised he'd led a charge against my family.

"What about you and Maeve? Is she…Are you…?" I left the question hanging, unsure how to ask Jaylan if I'd ruined his chances with the woman to whom he'd been ready to propose marriage.

"I…haven't spoken to her since everything happened," he said.

I dropped my eyes, unable to meet his gaze. "I'm sorry."

"It's not your fault," he said, but the denial sounded obligatory.

Silence stretched between us for a few seconds before I spoke again.

"I hope they gave you comfortable rooms here."

Jaylan smiled wanly. "Brix and I are living like kings compared to what we're used to. The Citadel will need to restock its pantry when we leave."

"It's good to know Brix's appetite is still intact at least. Where will you go if you can't go back to Fernweh?"

"I have no idea," Jaylan said. "We haven't thought that far ahead yet. Lord Bressen said we could stay here or in Solandis as long as we needed."

"You can just call him Bressen now. You're going to be family soon."

Jaylan shook his head in bewilderment. "I still can't believe the Nemesis Incarnate is going to be my brother-in-law. When I was little, I used to make Mom check under my bed at night to be sure he wasn't hiding under there ready to grab me."

I couldn't hold back a bark of laughter. "I dare you to tell him that."

"Absolutely not. I'm still intimidated by him as a grown man. I'm not about to tell him he gave me nightmares as a kid."

I frowned. "You're still intimidated by him?"

"A little. I'm coming around to the idea he's not really the monster we were led to believe, but I can't really see me and him having an ale at the tavern together anytime soon. There's still something I find… overwhelming about him. Like I'm afraid of being near him too long."

I understood what he meant. I often felt Bressen's power pulsing around him, and while I found it comforting, I could see how it might bother others. He'd also cultivated such a mythos of terror about himself that most people were afraid to be near him for more than a few minutes.

"How is Brix getting along with Bressen?" I asked. Even if Brix wouldn't talk to me, I hoped maybe he was warming up to Bressen.

"You know Brix. He has no fear regarding the things that come out of his mouth. He spends most of dinner peppering Lo…uh, Bressen with questions about everything under the sun. I'm sure everyone else thinks he's insane, but Bressen's been patient with him."

Relief warmed me. I'd need to thank Bressen later for indulging Brix.

My stomach grumbled, and I remembered I hadn't eaten for days. Almost as quickly, a lead weight settled there as I realized I'd have to go down to dinner tonight now that I was awake. I'd have to see Axenus.

No, I couldn't do it. Not yet. I'd ask for my dinner to be sent up to the room tonight, and perhaps for the near future. Brix didn't want to see me anyway, and I wasn't prepared to face Axenus after what I'd done to him. I could only guess what Aidan might think of everything, especially after the last conversation I'd had with him in the Great Chamber.

"Will you try to convince Brix to speak to me?" I asked Jaylan.

"I've been trying. He'll come around. He refuses to come see you when I check on you, but he always asks about you when I return. He still loves you. He just doesn't know what to do with his anger."

I sighed. Unfortunately, I'd known exactly what to do with my own anger when I'd seen the vineyard. Maybe it was better if Brix directed his frustrations at me. There were far worse ways he could deal with them.

Jaylan stayed to talk to me for the next hour, and I tried not to let the ache in my chest show when he finally rose to leave. I hugged him and sat back down with a book to wait for Bressen.

I wasn't sure if 'house arrest' meant I was confined to my room or just the Citadel, but I wasn't ready to venture out just yet anyway.

I'd only read a few dozen pages when Bressen returned hours later. I'd spent most of my time staring into the flames in the fireplace as images of the vineyard and Eddin's tavern burning played through my head.

Bressen wasn't happy when I told him I wasn't going down to dinner. He tried to convince me to come, but I refused, and the tray of food I'd ordered from the kitchen arrived just then. He relented and let me stay in the room, but I knew this was a fight we'd have again.

When we went to bed later that night, Bressen curled himself around me as usual, and I nestled into him. My body went rigid, though, as he gently pulled my hair away from my neck and kissed my shoulder. When one of his hands moved down my thigh, I laid my own hand on top of it to stop its slide. Bressen tensed for only a moment before he pulled his hand back and wrapped his arm around me to pull me closer instead.

I was confused by the relief I felt when he didn't press me about my lack of ardor, but I just relaxed against him and drifted off to sleep.

Mercifully, Bressen didn't question me about my rejection of his advances the next day, nor did he say anything the following day when I once again only allowed him to hold me in bed. I didn't let myself think about why I couldn't or wouldn't let him touch me intimately, even as I fell asleep each night with the proof of his desire pressed against me.

For nearly a week I awoke each morning with Bressen's body making its silent plea to enter mine, but he never pushed me. He never asked why I wouldn't let him touch or kiss me beyond the chaste cuddling we did each night, and in truth, I didn't have an answer for him.

I had no idea why the thought of Bressen's sensual touches now sent panic racing through my body.

# Chapter 14

I continued to eat my meals in our room for several days until Bressen finally put his foot down and told me it was time to stop hiding and start eating in the dining room again. He also told me I needed to resume my magic lessons with Axenus.

I balked at both decrees and argued with him for an hour, but he was immovable, and I went to sleep on my own side of the bed that night, shunning the feel of his body against mine for the first time ever.

When I awoke the next morning once again wrapped in his arms, my first thought was to rail at him for forcing his touch on me. Then I realized I was on his side of the bed and not the other way around. I'd somehow made my way across the bed toward him in the middle of the night where he'd accepted me, literally, with open arms.

Unfortunately, I didn't think I'd get the same reception from Axenus or Brix when I saw them again today for the first time since Fernweh.

I dreaded every step down to the dining room that morning for breakfast. Bressen was by my side, his hand in mine as we entered, but I breathed an audible sigh of relief to see Axenus wasn't there.

I received a warm welcome from Jasper, Jaylan, and Aramis as I entered, and a neutral one from Aidan. Maziren looked even more ready to spring across the table and attack me than she normally did.

I looked hopefully to Brix, but he turned his head away a second after our eyes met, and my heart twisted. Bressen's hand tightened around mine, and I felt his ire spike at Brix's dismissal of me, but he mastered himself and led me to the sideboard to get some food.

I understood Brix's anger. It had been a week since the incident in Fernweh, and I was slowly coming to terms with the loss of our vineyard. I'd given up my place there when I agreed to marry Bressen, and soon I'd have a vineyard of my own in Solandis, but the one in Fernweh had been my home for more than two decades, and I felt its loss acutely. If I could feel that way about a place I no longer had any claim to, I couldn't imagine what Jaylan and Brix were going through.

Jaylan had come to visit me every day this week, but I could barely look at him most of the time. He assured me he didn't blame me for anything as Brix did, but I'd noticed a new wariness in his eyes that hadn't been there before. He'd only ever seen me use a fraction of my powers and never violently, but I'd tried to kill at least three people rather horribly that day in Fernweh. I didn't need to read his mind to know that he'd forever see me differently now.

I didn't count Axenus as one of the people I'd tried to kill. I'd been trying to render him unconscious when I cut off his air so he couldn't use his power to stop me, but I'd never intended to hurt him. Whether he saw it that way or not was another story. Bressen promised me that Axenus bore me no ill-will, but I knew something had changed between us.

"It's good to see you up and about," Jasper said to me as I sat down at the table. "We were all starting to worry about you."

I looked doubtfully at Aidan and Maziren, whose expressions clearly told me they didn't share Jasper's concern. But the scoffing sound I heard next didn't come from either of them.

I looked at Brix to see him shaking his head. Shame washed over me, but it was quickly replaced by anger.

"If you have something you want to say to me, Brix, just say it," I snapped at him, and the entire table went silent.

He scoffed again. "No, I have nothing to say to you, Cyra."

I opened my mouth to retort but snapped it shut again when I saw the tense expressions on everyone's faces. I wasn't going to ruin their meal by fighting with my brother.

"It *is* good to see you join us, Cyra," Aramis said kindly to me, and I thought I saw Brix wince, as if my father's words had stung him.

I smiled wanly and bit into my biscuit. It was like ashes in my mouth.

*Where's Axenus?* I asked into Bressen's mind.

*I think he had breakfast early so he could swim before your training. Don't worry. He's not trying to avoid you.*

I went back to eating, and the table fell silent again, but a moment later Brix pushed his chair back and picked up his plate. There was still food on it, which was unheard of for Brix.

"Where are you going?" Jaylan asked him, apparently noticing the same thing.

"I've lost my appetite," he said.

"Sit down," Jaylan ordered him, but I didn't need Jaylan to fight this battle for me.

"What exactly is your issue with me?" I asked, rising as well. "It's not my fault the people of Fernweh hate perimortals."

"It goes far beyond that," Brix said, giving me his full attention for the first time since I'd walked in. "Did you know Brune had a brother who died in the battle at Gendris?"

"Brix!" Jaylan said, trying to silence him, but I stilled as I remembered the man I'd nearly killed in Fernweh.

"When they found his brother's body, half his bones were broken," Brix went on. "He was one of the soldiers that tried to fight Samhail."

My breath caught in my throat. I hadn't known that. It made Brune's hatred of me a little more understandable, but only partially.

My eyes narrowed as I remembered that day.

"Then Brune's brother was also one of the soldiers that cheered when Jerram and Glenora were torturing Bressen," I shot back.

I'd been tortured some as well, but it was Bressen's pain the crowd had cheered the loudest. I didn't look at him now to see what his reaction was, but Brix's eyes darted to Bressen at my words.

"He tried to help overthrow the Triumvirate," I went on.

"He was following orders," Brix grumbled.

"Regardless, it's not my fault Brune's brother is dead," I said. "And it's not my fault the vineyard is gone. Jaylan doesn't blame me, and he has more reason to do so than you do. Rodrick doesn't seem to blame me either. He was there to support you that day."

Brix barked out a mirthless laugh that took me by surprise.

"Is that why you think Rodrick was there?" he asked incredulously.

Jaylan shot to his feet. "Brix! Shut up now."

"I'm sorry, Jaylan," Brix said resolutely, "but she needs to know why Rodrick was really there."

"No, she doesn't," Jaylan hissed.

I went still again. "What are you talking about? If Rodrick wasn't there to show his support, then why was he there?"

A sense of foreboding settled in my stomach as I looked between my brothers, but I needed to know the answer to this question.

"I'm warning you, Brix, keep your mouth shut," Jaylan said. He grabbed Brix's arm, but Brix didn't stop.

"Rodrick was there to tell Jaylan that things were over between him and Maeve."

My eyes snapped to Jaylan before the floor seemed to shift under me, and my knees buckled. Bressen's hands gripped my shoulder and arm as I fell back into my chair.

"We should go," Jasper suggested softly to Aidan and Maziren.

"Yes, why would you want to stay to hear how us mortals are affected by the decisions you perimortals make?" Brix snapped at Jasper.

His words cleared my head immediately.

"Brix, yell at me if you want, but you'll show everyone else in this room respect!" I yelled, launching myself back out of my seat. "Jasper is mortal like you."

"He might as well be perimortal," Brix shot back. "He's part of their world. He enjoys their privileges. *Your* privileges."

"I'm so sorry for this," I said to Jasper.

"Don't apologize for me," Brix said angrily. "I'm only speaking the truth. You should be in prison right now, but you're not, either because you're some big, powerful perimortal, or because *he* pulled some strings to keep you out. Probably both."

He jabbed a finger at Bressen, and I felt Bressen's power pulse.

Brix must have felt it too because he winced and seemed to consider that maybe he'd gone too far.

I lowered myself back into my seat again. I couldn't argue with Brix. He was right that I was only free because of who I was and who I knew.

"Is what Brix said true?" I asked Jaylan quietly. "Was Rodrick there to tell you to stay away from Maeve?"

Jaylan only closed his eyes.

Brix started to interject again, but Jaylan silenced him.

"Shut up, Brix," he said in a tone I'd never heard him use before. "You wanted me to tell her, so let me tell her."

Brix looked a little shocked at Jaylan's tone, but he fell silent.

Jaylan turned to me, and the sadness in his eyes squeezed my chest.

"Rodrick didn't come to tell me to stay away from Maeve," Jaylan said, pain lancing every word. "He came to deliver a message from her. She doesn't want to see me again."

A strangled cry forced itself past my lips, and acid burned in my chest as I swallowed down bile.

"Oh gods," I whispered, forcing the words past the lump in my throat. "Jaylan, I'm so sorry."

I'd always liked Maeve. She was shy and sweet and probably the closest thing I could claim to a female friend in Fernweh. I never could've foreseen that she'd reject Jaylan like this.

"He'd almost gotten Rodrick to agree to let him talk to Maeve when you arrived," Brix spat out, and anything left inside me that wasn't yet broken shattered at the words.

"Leave it alone!" Jaylan said.

He stepped toward Brix, and even though our younger brother was stronger and taller by a couple inches, Brix actually retreated a step.

"Is that true?" I asked Jaylan.

He only looked at me, but I saw the confirmation in his eyes.

I rose once more and felt Bressen tense next to me. I was grateful he hadn't jumped into the argument. It would only have made things worse with Brix. I felt his power trying to cocoon around me now, but I pushed it back with a pulse of my own, the first time I'd ever done so, and I sensed Bressen's surprise.

"If you'll all excuse me, I should go," I said.

"Cyra, don't," Aramis said. "Brix doesn't speak for everyone here."

Hurt flashed across Brix's face again as he looked at Aramis. Jaylan had told me that Brix was getting close to Aramis, that he'd latched onto him as a father figure, and Brix seemed surprised that Aramis was supporting me. I'd have been grateful except that I was sure Brix would only use this as more reason to hate me.

"I'm sorry, but I need to go," I said as I stepped out from behind my chair. I turned to Bressen. "Please extend my apologies to Axenus, but I'm going to miss our lesson today. I don't feel very well."

*Cyra…*

Bressen's voice was coaxing in my mind, but I threw up my mental shield, and he flinched back.

I turned without another word and strode out of the dining room toward the sanctuary of our suite. I was prepared for Bressen to try and stop me, but he let me go, and I wasn't sure whether to be relieved or upset by that.

Back in our room a few minutes later, I slammed the door behind me and began to pace wildly. My hands shook with an emotion I couldn't pinpoint as my quick strides took me back and forth across the floor in a circuit that nearly made me dizzy. Tears had threatened half a dozen times since Brix first laid into me, but I'd managed to force them back each time. My eyes had been painfully dry on the walk up here, but I couldn't hold back any longer.

The tears rushed out in a deluge, and I wiped furiously at the great salty rivulets as they streamed down my cheeks. Brix's treatment of me had been upsetting, but it wasn't what tore me up inside.

Jaylan had lost Maeve, and he hadn't told me. He'd kept it a secret this whole week, letting me feel sorry for myself, and never once hinting that things were over between him and the woman he'd hoped to marry. I'd always thought he and I could tell each other anything, and this was yet another knife to my heart.

A gentle knock sounded on the door, and I willed my tears back as I strode over to open it. I expected to find Jaylan outside, but it was Aramis.

"May I come in?" he asked.

I moved aside to let him pass.

"Is this where you tell me to give Brix time?" I asked bitterly as I closed the door behind him. "That he's just angry and doesn't know where to direct his rage, and that I should just bear with him until he realizes I'm not the one he's really angry at?"

He smiled indulgently. "It sounds like you already know all that."

"Then why are you here?" I asked, my voice harsher than I'd intended.

"To offer you a friendly ear or perhaps a fatherly hug. Unfortunately, my healing powers don't work on wounds of the soul."

I rolled my eyes, but the corners of my mouth tugged upward in appreciation of his concern.

"Are there perimortals that can heal soul wounds?" I asked seriously.

"Not that I've ever heard of," Aramis said. "The only thing I know of that can help heal those wounds is love."

I rolled my eyes again.

"I know that sounds trite, but it's true," Aramis said. "And you have lots of people who love you, Cyra. Jaylan loves you. Bressen loves you, and, for what it's worth, *I* love you."

I gave him a frustrated look. "It means a lot that you love me," I said. "I know I've had a hard time trying to wrap my head around who you are and what you mean to me — or what you *should* mean to me — but don't mistake those difficulties for indifference. I value having you in my life now, and I appreciate the time you've given me to adjust to the situation."

Aramis nodded in understanding.

"It's just not fair," I went on, trying to keep my voice from breaking. "I can't help what I am or how people react to me. I know I didn't do myself or perimortals in general any favors by going after those men in Fernweh, but I thought that of all the people I could count on to stand by me, I could count on my brothers." I shook my head. "Brix and I used to be so close."

"You will be again," Aramis promised. "Take it from me, family relationships can be complicated things."

I met his eyes, and a question suddenly burned in my mind. "When was the last time you saw my aunt?" I asked, and Aramis stiffened.

My aunt, my mother's sister, had been the one to send the authorities after Aramis when he fled with me as an infant. She was the reason he'd felt compelled to leave me in Fernweh and the reason he'd ultimately spent two decades in Revenmyer.

Aramis exhaled deeply. "Not since the end of my trial when they hauled me away to Revenmyer," he said. "I…might have threatened to kill her if I ever got out."

My brows shot up, and Aramis shrugged.

"I was a little upset," he said.

"Do you think you'll ever see her again?" I asked.

"If the gods are good, no."

I felt a little ashamed of myself. Aramis had been through so much more than I had, and – threats of killing my aunt aside – he'd handled it so much better than me.

I knew Aramis had his demons. He never put up a mind shield, and I could sense the lingering turmoil inside him whenever I let my powers reach out, but he didn't let those demons control him. He hadn't let two decades in Revenmyer turn him into either a shell or a monster. Since being out, he'd gone back to being a healer, and he was trying his best to be a father to me. And to Brix, it seemed.

The click of the door opening drew my attention, and I turned to see Bressen poke his head into the room.

"Can I come in?" he asked.

"Please do, Lord Bressen," Aramis said. "I should get back to breakfast." He turned to me again. "Remember that you're loved. Brix was out of line, and yes, his anger is misplaced, but he's your brother, and he'll remember that eventually."

I nodded, and Aramis leaned in to press a gentle kiss on my forehead. Part of me wanted to ask for the fatherly hug he'd offered earlier, but I refrained. Being around him made me feel like I'd lost my memory. There was a tug in my heart that told me I knew him, that he was someone important to me, but my mind still insisted he was a stranger.

Bressen waited for Aramis to leave, then closed the door and came toward me. His pace was unhurried, as if he was afraid I might bolt if he approached too quickly, but there was no mistaking the focus in his eyes that rooted me to the spot. I was a rabbit, hoping that if I stayed perfectly still, the predator loping by wouldn't see me.

Bressen stopped in front of me, seemingly at ease, but I knew every muscle in his body was wound tight. He wanted to reach for me, to pull me into his arms, but I'd shied away from his touch all week, and he didn't want to risk it. I knew it hurt him every time I rejected his embrace, but I couldn't help it. Anxiety rose in me whenever he was close by so that I nearly shook with nervous energy.

"Did Aramis say anything to help?" Bressen asked.

I shrugged. "I suppose."

"Brix was out of line. He had no right to-"

"Brix isn't the problem," I said, cutting him off as I hugged my arms across my chest. "I'm more upset that Jaylan didn't tell me about Maeve."

"He didn't want you to feel worse than you already do."

"I know. I just…it hurts that he tried to hide it, that he thought I was so fragile I wouldn't be able to take the news."

"Or perhaps it's just too painful for him to talk about right now," Bressen suggested. "Maybe he was protecting himself, not you."

I blinked. That was certainly possible, and the fact that I'd assumed Jaylan's grief was about me only made me feel worse.

"I haven't handled any of this well," I said, shaking my head. "I thought I was stronger than this."

"Don't punish yourself," Bressen said.

He reached up to touch me, hesitated, then grasped my arms anyway.

"You've been through a lot in a very short time. No one is going to blame you for reaching a breaking point," he said gently.

"Aramis was in Revenmyer for twenty-two years, and he's fine."

Bressen let go of me.

"You can't compare yourself to Aramis," he said. "Revenmyer is… well, Revenmyer is something else altogether. Everyone reacts differently to being there depending on their experiences. Aramis was a good man who was falsely imprisoned. Revenmyer uses people's own fears and depravities against them. The worse the criminal, the more they suffer, but Aramis was never a criminal. I have no doubt he suffered, but not in the same way some of Revenmyer's other inmates do."

Bressen brushed a strand of hair behind my ear, and I flinched away from his touch without thinking. His expression remained neutral as he lowered his hand, but I felt the pain of the rejection spike through him.

"What is Revenmyer like?" I asked, trying to distract him.

He shook his head. "That's not something you need to hear about right now. I'll tell you someday, but not now."

"When did you first see the prison?" I pressed. "Did you see it before your father…"

I'd been about to ask him if he saw the prison before his father died, but it suddenly seemed like such a callous question. I didn't even know how his father had died. The man had been the warden of Revenmyer before Bressen, and for all I knew, his death had something to do with the prison.

"I was seven when my father first brought me to Revenmyer," Bressen said, answering anyway.

I gaped at him. "What?"

He shrugged. "The prison has been my family's responsibility for many centuries now. He knew it would be my responsibility one day, so he began my training early."

"But seven?" I asked incredulously. "What kind of parent takes their child to visit a prison for Thasia's worst criminals when they're seven?"

Something flashed across his face, and I instantly regretted my words. Bressen had been close to his father, and I'd just questioned the man's fitness as a parent.

"I'm sorry. I didn't mean that how it sounded," I said.

"It's fine. It's not something most parents would do, but my father was never one to hide anything from me or gloss over the realities of the world. To be honest, I'm glad he showed me what the prison was like when I was that young. I think it might almost have been harder to handle if he'd waited until later to show me what things were really like there. Children can probably handle more than we give them credit for, and I think my father knew that."

Bressen smiled as if remembering something.

"What?" I asked.

"When I was nine," he said, "I caught two of the servants at the Citadel having sex in an empty room."

My brows shot up. "Oh my."

"I was still too young to know what they were doing, and I actually thought the man might be hurting the woman the way she was moaning and whimpering. Then she saw me and screamed."

"What did they do?" I asked. "What did *you* do?"

"They stopped and pushed past me out of the room, and I went to my father to tell him what I'd seen. I was worried for the woman on some level, but I was also curious."

My mouth worked as if to say something, but I wasn't sure what.

"I tried to explain things to my father," he went on, "but he was clearly confused since I wasn't explaining it well, so I put the image into his mind of the couple fucking."

My mouth dropped open, and Bressen chuckled.

"You should have seen the look on his face when he realized what I'd witnessed," he said.

"What did he tell you was happening?"

"The truth," Bressen said. "He sat me down and explained sex to me then and there. Again, many parents might have tried to lie or explain it away, but my father was always honest with me."

There was amusement in his eyes before his face clouded over.

"What is it?" I asked.

He looked away. "My father was always honest with me, but I didn't return the favor when it counted. There was something I should have told him that I didn't, and I've regretted it ever since."

I waited for him to volunteer the story, but he didn't.

"How…how did your father die?" I asked instead. "I don't want to pry, but I know so little about you and your family."

Bressen sighed. "It's a rather sordid tale. My father and uncle killed each other in a fight."

"Oh gods," I said, putting a hand to my mouth. "Why were they fighting?"

He paused, then said, "It's not important. It's a fight that should never have happened. In fact, it might not have happened at all if I'd been honest with my father. By the time I tried to stop it, it was too late."

Bressen opened his jacket and pulled one side of his shirt up to bare his torso just under his ribs. There was a scar there I'd seen before, one that looked a little like a star. I'd touched it just before we had sex the first time when I'd been exploring his body, and I remembered him flinching when I brushed my fingers over it. I hadn't thought to ask at the time what it was from.

"My uncle gave me this when I jumped in front of his sword to try and save my father," he said. "Unfortunately, it was too late. My father was already mortally wounded, and we couldn't get a healer there in time."

I tried to swallow past the knot in my throat, but it remained lodged there. All I could do was reach out and brush my hand gently over the scar again. Bressen didn't flinch this time.

"My uncle was shocked when he accidentally ran me through," he went on, "and his distraction gave my father the opportunity he needed. My father used his last bit of strength to kill my uncle, and then all three of us collapsed. I was the only one to get back up."

"I'm so sorry," I said, my voice more a rush of air than a whisper.

My hand lingered on the scar as the desire to touch him for the first time in days swelled inside me. I ran my thumb lightly across it, and Bressen inhaled more deeply.

I raised my head to look at him. His eyes seemed to almost glow when they met mine, and my lips parted unconsciously. His pupils flared, and then his hand was at my back, pressing me against him. My fingers still rested over his scar as his arms snaked around me and one hand threaded up into my hair to grip the back of my head.

Bressen lowered his head slowly, giving me every chance to stop him. I didn't move, but a tempest roared inside me as desire warred with alarm. It had been more than a week since Bressen had kissed me with more than just a brush of his lips across my temple or forehead, and my body ached to bring his mouth crushing down onto mine. Behind that desire, though, was a blazing, blinding panic that screamed at me to push away and run for it. It was an irrational fear that told me Bressen was a threat from which I needed to flee far and fast.

Lightning struck through my veins as his lips met mine, but whether the sensation was predominantly one of pleasure or pain I wasn't sure. All I knew was that I couldn't move. Conflicting forces held me prisoner as Bressen's tongue coaxed my lips apart. I tried to remain perfectly still because I knew if I moved, I'd run.

The groan that rumbled in Bressen's throat was born of pure need, but my answering whimper was a plea. To stop? To deepen the kiss? To throw me on the bed and make my body remember his? I didn't know.

An ache started to pulse behind my eyes, and I furrowed my brows against it as Bressen pulled me closer, his kiss becoming more urgent. I forced my hand to slide up under his shirt so that it rested lightly over the hard swell of his chest muscle, and I stroked my thumb over the tight bud of his nipple. He groaned again, and his fingers tightened almost painfully in my hair as his mouth pressed down harder onto mine.

Pain suddenly stabbed through my head as if someone had shoved a dagger through my eye, and I shoved away from Bressen with a cry.

"Cyra, are you alright?" his voice swirled with concern and yearning. "Did I hurt you?"

"No," I lied shakily. "No, I just…have a headache."

We were both breathing hard, him from thwarted desire and me from pain and panic.

"I'm sorry," I said. "It just came on suddenly. I think I need to rest."

Bressen nodded, and his hands receded from around me like the tide.

"Get some rest," he said. "You have training with Axenus tomorrow."

I opened my mouth to protest, but he held up a hand to stop me.

"He told me to tell you that he's not accepting any further excuses, and that he'll drag you if necessary."

I snapped my mouth shut and frowned.

"I'm just the messenger," Bressen said.

Fine. I could only avoid Axenus for so long, and tomorrow was as good a day as any for my reckoning with him.

# Chapter 15

I stood outside the doors of the Great Chamber at nine o'clock with a knot in my stomach, every muscle itching to turn and flee back to my rooms. I'd almost decided to creep away when Axenus's muffled voice called out from inside the chamber, making me jump.

"Stop stalling and come inside, or I'll douse you in cold water again."

I swallowed and put a hand on one of the doors. Both of them swung open to admit me, and my eyes immediately fell to the floor as I walked slowly into the chamber.

I'd seen Axenus standing in the middle of the room when the doors first opened, but I couldn't bring myself to look at him as each step carried me closer. I might as well have been marching toward my execution. I forced myself to come within a few yards of him before my feet refused to take me any farther.

"I'm sorry," I croaked out as soon as I stopped. "I won't make excuses for what I did to you in Fernweh. The best I can offer is to beg your forgiveness and do whatever I possibly can-"

"Cyra," he cut me off, but his voice was soft and devoid of anger.

I swallowed and waited for him to continue. I saw his boots approach as he stepped to within a few feet of me.

"Cyra, look at me please," he said, and I dragged my eyes up to meet his cerulean ones.

His expression was easy, but somehow that only made my insides clench more.

"I forgive you," he said. "That woman I saw in Fernweh wasn't really you. I know that."

I huffed a mirthless laugh and looked at him incredulously. "How can you say that? That woman you saw in Fernweh is who you've been trying to make me into this whole time, isn't it?"

His eyes narrowed sharply. "No," he said emphatically. "No, not at all. I've been trying to teach you to be someone who can act for her own good and the good of those around her, but I definitely haven't been trying to turn you into someone who can kill with no conscience."

I winced, but I just shook my head and looked away from him.

"Then you failed," I said coldly as tears threatened in my eyes. It wasn't fair to blame him, but I needed to lash out…like Brix had.

Axenus stepped forward and tried to turn me back toward him with a hand to my cheek. When I resisted, he grabbed my chin and forced my face around.

"Stop," he said sharply. "The woman you were that day in Fernweh was in pain. She was someone who wanted vengeance and didn't care who she hurt in that pursuit, but I know that's not who you are."

"And how do you know that? How do you know you haven't just been peeling back the layers of the monster I've always been underneath?"

Axenus let go of my chin and looked at me for a long time. I started to think he wasn't going to answer me when he finally spoke.

"Because I know what it feels like to be where you were, and because I've seen true monsters, and you aren't one of them. You wouldn't be this upset about what happened if you were."

I wanted to argue with him, to insist I was indeed a monster, but there was something in his voice and the way he looked at me, almost as if he was seeing past me to something else, that kept me silent. I had no idea what horrors lay in Axenus's past, but I didn't doubt him when he said he understood how I felt.

"How do I build your trust again?" I asked him.

He smiled at me. "You never lost it. It's trust in yourself we need to build again."

"How do I do that?"

He gave me a look I knew immediately meant I wasn't going to like what he had to say.

"I want you to fill my lungs with water," he said.

I felt the color drain from my face, and I took several steps back.

"No! Don't make me do that!" I said as I shook my head violently.

"Cyra," he said in a tone of reason.

I shook my head more and took another step back from him, but he stepped toward me again. I tried to back further away, but his long legs closed the distance between us, and he grabbed one of the hands I held out to ward him off. I tried to yank free from his grasp, but he held my wrist firmly and pulled me toward him.

He waited patiently for me to realize I wasn't going to be able to free myself. When I finally stopped struggling, he brought my hand up to his neck to place it on his pulse.

"Can you feel my heartbeat?" he asked.

I swallowed and nodded as I felt the beat of his heart nudge the tips of my fingers.

"I'm alive," he said. "I'm fine. You didn't hurt me the other day."

"I did hurt you, and I don't want to hurt you again."

"You won't. You've done this before."

I looked at him pleadingly.

"I trust you, Cyra. Now trust yourself."

I closed my eyes and exhaled deeply, focusing on the steady thrum of his pulse under my fingers. I let it try to calm me with its rhythm since my own heart was running a race in my chest.

"You're sure?" I asked, exhaling shakily as I opened my eyes.

"Yes."

I took in a deep breath and carefully started to fill Axenus's lungs with water. He didn't move a muscle as I sensed the water rise inside his chest, and I stopped just before his lungs hit their capacity. Then I slowly pulled the water back out. All the while, the drum of Axenus's heartbeat kept me anchored.

I found him looking at me when the last of the water was out of his lungs. He nodded and released my hand.

"See?" he said. "Still alive. You used your powers on me, and you didn't turn into a bloodthirsty monster."

I let out the breath I held, and my shoulders relaxed as I stepped back.

"You still want to train me?" I asked.

"Of course," he said. "Like most perimortals, your powers are more volatile when you're feeling strong emotions. You've gotten over your reluctance to use them to hurt someone, although not in the way I would have preferred. Now we need to swing back the other way, and you need to learn to control them when your emotions are surging."

"That doesn't sound like it's going to be fun."

"It probably won't be," he said, "but it's what we need to do next."

I sighed and was about to ask him how we'd start when I heard the doors to the Great Chamber open. Axenus and I both turned to see who had entered, and my heart jumped into my throat to see the huge figure filling the doorway.

The man seemed impossibly tall, but I knew that the body packed with lean muscle standing there was all-too real. His stark-white hair was longer than I remembered, and he wasn't wearing his black leather armor or the two deadly-sharp blades that normally crisscrossed his back. His face was the same, though. Midnight blue eyes fixed on me from under sharp brows, and one side of his mouth ticked up, suggesting a smile was trying to force its way onto lips that I knew were surprisingly soft.

Gods above, I hadn't realized how much I'd missed him until now.

"Sorry to interrupt," Samhail said, "but Bressen told me you'd be here. I wanted to stop in to see how my replacement is working out."

I tried to swallow down the lump in my throat at the sight of the man who'd become my friend, my rock – both figuratively and once literally – when my world had been thrown upside down. Samhail had protected me, counseled me, and kept me sane during the uncertainty of my confinement when I'd first been brought to the Citadel, and I loved him almost as much as I loved Bressen.

I clamped a hand over my mouth to hold in a cry as tears sprung to my eyes. I'd needed him, and having him back now after not seeing him for two months snapped what little control I had left.

I broke into a run across the room and launched myself into Samhail's waiting arms, not caring what Axenus thought. Samhail picked me up so my legs hung in the air while his arms wrapped around me tightly in a perfect hug. I burst into full-on sobs as one strong arm held me against him while his other hand stroked my back gently.

"Why are you crying?" Samhail asked me as his stroking changed to light pats.

"You finally learned how to hug!" I cried into his neck.

His chuckle rumbled against me as he set me back down on the floor and pulled away. I let go of him to wipe furiously at the tears in my eyes.

"When did you get back?" I asked.

"Only about half an hour ago. I was in with Bressen just now. When we finished up, he told me where to find you."

Samhail looked over me at Axenus who was standing with his arms crossed over his chest where I'd left him. He started toward the merman, and I followed.

"Samhail," Axenus said as we approached, and his voice was suddenly full of the kind of male swagger that told me he and Samhail were either friends, rivals, or friendly rivals. "It's been a while. You seem shorter than I remember."

Samhail came up to stand a few feet from Axenus and crossed his arms over his own chest. Axenus was about Bressen's height, and Samhail towered over him by almost half a foot.

"Axe," Samhail said, drawing himself up to his full height. "I'm still long where it counts."

My mouth fell open at the innuendo, but Axenus just rolled his eyes.

"I'll take your word for that," he said, and the two men uncrossed their arms to grasp hands in a hearty handshake.

"I hear Cyra tried to kill you last week," Samhail said as he let go of Axenus's hand. "Are you really that bad a trainer?"

I made a noise that was part gasp and part choke, but they ignored me, apparently not done with their ritual pissing contest. In truth, it was fascinating to watch, given that neither man acted like this when Bressen was around. They were both deferential to Bressen, but apparently this display of dominance was standard practice between the two of them.

"Better than you, I'd say, since Bressen called me in to clean up your mess," Axenus said. He looked at me and nodded at Samhail. "Have you really never tried to kill him before? I find that hard to believe."

I opened my mouth to respond, but Samhail beat me to it.

"She *has* tried to kill me actually," he said. Then he added to me, "I see they haven't fixed the crack in the training yard wall yet."

I blushed. "First of all, you deserved that," I said. "Second, if you're going to count that as an attempt to kill you, we should also count the time you pushed me off a cliff as attempted murder as well."

Axenus's eyes flew open in surprise. "I haven't heard any of this. What happened to the training yard wall?"

"Cyra threw me into it," Samhail said casually.

Axenus blinked. "She what?"

"It was a forcefield," I told him. "Samhail was being an ass, so I pushed him."

"Ah, I see. Understandable," Axenus said. He turned to Samhail. "She likes your forcefields."

Samhail grinned wickedly. "Of course she does. Who doesn't?"

I threw him a glare but then looked away so Axenus couldn't see how red my face was.

"Do I get to hear what Samhail did to make you push him into a wall?" Axenus asked me.

"No," both Samhail and I said together, and Axenus looked a little taken aback.

He paused a moment before trying again. "How about the cliff? Why did he push you off a cliff?"

"You're familiar with the Soundless Woods?" Samhail asked, and Axenus nodded. "Ever encounter the fog there?"

"No, but I've heard about it. I take it you ran into the fog?"

Samhail nodded. "The only way for us to get away was to jump off the cliff that borders the woods on its eastern side. Cyra exaggerates when she says I pushed her off. I grabbed her and jumped off."

"He's leaving out that I didn't know he had wings at the time," I said.

Axenus chuckled. "Ah, I can see how that might make your life flash before your eyes. It sounds like the two of you have had a few adventures together."

"You have no idea," Samhail said with another grin, and I had to look away again as my face flushed brightly once more.

"But enough about that," Samhail went on. "What have the two of you been up to in training?"

"Here to get some pointers?" Axenus asked him.

"Here to show you how it's done," Samhail answered.

I rolled my eyes and sighed as both men crossed their arms again.

"Well, a week or so ago," Axenus said, "we were working on bringing out Cyra's killer instincts. If recent events are any indication, I'm an excellent teacher."

I gave Axenus a wounded look, and his face softened as he realized he'd gone too far.

"I'm sorry," he said, lowering his arms again. "I shouldn't joke."

"It's fine," I said, sighing. "I let myself go over the edge, and I need to face that. It's not your job to coddle me."

"No," he said, "but I don't need to exploit what happened just to prove something to this lout." He jabbed a thumb at Samhail.

Samhail uncrossed his arms as well, looking contrite. "I didn't come down here to make trouble," he said. "I came to see if I could help."

Axenus looked thoughtful. "You *would* make a good target. I've been letting Cyra practice on me, but it would be nice to hand that task off. Unless you're not up to it, of course."

Samhail glared at Axenus, but all of us knew he wouldn't decline now.

"What are you working on?" Samhail asked.

"We need to work on Cyra's control, and if we have you here today, it might be a good time for her to get some practice using the powers she syphoned from you. You can teach her how to use them more effectively. It might be a nice change of pace for her to be able to practice against someone who won't get her wet."

My eyes flared at his choice of words, but Samhail didn't miss a beat.

"Awfully presumptuous of you to think I won't get her wet, Axe. I'm sure I can get her wetter than you."

I made a choking noise and looked incredulously at Samhail, but he just winked at me.

Axenus didn't even glance at me before firing back. "Cyra can confirm I've gotten her soaking wet before."

"The two of you are unbelievable," I cut in before Samhail could respond. "That's enough innuendo out of the both of you, or I'll start cutting off people's air."

Axenus winced a little, but I shot him a look that said he deserved it, and he gave me a small nod of acceptance.

"Sorry," the two men muttered together.

"Great," I said. "Now, if you two juveniles are done, let's get started."

# Chapter 16

The three of us spent the next couple hours working mainly with Samhail's summoning and forcefield powers. I'd never realized just how unrefined my technique was until Samhail showed me the various ways I could concentrate or narrow the powers to do specific things or to hit smaller targets. Uncultivated, Samhail's fields were a blunt force that knocked down anything in their path, but with some control, they could be used in a more focused way. We gathered a few objects from the surrounding rooms, and I practiced knocking smaller and smaller items out of Samhail's hands or off the table without disturbing anything else.

Once I'd gotten the hang of focusing the forcefields, Axenus explained how I could apply the same principles to my wind power. With enough practice and control, he said, I could focus my wind into a compact enough form to use it as a whip. An air lash, he called it. I tried that for a while, but although I was able to focus my air a bit, I couldn't get it tight enough or fast enough to generate the force of a whip.

I was exhausted almost two hours later when Axenus finally stopped us, but I felt as though I'd made quite a bit of progress. Having Samhail there had helped immensely. Axenus had given me a little confidence back this morning, but I always felt safe around Samhail, and his presence had a calming effect on me that I'd desperately needed for this first time back.

"I need to update Bressen on your progress," Axenus said. "I'll leave you and Samhail to catch up."

"Thank you," I said sincerely to him, and he nodded, understanding that it was thanks for continuing to work with me despite what I'd done.

Samhail waited until Axenus left before turning to me.

"How are you doing?" he asked me seriously.

A hundred possible ways to respond to his question flitted through my head, but I settled on, "Better now that you're here. I missed you."

Samhail smiled. "I missed you too."

"Brix won't speak to me," I went on. "He blames me for the vineyard, for just being perimortal. Jaylan also lost the woman he was going to marry, and I didn't find out about it until yesterday. Out of everything, I think those two things hurt the most."

Samhail just nodded, waiting for me to go on.

"How much did Bressen tell you?" I asked him.

"Everything, I assume," he said. "That you tried to make three men walk into a burning building, that you tried to choke Eddin and Axenus to death…and that he had to break into your mind to stop you."

"I wasn't trying to kill Axenus, just…keep him out of my way."

"I know the feeling," Samhail chuckled. He nodded his head toward the door. "Shall I walk you back to your quarters?"

I nodded and fell into step next to him as we headed out of the Great Chamber and back toward the rotunda. He had to walk slowly so I could keep up with his long strides.

"How do you know Axenus?" I asked him.

"We met through Bressen shortly after the two of them met."

"That's a rather vague answer," I observed.

He was silent a moment. "Did you ask Bressen how they met?"

"Yes, but he's been just as cagey about the details as you," I admitted. "Axenus said he owes Bressen a debt, but neither will tell me what kind of debt. It must be something horrible if no one wants to tell me."

"Bressen saved Axenus from a very…unfortunate situation," Samhail said, using the same word Bressen had. "There were also far-reaching consequences, but that's all I'm at liberty to tell you if neither Axenus nor Bressen has shared more with you."

"Fair enough," I conceded. "You seem to know him well in any case."

"I consider Axe a friend," Samhail said. "He's not like a brother to me as Bressen is, but there was a time the three of us were fairly close."

"Was he…I mean, did you…The three of you…," I stammered, not knowing exactly how to ask the question of Samhail. He just looked down at me, letting me flounder for a few more attempts before finally having pity on me and voicing the question he knew I was trying to ask.

"Did Bressen and I ever share women with Axenus?" he offered with a half-smile, and I nodded.

"I didn't," he said, "and I don't think Bressen did either, but I never asked him."

"So no foursomes then?" I asked innocently.

Samhail gave me a wry look. "That might be one too many cocks in the room for me. Bressen is one thing, but I'm not sure I'm patient enough to share with another man."

"You and Axenus seem competitive," I ventured. "I thought I might need to break up a brawl."

He chuckled again. "We're not that bad, but the two of us can't seem to help posturing when we're around each other. We've never gotten into a fight, though. Not a real one anyway."

We walked in silence for a few seconds before Samhail spoke again.

"Why so many questions about Axenus? Planning your next Harmilan already?" he asked.

I made an indignant noise and punched his rock-hard arm, which only hurt my hand.

"Jealous?" I asked. "Afraid you might be replaced?"

He snorted. "As if you could ever replace me."

We were almost to the door that led to the rotunda, and while I headed straight for it, Samhail steered toward the stairs that led to the guest wing of the central building. He stopped when he realized I wasn't following him, and we looked at each other a moment.

Samhail huffed a laugh. "Force of habit. I forgot you don't live in the guest wing anymore."

He headed back toward me, but the sound of footsteps on the stairs made us both turn again. A moment later, Brix appeared. He stopped and jolted back when he saw Samhail.

"Brix, good to see you again," Samhail said to him, although his tone wasn't exactly friendly.

Brix didn't answer, and his eyes met mine instead. He opened his mouth to say something, thought better of it, then just hurried past us to head down one of the other halls into the central building, probably toward the kitchen if I had to guess.

My heart twinged at his dismissal, but there'd been something different in his eyes for a few seconds before he'd hurried off. It was the first time he hadn't looked angry at me.

I met Samhail's gaze, and he raised a brow at me, but I just shook my head. He shrugged and opened the door into the rotunda that led to the lords' wings of the Citadel.

"You don't have to escort me all the way back if you'd rather rest," I offered, but Samhail just stood waiting for me.

"How are things in Derridan?" I asked as I went through the door.

"Better now that Aidan has taken control," he said, "but still a little precarious. It was all I could do to keep order there until the selection trials were over. I even had to shift into my gargoyle form a few times."

"That bad?"

"I went through a lot of pants that first week or two," he said, sighing.

I couldn't help the laugh that bubbled up. Unlike other perimortal shapeshifters whose clothes usually transformed with them, Samhail's clothes ripped off him when he shifted into a gargoyle, so he needed to find spare garments once he changed back into his human form. I hadn't realized when I first met him that his shirts and leather armor all had slits in the back to allow his giant bat-like wings to spring free when he manifested them. Luckily, Samhail was an imposing-enough figure on his own that he didn't normally need to use his gargoyle form, although clearly his time in Derridan was the exception.

"What do you think of Aidan?" I asked him.

"He seems competent. I didn't get to know him well, but I already like him better than Jerram."

"That was a low bar to overcome," I said, and Samhail grunted.

"Do you need to go back to Derridan?" I ventured.

"I shouldn't have to. They have Aidan, so they don't need me, nor do I think Aidan would appreciate my presence. It would be too much like having Bressen hanging over his shoulder."

"Are you staying around then?" I asked casually.

Samhail gave me a knowing smirk, and I punched his arm again then winced at the pain in my hand, apparently not having learned my lesson.

"Don't let it go to your head," I said. "I just don't have a lot of people to talk to when Bressen is busy."

"So you only want me for my scintillating conversation?"

"Were you hoping I just needed you to stand around and look pretty?"

"You have Axenus for that."

I chuckled. "Seriously, how long are you staying?"

"At least until the wedding," he said.

I stopped walking suddenly. With everything that had happened, I'd almost forgotten Bressen and I were supposed to get married in two weeks. We'd be here at the Citadel for another week to help Aidan get settled into his role as a Triumvirate lord, then we were returning to Solandis to prepare for the wedding.

Samhail stopped and raised a brow at me. "Did you forget?"

I nodded slowly. "There's…there's been a lot going on. What if Brix won't come?"

Samhail's face softened. "He'll come. I know he will."

We were nearly to the door that led to Bressen's suite of rooms, now also mine, so we walked the rest of the way, and I led Samhail inside. The suite opened into a sitting area, and a door to the right led to our huge bedroom with an attached bathing chamber. There were doors to several other spaces off the sitting room that led to a war room, a private dining room, and Bressen's study. The last also had a door directly into the hall.

I couldn't help glancing at the bedroom as Samhail stepped into the suite, and I was afraid for a moment he might have had a very specific reason for coming all the way back here with me. I exhaled a sigh of relief when he just went over to the large sofa and dropped into it.

It had been just over a week since Bressen and I had last made love. It was the longest stretch we'd gone without sex since we'd first slept together, and considering we used to have sex multiple times a day, this was a significant dry spell for us. I knew Bressen was giving me time and space to sort myself out, but I suddenly wondered what Samhail's expectations were. For the moment, he didn't seem to have any, and I sat down in a chair across from him.

"You probably shouldn't have been so suggestive in your remarks to Axenus," I said to him. "He's going to suspect something."

"Axenus expects comments like that from me," Samhail said. "He'd be more suspicious if I didn't make them."

"If those are the things you say when there's someone else in the room, I can't imagine what men say when they're alone together."

Samhail smirked. "I heard some things when I was a soldier that shocked even me, but trust that I'd never let a conversation about you get out of hand."

I smiled weakly and shifted in my seat.

"Is everything alright?" he asked. "You seem…restless."

I let out a long breath. He was right. A jitteriness had taken root in me as we'd walked back from the Great Chamber. I'd managed to forget about everything for a while during training, but it was all coming back to me now, and I suddenly felt very alone and exposed.

Samhail's arm was slung over the back of the sofa, and I eyed the open space under it against his side. I had the overwhelming desire to tuck myself up against him, but I wasn't sure what Samhail would think if I did that – or what Bressen might think, for that matter – so I just looked away.

"Cyra?" Samhail asked when I didn't say anything.

I shook my head. "I don't know what's wrong with me. I'm having a lot of trouble getting comfortable with myself." My eyes darted to the space next to Samhail again, and I felt its pull.

He saw my glance and patted the spot in invitation.

I only hesitated a moment more before getting up and going over to sidle up next to him. I tucked myself under his arm and laid my head against his chest so I could hear his heartbeat against my ear. Samhail draped his arm heavily over my shoulder, and I sighed at the feeling of being sheltered against him.

"I should let Bressen know we're back," I said, and Samhail made a noise I took to be affirmation.

I was fairly sure Bressen was just next door in his study, but I sent him a mental message telling him Samhail and I were in the sitting room waiting for him. I got a message back almost immediately that he'd see us in a little while so we could all go down to lunch together. I knew Axenus was probably in with him, so I didn't bother him again.

Instead, I nestled closer into Samhail's side and shut my eyes. Samhail didn't move, nor did he say anything else. I'd seen him sit completely still for hours at a time – "still as stone" he'd called it – and indeed, he didn't move at all as he simply sat with me curled up against him. I barely moved either, content to soak in the feel of his strong body.

I sometimes wondered what might have happened between me and

Samhail if I'd never met Bressen. I'd met Samhail first, and there'd been a clear spark between us that we'd explored a little in the days before we arrived at the Citadel, but it had dimmed somewhat when I met Bressen.

My connection with Bressen had been instantaneous, even if I hadn't recognized it for what it was at the time. We'd been pulled toward each other from the first moment he'd shown up in the Great Chamber just in time for my interrogation with Jerram and Ursan. Samhail had been more overt in his support of me, but Bressen had also been steadfast in trying to help me, although his efforts had been more subtle in order to keep Jerram and Ursan from becoming suspicious.

When Bressen and I had finally given in to our desires, a part of me had mourned leaving Samhail behind, which is why it had meant so much to me on the Harmilan when Bressen had offered to invite Samhail to join us. That night had satiated me where Samhail was concerned for the time being, but recent events seemed to have rekindled that old need, and I guiltily indulged the desire to be close to him as we waited for Bressen.

Thirty minutes later, Bressen and Axenus emerged from the side door that led to Bressen's study. Neither Samhail nor I had moved since I'd curled up against him, and that was how Bressen and Axenus found us as they entered the sitting room.

Axenus paused in surprise to see Samhail and I nestled together, but Bressen showed no sign he was bothered by what he found.

I unfolded myself from Samhail and got up to meet Bressen as he approached. I felt stiff from not having moved in so long, but my body loosened as Bressen pulled me against him and kissed my forehead.

"Axenus said you made good progress with Samhail's powers," he said to me. He looked past me to Samhail. "He has some notes on how *you* might improve, though."

Samhail grunted and shot Axenus a look that suggested where he could shove his notes.

"I call it as I see it," Axenus said with a shrug.

"Will you be joining Bressen and I for some sword and combat training later, Axe?" Samhail asked. "I'm sure I'll have some 'notes' for you myself."

"Are they always like this?" I asked Bressen.

He gave an exaggerated sigh of weariness. "No, they're usually worse." He winked at me. "Let's go down to lunch. Maybe we can shove some food in their mouths long enough to get a few minutes of peace."

Bressen took my hand and led me toward the door. Samhail and Axenus fell in behind us, and the four of us made our way toward the main dining room.

I made a mental note to take a little walk on the battlements around the yard later today. If Bressen, Samhail, and Axenus were all going to train together, I wasn't going to miss it.

# Chapter 17

The one good thing about sitting on the ground in the snow, I thought the next morning, was that the cold now seeping through my pants was helping to ease the pain in my tailbone. Hopefully it would also minimize the size of the bruise I'd have to heal there later as well.

"Remember yesterday when I said I missed you?" I asked as I glared up at Samhail from the ground. "I take it back."

The smile he gave me said my misery was only feeding his amusement.

I'd been eager to restart my combat training with Samhail now that he'd returned, but it took me less than twenty minutes into our first session to regret that.

Axenus let me train my magic in the Great Chamber so I didn't have to brave the winter weather, but Samhail had flatly refused when I suggested we also use the space for our combat sessions. Consequently, I not only had to make sure I dressed warmly enough so I didn't freeze to death out in the yard, but I now had to sprint across the Citadel from the Great Chamber to the yard in order to make it in time to meet Samhail. He hadn't been pleased to lose his nine o'clock time slot, and he took it out on me by insisting I meet him directly after I was done with Axenus. He'd also expressly forbidden me to use a portal to get there on time.

Thankfully, Axenus had enough mercy to let me go five minutes early so I could make it to the yard, because Samhail himself had no mercy whatsoever. I might have complained about Axenus, but the merman was a joy compared to Samhail.

"Did you practice at all while I was gone?" Samhail asked as he stared down at me. "It's like we're starting from the beginning."

He didn't extend a hand to help me up, and I knew by now not to expect one from him. Instead, I picked myself up off the ground and immediately got back into my fighting stance, knowing he could attack at any moment once I was back on my feet.

Almost immediately I had to duck to the side to avoid the hand-held training pad Samhail swung at me. I came up quickly and threw an elbow into his stomach, making him grunt. I spun away from him and resumed my fighting stance, keeping my feet nimble and ready to move again.

"You rely too much on your elbows," Samhail said as he rubbed the place I'd hit him. "Using your elbows means having to get in closer to your opponent to make the hit. Work on using your fists more."

"It hurts less to hit you with my elbows," I said, not taking my eyes off him. "Your muscles are too hard. I feel like I'm going to break my hand, and I can't seem to hit you hard enough to do any damage anyway."

Samhail looked surprised for a second before he chuckled. "My muscles are too hard?" His look turned wicked. "I never thought I'd see the day you'd complain about any part of me being too hard."

My cheeks already stung from the cold, but I felt them flame hotly.

Samhail had warned me shortly after I met him that gargoyles were a "lusty bunch," and I was no stranger to his heated looks and innuendos. I was used to his teasing, and Bressen didn't seem to mind that Samhail did it, so I usually let it roll off me easily enough.

But that was back when I was still having sex daily.

Bressen had tried to initiate something again last night, but I'd tensed up when he did, and he'd withdrawn his hands.

While my body continued to reject Bressen's attempts at intimacy, that didn't mean I craved sex any less. I was used to having regular climaxes, and the need to feel a release had been building up in me for the last week. I'd gone back to pleasuring myself when Bressen wasn't around to take the edge off, but my own hands just didn't compare to his. Yet when he tried to touch me, I only felt the overwhelming urge to escape.

It hurt Bressen deeply when I pulled away. I could feel it in his mind, which he kept wide open to me, but I was powerless to stop myself. I kept my own mind carefully closed off. I'd thought at least half a dozen times about discussing the issue with him, and I suspected he wanted to do the same, but neither of us had yet broached the subject.

Unfortunately, that now left me desperately needing sex as I engaged in physical training with a very large, very attractive man who spoke fluent innuendo like it was a second language.

I swallowed hard and pressed my thighs together at Samhail's comment, which didn't go unnoticed by him. He swore violently and turned to stalk away from me for a moment before coming back.

"Gods dammit, Cyra. You're killing me. I can practically smell your need. You're not usually this…" He trailed off, dragging a hand through his long white hair. "What's going on between you and Bressen?"

I tried not to look away, but I couldn't manage to keep my eyes on Samhail's. "Nothing is going on between me and Bressen," I said.

He gave a short laugh. "And that seems to be the problem. How long has it been since the two of you fucked?"

My mouth fell open at his audacity, but I clamped it shut again. He just looked at me, waiting for an answer.

"That's none of your business," I said finally.

"Maybe not, but you're my friends, and there's obviously something wrong between the two of you."

"What did Bressen tell you?"

"Nothing. I asked, and he fed me the same bullshit you just did. That's not like him."

"I don't know what to tell you," I said. "Honestly, I'm not sure what's wrong with us."

"Have the two of you tried talking to each other about it?"

I didn't say anything, but my silence was answer enough for him.

"Cyra, the two of you need to figure this out because I can't be near you if you're going to walk around looking and smelling like that. I won't touch you unless I'm invited, but there are limits to what I can endure, and right now I just want to bend you over-"

"Don't say it!" I managed to get out before he could finish. If he said what he wanted to do, my knees would buckle.

I forced myself to look at Samhail's face, because if I looked down, I knew that more than just his stomach muscles would be hard, and seeing the proof of his own need would make everything far worse.

Samhail and I may have had sex together on the Harmilan, but Bressen had been there as well, and he'd been willing to share me at the time. That was before Bressen had proposed. While there might have been some leeway between me and Samhail before that, there wasn't any now. Neither I nor Samhail would do anything with each other without Bressen's full knowledge and consent.

"I'm sorry," I said. "I'll try to stop smelling like…"

*Like I need to be fucked. Hard. A lot,* my mind supplied.

Samhail exhaled and approached me carefully. I forced myself not to step away from him as he held up his hands, intending to put them on my shoulders. Thankfully, he thought better of it and lowered them.

"You need to talk to Bressen," he said. "Well, really you need to fuck him, but maybe talk to him first. Please. For all our sakes."

I opened my mouth to say something – I wasn't sure what – but a voice from the doorway startled both me and Samhail.

"Am I…interrupting?" Jasper asked, looking from me to Samhail. The lord consort was dressed for the cold weather and had a sword sheathed at his side.

Both Samhail and I instantly took a step apart.

"Not at all," Samhail said to him genially. He motioned to Jasper's sword. "Were you planning to get some practice in?"

"I was," Jasper said. "Aidan is busy, so I was hoping there might be someone in the yard I could challenge." He looked apologetically at Samhail. "Unfortunately, I'm not nearly skilled or insane enough to ask you, so I'll just use the practice dummy."

"Actually," Samhail said, "I have to cut my training with Cyra short. Something…came up, and I need to go. Perhaps you could practice with her. She's still learning, but she's good enough to give you a workout."

*Be careful,* I said into his head. *That sounded almost like a compliment.*

Samhail didn't react, but I knew he heard me. He usually kept a mind shield up as a matter of practice, but he always left a small sliver open for me and Bressen in case we needed to send him a message.

Jasper looked at me with interest. "I'd be happy to do some training with Cyra. If she'll have me."

I smiled warmly at him. "Of course."

"Then I'll leave Cyra in your hands," Samhail said to Jasper. "Do *not* go easy on her."

Jasper chuckled. "Are you going to save me from her fiancé if something happens to her?"

"I'll personally guarantee your safety," I assured Jasper.

Samhail looked at me once more before giving me a curt nod and heading toward the door to the yard. He tossed the training pad he'd been holding in front of his groin to the side as soon as he was facing away from us, and I turned back to Jasper to find him watching me intently.

"Is everything alright?" he asked when Samhail was out of earshot.

"It's fine," I said, forcing my voice to sell the lie. "Why do you ask?"

"It looked like you and Samhail were having a fairly intense discussion when I arrived. You certainly weren't training."

I flushed but forced myself not to look away. "Samhail and I are friends. We do talk occasionally," I said more defensively than I meant.

Jasper gave me a look that said he knew that wasn't the whole story.

"Samhail doesn't strike me as much of a conversationalist," he said.

I raised my chin a notch. "There's nothing going on between me and him, if that's what you're suggesting."

"But there was at one time, wasn't there," Jasper said.

It wasn't a question, and I was so shocked by the statement I couldn't do anything but stare at him.

"No!" I insisted, perhaps too vehemently. "Of course not. Why would you think that?"

He gave me a knowing look. "I have eyes, and I'm not an idiot."

"I…"

"Cyra, it's alright. I'm not going to tell anyone," he assured me.

I arched a brow at him. "Not even Aidan?"

He looked at me seriously. "Not even Aidan. He has his own theories about what's between you and Samhail, but I have no intention of confirming or denying them for him."

I waited for the rosy hue of the lie to bloom on Jasper's skin, but it remained its normal shade.

"You're telling the truth," I said. "Why wouldn't you tell Aidan?"

Jasper shrugged. "Who we love is our own business. There's no practical reason Aidan needs to know. You do love Samhail, I assume?"

Once again, I was shocked into silence before I managed to speak.

"I do love him," I said, "but what I think you're asking is if I'm *in love* with him."

"And you're not?"

I thought a moment. I loved Samhail dearly as a friend, and yes, I still desired him on occasion, but what I felt for Samhail was very different from what I felt for Bressen.

I could see myself building a family with Bressen someday. I couldn't see myself doing the same with Samhail. I liked spending time with him, and sex with him was incredible, but he wasn't Bressen. Samhail wouldn't have flown me to a vineyard in Hiraeth and spent the whole day following me around while I compared notes with the winemaker. Samhail wouldn't stay up half the night talking to me after sex because he wanted to know absolutely everything about me. Samhail looked at me with lust, but he didn't look at me with longing the way Bressen did. For Bressen, I was the riddle he wanted to solve, the wine he wanted to get drunk on, and the dream he wanted to have over and over again without ever waking up.

Samhail cared about me deeply, and I cared about him just as much. But he wasn't the air I breathed like Bressen was, and it was only now I realized just how much I'd been suffocating this last week.

I went over to one of the benches on the side of the training yard and sat down heavily, putting my head in my hands. Jasper followed and sat down next to me.

"I met Samhail before I met Bressen," I told him, "and there was a brief time in those few days that I could see myself being with him. I won't deny there's a physical attraction between us. After all, he's rather…" I searched for the right word to describe Samhail's rugged splendor.

"Breathtaking?" Jasper supplied.

I laughed. "Yes, that would describe him. Is that a personal opinion?"

Jasper sighed. "I love Aidan, but let's just say I've had some fantasies."

I smiled. "Your secret's safe with me."

"So I don't want to pry," Jasper said, "but I'm going to. What were you and Samhail so serious about when I arrived? Is he in love with *you*? Is that the issue?"

I shook my head, no longer surprised by Jasper's bold questions.

"No, nothing like that. Bressen and I have just been a little off since Fernweh. Samhail was encouraging me to talk to him."

Jasper waited for me to go on, but I wasn't ready to go into detail, even if I did trust he wouldn't share it with Aidan. Something had started to clench painfully in my chest as I realized how much I missed being with

Bressen this week.

"I'm sorry," I said. "That's all I can share right now."

"Fair enough. If you ever do need to talk, I'm probably the last person you should ask for advice on love, but I'm happy to offer it anyway. I recommend doing the opposite of anything I tell you."

I smiled again. "Thank you. I'll keep that in mind."

Jasper stood. "So would you like to practice some sword fighting? Or we can just head inside and start our lesson early if you want."

Unbeknownst to anyone else, I wasn't just training with two people, but three. After magic lessons with Axenus and now fighting lessons with Samhail, a few hours of my afternoon were spent with Jasper while he taught me how to dance. Of my three teachers, he was by far the most patient and understanding, and I was already progressing quickly in my dancing, despite having lost a week hiding in my room.

I was taking lessons so I could dance with Bressen at our wedding without him assisting me, yet I hadn't been able to let him make love to me for more than a week. What would happen if we got married, and I still wasn't able to have sex with him? Even worse, what if he refused to marry me because I wouldn't let him between my legs?

I shook the thoughts away. I couldn't think about that right now.

"Let's start our dance lessons," I said to Jasper. "I'm tired of the cold."

"For what it's worth," he said as I turned to open a portal into the Great Chamber, "I agree with Samhail. If you and Bressen are having issues, you need to talk to him. The longer you let it go, the worse it's likely to get."

"How comforting," I said with mild sarcasm as the portal glowed to life in front of us.

Jasper gave me a wry grin. "You'll get only the truth from me."

I stepped through the portal and closed it after Jasper came through.

"Since you're willing to be so truthful," I said, "will you answer a question for me?"

"Of course."

I paused, unsure of how to ask now that I had his permission.

"Aidan is perimortal," I said finally. "But you're not. How is that going to work...later?"

The smile he gave me said I wasn't the first person to ask him this.

"Truthfully, we're not sure how it's going to work," he said. "We'll walk that road when we come to it. Until then, we're just taking it day by day and enjoying our time together. It's not easy for either of us, knowing what's coming, but you can't choose who you fall in love with, and it was our fortune in life to find each other and fall madly in love. All we can do is make the most of that gift and enjoy our time while we have it."

Regret pooled in my stomach, partially for the pain he and Aidan would eventually endure as the price of their complicated situation, but also because I felt the distance between me and Bressen even more acutely now. He and I were both perimortal, and we likely had hundreds of years left together, but that didn't make any single day less precious, and I felt the wasted time of the last week like a leaden cloak.

I would talk to Bressen, I resolved as I took Jasper's hand and got ready to dance. I would stop putting it off and talk to him tonight.

# Chapter 18

"Can we talk?"

I jumped at Bressen's voice directly behind me as I sat brushing my hair that night. I hadn't heard him approach, nor had I seen him in the mirror since my mind had been somewhere else. I noticed in the reflection that he was shirtless and only wearing the loose pair of silky black bedtime pants that hung low on his hips. My body tingled in anticipation, but seconds later, a now-familiar nervous tremor replaced the tingle.

I swallowed and started to rise. "Of course," I said.

Bressen put his hands on my shoulders and pressed me lightly back down onto the seat. He slipped the brush from my hand and began to run it gently through my hair. I closed my eyes and tried to enjoy the feel of it on my scalp, but that familiar panic I'd been wearing all week lay heavily on me. I'd resolved earlier in the day to talk to Bressen about our issues, and I'd been trying to work up the courage all evening, but I still hadn't managed to make myself do it.

Bressen, it seemed, had taken the decision out of my hands. I should have been relieved he'd made the first move, but I was fighting the urge to get up and run.

My heart thudded clumsily in my chest as I waited for Bressen to go on, but he didn't say anything for almost a minute as he ran the brush carefully through my long dark strands. His hands gathered the locks, drawing them back from my shoulders, and I knew the graze of his fingers across the bare skin of my neck was deliberate. Gooseflesh rose on my arms at his whisper-soft touch, and I saw him smile softly in the mirror. Bressen knew an infinite number of ways to seduce me.

"Axenus is concerned you're struggling," Bressen said finally.

I frowned. That wasn't the topic I'd been expecting.

"Axenus promised to express any concerns directly to me before letting you know of them," I said in annoyance.

"He's not concerned with your progress in training," Bressen clarified. "He's concerned with your mental state. I believe that's something he's told you in his own way."

My head wagged from side-to-side as if to say that was one way to interpret his words.

"I'm concerned as well, and so is Samhail."

I narrowed my eyes. "Did the three of you have a meeting about me today?" I asked, my annoyance increasing.

"Not together. Axenus and I discussed your progress in our meetings yesterday and today as we normally do. I asked Samhail back to my study to talk after we trained this afternoon. He got to observe you with Axenus yesterday, and then he worked with you himself this morning. I thought he might have some insights. As it turned out, he was eager to talk about you…and me."

I waited for Bressen to mention finding me curled up against Samhail before lunch yesterday, but he didn't.

"And what insights did Samhail have to offer?" I asked snappishly.

"He agrees you're struggling, for one," he said.

"Well, it's nice to know the three of you are on the same page about all this," I said sarcastically as I stood to face him. "I suppose I should feel privileged that Samhail and Axenus actually agree on something."

Bressen winced at my anger, but his face was serious when he asked, "Do you disagree you've been having a hard time since Fernweh?"

I just pressed my lips together. I couldn't argue with their assessment. It just made me angry they'd all decided this without bothering to include me in the conversation. I thought Bressen at least knew better than that.

"I want to help you," Bressen said. "Let me help you."

"You're already helping me," I insisted.

"How?"

I didn't answer because I didn't know. I rarely saw Bressen during the day, and while I spent my nights in his arms, we both knew there was something off between us.

"There's a problem," Bressen said. "I can feel it between us, and I want to do whatever I can to fix it."

I shook my head. "There's nothing wrong between us. We're fine."

I knew without looking in the mirror that my own skin was glowing red with the obvious lie. I'd resolved today to talk to Bressen, but faced with the opportunity to do so now, that resolve had fled.

Part of it was anger. I felt attacked and at least a little embarrassed that these three men I trusted not only knew something was wrong with me, but they'd discussed it among themselves. It put me on the defensive.

"We're fine? Is that so?" Bressen asked, raising a brow.

He dropped the brush on my dresser and dragged me forcefully against him. His hands splayed across my back and shoulder blades as his mouth came down on mine in an urgent kiss. My body quaked at the heat that suddenly shot through me, and for a brief moment I leaned into him, letting his lips ravage mine. He started to draw my silk nightgown up my thighs, but then something snapped in my head, and I wrenched my mouth back from his.

"No!" I cried, and my heart sank at the sudden reflex to retreat from him. My eyes met his, and I saw there was hurt but not surprise in them.

"There is something wrong," he repeated as he held me against him.

I shook my head vigorously. "No, there's nothing wrong," I insisted.

Denial was my shield as I pressed forward again and crushed my mouth back into Bressen's. I threaded my fingers through his hair, gripping hard, and he groaned as he swept me off my feet to carry me to the bed. He tossed me down roughly, his body following immediately to cover mine, as if he feared any space between us would give me room to reject him. Need pulsed between my thighs, and I wrapped a leg around his hip as I tried to quash the nervous tremor rattling through me.

Bressen's eyes were turquoise gems as he grabbed for the fabric of my nightgown to yank it up again, and I arched my hips up to allow him to pull it out from under me.

His lips ground into mine, but a jolt of pain shot through my head, and I screamed as my body bucked under him like I'd been hit with lightning. I pushed him away without thinking, and he looked down at me. Again, there was no surprise as he lay over me breathing hard.

"I…I don't know what happened," I said. "I felt pain. In my head."

Bressen went still for a moment before bringing his forehead down to rest on mine. "I hurt you," he said as he cupped my cheek. "I hurt you when I broke into your mind, and now you're rejecting me."

I shook my head again emphatically. "No, I'm not rejecting you."

"Not on purpose, but your mind is," he said.

Bressen pulled my nightgown back down over my hips before drawing me against him, and I nestled my head into his chest.

He was right. I hadn't made the connection before, but it made sense that the pain I'd experienced when I forced him to break down my mind shield last week was causing me to unconsciously push him away.

"What do I do?" I asked, my voice breaking a little.

"It's not what *you* need to do," he said. "It's what *we* need to do."

"So then what do we need to do?"

Bressen didn't answer for a long while. I was about to repeat my question when he spoke.

"You feel safe with Samhail," he said.

I jerked my head up and frowned at him. "What does that mean?"

"When Axenus and I came out of my study the other day, you were curled up against Samhail," he said, and I felt a sudden apprehension.

"Are you angry at me for that?"

Bressen seemed to consider this. "No," he answered finally. "You've always been close to Samhail. I know and understand that. I suppose I'm just disappointed or even afraid that you seem more inclined to seek comfort from him right now than from me."

"Nothing happened," I said. "We just sat there waiting for you. I don't think either of us moved."

Bressen smiled sadly. "I know. Samhail said as much, and I don't begrudge you seeking comfort from him when I'm not available. The issue is that you're reluctant to seek the same comfort from me when I'm here."

"So what do I…what do we do?" I asked.

Bressen paused again. "I've asked Samhail if he would be willing to join us again…in bed, and he agreed."

"What?" I bolted upright into a sitting position.

Bressen sat up as well so he was facing me.

"It would be entirely up to you whether you want him to join us," he said quickly, "but I think having him here might help you feel safe."

"Why would you think that?" I asked. I couldn't deny a small part of me was suddenly thrilled at inviting Samhail back to our bed, but another part of me balked at the idea, or rather, balked at the idea that Bressen thought this was necessary to get us past this issue.

I loved Bressen. I knew without any doubt whatsoever that I loved him, and it hurt me that he believed we needed Samhail to save us. That alone was almost enough to make me reject the offer, but something kept me from saying the words.

"You don't have to decide right-" he started to say, but I cut him off.

"You can invite Samhail. Tonight, if he's available."

I couldn't tell if the look on Bressen's face was disappointment or relief, or perhaps a mixture of both, but he nodded.

My heart raced as I felt the faint prickle at the back of my neck that told me Bressen had sent his invitation to Samhail.

I wasn't entirely sure why I'd said yes. I couldn't deny I still desired Samhail, but my agreement to let Bressen invite him to our bed tonight seemed more like an attempt to prove to Bressen he was wrong, that I didn't in fact need Samhail.

Yet despite all my protests, there was indeed something wrong between us. I'd pulled away from Bressen twice just tonight when he'd tried to touch me, and the issue was undoubtedly due to the pain he'd caused me when he'd broken into my mind to keep me from killing Eddin. I didn't know how to come back from that, but maybe Bressen was right and having Samhail here would help. Maybe being with Samhail again was what I needed to convince both my body and my mind to move on.

Bressen lay back down on the bed, drawing me with him. I let him pull me against him, and I rested my forehead on his chest as we waited for Samhail. Bressen said that Samhail had agreed to come, but he might have changed his mind since then.

"What do we do if this doesn't work?" I asked.

"We try something else. I don't know what, but we'll keep trying until we find something that helps." He paused, then added, "I love you."

"I love you, too," I said emphatically and meant it. I sat up and looked down at him. "You believe that, don't you?"

"I do," he said. "I can feel that you still do."

I touched my hand to his cheek and stroked my thumb against the black stubble that was always just barely there. "I'm glad. It's important that you know that."

Any response Bressen might have made was interrupted by the whoosh of leathery wings from the balcony, and we both turned to look that way. Samhail's huge form filled most of the doorway while his wings, which were slightly splayed out behind him, filled the rest of it. A moment later the wings had folded into nothingness behind him as he pulled them back into his body and came forward into the room. Bressen rolled off the bed to meet Samhail, and I followed him.

"Thank you for coming," Bressen said to Samhail as the two men grasped each other by the forearm.

"I'm always honored to receive an invitation from the Lord and Lady of Hiraeth," Samhail said. "I'm just surprised to receive another so soon. Can I assume my performance on the Harmilan was above average?"

He cocked his head to grin at me, and I knew he was trying to downplay the real reason we all knew he was here. Not that I was going to let that stop me from responding to his brag.

"It was adequate," I said, and because I knew it would rankle him, I added, "We asked Axenus first, but he was busy tonight."

Bressen and Samhail glanced at each other quickly, and I wondered if I'd said something wrong. Samhail chuckled a moment later, though.

"I suppose I deserved that," he said.

I stepped toward Bressen and Samhail, some of the apprehension I'd felt earlier melting away. Now that Samhail was here, this all felt familiar, and I took each of them by the hand to pull them toward the bed. Samhail stepped forward at my urging, but Bressen didn't, and I stopped as I met with his resistance.

"What's wrong?" I asked him.

"I thought we'd do things a bit differently this time," he said carefully.

I furrowed my brows at him. "Differently how?"

Bressen looked between me and Samhail. "I thought perhaps the two of you could be together…without me. I can sit and watch for a while."

Samhail and I exchanged apprehensive looks.

"I know that's not exactly what I told either of you," Bressen said, "but I think perhaps things might go smoother without me to start."

"No," I said letting go of Samhail's hand and taking both of Bressen's in mine. "No, I need you both."

"I can join later," Bressen said, and my heart broke a little at the look in his eyes. I started to protest some more, but he cut in before I could.

"I enjoy a little voyeurism now and then," he said, "if it's alright with the two of you, of course. Perhaps it's what I need right now."

I opened my mouth but shut it again. He was framing the voyeurism as his own need to make me agree to it.

"I only have one request," Bressen said. "I ask that you both leave your mental shields down. I'd prefer not to have any barriers between the three of us this time."

I looked back at Samhail, and his body was rigid. This would be much more difficult for him than me. As far as I knew, he'd kept a relatively impenetrable shield up ever since Morland had taken over his mind in the war with Rowe. Morland had been a mind wraith like Bressen, and he'd nearly succeeded in forcing Samhail to kill Bressen. I knew that taking his mind shield down after so long wouldn't be easy for Samhail.

It was a few seconds before Samhail spoke. "If Cyra is alright with it all, then so am I."

Bressen looked at me questioningly.

"If this is how you want it," I said.

Bressen seemed to relax, and he leaned in to kiss me gently. "I'll be just over here." He motioned to a chair off to the side of the bed that he often sat in to put on his boots. "Enjoy yourselves."

Bressen stepped away from me then and sat down in the chair, crossing one leg over the other.

I just stared at him, my eyes locked with his as I struggled to find something to say to him, to apologize, to make him change his mind, but I couldn't find the words. His gaze held mine for several seconds until his eyes lifted to something over my shoulder, and I felt Samhail behind me.

I tried to read the expression on Bressen's face as he looked at the man he considered a brother, but I couldn't decipher the mix of emotions there. I tried instead to read his mind, but that seemed just as jumbled up with hope, sadness, fear, and several other emotions vying for dominance.

But I also felt his trust, both in me and Samhail. Bressen trusted that Samhail could have my body tonight, while he himself would always have my heart and soul. He trusted that Samhail and I could be together and not let it destroy our bonds with him, and I desperately hoped his trust wasn't misplaced.

I let out a ragged breath as Samhail's hand rested lightly on my hip. He didn't try to pull me away, but I recognized the urging in his gesture.

*Are you sure?* I asked Bressen through our connection.

*Yes*, was all he said, and the word echoed in my mind.

I didn't know exactly how this was supposed to work, whether it would indeed help things or only make them worse, but I was willing to try either way. In truth, I couldn't have stopped what was going to happen if I wanted to. My body was strung like a bow right now, and the added tensity in the room was an unexpected aphrodisiac. My skin cried out to be touched, and if my body wouldn't let Bressen satisfy its craving, then Samhail would have to try.

I nodded to Bressen and turned to face the beautiful giant behind me.

# Chapter 19



*Are you sure?* Cyra asked into my mind.

*Yes*, I answered before I could give myself a chance to rethink it.

Yes, I was sure something had to change between us before we could move forward. Yes, she still had unresolved feelings for Samhail even though I knew without a doubt she loved me. And yes, I was willing to let this man, the brother I trusted so much, have the woman I loved if it would somehow help her find her way back to me.

But no, I wasn't sure it would work.

Scratch that. It had to work because I couldn't continue to be near Cyra, to sleep with her wrapped in my arms, to breathe in her scent, and to see her smile and hear her speak day after day without being with her.

It was physically painful to be so close to her without being able to touch her, to kiss her, to bury myself inside her. My cock was semi-hard with my need for her nearly all hours of the day. The only relief I got was at night when I dreamed of fucking her, when the feel of her writhing in pleasure beneath me seemed so real I'd actually woken the other night to find the front of my sleeping pants soaked with my seed. I'd slipped carefully out of bed to clean myself up, only to harden once again when I crept back under the covers, and she'd nestled up against me.

Yes, something had to change because I was dying without her.

Cyra gave me a small nod and turned to face Samhail. He'd come up behind her to put a hand on her hip, and I suppressed the urge to shoot off my chair and tear his hand away. He and I had shared women before, lots of them, but I'd never felt at all possessive of any of them. Only Cyra. I wanted to hit him, but I reminded myself that I'd asked him to do this.

To be sure, it hadn't been hard to convince him. I knew he desired Cyra, that he'd hoped to become her lover before she met me, but he'd confessed to me one night after we'd had a few drinks that he knew she and I were meant to be with each other the first time he saw us together. He'd been grateful for the one night on the Harmilan I'd been willing to share her, and he was shocked today when I'd asked him to our bed again. It had been on the tip of his tongue to refuse, but I'd begged him. And I never begged for anything.

I'd been the one to ask him to come back to Callanus in the first place. He'd been hired to do a few jobs out in Derridan after Aidan had been selected as lord, but I'd sent him a message the other day asking him to return. I'd explained the situation and told him Cyra wasn't doing well.

She needed a friend, I'd told him. She needed *him*.

He'd said he could be here within twenty-four hours. He'd finished his latest job quickly and sent a message to Phaedrus. The priest had portaled him back early yesterday morning.

Cyra's joy when he'd interrupted her lesson with Axenus had reached me all the way across the Citadel, and I'd breathed a sigh of relief. It was the first time I'd felt happiness from her since Fernweh, and I knew I'd made the right decision to call Samhail back.

He could help her. I wasn't sure how, but I knew he could.

The question of how had been answered only a couple hours later.

It had taken all my self-control not to react yesterday when I'd come out of my study with Axenus to see Cyra tucked under Samhail's arm on the sofa, but seeing them together had been a revelation.

She felt safe with him, I realized.

*Safe from you*, a cruel voice in my head said as I'd watched them.

I'd hurt Cyra. I'd acted only to stop her from turning into a cold-blooded killer and thus losing her in a different way, but that didn't change the fact that it had been excruciating for her when I'd broken into her mind. I'd let myself feel her pain when I did it, and I didn't blame her for being wary of me after that, either consciously or unconsciously.

The more powerful the perimortal and the stronger their mind shield, the more it hurt them when I had to break past it. And Cyra was a very powerful perimortal, even if she didn't realize the extent of her abilities.

After only a few months, Cyra's mind powers nearly rivaled my own. She'd progressed by leaps and bounds under my training, but she didn't yet realize just how much effort it was for me to shield against her. It was like trying to keep someone out who had a key to the door of my mind. She had only to twist the key, and my mind would open wide for her.

But using my power against her in Fernweh had fundamentally damaged the connection between us, and now I needed to repair it.

It didn't surprise me that she'd gravitated to Samhail, given the rift between us. He'd always protected her, but more importantly, Samhail knew what she'd gone through. Morland had broken into his mind twenty-five years ago and taken control of his body, and that had left its mark on Samhail. Now he and Cyra shared the experience of having their minds violently broken open and violated. It was no wonder she'd sought comfort from him.

My eyes met Samhail's over Cyra's shoulder now. We'd been here before, me sitting off to the side watching while he took a woman, but this time would be very, very different.

Voyeurism wasn't new to me. I enjoyed watching, but I especially enjoyed watching Samhail. He was a powerful man, capable of so easily hurting a woman if he wasn't careful, yet he never had, and I admired his control. Somehow the man managed to fuck hard without hurting his partners, and I loved watching him drive into them as they thrashed with ecstasy beneath him. It made me hard as all hells to see it, and I often took the women he'd been with after he did.

I had in the past anyway. I'd never take another woman again as long as I had Cyra.

If I somehow managed to keep her.

I felt Samhail drop his mental shield, and his desire for Cyra flooded my head, nearly making me dizzy. I wasn't actively reading his mind, but my powers were so potent that if people didn't have a mind shield up, impressions of their thoughts and feelings always bombarded me, and I had to block them out with a shield of my own.

The only time I'd ever been powerless to block someone out was when I'd first met Cyra. I'd tried to keep a shield up around her when we first met for my own self-preservation, but the pull to connect with her had been impossible to resist. It was like her mind wrapped around my own, coaxing it open, drugging me with her essence, and making me yield to her will. It was absolutely maddening.

Samhail looked at me, and I knew what he was waiting for. It was a bit of a tradition with us for me to give him an 'order.' It was usually something along the lines of, "Make her moan," or, "Make her scream," or, "Make her come undone." Now, as I met the eyes of my brother in all but blood, I issued my order to him.

*Make her happy*, I said into his mind.

His eyes flared briefly, but he nodded the barest amount and looked down at Cyra as I tried to settle in to watch. This time would be agony, but I deserved it. This was my punishment for the pain I'd caused her, and I was very good at punishing those who deserved it, especially myself.

Cyra took Samhail's face between her hands, and he and I both tensed. I felt his unease mingle with my own at the tender gesture, but she held his face only a second before moving her hands down.

Samhail's mind eased as Cyra dipped her hands to his chest and then continued down over his abdomen, her touch turning from sentimental to sensual. I felt her pleasure at the way his muscles clenched under her fingers, and I fought a smile. She liked eliciting reactions like that from both of us. I doubted she even realized the myriad ways she teased me in bed until I was ready to rut her like some feral beast. It was only a century or so of learning restraint in all parts of my life that kept me from savaging her when we were together.

Both Samhail and I inhaled sharply as Cyra wrapped her hand around his cock through his pants and then pressed her breasts against his chest. I felt his desire surge, and my jaw popped as I clenched my teeth hard, but I forced myself to release the tension. I needed to get a grip on myself, or this would be over before it started.

Cyra turned toward me as if sensing my turmoil, but Samhail put his fingers on her cheek and turned her face back to his.

"If we're going to do this," he told her quietly, "then I need you to look at me, not at him, when your hand is wrapped around my cock."

His words went straight to my balls, and I saw Cyra press her thighs together. They'd aroused her as well.

She started to apologize, but Samhail brought his mouth down on hers to cut off the words, and I jerked as arousal mixed with a hint of crazed fury and flooded my body. I felt Cyra's own tension snap as he ravaged her mouth, and she melted against him. She untucked his shirt, and he helped her pull the garment the rest of the way off to reveal the broad expanse of his muscled chest. Then he slipped the straps of her nightgown over her shoulders so the silk fell down her body, leaving her naked. As many times as I'd seen her this way, completely bare, she always took my breath away. I ached to trace the curves of her body, to grip her narrow waist and press the gentle swells of her beautiful ass against me.

"Still stunning," Samhail told her, voicing my own thoughts.

Cyra trembled at the heat of Samhail's gaze on her bare skin, and I let myself slip briefly into her mind to feel the coil of need between her legs.

"Do you want to lead, or should I?" Samhail asked her.

His restraint was nearly palpable, even without me having to read his thoughts. He wanted to throw Cyra onto the bed and take her hard, and I wanted to see him do it.

Part of me did at least. The other part wanted to be the one to throw her down and drive into her.

"I was told last time that there were no leaders here. If you want to do something, do it," she told him, and I smiled at the reminder of what I'd said to her the first time we'd done this.

Samhail took her hand to lead her to the bed, then grabbed her by the waist and tossed her down on top of it. She squeaked in surprise, and the noise made my cock twitch. Gods, I loved her noises.

Samhail finished undressing, and anticipation shot through me as I took in his huge cock already standing erect. I didn't actually envy him the size of the appendage between his legs. There'd been a couple times he was too big for the women he tried to fuck. Those times we'd either had to switch bedpartners, or if there was only one woman, he'd watch me take her instead while he stroked himself to completion.

Cyra reached for Samhail as he prowled onto the bed over her. She tried to stop him when he pushed her legs open and lowered his head between them, but he threw her own words back at her, insisting that he'd been told he should do whatever he wanted to do.

Every muscle below my waist tensed as Samhail's head disappeared between Cyra's thighs. She cried out, fisting her hands in the covers, and I uncrossed my legs as my cock hardened painfully.

Samhail was an absolute master with his tongue. I was talented myself and could usually make a woman come easily that way, but the way women reacted to Samhail when he feasted on them was something else entirely. I'd asked him several times — sometimes jokingly, sometimes seriously — to tell me his secret, but he'd always refused with a grin.

Samhail stroked Cyra's breasts as he held her down. She looked ready to unravel, and I allowed myself to feel her pleasure. I needed to remind myself why I was doing this.

Cyra was close to a release already. Between Samhail's skill with his mouth and a week of celibacy, he'd driven her quickly to the point of near insanity, and I felt her teetering on the brink.

"Samhail I'm-" Cyra tried to speak, but her body arched up, and she screamed before she could finish. I let her climax wash over me for just a moment before I shut out her mind. I'd spill myself in my pants again if I let myself feel everything she was feeling. Just seeing her ecstasy made me strain against the fabric, and I shifted in my seat to ease the pressure.

Gods above, he hadn't even entered her yet, and I was already about to explode.

"Samhail," she breathed, and pain stabbed through me as I wished it was my name on her lips.

"I just wanted to get that first one out of the way," Samhail told her. "I want to take my time with you, and that's easier to do if your body isn't trying to fly off the bed."

She started to retort, but he silenced her with a merciless kiss. She gripped his biceps, and I knew his tongue was deep inside her mouth, battling with her own. If the sharp breath she inhaled through her nose was any indication, it was a battle she was losing.

Samhail reached a hand between their bodies, and the way she moaned and arched against him told me he'd slipped a finger inside her. He'd gotten over his initial hesitation and was in full control now as he dominated her, pushing her pleasure to greater and greater heights.

"Ready for me again already, I see," he said.

Cyra seemed to tighten her grip on the back of his arms, and I felt in her mind that he'd plunged a second finger inside her and was stroking her slowly.

"Are you going to fuck me or just tease me?" she growled at him in a voice I'd never heard her use before. The savage need in her words hit me straight in my balls again, and I swallowed back a groan.

"Maybe a little of both," Samhail said against her ear, but I felt his surprise at her tone. It was followed quickly by his arousal. He'd heard the need in her voice, and it was taking all his strength not to drive himself into her and fuck her like a wild animal.

Instead, Samhail withdrew his fingers and settled himself between her legs. She gripped his shoulders, digging her fingers into the muscles there as he pushed into her, and anticipation made every part of my body seize up as I watched him press forward, penetrating her, inch by inch. She groaned when he was fully inside her, and I jolted at the surge of ravenous hunger it made me feel.

Regret plucked at a string deep in my mind as I wished fervently it was me inside her, but I tamped it down and tried to breathe.

### Cyra

I felt the inadvertent tug on my mind as Bressen's desire rose while he watched Samhail sheathe himself into me. It was a heady mix of hunger, excitement, and something else I was having trouble putting my finger on. Regret perhaps?

My eyes met Samhail's, and I refocused my attention on him as he began to move. As he'd warned me, he was in no hurry, and each thrust was slow and aching as I felt every inch of him slide into me and then withdraw.

I tightened my inner muscles around him as he pressed into me the next time, and he growled deep in his throat. He'd still been bracing himself above me on his hands, but he lowered himself so he was on his elbows and our bodies were pressed more tightly together. I wrapped a leg around his hip to pull him toward me. He was driving me mad with his leisurely pace.

"You're trying to make me go faster," he rasped into my ear, "but I plan to enjoy you slowly."

He didn't mean it as a challenge, but I took it as one, and I locked my other leg around his waist to pull him toward me. I tightened my inner muscles around him again as he slid in, and Samhail groaned loudly before lowering his body against mine a little more.

"Fuck, Cyra. That's not fair, but I have more self-control than that."

He grazed my neck with his teeth and my body bowed up into him as the sensation sent shivers of pleasure over my skin.

"Talk about not playing fair," I gasped. "Are you trying to make me come apart?"

His answer was simple. "Yes."

Samhail rocked his hips in a way that sent a stab of pleasure shooting through me, and I pulled his head down to crush my mouth into his. His huge body pressed against me leaving little room to move. I enjoyed the feel of his weight on top of me, but it hampered my ability to increase our friction, and his unhurried thrusting was a sweet torture as I tried unsuccessfully to urge him faster. I loved Samhail's strength and dominance, but he was holding back, and I needed him to unleash himself. Gods above, I needed him to fuck me harder, but no one could make Samhail do anything he didn't want to do.

Or perhaps I could...

The thought flashed in my mind that Samhail's mental shield was down, and I let myself consider for half a second that I had the ability to urge him faster if I wanted. I could do it subtly, so he wasn't even aware of what was happening, but I dismissed the thought the next second, recognizing it for the violation of trust it was. Samhail would never forgive me if I took over his mind, especially for something like that.

As I considered the idea, though, my mind connected for just a moment with Samhail's before I could stop it, and the one thought I did see in his head sent a chill through me.

*Savor this last time.*

That's what Samhail was thinking. It was why he insisted on making love to me slowly. He was drawing out this time as long as possible because he knew it would be our last.

Tears gathered in my eyes as I realized he was right. I loved Samhail in my own way, but I'd known since I met Bressen that he was the one I was meant to be with, and holding onto Samhail wasn't fair to any of us. Samhail would always be my friend, but after tonight, he could no longer share my bed. I wondered if Bressen knew that as well, and it had always been his plan to let Samhail and I have this last night together.

"Am I hurting you?" Samhail asked, his voice etched with worry. He'd stopped moving altogether, and he wiped a thumb across the moisture in the corner of my eye.

"This is our last time together, isn't it," I whispered, my voice cracking. "I'm sorry. I saw it in your mind. I didn't mean to."

His face went serious. "Yes, I think this is our last time," he said.

I closed my eyes tightly, and a tear trickled down my face into the hair at my temple. Samhail quickly wiped it away.

"Don't do that," he said. It was an order, but I heard the plea beneath.

Samhail rolled to the side then, bringing me with him so I was now straddling him. I moaned as the new position pressed me down onto him further. He rested his hands gently on my hips, and I looked into his face.

"You move," he said. "Go as fast or slow as you want."

Excitement shot up my body at the heat in his eyes, and I leaned forward to brace my hands on his broad chest. I slid myself up his length, then eased back down him just as slowly as he'd been doing, no longer so eager to push us faster or harder.

Samhail shut his eyes and groaned as I moved again. I let my breasts graze his chest, and my nipples tightened almost painfully. I touched his cheek, and he opened his eyes to lock them with mine as I moved myself slowly up and down him while his hands guided my hips. He thrust up to meet me, and we both gasped in pleasure as we tried to resist the ravenous pull to unleash ourselves and let the chaos of our ecstasy take over.

Soon it became nearly impossible to maintain our languid pace, and I pressed myself down onto him more urgently as exquisite tension built in my core. Samhail's hands tightened on my hips as he slammed me down fiercely onto him, eliciting increasingly feverish cries from me.

"Gods dammit, Cyra!" he ground out. "Those noises are going to fucking undo me."

His hips bowed off the bed so he was fully buried inside me, and he roared his release with several more upward thrusts that brought me the rest of the way to my own climax. Rapture overtook me as the force of my pleasure speared through my body, and I threw my head back with a cry before falling forward to sprawl across Samhail's chest. One of his rough hands rested across my back, tangling in the mass of my hair, and

I lay there listening to the beat of his heart as my head rose and fell on his chest under his own heavy breathing.

It was a couple minutes before I managed to lift myself up and kiss Samhail softly on the lips.

"If that was our last time, then it was a good one to end on," I said softly. I blinked to force the tears back from my eyes.

"It was," he agreed and pulled me back down for another tender kiss.

I swallowed back a lump in my throat as I started to lift myself off him. His hands wrapped around my waist to help guide me, and the memory of the first time his hands had circled my waist back in Fernweh months ago nearly knocked the wind out of me. At the time, he'd been taking me away from my home and my family, and I'd hated him as he'd tried to lift me up into his saddle. I'd snapped at him that I knew how to mount a horse.

What a long, long way we'd come from that time.

Samhail wasn't leaving, I reminded myself. He'd still be in my life. It was just that this part of our involvement was ending. He was a gentle and skilled partner, but so was Bressen, and Bressen needed me now more than Samhail did. And I needed Bressen. I needed him so badly that the two climaxes Samhail had just given me seemed like lifetimes ago.

My eyes went to the chair where Bressen still sat watching us silently, and my breath hitched in my throat. His legs were splayed apart, the bulge at the front of his pants telling me he could no longer keep them comfortably crossed. Desire raged in his eyes, which had turned to a deep teal instead of their usual bright turquoise, and I felt the overwhelming need to touch him. I looked at Samhail and opened my mouth, but he knew before I said anything what I had to do.

"Go to him," Samhail said, nodding toward Bressen. "He needs you."


*Bressen*

Cyra got off the bed to close the space between us. The sway of her hips and the slight bounce of her perfect breasts nearly undid me, and my fingers closed on the arms of the chair until the wood groaned. Even more alluring than her body was the look in her eyes. It was a look I hadn't seen in more than a week, and it made my heart swell with joy and relief.

She wanted me.

Cyra tugged at my wrist. "It's time."

I hesitated for a moment but finally yielded my death-grip on the chair and rose to let her lead me toward the bed, every step torture as my cock pressed against my pants.

Samhail started to get up, but she held out a hand to stop him. "Stay. If neither of you mind, I'd like you to stay," she told him.

Samhail and I exchanged looks, but he nodded and shifted over.

*You don't have to stay if you don't want to*, I said into his mind.

I knew that watching me with Cyra wouldn't be like the other times we'd shared women for Samhail either. He cared for her, and I suspected that seeing me take her might be almost as difficult for him to watch as it had been for me to watch him with her.

*I'll stay unless you want me to go,* he thought back as I read his mind.

*Stay then*, was all I said, and he gave me the hint of a nod.

The feel of Cyra's hands running up my chest brought my attention back to her, and I willed myself not to move. I had to stay calm, or I'd end up hurting her with my ferocity.

"Are you alright?" she asked, frowning a bit.

I nodded. "Are you? That's more important."

"My happiness isn't more important than yours," she said. "I'm grateful you let Samhail and I have this last time together, and I don't want you to regret giving it to us."

I blinked at her words. The thought that this might be the last time I had to share her with Samhail made my heart light. At the same time, I knew if she wanted him again, I'd never deny her. If she changed her mind and asked me to call Samhail to our bed in the future, I'd do whatever I needed to do to get him there, beg, threaten, take over his mind if I needed to. Well, maybe not the last, but everything up to that point, because there was nothing I wouldn't do for her.

"I don't regret anything that makes you happy," I said, the words barely getting past the dryness in my throat.

She smiled and ran her hands down my chest. "Let me make you happy now."

She found the drawstring at my waist and untied my pants before guiding them down my legs. I stepped out of them, and my breath hitched as she knelt in front of me. I let myself slip into her mind for just a moment, but the anxiety that had plagued her all week didn't come.

A thousand and one thoughts ricocheted through my head as I looked down at her, and then my mind went completely blank as she slipped her mouth over my cock.

My knees nearly gave out as she ran her tongue over the head, and her name rasped from my throat as if I'd swallowed sand. She wrapped her hand around my base and plunged her mouth forward again as a groan tore from me. My hands found her hair, and I had to force myself to hold her gently and not thrust deep into her throat. I wasn't even sure how I was still standing as her mouth and tongue nearly made me lose my mind.

It seemed like only seconds before Cyra was driving me toward my release, but I didn't want my first climax with her in a week to come this way. I pulled myself back from the precipice I'd been about to plummet over and pushed her back.

"Let me be inside you," I said, my voice still nothing but gravel.

Cyra pulled her mouth from around my cock and let me help her stand, but she was the one to pull me to the bed and push me down into the space where Samhail had been. I couldn't move as she climbed onto the bed and straddled me.

"Cyra," I breathed before her mouth claimed mine for a searing kiss.

I let my fingers skim lightly up her back and then down again over her gorgeous ass. Sometime in the near future I'd put her on her hands and knees in front of me and take her from behind so I could watch my cock slide in an out of her between those perfect swells, but not right now. Right now, I needed to be face-to-face with her. I needed to see the desire in her eyes, to see her lips part as she moaned, and to see her breasts bob as she rocked above me.

Cyra moaned softly as she ran her slickness over my cock, and it was reflex to lock my arms around her and move her back and forth along my length. What I really wanted to do was plunge myself into her and fuck her like a madman, but our bodies were just getting reacquainted after a long absence, and I wouldn't push her beyond what she was ready to do.

As if sensing my need, Cyra moved up my body so her warm, wet slit was lined up with me. I waited for her to ease herself down, but she speared herself onto me in one swift, brutal thrust instead, and I saw stars as the raw pleasure of finally being sheathed inside her banished everything else in my head.

"Nemesis take me!" I swore as Cyra began to move on top of me, and my hands clamped down on her thighs. I tried to keep my grip light so I didn't bruise her, but I couldn't even wrap my mind around how good it felt to be inside her again, to watch her riding me.

She pushed down harder and faster, and the next words left my mouth on a groan. "Cyra, I don't know how long I can last. It's been-"

The rest of the thought was cut off in my throat as she thrust herself down onto me with wanton demand, and my head jerked back against the bed. Gods above, I was going to die. I'd almost come the moment she took me inside her, but I was trying to hold back my climax to keep our time from ending too soon. I'd be ready to take her again within minutes once we were done, but I'd waited too long for her soft body to be wrapped around mine. I couldn't let it be over so quickly.

Cyra leaned forward to whisper in my ear. "Come for me, my love."

My restraint snapped like a twig at the words, and I grabbed her to flip her beneath me as a growl that was more animal than human ripped from my throat. Cyra wrapped her legs around me, and I drove into her brutally as each thrust pushed her up the bed. She grabbed the covers to try and hold us in place, but her attempts were no match for the strength of my thrusts. A small voice in the back of my head screamed at me to pull back so I didn't hurt her, but I felt only pleasure from her through the wide-open channel between our minds.

Cyra clenched around me, and I exploded inside her, shooting my hot seed into her so hard I was surprised she didn't flinch. She crushed her mouth against mine and screamed her own climax into me, and I absorbed the sound as starbursts flared behind my eyes. Somewhere in the universe, entire worlds lived and died in the seconds that we clung to each other during the throws of our release, and in that moment of pure blinding bliss, I was certain I'd been sent straight to the third tier of the Heavens.

My arms went limp, and I collapsed on top of her. I tried to hold my weight up, but my limbs no longer obeyed me. My efforts were in vain anyway as Cyra only tightened her arms and legs around me, preventing me from pulling away from her. I had to be nearly crushing her, but neither of us seemed to care.

I managed to lift my head to look down at her, and my mouth parted as if to say something. I had no idea what. Words failed me as I looked into her brilliant silver eyes that now glowed in a way I hadn't seen in days.

A deep groan from beside us drew our attention.

On the bed next to us, Samhail jerked his hand over his long cock as his lips drew back from his teeth in an expression raw with need. He thrust his hips up as a jet of seed pumped from the head of his hard shaft to land on his chest, and he gave his cock several more tugs to milk the last few bursts from it before his body eased back onto the bed.

He looked over at us after a few heaving breaths, and I smiled at him, almost laughing. Samhail wasn't much of a voyeur himself, but I saw in his still-open mind that watching Cyra and I fuck with wild abandon had turned him on immeasurably.

He only shrugged as he looked at us before saying, "I hope that was as good for you as it was for me."

# Chapter 20

Several days later, the last of the lingering tension that had been coiled in my body these two weeks released itself as I stepped through the portal into Solandis and the cool salt air hit my nose. Bressen was at my side a moment later, and I felt both his body and mind ease as well.

Bressen far preferred to be here at his home in Solandis than in Callanus, and I'd learned early on that he spent less time in Thasia's capital than other lords typically did. I was glad to be away from Callanus as well and all the politics and responsibilities that came with living in the city.

It had been five days since our night with Samhail, and things were better between me and Bressen. We still weren't completely back to normal, but the night had helped break down some barriers.

Bressen and I slept entwined in each other's arms as we had before the incident in Fernweh, and I found myself once again aching to be close to him, to seek comfort and protection in his arms. When we kissed, I no longer felt pain or the need to pull away, and my desire for him had returned with a vengeance.

Unfortunately, further sex had been put on hold when my cycle arrived the day after we'd been with Samhail. Perimortal cycles were notoriously irregular, and I hadn't had one in almost nine months, so I'd been due. The irregularity was part of the reason perimortals had so much trouble conceiving children. I'd once had my cycle three months in a row only to not have it again for a year and a half.

To my surprise, the start of my bleeding hadn't dissuaded Bressen one bit from wanting to get between my legs. He'd been eager to fuck me regardless, but perimortal cycles were also very uncomfortable, and I'd spent most of the last few days in bed with cramps, back pain, and nausea. I'd even canceled my trainings with Axenus and Samhail all week. Aramis had given me a tea that helped with the pain, but it could only do so much.

Today was the first day I'd felt somewhat back to normal, so Bressen had decided it was as good a day as any to move back to Solandis.

We both needed to get out of the Citadel. We associated it too much with recent pain, and I knew we both hoped that moving back to Solandis for a while would help us move forward. Aidan had settled into his role as a Triumvirate lord, and there was no immediate business that needed the lords' attention. It was also a week before our wedding and there was a lot that needed to be done.

I inhaled deeply and savored the feel of the ocean breeze on my face. The air bore a slight winter chill, but unlike Fernweh and the rest of the outer lands, which could see snow, ice, and temperatures well below freezing throughout the winter, Bressen told me that the coast of Solandis experienced milder winters with far less snow and occasional warm spells that were brought in by temperate fronts off the water. It was a welcome change for someone like me who wasn't particularly fond of cold weather.

It was the proximity to the ocean I loved most about Solandis, though. Bressen's manor house, Tide's End, was built on a bluff overlooking the water that eased down into a wide expanse of beach.

I'd always loved going to the shore with my family as a child, but that had stopped after my parents died, and I hadn't realized just how much I missed those trips until I saw Tide's End. It had been delightful to learn my new home would be located right on the water. Our bedroom, in fact, had a huge balcony that opened over the edge of the bluff.

The first time I'd seen Tide's End was actually in Bressen's dream a week before I'd met him. I'd somehow managed to not only dream walk into the unconsciousness of a man I'd never met before, but I'd apparently let myself right into his house as well. Just before he'd found me in the dream, I'd been staring out a huge window that overlooked the ocean, the water bathed in the pale blue light of the full moon.

It had been surreal when I'd found that window in the real house.

I'd been to the house a few times in the last months, but only for a day or two. This would be the first time we'd be staying for an extended period, and I'd purposely opened my portal in front of the house rather than inside it so I could smell the salt air when we came through.

From the expression on Bressen's face, he approved of my choice. He slipped his hand into mine and brushed a kiss across my knuckles before we stepped to the front door where his steward Ferris awaited us.

"Welcome home, my lord, my lady," Ferris said, bowing low at the waist. "Your rooms and the guest rooms are ready."

Ferris was a tall man, although not as tall as Bressen. He had a thin, lanky frame, and his angular face was framed by sandy blond hair that just brushed his shoulders. He was half perimortal and had a small amount of summoning power he could use to retrieve smaller objects.

We all turned to the portal as Samhail and Axenus came through. They'd both agreed to accompany us back to Solandis to help me keep up my lessons now that I was feeling better. The Aspan Ocean off Solandis was actually Axenus's home, so convincing him to come hadn't been hard.

As for Samhail, he'd considered it a given he'd be coming. I'd been afraid it might be awkward between the three of us after our second night together, but if Bressen or Samhail were bothered, neither showed it.

As before, Samhail had stayed that whole night, and he and Bressen had woken me twice more to make me scream with pleasure. Unlike the Harmilan, though, Bressen had been the only one to take me again while Samhail seemed content to play a supporting role. He'd spent the night teasing and sucking my breasts or massaging my clit while Bressen fucked me, and I'd lost track of how many times I'd climaxed by the end. Samhail had been achingly hard by morning, and I'd taken him into my mouth one final time – our last, *last* time we'd joked – to make him spill himself down my throat as Bressen drove into me from behind.

Samhail had kissed me on the cheek before leaving that morning, and that had been that. It remained to be seen if we could just be friends. We had yet to put anything to the test since my cycle had started shortly after.

"Master Samhail," Ferris said, bowing as the warrior approached. "It's good to see you again."

"Thank you, Ferris. It's good to see you as well," Samhail said. He had a set of saddlebags and a canvas rucksack slung over his shoulder.

"Your usual quarters on the third floor of the east wing are ready," Ferris said, and Samhail nodded his thanks before striding into the house.

"And this is Axenus," Bressen told Ferris as the merman came up.

"Master Axenus," Ferris said. "It's an honor. If you'll follow me, I can show you to your rooms."

"Actually, if it can wait a little while, I'd like to take a swim first," Axenus said, eyeing the water. "It's been a while since I've been back in the ocean, and it's calling to me."

"Of course, sir," Ferris said. "I'll await your return."

Axenus turned and hurried down the stairs to head toward the beach.

He needed to be in the water every few days to maintain his ability to shift into his mer form. Fresh water would suffice, and he'd swum daily in the Scion River that ran through Callanus, but salt water was better, so I wasn't surprised the first thing he wanted to do was jump in the ocean.

Several pairs of guards stepped through the portal next, each carrying a trunk between them. The first three sets of guards marched straight into the house, heading directly to the rooms I now shared with Bressen. The fourth set of guards stopped in front of Ferris with their trunk.

"Master Axenus's things," said one of the guards.

"Third floor, west wing," Ferris told them, and the guards moved past him into the house.

Finally, three stable hands stepped through, one leading my gray mare, one leading Samhail's giant black stallion, and one leading Bressen's white stallion. They headed for the stables, and I closed the portal after them.

I felt a twinge of pain as the Citadel disappeared from view. Brix had declined to come with us, so Jaylan had opted to stay with him in Callanus for now. Brix hadn't been as openly hostile to me this week, but he also hadn't made any overtures of peace either. I hoped that some time away from me might give him the space he needed to sort himself out.

"The four of us will take dinner at seven," Bressen told Ferris as we all turned to head into the house. Our footsteps sounded softly on the marble floor as we entered the large foyer. A huge crystal chandelier hung from the domed ceiling while staircases curved up on either side of the space leading to the living areas on the upper floors.

"My lord," Ferris said hesitantly as we crossed the foyer, "we have one more guest who just arrived a little before you did."

Bressen stopped short, making Ferris and I pull up as well.

"Who?" Bressen asked, his eyes narrowing. "And why wasn't I told?"

"Her arrival was unexpected," Ferris said apologetically.

Bressen's body went rigid. "Ferris, tell me it's not-" he started to say, but he was cut off by a bright female voice from the top of the stairs.

"Bressen! There you are!"

Bressen and I both turned to see a woman in a flowing light blue gown descending the staircase toward us. She looked to be in her late thirties, and her pale blond hair was pulled into a neat chignon at the back of her head. Her stride was purposeful, her posture regal as she held her hands out wide in a welcoming gesture. She was stunningly gorgeous, and jealousy immediately prickled against my scalp until she got closer, and I recognized her bright turquoise eyes.

My head snapped to Bressen, but his attention was on the woman as a muscle ticked in his jaw.

The woman reached us and wrapped her arms gently around Bressen to pull him into what I could only describe as an elegant hug. He smiled tightly and hugged her back, a definite reticence in his embrace.

"Mother," Bressen said as he pulled back. "What are you doing here? You weren't supposed to be here until the day before the wedding."

Mother. This woman was Bressen's mother.

I knew Bressen's father had died about twenty years ago, but I'd never even thought to ask him about his mother. Our meeting and courtship had been such a chaotic whirlwind, I hadn't had a chance to ask about such mundane things as who Bressen still had for family. Part of me just assumed he didn't have any living relatives, since he'd never mentioned any, but here was his mother. I wasn't sure if I was more annoyed I hadn't thought to ask him about her or that he hadn't volunteered anything.

"I came to help you prepare for the wedding," his mother said. She swung her gaze to me. "And, of course, to meet my new daughter-in-law."

"Of course," Bressen grumbled. He turned to me and put an arm around my waist to pull me against him in what I'd come to recognize as a gesture of protectiveness and possession. "Mother, this is my fiancé, Cyra, formerly of Fernweh in the Polaris territory. Cyra, this is my mother, Lady Andromeda of Laycan in Hiraeth."

I wasn't sure what the protocol was to greet the woman, but with Bressen holding onto me, the only thing I could do was incline my head to her. I didn't offer my hand – I'd become wary of doing so – and Andromeda didn't offer hers, so we just exchanged polite nods.

"Lady Andromeda, it's wonderful to meet you," I said, trying to mask the unease I felt. Bressen's reaction to her had set me on edge, but there was something about the woman herself that prickled my own senses.

"You as well, my dear," Andromeda said. "I wish I could say my son has told me all about you, but alas, most of what I know I've learned through the social gossip scene." She looked pointedly at Bressen. "Including the fact you were engaged."

I looked up at Bressen, my face conveying my surprise that he hadn't told his mother we were engaged.

*I'll explain later*, he said into my mind.

"I was a little busy dealing with a coup and the possible dissolution of the Triumvirate," Bressen said to his mother, his hand tightening on my waist, "but the next time the government is ready to fall and the country is in chaos, I'll be sure to let you know my wedding plans first."

I gasped at the biting sarcasm, but Andromeda waved away his tone.

"Still overdramatic as ever," she said with a sigh.

I blinked. Bressen had moments of showmanship, but I'd never call him overdramatic.

Bressen sighed. "I'm sorry you didn't hear about the engagement directly, Mother, but in my defense, there was a lot going on at the time."

Andromeda smiled. "I'm sure there was," she said, her tone suggesting it still wasn't an acceptable excuse. "So when will Cyra and I have some time to get to know each other?"

Bressen's body tensed even more against me.

"I'm sure we can find time at some point. You're welcome to join us for dinner if you'd like. You can speak to her then," he said.

"I'll certainly join you for dinner," Andromeda said, "but I was hoping for some private time to get to know Cyra as well."

"Cyra will be extremely busy this week," Bressen said, "hence the reason I suggested you not come until the wedding. You can get to know her after we're married."

Andromeda's mouth tightened into a thin-lipped smile. "Of course," she said in an overly polite voice.

"Lady Andromeda?" Samhail's deep voice sounded from the top of the stairs, and we all turned to see him descending toward us.

"Samhail," Andromeda said, her voice again bright. "I should've known you'd be here."

"Someone needs to keep Bressen out of trouble," Samhail said lightly as he approached us and took Andromeda's hand to kiss it. His tone was teasing, but he flashed Bressen a look that said he wasn't happy to see Andromeda either.

"Keep him out of trouble?" she asked incredulously. "I seem to recall you're the one always getting him into it."

"I knew it was one of the two," Samhail said without missing a beat.

"Your timing is perfect, Samhail," Andromeda continued. "Would you escort Cyra up to her rooms? I need to speak with my son alone."

I raised a brow at her high-handedness. I wasn't officially the Lady of Hiraeth yet, but I wasn't going to let this woman order me around in my own home, Bressen's mother or no.

"I don't have time to speak with you now, Mother," Bressen said before I could tell Andromeda what I thought of her idea. "I need to get Cyra settled in, and then I have a lot of work to do. Ferris undoubtedly has a long list of things he needs to speak to me about."

"A huge list," Ferris confirmed, obviously familiar with the steps of this little dance.

"It's fairly urgent I speak with you," she insisted.

"Perhaps before dinner," Bressen said.

He took my hand and led me toward the stairs. I felt a tingle at the base of my neck and saw Samhail nod almost imperceptibly in apparent acknowledgement of whatever Bressen had just told him.

"Lady Andromeda, have you met Axenus yet?" I heard Samhail say as Bressen and I climbed the stairs. "I think he went down for a swim in the ocean. If we hurry, you can catch him before he puts his clothes back on."

My head whipped around to watch Samhail lead Andromeda to the door. I'd learned Axenus needed to strip off his clothes in order to change into his mer form, but Samhail couldn't possibly mean to...

"He wouldn't-" I started to say, but Bressen cut me off with a sigh.

"He would."

I shook my head. "Honestly, Samhail and Axenus have the strangest friendship I've ever seen. They *are* friends, aren't they?"

"I'm still trying to figure that out myself," Bressen sighed.

We continued all the way up to the fourth floor of the house, which was entirely dedicated to our private quarters.

"I didn't realize your mother was still alive," I said as we headed toward our bedroom. "I'm sorry. I should've asked. You never mentioned her, so I just assumed…" I trailed off.

"As you can probably tell, I don't get along with my mother very well," Bressen said. "I'm sorry I didn't tell you about her before now. I should've prepared you to meet her, but part of me was hoping she wouldn't even come to the wedding."

I waited for Bressen to offer more, but he didn't go on. I was working up the courage to ask him about it when he suddenly pressed me up against the wall next to our bedroom door and brought his lips down on mine for an urgent kiss. I wasn't sure if he'd sensed my question and wanted to head it off, but if so, it certainly worked. All thoughts of his mother flew out of my head as his tongue delved into my mouth and my knees went weak. I whimpered softly when he pulled away seconds later.

"No more about my mother," Bressen rasped against my ear. "I need to fuck you. Are you feeling up to it?"

I nodded eagerly. "Yes." The word came out as a breath.

Bressen took my hand to pull me toward our room. He threw open the door, and we hurried inside only to stop dead when we saw the young woman rummaging through the trunks the guards had brought up. She looked startled at our entrance and quickly stood up straight.

"And who are you?" Bressen asked her, his tone somewhere between curious and wary.

"Apologies, my lord," she said, bobbing a curtsey. "I'm the new lady's maid. You can call me Leeda."

The woman was about my height with olive skin and flat brown hair. Her figure was somewhere between curvy and plump, and her eyes seemed just a bit large for her face, which made her look perpetually surprised, even after she'd recovered from the shock of having me and Bressen catch her in our trunks.

"Ah, of course," Bressen said. "As usual, Ferris is on top of all the details. What are you doing in our trunks?"

"I was…putting your things away," Leeda said, seeming unsure now if she was supposed to be doing this.

I furrowed my brow as I thought Leeda's skin emitted a faint red glow, indicating she was lying, but it was there and gone in an instant. Maybe I'd imagined the red glow, or perhaps its brief appearance was an indication of a half-truth on her part.

"Hello, Leeda," I said, smiling at her. "I'm Cyra. It's nice to meet you."

Leeda bobbed another curtsey. "Should I leave?" she asked, looking between us.

"No, please stay and finish what you were doing," I said without thinking, then caught the flash of disappointment on Bressen's face. "I mean-," I started to correct myself, but he held up a hand to interrupt me.

"It's alright. I should check in with Ferris and then see what my mother wants," he said. "There's only so long Samhail can keep her busy before he'll want to beat his head against a wall. Axenus also has no idea what he's in for, so I should go see if he needs to be rescued as well."

He pulled me against him and closed his mouth over mine for a deep, penetrating kiss. Lightning shot straight through my veins, and I now thoroughly regretted telling Leeda to stay.

Bressen wasn't usually quite so bold when we had an audience – except maybe in front of Samhail – but I supposed his mother's unexpected arrival had unsettled him, and he was trying to ground himself. Rather than feeling embarrassed about our shameless show of affection in front of Leeda, I kissed him back with a fervor I hoped told him I was here for whatever he needed.

When we finally broke the kiss, Bressen laid his forehead on mine.

"Nemesis take me," he breathed. "I needed that. I'd hoped to be working on your third climax by now, but it looks like that will have to wait a bit longer."

I shivered with elation at the promise in his words. "Soon," I said. "For now, take care of whatever you need to take care of."

"You'll be alright here by yourself?"

"I won't be by myself. Leeda and I will get to know each other a bit," I said, nodding my head at the maid.

Bressen and I both turned to look at Leeda, who quickly ducked her gaze back to the clothing she'd been pulling out of the trunks. She'd clearly been watching us, but I didn't mind. Maybe I'd gotten used to having people watch me during intimate moments after that last time with Bressen and Samhail. There was something…thrilling about it.

Bressen kissed me again, more tenderly this time, before he pulled away and headed for the door. "I'll see you at dinner, if not before then," he said, and then he was gone.

I walked over and sat down on the bed to watch Leeda. I wanted to help her, but I'd found that the Citadel staff were uncomfortable when I tried to do things like that. For better or worse, they preferred to separate themselves from me and the lords.

Raina had been the exception. She'd embraced a friendship with me after some resistance, but in fairness, I'd only been a winemaker at the time I met her, not the Lady of Hiraeth.

"Tell me about yourself, Leeda," I said. "Where are you from?"

"I'm from Rowe originally, my lady," she said without looking up.

My eyes widened in mild surprise. "Really? What brings you all the way out here?"

Leeda shrugged. "Opportunity. I'll travel for work if the job is right."

"And coming all the way to Solandis to be my lady's maid was right?"

Leeda glanced at me quickly and smiled. "Very much so, my lady."

I watched her carefully, but so far everything she'd said was true. Whatever I'd seen before must have been a trick of my eyes. Still, I let my mind reach out toward hers.

As we'd begun to train my mind powers, Bressen had impressed on me the importance of staying out of people's heads unless they gave you good reason to want to know what they were thinking. Our own private thoughts and feelings needed to remain as sacred as possible, he said, and I'd agreed. I'd been angry to think he was reading my thoughts early on in our relationship, and it wasn't until later when I'd confronted him about it that he'd told me it felt like my mind had been inviting him in.

I convinced myself now that the red glow I'd seen on Leeda and the fact that she'd be around me at some of my most vulnerable moments was reason enough just to check to be sure she wasn't hiding anything.

I thought I saw Leeda pause briefly in her work when my mind connected with hers, and I wondered if I hadn't been as subtle in my attempt as I'd hoped, but she didn't say anything.

Nor did I see anything of concern. I didn't probe very deeply, wary of being too invasive of her thoughts, but my quick search of her mind told me Leeda was, as far as I could tell, exactly who she claimed to be.

I was thinking of other things to ask her to get to know her more when she rose with an armful of clothes and quickly disappeared into the closet to put them away. I had a feeling she was hoping I wouldn't ask her anything else, and I sighed. I missed Raina.

I'd heard ladies and their personal maids sometimes formed close friendships because they spent a lot of time together, but it didn't seem like Leeda was interested in forming any kind of bond. I'd respect her preference if she just wanted to do her job. Perhaps it was for the best anyway. Now that I was living in the same rooms as Bressen, I had far less private time than I had when Raina and I were together at the Citadel. Bressen himself didn't keep a personal valet, and I had plenty of experience taking care of myself.

It was more the companionship I missed. I'd never had female friends growing up – or really any friends besides my brothers – and I'd liked having Raina to talk to.

I got up from the bed and went over to the writing desk set against the wall. I opened drawers until I found a pen and a few small rectangular sheets of paper that had a slightly golden hue to them. I took one of the message leaves, thought for a moment, then wrote a note to Raina.

*Dear Raina,*
*When were you planning to arrive for the wedding? Will the High Council let you come early? I just met the mother-in-law I didn't realize I had, and my new lady's maid is not nearly as charming as my last one. Please advise.*
*Love, Cyra*

I held the piece of paper up between my middle and pointer fingers, whispered Raina's name, and the paper disappeared in a puff of smoke.

Almost immediately, I felt bad about imposing my problems on Raina. She had her own issues to worry about in Polaris, and I nearly grabbed another message leaf to tell her to ignore my first one, when her response puffed into existence in front of my face.

I plucked the message leaf out of the air and read it.

I smiled and felt an instant sense of relief that Raina would be arriving tomorrow. I held the leaf out in my palm, and a small flame quickly curled the paper into ash that I swept into the fireplace. The last thing I wanted was for Leeda to find the message and be offended.

In any case, I wasn't planning to spend the rest of my day stuck in this room, especially if Leeda didn't want me here. Now that I was back in Solandis, a walk on the beach was just the thing I needed. Hopefully Axenus had finished his swim and would be dressed again by the time I walked down to the sand. I – unlike Samhail – had no desire to surprise him while he was naked.

I spared a glance into the closet to see that Leeda was still putting clothes away, seemingly as slow as she could.

"I'm going for a walk," I called in to her. "I'll be back by half past six to dress for dinner."

"Of course, my lady," Leeda said, coming to the door of the closet.

I wondered if it was relief I heard in her voice.

"Is there something in particular you'd like to wear?" she asked.

I thought for a moment. "There's an emerald silk dress you can lay out for me."

"Yes, my lady."

The emerald dress was the only truly nice thing I'd brought with me from Fernweh. It wasn't ornate, but I'd worn it my first night in Callanus to dine with the lords of the last Triumvirate, and then also the day after the coup when Bressen had announced our engagement to the people. The dress had come to symbolize strength and power for me, and I had a feeling I was going to need both to survive a week with Bressen's mother.

# Chapter 21

Before heading down to the beach, I made my way to the library on the second floor. I figured I would bring a book with me in case I wanted to stop and do some reading before coming back to the house.

Even though I'd only been to Tide's End a few times, I had a good handle on the lay of the house. Bressen's private quarters took up the entirety of the fourth floor and – much like our suite at the Citadel – included our bedroom, a bathing chamber, a sitting room, Bressen's study, and a large meeting room that, under extreme circumstances, might be called a war room. Several guest quarters were on the third floor, and most of the second floor was taken up by a library, a leisure room, and a solarium. The main floor included the foyer, the kitchens, the main dining room, a modest ballroom, and the quarters for the live-in servants. Below the main floor was a basement that housed the pantry, a wine cellar, a small armory, and a few storage rooms. Even further below that was a subbasement with holding cells for prisoners, which seemed strange for a private residence, but which I imagined were used only for emergencies.

I strode down the hall of the second floor and was a bit surprised to find the door of the library closed. I started to open it but froze as I heard voices inside. On instinct I raised my mind shield and leaned closer to listen, finding that I could hear just well enough to make out what was being said through the crack.

"She seems like a lovely girl," Andromeda was saying, "but she's not an angelus."

I'd been surprised to learn shortly after I'd met Bressen that he wasn't fully human, but demi-human. Like Samhail, he could manifest wings, but whereas Samhail's gargoyle wings were leathery and bat-like, Bressen's were sleek feathered ones. He'd told me that his kind, angelus, had the ability to harness extremes of light and dark, but I had yet to fully understand what that meant.

"I'm well aware she's not an angelus," Bressen answered, a hard edge to his voice. "And she's much more than a 'lovely girl.' She's a beautiful, strong, remarkable woman that I happen to be very much in love with."

My heart swelled to hear Bressen's words, and I smiled, but that smile faded a moment later at his mother's response.

"That's all well and good," she said, "but you can't actually marry her."

I blinked, not sure I'd heard her correctly.

"I can and I will," Bressen replied without hesitation.

"Your children won't be angelus," Andromeda said. "You know both parents must be angelus for the child to be."

"Again, I'm aware," Bressen said, "but it's extremely premature to be discussing children Cyra and I might have. We aren't even married yet."

"And you never will be," she said. "Angelus are nearly extinct on the continent. You have an obligation to do what you can to help prevent that, and that means marrying another angelus."

I clamped my hand over my mouth to stifle the gasp I'd been about to make. I wasn't sure what shocked me most, the news that angelus were nearly extinct, or Andromeda's adamant declaration that Bressen and I would never marry.

"I have no such obligation," Bressen said, his voice even colder than before. "I'll marry whomever I want."

"So you want to see us die out?" Andromeda asked in indignation.

"No, of course not, but I won't sacrifice my personal happiness for what will only be a small bandage on a much larger problem. Me marrying another angelus won't suddenly replenish our diminishing population, especially since such a union might at most only produce one or two children. At this point, it's almost inevitable our kind will die out eventually, but I won't let you hold me responsible for that."

My heart clenched. Gods above, this couldn't be happening.

There were a few seconds of silence before Andromeda spoke again.

"You're right. Marriage to another angelus wouldn't be enough. Maybe you don't have to actually marry one, then. If I could find a few females of our kind who were willing to bear children without being married, perhaps you could simply-"

I inhaled sharply as a surge of Bressen's power reverberated out of the room in pulsing waves, shaking the entire house as it went. My hands flew up to cover my ears as they popped under the pressure, and my heart stuttered as the surge reset my heartbeat.

Inside the room, there was a soft cry that I assumed was Bressen's mother, then there was dead silence on the other side of the door. I knew without seeing it that Bressen's eyes were now burning scarlet with rage. I could barely hear him when he spoke again, but the menace in his voice was clear enough.

"I know you're not suggesting I betray my wife and our marriage bed so you can use me to sire angelus," he said more coldly than I'd ever heard.

"I'm only suggesting-" she started to say carefully, but he cut her off.

"Do you also plan to collect stud fees for me as well?" he snapped.

Something prickly crawled its way down my spine as fear for Bressen's mother rose within me. As much as I didn't like the woman, especially after those comments, I was almost afraid of what Bressen might do next.

"You're being dramatic again," came her reply, her scolding tone back.

There was a pause. "I'm only going to say this once, Mother, so I hope you're listening," Bressen said, his voice still just barely discernable. "I'm marrying Cyra, and she's the only woman with whom I will have children, if or when we so choose. You can either accept that and come to the wedding, or you can leave now."

"Your father would have wanted-" Andromeda started to say, but he cut her off again.

"Don't you dare finish that sentence!" he hissed, and another smaller surge of his power rumbled through the house.

"I'm only saying-"

"My father would have wanted me to be happy," Bressen said, "and Cyra makes me happy. She makes me happier than I've ever been in my life, and my father would have loved her for that, as I do."

Bressen's voice broke as emotion replaced the cold menace.

"Bressen-"

"We're done here. You can show yourself out."

There was silence again, and I realized a second later that Andromeda was likely leaving the library.

I hurried down the hall, trying to run on my toes to keep silent, but I stopped as I reached a small alcove in the opposite wall where a seating nook extended out from the house at a window. I tucked myself inside it and managed to put up an obfuscation glamour just as the door swung open. The glamour would make me mostly invisible if she came this way.

Andromeda exited the room and – to my relief – turned down the hall in the opposite direction. I waited for her to disappear around the corner and was about to step out when Bressen walked into the hall.

Gods damn me.

I pressed myself back into the alcove again and sent a silent prayer up to whichever of the Trinity might be listening that Bressen would turn down the same way as his mother.

He didn't.

I stayed perfectly still in the alcove as Bressen approached, but I knew more certainly with each step he took that he knew I was here. Sure enough, he stopped when he got to the alcove, and his eyes scanned the space as if searching for something. I was about to reveal myself when his hand shot out and wrapped around my waist to pull me against him. A squeak escaped my lips, and the obfuscation glamour fell away.

Bressen's eyes refocused to meet mine now that I was visible. "I found you," he said lightly. "Is it my turn to hide now?"

Bressen's head dipped down to trail kisses up my neck, and the shiver of pleasure they evoked made me arch against him.

"Let me guess," I said breathlessly. "You could smell me?"

Bressen pressed his face into my hair and inhaled deeply.

"Mmm, still almond and jasmine. But no. I sensed you were nearby when my power surges passed over you. Is there a chance you didn't hear any of that?"

I smiled sadly and shook my head.

He sighed. "Of course you heard. You're an expert eavesdropper."

"Not that expert. You've caught me twice now."

Bressen brushed a lock of my hair back over my ear and let his fingers trail down my face. "I want you to forget everything you overheard. My mother was egregiously out of line."

"She doesn't want us to marry," I said, needing to state the obvious.

"Her objection has nothing to do with you personally, and it doesn't matter anyway. All that matters is that I love you, and I don't give a fuck what my mother thinks."

"It still would have been nice to have her like me."

Bressen laid his forehead against mine and brushed my cheek with his thumb. "She doesn't dislike you. Not exactly, anyway. And once we're married, hopefully she'll take the opportunity to actually get to know you."

"You mean when she's not loaning you out as a breeding stud?"

Bressen sighed heavily. "I was especially hoping you didn't hear that part. You know I'd never, ever do anything like that to you, right?"

"I know."

"Then put it out of your mind and forget about my mother."

"Why didn't you tell me angelus are nearly gone?" I asked.

"Because that doesn't matter either," he said. "It's not something you or me or anyone else can change, despite what my mother thinks. Within the next few hundred years, angelus will likely die out. The fact that both parents must be angelus, along with the abysmal birth rates perimortals have in general, means we're unlikely to rebound."

"But-"

"And what my mother also left out is that the possibility of conceiving children is even more diminished if both angelus are of the same alignment," he went on.

I frowned. "The same alignment?"

Apparently deciding this would be a longer conversation than he expected, Bressen sat down on the seat in the window alcove and pulled me onto his lap.

"You remember I told you angelus are beings that hold the capacity to harness both darkness and light?" he asked.

I nodded.

"Well, as you may have noticed, my powers skew more toward darkness, as did my father's. My mother, on the other hand, is an angelus of the light. She can wield sunfire."

"Sunfire?"

"It's a powerful kind of magic that, when used as a weapon, can make one feel as though they're on fire without actually burning them," he said.

I stared in horror. "How does that make her an angelus of the light?"

"Don't mistake light and dark for the same as good and evil, as I once did," he said. "Angelus of the light are not automatically good people, just as I hope you've discovered angelus of the darkness are not all evil."

I thought about that a moment. "No, they aren't evil," I agreed. "It's been my experience that they're more wicked than anything."

Bressen's eyes smoldered. "And what do you know of wickedness?"

"I know quite a bit. My fiancé is exceedingly wicked."

"Is he?" Bressen asked huskily. "What does he do that's so wicked?"

Bressen pulled me against his groin, and I felt his hard arousal pressing at my backside. I exhaled and rocked my ass in small circles against him.

"Fuuck," he breathed, drawing out the word. He tightened his hold on me and pressed his face into the crook of my neck. "Which one of us did you say was the wicked one again?"

I smiled as I took Bressen's hands and gently pulled them away from my body. Reluctantly, he let me go, and I slipped off his lap so I was on my knees facing him.

"Cyra," he whispered, his eyes flaring as he realized what I intended.

I nudged his knees apart so I could move between them, and his gaze became hooded as I undid the fastenings of his pants. I peeled back the flaps and reached in to pull out his cock. He leaned back and groaned as my fingers wrapped around him. I ran my hand up over the head of his shaft, and our eyes locked as I began to lower my mouth toward him.

Someone cleared their throat behind us, and I froze.

"Are we interrupting something?" came Samhail's amused voice.

"Fuck," Bressen growled again in a very different tone.

I shot to my feet and whirled to find both Samhail and Axenus in front of the alcove. Heat of a different kind flamed inside me, and I was sure my skin must be the color of red wine.

"Fuck," I echoed as I looked at the two of them.

Samhail raised a brow at my language while Axenus gave me an apologetic smile.

"Have I ever told the two of you that you have shit timing?" Bressen asked as he stood and refastened his pants.

"We were just coming to find out why the house shook twice a few minutes ago," Samhail said. "It's not our fault the two of you decided that, in a house with this many rooms, the middle of the hall would be an ideal place for Cyra to-"

"Do not finish that sentence, or I swear I'll make you regret it," I cut in warningly.

Samhail smirked. I'd threatened him like this before, and we both knew I still didn't have a way to make him regret anything. Luckily, he had enough courtesy not to test me.

"So should we be concerned about the power surges?" Axenus asked.

"I was just having a conversation with my mother," Bressen said.

Samhail narrowed his eyes. "Are you sure we shouldn't be concerned? Is Andromeda still in one piece?"

"For now," Bressen said. "She had the temerity to tell me I wasn't allowed to marry Cyra because she's not angelus."

Both Samhail and Axenus looked shocked.

"Don't forget her plan to loan you out for studding, regardless of whether we're married or not. That was my favorite part," I offered nonchalantly.

Samhail and Axenus gaped at me.

"She said all this in front of you?" Axenus asked me, aghast.

"No, my little spy has a bad habit of listening at doors to exchanges that weren't meant for her ears," Bressen said, his tone light.

"I understand the power surges now," Samhail said. "What are you planning to do?"

"I don't plan to do anything but marry Cyra at the end of the week," Bressen said. "My mother's been told her options are to accept my decision and attend the wedding, or she can leave."

"My money is on secret option number three," Samhail said. "She goes behind your back and tries to convince Cyra to let you go."

Bressen sighed. "It crossed my mind she might do that as well." He turned to me. "Please, do not agree under any circumstances to speak to my mother alone this week. If I need to, I'll have Ferris assign a guard to follow you around until the wedding."

My brows shot up at the suggestion.

"Thankfully, it won't be necessary for me to tell you how out of the question that plan is," I said. "As it happens, I sent a message to Raina a little while ago asking her to come early. She arrives tomorrow after lunch. If anyone can keep me safe from your mother, it's her."

Bressen visibly relaxed at the news. "That's perfect."

"Raina? Your former lady's maid?" Samhail asked, and I nodded.

"The girl who hid behind you or in the bathing chamber every time I used to come to your room?" Samhail pressed. "She's the one who's going to keep you away from Andromeda?"

I smiled. "Raina doesn't hide from anyone anymore. You might want to watch yourself around her now."

Samhail quirked a brow. "Well, now I'm intrigued."

I narrowed my eyes at him, and he winked. I wasn't sure if that meant he was kidding or if it was a wink that promised mischief. For that matter, I wasn't sure how I felt about the idea of something happening between Samhail and Raina. Samhail and I had decided we shouldn't sleep together anymore, so I had no romantic or sexual claims on him, and I had no reason or right to be jealous where he was concerned, but I couldn't help disliking the idea of him and Raina together.

"I don't imagine Andromeda is planning to leave anytime soon then?" Axenus said, steering the conversation back around.

Bressen shook his head. "My mother doesn't give up easily." He turned to me. "Until the wedding, if you're not with me, Samhail, or Axenus, then make sure you're with Raina."

"I'm not going to make Raina guard me the whole time," I said.

"She doesn't have to," Bressen said. "You just need to spend your free time together doing…whatever it is young women of your age do in their free time." He sounded genuinely ignorant of what that was.

I smirked at him. "So drinking, gambling, and fighting then?"

"If that's the case, I volunteer to go with them," Samhail said.

I shot him a withering look, but he just smiled and shrugged.

"I'm serious," Bressen said to me. "Stay close to Raina and stay away from my mother, or I'll put a guard on you whether you like it or not."

"Fine. I promise," I said, giving him a frown.

"Do you expect trouble tonight?" Axenus asked.

Bressen shook his head. "No, I won this first round with my mother. She'll retreat to rethink her strategy. Just don't be fooled by it. She's a viper waiting to strike when your guard is down."

I really had to ask Bressen more about his mother soon. I wanted to understand what had happened between the two of them to warrant such a characterization.

In any case, Raina would be arriving tomorrow, and we wouldn't spend much time apart anyway. I missed her, and I was looking forward to getting as much time with her as possible. I'd still be spending my mornings training with both Axenus and Samhail, but then Raina and I would have the afternoons and evenings to ourselves.

Andromeda may be a viper, but I'd have a peregrine falcon on my side ready to squeeze the snake under her talons.

# Chapter 22

"She said *what?*" Raina nearly shrieked the next afternoon when she and I were alone in my chambers. We were waiting for the seamstress to arrive with my wedding dress for the final fitting, and I was filling her in on what I'd overheard Bressen's mother say yesterday. We hadn't even gotten to the worst of it yet, and Raina was already furious on my behalf.

"She actually dared to tell Bressen he wasn't allowed to marry you?" she asked indignantly. "I assume he told her to go fuck herself?"

I smiled. "Not in quite those words, but yes. So then she decided he didn't actually need to marry an angelus woman. He just needed to fuck a few to impregnate them."

I usually swore only rarely, but Raina's much more liberal use of expletives tended to wear off on me when she was around. Still, I'd never have the nerve to utter half the string of filthy curses that came out of her mouth now at that tidbit of news.

"Raina!" I admonished, feeling my face redden at her language. I'd never even heard Samhail use such language, and I'd overheard him say some shocking things when he didn't realize I was around.

"I'll kill her," Raina said. "I don't care if she is his mother."

"No, you won't," I said reasonably, chuckling. "You're going to smile at her and be polite and pretend that you don't know she wants to prostitute my husband to other women."

"Cyra, you seem to think that I'm nice like you," Raina said just as reasonably. "I'll take my talons to her face."

"I wouldn't recommend it. Bressen said her power is sunfire? It sounds rather painful."

Raina shook her head. "I've never heard of it."

I was about to explain when a knock sounded at the door, and I stood up to answer it. I let the dressmaker in, and Raina and I cut our conversation short as they both helped me into the unbelievably gorgeous gown I'd be wearing to marry Bressen in less than a week.

As long as his mother didn't have a say.

The gown was made of a shimmering white fabric that hugged my body until it reached my knees where it flared out like the petals of a flower. Delicate straps held it at my shoulders, and my back lay bare to almost my waist, covered only by strands of tiny sparkling gems and pearls that hung loosely between my shoulders and tickled my skin when they swayed. More tiny gems and pearls were sown all over the dress as well, so there wasn't one part of it that didn't twinkle and flash. All the gems and beading should have made the gown heavy, yet it was impossibly light.

"You're going to look absolutely exquisite!" Raina said as I turned to face her. I held my arms out a little to avoid being poked by the pins the seamstress was now sticking in the gown to mark the areas it still needed some adjustment.

"I'm not sure why this is even necessary," I said, flinching as one of the pins poked me in the waist. "At the Citadel, the clothiers just sent dresses and garments up to my room without any need for fittings, and everything fit just fine."

"Yes, but this is your wedding dress," Raina said. "This is different. It needs to be perfect."

I looked at Raina's own deep crimson gown. Since moving to Gendris, her wardrobe had changed significantly. The High Council had encouraged her to wear more courtly attire as part of their plan to hold her up as their figurehead, and it hadn't taken any arm-twisting for her to agree. She'd happily exchanged the cottons and rougher fabrics of her former maid's attire for the silks, satins, and velvets that befit her status as daughter of the late Lord Ursan. Raina's tastes ran toward bold, warm colors like what she now wore, in contrast to the cooler shades of blues, greens, and lavenders I preferred.

"At least the gown will be perfect, if not the person wearing it," I said.

Raina gave me a look of frustration that told me she wasn't going to indulge any self-pity, particularly about Fernweh.

"If you're waiting for me to tell you that you're perfect, you're going to be waiting a long time," she said. "You're not perfect, and you never will be, so just let the dress have its moment. We all make mistakes. Stop dwelling on yours."

I gave Raina an exaggerated frown. "You know, I miss that shy lady's maid who always told me what I wanted to hear and wasn't so quick to shove the unpolished truth down my throat," I teased her. "Whatever happened to her? I could really use some coddling right now."

Raina rolled her eyes. "That lady's maid died when Ursan did."

That wasn't quite accurate. Raina had still been shy enough when the High Council of Polaris had come to collect her after Ursan's death, and she'd remained that way for a couple weeks into her stay in Gendris before she'd had enough. They saw her as no more than a servant, so after two weeks of bearing their cups and listening to them make plans for her father's territory that didn't involve finding a new lord or lady to replace him, something had snapped in Raina, and she'd put her foot down.

Well, actually she'd put her feet up. According to Raina, one day she'd simply sat down at the head of the table during a council meeting – none of the members had yet claimed that place of honor – and she'd put her feet up on the table. She'd been met with stunned silence before everyone at the table erupted at once, yelling at her to take her feet down or asking her what in the three hells she thought she was doing. Raina had just sat there for a moment before taking her feet down from the table and laying out the new world order.

She'd heard enough those weeks to know that the High Council needed her cooperation if they wanted to maintain their power indefinitely. If Polaris didn't appoint a new lord or lady soon, the people would begin to clamor for one. The council's plan had been to give the people Raina for the time being to appease them while they continue to manage things from behind the scenes.

Raina had decided she wasn't interested in letting them pull her strings like a puppet while still keeping her as a servant. She'd insisted that if she was going to play the Lady of Polaris for them, she was going to live like the Lady of Polaris, or she'd refuse to cooperate when they trotted her out for functions.

Raina didn't necessarily want to rule the territory or ascend to the Triumvirate. She just didn't want to be a servant anymore, and this solution gave both her and the council what they wanted for the moment.

It remained to be seen how long Bressen and Aidan would let the High Council get away with this workaround. So far, Bressen hadn't pushed them, but I knew his patience was running out. There was only so long the council could play this game before they threatened the larger institution of the Triumvirate. They'd need to make a decision soon to either allow Raina to ascend the seat or to find someone else.

"How are things going with the High Council anyway?" I asked. "Are they still trying to keep you out of meetings?"

"They only tried a couple times," Raina said, "but I pointed out that if they wanted me to represent Polaris at public functions, I needed to know what was happening in the territory in case anyone questioned me. That and I threatened to not play along with their little game if they didn't let me sit in."

Raina had come so far since her days as my lady's maid, not just in social station, but in confidence and poise as well. She in no way resembled the girl who'd hid behind me when Samhail was in the room or who would wring her hands in worry when I suggested we do something halfway daring. In truth, I could see how Raina had always had the potential to become the young woman she was now. She'd come to the Citadel to meet her lordly father against her mother's wishes, she'd played strip poker with the fortress guards, and she'd taken on Ursan when he tried to attack me after finding out Bressen and I were together.

"Do they ever let you make suggestions?" I asked.

"They've been polite enough to let me speak when I have an idea," Raina said, "but then they usually ignore whatever I said and go back to arguing. Of course, ten minutes later one of them will inevitably suggest exactly what I said, and then suddenly they're all on board with it."

"Is there any chance they'll let you ascend to the Triumvirate seat?" I asked as the seamstress began to carefully peel the heavily pinned gown off me so she could take it back to her workshop and put actual needle and thread to it.

Raina sighed. "I have no idea. It could go either way at this point."

"Would it help if Bressen backed your claim?"

"I don't think so. They seem extremely resistant to help or advice from anyone outside themselves, and I imagine that would go double for anyone outside Polaris. Bressen and Aidan should certainly keep the pressure on them to choose someone to ascend to the seat, but putting their weight behind me in particular is only likely to backfire."

I was naked now except for my undergarment, and Raina got up from her seat to grab the dress I'd been wearing earlier off the back of a chair. She brought it over to help me get into it, and I raised a brow at her.

She shrugged. "Force of habit," she said and slipped it over my head.

I thanked the dressmaker, and she hurried out the door, promising to return with the finished gown the day before the wedding.

"You know you'll outrank me if you ascend to the Triumvirate," I told Raina, and her hands froze as they buttoned the dress up my back.

"Nemesis take me," she breathed. "I don't think I actually realized that. I'm so used to thinking of you and Bressen as a pair that it never occurred to me you aren't really part of the Triumvirate."

"I think Bressen forgets that too. Aidan didn't really appreciate seeing me in one of the Triumvirate seats the day we met him."

Technically I outranked both Raina and Bressen if you considered my status as a Hand of the Trinity, but at the moment that was an archaic title with no real authority behind it. As much as I wanted to tell Raina what we'd learned, Bressen was adamant that only me, him, and Phaedrus should know about it right now, and I respected his desire for caution.

"Bressen can get away with a lot of things that other lords can't," Raina said. "For that matter, so can you."

She stopped when she saw me blanch. Technically I was still supposed to be under house arrest for what I'd done in Fernweh, yet nothing about my life had really changed. I wasn't even sure I was allowed to leave Callanus, but no one had questioned us about moving to Solandis.

"I'm sorry," Raina said quickly, "I didn't mean-"

"It's fine," I said. "It's not as though everyone isn't aware of the special privileges people in positions of power receive. If I wasn't such a coward, I'd just turn myself in and serve my sentence."

"It's not that simple," she said.

"It feels like it is."

"If it bothers you that much then just find a way to make up for it. Doing something good to make up for whatever crime you think you committed is a better solution than having you sit in jail."

"That's actually a great idea," I said. "You're good at this. I hope the

High Council get their heads out of their asses soon and recognize that."

Raina smiled back, but there was a knock at the door before she could respond. She answered it, and I looked around her to see who it was.

"Leeda," I said. "What are you doing here?"

"I was told you were up here, my lady. I came to see if you needed any help," she said as she stepped into the room.

"Is this my replacement?" Raina asked as she closed the door and looked Leeda over with interest.

I saw a look of annoyance, or perhaps defiance flash in Leeda's face, but it was there and gone in an instant. I had the urge to read her mind to see what she was thinking, but I tamped it down.

"I'm Lady Cyra's handmaid," Leeda said to Raina. "Who are you?"

Raina raised a brow and turned to me. "Was I this cheeky when I was your lady's maid?"

"No," I said. "You were much worse."

Raina stuck out her tongue at me and turned back to Leeda. "It's nice to meet you, Leeda. I'm Raina, former lady's maid to Cyra and current heir apparent to the Triumvirate seat of Polaris."

Raina held out a hand to shake Leeda's, but Leeda flushed and dipped into a deep curtsey instead.

"Please forgive me, my lady," Leeda said. "I meant no disrespect."

"Tell me, Leeda," Raina said, ignoring her apology, "has Lady Cyra asked you to sneak her out of the house yet so she can go drinking?"

"Raina!" I admonished her.

Leeda's brows went up in surprise, but she didn't seem scandalized as I'd expected.

Raina smirked. "Am I the only one you've tried to get into trouble?"

I gave her an exasperated look before another knock at the door drew our attention.

"I don't remember you being this in-demand when I was with you," Raina said to me as she opened the door again.

Ferris entered and bowed to me. "My lady, my apologies for intruding. There's a woman here to see you. She claims to be your aunt."

# Chapter 23

I stopped breathing and stared at Ferris. My first thought was that what he'd said was impossible. Neither of my parents had a sister. Neither of the parents I'd known in Fernweh did, in any case.

The woman who'd given birth to me did, though.

I groped behind me for somewhere to sit, and Raina grabbed the nearest chair to shove it under me just as my legs gave out. Then her hand was in mine.

"Cyra? Do you know this woman? Should I have her sent away?"

My mouth moved, but I couldn't get my voice to form words. I looked at Ferris who stood waiting for my answer as to what I wanted him to do.

"Show her into the great room," I said. "I'll be down in a minute."

Ferris turned to go, but I called him back, and he turned once again.

"Send a message to Aramis to let him know my aunt is here," I said, and he nodded.

I could've sent Aramis a mental message myself, but I couldn't seem to clear my head enough to remember how to do it.

"And to Lord Bressen as well?" Ferris ventured.

I paused before nodding. Here again I could have sent my own message, but I still couldn't wrap my head around who was waiting for me downstairs. Bressen could usually sense when I was upset, though, so he was likely already on his way.

Ferris bowed and left.

"Cyra?" Raina tried again. "Who is this woman?"

I looked at her finally, and sucked in a deep breath, as if I suddenly remembered how lungs worked.

"I think…she's my birth mother's sister. She's the woman responsible for putting Aramis in prison and the reason I grew up in Fernweh."

Raina gasped and knelt down next to me. "You're not really going to see her, are you?"

"I have to."

"No, you don't. You can send her away. I'll go down and tell her to fuck off myself."

I shook my head. "No, I'll see her." I rose unsteadily from the chair.

"Cyra, are you sure you want to do this?" Raina asked, rising with me.

"Come with me?" I asked Raina.

"Of course," she said, slipping an arm through mine.

I started to walk, and Raina put an arm around my back as we headed down toward the great room, leaving Leeda alone in my chambers. I let Raina help support me until we got to the entrance of the leisure room and then I pulled my arm out of hers and stood up straight. I was going to walk in under my own power and not let this woman see how much her presence affected me. I nodded to Raina, and she stepped back, understanding that I needed to present a strong façade.

"I'll be right behind you," she said softly.

I took a deep breath and was about to step into the room when an idea occurred to me. I'd never tried to do it before, but now seemed as good a time as any. I put up a halo glamour like Bressen often used when he wanted to make an impression. I wasn't sure if I'd done it right, but when I looked at Raina, she gave me a quick tilt of her head that told me she was impressed. With that, I turned and strode inside.

The woman had her back to me at the far end of the room where she stood near the fireplace. It was the same place I'd first met Aramis a few months ago, twenty-two years after this woman had made sure he went to prison for my supposed murder.

I opened my mouth to address the woman as I got closer, but it occurred to me that no one, including Aramis, had ever told me her name.

"You asked to see me?" I said as I approached.

The woman swung around, and I stopped in my tracks, almost causing Raina to crash into me. She pulled up in time, though, and the two of us stared at the woman near the fireplace.

She appeared to be only a few years older than me, and that likely exacerbated her uncanny resemblance. She wore her hair up on her head while mine was down today, but it was the same deep brown. Her eyes were also brown, whereas mine were silver-gray like Aramis's, but that was perhaps the most noticeable difference between us. There was no mistaking that this woman and I were related, and I might have thought her to be my mother if I didn't know my mother was dead.

The woman took in the dark halo I wore, but she didn't look away as I'd intended. Instead, she held my gaze, and we stood staring at each other for several long moments before tears welled in her eyes.

"Cyra," she breathed, her voice cracking a bit. "Is that really you?"

She took a step toward me, but I stepped back, and she froze.

"Who are you?" I asked.

The woman looked shocked, as if it was perfectly obvious who she was, but she nodded. "My name is Calanthe Thornwyst. I believe my sister Lillian was your mother, and that I'm your aunt."

I was surprised to hear her use a surname. The use of surnames in Thasia wasn't terribly common, even less so in places like the outer lands. Outside of major cities like Callanus or Gendris, people simply identified themselves by their given name and the town or city in which they lived. Aramis had told me my mother's family was powerful, though, so it made sense its members might use their surnames more readily in order to enjoy the benefits that came with the affiliation.

"And what is your business here in Solandis?" I asked her.

She seemed taken aback for a moment. She'd obviously expected our familial relationship to be reason enough for her visit, but I wasn't feeling magnanimous. I was certain it was no coincidence that she'd suddenly sought me out when I was days away from marrying the most powerful man in the country. She'd undoubtedly seen an opportunity to connect herself and her family to Bressen, but she was going to be disappointed. I had no intention of letting her into our lives. Into *my* life.

"Cyra-"

"My lady," I corrected her. "It may not be official for a few days, but you can call me 'my lady.'"

Calanthe's mouth snapped shut, but she nodded again before saying, "My lady, my business is that I've come to meet the niece who was stolen from me two decades ago, the niece I thought was long dead. I only learned of your existence when your engagement to Lord Bressen was announced and-"

"And you thought you might seek me out to connect your family with the Lord of Hiraeth?" I finished for her.

She blinked, then shook her head vigorously. "No!" she insisted. "Not at all. I came to meet you, to get to know you, and to give you the family you should have had before Aramis stole you away."

"Aramis is my father," I snapped at her. "He had every right to take me wherever he wanted. You had no right to have him hunted down for doing what he saw fit."

She shook her head again. "You don't understand. Aramis wasn't in his right mind when he took you. He was grieving Lillian's death, and we feared he might hurt you. We had to go after him for your own safety."

"My own safety?" I choked. "Being raised by my father might have been good for my safety, but you took that away from me when you had him pursued and then imprisoned."

"Calanthe!" Aramis's voice carried across the room, and we all turned to see him standing in the doorway.

"Aramis?" Calanthe said as her eyes flared wide.

Aramis stalked into the room toward us, his gaze fixed on my aunt, and I imagined that if he had Bressen's powers, his eyes might have glowed red with fire right about now. He stopped next to me and stared Calanthe down as she continued to look at him in shock.

"Aramis," Calanthe said. "How did you-"

"How did I get out of Revenmyer?" he supplied before letting out a mirthless laugh. "As it turns out, I didn't murder my daughter after all."

A chill ran up my spine at the venom in his words. I had reason to be angry with Calanthe, but Aramis had every right to be outraged with her.

Calanthe flinched at Aramis's words and lowered her head. "I can see that," she said softly, "and I'm sorry I thought you did."

"Sorry?" Aramis spat. "Sorry doesn't make up for the two decades I spent in Revenmyer. Sorry doesn't make up for the two decades I lost being with my daughter!" His voice had begun to crack.

Calanthe kept her eyes down and nodded. "I know, but I'd like to try and make up for that now if I can."

"You can't!" Aramis raged. "You can't make up for me losing the chance to see Cyra grow up, to be a father to her. You took that away when you sent the authorities after me, and I'll never forgive you for that."

Aramis's voice shook violently, and I laid a hand gently on his arm.

He startled at the touch but then placed his own hand on top of mine, accepting the comfort I offered.

Calanthe nodded. "I understand." She turned to me. "Is it possible that you…your ladyship, might find it in your heart to forgive me?"

I was shaking my head before she finished. "No. I can't either."

Power suddenly filled the room, and I knew without looking that Bressen had arrived. The air seemed to be heavier, and the small hairs on my arms rose.

We all turned to see Bressen striding across the room toward us. He took in the halo glamour around me as he approached, and a smile quirked briefly at the corners of his mouth. He gave me an appreciative look before turning his attention to Calanthe.

Bressen stopped behind me so he could look over my shoulder, and I felt both his warmth at my back as well as his power surrounding me. His unyielding strength seemed to flow through me, and it was a strength I desperately needed right now. My hand was still on Aramis's arm, and the three of us stood together presenting a united front. A family.

"Is everything alright?" Bressen asked, his Hiraethian accent like silk.

Calanthe watched Bressen with wide, doe-like eyes, and I thought she might bolt for the door at any moment.

"This is Calanthe Thornwyst," I said to Bressen. "She's my mother's sister. She came to congratulate us on our wedding, but she's just leaving."

Calanthe's eyes darted to mine, and I saw the hurt in them, but I didn't care. I wasn't feeling merciful or forgiving.

"Ah, it's good to meet you, Calanthe," Bressen said pleasantly. "Are you related to Lord Byron Thornwyst?"

"He's my father," she answered, and I started in surprise.

A grandfather. I had a grandfather.

"Thank you for your well wishes, Lady Thornwyst," Bressen continued, his words like poisoned honey. "We appreciate it. I can have someone show you the way out."

Calanthe pursed her lips slightly, but she accepted the dismissal and gave Bressen a low bow. "My lord," she said, "I'm honored to meet you. I wish you and my niece all the best in your life together."

Ferris appeared beside us with two guards, and Calanthe gathered up the cloak she'd thrown over the back of a chair before following them out. Ferris turned to go as well, but Bressen called him back.

"That woman isn't allowed in this house again," he told the steward, "and the next time someone shows up claiming to be a long-lost relative, you come to me first before bothering Lady Cyra."

"Ferris, please disregard that second part," I told the man. "If anyone comes looking for me, you can come straight to me."

Ferris looked nervously from me to Bressen, clearly uncertain whose orders he should obey in this case. I felt a hint of frustration from Bressen, but I caught his nod to Ferris.

"As Lady Cyra wishes," Bressen said to him.

"Yes, my lady," Ferris said. He nodded to me and hurried away before he could get caught between us again.

I turned to Bressen. "I appreciate your desire to shield me, but I don't need you to regulate my visitors."

He pushed a heavy breath out through his nose but nodded. "My apologies. You're right. I'll let you decide who you want to see."

"Thank you."

"Are you alright?" he asked.

I looked at Aramis. He stood next to us still seeming a little dazed, but his eyes met mine.

"We were a little taken off-guard," I said, "but I think we're fine."

Bressen looked at my father. "Aramis?"

Aramis nodded his agreement. "I need a drink, though," he said.

"I second that," I admitted.

"I've never turned down a drink in my life, and I won't start now," Raina said from behind us.

Bressen nodded and moved to a large cabinet on one side of the room. He opened it and pulled out two bottles. "Wine or liquor?" he asked.

"Liquor," me, Raina, and Aramis all answered together.

Bressen looked a bit surprised by the unanimity, but he put the wine back and pulled out four glasses. He poured amber liquid into them and handed them around to us.

I took a sip of mine and shuddered as the strong spirit burned its way down my throat. I rarely drank anything stronger than wine, but I felt the need for something with a little more kick this time.

Aramis threw back his glass to drain it before setting it down on the table. "If you'll forgive me, I need to go home," he said.

"Of course," I told him. "Let me know if you need anything. Do you want a portal?"

He shook his head. "I think I need to walk, but thank you."

I nodded and moved forward to hug him. Aramis wrapped his arms around me and kissed my forehead before turning to head out. My affection was still tentative with him, but our hugs were getting less awkward as time went on.

"I'll take this up to my room," Raina said, raising her glass. She looked at me. "Come find me if you need to talk."

I nodded, and she strode from the room leaving me with Bressen.

"Are you really alright?" he asked.

I shrugged. "I don't know. I'm still a little in shock."

Bressen drew me against him, and I laid my head on his chest. His musky, hot cinnamon scent drifted up my nose, and I let it calm me.

"Is there anything I can do?" he asked.

I shook my head against him. "Not unless you can rewrite the past so Aramis didn't spend the last twenty-two years in prison."

I felt his chin on the top of my head. "I'm afraid that's a bit beyond my powers. I can make him forget those years. Three hells, I can even implant twenty-two years of new memories if Aramis so desired, but I can't change what actually happened, either for him or for you."

I sighed. "Honestly, I'm not sure I'd want to change anything even if I could. It's not fair that Aramis and I never got to be together, but I don't know that I'd trade the family I have for the one I could've had. The thought of never knowing Jaylan, Brix, and my parents hurts my heart."

Bressen's arms tightened, and I lifted my head, sensing an opening.

"What happened between you and your mother? Why is your relationship with her so strained?"

Bressen grimaced, and he was quiet for several moments. I had the feeling he was trying to decide how much to tell me.

"My mother has always been a bit difficult to get along with, at least for me," he said finally. "As you can tell, she's a relentlessly practical person and dogmatic in her beliefs about how things should be. She was never terribly nurturing. I was always closer to my father, so that made it much worse when I learned she'd had an affair."

"She cheated on him? I'm so sorry."

"For some reason, my father loved her desperately, and it broke him to learn of the affair." He paused, seeming to stare off into nothing. "It eventually led to his death, and I've never forgiven her for that."

I swallowed down the lump in my throat and shook my head. I could see why Bressen couldn't bring himself to forgive her. I wrapped my arms around him tighter, and he laid his head on top of mine again.

"Thank you for telling me," I said.

He didn't say anything else as we stood wrapped in each other's arms. That his mother had suggested he bed other women even after marrying me seemed all the more incredible now that I knew of her own infidelity. She was still clearly oblivious to the effect her affair had on Bressen.

I pulled back and looked at him in alarm. "Samhail and I…," I said, suddenly worried that he felt as though I'd cheated on him.

"Had my blessing to be together," he assured me. "Infidelity is an offense of deception and stealth, not of sex per se. It's not a betrayal of the body, but a betrayal of the mind and heart. If I willingly let you be with Samhail, it's not infidelity."

I nodded, but my mind was still trying to wrap itself around all this. For an angelus like Bressen, whose kind seemed to embody the extremes of darkness and light, he often saw things in such subtle shades of gray that it bewildered me sometimes.

"I don't ever want to hurt you like that," I whispered to him.

He smiled. "I know you won't."

I hugged him tighter and wondered again how I could be worthy of this man, of his trust and faith in me. I didn't know what I'd done to deserve such good fortune, but I vowed that I'd do everything in my power from here on out to make sure I deserved his love.

# Chapter 24

"Get your cloak, and put this on," Raina said as she entered the sitting room three days later to find me on the sofa. She pressed something metal into my hand, and I held it up to find a delicate filagree mask that would cover the top half of my face.

It was the evening before the wedding, and Raina had told me earlier in the day she wanted to do something special with me that night to mark my last hours of "freedom," as she'd called them.

"What's this for?" I asked, putting my book down to study the mask.

"So you're not recognized tonight when we go out," Raina said. "I have one too."

Raina held up her own mask that matched the sparkling plum-colored gown she wore. The dress hugged her curves and pressed her ample breasts into two tantalizing mounds above the bodice. It definitely wasn't an outfit for the quiet night I'd been anticipating.

Bressen was finishing up some territory business while also overseeing the final preparations for our wedding tomorrow, so he'd told me not to expect him until late. I'd thus assumed Raina and I might have a nice dinner and spend the night talking as usual, but apparently that wasn't Raina's idea of special.

"Exactly where are we going?" I asked.

"We're celebrating your last night as an unmarried woman," she said, "and I plan to take you to some less-than-appropriate places."

I shook my head. "Didn't you learn your lesson the last time we went out together?"

Raina waved a dismissive hand. "You're far more powerful now than you were then, and I'm less timid as well." She lifted the hem of her skirt to reveal a dagger strapped to her thigh.

"Raina!" I gasped. "Do you even know how to use that?"

She shrugged. "You stab people with the sharp end. What more do I need to know?"

"A lot," I said. Having trained with Samhail, I knew there was far more to fighting than just her 'stab people with the sharp end' approach.

"Do you have a dagger you can bring?" she asked, ignoring me.

"I can get one from the armory if necessary, but-"

"Perfect," Raina said. "Go get one."

"Not until you tell me where we're going."

"We'll start at a tavern for old times' sake," she said, "but after that it's a surprise."

I wasn't sure I was willing to trust Raina's idea of a surprise, but she just crossed her arms over her chest, and I sighed.

"Fine. Wait here," I said.

I opened a portal down to the cellar of the house and returned a minute later with a dagger and thigh sheath in hand. Raina had already pulled a deep jade gown from my closet that was cut daringly low in the bodice and slit high up the thigh. Why I even had a dress like this I wasn't sure, but I wasn't surprised it was the one Raina gravitated to.

"I thought the idea was not to draw attention to ourselves," I said to her as she helped me into the dress and strapped the dagger to the thigh opposite the slit. "This dress is certainly going to draw attention."

"The idea is not to be *recognized*," she corrected me, "but we most definitely want some attention."

"Those goals seem a bit adverse to each other."

"It's possible to create a little interest and intrigue without letting people know who we are," she insisted.

"I should let Bressen know where we're going."

"No, you shouldn't," Raina said emphatically. "If he doesn't try to talk you out of going, he'll send guards – or worse, Samhail – to keep an eye on you, and that would defeat the purpose of this night. At the very least, he'll have Samhail watching us from the shadows all night."

"Samhail isn't really the type who stays hidden well," I pointed out.

"Exactly. And you won't be able to relax and have fun if you see that gargoyle hovering over your shoulder everywhere, so get ready and let's go. You said Bressen was working late, so we'll probably be back before he even notices you're gone. What's the worst that could happen?"

I gave Raina a meaningful look.

"We already had our bad luck for the year," she argued. "We can't possibly have trouble a second time out."

I groaned. "You just had to jinx us," I said. "Bad luck seems to follow me. You may recall I was attacked by bandits both times I went riding."

"Well, we're breaking your streak tonight," she said.

A knock sounded at the door to the bedroom, and Raina and I froze to look at each other. We relaxed when Leeda poked her head in.

"Does my lady need any help?" Leeda asked.

"Yes," Raina answered for me. "Can you put some color on her lips and a touch of shadow on her eyes while I fix her hair?"

Leeda came in and went immediately to the makeup on my vanity to get to work. I sat still as the two of them quickly turned me into a more sultry version of myself.

"Where are you off to tonight, my lady?" Leeda asked.

"We're just going into the city for a drink or two," Raina answered

"Oh? Which tavern?" Leeda asked.

When Raina wasn't as quick to answer, Leeda added, "Being new to the city, I'm always looking for new places to try."

"The Silver Horse is nice," Raina told her. Then she stepped back to look at me. "There, all done. Thank you for your help, Leeda."

Leeda bobbed a curtsey but didn't move.

"You can go now," Raina told her, but Leeda only looked to me.

I nodded. "We're all set. Thank you for your help."

Leeda paused another second, but then she gave a quick bow and left.

"Now open a portal near the Tryst and Vine," Raina said when the door had closed behind Leeda.

"But I thought you said-"

"I recommended the Silver Horse to her," Raina cut in. "I didn't say that's where we were going. Now she can't tell anyone where we are."

I sighed but opened a portal into a side alley near the tavern, and we stepped through. I closed the portal behind us, and we walked out onto the busy street, then around the corner to the tavern itself. I stopped when I saw the garland of bay laurel leaves over the doorway.

"Raina, are you sure you want to go here?" I asked. "The garland is to ward off perimortals."

"Not exactly," she said. "Do you see the dried turrow berries interwoven in it? That's a code. Trust me, it's open to perimortals."

I looked again and noticed the red berries tucked among the leaves.

"Exactly what are the berries code for?" I asked her suspiciously.

She only grinned at me. "You'll see."

I had a feeling I was going to regret this, but I followed her inside, and we went directly to the bar to order. I'd brought a small coin purse with me, but Raina insisted on paying for our drinks.

To her shock, Ursan had left Raina a large part of his fortune when he'd died. On top of that, Glenora's treachery had negated her own claim to the rest of her husband's wealth, so that half would likely fall to Raina as well, unless Glenora's child was Ursan's. In any case, Raina had started to enjoy having lots of money.

Being wealthy was a new feeling for me as well. My brothers and I hadn't been poor, but we also hadn't had a lot of extra funds to use for frivolous or extravagant things. As the Lady of Hiraeth, though, I'd be a very wealthy woman. I didn't know exactly how much money Bressen had, but it was enough that he hadn't placed a limit on what I could spend when redecorating his wing in the Citadel. Still, I'd been frugal thus far.

Once Bressen bought me the vineyard he'd promised, I'd have my own account linked to its profits, but for now I was still reliant on him for anything I needed. Not that I needed much. My food, clothing, and shelter were all provided, but he'd still given me access to his accounts to use for anything else I wanted.

The tavern was busy tonight, but Raina and I found a table in the corner where we remained unnoticed as we talked and drank. I hadn't eaten a big dinner, so I was already feeling the wine.

"Now that Damian is out of the picture, do you have your eye on anyone?" I asked Raina. "You haven't really been taking the guards in the palace to bed, have you?"

She'd suggested as much at Aidan's ball, but I'd forgotten to ask her about it since then.

Raina gave me a wicked grin. "And why not?" she asked. "I just need someone to help me…relieve tension every now and again, so I found a palace guard willing to help."

"Raina!"

"He has the most perfect ass I've ever seen," she said unrepentantly.

"When I asked if you had your eye on anyone, I was thinking one of the lords of Polaris," I told her. "You need to be careful about who you spend your time with now that you're being considered for a Triumvirate seat. If the High Council finds out-"

"I know, I know," Raina said, waving a hand. "Gods forbid I do anything to remind them I'm the lowly bastard of a lady's maid."

I gave her an apologetic look. After Ursan's death, she'd been thrust into the middle of a political maelstrom and now had all her actions and movements carefully scrutinized. While Raina had adapted quickly enough to court life, I suspected she might be just as happy falling back into anonymity.

"I'm sorry," I said. "I know you didn't ask for all these rules and restrictions. I just don't want you to get into a situation that's going to make things even more difficult for you."

She sighed. "I know, and I appreciate you looking out for me. The uncertainty is just getting to me."

"I understand," I said. "Just take my unsolicited advice and try to look for someone more suitable to your new station. No offense to this guard and his perfect ass."

Raina opened her mouth to speak, then closed it.

"What?" I asked.

"Forget it. It's nothing."

"Oh no. You're not getting out of it. What were you going to say?"

"Alright, fine," she said. "I was just wondering if Samhail would be considered more appropriate to my station."

My eyes widened, and I was sure I'd lost the ability to blink.

"I mean, now that I'm no longer afraid of him, and since you never fucked him," she went on, "I have to admit that Samhail is delicious."

I remembered how to blink then and did so very rapidly.

"What do you think?" Raina asked, finally looking up at me.

It was my turn to imitate a fish gasping on land.

Raina arched a brow at me. "You didn't fuck him, right?"

My mouth snapped shut, and I swallowed.

Her eyes widened. "Nemesis take you! You did, didn't you!" she said.

I couldn't tell if she was impressed or angry.

"Raina, I-"

"When?" she cut in. "Before Bressen? Why didn't you tell me?"

Her tone was hurt, and I shook my head vigorously. "I-"

"Have you been cheating on Bressen?" she asked, her voice rising dangerously high, even in the noisy tavern.

"No! Of course not!" I said quickly. "And keep your voice down."

"Then you better start talking," she said, lowering her voice.

"I've been trying to. Yes, I slept with-"

"Fucked," she corrected me.

"Fine. Yes, I fucked Samhail. It was on the Harmilan."

Raina let out a long breath as her eyes bore into me. "Alright, but you were already with Bressen by then, weren't you? Does he know?"

"Yes, he knows," I said hesitantly, "…because he was there with us."

Raina stared at me blankly for a few seconds before what I was saying clicked into place. Then her eyes widened so much I was afraid they might fall out of her head. She took a sharp intake of breath, and I quickly reached over the table to put my hand on her mouth.

"Don't scream," I said. "I'm sorry I didn't tell you, but it needed to be between the three of us, at least for a while. I was having enough trouble making sense of it myself."

Raina pulled my hand off her mouth. "All the more reason you should have told me," she said. She grimaced, but then her face softened. "I guess I understand why you didn't tell me. Was that the only time?"

My face flushed, and I looked away.

"Gods damn you!" she said loudly.

I tried to put my hand over her mouth again, but she batted it away.

"Sorry," she said.

"The second time was very different," I said, and something in my look made her pause because she nodded for me to go on.

I took a deep breath and told her how Bressen and Samhail had shared women in the past. Then I explained about the last time the three of us had been together and how it had gotten me past the issues I'd been having being intimate with Bressen.

She listened quietly, nodding every now and again, and I poured everything out to her, every detail I'd been afraid to speak out loud for fear that she or someone else might judge me, and I felt a strange weight lift as I laid everything bare before her. I was tempted to read her mind to see what she was thinking, but I refrained.

My wine was gone when I finished speaking, as was Raina's, and she sat staring at me for several long moments.

"Please say something," I begged her when I could bear her silence no longer. "Do you hate me?"

My words seemed to shake her from her trance, and she reached a hand across the table to lay it over mine.

"No, I don't hate you," she said. "I wish you'd told me all this much sooner, but I don't hate you." Then she added, "Although I'm annoyed you quashed any further fantasies I may have had about Samhail."

I let out a strangled laugh. In truth, I'd wanted to tell Raina all this for a while now, but I'd been too afraid of her reaction. It meant a lot to me now that she wasn't judging me for what I'd done and that she wasn't angry with me for keeping this a secret from her for so long.

Raina shook her head, still a bit dazed. "I had a feeling Samhail was adventurous in bed, but who knew Bressen was such a libertine."

I just smiled at her. She had no idea.

"Is there anything else I should know?" she asked, eyeing me.

I paused. "Actually, yes."

"There's more?" she asked incredulously.

"Yes, but you have to swear that you won't breathe a word of this to anyone, especially the High Council," I said. "This is incredibly sensitive information that Bressen hasn't even told Samhail. I shouldn't be telling you, but I feel like I owe you for keeping secrets about Samhail."

"Cyra, you don't owe me anything," she said, "and I'm sorry for making you feel guilty. You had good reasons for not sharing some things, and you don't have to tell me this if you don't think you should. But if you choose to tell me, I promise I won't say a word to anyone."

With this information, I wasn't going to take any chance of being overheard. "I'm going to say it into your mind," I told her.

She raised a brow. "It's really that secret?"

I nodded, and Raina motioned for me to go ahead.

I spoke into her mind then, telling her everything Phaedrus had told Bressen and I about who and what I supposedly was. She leaned back when I was done, her eyes impossibly wide again.

"Fuck me," she whispered.

"You understand why you can't breathe a word of this to anyone?" I asked, and she nodded solemnly.

"Thank you for telling me. Your secrets, all of them, are safe with me," she said. "I don't know about you, but I need another drink, and I think it's time to proceed to phase two of the night."

"Phase two?"

Raina went to the counter and ordered another glass of wine for each of us. "Follow me," she said after she handed me my drink.

I followed her as she ducked behind a curtain next to the bar and we emerged into a hallway. There was a large man on the other side who straightened as we slipped through the curtain, but he relaxed when Raina flashed something at him, and he nodded.

Raina swept down the hallway with me in her wake before she descended a set of stairs. At the bottom, there was another long hallway where an even larger man stood guard in front of a door. Raina marched straight up to him and held out some sort of coin that was either foreign or perhaps specially made for this place.

The man took the coin and looked me and Raina up and down carefully, his gaze lingering on our breasts above the low-cut bodices of our gowns. I wondered if he would try to check us for weapons, but he must've decided we didn't pose a threat because he stepped aside a moment later and opened the door for us.

I entered the room after Raina but pulled up short as I gawked at our surroundings. Yes, we were in a less-than-appropriate place indeed.

# Chapter 25

I didn't know where to look first as I took in the room we entered while the guard closed the door behind us. The decor was lavish, if a bit gawdy, but the entire area screamed with the promise of excitement. The walls were bright blue and hung with tapestries or paintings. Upon closer look, most of the people in the paintings were naked, and some were even engaged in various lascivious acts that made me blush.

Giant dark red velvet curtains were gathered near the walls at various intervals, and I saw that they could be pulled along a track in the ceiling to section off the room. There was a bar counter for ordering drinks off to one side, and dozens of round tables dotted the huge space.

The tables were all packed with extravagantly dressed people playing cards. Most wore bold colors and lots of jewels, even the men. The women's dresses were just as daringly cut as the ones Raina and I wore so that we no longer stood out quite so conspicuously. We also weren't the only ones wearing masks.

"Raina, is this a gambling den?"

"A secret, underground, very exclusive gambling den," Raina said, grinning. "I figured we'd put all those poker lessons to good use."

I looked at her in alarm. "Raina, I'm not good enough to play with these people. Where would I even get the money to play?"

I'd gotten a glimpse of the brightly colored chips on the tables, and while I wasn't entirely sure what each one was worth, it was clear there were huge sums of money in play.

"You said Bressen gave you access to his accounts," Raina said. "Just borrow a little from one of those."

I looked at her incredulously. "You want me to gamble with Bressen's money without telling him? You remember who he is, right?"

Raina waved a dismissive hand, and I had the urge to shake her.

"Yes, and I remember he has trouble denying you anything," she said. "He may not be thrilled when, or *if*, he learns what you've done, but I doubt you'll get anything more than a stern look from him. For that matter, feel free to blame everything on me. I'll take his wrath if need be."

Raina wasn't entirely correct that the only thing I'd get from Bressen was a stern look. When Bressen was frustrated with me, he often took me to bed where he liked to fuck me hard. Not that I minded. Part of me wondered if I sometimes took risks just to goad him. It was in fact probably the idea of Bressen's 'punishment' that had me nodding my agreement to Raina.

"Alright, fine. Let's do it," I told her. "As long as I can blame you for everything."

"Agreed," Raina said as her face split into a grin.

She took my hand and led me toward a desk near the side of the room. A young man sat there while a slightly older, much more well-dressed man stood behind him.

"We'd like to buy in," Raina told the older man.

To my surprise, he didn't bother to ask who we were.

"Accounts?" was the only thing he asked.

Raina handed the younger man a slip of paper that I imagined had the number of her private bank account on it with the money she'd inherited from Ursan. The man checked the number against his ledger and nodded.

"How much?" the younger man asked.

"Ten thousand," Raina said, and I gasped.

"Are you mad?" I hissed under my breath.

She just winked at me.

"Have you been here before?" I asked.

Raina shrugged. "Once or twice."

The younger man made some notes in his ledger and reached behind him to grab several stacks of colored chips. He put them into a box and handed them to Raina. Then he turned to me.

I sighed heavily as Raina slipped a blank piece of paper into my hand. There was a pen on the desk, and I thought for a minute before writing down the number to one of Bressen's lesser-used accounts. If I lost all the money, I hoped I might have enough time to find a way to replace it before he noticed it was missing. I handed the paper to the man and watched as he searched his ledger.

Seeming to come up empty, he asked, "Is this your first time here?"

“Yes.”

“And to whom does this account belong?” he asked.

I paused. “It’s my fiancés, but I have permission to draw from it.”

The man looked at me, and I understood he was waiting for an actual name. Dammit. So much for staying anonymous.

I sighed again. “The account belongs to Lord Bressen.”

Both men jolted as they took a closer look at me, trying to see behind the mask I wore.

“My lady,” the older man said tentatively, “we’ll need to verify this account and confirm you have access to it.”

“Of course,” I said, suddenly uncertain that Bressen had given me unlimited access to all his accounts. Maybe it was only the main expense account he’d allowed me to use? What would happen if they looked into this account, and I didn’t have permission to use it? Would they call the authorities? Or worse, would they call Bressen?

The older man opened a door behind the desk and disappeared into a back room with the slip of paper I’d written the account on. It was nearly five minutes before he returned again, but he handed the paper to the other man and nodded.

“She’s approved for any amount,” he told the younger man, and I let out a deep sigh of relief.

Whether that approval remained in place after Bressen learned of this was another question entirely, and the idea of starting out our marriage this way suddenly left me cold. I was about to tell the man I’d changed my mind when he handed me a box of chips.

“Ten thousand?” he asked, apparently assuming I’d follow Raina’s lead. I took the box with trembling hands and vowed inwardly that I’d play as conservatively as possible.

“There’s just one other thing, my lady,” the older man said. He seemed afraid to broach the topic, but I nodded encouragingly, and he held up a pewter-colored bracelet.

I didn’t understand what the bracelet had to do with anything, but Raina gasped.

“You can’t be serious,” she said to him in indignation. “Are you implying the future Lady of Hiraeth would stoop to cheating?”

"Cheating?" I asked, my gaze swinging to her. "What do you mean? What is that thing?"

Raina looked at me in shock that I didn't know what the bracelet was, but it was the older man who answered.

"This is a caronium cuff," the man said. "It will temporarily suppress your powers. I believe you have the ability to read minds?"

I blinked, shocked both that he knew that and that it hadn't even occurred to me I could use my mindreading abilities to cheat at cards.

"There's no offense meant, my lady," the man said, sounding genuinely sorry, "but if you're going to play, you'll need to wear the cuff. It doesn't lock, so you can easily take it off, but you'll need to keep it on at all times while you're down here."

Raina opened her mouth to argue with him further, but I put a hand on her arm. "I'll wear it," I said and took the cuff from him.

I snapped it onto my wrist and waited for something to happen, but I didn't feel any different.

The older man stepped ahead of us then and motioned to follow him.

"Let me show you and your friend to a table, my lady," he said.

Raina looked at me meaningfully, and I could tell she'd never been personally escorted to her seat.

The man brought us over to a table with only one seat open, but he inclined his head to one of the men at the table in a gesture that indicated the man should move. Reluctantly the man picked up his chips and moved to another table. With two chairs now open, Raina and I sat down. Before leaving, the older man leaned down and whispered something into the dealer's ear, and I sighed inwardly as the dealer's eyes flicked to me.

"Welcome, ladies," the dealer said as the other man left.

Raina had taught me a couple different versions of this game, and this version was probably the easiest one I knew, although the one I'd practiced the least.

I received my cards and looked at them carefully. They were two low cards in the same suit. The dealer flipped three cards, and two were in my suit. I only needed one more to have a good hand.

Everyone bet, and the dealer turned a fourth card. It wasn't my suit, but a reckless urge hit me, and I stayed in. Relief hit me first, then elation as the fifth card was turned and it was in the same suit I had. The other players turned their cards over, and I saw I'd won the hand. Raina and I exchanged glances as I pulled the pot of chips toward me.

As the dealer reshuffled the cards, I suddenly had a strange feeling, as if someone was watching me. My stomach lurched as I looked around to see if Bressen had already found I was gone. As I scanned the room, a consciousness seemed to call to me, and my eyes soon locked with the deep brown ones of a woman who looked uncannily like me.

I grabbed Raina's wrist, and she flinched.

"Cyra? What's wrong?" she whispered.

I nodded toward the woman across the room. "My aunt is here."

Raina's head snapped to where I indicated, and her eyes narrowed. "What in the three hells is she doing here?"

"Playing cards, like everyone else," I said numbly.

"You can probably have her removed if you want," Raina suggested. "They know who you are. If you asked them…"

I shook my head. I wasn't going to be that petty. As long as she stayed away from me, I'd leave her alone.

"It's fine," I said. "She can stay."

Across the room, Calanthe smiled weakly at me and went back to her cards, as if she sensed my acquiescence.

An hour later, my luck had long since turned after that first good hand. My stack of chips was considerably smaller than when I'd started, although not nearly as small as it probably should've been, and I wondered just how hard the dealer was working to keep me from losing worse than I was. Raina, on the other hand, had nearly doubled her chips, and I resolved to ask her later if she had some mindreading abilities of her own.

"I need another drink," I said, getting up from the table. What I actually needed was to take a break before I lost any more of Bressen's money. "Do you want anything?" I asked Raina.

She shook her head, and I went up to the counter where a man was pouring drinks. I ordered another wine and was about to leave when a voice just over my shoulder startled me.

"You can put that on my tab."

I swung around to see an attractive man with light brown skin, golden eyes, and burnt auburn hair standing very close to me. He wasn't touching me, but only just barely.

"I appreciate the offer," I said, stepping back, "but I can buy my own drinks."

"I insist," he said. He held up a hand to cut off any protest I might make. "I expect nothing in return, I promise. I don't believe I've seen you here before, so consider it a welcome drink."

"This is my first time," I admitted.

"A toast to celebrate then," he said and held up his own glass. I clinked mine against his, and we drank.

"You're a mind wraith I see," he said, pointing to the caronium cuff on my wrist.

I looked at the cuff and gave a small laugh. "Something like that."

"I'm a fire elemental myself," he said as he called a small flame to his hand. He looked at me as if I should be impressed.

"That's a neat trick," I said, feigning interest. I really wanted to call my own flame to wipe the smug look off his face, but I remembered that the caronium cuff would prevent it.

"My name is Heren," the man said holding out a hand to me.

I hesitated only a second before shaking it. I already had elemental fire, so I couldn't take any power from him that I didn't already have. In fact, if I understood him correctly, he wasn't even a poly-elemental. Fire was his only element, so my own elemental powers already surpassed his. For that matter, it occurred to me that I probably couldn't syphon his power while I was wearing the caronium cuff.

"I'm Cyr…Serena," I said.

The man smiled at me, as if he knew I'd just given him a false name.

"It's nice to meet you, Serena. What brings you out tonight?"

Despite myself, I found him charming, and I reasoned that it couldn't hurt to at least talk to him.

"My friend brought me," I said, inclining my head toward the table where Raina sat behind a pile of chips. "She said we're celebrating."

Heren looked over and nodded. "Ah, yes. Rebeka," he said. "I met her earlier this week."

I started in surprise to hear that Raina had been here this week. She must have come here after leaving my quarters one night. Or perhaps every night.

"Yes, Rebeka is a much better player than I am," I said as evenly as I could while I regained my bearings.

"So what are you celebrating?" he asked, taking a sip of his drink.

I held up my hand to show him the large emerald ring Bressen had given me.

"Ah, recently engaged I see," he said.

If he was disappointed by the news, I couldn't tell.

"That's quite a stone. When's the day?" he asked.

"Tomorrow," I said.

This time he did look surprised. "That soon? That doesn't leave you much time left," he said.

"Time left for what?" I asked.

His expression turned to one I recognized well as he looked at me from under heavy lashes with undisguised lust. I thought for a moment he might actually grab me and kiss me, since that's normally what Bressen would do while wearing that look, but he didn't move.

"Time left for you to have some fun," he said. "A lot of men I know use the night before their wedding as an opportunity for one last time between the legs of a woman other than their wife-to-be. I assume it must be similar for some women."

I just stared at him, my mouth hanging half open. That wasn't something I'd ever heard before, and I was about to tell him so when my gut suddenly felt like I'd been punched. Was Bressen really working late tonight, or was he out somewhere with Samhail looking for a woman to spend the night with? I shook the thought away.

No, Bressen would never…He'd promised.

"Are you suggesting…?" I started to ask.

"I'm not suggesting anything," he corrected. "I'm stating outright that I'm available if you want someone new between those beautiful thighs tonight. I'm not too humble to admit that I'm very skilled with my tongue." He paused. "I assume since you're new you don't know about the rooms in the back?"

He inclined his head toward a curtain at the very rear of the room that I hadn't noticed. Gods above, were there actually rooms for sex in the back? Did Raina know about them? Had she…ever used them?

Heren reached out a hand as if he meant to stroke the bit of my bare thigh that peeked out from the slit of my dress. I stepped back quickly, and he held up his hands in a placating gesture.

"My apologies," he said, lowering his hands. "I meant no offense. I was merely hoping to be of service to an exquisite creature such as yourself."

I huffed a small laugh. I really wanted to tell him who my fiancé was to see if he still felt he could be of service to me, but too many people here already knew who I was, so I bit back the comment.

"No offense taken," I said, "but I assure you my needs are well met."

Heren nodded, and I saw his disappointment. Allowing myself to feel a small bit of sympathy for him, I added as kindly as I could, "Under different circumstances your offer of 'services' might be tempting, but I don't anticipate needing them tonight or anytime soon."

He inclined his head. "You can't blame a man for trying, but I'll leave you to your cards. May you have more luck tonight than I did."

I gave him a wry smile and headed back to my table. I sat down just as the last hand ended, and Raina looked mournfully at the pile of chips being pulled away by one of the other players. It seemed her luck might have turned as well.

"I see you met Heren," she said.

"Indeed. He invited me to go into a back room. Apparently, it's the thing to do the night before one's wedding."

Raina stopped restacking her chips and looked up at me. "Is it?" she asked, genuinely surprised. "I wasn't aware."

I shrugged. "For men anyway. Did you know about the back rooms?"

Her answer was cut off by a loud thud followed by a muffled scream that sounded from outside the main door. All activity in the room died as everyone's attention swung toward the entrance.

Several heartbeats passed before the door crashed open, and I stared in horror as the stuff of nightmares poured through it.

# Chapter 26

I couldn't move as I took in the dozen or so creatures that crashed into the room, overturning tables and attacking patrons. They were human in shape, but their skin was a familiar midnight blue, and they didn't have faces except for what seemed to be shining yellow eyes. Their hands ended in sharp pointed claws that looked as though they could easily tear flesh. Indeed, one man seated at a table near the door sprang up from his seat only to have the creature slash him across the stomach with those claws, and he went down with a gurgled scream.

Raina and I both shot to our feet and pulled our daggers.

"What the fuck are those things?" Raina asked, her face aghast.

"I have no idea. Stay here," I said and started to move toward the door, but Raina followed me.

"Fucking hells I will," she said.

I was about to argue when another person screamed as a creature's claws slashed through them, and I launched myself toward the fray.

One of the creatures met me halfway across the room, and I dodged the swing of its claws, then slashed out with my dagger. The blade skirted across the creature's chest as if it were wearing armor, and I swore under my breath. I dodged another swipe from its claws as muscle memory from Samhail's training took over, and then I tried stabbing it in the stomach. This time the blade penetrated its flesh, but not very far. The creature's body was dense so it could only be pierced with great effort.

I pulled the blade back out and watched in shock as the wound healed over seconds later.

"Raina!" I shouted. "They're skin is like armor, and they can heal themselves!"

I kicked the creature in the stomach and then came down with my dagger, aiming for its neck. Perhaps if I could hit it somewhere vital, it would die before it could heal.

I drove the blade down as hard as I could, and my knife punctured the creature's skin enough that the blade sunk into its neck up to the hilt.

It let out a high-pitched screech that hurt my ears, and it tried to claw at my arm, but I didn't dare remove the blade until the thing stopped moving. I followed it down to the floor as it fell, keeping my blade lodged firmly in its throat and trying to ignore the warm blood coating my hands.

Finally, the thing stopped moving, and I relaxed. I cried out a second later, though, as the blue from its skin seemed to drip off the creature and puddle under what now appeared to be a normal human man.

I gasped and scrambled away from it as I remembered the puddle of blue liquid I'd stepped in at Bronwyn after the village had been attacked. The injured man's words came back to me.

*Demons. Two of them. Like dark blue shadows with no real faces. Just…glowing yellow eyes.*

These things were what he'd seen, but they weren't demons. They were people who'd been taken over by some kind of entity, a parasite.

My stomach threatened to empty as I realized I'd just killed my first human. The man's eyes were dull and vacant as I stared down at his lifeless body, and I swallowed the bile that rose in my throat. I'd been ready to kill in Fernweh, but now, faced with the aftermath of actually taking a life, I felt sick.

Someone screamed nearby, and I remembered that there was still a battle going on. I shoved down the horror at what I'd done. There was no time to mourn now.

I turned to search the chaos of the room for Raina and found her backed up against a wall battling one of the creatures. I was relieved to see that she'd undersold herself with her comments about the dagger. Raina knew how to fight. Not as well as I did, but someone had clearly shown her how to wield the blade she held.

My smile lasted only a second before the creature grabbed Raina by the neck and threw her against the wall after her dagger just glanced off its skin. The creature pulled its arm back to swipe its sharp claws across her chest, and I knew I'd never reach her in time.

Without thinking, I flung out a hand and loosed a forcefield that hurled the creature back several feet. Raina's eyes met mine, her gratitude evident. Then both of our brows furrowed at the same time as our gazes dropped to the caronium cuff still on my wrist. The cuff was supposed to suppress all my powers, not just my mind reading. Either this one wasn't working…or the cuffs didn't work on me at all.

I ran to Raina. "Are you alright?" I asked her.

"I'm fine. Thank you."

Across the room, fire erupted around one of the creatures, and it screamed in pain. Heren stood before the creature, obviously having ignited it with his flames.

Just as I started to consider fire as an option, the creature fell back against one of the velvet curtains, and it was set ablaze. Within seconds, flames had climbed up the curtain, and smoke started to fill the room.

"Dammit!" I swore and threw out my hand to send a deluge of water down onto the curtain.

"No fire inside!" I shouted to Heren. "You'll kill us all if the room goes up in flames!"

He looked back at me in shock, and I remembered belatedly that he thought I was only a mind wraith. He also looked frustrated to have his one weapon taken away, but he nodded.

"Cyra!" Raina yelled from next to me.

I swung around to see that one of the creatures was almost on top of me, its claws already swinging out toward my chest. I didn't have time to react, and a scream caught in my throat as I braced to feel the burn of those claws across my skin.

The blow never came as the creature was suddenly jerked backwards. Tentacles of some kind had wrapped themselves around its neck and were slowly squeezing tighter, cutting off its air. I looked behind it to see Calanthe standing with her hands extended. The tentacles were vines, I realized, and Calanthe was controlling them. The vines pulled the creature back even further and continued to wrap around its body and neck, squeezing and tightening as they slowly crushed it to death. It was several more seconds before the creature's body went limp, and the blue substance dripped off the human form to pool beneath it.

The vines retracted back down from where they'd pushed up through the floor, and the body crumpled into a heap in the puddle.

My breaths were heaving and ragged as I met Calanthe's eyes and nodded my thanks. She nodded back before moving off to intercept another creature.

I looked out over the room. While some of the patrons were trying to fight the creatures, most were losing their battles. Only one young man seemed to be holding his own. He fought with the kind of skill I'd only ever seen from Samhail and Bressen, and I couldn't help watching him for a moment. He'd apparently figured out the creatures could heal themselves because he stabbed one through the neck, then waited until the blue had dripped off the body before withdrawing his dagger and looking for his next opponent.

I scanned the room some more, and my gaze snagged on Heren again, but I screamed when I saw blood coating his stomach where a creature had slashed him. It had him pinned against a wall with its clawed hand pressed to his wound, and I watched in horror as a midnight blue coating began to crawl over Heren's skin like liquid. Seconds later, he was encased in a shell of blue like the creature, and his eyes flared eerily yellow.

Gods above. The creatures could infect others.

I swung around to face Raina. "I need to call Bressen," I said to her. "We don't have the right weapons to fight these things."

Raina had been watching the same thing I was, and I saw the disbelief and revulsion on her face.

"Call him," was all she said, her voice unsteady as she stared at Heren, who'd now joined the fight on the side of the creatures.

In fact, I noticed now that there were more creatures than we'd started with and almost no bodies on the ground. The creatures were making more of themselves.

I needed Bressen and Samhail here right now, and my mind reached out to Bressen. His panicked voice filled my head.

*Cyra, where are you? Why haven't I been able to reach you?*

His second question caught me off guard. My only thought was that I must have unconsciously put up a mind shield. I always left a sliver open for Bressen to send me a message, but perhaps I'd been too distracted by the attack to realize he'd been trying to call to me.

*I'm in the city*, I answered. *I don't have time to explain now. Raina and I are in huge trouble. Some kind of creatures are attacking. Bring weapons.*

*Samhail is with me*, he said. *We're in the sitting room. Open a portal.*

I immediately drew a circle in the air, then widened the portal as it blazed open. I stepped back quickly as Bressen and Samhail barreled through it, then closed it behind them.

The two men looked stunned as they took in the chaos before them.

"Gods above, what the fuck are those things?" Bressen breathed.

"I don't know," I said, "but their skin is almost like armor. It's hard to pierce, and if you don't kill them, they just heal. They're some kind of human-monster hybrid. If you kill the human, the creature seems to die, but don't let them scratch you. The blue stuff can seep inside the wound and take over your body."

Bressen and Samhail had both been surveying the room as I explained all I knew as quickly as possible, but their heads snapped back to me at that last bit.

"What?" Bressen exclaimed in disbelief.

"Fuck me," Samhail growled.

A scream sounded across the room, and Samhail hurled himself toward it automatically, drawing his swords as he went.

Close by, several creatures charged at me, Raina, and Bressen. Their numbers had almost doubled now since they'd turned many of the patrons into more creatures, and I spared a second to wonder if my aunt was now one of them. The thought was surprisingly painful. While I was still angry at her for what she'd done, she was my mother's sister, and I felt a reluctant familial pull toward her.

Next to me, Bressen caught the wrists of a creature as it reached out for him. He managed to hold it back from clawing him, but I didn't wait to see if he'd be able to throw it off. I lunged toward the creature and plunged my dagger through the side of its neck. Blood, red and human, sprayed out from the wound splattering both Bressen and I in the face. Our eyes met over the creature's shoulder, and I saw both fear and pride in his expression as the body sank to the floor in a heap before first its life and then the parasite seeped from it.

Bressen's eyes remained locked with mine, and he reached up to brush the blood from my cheek. I was sure he'd only managed to smear it, but there was no time to worry about that. He tore his gaze from mine and called to Samhail.

"Samhail! I can't connect to their minds!"

A dozen or so feet away, Samhail slammed one of the creatures against the wall by its throat and drove one of his swords through its heart. His iron grip on its neck had likely killed the thing when it hit the wall, but the sword sealed its fate, and the creature fell limp as the blue drained away from its skin to puddle on the floor below it. Samhail wrenched the sword free from the body of what was now just a man and tossed the blade to Bressen before retrieving his other sword from a nearby body.

Bressen caught the sword and immediately slashed it across the body of a creature that was charging us. The blade was razor sharp, but it still only made a shallow cut that healed almost as soon as it appeared.

"They heal instantly," I reminded Bressen as I pulled Raina with me behind him. I was more than willing to fight, but the daggers Raina and I had brought were too ineffectual against these creatures. As long as Bressen had one of Samhail's swords, it was best to stay behind him and watch his back as he fought.

Bressen's next swing was to the creature's neck, and the blow cut through its throat about halfway before stopping. It was enough, and the creature went down as Bressen pulled the sword free.

"We're going to have a long conversation after this about how you ended up here," Bressen said, glancing over his shoulder at me.

"It was Raina's idea," I said as I used a forcefield to throw back two more creatures who were attacking from the side.

Raina let out an indignant squeak. "I was kidding about taking the blame!" she yelled back at me.

Bressen pressed forward to thrust his sword at another one of the creatures as it swiped at him. The blade found its mark just below the thing's heart, but not before it managed to slash Bressen's arm with its claws. He grunted in pain and withdrew the sword, but the creature wasn't done. With its last bit of life, it reached out and laid its hand over the wound it had made.

I screamed as Bressen's body seized and pure terror washed over me. I sent the creature flying back with a forcefield, but a blob of whatever the creature was made of remained on Bressen's arm. It looked as though part of it had already seeped into him as his arm began to turn dark blue.

"No!" I screamed, and panic made me dizzy as I clamped my hands down on Bressen's wound and tried desperately to pull the blue substance back out as I'd once pulled the poison from his body. Slowly, ever so slowly, I felt the thing receding. I used all my strength to draw it out until I was absolutely certain I had the last drop, and then I flung the substance to the side where it splattered against the wall.

As soon as the parasite was away from him, Bressen's body unseized, and he sank to his knees. I dropped down beside him and laid my hands on his arm to heal his wound. When I was done, I grabbed his face between my hands.

"Are you alright?" I asked urgently.

His skin had gone pale, and his normally brilliant turquoise eyes were a bit glazed, but he nodded.

"I think that's the most disturbing thing I've ever felt," Bressen said as he got to his feet. "It was like the creature was trying to take over both my mind and my body. I think I understand how others feel when I do that to them now."

I only grasped his face again, and he brought his hands up to hold my wrists. He jerked back a moment later as his eyes fixed on the caronium cuff I hadn't bothered to remove.

"Nemesis damn me!" he said. "Why the fuck are you wearing that?"

"Oh, I forgot about it," I said, pulling the cuff off. "They told me I had to wear it so I couldn't use my mindreading powers to cheat, but it doesn't seem to work."

"I assure you, it works just fine," he said, his brows pinched. "Are you saying you still have your powers with that thing on?"

I nodded. "Yes, you just saw me use my forcefield, right? I was wearing it when I opened the portal. Why?"

"Because I could feel it try to suppress my power the moment I touched it," he said. "You really didn't feel anything when you were wearing it?"

I shook my head.

"Gods above," Bressen said. "Either you're immune to caronium because you're a syphon or maybe your negation powers are pre-empting the cuff's power."

"Less talking, more fighting!" Raina yelled beside us, and both Bressen and I turned back to the fight.

Bressen picked up his sword again and threw out an arm to shepherd me and Raina behind him before he swung it in a wide swipe to drive back three creatures that were attacking. I threw one back with a forcefield to give us a few extra seconds while Bressen ran the closest one through with a blade to its heart. He waited for the dark blue substance to leak from the body before withdrawing his sword and turning to swing at the neck of another creature.

I saw a head go flying out of my periphery as I focused my attention on the third creature that was advancing again on me and Raina. I raised my dagger, ready to stab it in the neck, when something huge moved behind it. A second later, the blade of a sword punched through the creature's stomach before being dragged upward through its chest, creating a huge gash in the thing's torso. I gasped as the blue trickled away to reveal a woman beneath this time, and her body hit the floor with a thud as the blade withdrew.

My eyes refocused on Samhail, who'd been behind her.

"Are you alright?" he asked, and both Raina and I nodded.

I realized how quiet the room had gotten as I took in the carnage. Bodies lay everywhere in pools of dark blue sludge that swirled together with crimson blood.

My gaze couldn't help drifting to the first man I'd killed. I had no idea who he was, but I'd taken his life – his and another's – and I knew I'd never be the same. It didn't matter that they'd been some kind of horrible creatures at the time. The bodies that lay on the floor now were human.

"I really thought you were kidding when you said you and Raina would be drinking, gambling, and fighting," Bressen said coming up next to me.

I tried to laugh, but it came out as a sob instead, and Bressen quickly drew me into his arms.

"I killed two of them," I whispered to him. "They were human."

Bressen eased his hold on me and pulled my mask off, which I'd somehow forgotten I was still wearing. I tried to will back the tears that threatened, but a few trickled down my cheeks.

"You did what you had to do," he said softly into my ear. "But what in the three hells were you doing here in the first place?"

Bressen pulled back to look at me, and I prepared to take full responsibility for the outing, despite the blame I'd thrown at Raina earlier.

"It was my fault," Raina said next to me. "I took Cyra out to celebrate. I've been teaching her to play cards, and I thought this would be fun."

"Why didn't you tell me where you were going?" Bressen asked me.

"We were afraid you'd try to send guards with us," I said, although in hindsight, the guards would've been helpful.

Bressen exhaled deeply. "I absolutely would have sent guards with you, and this is why."

"You were afraid we'd be attacked by horrific blue human-monster hybrids?" I tried to joke, earning me a glower from Bressen.

"Gods above, Cyra," Bressen said, "do you enjoy driving me into an early grave? I aged a hundred years when I found you gone and couldn't contact you."

I opened my mouth to apologize, but Bressen's lips crushed down brutally onto mine, and I knew I'd been right to expect some kind of punishment later. My body would absorb his worry and frustration soon enough, and I wondered what it said about me that the idea sent a thrill straight down to my toes.

Bressen pulled back from me again. "Was this dress part of the plan for the evening, or were you wearing it to distract me when I finally found out where you went?" he asked.

I turned to Raina to see if she'd volunteer an explanation, but she was frowning at Samhail, who appeared to have fixed his eyes on her cleavage. Raina shocked us all by putting a finger under Samhail's chin to tip his head up, so he was looking into her face. She had to reach high given his height compared to hers.

"If you're looking for my eyes, they're up here," she said, but her tone was teasing despite the admonition.

Samhail recovered enough from his surprise that she'd dared to touch him to quirk an amused brow at her.

I fought down a pang of jealousy at the look I thought I saw pass between the two of them. Perhaps it didn't matter after all to Raina that Samhail and I had been together, and I tried to make my peace with that.

"My lord?" a voice came from behind us, and we all turned to see the older man who'd helped me and Raina earlier. He and the younger man had likely slipped into the back room to hide when the creatures attacked.

"Are you the owner of this…place?" Bressen asked the man with that authority he exuded so well.

The man swallowed before giving a small bow. "I'm the manager, Lord Bressen. Lord Carlyle is the owner."

Bressen frowned but then nodded, apparently recognizing the name.

He turned to me. "Go back to the house, please," he said. "Samhail and I need to figure out what in the three hells happened here and what these creatures are. Will you be alright by yourself until I get back, or do you want me to ask Axenus to stay with you?"

I looked at Raina to gauge her state of mind, but she shook her head the barest amount.

"We'll be fine," I said, and Bressen nodded.

"Your ladyship," the manager said from behind Bressen, "we will, of course, return the entire ten thousand to your account with our apologies for the disruption."

My eyes widened as they locked with Bressen's, and he arched a brow at me. I opened my mouth to explain, but I had no idea what to say. He spoke before I could decide on something.

"Only ten thousand?" he said to me, humor and something dangerous dancing in his voice. "I thought I said to take at least twenty thousand."

I swallowed as Bressen looked at me like a lion toying with its prey.

"Twenty seemed excessive," I choked out.

He smiled wickedly before wrapping an arm around my waist to pull me against him again. He kissed me hard as he held me there, and I had to gasp for breath when he finally lifted his lips from mine.

"We will definitely speak about this later," he whispered in my ear, and all the muscles below my waist clenched at the promise in his words.

"Will this conversation involve parts of you inside of me?" I asked so only he could hear, and I felt his body twitch against mine.

"It will involve parts of me deep, deep inside you," he rasped softly. "The conversation is likely to be long and hard. And very rough."

I swallowed and pulled slowly away from him. There was an almost unbearable tightening between my legs, and I needed to get distance between us before I went mad. One issue or another had kept us from having sex again since that night with Samhail, and I knew we were both ready to splinter.

Raina's hand on my arm brought me back from my daze of arousal, and Bressen reluctantly let go of me.

"We better get back to the house before the two of you traumatize this poor man any further," she said, pulling on my arm as she nodded toward the manager.

I nodded and turned to go before suddenly remembering something.

"Wait!" I said. I swung around and surveyed the room frantically, but I didn't see who I was looking for. "Calanthe!" I called out, my voice laced with concern. My eyes skimmed over the bodies on the floor, equally afraid to find her as not to find her.

"Calanthe!" I called again, taking a few steps toward the door. It was too much to hope she'd managed to slip out and escape. For a moment all was quiet, but then my aunt stepped out from a small alcove near one of the curtains, and I released the breath I'd been holding.

Whether she'd taken up the hiding place during the attack at some point or only ducked into it when Bressen appeared, I wasn't sure, but I walked toward her now in relief. I sensed Bressen following behind me. Calanthe looked wary, but she held her ground as we approached.

"Cyra?" Bressen asked as his hand rested on my hip. "Is everything-"

"She saved my life," I said, and his hard expression softened instantly.

"Thank you," I said, turning back to my aunt. I reached out to take her hands but pulled back again as I remembered that touching her would syphon her power. It appeared to be some sort of plant manipulation if the vines were any indication.

Calanthe understood my hesitation and grabbed my hands anyway. "You're welcome," she said. She looked down at our clasped hands. "Consider it a wedding gift."

I tried to swallow down the sudden lump in my throat. "Come to the wedding," I told her. "Tomorrow at the house at four o'clock."

Calanthe's eyes widened and her mouth dropped open. "But Aramis…," she said, looking at me uncertainly.

"I'll explain things to him tomorrow morning," I said. "He may not be ready to forgive you, but he won't object if I ask him to let you come."

"Thank you," Calanthe whispered as tears fell freely down her cheeks. "I'll do whatever I can to make up for my past mistakes. To both of you."

She hesitated but then stepped forward to pull me into a hug. She squeezed me tightly before stepping back to get her sniffling under control. She looked at Bressen as if to be certain she'd be welcome, and he nodded at her.

"My wife-to-be has spoken," Bressen said with a smile, "and we all know she's the true authority here in Solandis."

Calanthe smiled back, and Bressen and I returned to where Raina and Samhail waited for us. I glanced around the room, looking for the young man who'd fought so skillfully against the creatures, but I didn't see him. I sent a prayer up to the Trinity that he was alive and safe somewhere.

I opened a portal, and Bressen gripped my shoulders to face him.

"Try to behave yourself for the next couple hours," he said and kissed my forehead. "I'll be home as soon as I can wrap things up here."

As much as Bressen might tease me about being in charge, this was the part of his responsibilities as Lord of Hiraeth that I had no desire to claim. I didn't envy him the next few hours he'd spend trying to help identify the victims and figure out exactly what had happened.

I was having enough trouble dealing with my own part in the incident. I'd never forget the faces of the men I'd killed, nor was I likely to forget Heren and how he'd looked as he'd been taken over by the creature. I didn't know what had happened to him, but I guessed that he'd likely fallen under Samhail's blade. I couldn't look for his body among the fallen.

Tomorrow, or maybe in a few weeks, I'd remind Raina that she'd asked about the worst that could happen tonight, but for now my heart was too heavy to tease her as we stepped through the portal back into my bedroom at Tide's End.

I also had a lot of questions for Raina about how she spent her free time and how often she snuck out late at night without telling anyone. In just a couple months, she seemed to have changed dramatically from the shy girl I'd first met in Callanus. Now she was taking late-night forays into the city, gambling in underground dens, and the gods only knew what else.

I was too exhausted to think about any of that now, though. Back in my room, Raina and I changed out of our gowns, bathed, and crawled into the bed I shared with Bressen. She'd stay with me at least until he returned so we didn't need to be alone.

There was much I'd have to deal with soon enough, but for now, my weary mind was easily persuaded to succumb to sleep. After all, tomorrow was my wedding day, when I'd become Bressen's, and he'd become mine.

Nothing could be wrong in the world after that.

# Chapter 27

The day of our wedding dawned crisp but clear and sunny. I didn't know what time Bressen had returned last night, but I awoke to find his arms around me and his warm breath fluttering the whisps of hair near my ear. Raina had apparently returned to her own bed sometime during the night, and I snuggled back against Bressen. Almost immediately I felt his hard arousal against my backside.

"Are you ready to take your punishment?" he drawled as he ground himself against me.

Heat shot straight to my core, and I groaned, but a small part of me that enjoyed the torment decided to draw it out a little longer.

"We've waited this whole last week," I said. "We might as well wait another few hours and have a proper wedding night."

Bressen growled his displeasure. "You just want to see a lord beg."

I smiled and turned to face him, then pressed on his shoulder to urge him onto his back. I pulled the covers away to reveal his swollen cock.

Bressen's eyes were dark as they found mine, his breathing already ragged. I moved down his body and wrapped my hand around his base before slipping my mouth over the length of him. He groaned loudly, and his hips jerked up in soft thrusts as I moved my mouth, taking him deep into the back of my throat.

"Fuck, Cyra," he breathed as his hands threaded through my hair.

My answer was to press my mouth down harder onto him, and his hips jerked again. I knew his body enough to know when he was close to his release, and I moved faster over him. A low rumble started in his throat as his hips arched again, and he let out a roar a minute later as he came, his hot seed spilling into my throat as I swallowed him down. I pumped my mouth a few more times until his body relaxed beneath me.

Bressen lay panting as I curled up against him again.

"Your turn," he said as he moved to shift our positions, but I stopped him with a hand on his shoulder.

"Tonight," I told him. "You can do anything you want to me tonight."

He groaned. "You'll make me come again with promises like that."

A knock sounded at our door, and Leeda's voice floated through. "My lady, are you ready to get up?"

"In a minute!" I called back as Bressen grumbled.

It was a little tricky to have a handmaid now that Bressen and I lived in the same quarters, but we'd worked out a schedule that largely allowed Leeda to avoid being here when Bressen and I were together. He was only still in bed now because he'd gotten home so late last night.

Bressen swung himself out of bed and strode across the room naked toward the closet to find some clothes while I grabbed my robe off a chair and tied it around me. I went to the door to let Leeda in.

Despite that first day when she'd seemed anxious to get rid of me, Leeda had been strangely underfoot the rest of the week. She seemed to pop up randomly when I was with Bressen or Raina, and more than once I'd opened a door to find her just on the other side, seemingly in the process of cleaning something.

Leeda went straight to the bathing chamber to prepare my bath, and Bressen emerged from the closet a minute or so later, fully dressed, and looking perfectly put together as always. I had no idea how he did that with such ease. Even with Leeda's help, it took me a minimum of twenty minutes before I felt presentable.

Bressen pulled me into his arms and kissed me. "I probably won't see you until the wedding," he said. "I have to take care of a few more things related to the attack last night, and then I'll be in Samhail's room getting ready. Just call if you need me for anything."

I smiled to imagine Samhail of all people trying to help Bressen get ready, but I smiled even more to imagine Bressen, already devastatingly beautiful as he was, putting on his finest clothes to look his best for me.

"I'll be fine," I said. "I have to go talk to Aramis about Calanthe and then let Ferris know not to turn her away when she arrives."

He looked at me solemnly. "You're sure about this?"

"You'd be attending a funeral today instead of a wedding if it wasn't for her," I told him seriously.

He winced, but nodded and then kissed my forehead. "Good luck with Aramis. I suggest telling him the same thing you just said to me if you want any hope of convincing him to be okay with this."

Bressen kissed me one more time, and then he was gone. I turned to find Leeda watching me from the doorway of the bathroom and had the strange sense she'd been there for a while. Maybe after the wedding I'd consider breaking my vow about not reading her mind again to see what she was thinking, but right now I had more important things to deal with.

At three o'clock, I was back in my room trying desperately to calm the nervous jitter that was vibrating in my chest. I was already in my wedding gown as Raina and Leeda tried to coax my waves of dark hair into some kind of elegant coiffure on top of my head. They were having only minimal success at the moment.

My talk with Aramis had gone about as well as I could have hoped. He wasn't thrilled by the idea of having Calanthe here, but I'd taken Bressen's advice and used the same line with him about attending a funeral rather than a wedding, and he'd reluctantly conceded. Part of me felt bad for asking him to accept her presence after all she'd put him through, but I couldn't in good conscience not invite her to the wedding, considering that she was the only reason I was here right now.

"This would be easier if you'd stop vibrating in that chair," Raina grumbled through the jeweled comb she held in her mouth. Leeda plucked the comb from between her teeth and stuck it in my hair where Raina was holding it.

"In hindsight, that third cup of coffee at lunch was a bad idea," I said.

A knock sounded at the door before Raina could comment, and she went over to open it.

I couldn't see who it was, but I heard Andromeda's voice a second later. "May I have a moment to speak to my daughter-in-law-to-be?"

"She's not here," Raina said, not even trying to hide the lie.

A pause. "Please?"

Raina looked at me, and I nodded after a moment. Raina opened the door and stepped out of the way so Andromeda could enter.

"Alone," Andromeda said as Raina started to move back toward me.

Raina didn't even look at me this time. "No," she said. "If you have anything to say to Cyra, you can say it in front of us."

My heart warmed at Raina's unwillingness to leave me alone with Andromeda. It was too much to hope that Bressen's mother had changed her mind and was here to welcome me to the family.

Andromeda didn't bother to answer Raina. She simply looked at me.

"Please?" she asked again, her tone anything but pleading. I was actually impressed at how much entitlement she infused into the request.

I sighed and nodded to Raina. I was sure I could handle Andromeda at this point. The wedding was in an hour, and there was nothing she could say to convince me to call it off.

Raina gave me a look that begged me to reconsider, but I just nodded again. She exhaled in defeat and turned to leave the room. "We'll be just outside," she said as Leeda followed her.

The door clicked shut behind Raina and Leeda, and I turned my attention to my reluctant mother-in-law.

"What can I do for you, Lady Andromeda?" I asked, trying to smile at her but only partially succeeding.

"You can tell my son you've changed your mind and can't marry him," she said without missing a beat.

My heart sank to hear her say the one thing I'd been hoping she wouldn't. I was expecting some version of this request, but it still shocked me to hear her state it so baldly.

"Excuse me?" I said, buying myself a few seconds to accept that she really wasn't going to accept my marriage to Bressen.

"I have nothing against you personally, my dear," Andromeda said, completely unconcerned by any offense she may have given, "but I can't let you marry Bressen."

"That's not up to you."

"Do you know what an angelus is?" she asked me, sitting down in one of the chairs without being invited.

"They're beings with the capacity to harness that which is most light in the world, but also that which is darkest," I said, parroting back what Bressen had once told me when I'd asked him what an angelus was.

Andromeda rolled her eyes. "A textbook answer," she said dryly, "but do you know what that actually means?"

I opened my mouth but then closed it again and shook my head.

"Angelus provide balance in the world," Andromeda said. "Many things are meaningless without their opposite. For instance, how does one know they're happy if one has never experienced sadness? Being satiated is all the sweeter for having known hunger. The sun shines brighter after the rain, yet as a winemaker, you of all people know that the rain is welcome when the sun has shone for too long and dried out the land."

I pursed my lips. "What's your point?"

"My point," she said, "is that angelus serve an important purpose in the world, but our numbers are dwindling. Unfortunately, a new angelus can only be born to two angelus parents."

I furrowed my brows. I understood the need for balance between light and dark, or between any opposites really, but I didn't understand how angelus affected that balance either directly or indirectly. It was on the tip of my tongue to ask her to explain, but I stopped myself. It didn't matter. There was nothing she could say to make me reconsider marrying Bressen.

"So you want me to sacrifice my own happiness and Bressen's for …what?" I asked. "The possibility Bressen may eventually find an angelus woman to marry and then spend decades trying to have a child?"

"The possibility of one angelus child is better than the certainty of none," Andromeda countered.

She wasn't wrong, and I had no real argument against that.

"And if I refuse to let him go," I asked, "will you try again to talk him into fucking other women in the hopes he may impregnate one?"

Shock crossed her soft features, and I wondered if she was more surprised by my language or that I knew what she'd tried to do.

"Bressen told you about our conversation?" she asked in surprise.

"I overheard it."

She nodded. "I see. And knowing what's at stake for us is still not enough for you to make this sacrifice?"

"Why is it my sacrifice to make?" I asked. "I don't want angelus to die out, but I don't see how I'm supposed to make a difference in the grand scheme. Angelus need far more to survive than I alone can give them."

"That's true," Andromeda said. "If you were to step out of the way, it's possible Bressen might only ever sire one or two angelus, and that wouldn't be enough to bring us back from the brink. Yet it would help, just as the sacrifice of another angelus somewhere in the world might add one more to our number. As a lord and the most powerful of our kind, Bressen has an obligation to set an example. Marrying you is a betrayal of that obligation, and I need you to help him see that."

"I'm sorry," I said, shaking my head. "I can't do that."

She paused then asked, "Do you know how my husband died?"

I blinked at her pivot in topic and furrowed my brows as I recalled my conversation with Bressen about his father's death.

"Bressen said his uncle killed his father," I ventured.

Andromeda smiled sadly. "Yes. Garreth, my husband, and his brother Tymon killed each other in a fight over me."

My eyes flared. "What? Why?"

Then my eyes went wide as I remembered what Bressen had told me about his mother's affair, and everything suddenly fell into place.

"Oh gods," I whispered as my hand flew to cover my mouth.

"Garreth and I were relatively young when we met," Andromeda went on. "We began trying for a child almost immediately after we married, but decades passed, and I didn't get pregnant. We saw several healers in the hope they could help us, but the news was always the same. Garreth's seed wasn't strong enough, and the chances were extremely remote we'd be able to conceive. Garreth wanted children desperately. We both did. Not only that, but as the Lord of Hiraeth, Garreth needed an heir. I felt the pressure to help give him that heir, as well as to add to our numbers."

"You had an affair with Tymon," I concluded.

"I did," she said. "A rather lengthy one in fact. It took us nearly twelve years to conceive Bressen. Luckily Tymon had the same dark angelus features as my husband, so I was able to convince Garreth a miracle had happened and Bressen was his."

I thought I might vomit. Andromeda's affair hadn't been brief. She'd cheated on her husband for more than a decade. Even more sickening was that the man Bressen thought was his uncle was actually his father.

"Does Bressen know all this?" I asked, swallowing down my nausea.

"He knows Tymon and I had an affair, and that Garreth challenged Tymon to a fight because of it," she said, "but I don't believe he ever learned Tymon was his true father."

"And you're sure that's the case?" I asked.

"Yes, I'm sure Tymon was Bressen's father. I brought Bressen to a healer as a baby, and she was able to compare his blood to Tymon's. As much as I might wish it otherwise, Bressen was not Garreth's."

I fell into a chair, unable to stand anymore.

"Did Tymon know Bressen was his?" I asked.

"Of course," she said. "He knew why I started the affair with him. He had no desire to be a parent, so he left that to Garreth when Bressen was born. He and I just shared a desire to create more angelus."

*Create more angelus.* She spoke about having children with such detachment, and everything Bressen had said about her relentless practicality and her lack of nurturing came back to me. I couldn't imagine what it must have been like for him to grow up with her as a mother.

"When Garreth learned of the affair, he attacked Tymon," Andromeda went on, almost as if she remembered the fight fondly, "Garreth was already gravely wounded when Tymon went in for a killing blow. Bressen had learned of the fight somehow and arrived just in time to throw himself in front of Garreth. I assume you and my son already know each other intimately, so perhaps you've seen the scar just below his ribs. That was the thrust from Tymon's sword meant for Garreth. Bressen took it instead."

I frowned as something occurred to me.

"Bressen is a hundred and seventeen years old," I said, "and his father died twenty years ago. Why did it take Garreth ninety-seven years to learn about your affair with Tymon?"

"Because I only tried to stop the affair with Tymon twenty years ago," Andromeda answered coolly.

"What! Why would you keep an affair going that long?"

"I told you," Andromeda said. "Garreth wanted children. Not just one child, but many, and I felt an obligation to help create more angelus, so Tymon and I kept up our affair for almost a century."

I would have fallen out of my chair if not for its arms.

"Unfortunately," she went on, oblivious to my horror, "Bressen was the only child I ever had. I got pregnant one other time, but I miscarried. Twenty years ago, I told Tymon it was finally time to stop our affair since it seemed unlikely I'd have another child. By then, however, he'd fallen in love with me. He refused to let it end, so in what I can only assume was an attempt to force me to take him back, he told Garreth about the affair."

I shook my head. She hadn't even loved Tymon. The affair had been entirely for the pragmatic purposes of having children. No wonder she thought nothing of whoring Bressen out to other women.

"Tymon was stunned when Bressen jumped in front of his sword," she went on relentlessly. "He stopped to help Bressen, the son he could never acknowledge, and his distraction allowed Garreth to stab him through the neck with his last bit of strength. I'd already called a healer when I learned of the fight, but Garreth and Tymon were both gone by the time she arrived. She was only able to save Bressen."

I squeezed my eyes shut and willed my already roiling stomach not to send up the few bites of food I'd managed to eat earlier.

"So you see," Andromeda said, "you're not the only one to sacrifice for the good of the angelus race. I lost both my husband and my lover for that sacrifice, and as you can probably tell, the whole tragedy has done nothing to endear me to my son."

My eyes flew open as I tried to comprehend what I was hearing. Nemesis take her, was she actually trying to...

"Are you suggesting that having a nearly hundred-year affair with your husband's brother was a sacrifice on your part?" I asked in disbelief.

"It was," she insisted, her voice growing hard. "Don't you think I would have preferred to have children with my own husband, with the man I married and fell in love with? Of course I would have preferred that, but that wasn't going to be possible. So I did what I had to do to give Garreth his heir and add one more angelus to the world."

I just stared at her, slowly shaking my head.

"You're absolutely mad," I said quietly. "Surely there were other options aside from betraying your husband with his brother."

Andromeda shrugged. "If there were, I didn't see them."

I shook my head again as I rose, anger steadying my legs, and my voice was colder than I'd ever heard it when I spoke.

"You should leave now," I said. "I'd prefer you go and not even attend the wedding, but for now I'll settle for you getting out of my sight."

Andromeda stood, seemingly unphased by the fury in my voice.

"It sounds like you won't call off the wedding," she said.

I raised my brows at her. "There was never any chance in the three hells I'd do that," I told her.

"That's unfortunate. I was hoping I wouldn't have to do this."

"Do what?" I asked, narrowing my eyes.

Andromeda held up her hands in front of her chest, and a bright fiery ball formed in the space between them.

"Don't worry," she said, "I just need you out of the way for a while until Bressen believes you've left him."

And then she attacked.

# Chapter 28

Sunfire.

I'd never seen it before, but I knew that's what it was the moment I saw the light form between Andromeda's hands. The reasonable part of my brain told me she couldn't possibly mean to attack me. My next thought was that I couldn't attack Bressen's mother, but then the words Axenus had said to me the day I'd first met him came back to me: *You must learn to be willing to attack, even if you're not sure the threat is real.*

Before I realized what I was doing, I held out a hand and loosed a forcefield at her, just as she sent her sunfire toward me. The forcefield did nothing to the sunfire itself, which sent an instant sensation of burning through my entire body, but it did knock Andromeda backward. She cried out as she was thrown across the room where she hit the wall with a thud and slid to the floor. I just stared at her where she lay looking up at me while my body tried to banish the momentary agony of her sunfire.

I knew some people didn't necessarily get along with their in-laws, but this was ridiculous.

"That was a mistake, my dear," Andromeda said as she picked herself up. Before I could recover myself enough to react, Andromeda drew another ball of sunfire and sent it shooting straight for me.

The ball hit me in the center of my chest, and I screamed as the feeling of being engulfed in flames consumed my body. I was only vaguely aware that no part of me or my clothing was actually on fire, but that knowledge did nothing to alleviate the excruciating pain that coursed through me. My own flames had never burned me, but Andromeda's sunfire scorched every part of me, and my mind longed for the respite of unconsciousness.

I fell to my knees still screaming as the door flew open, and Raina rushed in. I wasn't completely sure what she saw, but she grasped instantly that I was in danger and that Andromeda was the cause. She shifted into her peregrine falcon form and shot straight for Andromeda, who shrieked as Raina's sharp talons and beak tore at her face.

Andromeda's sunfire died out, along with the pain, as she redirected her efforts to warding off the angry raptor. I inhaled a deep, gasping breath and tried to focus on Raina. I needed to help her before Andromeda hurt her too, but I was still on my knees when a huge form entered the room.

"What in the three hells is going on?" Samhail's voice boomed across the room. I wasn't sure how he'd gotten here so fast, but I suspected Raina might have sent Leeda to find Bressen as soon as they left the room.

I continued to gasp for breath on the floor as my hands shook violently, but Raina abandoned her attack and shifted back into her human form to answer Samhail.

"She was attacking Cyra," she told him. "Some kind of fire."

"Lying bitch!" Andromeda spat at Raina, wiping at a scratch on her face that dripped blood. She turned to Samhail. "They both attacked me!"

Samhail looked at me where I still knelt on the floor gasping.

"Sunfire," was all I managed to say, but Samhail understood.

"Lady Andromeda, tell me you didn't just attack Cyra with sunfire," Samhail said. His tone was a mix of incredulity and pleading, as if he didn't want to believe she could possibly be that foolish.

Andromeda paused, apparently weighing whether or not she could convince Samhail that Raina and I were actually the aggressors.

"I'm sorry, Samhail," she said finally. "I have to do what I need to."

She drew her sunfire again, but Samhail was faster, and his forcefield sent her back into the wall again before she could release it on him. Andromeda recovered quickly, though, and her next attempt at sunfire hit Samhail before he could act. His roar of pain reverberated through the room, and both Raina and I launched ourselves at Andromeda. We reached her at the same time and each grabbed one of her arms to pull them to her sides and stop her flow of sunfire to Samhail. Half a second later, I remembered to also negate her power.

It occurred to me that I'd also just syphoned her sunfire as well, but my only real thought was that I had to stop her from hurting Samhail.

"My power!" Andromeda cried as she felt me snuff it out.

Samhail's roaring stopped, and he sank to one knee as Raina and I tried to hold a struggling Andromeda fast.

Power suddenly pulsed through the room as Bressen entered with

Axenus and Leeda on his heels. His gaze swept the space, taking in Raina and I on the floor holding Andromeda, and Samhail on one knee across the room trying to catch his breath. His eyes snapped back to his mother and blazed red.

"You have five seconds to explain yourself, Mother," he said, and the quiet fury in his voice sent a shiver down my spine.

I thought Andromeda might try to claim again that we'd all attacked her, but she seemed to know Bressen wouldn't entertain such a notion.

"I did it for you," she said to him. "I did it for all angelus kind. You can't marry her."

The look in Bressen's eyes and the second pulse of power that punched through the room made both Raina and I stand up and back away from Andromeda. Free of our hold, Bressen's mother stood to face her son, chin high.

"Someone tell me what happened," Bressen snarled, his eyes never leaving Andromeda.

Samhail spoke up first as he got back to his feet. "I wasn't here for the first part, but I'm told Lady Andromeda attacked Cyra with sunfire. When I arrived, Raina was in her falcon form trying to defend Cyra. When I questioned Lady Andromeda, she attacked me with sunfire as well."

Bressen's gaze shot to me, looking me over for injuries. I saw the question in his eyes when they met mine again, and I nodded my confirmation of Samhail's summary.

Bressen's gaze returned to his mother, and his eyes flared into fiery red orbs. I didn't think I'd ever seen them quite so red before.

"You dare attack my fiancé in my home before our wedding?" he asked, the cold fury back in his voice.

"I did what I needed to do," Andromeda said. "I've always done what I thought was best for you, even if it's not what you wanted."

"Not today you won't," Bressen said. "Samhail, please find my mother a cell in the basement until I have time to deal with her."

Raina and I both gasped, but Samhail didn't hesitate as he stepped forward to grab Andromeda by the wrist.

"Bressen, no! You can't be serious!" Andromeda shrieked as Samhail pulled her toward the door.

"I told you before that you had two choices," Bressen said to her. "You could leave, or you could stay without making trouble. You chose neither of those options, so now I'm choosing for you."

"Wait! You can't do this!" she yelled. "I'm your mother!"

Bressen didn't move at all as Samhail dragged Andromeda toward the door, but she grabbed the collar of Bressen's jacket as she went by and jerked him forward.

"Wait! There's something you need to know about your father!" she screamed as she held fast to his jacket.

My eyes widened. Gods above, I wasn't going to let her confess *that* to Bressen an hour before his wedding.

"No!" I yelled, shooting forward. I wasn't sure what I planned to do, whether I only meant to pry her hands from Bressen's jacket, or whether I meant to throw my hand over her mouth to stop her from speaking, but I had to do something to keep her from saying what she meant to say.

"Stop!" Bressen roared, and everyone in the room froze at the menace in his tone, including me and Samhail.

"Bressen, please," Andromeda whispered. "You need to know about your father. You need to understand what I did and why."

Her eyes had started to glisten with tears, but Bressen's still glowed like fire. I'd never seen his eyes blaze for this long.

Bressen narrowed his gaze as he spoke, and his voice seemed to almost chill the air in the room itself.

"I know," he said to his mother. "Do you really think I don't already know what you want to tell me? Do you really think it's going to make a difference? I'm a fucking mind wraith, Mother. Did you really think you'd be able to keep such a secret from me?"

Andromeda's mouth fell open as she struggled to find words. "How long?" she asked finally.

"Decades. Long before that fight," he said, and pain etched his face. "I should have told him long before then, but I was giving you the chance to stop on your own and tell him."

Her face was stricken. "And you still threw yourself in front of-"

"Garreth was my father," Bressen cut in before she could finish. "He's the man who raised me, the man that made me who I am today." He paused. "In the end, it wasn't even the affair that broke him. It was learning that I wasn't…"

His words seemed to choke off, and I wanted to go to him, to wrap him in my arms and soothe his hurt.

"Garreth was the only father I'll ever have," Bressen finished.

Samhail's eyes jerked to me, and I saw the question in his face. I was sure he knew exactly what fight Bressen was talking about, and I nodded once to confirm what he must be asking. His expression darkened, and Andromeda winced as his hand tightened on her wrist.

Andromeda opened her mouth to say something, but Bressen spoke before she could. "Get her out of my sight," he said.

Samhail pulled his mother away, and her hand fell from Bressen's jacket, as if his words had taken away any strength she had left to hold him. No one moved until she was fully out of the room, and only then did everyone seem to take a collective breath.

Bressen immediately closed the distance between us, and I took a step back at the intensity I saw in his eyes. They were finally turquoise again, but I could feel his rage still simmering below the surface. He only grasped my arms gently and looked me over.

"Are you alright?" he asked, worry still prickling his words.

A slightly hysterical laugh fell loose from me. "I can't say sunfire was a fun experience, but I'll live."

Bressen didn't laugh but pulled me to him for a crushing embrace.

"I'm so sorry," he whispered in my ear. "I underestimated how far she'd go to dissuade you from marrying me."

I nodded against his chest. I'd start crying if I said anything else, so I remained silent as I tried to swallow down the knot in my throat.

Bressen leaned back to look at me. "Tell me what I can do."

I tried to swallow the lump a few more times, but it was several seconds before I could get my mouth to open, and then a few more seconds before I could force sound out.

"I just need a few minutes alone," I said, my voice barely a whisper.

Bressen stiffened, and I knew he wanted to do anything but leave me alone right now. He wanted to be able to help me, to fix things, and it wrenched at me to push him away like this, as I had after Fernweh.

I wanted to be able to accept his comfort – to comfort him back for all he'd endured – but I just needed to be alone for a few minutes. I needed it to be quiet so I could think, so I could make sense of what had just happened and everything I'd just learned.

"I'm sorry," I said, needing him to understand this had nothing to do with him. "I just…"

"Take the time you need," Bressen said, his tone committed to patience. He kissed my forehead and left the room as Axenus fell in behind him.

"Cyra?" Raina said, and I looked up at her.

"I just need a few minutes alone," I repeated to her.

She looked surprised that I included her in the people to leave.

"Are you sure?" she said. "I can-"

"Please," I said. My voice had started to break, and if I had to say anything else, I was sure I'd burst into tears.

Raina paused for several seconds before she finally nodded and turned to leave, ushering Leeda out and closing the door behind them.

The moment the door shut behind Raina, the air seemed to leave the room, and I doubled over to gasp for breath. I sank to my knees, trying desperately not to start sobbing uncontrollably. Andromeda's sunfire had been excruciating physical pain, but it was nothing compared to the mental pain of everything else, of learning about Bressen's father, of his mother's rejection of me, and of watching him order her to be imprisoned.

Andromeda had gone to unbelievable lengths to keep me from Bressen, and part of me couldn't help wondering if it was a sign. If all of it was a sign. Fernweh, Brix blaming me, the way my body had rejected Bressen, the attack of the creatures last night, and Andromeda. It felt like every force in the world was conspiring to keep me from marrying Bressen, and I was starting to wonder if I should give up.

I wanted to marry him more than anything I'd ever wanted in my life, but it seemed almost foolhardy to keep pushing for it when everything was fighting against me. Maybe I just wasn't meant to be his wife. Maybe the universe was trying to tell me I wasn't worthy of him.

It felt like there was a yawning chasm between me and Bressen, and the thought sent another wave of stabbing pain through me. I doubled over further as I gave in to great choking sobs.

Suddenly I couldn't be here anymore. I needed to get out of the house, if only for a few minutes. I wasn't ready to call off the wedding, but I needed some time to get my head on straight, and I couldn't do that here.

I picked myself up off the floor and drew a circle in the air. I wasn't even sure where I was going as the delicate blue glow of the portal flared up, and I threw myself through it, then turned quickly to close it behind me before anyone could see where I'd gone.

I felt guilty instantly as I realized everyone would likely assume the worst, that I'd gotten cold feet and run off. Well, that was really what I'd done, wasn't it? Even if I had every intention of returning?

I did have every intention of returning, right?

I just needed a few minutes, just a few minutes to collect myself, then I could get married. I'd beg Bressen's forgiveness when I got back.

I fought down another wave of sobs that threatened as I realized what he'd think when he couldn't find me. Maybe I could pull myself together quickly enough that he'd never even know I was gone.

I inhaled deeply and lifted my head to see where I was.

# Chapter 29

I recognized the room instantly. The hard, cold marble of the Priory's main hall held in the winter chill despite the oil lamps burning all around, and the silence seemed to pulse with a life of its own in the huge empty space. I suddenly wished I'd taken a moment to grab my cloak before leaving as I rubbed my hands over my bare arms for warmth.

Gods above, what had made me come here of all places?

The room was hardly comforting, especially given some of my experiences here, but at least it was quiet, and I was alone. I walked to the Triumvirate chairs on the side of the dais and sank down into Bressen's. The most senior member of the Triumvirate always took the middle chair, and with Jerram and Ursan gone, that was now Bressen. He'd only started to use this chair recently, but the faint smell of his musk and hot cinnamon scent still wafted up to my nose, making my stomach clench painfully.

I looked around the room slowly before my eyes stopped on the giant statue of the Nemesis holding its scales.

I'd never been a particularly religious person. Worship of the Trinity had been informal at best in Fernweh, but I wondered if my mind had somehow decided I needed to be here right now. Bressen himself was known as the Nemesis Incarnate, so perhaps it was fitting that I'd been drawn here to where the Nemesis, or at least its effigy, loomed over me.

I sighed. I was supposed to be getting married in a little over half an hour and I'd just taken a portal halfway across Thasia to sit in an empty building where I'd once been attacked by tigers. I was being stupid. I needed to get back to Solandis before Bressen went crazy looking for me.

I was about to stand up when a familiar voice rang out across the hall.

"My lady? My lady, what are you doing here? I thought you were in… isn't it…aren't you…," Phaedrus stumbled over his words in several attempts to get to his question as he hurried toward me.

"Isn't today my wedding day?" I supplied for him. We both looked down at the shimmering gown I was wearing. "Yes, it is."

Phaedrus slowed as he neared me. "What are you doing here? Is Lord

Bressen with you?"

I shook my head.

"Does he…know you're here?" he asked more carefully.

I shook my head again, and a look of panic crossed Phaedrus's face. I could see him already considering how angry Bressen would be with him for not immediately sending me back to Solandis.

I sighed again. "I'll go back. You needn't worry about what Bressen will do. I just needed a little space to breathe for a minute."

Phaedrus flinched as he realized I knew what he'd been thinking, but his face softened a moment later. "May I sit?" he asked.

I nodded to the Triumvirate chair next to me, and Phaedrus sat down. He reached out, hesitated, then took my hand gently in his own.

"Is there something you need to talk about?" he asked.

"No," I said, then reconsidered. "Yes. I mean, I don't know."

"It's natural to be a little nervous on your wedding day," he ventured. "Can I ask what's troubling you the most? Are you worried about becoming Lady of Hiraeth?"

I shook my head.

"Is it…the wedding night?" he asked cautiously, and I pitched forward in my chair as I almost choked on my sharp laugh. I was a bit nervous about the wedding night, but not in the way Phaedrus was thinking, and I shook my head forcefully as I tried to clear my throat.

"Nothing like that," I said. "I'm just…confused."

"Confused about how you feel?" Phaedrus asked.

"Confused about how I feel, about how Bressen feels, about why every force in the world seems to be working against us right now."

Phaedrus frowned. "Why are you confused about how Lord Bressen feels?" he asked. "If you'll allow me to say so, my lady, it seems fairly obvious to me how he feels."

I didn't say anything as I tried to figure out how to explain the situation without having to mention the nights with Bressen and Samhail. Truth be told, part of me didn't understand why Bressen had agreed to them. Most of the time he was possessive of me, yet he'd agreed to let Samhail have me twice. The first time had been early in our relationship, and sharing had been normal between him and Samhail, but this last time had seemed more like a sacrifice for Bressen. I didn't fully understand why he'd let me and Samhail be together.

"It's just been a rather emotional few weeks for me," I said, waving a hand. "The loss of our vineyard. My attempts to hurt people. When Bressen had to…" I trailed off.

"When he had to break into your mind?" he offered, and I nodded.

"My brother is also mad at me. I don't think he's coming to the wedding. I just met my aunt for the first time after twenty-two years. She looks just like me, just like my mother, and she and my father don't get along. Also, Bressen's mother doesn't seem to like me very much."

The last was a significant understatement, but I didn't want to go into the details of Andromeda's attack on me just now.

Phaedrus squeezed my hand a little. "That's a lot to have hanging over you," he said kindly. "Do you still want to get married?"

I found myself nodding before I'd even considered the question. "Yes. Very much so. I just needed some space to think."

"To think about what?" Phaedrus asked.

When I didn't go on, he asked, "Do you love Lord Bressen?"

I looked up at the hint of nervousness in his tone.

"Of course," I said quickly, then amended myself. "I mean, I'm almost certain I do. I've never been in love before, so I'm not sure what it's supposed to feel like."

Phaedrus smiled. "Are you familiar with the myth of the origin of love?" he asked, and I shook my head.

"According to some of our much older texts on the Trinity, ones we don't really use anymore," Phaedrus said, "humans didn't really look like we do now when the Creator first made us. One text in particular describes us as previously looking like two humans stuck together with two heads, four legs, and four arms."

I raised a brow at him. "That's ridiculous."

He shrugged. "Agreed, but according to this text, there were three different kinds of humans. The Souls of the Sun looked like two men who were stuck together, while the Souls of the Earth looked to be made of two women. Then there were the Souls of the Moon, who looked like one of each, a man and a woman pressed together."

"I suppose there's a reason we don't look like this anymore?" I asked.

"There is. According to the texts, we were very powerful beings, especially the perimortals. Just imagine, for example, what you and Bressen would be capable of if you were one person with all of your combined powers."

I nodded. My range of abilities with Bressen's level of power would make a formidable being indeed.

"We were also very defiant beings, though," Phaedrus went on, "and the Trinity weren't happy with us. We weren't worshipping them as we were supposed to, since we were too wrapped up in ourselves, so the gods of the Trinity got together to discuss what to do. The Nemesis wanted to punish us for our insolence. The first suggestion was to kill us all and start over, but the Protector had a different idea. The Protector suggested they split us all down the middle, that they sever us in half so that each human was now two separate beings."

I stared at him. "Why? What would that accomplish?"

Phaedrus held up a finger to indicate he was getting to that.

"The Trinity all agreed to try this idea, so the Nemesis took each of us and split us down the middle so that each half had a head and two arms and two legs. The Protector then sewed up the wound by threading us up the middle, pulling the string tight, and tying it off right about here."

He pointed a finger to his navel.

I smiled. "So our navel is where the Protector sewed us up?"

"That's what the ancient Arystrians believed, yes," Phaedrus said.

"What does all this have to do with love?"

"Everything," Phaedrus said. "After being torn in two, humans suddenly felt incomplete, no longer whole. We wanted to rejoin ourselves, and that yearning to do so was the birth of love. But to make sure we relied on the gods to fill the void we felt, the Creator called a giant storm to blow us all around the world so we couldn't immediately find our partners. We were lost without our other halves, so we once again turned to the Trinity."

I considered this. It was certainly true that when I felt like I was missing something I always tried to find something else to take its place.

"What the gods didn't count on was that most humans never gave up trying to find their mate," he went on, "and many did eventually succeed in finding that other half. They didn't have the power to put themselves back together, so they did the next best thing."

"They got married?" I ventured.

"They made love," Phaedrus said, making me blink. "According to the myth, having sex is our attempt to join our bodies back together. It isn't possible to physically reconnect ourselves permanently, but we can at least do it temporarily. For some humans this wasn't enough, though, so they found a way to symbolically rejoin their souls as well."

"Marriage?" I ventured again.

"Marriage," Phaedrus confirmed. "This myth isn't part of our current official doctrine, but you can see vestiges of it in things like the Harmilan."

I frowned, but then I raised my brows as I saw the connection.

"The Harmilan has evolved over the centuries as a celebration of the Trinity and the Triumvirate joining for the good of all humanity, but the roots of the Harmilan are much humbler," Phaedrus explained. "In my research I've found that the Harmilan began as a way for humans who'd found their other half to celebrate that success by trying to make themselves whole again, or as whole as they could reasonably be. It's why many people celebrate the Harmilan with either sex or marriage or both."

I gave him a dubious look. "So all that promiscuity on the Harmilan is just humans trying to merge again with their other halves?"

He smiled and winked. "Sometimes it takes a few tries to find your mate. People may need to have sex with dozens of others before they find the one who fits them just right."

"But doesn't that make the Harmilan an affront to the Trinity? It's as though people are flaunting that they found their other half and are rejoining themselves. If the Trinity tore us apart to make us dependent on them, then marriage seems like we're abandoning them again, no?"

"That's often what happens when you lose the original meaning of a ceremony," he said. "It becomes a patchwork of old and new stitched together in a way that sometimes makes sense and sometimes doesn't. The Harmilan takes all forms of joining – marriage, sex, and connection with the gods – and rolls it all into one." He paused. "Do you want to know a secret?"

"Always," I said, intrigued by the sly smile that crept onto his lips.

"The vows that the lords recite when they're first sworn into the Triumvirate and the ones they say during the Harmilan are taken from the same part of the ancient text that contains this myth," he said.

I looked at him questioningly.

"The myth explains the origin of love," he prompted.

My eyes widened. "Are you saying that the Triumvirate vows are…"

"Ancient marriage vows," Phaedrus finished.

I clamped a hand over my mouth to hold in the squeal of laughter that threatened to echo across the chamber.

"The wording is vague enough that the vows serve a dual purpose," he said, "but their original intent was for nuptials."

"So, if what you're saying is true," I said seriously, "then I can't marry Bressen because he's already married to Aidan?"

Phaedrus's mouth fell open, and he started to shake his head in panic. "No, that's not at all-"

"I'm kidding," I said, and Phaedrus let out a relieved sigh.

"What do you think?" he asked. "Do you understand love now?"

"So everyone has a soul mate, and you think Bressen is mine?"

He shook his head. "Not quite. A soulmate has often implied two independent souls that belong together, souls that find each other and bind themselves to create something new. The origin of love story describes a single soul that's been sundered. It's one soul that can only be fully whole again when it finds its other half, and the two halves heal by putting themselves back together. What I'm asking is if you think Lord Bressen is your other half. Is he the one you feel whole with? Are the two of you more complete with each other than without?"

I was quiet for a moment, but I had my answer well before Phaedrus finished speaking. Even before Bressen and I had met in person, we'd been drawn to each other. We'd appeared in each other's dreams a week before ever setting eyes on each other, and from the moment we'd met, our bodies had gravitated together, as if drawn like magnets.

I thought back to those first few weeks at the Citadel where I'd often felt myself leaning toward Bressen when he was close by. Several times we'd found ourselves alone together and seconds later our bodies had suddenly been touching. I'd thought at the time that Bressen was simply well-practiced at seduction, but if I was honest with myself, it hadn't been entirely his fault we always ended up pressed together. I'd been just as guilty about closing the distance between us as he had.

I was attracted to Samhail, but he didn't pull me toward him the way Bressen did. Bressen and I were indeed two halves that only felt whole when we were together, and I suddenly wondered how we'd managed to stay away from each other so long these last few weeks. I could already feel my body pulling me back toward him.

It wasn't just our bodies, though. The morning after the Harmilan I'd confronted Bressen about how he was always reading my mind, and he'd been surprised to learn I hadn't been letting him in on purpose. He confessed that it felt like my mind was constantly calling to him. He said he'd never experienced anything like it before.

Ridiculous as it sounded, the myth about eight-limbed bodies with two heads nevertheless explained the pull Bressen and I seemed to feel – mind, body, and soul – when we were near each other.

A smile tugged at my lips as I imagined me and Bressen stuck together at the navel as one being. He was much taller than I was, and I saw him walking around while my feet dangled in the air, never quite touching the ground. I had to press my lips together to keep from laughing, but then an ache formed in my stomach.

"Yes, he is," I said to Phaedrus. "Bressen is my other half."

"Are you ready to go back then?" he asked quietly.

"I am," I said, standing up from the chair, "but I have a favor to ask."

"Anything, my lady," Phaedrus said, standing as well.

"Come with me to Solandis. I'd like you to perform the marriage ceremony for us."

Phaedrus's mouth fell open. "My lady, I couldn't…that is, it would be an honor, but don't you already have someone?"

"I'm sure we do, but I'd rather have you perform the ceremony."

"I…I don't have my ceremonial robes," he said weakly, as if offering me an opportunity to withdraw my request.

"Then it's lucky you know how to call portals and can retrieve them from your quarters in all haste," I said.

Phaedrus straightened. "Of course, my lady. I'll be right back."

He quickly drew a portal and stepped through it the second it opened. A minute later he was back with a fine set of robes draped over his arm.

"There might be some…awkwardness when we get back," I warned as he closed his portal. "I may have forgotten to tell anyone I was leaving."

He paused. "Understood," he said finally, but he looked as though he'd rather do anything than face the panicked and angry Bressen we both knew must be waiting back in Solandis. In truth, I wasn't looking forward to facing that Bressen either, but I took a deep breath and drew a circle in the air to call a portal back to Solandis.

Bressen was the first thing I saw when our room appeared again through the portal. He swung around when it opened and his mind once again sensed mine. I'd been too far away before.

His face was paler than I'd seen in a long time, and I swore I saw the flash of embers in his eyes, followed by relief.

My smile was apologetic as Phaedrus and I stepped through the portal.

"I'm sorry," I said as I locked eyes with Bressen. "I needed to pick up one more wedding guest."

# Chapter 30

There were several others in the room when Phaedrus and I entered. Samhail stood off to one side with his wings out, and I knew he must have been out searching the grounds for me. Raina, Leeda, Aramis, Jaylan, and Axenus were there as well.

I moved aside so Phaedrus could step hesitantly toward Bressen. The priest dipped into a deep bow but didn't say a word.

"I hope it's alright if Phaedrus performs the ceremony," I said to Bressen. His eyes hadn't left me since I'd entered, and I wasn't sure if the tension in his posture meant he wanted to embrace me or throttle me.

Bressen's throat bobbed once as he swallowed and then nodded, acknowledging my request. No one in the room moved, and I decided that the silence I'd encountered in the Soundless Woods months ago with Samhail was a cacophony compared to this. This was truly a silence so profound it could drive one mad.

"I need a word alone with Bressen please," I said to the others.

There was a short pause before Samhail moved wordlessly toward the door. Everyone else fell in after him, including Phaedrus, who couldn't seem to get out of the room fast enough.

I closed the portal behind me and waited for the last person to exit before walking carefully toward Bressen. He didn't move, and I stopped a foot or two in front of him. His turquoise eyes bore into me, and I still couldn't tell whether it was fear, rage, or something else that had control of him right now. If he was furious with me, he deserved to be, and I'd let him do or say whatever he needed to.

"I'm sorry if I frightened you," I said, needing to break the silence. "I didn't mean to hurt you."

Bressen just looked at me. I reached up a hand to touch his face but stopped short. I was afraid he might push me away if I tried to touch him.

"I...I know I haven't handled everything that's happened very well," I said. "I was just overwhelmed all of a sudden, and I needed to be alone for a few minutes. I always intended to come back."

Still Bressen didn't move.

"Please say something," I whispered. "Yell at me if you need to-"

My plea was cut off when Bressen reached out and dragged me against him to pull me into a crushing embrace. He buried his face in the hair near my temple, and I heard the raggedness of his breathing in my ear. I brought my own arms up to wrap around his waist and leaned into him as closely as I could, infinitely relieved he hadn't pushed me away.

"I've never been so scared in my life when we couldn't find you," he whispered. "Not even last night."

My heart twisted in my chest to remember that this was the second time in less than a day I'd disappeared on him with no warning, and I resolved to never, ever do it again. "I'm sorry," was all I could say.

"I couldn't connect to your mind. We didn't know if you'd run away or been taken," Bressen went on. He set me away from him to look me over as if to be sure I was alright.

"Taken?" I asked. "Who would have taken me?"

Bressen shook his head. "It doesn't matter. You're safe."

He cupped my face in his hands, and I saw the desperation still in his eyes, the look that said he wasn't quite ready to believe yet that I was back.

I lifted my face up to his and brought my own hand to his cheek. He took the offering and lowered his mouth to mine to kiss me urgently, still holding my face captured between his palms. Finally, he pulled back and rested his forehead against mine.

"Cyra, you don't have to marry me if you don't want to. I'll…I'll find a way to be okay with that. I'll…I can…"

His voice cracked, and he trailed off. I looked up and was shocked to see tears streaming down his face.

I shook my head violently. "No! I do want to marry you!" I assured him. "I've never been more certain of that than I am right now. I don't know what was wrong with me before, but I've cleared my head, and I'm ready to get married. I'm so sorry I made you worry."

"Why did you go to the Priory?" he asked as his hands snaked around my body again, holding me tight.

"I don't know. I just opened a portal and that's what was on the other side. I'm glad that's where it took me, though. Phaedrus found me, and he helped me put a few things into perspective."

"Then I owe Phaedrus my undying gratitude. Is that why you brought him back here?"

I nodded. "It felt like the right thing to do."

"You seem to allow anyone but me to help you lately," Bressen said sadly, and my heart broke all over again. "At some point in the future, I hope you'll want to come to me for help."

"Not in the future. Right now," I said emphatically. "I don't plan on coming to anyone else but you from here on out."

I saw the question in his mind and shook my head. "Not even Samhail. And while we're on it, you are the only man I want in my bed from now on as well. I don't want you to be generous about sharing me anymore. I want you to be selfish and possessive and to growl at other men if they even look at me too long," I insisted, the urgency in my voice growing with every word.

Bressen blinked at me. "You want me to growl at other men to keep them away from you?" The hint of a smile finally started to curl his lips.

"Or snarl if you prefer."

"Exactly what did Phaedrus say to you?" he asked incredulously.

"Have you ever heard the myth of the origin of love, about how we all used to have two heads, four arms, and four legs until we were all cut in half because the Trinity was angry at us?" I asked.

The shock on Bressen's face said this was the first he'd heard of it.

"Phaedrus can explain it sometime," I said. "For now, the only thing you need to know is that you're my other half, and I plan to spend the whole night trying to stick us back together."

Bressen's brows furrowed as he tried to figure out what in the three hells I was talking about, but I just reached up and kissed him. He didn't need any more urging than that, and then our mouths were moving hungrily against each other as we tried to press our bodies as close as we could, our hands moving over each other. I smiled against Bressen's lips as I couldn't help remembering the myth.

"Why are you smiling?" he asked.

"Because I love you," I said. "Are you ready to get married? We're about to be late for our own wedding."

"Let them wait," Bressen said and kissed me again.

I pressed myself up against him as my lips ground into his, and I couldn't help noticing how perfectly our bodies fit together, almost as though they'd been made that way as complimentary pieces.

At least, that's what I convinced myself. Even if our bodies didn't fit together perfectly, I knew that our minds and souls…our *soul* did.

I felt Bressen's hard length against my stomach and looked up at him. "That might delay us a little more than we can afford."

Bressen opened his mouth, presumably to tell me he didn't care, but there was a knock at the door, and it swung open before we could answer.

Bressen looked like he was about to begin practicing his growling, but he stopped when we saw who entered.

"I was told to let you know that it's time," Brix said hesitantly from where he stood half in the door.

Just outside, I saw that everyone hadn't gone far. I didn't know when Brix had joined the group, but they'd apparently sent him in as the sacrificial lamb to gauge the situation.

"Brix," I said, not daring to believe he was actually here.

Bressen gently removed my arms from around him in tacit urging for me to go to my brother, and I crossed quickly to him. Brix stepped further into the room, but I pulled up short just as I reached him.

"I'm sorry," Brix said. "I shouldn't have blamed you for what happened to the vineyard. It wasn't your fault. I was angry, but it was wrong of me to take that out on you. Can you forgive me?"

I pulled Brix into a hug the second he finished speaking, and he wrapped his long arms around me tightly.

"I'm sorry," he repeated.

"You're forgiven," I said as tears rolled freely down my cheeks.

Raina and Leeda would have their work cut out for them to fix my makeup before I'd be presentable again, but I didn't care. Brix was here.

As if summoned by my thoughts, Raina's voice rang out from the doorway. "Now that we have everyone we need for this wedding, can we get on with it?"

Bressen came toward us, having taken the opportunity while I was with Brix to fix the problem in his pants.

"My makeup may need a little fixing first," I told Raina.

She grimaced. "Maybe just a little..."

Twenty minutes later, Jaylan's hand was warm in mine as we stood at the end of the aisle waiting to begin the ceremony. Several yards away, Bressen waited under an arch that dripped heavily with pale lavender clusters of wisteria and deep purple clematis flowers while waves sprawled over the white sand on the beach behind him. Phaedrus was to his right directly under the arch while Samhail stood just behind him to his left, wearing what appeared to be a new black jacket. Raina waited ahead of me, ready to head down the aisle first while Brix, Aramis, Axenus, Calanthe, Aidan, Jasper, and Maziren stood to either side before the arch.

The ceremony would be small, although nobles from prominent families around Solandis and a few other areas close to Hiraeth had been invited to the reception.

Jaylan patted my hand, which rested on his arm, and I smiled up at him. There'd never been any doubt in my mind that he'd be the one to walk me down the aisle today. I may have recently reunited with Aramis, but Jaylan had helped raise me, even before our parents died, and I couldn't imagine being here with anyone else. I knew it pained Aramis to cede this fatherly right to Jaylan, but he'd understood when I told him.

Bressen had enlisted a priest from the temple in Solandis who could create atmospheric bubbles to form one here on the beach for the ceremony, so despite the winter wind that whipped all around us not far away, the air inside the bubble was calm and warm. The priest was an elemental, and the bubble was just a combination of various air magics that first formed a shield and then tempered the air inside. I made a note to have him teach me how to do it all later.

I'd felt a little bad when I learned the man was also the priest who was supposed to perform our ceremony before I'd recruited Phaedrus, but he seemed more than happy to defer to my choice. The priest didn't enjoy attention, he'd said, so he was relieved to have Phaedrus step in, especially given the added pressure of marrying the Lord of Hiraeth.

Calanthe had applied her magic to the flowers in my bouquet and Raina's, and what we held now were masterpieces of floral arrangements.

Calanthe was also responsible for all the flora that decorated the bubble, from the wisteria and clematis covering the arch, to the jasmine twining around the decorative columns circling the area that gave the bubble its heavenly scent.

My stomach fluttered as the delicate strains of a harp floated through the air, and Raina began her slow promenade down the aisle. She took her place on the other side of Phaedrus before the harpist lifted the music to something more joyous, and the steady pressure of Jaylan's arm invited me to move forward.

I looked up and caught Bressen's eyes. He was smiling, but I could feel his lingering fear that something would happen to keep the marriage from taking place. He wouldn't relax until the vows were spoken and the ceremony was over, and I felt a stab of guilt at the part I'd played in his worry. It was his wedding day too after all, and I'd tarnished it by all but ensuring that his fear would be the only thing he'd remember about it. I vowed with each step I took toward the arch that I'd make it up to him later, that his wedding day would pale in comparison to his wedding night.

*I love you.* I sent the words down the aisle ahead of me into Bressen's mind, and the tense edge of his expression softened.

*I love you, too.* His answer came back a second later, full of relief. *You look…I can't even express how beautiful, how perfect you look.*

*You saw me in this dress earlier*, I reminded him.

*Yes, but I'm just now really, truly seeing you. Please tell me this isn't a dream, because if it is, I refuse to wake up.*

We were there at the arch before I could answer, and I was standing before my husband-to-be. Bressen had always been a stunning man, but he looked absolutely resplendent in a form-fitting jacket that shimmered ever-so-slightly in the sun from the delicate silver fibers woven into it. A turquoise vest the color of his eyes rounded out his ensemble, and I bit my lip at how incredible he looked.

Bressen shook Jaylan's hand before Jaylan slipped my own hand into Bressen's. The relief I felt in the strength of Bressen's fingers when they twined in mine nearly made me lightheaded as we turned to Phaedrus.

*Will you be doing the ceremony in the common tongue or in ancient Arystrian?* I asked Phaedrus mentally as he was about to speak, and he choked on whatever he'd been about to say. He coughed several times before getting himself under control and clearing his throat.

"My apologies," Phaedrus croaked to the crowd. "Just a small tickle in my throat."

I smiled as Phaedrus's dark skin took on a reddish glow at his lie. I looked at Bressen, and he quirked a brow at me, obviously aware I was the cause of Phaedrus's sudden fluster.

*I'll explain later*, I said into Bressen's mind.

Phaedrus began to speak in the common tongue, and this time he didn't even blink when I sent the word *"Coward"* lightly into his head.

In truth, I didn't even hear the words of the ceremony. From the moment it started, I lost myself in Bressen's gaze. I'd always loved his eyes, and I couldn't seem to tear myself from them. I wanted to fall into them like pools of water.

Logically it was impossible that Bressen and I had started out as a singular being that had been cleaved in two. He was almost a century older than me, so we hadn't been created at the same time, but the logistics of the myth mattered little to me. I knew in my heart we were like the Souls of the Moon who were only whole when we were together. The first time we'd seen each other in our dream had been by the light of the full moon, and that was all I needed in order to make the myth true in my mind.

Phaedrus pronounced us husband and wife, and Bressen's arms slid around me to pull me against him as his lips claimed mine in a kiss so full of heat that I was sure our guests must be scandalized.

Neither of us cared. I felt our minds connect, not with words, but with the understanding that we'd never be apart from each other again, even if we were separated by distance. In that instant, despite being two bodies, I knew we were one mind and one soul.

Our lips parted, and I found Bressen's eyes again before my vision went a blinding white. My body seized up against his as the world tilted sideways, and my last thought before my mind was no longer my own was that the gods must be punishing me by splitting me in half once again.

# Chapter 31

I had no sense of how much time had passed when my eyes fluttered open again after the barrage of images finally stopped charging through my head. I could hear the terror in Bressen's voice as he called my name, and I realized I was on the ground gripped in his arms. My vision was still too bright to see much, but I could make out enough to tell that several people were bent over close around me.

"What's wrong with her?" Bressen demanded.

A blurry form in front of me shook its head before Aramis's voice floated to my ears. "Nothing as far as I can tell. I'm not detecting anything physically or mentally wrong with her."

"Check her again," Bressen snarled. "A person doesn't go rigid like that and pass out when there's nothing wrong with them."

"It…It looked like she was having a vision," Phaedrus offered, seeming hesitant to draw Bressen's attention.

"It *was* a vision," I confirmed weakly as the world rematerialized.

"Cyra!" Bressen crushed me against his chest. "Thank the Protector you're okay!"

Okay was a relative term. I was awake and alive, but my head was pounding, and nausea churned violently in my stomach as the images from the vision flashed through my head again.

"I'm going to…," I started to say as bile rose in my throat.

I just barely managed to push away from Bressen and turn myself over before I heaved the meager contents of my stomach onto the sand. Bressen's hand ran over my back in slow circles as I tried to spit out the acrid taste in my mouth.

"I'm taking Cyra back to the house," Bressen said. "The rest of you should go to the reception. Tell them Cyra isn't feeling well."

"No," I said reaching back to grab his jacket. "I can go. I'm fine."

I still felt awful, but this was my wedding day, and I'd already spent the first half of it in distress. I wasn't about to miss the second half of it.

"You're not fine," Bressen said. "You need to rest."

"

"My lord," Phaedrus said carefully. "If Lady Cyra had a vision, she should tell it to someone right away before the details are lost. It could be important."

"I don't care about-," Bressen started to yell at Phaedrus, but I stopped him with a gentle hand to his cheek.

"Let me tell it before I lose it," I said.

Bressen hesitated but then slipped his arms under me and lifted me up. "Fine. We'll hear the vision, but I'm still bringing you back to the house. We'll join the reception later if we can. Phaedrus, can you summon a portal to my chambers?"

Phaedrus nodded. "Of course, my lord."

"Phaedrus, Samhail, and Axenus, come with me," Bressen said as he stepped toward the portal that now glowed with a blue outline in the air.

"Bressen," Aidan said, stepping toward us. "With all due respect to you and Cyra, this feels like something I should be privy to as well."

Bressen's jaw tightened, but he nodded. "Fine."

"Then I should come too," Raina argued. "To represent Polaris."

"No," Bressen said flatly, and Raina blinked at him.

"Bressen, let-," I started to say, but he cut me off.

"Aidan is a Triumvirate lord. He has a right to hear what you saw if it affects the realm, but Raina isn't part of the Triumvirate. If the High Council gets off their asses and makes her part of it, then she's welcome to join discussions like this in the future, but not until then."

I frowned at Bressen, but I knew why he'd drawn this line in the sand, almost literally. If the High Council wasn't given an incentive to replace Ursan, they'd put it off indefinitely. The council could rule Polaris if they wanted, but they couldn't force their way into the Triumvirate. In the end, nudging their hand might actually benefit Raina, so I let the matter drop and gave my friend an apologetic look.

She frowned, but her eyes softened again as I caught her gaze. I knew her desire to come had more to do with worry for me than with anything having to do with the Triumvirate. She'd only used that as a bargaining chip to go with us.

"I'm okay," I told her. "We'll be back soon."

Raina didn't have time to answer before Bressen turned and strode through the portal into the rooms I shared with him. He made straight for the bed to lay me down, but I stopped him.

"No," I murmured against his chest. "Let me sit."

"You should lay down," he argued.

"Please, I want to sit."

Bressen sighed and changed course to head toward the chairs next to the fireplace instead. He set me down gently in one of them and knelt beside me.

"How are you feeling?" he asked.

"Better," I lied.

"Liar," he said, half amused, half annoyed.

There were four chairs near the fireplace, and Aidan and Axenus took the two across from me and Bressen. Samhail stood behind them with his arms crossed over his chest, eyeing me as if I might suddenly sprout wings and fly away. Bressen stood up from where he knelt, then eased himself down into the chair next to me.

"Phaedrus, you've worked with the seers at the Priory before," Bressen said to him. "Can you lead Cyra through what she saw?"

Phaedrus had been hanging back, but he pulled a smaller chair from the game table over so he could sit down next to me.

I'd known there was a possibility that I'd syphoned this power from Jemma, a priestess at the Priory, before she'd been murdered, but this was my first confirmation.

"Cyra," Phaedrus said soothingly, "I want you to take a deep breath and then tell us the first thing you remember seeing."

I tried to think. There'd been so many images in my head so quickly, I could hardly make sense of them all. Which one had been first? I wasn't sure why it mattered, but I trusted that Phaedrus knew what he was doing.

"A man without a face," I said after a few seconds, wincing as the image swam into my mind. "I'm fairly sure it was a man without a face."

"Without a face how?" Phaedrus asked. "Was his face in shadow? Was it unfocused?"

I shook my head. "No, his face was gone. As if it had somehow been …destroyed."

All the men shifted around me, and Axenus voiced the thought they must have had. "That's not an auspicious start."

Phaedrus shook his head. "No, an image like that doesn't usually bode well for the rest of the vision. What came next?" he asked.

"Another man," I said, "but I can see his face this time. He looks gaunt. His eyes are sunken. He's young, maybe around thirty with dark blonde hair."

Bressen sat forward in his chair suddenly. "Let me see."

It was more of an order than a request, but there was something in the urgency of his voice that made me obey. I sent the image of the man into his mind, and he swore violently.

"Sandrian," he said. "She saw Sandrian."

Samhail let out a growl and began to pace.

"Sandrian?" I asked. "Isn't he in Revenmyer?"

Bressen shook his head. "He escaped a few months ago. Samhail and I were trying to track him down before the coup."

"Why didn't you tell me?" I asked.

I looked at the others. Phaedrus and Axenus both looked as shocked as I did, but Aidan's face was passive. Bressen must have filled him in on Sandrian's escape after Aidan was sworn into the Triumvirate, and I suddenly remembered a conversation between Bressen and Samhail a week or so after I'd first arrived at the Citadel.

*"And the other thing we discussed earlier this morning? Were you able to confirm...?"*

*"Gone."*

*"How?"*

*"I don't know yet. They found the issue and took care of it, but we're not sure how it happened in the first place."*

*"And you're certain he's gone?"*

*"Yes."*

I'd learned later from a guard Raina knew that a prisoner had escaped from Revenmyer, but I had no idea they'd been talking about Sandrian.

"Nemesis damn me," Samhail said. "Could the faceless man be Morland, then?"

"Possibly," Bressen said, "but he's been dead for twenty-five years. Why would he appear in Cyra's vision?"

"Because he's not dead," I said. I didn't know what made me say it or how I knew it, but I could feel the truth in the words as I said them.

Samhail stopped dead, and Bressen's back snapped straight.

"Impossible," Samhail growled. "I put a spear through his head."

"Cyra, why do you think he's alive?" Bressen asked me.

He was trying to keep his voice gentle, but the underlying urgency of his question made his tone harsher than I'm sure he wanted. He laid his hand over mine on the arm of the chair to soften the ask.

"I don't know," I said. "I don't remember seeing anything specific in the vision. I just know that when you said he was dead, something inside me said that wasn't true. Morland is somehow alive."

"I stood over his body myself. He was dead," Samhail said, and I flinched at the severity in his voice. He'd never used such a tone with me.

"I don't know what to tell you," I said defensively. "He's alive. I don't know how I know, but I know."

"Let's hear the rest of the vision," Phaedrus suggested before Samhail could argue more. "Maybe something else Cyra saw will explain things."

Samhail just looked away and began pacing again. Phaedrus nodded at me to go on, and I searched my mind for the next image.

"Stalwart," I said as the word rose from the depths of my mind.

"Stalwart?" Bressen asked. "What's stalwart?"

I furrowed my brow. "It was the word. I saw it as if it was painted on something, like a piece of wood."

"That sounds familiar for some reason," Axenus said, "but I can't figure out why."

"Wait, it wasn't just stalwart," I said as the vision seemed to clarify in my mind. "It was…'The Stalwart.' I can see the words, but it's as if they're murky somehow. Blurry, like they're underwater."

"It sounds almost like the name of a ship," Aidan offered.

"Yes!" Axenus said, his face blooming with recognition. "That's exactly what it is. Or more accurately, it's a shipwreck far into the Carkinos Ocean. I've never seen it myself, but I know others who claim they have."

"Why would Cyra have a vision about a shipwreck?" Aidan asked.

Axenus surveyed the rest of us. "None of you recognize the name?"

"Why don't you enlighten us?" Bressen said to him, failing to contain his impatience.

"*The Stalwart* was the ship carrying Praya of Gonderil before it went down in the middle of the ocean during a storm," Axenus explained.

Only Phaedrus gasped as the rest of us continued to look perplexed.

"Keep going," Bressen prompted when we didn't catch his meaning.

Axenus sighed. "Are Phaedrus and I the only ones who study history?" he asked, but he held up his hands in surrender and went on when Bressen and Samhail both growled at him. "Praya was the last known syphon on the continent. She was supposedly killed when her ship, *The Stalwart*, went down during a storm as she was fleeing for her life."

Everyone had gone still. Even Samhail had stopped his pacing again.

"Supposedly killed?" Aidan prompted.

"The ship went down far out in rough waters, so it was assumed she died," Axenus said, "but Praya was the most powerful being on the continent at the time. She undoubtedly had prodigious elemental powers, and some have theorized that she herself caused the storm and staged her own death to finally be free of the persistent attempts to kill her."

"And people have claimed to see this ship?" Bressen asked.

"Well, merpeople," Axenus clarified, "but yes. I know at least one merman who told me he'd seen the carcass of the ship on the floor of the ocean. Whether that's what he actually saw I can't be sure, but it's what he believes he saw."

"But that shipwreck would have been four hundred years ago," Aidan said. "Surely the ship would be rotted into nothing by now."

"If Praya was as powerful as she was said to be, it's possible she had protections on the ship that might have preserved it," Axenus argued.

"But what does it mean?" Samhail asked. "Why is Cyra having visions about it?" He clamped his large hands onto the backs of Aidan and Axenus's chairs and leaned in. Both men seemed a bit uneasy to have him looming over them in his current mood.

"It can't be a coincidence that Cyra is the first syphon in four hundred years, and she had a vision about the last known syphon," Aidan said.

"She didn't have a vision about Praya. She had a vision about her ship," Samhail snapped at Aidan, then added, "my lord."

I'd never seen Samhail quite this rattled before. He clearly hadn't recovered yet from my news that Morland, the man who'd taken over his mind twenty-five years ago, was still alive. I knew how much those memories haunted Samhail, and I didn't blame him.

"Did you see why the ship is significant?" Phaedrus asked me.

I tried to focus on the vague feelings and impressions I'd gleaned when I'd been inside the vision. "It feels as though Sandrian and Morland are looking for something," I said, somehow knowing I was right. "They want something that was on the ship."

"Like what?" Bressen asked.

I shook my head. "That I don't know."

Bressen looked at Axenus. "You're our expert on Praya. What could have been on that ship that Sandrian and Morland might want?"

Axenus blew a hard breath out through his mouth. "It could be any number of things. Praya both collected and created a number of powerful magical items during her time, which were then rumored to have gone down on the ship with her. Sandrian and Morland may even be looking for her bones in the hope that some of her power is still infused in them."

My eyes rounded in horror. I had no idea what anyone might do with Praya's bones, but I shuddered to think that hundreds of years from now, someone might try to dig up my own bones to see if they still contained any of my power.

"What kind of magical items?" Aidan asked.

"Well, there were rumors of a sword that inflicted unhealable wounds, or a spyglass that could see across continents," Axenus said, "but Praya's necklace was probably the most infamous of the items."

"Necklace," I said. The word sparked an image in my mind, and everyone looked at me.

"Does that mean something to you?" Phaedrus asked.

"Maybe," I said. I turned to Axenus. "Did the necklace look like a collar? Gold with five large jewels set into it? I remember seeing something like that in my vision."

"I'm not sure," he said. "I've never heard a description of it."

"What was this necklace supposed to do?" Bressen asked.

Axenus looked uneasy. "It…the necklace was a prison."

"How can the necklace be a prison?" Samhail asked.

"According to legend," Axenus said, "the kings and queens around the Arystrian continent feared Praya had ambitions to take over their lands and rule all of Arystria herself. They pooled their resources and hired three of the most powerful and dangerous perimortal warriors and assassins of the time to kill her. Somehow Praya knew they were coming, so when the warriors attacked, she was able to overpower them. It was said she trapped them inside the jewels of her necklace and wore them around her neck every day thereafter as a reminder to them and the rest of her enemies how powerless they were to stop her."

"Gods above," I whispered.

"She would've been wearing this necklace when her ship went down?" Bressen asked.

Axenus shrugged. "Presumably."

"Why would Sandrian and Morland want this necklace?" Aidan asked. "What could they possibly hope to do with it?"

Bressen and Samhail exchanged dark looks before Bressen spoke.

"Sandrian was imprisoned in Revenmyer for twenty-five years before he escaped," he said. "One possibility is that he wants revenge on me for that and hopes to trap me in the necklace."

I gasped. "No! He couldn't do that, could he?" I looked at Axenus, waiting for him to deny the possibility.

"I'm not sure," he answered. "There's no clear information on how the necklace might work. For that matter, the necklace itself is only a legend. No one is certain it really existed."

"Did you get any sense of this sword Axenus mentioned?" Bressen asked me. "Sandrian would be interested in a powerful weapon like that."

I thought for a moment but shook my head. "I don't remember a sword in the vision."

"I'm not sure the sword still exists," Axenus said. "The stories say Praya's lover cut himself with it one day while sharpening the blade. Not even Praya's own magic was able to heal him, and he bled to death. In her grief, Praya supposedly had the sword destroyed."

I looked at Bressen, trying not to imagine what it would be like to lose him. I was certain if something ever happened to him, I would wreck destruction on the world like no one had ever seen.

As if sensing my roiling thoughts, Bressen turned to me. A flicker of understanding crossed his face, and I felt the comfort and love he sent into my mind to try and soothe me. His arm twitched, and I knew he was aching to pull me into his lap.

"No sword then," Bressen said. "Is there anything else?"

Twin rings flashed in my mind suddenly. I'd nearly dismissed them, assuming at first they were simply the wedding bands Bressen and I had just exchanged, but something made me pull the images back again, and I frowned. The rings in my head were plain yellow gold circlets, whereas the wedding bands Bressen and I now wore looked nothing like that. Bressen's ring was a circle of black gold, while my white gold band was set with small diamonds all the way around it.

"I see two rings," I said. "Two simple gold bands, identical as far as I can tell, but there's something significant about them."

"More magical items?" Bressen asked, looking to Axenus.

"Possibly, but I don't remember any stories about rings related to Praya, so I couldn't tell you what they do, if anything."

"Jewelry and weapons," Samhail said wryly. "No one ever creates a magical spoon or a magical garden trowel. It's always jewelry or weapons."

"It's for practical purposes," Phaedrus offered helpfully. "Jewelry and weapons are easily carried on one's person without arousing suspicion. It's harder to explain carrying around a garden trowel."

The look Samhail gave the priest wasn't menacing, but Phaedrus still bowed his head and shrank back a bit under the gargoyle's potent gaze.

I closed my eyes, trying hard to think if there was anything else. I jolted suddenly in my seat as the last few images of my vision flashed through my mind again.

"Cyra?" Bressen asked. His warm hand rested over mine as I tried to simultaneously retain yet banish the images I'd just seen.

"I was surrounded by darkness, but I could see black eyes," I said, my voice trembling slightly. "Something was rising up from a dense pool of darkness. Then there was a storm, a raging storm." I furrowed my brows. "And then the Triumvirate seats…I think. They looked like the ones in Jemma's old vision, except there were two figures in them instead of one."

"You saw the seats from Jemma's original vision?" Bressen asked.

I nodded. "When Jemma touched me that day Ursan and Jerram brought me to the Priory, I saw everything she did until she cut the vision off early. I saw the three chairs with one figure in them, although to be honest, they didn't really look like the Triumvirate seats in the Great Chamber. In any case, I just saw the three chairs again, but now there are two figures in them."

Aidan and Bressen exchanged glances.

"There are two of us now," Aidan said. "I suppose that's reassuring."

Bressen's gaze met mine, and dread suddenly gathered in my stomach. There'd been something else in the vision, something horrible and chilling, but my mind seemed unwilling to let me remember what it was.

"Something else?" Bressen asked, canting his head at me in question.

"There is, but I can't recall it. My mind seems to be blocking it."

"Maybe I can see it?" Bressen suggested.

He wanted to read my thoughts, but something in my head balked at the idea of giving him such deep access so soon after he'd broken into my mind in Fernweh. There was something important about this last part of the vision, though, so if there was any chance he could help me uncover it, I had to take it.

I nodded and tried to relax as I felt his presence in my mind. Anxiety vibrated in my chest, but I tamped it down, willing my hands not to shake.

I exhaled in relief as Bressen withdrew moments later.

"There's something there, but I can't seem to access it either," he said. "With enough time, I could probably delve deeper and pull it out of your mind, but I get the sense you're not ready for that yet."

I gave him an apologetic look, and he squeezed my hand to let me know it was fine.

"So what do we do with all this information?" Aidan asked.

"If Sandrian and Morland are looking for this collar and these rings, we need to get to them first," Bressen said. He turned to Axenus. "Do you think you can find out if there's any truth to the stories you've heard about where *The Stalwart* went down? If the wreckage is still there, we need to search for it."

"And how would we do that?" Aidan asked.

Bressen looked at Axenus, who nodded.

"Yes." Axenus answered Bressen's unspoken question. "I can go down and look."

Aidan eyed Axenus as if just now noticing the slight iridescent sheen to his skin.

"I can go with, Axenus," I said.

Five pairs of eyes shot to me before Axenus's voice split the silence.

"No, it's too dangerous," he said.

I raised a brow, and he added, "It's too dangerous, *my lady*."

"More to the point," Aidan said, "how would you breathe?"

Bressen too seemed interested in the answer, and the expression on Axenus's face told me he might have forgotten to mention this potential ability to Bressen.

"It's not entirely certain I can breathe underwater," I said carefully, "but in theory, I can continually replenish the air in my lungs using my elemental powers. I think I did it once before while taking a bath. Axenus and I just haven't had a chance to test it out yet."

Bressen shook his head. "Regardless, I agree with Axenus that it's too dangerous for you to go down with him."

"Your opposition is noted," I said smoothly, "and I'll take that into consideration when I decide whether or not to accompany him down to the ship, if we find it."

I locked eyes with Bressen, daring him to object, and I felt everyone watching as he and I stared each other down. I knew he was desperate to keep me out of harm's way, but he'd promised me when he proposed that I'd be his partner in all things. He couldn't just forbid me from going down to the shipwreck, but I'd just challenged his authority in front of Samhail, Axenus, a priest of the Priory, and another Triumvirate lord. What he did now would affect not only how they saw him, but his relationship with me. I regretted backing him into a corner, but it seemed inevitable that his promise to me would be tested like this.

Bressen exhaled slowly and nodded. "If you and Axenus determine that you can in fact breathe underwater," he said tightly, "you should also consider whether or not your abilities will also allow you to make such a deep dive under unfamiliar conditions."

*And I will lock you up later on to keep you from going if I think you're being foolhardy in your decision*, he added into my mind. *I'll gladly let you hate me if it keeps you safe.*

I ignored his words and turned to Axenus. "I have every confidence Axenus can prepare me to go with him."

Axenus's head jerked toward Bressen, and he opened his mouth, but nothing came out.

"Axenus will be leaving tomorrow to see if he can find the location of *The Stalwart*. He won't be around to help train you," Bressen said lightly, and I knew he was suppressing the urge to smile in victory.

"I'll just have to practice on my own until he returns then," I said.

The slightest furrowing of Bressen's brow was his only reaction as the silence in the room stretched on.

"There's nothing more we need to decide now," Bressen said finally. He turned his attention to the other men in the room. "Unless Cyra can remember anything else about the vision, you should all return to the reception. My wife and I will follow shortly."

Recognizing the dismissal, Axenus, Phaedrus, and even Aidan all rose from their chairs. Samhail paused where he stood, but the slightest nod of Bressen's head had him turning with the others to leave. Phaedrus created a portal, and the four men stepped through it into the reception before Phaedrus closed it behind them, leaving Bressen and I alone.

"I could have sworn our marriage vows contained a provision about the wife obeying her husband in all things," Bressen said wryly.

"I made sure Phaedrus left that part out," I said.

He heaved a beleaguered sigh. "Why do you want to go down?"

"Because it's not right to make Axenus go by himself, and I'm the only one who can possibly go with him."

"We don't know for sure you can breathe underwater yet, and even if you can, going down that far will be extremely dangerous. You might not be able to withstand the pressure of the water for one."

"That's a chance I'll have to take," I said. "This isn't Axenus's fight. We can't ask him to put himself at risk if we're not willing to take the same risks ourselves."

He sighed again. "True. I just wish anyone else but you could go."

I stood up from my own chair and eased myself down onto Bressen's lap. I curled up against him as he wrapped his arms around me and leaned back in the chair. My head tucked into the crook of his neck, and I inhaled his musk and hot cinnamon scent.

"I can't lose you," he said softly. "I spent that half hour you were gone today trying to convince myself I could let you go if you decided you didn't want to marry me, but this is different. If something ever happened to you..."

"I'm so sorry I made you think I didn't want to marry you," I said. "I don't think I've ever wanted anything more than just to be with you."

Bressen's arms tightened around me, and I nuzzled my head into his shoulder. His lips grazed my forehead, and I lifted my face to his. One of his hands cupped my cheek, and he leaned in to kiss me.

"We should get to the reception," I whispered against his lips.

"Do we have to?" he whispered back.

"There's still plenty of night left. I promise we'll get to everything you want to do."

"I doubt that. There's a lot I want to do with you, and we're already behind schedule." He nuzzled my temple.

"We have the rest of our lives to catch up."

"Fine. We'll go for a couple hours, but I'm going to keep you in bed all day tomorrow, and possibly through next week as a trade-off."

"I'll agree to that," I said with a grin.

Bressen stood up from the chair, taking me with him. He kissed me again before setting me on my feet, and I turned to open a portal.

Heads turned toward us as it opened into the reception tent, and a cheer went up from the guests gathered there. Bressen took my hand, and we stepped through together to meet friends, family, and the nobility of Hiraeth for the first time as husband and wife.

# Chapter 32

*Are you sure you want to do this?* Bressen asked as we stepped into the tent. *We can make a quick circuit and leave if you're not up to this.*

*I'm not missing my wedding reception*, I thought back. *Also, I'm hungry.*

He sighed in my mind. *We have to dance first. It's considered good luck.*

I'd almost forgotten about the dance, but I smiled and took his hand to pull him out into the middle of the floor. We took our positions, but his brow furrowed as his power scraped against my mind shield.

"Cyra, you have your shield up," he said as the music started. "I can't give you the steps if your shield is up."

"No, you can't," I agreed with a grin.

"But…" his voice trailed off and his eyes narrowed even further as understanding dawned on him. "Did you…?"

He couldn't finish the question as the music swelled, and we began to move. Bressen took his first steps, and I followed perfectly along, my feet doing exactly what I needed them to do at exactly the right time. It was just like the other times I'd danced with Bressen where our bodies moved as one, perfectly in sync with each other, except this time I had control of my own movements without any help from him.

Bressen's eyes never left mine as we whirled around the floor, oblivious to everyone else around us. His eyes sparkled with delight as he realized I not only knew the dance, but that I could dance it just as well as him. I'd been a little worried he might be upset at my newfound dancing ability, given how I'd acquired it, but he seemed to love that I'd learned.

As the music faded off, I sunk into a deep curtsy, and the room erupted in applause. Bressen tugged on my hand to pull me up, and then his arms were around me. He lifted me into the air so my feet hovered above the ground, and his lips closed over mine before he let my body slide down his until my feet once again touched the floor.

"Jasper," he said as we stood there, and I blinked in confusion for a moment before I realized what he was saying.

I nodded. "Yes, Jasper's been giving me lessons."

"I'm not sure if I should kiss the man or punch him," Bressen said.

"Just thank him," I said with a smile. "He's been giving up a couple hours of his afternoons for days to help me be ready in time for this."

"Has he been coming to Solandis, or have you been sneaking off to Derridan?" Bressen asked as he took my hand to lead me to the table set up at the head of the tent for us.

"A little of both."

"Does Aidan know?"

"No, so for Jasper's sake, please don't mention it to him."

"Your secret is safe with me," he said as we sat down. "Although I now wish I'd been the one to teach you."

"There are still plenty of dances I need to learn if I'm going to be Lady of Hiraeth," I said. "I'm sure Jasper won't mind getting his afternoons back if you're willing to step in."

"I think I can arrange that," Bressen said. He leaned in to brush a kiss lightly on my lips.

Servants arrived a moment later with the first course of our meal, and I eagerly dug into the prawns in garlic butter on my plate, then washed them down with a sip of white wine.

"It's not safe for my brothers to go back to Fernweh," I said as I swirled the wine in the glass. "Maybe I can convince them to stay here in Hiraeth and work on the new vineyard if the deal ever goes through."

"We'll figure something out," Bressen assured me.

"My lord, my lady."

Our attention was drawn by the appearance of a man who looked to be in his fifties. I didn't recognize him, but his elegant clothes and the fact that he'd been invited at all told me he was likely one of Hiraeth's nobility.

I went rigid as Bressen addressed him.

"Lord Carlyle," Bressen said smoothly. "I was wondering if you were going to join us tonight."

"I wouldn't dream of missing such an important event," Carlyle assured him with a simper. "I just wanted to express my deepest apologies to both you and Lady Cyra in person for the unfortunateness last night. I'm so grateful your ladyship didn't come to any harm."

"You should be grateful indeed," Bressen said. "It would've been a shame if you'd spent tonight in Revenmyer instead of here with us."

Carlyle paled visibly, but I was impressed that he managed not to flinch or even let the smile fall from his face.

"Of course, my lord," he said, his voice no longer quite so steady. "Thank you for your understanding, and please let me know if there's anything I can do to make up for what happened at my club."

"Rest assured, I'll call on you if I need anything," Bressen said.

Carlyle slunk back the way he'd come, but other nobles were making their way toward us now, emboldened by Carlyle's attempt to curry favor with Bressen.

"It wasn't nice to scare him," I chided Bressen gently. "The attack wasn't his fault."

"Carlyle knows I was kidding about Revenmyer," Bressen said, his easy smile drawing in the approaching lords and ladies like the bright colors on a poisonous serpent. "He knows that if anything had actually happened to you last night, he'd be dead already."

My head snapped to Bressen. His face still wore an expression of light cheeriness, but there was no red glow on his skin to suggest an untruth.

"You wouldn't have," I said.

"I would," he insisted. "Any rules of morality I live by are moot where your safety is concerned, so it's lucky for Carlyle you weren't hurt."

Bressen turned to face the next lord who approached, congratulations and well-wishes tumbling from the man's lips well before he reached us. I sighed to see at least twenty more nobles lined up behind him.

"This is going to be a long night, isn't it," I said.

"I told you we should have skipped the reception," he said. His smile never wavered, but he was suddenly wearing his halo glamour.

Thankfully our next course arrived at that point, and I let Bressen handle Hiraeth's nobility as I dug into the herb-crusted boar with wild greens, pistachios, and pomegranate seeds on my plate. I looked up only long enough to nod my greeting to each lord or lady who approached.

Bressen was able to eat a bit as well since the nobles seemed more than happy to do all the talking. He could get at least a few bites in before thanking them for coming and then dismissing them so the next person could step forward, although none dared to get too close to either of us.

By the time dessert arrived, both my energy and my attention was flagging, and I desperately needed to get up and move. I hadn't talked to any friends or family yet, and I wanted to make my rounds.

"Go," Bressen said softly to me. "I'll shoo the rest of them away soon and join you."

I kissed him, then fled before the next noble could claim my attention.

I made straight for the side of the open tent where I'd noticed Samhail standing sentinel the entire time. He stood stone-still with his arms crossed over his muscled chest watching the crowd. The gentle blowing of his long white hair in the breeze off the ocean was the only thing about him I'd seen move all night.

"Stop guarding and go enjoy yourself," I said, drawing up next to him.

He tilted his head to side-eye me. "Do I strike you as the sociable dancing type?" he asked.

I curbed a grin as I pictured Samhail whirling around the dance floor.

"Do gargoyles even have weddings?" I asked, curious now.

"Not like this," he said. "Gargoyles value strength and power, so we're usually mated when one of us claims the Right of Primacy over another."

I frowned. "Right of Primacy?"

"When a gargoyle claims the Right of Primacy, and their potential mate accepts the claim, it binds them to each other much like marriage."

"So claiming the right is like proposing?" I asked.

"More or less," he said. "If the potential mate refuses the claim, they have to defeat the claimant in combat to break the bond."

I blinked at him. "Wait, so if you tried to claim someone by this right, and they didn't want to be bonded to you, they'd have to kill you?"

"Not kill, just defeat," he clarified. "But yes. It almost never happens anymore because the claimant usually makes damn sure their potential mate is willing before they make the claim, but it's not unheard of."

I just stared at him for several long moments before shaking my head. "I really need to learn more about gargoyle culture. It sounds fascinating."

He huffed a laugh. "I think the word you're looking for is disturbing."

I smiled. "You don't have to dance, but go get some dinner at least."

Samhail didn't stop scanning the crowd as he spoke. "I had a big meal earlier. I'm fine."

I put a hand on his arm and waited until he finally looked down at me.

"Nothing is going to happen. Sandrian isn't out on the beach waiting to attack," I said gently.

He didn't respond.

"I'm sorry about Morland," I said. "I hope I'm wrong, but-"

"It's fine," he said. "I handled him once, and I can handle him again. I'm stronger now. More prepared."

A few seconds of silence went out with the ocean tide.

"Are you alright?" I asked finally. "That is…are *we* alright?"

The question shocked him enough that he turned to look at me fully. "Why wouldn't we be alright?" he asked, frowning.

Because I'd met him first, and there'd been a spark. Because we were, or had been, lovers. Because even though we'd decided to end our physical relationship, there was still something unspoken between us.

That's what I wanted to say to him. What I actually said was, "I don't know. I just wanted to be sure. I don't want you pining over me."

I said the last teasingly, and Samhail's lips twitched before he answered me seriously.

"Cyra, nothing makes me happier than to see you and Bressen marry each other. I have no doubt you were meant to be together, and I told you before that I'd never dream of coming between that." He paused. "Are you happy with him?"

I nodded. "Very much so."

"Then I'm happy for you."

I wiped at the moisture gathering in the corners of my eyes, and Samhail rolled his own.

"Now that you're married, hopefully we can stop having these conversations," he said. "I don't handle tears well."

"We'll add it to the list of things you don't handle well," I said, then counted them off on my fingers. "Tears, hugs, apologies, caring…Am I missing anything?"

"You're still a maddening woman," he said, reiterating what he'd told me our first night traveling together from Fernweh months ago, but the hint of a smile curled his lips.

I tugged on his finely embroidered jacket until he leaned down enough for me to kiss his cheek. "I love you," I told him. "Just accept that and don't get uncomfortable about it."

"Yes, my lady," he said, the corners of his mouth curling up even more as he straightened once again to resume his watch over the crowd.

I sighed and headed to where Raina and Calanthe were talking near the table that held the High Council members from Polaris. Raina and Calanthe turned their attention to me as I approached, but members of the High Council cut them off, all of them rising from the table at once to surround me with congratulations and inquiries about my well-being. I spared a few seconds to assure them I was fine before I excused myself and pulled Raina and Calanthe away.

"Cyra, are you alright?" Raina asked as I hugged her and Calanthe.

"I'm fine," I said. "Just a little vertigo-inducing vision."

"What did you see?" Raina asked, and I gave her a brief summary.

"Gods damn me," she said when I'd finished, and I just nodded.

"Why did the vision affect you so much?" she asked. "Didn't you say you'd seen Jemma's vision as she was having it? It doesn't sound like the visions gave Jemma vertigo."

"No, she was fine," I said. "Maybe it was because this was my first or because visions were Jemma's primary power. She was probably used to the effects."

Raina grinned at me. "So you lost your seer virginity?"

I rolled my eyes at her.

"Well, congratulations, in any case," she said. "You look absolutely radiant despite everything that's happened today."

I sobered. "How was Bressen while I was gone?" I asked.

"I've never seen him like that," Raina said softly, as if afraid he might hear. "I've felt his power before, but it was nothing like what happened when we couldn't find you. It was almost like he was pulling the air out of the room. It was hard to breathe. I was sure we'd all just drop dead suddenly if bad news came back."

Calanthe nodded. "Whatever happened when he found you missing, we felt it down on the beach," she added.

I closed my eyes as my guilt pelted down on me like a waterfall.

"I'm sorry about that," I said. "I have a lot of work to do to make up for what I put him through. For what I put you all through."

"No one blames you for needing a little space after dealing with Andromeda," Raina said. "Not even Bressen, so don't beat yourself up."

I nodded and turned to Calanthe.

"How are you?" I asked her, needing to change the subject. "Aramis hasn't said anything to you, has he?"

She smiled sadly. "He hasn't said a word to me, but if his eyes were daggers, I'd have been dead shortly after I arrived. He's been careful to stay on his side of the tent, and I've stayed on mine."

I gave her a sympathetic look. "I hope the two of you get to a point someday where you can at least coexist peacefully," I said.

"I'm hoping for much more than that," Calanthe said. "I know it's going to take a lot of time and work, but I'd like him to one day be able to forgive me. I understand the enormity of my mistake now."

"I'll do what I can to help make that happen," I promised her.

I found Aramis across the room watching us, but he turned his head quickly when my eyes met his.

"I'd better go see him," I said. "Not only did I make him tolerate having you here, but Jaylan took away his job of walking me down the aisle. I think it's been a tough day for him."

Calanthe and Raina nodded, and I turned to make my way toward Aramis. I noticed when I was almost there that he was standing with Jaylan and Brix. The three of them had bonded since they'd met a few months ago, and Brix in particular had adopted Aramis as a surrogate father figure, if the stories Jaylan had told me were any indication. Jaylan also felt a connection with Aramis since they'd met back when he was five, and he gave Aramis a degree of fatherly deference as well.

"You've gotten into a bad habit of scaring the three hells out of us since you met Bressen," Jaylan said, pulling me into a hug when I came up to them. "I'm starting to think he's a bad influence on you."

I chuckled against his shoulder. "I think you should tell him that."

"Not for all the coin in the world," Jaylan said as he released me.

Brix pulled me into a nearly bone-crushing embrace when I turned to him, and I felt the rest of his apology in it.

"Congratulations," he said as we held onto each other for several long moments. "I hope you can forgive me for being such an ass."

"I'll think about it," I said, and he chuckled as we let go of each other.

Brix shook his head as he finally released me. "I still can't believe you married the Nemesis Incarnate. What's it like when he talks in your head?"

I smiled at Brix's fascination with Bressen. From the little I'd seen of their interactions, Brix seemed to view Bressen as one step below a god.

*Jaylan thinks it feels disturbing. What do you think?* I said into Brix's mind, and his eyes widened in amazement.

"Nemesis damn me, Cyra," Brix said in awe. "I forgot you can do it too. That feels so strange. Do it again!"

"Later," I said as I turned to address Aramis. "Thank you for everything. I really appreciate you allowing Calanthe to attend the wedding and letting Jaylan walk me down the aisle."

Aramis pulled me into a hug, and we held onto each other for what seemed to be the first true hug he and I had ever shared. There'd always been a certain awkwardness to our embraces since we met, as if we were trying to force ourselves to feel the father-daughter bond we should've had. For the first time now, I felt a real warmth toward Aramis as if my mind and body had finally taken their first steps toward accepting that he was family. Not just family, but my father, the man who'd given me life and then made an impossible choice to keep me safe.

Aramis and I finally pulled away from each other, both of us now holding back the tears gathering in our eyes.

"You look so beautiful," he said. "I can't believe the baby I left in Fernweh so many years ago is now married, and to a Triumvirate lord, no less." He shook his head in disbelief. "I thought I'd failed you when Lord Bressen first told me he'd found you. I thought my years in Revenmyer had all been for nothing when I learned that the Nemesis Incarnate himself had you in his clutches, but in truth, he seems like the best thing that could have happened to you. I left you in Fernweh to keep you safe, and when you finally left, you found the one person powerful enough to keep you safe from just about anything."

He smiled and tipped his head briefly. "Not that you need protecting. You've become a beautiful, powerful, amazing woman that's more than capable of taking care of herself, and I can't begin to tell you how proud

I am of you and how much I love you."

I was wiping my eyes before he finished, and I threw myself back into his arms. Aramis hugged me tightly, and I heard Brix sniffle next to us.

I started to tell Aramis that I loved him back, but the words lodged in my throat for some reason, and I swallowed instead. I was so close to being able to say them, but I couldn't. Not yet.

Instead I said to him, "I hope that one day I'll be able to repay you for all the sacrifices you made for me."

Aramis waved a dismissive hand as we parted. "Don't be ridiculous. You're my daughter. I'd do it all again in a heartbeat if I had to. But I do have a small request, now that you mention it."

"Anything," I said. "Name it."

"Your mother was a wonderful dancer, and I see you take after her. Will you do your lowly father the favor of granting him a dance with the new Lady of Hiraeth?" he asked teasingly.

"It would be my pleasure," I said, "although I only know a couple of dances so far."

"Shall we go make a request?" Aramis suggested.

We excused ourselves from Jaylan and Brix and went over to wait near the orchestra. Just as the last song ended, I hurried over to request the dance that Aramis and I had decided on. We took our places on the floor as the music started and were soon swirling around with the other couples.

The dance I'd done with Bressen was the one I knew the best, since Jasper and I had practiced that one the most, but Jasper had also taught me another simpler one, and I knew it well enough to do it competently, if not impressively.

"You remind me so much of your mother," Aramis said as we swung around the floor. There was still a slight break in his voice.

"I look like her?" I asked.

"Yes, Lillian and Calanthe looked a lot alike, and you take after them both, except for your eyes of course," Aramis said. "But I don't just mean how you look. Your mother was strong and confident, just like you, but she was also humble and kind. She had me wrapped around her little finger, and she kept me in line, just like you do with Bressen."

I scoffed. "I hardly keep Bressen in line. He's a lord, after all."

"Yet I've seen him defer to you time and again," he said. "You're not afraid to scold him, and I've seen the great Bressen of Hiraeth, Triumvirate Lord and Nemesis Incarnate, actually rein himself in when you do. You don't seem to realize how much power you have over him."

I frowned. While that was a heady idea, I didn't really want power over Bressen. I only wanted to be his equal, and only in some things. I wasn't a ruler. I wanted agency over my own life and decisions, but I had no desire to control Bressen or 'keep him in line,' as Aramis called it.

Aramis seemed to sense the direction of my thoughts. "That's not a bad thing," he said as we continued to twirl around the floor. "There are very few people or powers in this world that can keep a man like Lord Bressen in check, but it's good to have at least one thing that makes him pause, and you're that one thing for him. Don't regret that. Embrace it."

He was right. Every power needed some way to be put in check so it didn't become dangerous. It was the very reason Thasia had a triumvirate system to begin with, the idea that the three rulers could balance each other out. Someone with more ambition than Bressen might have refused to replace Ursan and Jerram when they died and converted the government to a monarchy, but Bressen had never considered it for a second. That he held himself in check as often as he did, given his immense power, spoke volumes about the kind of man he was, even if he himself thought he could do better sometimes.

The music wound down, and Aramis kissed my hand. "You should get back to your husband," he said. "It looks like he may need you."

I glanced toward the table where Bressen still sat with a line of nobles waiting for his attention. He looked up, sensing my gaze, and I nodded my head toward the edge of the tent where Samhail still stood watch. Bressen nodded back, and I made my way toward Samhail. If Samhail was committed to playing sentry, then we'd use that to our advantage.

"We may need your help making our escape," I said to Samhail as I stopped in front of him on my way out of the tent. We both glanced toward the table where Bressen had just risen and started toward us. Most of the courtiers had taken the hint and were drifting back to their tables, but a few stubborn ones attempted to follow Bressen.

"They won't get by me," Samhail promised.

"I know," I said, patting one of his arms still crossed over his chest.

I stepped out from under the tent, and its warmth evaporated as the chilly night air bathed my face. I let the change rouse me.

I felt Bressen's presence behind me before I heard him. My body usually sensed when he was near, but that feeling had taken on new meaning since talking to Phaedrus earlier today. The story of the origin of love couldn't be real, but it nevertheless explained so much, and wasn't that really the purpose of myths anyway? To explain the unexplainable?

I purred with contentment when Bressen's arms slid around my waist and shoulders, and he pulled me against him. I tipped my head to the side to bare my neck in invitation, and he accepted it gladly, running his lips over the delicate skin there before nipping my earlobe. The feel of his teeth brought gooseflesh to my arms, and I let out a longing sigh.

"Are you tired yet, or did you want to stay longer?" he asked me.

"I'm ready to leave whenever you are," I said. I was glad we'd made it to our own wedding reception, but it had been a long day, and I was starting to feel the first strains of exhaustion pull at me.

"I've been ready since we got here," he said. "I was told I shouldn't share you anymore, yet I've had to share you with all these people for the last few hours."

"There are occasional exceptions to the rule, but if you're ready to stop sharing me now, then I'm ready to stop being shared," I laughed.

"It's about time," he said, and I heard the whoosh of his giant feathered wings as they unfurled behind him.

"Shouldn't we at least-" I started to say, but he cut me off.

"No," he said as he scooped me into his arms and shot into the sky.

I stifled a shriek as we left our guests behind to continue their celebration without us. It was time for a long overdue night with my love.

My husband.

My soul.

# Chapter 33

Bressen set me down on the balcony of our bedroom moments later, and I turned in his arms to face him. We hadn't made love again since he'd invited Samhail to our bed, and the unasked questions of that night still hung between us. I'd broken something open this afternoon when I'd returned from the Priory, and the ache of deferred desire was heavy in the air as we stood pressed together, our breathing already starting to quicken.

"We can go to sleep if you're tired," Bressen ventured. An offer I knew he hoped I'd refuse.

I only fisted my hands into his jacket as I lifted my head.

"I want my wedding night," I said.

"Thank the gods," he breathed as he pulled me tighter. His lips grazed against mine, and I nipped at them, but neither of us made any more aggressive moves. We'd take this slow.

"Are you going to tell me what Phaedrus said to you?" Bressen asked as his lips teased my cheek.

"That's what you're thinking about now?"

He nodded his head against mine.

"Phaedrus told me," I whispered, leaning up to run my lips along Bressen's jawline against the hint of stubble there, "that you're already married."

Bressen's head jerked back as he looked down at me. "What?" he asked, confusion on his face.

I smiled. "You told me once that you knew enough ancient Arystrian to understand what you were saying on the Harmilan during the rededication ceremony, right?"

"Yes," he said, frowning. "So?"

"So you don't think the words from the Harmilan sound at all familiar to some of the things we said today during the wedding?" I asked.

Bressen's furrow deepened. "Exactly what are you saying?"

"I'm saying that the vows you took in Arystrian are ancient marriage vows from little-used religious texts that were repurposed for other ceremonies."

Bressen stared at me. "That's what Phaedrus told you that convinced you to marry me?" he asked incredulously.

"No," I said. "He told me a myth from that same text about the origin of love that said the gods once punished us all by splitting us in half, and that making love is our attempt to put ourselves back together."

Bressen's brows shot up, and I filled in the details of the story Phaedrus had given me. His face started to ease in understanding as I spoke, and by the time I finished, his expression was solemn.

"And this story made you feel…" He trailed off as his throat bobbed in a swallow. "It made you think I was the other half of your soul?"

I nodded, and Bressen's face broke in a way that made me sure he was about to cry.

"Cyra, I…," he said, but trailed off again. His hands came up to cup my face. "I'm honored you would consider me your mate, that you feel like we could be a single body, mind, and soul like that."

"Do…do you feel like that as well?" I asked him, suddenly uncertain.

"Since the moment I met you," he breathed. "Part of me has always recognized that I was never whole until you came into my life. It's why I couldn't leave you alone after we met, even though the gods know I tried."

Bressen had often ignored me in public for the first few weeks I knew him, but we'd nevertheless found ourselves alone together often enough due to one circumstance or another. He'd even vowed once to my face that he'd stay away from me, but that promise hadn't lasted long at all.

"Well, maybe I didn't try all that hard," Bressen corrected himself. "Somehow you kept turning up wherever I was or crossing my path. Eventually I gave up trying to avoid you, mostly because I didn't want to. I couldn't. Thinking about you kept me awake at night. Then eventually you kept me awake all night for completely different reasons."

He grinned wickedly at me, and I smiled at the reminder of how we'd both spent our days exhausted after finally consummating our relationship because we'd spent every night thereafter fucking each other until dawn.

"Should we try to press ourselves back together now?" I asked.

"Even if it takes all night," he said. "And if we don't succeed, we'll try again tomorrow."

Bressen shrugged his wings back into his body and took my hand to lead me to the bed, but I put a hand on his chest.

"Leave your wings out," I said. "I married an angelus. I want to make love to one."

Bressen chuckled, but he nodded and released his wings again so that they flared wide behind him. They'd been raven black when I first met him, but he'd shocked me by unfurling brilliant white ones the day after Jerram and Glenora's thwarted coup. They were black again now, so dark that they seemed to drink in the night.

"Why do your wings change color?" I asked him.

He ruffled them, and I lifted a hand toward them without thinking.

"Can I touch them?" I asked.

"If you want to," he said. "I can manifest them as either white or black. I'm a dark angelus, so they usually come out black if I'm not thinking about it, but I can make them white with a little effort. Angelus always have a dominant side, but we're diametric by nature."

I needed to ask him more about that later, but right now I had other more important things on my mind.

I started unbuttoning the shimmering black jacket Bressen wore. When I finished, I stepped around behind him and pulled it off his shoulders. It slipped right past the wings, as if they were ephemeral where they met the fabric. I looked again, and the wings seemed to come right out of his shirt, unlike Samhail's wings that needed holes so they didn't tear his clothes. I reached up to touch one of them near its base, and Bressen trembled a little.

"Does it hurt when I touch them?" I asked.

"No," he said. "If anything, it tickles a bit. I've never had someone touch them like this before. They're a bit more sensitive than I realized."

"You've never had sex with them out?" I asked, strangely comforted by that thought.

"No, not until they unfurled that first time with you," he said.

I smiled. "Good. Take off your shirt."

Bressen glanced over his shoulder with a look that told me I'd pay later for ordering him around, but he unbuttoned the shirt and took it off.

I bit my lip as I examined the spots where the wings flared out from his back just under his shoulder blades. I ran my hands along the expanse of hard muscles there, then touched the place where one of the wings emerged, running my thumb over the joint. I continued my exploration up the wing bone that connected to his back, and he inhaled deeply before trembling again. I ignored his reaction and traced my finger over the top of the wing until I got to the next joint.

I'd decided weeks ago after seeing Bressen and Samhail naked that I needed to learn the names of every muscle in their bodies, and I'd done so with the help of Aramis's healer training and a book on anatomy. Now, I decided, I needed to learn the names of all the bones, muscles, and feathers in Bressen's wings as well.

"When do I get to touch you?" he rasped out as I ran my fingers down his feathers.

"In a few minutes. I'm not done exploring your wings yet."

He growled.

"You're supposed to growl at other men, not at me," I chided him.

"You have one more minute," he said, "and then I won't be responsible for my actions."

"If you need something to do, get rid of those pants," I suggested.

Bressen attacked the fastenings of his pants, and I let out a delighted gasp of approval as the muscles in his back twitched and bunched with the effort. I pressed my palms against his skin and reveled in the feel of the steely muscles undulating beneath them.

Bressen toed off his boots, and I helped his pants down his legs so he could step out of them. This put my face level with his gorgeous ass, and I couldn't help nipping one cheek with my teeth before I stood up again. Bressen grunted and started to turn, but I stopped him by pressing his hips back around to face front.

"My minute isn't up yet," I told him.

Another growl rumbled in his throat, but he obeyed.

My hands came back up to run over his wings again, and I bit my lip as his muscles tensed and contracted at my touch.

"Are you sure I'm not hurting you?" I asked.

"Gods no, it doesn't hurt," he said through his teeth. "I've had healers touch my wings before, but it's never felt like this. There's something about your touch that drives me insane. I can barely control myself.”

I hummed a noise of approval and slipped my hands forward around his waist over the oblique muscles that dipped down toward his groin. Bressen exhaled sharply as I pressed against his back and my hands slid toward his cock.

“Why are you torturing me like this?” he ground out.

“If you think this is torture, I’m not sure you’ll be able to handle what comes next.”

I walked around in front of him and started to lower myself to my knees, but he caught my elbows and dragged me back up.

“Your time is up,” he said. “My turn.”

I drew in a breath to argue, but his mouth crashed into mine for a plundering kiss, and my body lurched toward his to seek support. His hands tangled in the strands of jewels and pearls hanging off the back of my dress as his hands sought my bare skin. Then they were at the straps that held the dress on my shoulders, and he guided them down my arms so the dress bunched at my hips. He popped the fastenings at my backside free, and the dress slipped the rest of the way to the floor.

Bressen dropped to his knees then, and I cried out as his mouth closed over one breast to suck greedily at it before moving to the other. My fingers threaded through his hair, gripping a handful as he bit gently on one nipple. His hand slid between my legs, and I almost yanked on his hair as two of his fingers slipped inside me, testing my readiness for him. He moved them in and out languidly before pulling them back out, covered in my slickness. It had been too long since he’d touched me like this, and I was ready to shatter.

“Perfect,” Bressen murmured as he slipped the fingers into his mouth to taste me on them, and I moaned a little at the look in his eye.

He caught me under my arms as he stood up and hoisted me into the air. Instinctively, I wrapped my legs around him, and he lowered me down right onto his waiting erection. It was the first time in a week and a half he’d been inside me, and the sound I made as my body closed around him was somewhere between a cry and a whimper.

Maybe it was wishful thinking from Phaedrus’s story, but I felt as though we fit together so perfectly, like a key in a lock. His body was hard everywhere mine was soft, as though we balanced each other out.

I wrapped my arms around his neck as I tried to press myself down further onto him, and we both moaned as the effort sheathed him into me to the hilt. One of his arms fastened around my waist while the other cupped me under my ass, and I rocked my hips against him.

"Fuck, Cyra. You're going to bring me to my knees again," he rasped as his lips ran along my throat. He thrust his hips up into me making me bounce on his cock, and I cried out, squeezing my thighs around him.

"Maybe that's where I want you," I said teasingly.

"Just the opposite," he said as he walked toward the balcony with me still wrapped around him.

"What are you doing? Where are we going?" I asked, the words coming out in a gasp. His walking was shifting me against him in a way that drove me wild with desire.

"You wanted to make love to an angelus," Bressen said, "so you're going to get the full angelus experience."

"What?" I asked, pulling back a little to look into his face.

I felt his obfuscation glamour fall over us as we reached the balcony, and cold air bit my skin as we passed through the barrier that kept the biting night air out of the room.

"You can't mean…"

"I do," he said. Then he added, "If you know how to make a bubble of warm air, I suggest trying one now or this may get a little chilly."

I'd never tried to do anything of the kind, but I attempted it now. I concentrated on the idea of warming the air around us, and a moment later a cushion of comfortable air enveloped us, blocking out the cold. Bressen smiled and pulled my mouth to his for another hungry kiss.

"Good girl," he breathed against my lips. "Now hold on tight."

I tightened my legs and arms around him again as he beat his huge wings, and we launched into the sky. I'd never noticed before how much jostling his wings caused until I could feel it where we were joined, and I moaned as each beat caused a small thrust between my legs.

Higher and higher we rose into the sky, a hundred feet, two hundred feet, three hundred feet up into the air, and I smiled against Bressen's mouth as I kissed him. I thought about all the people below celebrating our wedding, oblivious that Bressen and I were naked and enjoying our wedding night hundreds of feet above the house, the beach, and the tent. Even if they looked up into the sky, Bressen's glamour would keep us hidden from curious eyes.

"High enough?" he asked as he beat his wings to keep us in place.

Below us, the lights from the house and the tent glowed like stars against the dark landscape, and I gasped as every beat of Bressen's wings sent shivers of pleasure through me.

"I need to be higher," I whimpered against his mouth as I tried to rock myself against him, and he chuckled, understanding that I wasn't talking about how far up in the air we were.

I unwrapped one hand from around Bressen's neck and called my wind to create an updraft under us. Bressen's wings caught the draft, and he stopped beating them to simply let the wind hold us aloft.

Without the beating of his wings there was no more friction between us, but the wind freed Bressen to do other things. He moved both hands to grip my ass so he could move me up and down along his length while I used my legs to help thrust myself up and down. My breath came in ragged gasps against Bressen's cheek as I felt every inch of him slide in and out of me. His own hot breath caressed my shoulder, and his muscles flexed under my fingers and against my legs as he pulled me down onto him again and again so that a knot of tension tightened in my core.

"I feel like I was created to be inside you, Cyra," Bressen said through clenched teeth as I ground my hips against him. "You're so tight and sweet around my cock, it's like-"

"Like we were made to fit together?" I finished for him.

"Yes!" he groaned as he slammed me down onto him.

The thrust brought me so close to a release that I dug my nails into his shoulders. That only spurred him to drive into me again, and then I was falling over the edge as every extreme – hot and cold, hard and soft, light and dark – all seemed to pour through me at once.

We dropped in the sky as my wind faltered under the torrent of sensation gripping me, and I cried out in both pleasure and fright. We grabbed for each other as I renewed my wind and Bressen beat his wings again to catch the air. My heart hammered against my ribs as I felt the pulse of his release a second later, and he groaned into my shoulder.

We held each other there for nearly a minute as our panting breaths swirled together before being carried away on my wind. His arms were like steel bands around me, holding me against him, and I had my own arms wrapped so tightly around him that I doubted anyone would be able to pry me loose. For this time at least, it felt like we were one.

"Maybe it's time to go back down," Bressen finally said with a breathless chuckle.

"Probably a good idea," I said as the knot in my stomach from our sudden drop finally eased.

I pulled my wind, and Bressen brought us back down to touch lightly onto the balcony. The obfuscation glamour lifted as he walked me back inside to the bed, my arms and legs still wrapped around him. He lifted me off him and set me down on the floor. My legs felt unsteady to be back on solid ground, and I held onto him.

"I don't think it worked," Bressen said softly as he tucked a stray strand of my hair behind my ear and trailed his fingers down my cheek.

I frowned. "What didn't work?"

"Putting ourselves back together," he said. "We came close, but we still have two bodies."

"Should we try again?" I asked. "Maybe it wasn't the right position."

"I'm willing to do this all night if necessary," he said. "We'll try positions until we find one that works."

"What should we try next?"

I squeaked in surprise as Bressen turned me around and tossed me forward onto my stomach on the bed. He was on top of me a moment later, and his hand wrapped around the underside of my thigh to pull my leg up, opening me to him. I felt his cock, already hard again, press at my entrance from behind.

"How about this one?" he asked, and I winced a little at the strength of his grip on my thigh.

"It's not navel to navel, so I'm not sure it will work," I said, lifting my ass off the bed to try to push him into me further, "but we should at least try, if only to eliminate it as an option."

"As I recall, I also owe you some punishment," he said huskily.

The fingers of his other hand curled gently around my throat, and I swallowed against his palm.

"You do," I admitted, my voice shaking a little.

I smothered my cry into the bed as he speared into me in one stroke that buried him to the hilt. He'd just been inside me a minute ago, but he was big and my body always seemed to forget that when he withdrew.

"Are you ready to take your punishment?" he asked, and I whimpered as my muscles tightened at the growl in his voice.

I nodded, but he only pulled back so he was barely inside me.

"Say it," he rasped.

"I'm ready for my punishment," I whispered.

He slammed back into me fully, and I fisted my hands in the covers with a cry.

"Are you going to be a good girl and behave yourself from now on?" he asked. "No more getting yourself into trouble?"

I paused. "Yes," I said finally, and he chuckled.

"Why don't I believe you?" he asked before he shoved into me again.

I tried to bury my forehead in the covers, but he still held my neck, and he pulled me back. He adjusted his legs between mine to spread my knees wider, and I felt him sink deeper into me.

"Oh gods," I moaned.

"Do you want me to stop?" he asked as he withdrew completely.

"No!" I whimpered.

His lips and breath tickled my ear as he whispered, "Good. Because I wasn't going to."

He covered my hands with his own, and he curled his fingers through mine as he slammed into me as far as he could go. He began to thrust again with great punishing strokes as I screamed into the bed and pushed back against him, determined to help put us back together.

# Chapter 34

Bressen and I stayed in bed until lunchtime the next day, carefully testing different sexual positions to see if any worked to permanently join us back into one being, but alas, success eluded us.

On the other hand, I'd lost count of the number of times Bressen had made me climax by the time he finally threw off the covers and told me regretfully that he needed to eat something besides me. He also needed to check in with Ferris. If Axenus managed to find where *The Stalwart* was, we'd likely be gone for several days, and Bressen needed to make sure Hiraeth's affairs were in order before he left. His duties as lord didn't stop just because he'd gotten married.

"You're welcome to stay in bed all day if you want," Bressen told me as he got up. "You're going to need your strength for tonight. There are still a number of positions we haven't tried, and there's a few others I want to try again, just to be sure."

"Like that last one?" I asked.

He stopped to look back at me on his way to the closet. "Definitely that last one," he said before striding across the room naked.

I'd never seen a more perfect ass on a man, and I reveled that it was now all mine as I watched him go.

I sighed and swung my legs out of bed but stopped as the soreness between them made me wince. I'd only had sex once in the last couple weeks, and my body was letting me know it hadn't been prepared for last night's excess. The last time I'd been this sore was on the Harmilan, and that was because Bressen and Samhail had taken me multiple times, and then once together, Samhail in front and Bressen behind. They'd pushed my body further than it had ever been before, and I'd felt it the next day.

Sitting had been a problem that morning, and it was going to be a problem again now, but that was fine. The pain reminded me of what I'd done to feel it, and that only made me want to do it some more.

Bressen was dressed when I entered the closet to find my own clothes.

"Not staying in bed?" he asked, shrugging on a jacket.

My stomach rumbled before I could answer, and he waited for me while I got dressed so we could go down to lunch together.

Samhail and Raina were in the dining room when we entered, and I tried not to read anything into the way their bodies leaned in across the table toward each other like they'd been talking.

They looked up when Bressen and I entered, and I wondered if it was guilt I saw on Raina's face when she looked at me, or if I was just being paranoid. I was sure they hadn't spent the night together…right?

I resisted the urge to look into Raina's mind and find the answer.

"We didn't expect to see you today," Samhail remarked as he sat back, "but by the way Cyra is walking, I'm guessing she needed a break."

I glared at Samhail, but he only smirked at me. Raina tried but failed to hide her own smile.

"Actually, I was just hungry," I said, making an effort to walk more normally before I sat down and pulled a plate of sandwiches toward me.

I glanced at Raina, but her face betrayed nothing of what she'd been talking to Samhail about before we arrived. Maybe I was imagining things.

Regardless, it didn't matter. I was married to Bressen now, and I had no right to be jealous over anyone Samhail took to bed. He'd been in Seatherny for almost two months while the Derridan trials had been going on, and knowing what I did about his lusty nature, I'd be a fool to think he hadn't taken women to bed while he was there.

"You weren't at training this morning," Samhail said to me before popping the last bite of his own sandwich into his mouth.

"It's the day after my wedding," I said dryly. "I gave myself the morning off."

"Too bad I didn't give you the morning off as well," he said. "We'll meet after lunch, since I know Bressen has work and you no longer have dance lessons with Jasper."

My eyes flew open wide, and I nearly choked on my sandwich as I looked at him. "How did you know I had dance lessons with Jasper in the afternoons?" I asked him.

Samhail grinned at me. "Just because Bressen didn't know where you spent your afternoons doesn't mean *I* didn't."

I rounded on Bressen. "Did you have Samhail spying on me?"

He held up his hands in defense. "I'm not that foolish."

I waited to see if his skin would glow red to indicate a lie, but it remained its usual golden tan color.

"So you took it upon yourself to spy on me?" I asked Samhail.

"With Andromeda around, I took it upon myself to know where you were in relationship to where she was," he said seriously. "Unfortunately, I failed in that yesterday due to other priorities." He glanced at Bressen.

"I'm sorry," Raina said sheepishly. "I should have told you Samhail caught me by myself twice while you were with Jasper, and I wasn't good at covering for you. I just lied the first time-"

"Lied badly," Samhail cut in.

"And then the second time I just confessed where you were so he didn't get the wrong idea," she went on. "I swore him to secrecy, but I should've told you."

I opened and closed my mouth several times but didn't say anything. I wasn't mad at Raina so much as surprised to know she'd spoken to Samhail a few times when I wasn't around. It made her interest in him more understandable.

"So I was the only one who didn't know you were taking dance lessons with Jasper?" Bressen asked.

"You and Aidan," I offered.

"Yes, but I'm a fucking mind wraith," he said, shaking his head. "Nemesis damn me, I must be slipping."

"It would have ruined the surprise if you'd known," I said.

His face softened. "And it was a wonderful surprise."

"What do you want to do with your mother, by the way?" Samhail asked Bressen before he and I could get too lost in each other.

Bressen sighed. "Is Phaedrus still here?"

"No, he sent Aidan and Jasper to Seatherny this morning, then took a portal back to the Priory," Samhail said.

"Are my brothers still here?" I asked.

"They were having lunch when I arrived," Samhail said. "I think they were planning to stay at least until they saw you again." He looked back at Bressen. "You're going to send Andromeda home?"

"Yes. I'll have Phaedrus come back," Bressen said.

"I can create a portal for her," I offered.

Bressen shook his head. "No, I don't want her anywhere near you."

"I'll be fine. There's no need to call Phaedrus all the way back here. I can go with Samhail and open the portal," I insisted.

"I really should've made sure that part about the wife obeying her husband stayed in our marriage vows," Bressen grumbled.

I just smiled sweetly at him.

"Bring a caronium cuff for my mother," he told Samhail. "If she wants out of her cell, she'll agree to wear it for a month."

Samhail, Raina, and I all gaped at him as though he'd gone mad.

"She attacked the future Lady of Hiraeth," Bressen said coolly, seeing our looks. "She's lucky I don't leave her in that cell for the next month."

I opened my mouth but then closed it again, realizing I had no real desire to let Andromeda off too easily. If she wasn't Bressen's mother, the punishment would actually seem too light.

Bressen arched his brows in surprise at me, and I knew he'd been expecting me to argue with him.

I could let him have his way once in a while.

After lunch, Raina and I waited in the foyer for Samhail to bring Andromeda up from the holding cells in the basement while Bressen went to meet with Ferris. I told Samhail we could go down with him to get her, but he'd insisted we wait up here.

"Does he think I can't handle seeing a dungeon?" I complained to Raina as Samhail disappeared down the stairs.

She shrugged. "I have no idea, but to be honest, I'm perfectly fine waiting here," she said, giving a small yawn.

"How was your night after we left the reception?" I asked her, trying not to sound too curious.

"Not as good as yours I'm sure," she said, smirking at me. "You really were walking rather gingerly this morning."

I blushed but didn't let her change the subject. "So you didn't spend the night with anyone fun?" I ventured.

Raina cocked her head at me. "No. Why?"

"You and Samhail just seemed rather…friendly when we arrived at lunch," I said, deciding not to beat around the bush.

Raina's eyes flew open. "And you think I slept with him last night?"

"Keep your voice down!" I hushed her, looking toward the basement door where Samhail had disappeared.

Raina just stared at me.

"Are you actually jealous?" she asked finally.

"No, of course not. Well…maybe. I don't know."

"You do remember that you're married now, right?" Raina said.

"Yes, I know. I suppose I'm still just having trouble fully letting go of Samhail," I said, exhaling deeply. "For some reason, imagining him with someone else is making me crazy."

Raina crossed her arms over her chest. "Imagining him with *me* is making you crazy," she corrected.

I thought about denying it, but I couldn't. "Yes. I'm sorry. I don't know what's wrong with me."

"You really think I'd still jump into bed with Samhail after our conversation the other night?" she asked. Her tone was almost offended.

"I don't know what to think," I said. "You seem to have this secret life of drinking, gambling, and fucking that I know nothing about. That man I met the other night said he knew you, and I wondered…"

"If I fucked him?" Raina supplied. "Would it be a problem if I did?"

"No, not at all," I said. "I just wish I'd known about it. I had no idea you were sneaking out of the house to go to that gambling den all week. I guess I just thought we used to tell each other everything, and it turns out both of us have been keeping a lot of secrets."

Raina's expression eased and she uncrossed her arms. "You're right, and I'm sorry," she said. "Not that it matters now, but yes. I did fuck Heren, and several other men there." She shrugged. "I like sex, and I don't see why I should abstain from something I like if it's not hurting anyone."

I nodded my agreement.

"And to be honest," she went on, "I also don't see why you need to stop sleeping with Samhail if Bressen is okay with it. The problem isn't that you still want him. It's that you've chosen Bressen, but you don't want Samhail to have anyone else. That's what's not fair."

I dropped my gaze. "You're right. I'm being selfish and hypocritical."

"Look," Raina said, "Samhail isn't husband material. You and I both know that, but I don't think that's what you really want from him anyway. I assume he's good in bed?"

I nodded. "I swear his tongue is enchanted."

Raina closed her eyes a moment. "If you're not going to let me have him, you can't give me details like that," she said.

"Sorry."

"My point is," she went on, "you're a young woman, and you have both needs and eyes. It's not wrong to want Samhail. Just because you love Bressen doesn't mean you can't recognize how gorgeous Samhail is. But you have to be honest with both yourself and Bressen about what you want. If Bressen no longer wants to let you and Samhail be together, then you need to respect that and honor your marriage vows. If he's fine with it, then the only other person's consent you need is Samhail's."

I smiled wryly. She made it all sound so simple, but it hadn't seemed that way the last time I was with Samhail. For that matter, I wasn't sure I wanted to go back now that he and I had decided that last time had been our last time. It seemed better to just move on.

I was about to say as much when Samhail crested the stairs with Andromeda in tow. My gaze locked with my mother-in-law's — her turquoise irises a disturbingly perfect mirror of Bressen's — and I raised my chin defiantly.

"I suppose this was your doing?" Andromeda said to me, raising her wrist to display the caronium cuff locked onto it.

"Actually, that was Bressen's condition," I told her. "I just didn't argue with him about it."

"You may have married him, but he'll never truly be yours," she said. "He belongs to the angelus, and when he eventually gets tired of you — which he will — he'll realize I was right."

A snarl rose up in Samhail's throat, but I held up a hand to stop him from snapping at her.

"I don't know whether to be grateful or pity you," I told her. "Maybe both. If you hadn't had an affair, I wouldn't have Bressen. In truth, you're responsible for where we are right now. You lost your son by your own actions, and your refusal to accept that is just willful blindness. The tragic irony is that in attempting to create more angelus, you caused the deaths of two others."

Andromeda's mouth dropped open in outrage, and she started to speak, but I held up a hand again.

"Don't," I said sharply. "I have no desire to hear what you have to say, and if you speak, I'll make sure that stays on for a year." I pointed to her caronium cuff. "You know Bressen will agree in a heartbeat if I ask him for that."

Her mouth clamped shut so hard her teeth clicked, and I turned to open a portal into Laycan. A majestic house appeared on the other side of the glowing blue ring, and I stepped aside to give her room to pass. She went through the portal without another word, but she looked back through it at me. I didn't bother to catch her eye as I closed it behind her.

"Well done, Lady of Hiraeth," Raina said, smirking at me.

I glanced at Samhail, but he shook his head with a half-grin.

"I'm disappointed," he said. "I really wanted to see you slap her."

"Are you sure you won't stay?" I asked my brothers half an hour later when they tracked me down in the great room to say goodbye.

They weren't heading back to Fernweh, just the Citadel, but I wasn't ready for them to leave yet, especially after I'd just reconciled with Brix.

"Under the same roof as a newly married couple?" Jaylan said. "Not a chance."

"We heard what goes on at the Citadel," Brix added, "and that was before you were even married."

"Brix!" Jaylan hissed, but my cheeks flamed as hot as the third hell.

"What have they been saying at the Citadel?" I asked, mortified. I held up a hand a second later. "Never mind. I don't want to know."

I hugged my brothers and promised to visit a couple times a week.

"Think about my offer," I told Jaylan. "I'm not sure when the sale of the vineyard will go through, but I'll need help when it does."

"I'll help you get started when you're ready, but I don't think I can leave Fernweh for good," he said. "I have to go back at some point. I have to at least…try."

I knew what he meant. He needed to see if he could salvage his relationship with Maeve, and I didn't blame him. I'd fight to keep Bressen if I was in the same situation.

"When the time comes for you to return, I'll do what I can," I told him. "Or I'll stay out of the way. Whatever you think will help more."

Jaylan nodded and gave me another big hug before he stepped through the portal I'd opened back into the Citadel.

I turned to Brix, and he gave me a crooked smile.

"Do you forgive me yet?" he asked.

"There's nothing to forgive," I said seriously. "I grew up with you, remember? I've always known you were an idiot."

Shock blossomed on Brix's face, but then he chuckled.

"I suppose I deserved that," he said, still smiling.

I sighed and shook my head. "Pain and anger make people react in strange ways. At least you only got mad at me. I burned down a building and tried to kill three people. I'd say your reaction was more reasonable."

Brix nodded and pulled me into a crushing hug.

"Try to stay out of trouble," he said as he let go of me.

"I was about to tell you the same thing," I said, laughing. "You think about my offer as well. We can find something for you up here if you don't want to go back to Fernweh with Jaylan."

"I'll think about it," he promised.

He turned to the portal but stopped just before going through and looked back again.

"Cyra, can I ask you about something?" he said hesitantly.

"Of course."

"In Fernweh when I said it wasn't your vineyard anymore…"

I shook my head. "It's fine. You were right. It's not."

He smiled sadly. "It will always be partially your vineyard, but that's not what I was going to ask."

I looked at him expectantly, and he took a deep breath.

"When I said that, you turned to me, and I could see you were furious. I…I thought I saw something in your eyes."

My brows knit in question. "What did you see?"

"I thought I saw your eyes go red. Is that one of your powers?"

I just stared at Brix as every thought emptied from my head. I couldn't have moved if the ground had opened up to swallow me whole.

"Cyra?" Brix said, looking at me with concern now. "Is something wrong? Are your eyes not supposed to flash like that?"

My jaw flexed up and down, but no words came out. It was several seconds before I remembered how to speak.

"I…Are you sure it wasn't just a trick of the light?" I asked. "Maybe it was the flames from the building."

Brix thought for a moment. "I don't think you'd set the building on fire yet," he said.

I jerked my shoulders in a nervous shrug. "I'm not sure what it was then." I tried for a breezy, unconcerned tone, but my mouth had gone dry, and my voice was just a bit too high-pitched to pull off nonchalance.

Brix looked at me for a long moment before he gave me a small smile.

"I just thought I'd ask," he said.

I forced a smile onto my own face and nodded. He could see something was wrong but had apparently decided not to push me.

Brix stepped through the portal, and I closed it quickly behind him.

I walked to one of the armchairs on shaky legs and sunk into it.

Had Brix really seen my eyes flash red as Bressen's sometimes did when he was angry? If so, what did that mean?

I wasn't an angelus. Aramis would have told me if either he or my mother were one. Or both of them. That's what Andromeda had said. Both parents needed to be angelus for the child to be one.

I considered whether I should tell Bressen about this but decided against it for the moment. Brix hadn't been sure of what he'd seen, and we had enough to worry about already. We'd just gotten married and hadn't had a real chance to enjoy each other's company yet. I didn't want to throw one more thing on the pile for us to have to figure out.

I'd tell Bressen what Brix thought he saw…eventually.

Just not today.

# Chapter 35

I had no sense of time as I lay under the water in my bath later that night, filling and refilling my lungs with fresh air. It might've been twenty minutes, or it might've been forty-five for all I knew. I'd told Leeda to come get me after an hour, so I only knew it hadn't been that long yet.

Axenus had left this afternoon to see if he could find the exact location of *The Stalwart*. I wasn't sure how long we'd need to be underwater when we went after the collar and rings, so I was just trying to practice staying under as long as I could for now. I'd eventually need to practice out in open water, since the conditions in my bathtub would hardly be similar to those we'd face in the ocean.

For one, the water would be much, much colder, and I imagined it would also be dark, considering how far we might need to go down. As a merman, Axenus could adjust easily to the cold and the water pressure we'd face, but I didn't yet know how I might be able to do it myself. I'd also be swimming and would need to be able to refill my lungs without thinking about it so I could concentrate on doing other things.

I opened my eyes and saw a dark shape peek over the side of the tub and then retreat. The form wasn't Leeda's, and panic rose in my chest to think someone was in the bathing chamber with me.

I shot to the surface and held out a hand, ready to loose a forcefield at whoever was there. I inhaled air instinctively once I was no longer submerged, and I wiped quickly at the water running into my eyes with my other hand. Then I sank back in relief against the tub.

"Nemesis take you, Bressen," I gasped. "You frightened the three hells out of me."

He sat next to the tub in a chair with one knee crossed over the other and a faint grin on his face.

"My apologies," he said. "I was starting to doubt my power, so I wanted to check to make sure you were still alive."

"Your power?"

"I was keeping an eye on you to be sure you were still conscious," he said. "My power was telling me you were, but I was having trouble believing it."

"How long have you been watching me?"

I'd become sensitive to knowing when Bressen's mind was connected to mine, but I hadn't even felt he was in the room this time, let alone that he was checking to be sure I was conscious.

"Probably about twenty-five minutes or so," Bressen said.

"Twenty-five minutes?" I asked incredulously. "How did I not sense that you've been here for twenty-five minutes?"

He smiled. "I do still have some tricks I've kept to myself."

I frowned at him. "And what have you been doing here for twenty-five minutes while I've been underwater?"

"Just waiting," he said. "Well, waiting and imagining what I wanted to do to you when you finally came up."

I couldn't help the flutter in my stomach at both his words and the devilishly sensual look he gave me.

"Oh?" I said, biting my lip. "And what did you decide?"

His grin widened as his eyes dipped to the waterline where the mounds of my breasts arched just above the surface.

"I have several ideas," he said. "I was trying to narrow it down, just for the sake of time, but I know what direction I'd like to go now."

I arched a brow. "And what direction would that be?"

"I can show you if you want," he said, his eyes glinting with mischief.

He extended a hand to me, and I took it so he could help me stand in the tub. His eyes roamed over the curves of my body as the water ran down my breasts, hips, and legs, but they narrowed a second later.

"What?" I asked.

"What's that around your navel?" he asked.

I looked down, but it took me a moment to see what he was talking about. My skin was pale, and I could just barely see now that there was a patch of even paler skin that circled my navel in the shape of a crescent moon. I gasped and wiped at the skin to rub away the shape, but nothing happened when my thumb ran over it.

My eyes snapped up to meet Bressen's, and we both seemed to have the same idea at the same time.

"Do you have one?" I asked, but he was already tugging up his own shirt before I finished the question.

We both gaped at the pale crescent moon circling his navel, its presence so much more apparent against his golden skin.

"Gods above," I breathed. "Was that there last night?"

I'd taken him into my mouth at least twice on our wedding night, so my eyes would have been perfectly positioned to notice something so starkly visible on his body. I racked my brain to remember if I'd actually looked at his navel, or if I'd been too busy looking up into his eyes while I slid my mouth over his erection. I couldn't remember.

"I didn't see them last night," Bressen said. "Yours is harder to see, but I'd like to think I would have noticed mine at some point."

"It's…It's a moon," I said, my voice barely above a whisper. "What does it mean?"

We looked at each other, and I didn't need my mind powers to know we were both thinking of the story I'd told Bressen about the Souls of the Moon, beings that had once looked like a man and woman stuck together before the gods had sundered them.

"Have you ever heard of marks like this before?" I asked Bressen.

"No. Maybe Aramis has?"

Aramis was more than three hundred years old and had been a healer for most of that time. If anyone had seen such marks before, it would be him. For that matter, if Souls of the Moon really did exist, he and my mother had to have been one. They'd been devoted to each other, and like Bressen and I, they met in a dream before meeting in person.

"I'll ask Aramis when I see him next," I said.

Bressen reached for the towel on the back of the chair he'd been sitting in and helped me out of the tub. He wrapped the towel around me so my arms were pinned to my sides and his mouth descended on mine, capturing my lips for a hungry kiss.

"I don't need Aramis to tell me that this means we're meant to be together," Bressen said against my lips. "We are one soul, one mind, and even one body, if not in the literal sense."

I tried to move my arms so I could wrap them around his neck, but they were stuck inside the towel. Bressen only tightened his hold around me and captured my lips again as his tongue teased my own.

"Your arms stay in the towel," he said when he pulled back. "This is part of the fun."

He scooped me up to carry me out into the bedroom, but I was surprised when he set me down in front of my vanity instead of taking me to the bed. I frowned when he went back into the bathroom.

"Bressen? What are you doing?"

He came back a moment later with a second towel and began to gently dry my hair.

"You'll catch a chill if we don't dry your hair," he said.

My brows went up again, but I let him use the towel to take some of the water out. I was surprised again when he reached for my brush and started to pull it gently through the wet strands. He hit a few snags, but he was unexpectedly adept at getting the tangles out before he once again used the towel to dry my hair even more. I was thoroughly bewildered by the time he finally set my brush down and picked me up again, towel and all. He put me down on my feet next to the bed, and only then did he unwrap the towel from me and toss it aside.

"Get on the bed," he ordered, and the smolder in his eyes sent a shiver of anticipation through me.

"Yes, my lord," I said, and his gaze turned feral.

I sat down on the bed and pushed myself up the length of it so I was leaning against the pillows at the head. Only when I'd settled back did Bressen follow me, crawling toward me like a predator stalking its prey.

"Why am I the only one who's naked right now?" I asked.

"You're the only one who needs to be for this first part," he said.

"There are multiple parts?"

"Oh yes."

Bressen grabbed my ankles and yanked me back down the large bed toward him so I was no longer propped on the pillows but lying flat. I let out a shriek of surprise that turned into a moan of need as he ran his hands up the insides of my calves and then my thighs. His hands came back down to rest on my knees, and I swallowed as he pushed them up and apart, spreading me for him. His eyes never left mine.

"Bressen," I whispered, reaching for him.

He took my hand and placed it by my side, shaking his head. He was kneeling between my legs now, and my breath hitched as he pulled his shirt off to reveal the broad expanse of his muscled chest. My eyes lit on the pale moon around his navel before they dipped lower, waiting for him to remove his pants as well. His gaze found my own crescent moon, and he kissed it softly before lowering his head between my thighs.

Wetness instantly welled in my core, and my breath caught in my throat as Bressen looked up at me with his heavy-lidded turquoise gaze. Every muscle below my waist tightened in anticipation, and then his lips and tongue were on me, sucking and licking me as if he meant to devour me. I moaned and arched against him as he flicked at my clit, and he slipped a finger inside me to move it in and out as an accompaniment to the dance of his tongue. I writhed beneath him as he continued to feast on me, and my pleasure built quickly.

"Oh gods, Bressen," I gasped.

His tongue delved deep into my slit, pushing me close to my release. My body tensed as I prepared to be washed over the edge, but Bressen lifted his mouth, leaving me with nothing but sharp, aching need.

"Bressen, please," I whimpered. "I'm so close." My chest heaved with great ragged breaths, and I lifted my head to look down at him. His head hovered between my thighs as his gaze remained fierce and predatory but with the hint of a wicked smile on his lips.

"Bressen?"

"One of the things I love about you," he said softly, "is that you don't back down from a fight or a challenge." He lowered his mouth to lick lightly over my sensitive bud, and I jolted as pleasure shot through me.

"Bressen, please, I need you," I said, trying to writhe against his mouth, but he held my hips in place.

"When we first met, you always challenged me, and I loved it," he said. "I even accused you of courting danger."

I whimpered again, and Bressen slipped a finger inside me, moving it in and out at a tortuously slow pace.

"Do you remember?"

"I remember," I gasped.

"You faced Jerram after he drugged you, you asked Samhail to train you to fight, and you saved my life when Jerram and Glenora had me weakened and seconds away from death."

"Yes," I gasped, hoping that if I just agreed, he'd let me come.

I had no idea where he was going with this, but I didn't care. All my muscles seemed to seize up as he slipped another finger into me. He moved them leisurely inside, but the release I sought remained at bay.

He lowered his head again, and I arched off the bed as his lips closed over my clit. It was only for a brief second, and then they were gone again.

"I love that you're strong and brave and that you're willing to step up when something needs to be done," he said.

"Gods above, Bressen. Can't this conversation wait until we're done?"

Frustration gave my voice a gravel that vibrated in my throat.

"No, now is the perfect time to have this conversation," he said, and something in his tone made my body tense in a different way.

His tongue dipped back between my legs, and I cried out as the sweet agony pushed me once more toward my climax. But seconds before I snapped, Bressen again lifted his mouth, leaving me a hair's breadth from satisfaction.

"Bressen! Please!"

I was so close. If he breathed on me strongly enough I was sure it would send me over the edge.

I reached between my legs, intent on taking care of things myself, but Bressen grabbed my hand and pinned it to the bed next to me. My other hand shot out, but he withdrew his fingers from me to catch and pin that hand as well.

"As much as it would absolutely wreck me to watch you pleasure yourself," Bressen said, his voice hoarse with his own need, "I need another minute to finish this conversation."

"Bressen, please…," I begged.

"One more minute, and then I promise to give you what you need. Can you give me one more minute?"

I whimpered but nodded vigorously. "Yes."

"Good. Then think about what you're feeling right now. Do you feel that sensation that's both pleasure and pain? Torture and ecstasy?"

"What?" I asked, suddenly wary of what he was doing.

He ran his tongue up my slit again, and I struggled against his hold as a moan wrung itself from my lips.

"It's a feeling that you both want to draw out forever yet also drive toward releasing as quickly as possible. Do you know the feeling I'm talking about?"

"Yes!" I cried.

"That's the feeling I have whenever I see you rushing into danger," he said softly, and my breathing shallowed. "It's a feeling of being both amazed by you and your boundless capacity to surprise and impress me, but it's also that feeling of desperately wanting the danger to be over and knowing you're safe again. It all but drives me mad sometimes." His voice was barely a whisper, and I thought I heard it break toward the end.

"Bressen…"

His name was no longer a plea but a balm.

"I know I can't talk you out of going down to find *The Stalwart*," he said, "and part of me loves you all the more, knowing I can't, but I need you to understand what I'll be feeling up on the ship while I'm waiting for you to return."

I swallowed. "I understand," I said, the words barely a breath.

I almost apologized, but I didn't. I wouldn't apologize for who I was, but I did understand more fully now that my actions and decisions affected Bressen as well. I didn't think knowing that would make me choose any differently, but I loved Bressen, and I wanted to be mindful of what he was feeling.

To be sure, I'd need to speak to him about how he'd broached the conversation, but I did understand.

"Do you want to know what it feels like when you're safely back in my arms?" he asked.

"Yes!" I cried, unable to keep the desperation from my voice.

Bressen lowered his head, and I arched off the bed as his tongue and lips once again delved between my thighs. It took only seconds before I shattered beneath him, my scream of pleasure piercing the silence of the room and probably echoing down the halls. The noise tore from my throat and amplified the sensation at my core as I shuddered over and over again with the rapture that broke over me.

I was panting when my body finally settled back on the bed and I looked down at Bressen, who gazed up at me from between my legs. Whatever I'd planned to say was cut off as the bedroom door flew open and banged against the wall.

I lifted my head to see Leeda race into the room.

"My lady, are you-"

Leeda's urgent voice was choked off as she found Bressen and I on the bed, and her eyes widened.

"I…I heard a scream," she said softly.

"Everything's fine," I managed to say, my voice more of a croak.

Leeda nodded slowly and turned to go, but I saw her eyes dip to where Bressen still held my wrists pinned to the bed. She stopped, and her expression seemed to harden.

"Are you sure you're alright, my lady?" she asked, and I was surprised to hear the aggression in her voice.

Bressen turned to look at her over his shoulder, and I felt his own surprise mingle with amusement. It was indeed laughable that my lady's maid thought there was anything she could do to stop Bressen if I did need her help. Luckily, I didn't.

*Let go of my wrists*, I said into Bressen's mind, and his grip loosened enough for me to pull my hands free.

"Yes," I said to Leeda more steadily. "I'm fine. I promise."

It was another moment before she finally nodded, and I saw her hand ease on the fabric of her skirt. It looked as though she'd been about to pull it up, and I wondered if she had a dagger sheathed to her thigh.

I didn't begrudge Leeda carrying a weapon for protection, but I'd have to warn her against ever drawing it in Bressen's presence. That would only end badly for her.

Leeda finally closed the door with a soft click behind her, and I exhaled my relief.

"It seems I'm not the only one who's protective of you," Bressen said as he crawled up the bed to lay beside me.

"I forgot she was supposed to come get me out of the bath after an hour," I said. "She must've been nearby when I screamed."

Bressen reached up to my shoulder and brushed his fingers lightly down my arm, drawing up gooseflesh, a favorite habit of his.

"I'm sorry," Bressen said. "I was watching you underwater in the bath, and all I could think of was how hard it was going to be to watch you go into the ocean, of how much dread I'd feel until you returned and I knew you were safe again."

"So you decided holding my climax hostage was the way to address the issue?" I asked.

To his credit, Bressen flinched before admitting, "I suppose there was probably a more appropriate way to go about discussing it."

"I would say so."

"I promise I won't do anything like that again," he said, "and you're welcome to take your revenge on me if you like."

The contrition in his voice was sincere, and any lingering annoyance I felt toward him dissipated.

"I don't need revenge. Just promise not to do that again."

He nodded. "I promise. Can I do anything to make it up to you?"

I thought for a moment. "Yes, you can lay there and behave yourself."

He raised a brow as I put a hand on his chest and pressed him over onto his back. I followed him so I was straddling his legs before I went to work unfastening his pants. He lifted his hips just enough so I could slip them down his waist and free his cock, already swollen and ready.

There was a milky bead of liquid at the tip of his crown, and I flicked at it with my tongue before curling my fingers around his shaft. Bressen groaned and arched his hips. I ran my hand up and down his length as he continued to move, thrusting against my grip, but I put my other hand on his stomach and pressed down to stop him. He tried to reach for me, but I pulled back and wagged a finger at him.

"Oh no. You don't get to touch me," I said.

"I thought you weren't going to take any revenge," he rasped.

I canted my head at him. "Well, maybe just a little revenge."

I took his wrists in my hands and pinned them above his head as I climbed up higher on his body until I was hovering over the hard length of him. He grinned in amusement, allowing me the restraint. His grin turned to a grimace as I slid myself along his shaft to tease him. His cock jumped beneath me, and I reached down just long enough to guide him inside me before bringing my hand up again to hold his wrist down. He groaned loudly as I slid down onto him.

"Gods damn me, Cyra," he gritted out. "How do you feel so fucking good every time?"

"I'm a Hand of the Gods, remember?" I drawled, and his bark of laughter sent a sharp pang of need up my body. He'd given me a shattering orgasm minutes before, but my body wasn't done with him yet.

I slid slowly up and down his length as I ground myself against him. Bressen's hands twitched beneath mine, but I pressed my weight down harder. He honored my desire to restrain him, even though we both knew I had no real control over him. No physical control anyway.

I moved faster, pushing myself down harder onto him as I tried to bury him inside me as deeply as I could. He thrust up to meet me, and I let him, although I held his wrists firmly.

"I love it when you ride me," Bressen said as our breathing labored.

I let go of his wrists and sat back as I continued to grind myself into him. His hands closed over my breasts, and his gentle kneading sent shocks of bliss down my stomach to my core. I pressed my fingers to Bressen's chest, digging my nails into his muscles, and he groaned as his hands moved to my hips to help rock me on top of him.

Bressen broke first, and his cock throbbed as he spilled into me, a roar of pleasure escaping his throat. I was only a moment behind, and I pitched over on top of him as I cried out my release into the crook of his neck, afraid of drawing Leeda back again. He wrapped his arms around me and held me against him as his hips gave one last thrust that wrung another small cry from me before we both stilled, breathing deeply.

"Promise me," Bressen whispered, "promise me you'll come back to me safely, because I'll destroy this world if it takes you from me."

His voice was ragged, and his arms tightened around me, making it hard for me to breathe. I pushed back so I was looking down at him, and I was shocked by the intensity in his gaze. His words weren't hyperbole. He believed he'd tear the world down if he lost me, and I nearly reconsidered my determination to go down into the water with Axenus.

Axenus would accept it with good grace if I decided not to go, but my conscience wouldn't let me do that. Axenus might be a merman and infinitely better equipped to go down into the ocean to look for *The Stalwart*, but this wasn't his responsibility.

I stroked a hand down Bressen's cheek as his hands gripped my thighs so hard it hurt.

"I swear to the Trinity, I'll come back alive," I said solemnly.

Bressen sat up and his lips crashed into mine, the ferocity of his kiss acknowledging what both of us knew, that I had very little power to keep that vow if the Nemesis decided it was my time.

I felt Bressen's fear then. It seemed to settle on my skin like sweat, sticky and tight, and I vowed to myself right then that I'd do everything in my power to return to this man who held the other half of my soul.

Even if it meant defying the gods themselves.

# Chapter 36

It only took Axenus a week and a half to find the merman who'd seen *The Stalwart*. By the time he returned with the coordinates for its location, I'd managed to breathe underwater in my bathtub for almost two hours.

I'd also tried to swim in the ocean, but I'd only managed to stay under about fifteen minutes before I emerged shivering from the frigid water to find Bressen livid and pacing the beach. He'd wrapped me in a blanket, carried me back to the house, and forbidden me from training in the ocean until Axenus came back. I'd felt miserable enough that I'd agreed to wait, but luckily, the merman returned the next day, to Bressen's chagrin.

Being in the ocean had highlighted some of my other challenges besides breathing underwater, though. Another issue was that the salt stung my eyes when I tried to open them, but here again my elemental powers helped by allowing me to keep a thin layer of clean, fresh water between my eyes and the ocean.

The bigger problem was the icy chill of the water. Axenus's mer body adjusted automatically, but as a full human, I wasn't so lucky. It took some fast and fancy work by the clothiers in Solandis to make it possible for me to enter the water without my body shutting down. They made me a full body suit out of a fabric that was designed to help keep heat in. The water was still cold, but the suit at least made it bearable. I learned that my elemental magic could warm the water around me to a degree, much like I could warm the air, so that had helped as well.

To swim faster, the local cobbler had also made me a special pair of shoes with large webs of leather at the ends like fins. I looked rather ridiculous all dressed up between the shoes and the suit, but they were a necessary evil to allow me to stay underwater and move around fast.

Before stepping foot on a ship, Axenus and I spent several days in the water by Tide's End just letting me practice everything I needed to do to keep myself alive and functional underwater. It took hours for me the first day to learn to use several types of magic at once without thinking about it, and by the next day I'd forgotten how to do it and had to start over.

I got frustrated enough times to almost reconsider going on the trip, but Axenus had an infinite amount of patience, and his continued encouragement kept me going. I knew he was nervous about letting me come with him, but to his credit, he never tried to talk me out of it or suggest I give up when I got discouraged, and eventually I got the hang of everything.

When I finally mastered breathing and seeing underwater, and not freezing to death, Axenus declared me ready to try it all in deeper water.

Unfortunately, I learned on my first day out on a ship that I didn't have the stomach for sailing. We'd left a little after dawn to head out into open water so I could get used to swimming and using my powers in an environment that would mirror what we'd encounter while searching for *The Stalwart*, but the rocking of the ship had quickly made me queasy. Nothing we tried settled my stomach, and we'd had to return early. Bressen's fear had been palpable when he met us at the docks and saw Axenus carry me off the boat looking weak and paler than normal only a couple hours after we'd gone out.

Thankfully my father knew of a tonic that could prevent the nausea before it started, and my second day out with Axenus had been much more successful.

While I looked like something out of a carnival sideshow all dressed up in my body suit and fin shoes, Axenus was the exact opposite. I was awed to see him strip naked the first time we went into the water, and he dove in with a powerful grace I knew I'd never be able to imitate. Indeed, I followed him in that first day with something more akin to a bellyflop as I sat down on the side of the ship and rolled into the water.

Axenus was waiting for me below the surface, already in his mer form. What he looked like underwater literally took my breath away as I forgot to replenish the air in my lungs at my first sight of him. His tail was long and powerful with a short dorsal fin that ran all along it and even partially up the small of his back. The tail was deep blue, but there was an iridescent sheen to his scales that made them flash almost the same color as Bressen's eyes. Deep blue stripes and swirls covered his broad shoulders and muscled arms, and a few even ran over his sculpted chest. The markings looked like tattoos, but I guessed that – like the designs on

Samhail's forearms – they were probably characteristic of his kind.

I'd always thought Axenus was attractive, but underwater in his mer form with his dark red hair floating around his head, he was nothing short of stunning. He hadn't shifted into his mer form when we practiced at Tide's End, and all I could do for the first several seconds was watch as he swished his sharp-finned tail to keep himself in place in the current.

"Are you alright?" Axenus asked, and I was startled to hear his voice through the water. I nearly opened my mouth to answer but remembered in time that I couldn't.

Axenus had told me earlier I'd be able to hear him speak since his vocal cords could send sound through the water, but the words were slightly muffled because my human ears could only do so much to translate the sounds. To communicate back to him, I had to send messages into his mind, which I was able to do because he'd graciously agreed to keep his shield down when we were in the water.

"Remember to breathe," he said, pumping his tail once to bring him within reach of me.

I nodded, hoping he couldn't see me blush through the water. I assumed it was just a friendly reminder and that he didn't realize I'd actually stopped breathing when I first saw him.

"Are you ready to swim?" he asked, and I nodded again.

I took the hand Axenus extended and tried to kick my legs, but the resistance of the fin shoes was awkward, and I let go of his hand again so I could flail my arms and right myself in the water.

"Those will take some getting used to," he said. "Can I guide you until you feel more comfortable?"

I nodded, and he slipped one arm around my waist before taking my hand again.

"Kick slowly," he said. "I'll keep you balanced."

I kicked one leg and then the other. When I didn't somersault over in the water, I did it again and felt us glide forward.

"Very good," he said. "That was entirely you moving us."

I looked at him in surprise, but he just gave me a reassuring smile.

We practiced for nearly an hour more until I finally learned to swim forward quickly and in a straight line with little effort. Meanwhile, Axenus swum around me with easy grace, his powerful tail propelling him through the water as lithely as the fish we sometimes saw.

We went out again every day for a week so I could practice, going deeper each time, and Axenus finally declared that I was as prepared as I was going to be for our mission.

The declaration didn't make Bressen happy. After each day of training, we found him waiting on the docks pacing nervously until he caught sight of me. It wasn't until the third day that I finally thought to send him a mental message ahead of time to let him know we were heading back safely. We'd only barely managed to convince him he didn't need to come out with us for the trainings.

Leaving Bressen behind for the actual mission had never been an option, and I stood now at the prow of Bressen's fastest ship, my face tight from the fine sheen of salt that covered my skin after a week in the middle of the Carkinos Ocean. Thanks to Aramis's tonic, I could at least enjoy the way the ship cut nimbly through the water without spilling my guts over her hull, and I breathed in deeply as the salty wind whipped past me. I tried not to think that these were some of the last actual breaths I'd take for a while.

I jumped in surprise as steely arms slipped around my waist and pulled me up against a hard body. The smell of hot cinnamon and musk wafted by me quickly before being overwhelmed again by the briny air, and I relaxed against Bressen.

I hadn't heard him come up behind me. Living on the coast as he had for much of his life, he'd spent plenty of time on boats and ships, so his practiced steps were light and quick on the deck. He also didn't need to take Aramis's tonic the way I did, which made me jealous, since the tonic wasn't pleasant to drink.

"Are you sure I can't talk you out of this?" Bressen asked me, his lips warm against my neck just below my ear.

He'd asked every day since I'd insisted on doing this, and it might have started to annoy me by now if the question wasn't always accompanied by the sharp pang of dread I felt in him. He was terrified of what might happen to me, so out of respect for his persistent fear, I let him keep asking, even if I had to dash his hopes every time.

"I'm sure."

"Nemesis take you, Cyra," he said as he tightened his arms around me and buried his head in my neck. "You're intent on aging me before my time. I found a gray hair the other day that I'm sure is your fault. I shouldn't be getting gray hair for another three hundred years at least."

I turned in his arms to face him and took his head in my hands. I turned it one way and then the other as if looking for the offending hair. There wasn't one, of course, but I took one night-black hair between my fingers and plucked it from his head anyway.

"Ouch," he said, looking down at me with mock crossness.

"I got it for you," I said, smiling wickedly.

He smiled back. "But to what end? There'll just be another there tomorrow to take its place."

"It will make you look distinguished."

"You're a cruel woman," he said, but his voice was playful.

Bressen lowered his lips to mine, just brushing them at first, but it was only seconds before he deepened the kiss and pulled me up against him so I could feel his arousal against me.

"We should go down to the cabin so you can help me look for more gray hair," he whispered. "I thought I saw one between my legs as well."

"Oh really?" I managed to get out before his mouth roved over mine.

"Mmhhhmm," he murmured.

"You're insatiable," I chuckled as his lips moved to my neck, and I knew I only had seconds before he picked me up and carried me below.

Bressen and I had never been able to keep our hands off each other for very long anyway, but his need for me had grown twofold in the last week or so. To use an ocean analogy, Bressen had become my own personal barnacle, and I'd spent a considerable amount of time below decks with him in our cabin here on *The Maidenhead* since we'd come aboard. Not that I minded.

The name of the ship was another thing entirely. I'd given Bressen a reproving look when I'd first seen which ship from his armada he'd selected for us to use, but he'd only given me an apologetic shrug and told me it was the fastest one in his fleet.

It was also his men's favorite ship, he'd added after I'd sighed with resignation. "Let's take *The Maidenhead*!" was apparently a common cry among the sailors.

Bressen took my hand to lead me toward our cabin, but a light twisting sensation in my chest halted me in my tracks. He turned to look at me when his hand met with resistance.

"What is it, Cyra?"

"Stop the ship," I said, a little dazed at first.

"What?"

"Stop the ship!" I said as my head snapped up. "We're here."

I let go of Bressen's hand and ran toward the helm where the captain was at the wheel.

"We're here," I told the captain. "Stop the ship."

The captain just looked at me in confusion as Bressen and Axenus came up behind me.

"My lady," the captain said, "we still have almost an hour before we get to the coordinates I was given."

"No, my powers are telling me we're here already," I said.

"You're sure?" Bressen asked.

I nodded. "I felt the twist."

One of the other things I'd done the week before we sailed was go to the Priory to meet with one of the priestesses Phaedrus knew. Her power was the ability to find things that people were looking for, and she'd agreed to let me touch her and syphon the power for myself. Once I had her power, Phaedrus had arranged a small scavenger hunt for me around the Priory, and the priestess had helped me fine tune the ability so I knew what I was sensing and could use it to find the hidden objects. The twisting sensation in my chest, while a little disconcerting at first, was evidence that the object I sought was nearby.

The captain looked at Bressen, who nodded.

"Stop the ship," Bressen confirmed.

The captain immediately began to bear away and started barking orders to the crew around him.

"Could your source be wrong about the location?" Bressen asked Axenus.

"Possibly," Axenus said. "It's been decades since he supposedly found it. He could have been off on the location, or it's just as likely the currents moved the wreck or some of its cargo from their original position."

I looked at Bressen and saw he'd masked his dread behind a façade of confidence and authority, but he couldn't hide what was in his head from me. I put a hand to his cheek, letting my fingers brush lightly over the black stubble that roughed the skin of his face.

"I'll be fine," I said. "This will all be over in a couple hours, and then we can spend the rest of the trip home downstairs in the cabin."

His eyelids lowered over the smolder in his gaze. "If you make that promise, I expect you to keep it," he said. "Especially the part where you come back to me alive and unharmed."

"I promise," I said, fully aware Axenus was standing nearby pretending not to hear us.

"Then go get ready," Bressen said. "I need to remind Axenus what will happen if he doesn't bring you back safely."

His tone was light, and Axenus smiled at first, but the merman's face went serious as we both saw the brief flash of red in Bressen's eyes.

I turned Bressen's face back toward me. "I trust Axenus, and I know you do too," I said. "He'll get me back safely, so no threatening him."

Bressen shoulder's slumped as the fight left him. He nodded at Axenus, and the merman visibly relaxed.

Fifteen minutes later, I was in my diving suit and flopping my way across the ship, taking high steps to keep the fin shoes from catching on the deck. Axenus had already removed his clothing save for his pants, and he was waiting for me near the side of the ship where the gate had been opened for us. Bressen stood on the other side of the opening with the captain, his arms straining with tension where they crossed over his chest.

Aramis was there as well. He didn't really like sailing, but he'd readily agreed to come along when we told him what we planned to do. While I had healing powers, they wouldn't do much good if I was the one who needed healing. Bressen had in fact told me that if Aramis didn't agree to come along, he'd refuse to let me go.

I'd crossed my arms and asked how he planned to stop me, but he promised he'd find a way if it came down to it. Luckily, it hadn't.

"I'll go in first and make sure the immediate area is safe," Axenus said.

He turned away to strip off his pants. I shouldn't have looked, but I did, and Bressen growled into my head as I let my eyes roam for a moment over the merman's muscled ass. I turned to Bressen and gave him an innocent shrug that said I was sorry…but not very.

Axenus's dive was so smooth that there was barely a splash, and I had the sudden realization that this was it. We were finally doing what I'd trained for weeks to do.

It was several minutes before Axenus surfaced again, his deep garnet hair floating around his neck.

"It looks safe," he said, "but I don't see the shipwreck. I tried to go down a ways, but I couldn't find the bottom."

My heart sank. Axenus and I had practiced trying to mitigate the water pressure that would be pushing down on me if we had to go deep to find the ship. His mer body could handle significant depths, but my human one didn't handle the pressure as well.

We'd found that I could counteract the water pressure somewhat by causing the water above me to flow upward, thus creating a kind of lift, but we'd always been able to find the ocean floor where we were. If Axenus couldn't see the bottom, that meant I'd have to go deeper than I ever had before, all while maintaining air in my lungs, warming the water in my diving suit, and keeping the water flowing above me. The enormity of what I was about to do suddenly hit me, and I took a step back.

Bressen was at my side in an instant, his arms wrapping around me.

"You don't have to go," he said, hope coating his voice.

I shook my head. "I do. Axenus needs me to go down to find the collar and rings. He could be down there for hours trying to find them if I don't go."

"Cyra, you don't have to go," Axenus called from the water. "I can find what we need."

Bressen looked down at me, and the pleading in his eyes almost broke me, but I leaned up and kissed him tenderly.

"I love you," I said. "Don't worry."

His face fell, and I tried not to feel his worry twist in my gut as I sat down on the edge of the deck with my legs dangling over the side. A quick heave, and then I was in the water. Its icy chill closed over my head before I bobbed back up several seconds later, gasping at the shock to my senses. The water was like razor blades on my skin, and I quickly got to work trying to warm the water in my suit as I kicked lightly with my fins.

I took in quick, ragged gasps of air as I fought to control the chattering of my teeth, both from the cold and from fear. Bressen's apprehension seemed to mingle with my own as I tried to calm myself, and I saw Axenus give him a meaningful look.

"Breathe," Axenus reminded me as he swam up. "Breathe, Cyra."

I nodded and tried to inhale, but the cold air grated down my throat. The water pressed in on my chest, and I couldn't fill my lungs as I tried to suck in deep breaths.

Axenus took my hand and put it on his shoulder to help keep me above the water. His tail swished below the surface to hold us up, and I focused my gaze on the dark blue markings under my fingers as I concentrated on making my lungs work again.

A wave of calm hit me a moment later, and I knew Bressen was using his power to ease my mind, and perhaps his own as well. It worked, and my breathing became steadier as the knot in my chest uncoiled.

It was a couple minutes before I got my breathing under control, and I looked up to see Axenus watching me with concern.

"I'm ready whenever you are," I said to him. "I'm alright now."

"Are you sure?" he asked, sounding doubtful.

I nodded and looked at Bressen. His face gave nothing away, but I knew his insides were roiling, even if he'd somehow pushed his fear down to a place I couldn't feel it.

*I'm alright*, I said into Bressen's head. *I'll be back soon.*

*I love you*, was all he said in return, and I echoed it back to him.

"Let's go," I said to Axenus.

He nodded, and we sank beneath the surface of the water as the icy azure depths of the ocean swallowed us up.

# Chapter 37

I let the twisting sensation in my chest guide us as Axenus and I swam deeper and deeper into the growing darkness of the water. Axenus stayed by my side, beating his tail just enough to keep up as I kicked my flippered feet behind me. He could have pulled me down faster with him, but he'd told me during our training sessions it was better to go down and come up as slow as possible, so we were going at my pace, sluggish as it was.

*We're not going to be able to see soon if we go down any farther*, I said into his mind. It was growing darker the further we got from the surface, and the murky water wasn't helping our visibility any.

"I can help with that," he said, and he opened his palm to reveal a pale, glowing blue light. The light wasn't strong by any means, but it at least lit his face enough for me to see his features.

*What is that?* I asked, a little in awe of the swirling blue light.

"It's called phosphorescence," Axenus said. "There are several types of fish and other underwater creatures that produce it to make themselves glow, but most merpeople can also generate it to use as light as well."

*Can I create it?* I asked.

Axenus stopped swimming and turned to look at me. "I'm not sure. I don't know if the phosphorescence is part of my water magic, or if it's a merperson ability. If it's the former, then yes, you've likely syphoned the power to do it. Try."

I held out my hand and concentrated on manifesting the phosphorescence while also maintaining all the other things I was trying to do to keep myself alive underwater. To my surprise, a soft blue light bloomed in my hand, bringing Axenus's face into starker relief.

He smiled. "Nicely done."

He began swimming again, and I followed, trying to keep the light out in front of me. This, of course, made swimming even harder, and I realized with some trepidation that I was starting to tire. We'd trained for a long time each day this week, but we'd also taken breaks in between. This was the longest I'd spent swimming continuously at any time, and I was starting to feel the burn in my muscles.

*To the right*, I told Axenus as the twist in my chest tugged that way, and he shifted course to follow me.

I didn't know how far we'd gone down, but it was now too dark to see anything around us outside the glow of the blue light in our hands. Thankfully we didn't encounter anything more than a small school of fish that scattered in two directions when we swam into their midst.

*Can you sense if there's anything around us…like sharks?* I asked, voicing a question I should have asked long before now.

"Sometimes. Not always," Axenus said. "But if it eases your mind, there are very few sharks in this part of the ocean."

It did ease my mind as much as it could, but my relief was short-lived.

As if my question had drawn something to us, I felt the press of water against my body, like something large had swished its tail and the slipstream from the movement was hitting us. Axenus and I both stopped swimming, and our hands flew to the daggers sheathed at our sides.

*What in the name of the gods was that?* I asked.

*I don't know*, Axenus answered back into my mind, surprising me. I had no idea he could do that without mind powers.

*How are you able to speak into my mind?* I asked him.

*I'm not*, he said. *I'm just thinking, and you're reading my thoughts. I'm going to continue to communicate this way until we figure out what just brushed past us.*

*Why haven't we been doing this the whole time?* I asked.

*It's easier for me to just speak to you. It's less intuitive for me to think my answers, but I'm going to do it this way for now.*

We waited another minute, both of us tensed to fight as we tried to sense any other movement, but nothing emerged from the darkness.

Tentatively, we started swimming again.

It was only another minute before the twist in my chest coiled a bit tighter, and I made out a shape below.

*There*, I said, pointing, and we both directed our light out in front.

Only a few feet away, we could just barely make out the large wooden mast of a ship sitting crookedly in the water, and Axenus and I looked at each other with elation. We swam down, following the mast until the hull of a ship emerged in front of us. Axenus strengthened his phosphorescent light, and I tried to do the same as more of the ship became visible. It seemed to be on its side, but the mast had broken off and was propped against the hull, which is why it had been sticking up.

We'd found the ship but that seemed to be where our luck ended.

*It looks like it's buried in the sand*, I said, my stomach sinking.

I'd pictured a ship on the bottom of the ocean, half-rotted out, but still sitting upright so we could swim through it. I'd been gravely mistaken, though. The side of the hull was visible, but the rest of the ship was buried under sand heaped on it by four hundred years of shifting currents. It was possible that what we sought was too far buried for us to find, and the task before us suddenly seemed so much more monumental than it had a few minutes ago.

Axenus and I swam slowly along the length of the ship until something tugged in my chest, and I pulled up short. I ran my hand over the hull until I felt a tingling under my fingers.

*Something is here*, I said.

Axenus unsheathed one of his daggers and began to pry at the wood. After four hundred years underwater, the wood broke away easily, and between the two of us, we soon made a hole just large enough for me to slip through.

*We can widen the hole if you want me to go in*, Axenus said, but I shook my head. I was the one who had the power to find what we sought.

Fighting down my unease at the idea of being in a dark, enclosed space, I squeezed into the hole, letting the faint blue light illuminate the area. The inside of the ship was filled with sand as well, but it was more open inside than I'd anticipated. I still had to fight down the feeling of claustrophobia I felt, but it was at least manageable.

I let myself sink to the sand and ran my hand over it. The tingling in my fingers intensified, and I began to dig, pulling away big handfuls of sand with one hand while my other hand held the light. Axenus had extended his light down into the hole as well, and between the two sources, I just barely had enough light to see.

I worked for several minutes before my hand brushed something hard. I redoubled my efforts, and the lid of a trunk came into view.

I worked a few more minutes until I was able to get enough sand pulled away from it that I could find the seam of its lid. I hooked my fingers under it and said a prayer to the gods that it wasn't locked. By some miracle, it wasn't.

I opened the lid and let my light inside. The trunk contained the remains of what had probably been clothes at one time. I sifted my hands through the shreds of what was left, and my fingers tingled as they swept over something hard. My hand closed over the edge of a box that appeared to be just under a foot square, and I pulled it out, the sensation in my hand telling me I'd found what I was looking for.

I opened the box carefully and let the light spill over the object inside. The phosphorescence glinted off a metal necklace, a collar with five large jewels set into it. I had to remind myself not to gasp as some of the jewels closest to the light caught the glow and reflected it back as if lit from within. After four hundred years at the bottom of the ocean, the necklace still looked perfect.

I touched a finger to the collar but pulled it back as a surge of power shocked me. This was definitely one of the items we were looking for, and I held it up to show Axenus.

*I found the collar*, I said.

*Wonderful! Any sign of the rings?*

*Not yet.*

I closed the box and tucked it into a satchel that was slung across my torso. I reached my hand out again, running it over the inside of the trunk, but I didn't feel any tingling. I started to move, but the twist in my chest pulled me back in the opposite direction, and I swam that way instead, running my hands along the sand.

I'd only gone a few feet when I felt another tingle under my palm, and I stopped. I began to dig again, but I'd only taken a few handfuls of sand when something shiny kicked up and caught the light. I stopped, letting the sand settle again, then swept my light over the area.

Inspiration struck, and I called on my summoning power. Something flew up into my hand, and I turned it over to find a simple gold band in my palm. Nothing shocked me this time, and I tapped my power again to be sure this was what we were looking for. My palm tingled around the ring, and it warmed against my skin, confirming I'd found one of the pair.

*I found one of the rings*, I told Axenus before slipping it into my bag.

I reached out over the sand where I'd found the first ring and tried to summon the second one, but nothing happened. I broadened my senses, and the twist in my chest tugged me further into the ship. I swam along the sand some more, waiting to feel a tingle in my hand, but nothing came. I was almost to the end of the space when the twist in my chest suddenly pulled away in a different direction. I marshalled my searching power again, wondering if something had gone wrong, but the twist continued to pull me in the opposite direction. I began to swim again, but I pulled up short when the tug once more switched directions.

*It's moving,* I said to Axenus. *The second ring is moving.*

*What?* he asked, poking his head into the hole.

*The magic keeps shifting directions,* I said. *It must be moving.*

I felt Axenus's mental sigh. *Nemesis take me. A fish must have swallowed it. Come back up and we'll see if we can track it down.*

I swam back to the hole, and Axenus helped guide me through it.

*I'll try summoning it again*, I said, and I called the second ring to me.

Nothing happened for several seconds until something long and thin suddenly came shooting at me. I nearly shrieked as my hand closed around a slick, squirmy body, but I managed to stop myself in time. I let go of whatever was in my hand, and the blue light from Axenus's phosphorescence glinted off three bright spots on the wriggling thing.

The first two, I realized, were the eyes of a small eel that faced off against us, its mouth open wide in warning. The third glint came from something halfway down the eel's body.

*The eel!* I said, grabbing Axenus's arm and pointing.

*Gods damn me,* Axenus said. *The ring is stuck around its body.*

Not just stuck. Its body seemed to have grown into the ring. The eel must have swum through the ring when it was smaller, and the ring had gotten lodged around its body. As it grew, the ring remained, pinching the eel in the middle.

The eel tried to swim off again, but I summoned the ring, and the eel was dragged backward. Axenus grabbed the creature when it was within reach, but he flinched a moment later.

*The little bastard bit me*, Axenus said as he changed his grip so his hand was closer to the eel's head. *The ring is really stuck on him. I don't know if we'll be able to remove it without hurting him or worse.*

I looked at the little creature as it thrashed in Axenus's hand and wondered if my mind powers would work on it, when I remembered that I'd syphoned Ursan's ability to communicate with animals. I'd never tried to use that particular power before, but it seemed like a good time to try.

I wasn't sure where to start, but I reached out to the eel with my mind and sent soothing sensations toward it. It seemed to calm a bit in Axenus's grasp as I took the ring between two fingers and my thumb and tugged, but Axenus was right. The ring wouldn't budge.

*Did you do something to him?* Axenus asked, seeming surprised that the eel had stopped struggling.

*Ursan could communicate with animals*, I reminded him.

He nodded. *What do you want to do?*

*I want to try and get it off him without hurting him*, I said.

*How?*

*Do you think you can pull his body a little to make it leaner? Just enough to stretch him without injuring him?*

*I'll try. What are you going to do?*

*I'm not sure*, I said. *I wonder if I can somehow move the water both inside and outside the eel to help loosen the ring.*

Axenus inclined his head to indicate that might work. *That's a good idea. I can do that if you want. I'll hold the eel and try to manipulate the water. You keep him calm and pull the ring off.*

I nodded. *Let's try it. On the count of three…one, two, three.*

Axenus grabbed the tail of the eel in his other hand and stretched the creature out, pulling gently from both sides. I tried to convey to the eel what we were doing as I took hold of the ring to twist it gently. The ring loosened slightly from its body, and I pulled as firmly as I dared. Very gradually, the ring began to move, and inch by inch, I slowly shimmied it down its body. When it was fully loose, Axenus let go of the eel's tail, and I pulled the ring the rest of the way off. Axenus let go of the eel altogether and it shot off into the darkness.

I held the ring up, letting my power explore it to be sure it was what we sought. The same tingle and warming I'd felt before told me it was, and I slipped it into my satchel.

*We did it. I can't believe we found everything*, I said.

The elation of doing something that a small part of me had thought was impossible took over, and I threw my arms around Axenus's neck to hug him. He seemed surprised at first, but his arms came around me a moment later to return the hug.

*Let's get back up*, I said. *No offense to you and other merpeople, but I've had enough of being underwater for a lifetime.*

I heard Axenus chuckle through the water. *No offense taken. Let's get you back to the surface.*

I smiled as much as I could while keeping my mouth closed and began to kick. Axenus pumped his tail, and the two of us rose slowly upward. I still had no idea why the collar and rings were important, but we'd overcome the huge hurdle of finding them. Whatever came next would hopefully be the easy part.

I turned to look at Axenus swimming next to me, feeling the need to express to him the enormity of what we'd done.

Before I could fully form the thought in my mind, Axenus was yanked downward with such force that he was beside me one second and completely gone the next.

I almost screamed out loud but somehow managed to keep my mouth closed and yell to him through my mind instead. From the black void below me, Axenus's frantic words rose up through the water.

"Cyra! Swim for the surface! It's a kraken!"

# Chapter 38

For a long moment I just floated there as my mind refused to accept Axenus's words. There was no way I'd heard him right.

A kraken.

I didn't know exactly what a kraken looked like, but I knew it was supposed to be a huge sea monster…one that now had Axenus.

I snapped back to attention as dread chilled me far more than the icy water around me ever could.

At least twice before now I'd been told to run from danger, once by Samhail and once by Ursan. Both times I'd been torn about whether or not to obey. The first time, I'd ignored the order and ended up with a knife to my throat. The second time, I'd hesitated too long and lost my opportunity to flee.

This time I was near the bottom of the ocean using every last bit of magic I possessed just to keep myself alive. My strength was fading, my muscles were exhausted, and a monster had just grabbed my friend and yanked him down into the depths. There was no one to save me this time. No one would be coming down to help us – because no one *could* come down – so this time I didn't hesitate.

I turned immediately and swam back down the way the monster had dragged Axenus as fast as I could. I wouldn't leave him down here to die.

We hadn't risen very high yet, so I didn't have far to go before the outline of a massive shape emerged in my dim blue light.

The thing was beyond any horror I could imagine. The kraken was bigger than any creature I'd ever seen. Its roiling and undulating form looked purple in the pale light of my phosphorescence, but I imagined it must actually be a deep bloodred, since Axenus's hair looked a similar color down here. What appeared to be a beard of tentacles hung down below its eyes, while larger tentacles writhed beneath it like a giant octopus. Its black eyes caught just enough of my light that I could see how empty they were, and I suddenly remembered seeing these eyes emerge from a dark void in the vision I'd had. I'd foreseen this exact encounter, and I tried to recall if the vision had contained any clues as to how to get out of this.

A sickening shudder racked my body as I realized this creature had likely been lurking just out of sight around us while Axenus and I searched the wreckage of *The Stalwart*. I was almost certain it was what had caused the slipstream we felt on our way down, and I thanked the gods I hadn't seen it sooner, or I would've bolted for the surface right then and there.

Movement caught my eye, and I saw Axenus wrapped tightly in one of the creature's tentacles as he struggled to free himself. The thing nearly engulfed him, its giant suckers stuck securely to his body as his tail thrashed beneath him trying to loosen the monster's hold.

The kraken pulled him closer, and the tentacles on its face parted to reveal a gaping mouth with a sharp beak capable of crushing bone and snapping a man in half. One of Axenus's arms was pinned to his side while the other tried desperately to free the dagger at his waist that was partially covered by the giant tentacle wrapped around him.

I swam toward Axenus and unsheathed my own dagger as I went. Without even realizing how I'd done it, my phosphorescent light moved out in front of me to allow me the use of both hands, and I kicked hard toward Axenus, adrenaline overriding my exhaustion. My light drew his attention, and a look of horror crossed his face.

"Cyra! What are you doing?" he cried, the water doing nothing to muffle the panic in his voice. "Get to the surface! Now!"

*You're mad if you think I'm leaving you down here alone*, I said into his mind as I tried to mask my fear.

"Cyra, please!" he said. "If something happens to you, Bressen will never forgive me. I can't come back without you."

*And I won't come back without you either*, I said to him, my words edged with anger now. *I won't leave you down here to die!*

I reached him and raised my hand high before plunging my blade down into the tentacle that held him. The kraken screamed, a high-pitched sound somewhere between a whine and a shriek that echoed in the water and threatened to shatter my eardrums. It loosened its hold on Axenus just enough that he was able to pull his arm free along with his own dagger, and his blade followed mine into the flesh of the kraken.

The monster didn't scream this time, but one of its other tentacles slammed into my stomach, and a flurry of bubbles danced upward toward the surface as the breath was knocked out of me. I almost opened my mouth to inhale more air, but I remembered just in time to use my magic to refill my lungs instead.

The blow had pushed me back away from Axenus, and I swam toward him again. Axenus sliced his blade across the tentacle that still held him, but I heard his yell as the kraken squeezed him tighter. I seemed to feel rather than hear the crack of his ribs through the water, and his white-hot agony filled my mind. I kicked hard, trying to get back to him, but I was afraid to slash at the kraken again in case it broke more ribs.

"Go for its eyes," Axenus gritted out.

I changed course and swam toward the creature's face, toward its eyes, but also toward that giant snapping beak. I dodged as one of the smaller beard-like tentacles grabbed for me. I stabbed at it, and the dark blood that clouded the water told me I'd struck true. I started to swim again, but one of its larger tentacles wrapped around me, and I used all my strength to hold in my breath as it squeezed me painfully. I stabbed down with my dagger and prayed the creature's hold loosened rather than tightened. To my immense relief, the kraken's grip eased, but it didn't let go. Instead it pulled me toward its mouth.

"Cyra!"

Axenus's cry cut through the water, and I plunged the dagger into the tentacle again where I left it there this time. I turned both hands toward the kraken and sent a forcefield straight toward its face. The field pulsed through the water and kicked the creature's head back, but its force was blunted down here. The kraken seemed dazed for a moment, but then it roared and yanked me toward its mouth again.

Exhaustion overtook me. I'd been swimming and using multiple types of magic at the same time for what seemed like hours, and my body was weakening. I was physically exhausted, and my magic was fading. Whatever I'd had in reserve was spent with my forcefield. If I didn't get free from the kraken's grip soon, I'd no longer even be able to refill my lungs with air or keep the water pressure from crushing me, and I'd drown before the monster had a chance to eat me.

Cold dread seized me as I found myself within inches of the kraken's snapping jaw. I found the dagger still lodged in its tentacle and pulled it out so I could stab toward its face instead. The blade glanced off the kraken's beak and stuck loosely in the soft flesh at the edge of its mouth. I put my hands out to try another forcefield, but nothing happened, and I pressed my hand instead against the creature's face near its beak.

I was out of ideas. Daggers were doing little against the beast, and I was too weak to create a strong enough forcefield. I didn't have much else in my arsenal. Fire, air, earth…none of my elemental powers would do much. I was surrounded by water, but I had no idea what to do with it.

My thoughts strayed to Bressen, and I remembered the promise I'd made to return safely, a promise that had seemed certain minutes ago, but which now appeared to be one I'd have to break. Bressen had been terrified for me, and while I'd been afraid, I'd always been sure everything would be fine. My heart twisted painfully to think of Bressen on the ship and what he would do or feel when I never came back up. I felt a gut-twisting surge of guilt at what he'd go through because I'd stubbornly insisted on coming down here with Axenus.

I reminded myself that Axenus would be facing the kraken alone right now if I hadn't come, but that seemed to matter little now that we were both seconds away from death.

*Bressen, I love you.* I tried to send the message up through the expanse of dark water above me, praying it would reach the ship. *I'm so sorry.*

The kraken opened its jaws wide so I could see its purple tongue reach toward me. I felt the air begin to leave my lungs as my limbs went heavy.

"Cyra!" Axenus's voice penetrated my daze, but I couldn't answer.

I was right near the kraken's mouth now, staring into the dark void of its maw, and I put my hands out in one last effort to push myself away from that abyss inside. The water pressed down above me, and I knew that I'd soon be crushed to death if the monster didn't eat me first.

A second later, I felt my mind connect with Bressen's. He'd stayed out of my head so I could concentrate on my magic while I was underwater, but as death loomed and I reached out for him, he answered. I knew he could feel me fading, and his responding flare of agony and horror almost made me black out. I just barely managed to stay conscious as my body fought to keep me alive as long as possible.

*I'm sorry. I love you*, I said again to Bressen as my hands pressed against the slimy flesh around the kraken's mouth, and I waited to feel the crush of its jaws send me to oblivion.


### Bressen, minutes earlier

I paced the deck of the ship, not caring that I was in the way of the sailors as they hurried about their duties. I should have felt bad that they actually apologized to me when I bumped into them in my distraction, but it just seemed wrong that they could do something so mundane as work while Cyra was on the bottom of the ocean somewhere.

That I'd let her go seemed even more wrong.

It was taking all my effort right now to keep my mind closed off so it didn't try to reach out to her. As much as I wanted to assure myself she was okay, I knew she needed to concentrate on what she was doing. Axenus had impressed on me earlier how important it would be for me to leave her alone while they were down there. My first instinct had been to get angry at him, but I'd talked myself down. Despite our friendship, Axenus usually gave me a certain amount of deference, and I knew he would only have dared to give me an order – it hadn't been a request – unless it was a matter of vital importance.

Cyra needed to stay focused on what she was doing, he'd told me. The trip down would be extremely dangerous, and if she didn't direct her powers entirely toward keeping herself alive at the bottom of the ocean, the results could be catastrophic. He needed me to stay out of her head. He needed me to mask my worry for her so that she kept her mind on her task and not on me.

I'd wavered between thanking him for telling me this and wanting to wrap my hands around his neck and ask him why in the three hells he was letting her do this. He'd helped her train for it, for the gods' sake, when what he should have been doing was sabotaging her efforts so that she called it off and decided not to go with him.

But I knew Axenus well enough to know that the idea of sabotaging her had never crossed his mind, and I felt like a piece of shit that it had crossed mine. As much as I sometimes wished it was otherwise, Cyra wasn't mine to control. If anything, she was the one usually controlling me. The woman had me tied around her finger like a string.

Nemesis take me, how long had it been since she'd gone under?

I strode to the railing of the ship and leaned on it as I looked out over the water. It baffled me that my wife, my soul, was down there somewhere. I took it for granted that Axenus could survive underwater somehow, but the thought of Cyra doing it sent sharp dread coursing through my body. The only thing keeping me on the hair's breadth of sanity was the certainty that I'd feel if something was wrong with her.

I felt someone behind me, and Aramis appeared at the railing.

"Do you sense anything, Lord Bressen?" he asked, not looking at me.

For the first time it occurred to me to consider what he thought about all this. It was as much his daughter down there as it was my wife, and I suddenly wondered if he was angry at me for letting her go.

"No," I said, "and for now that's a good thing."

He was silent for almost a minute before he spoke again.

"Cyra said that the two of you met in a dream a week before meeting in person," he said. "Did she tell you that's how her mother and I first met as well?"

My head snapped to him, and he turned to face me.

"No, she didn't tell me. When did she learn this?"

"Just after she woke up. After Fernweh," he said.

I inhaled a deep breath. There'd been so much going on recently that it didn't surprise me she'd forgotten to tell me that. It made me think of something else, though.

"Did Cyra show you the marks we found after our wedding?" I asked.

Aramis frowned. "Marks?"

I untucked my shirt and showed him the crescent moon around my navel. His brows shot up when he saw it, and his gaze lifted back to mine.

"What is that?" he asked.

"That's what I was going to ask you," I told him.

Aramis knelt down to take a closer look, and I felt strange standing here on the deck with him staring at my stomach.

He lifted a hand to hover it over my navel.

"I don't sense anything strange about it," Aramis said, getting back to his feet. "It's nothing that my healing magic considers an issue."

"You've never seen anything like it?"

"No. Never. When did you say it appeared?"

"The day after the wedding sometime. We noticed them when Cyra was taking a bath."

He frowned again. "Wait, so Cyra has one as well?"

"Hers is harder to see against that pale porcelain skin of hers, but yes."

"Have you asked anyone at the Priory to look at it for you?"

"Not yet, but Phaedrus is on my list of people to consult."

"I'd be interested to hear what he has to say about it," Aramis noted.

"I'll be sure to-"

My words were cut off by a stab of fear deep in my core that was only partially mine. My hand flew to my chest as I almost doubled over with it.

"My lord?" Aramis asked, reaching for me. "Are you alright?"

"It's Cyra," I said as my breathing turned to ragged gasps. "She's afraid. No…she's terrified."

Aramis and I looked out over the water. It was tranquil enough, given that we were out in the middle of the ocean. The vast expanse of blue stretched out as far as we could see, its gently undulating surface now so at odds with the churning inside me that warned of a tumult far below.

I felt another jolt of fear, and I gripped the railing until my knuckles went white.

There were very few times in my life that I'd ever felt truly helpless. When my father had died, when Morland had taken control of Samhail's mind in the war, and more recently, when Glenora and Jerram had strapped me to a piece of wood, taken my powers, and made me watch them hurt Cyra. But those were nothing to how I felt now as I looked out over the water and knew there was nothing I could do to help the woman I loved against the bone-deep terror she was now feeling.

I couldn't imagine what she was encountering down there, and that was the worst part, that I didn't even know what was wrong.

"What do we do?" Aramis asked, his voice shaking with panic.

I raked a hand through my hair, probably pulling out some strands against the strength of my grip.

"There's nothing we can do," I ground out through teeth clenched so tight I'd probably chip them.

I debated letting my mind call out to Cyra, but I didn't dare, afraid that distracting her now would only make whatever was going on down there worse. Without knowing what was happening, I couldn't risk doing anything. I had to trust she had Axenus to keep her safe. I had to trust he was protecting her.

Minutes passed, but the fear I felt didn't abate. If anything, it only grew stronger. I raked my hand through my hair again and began to pace the deck. Aramis's eyes followed me, and I knew he was gauging my reactions, waiting to see any hint of a change in my demeanor that might tell him one way or another if Cyra was alright.

"Is something wrong, my lord?" the captain asked as he came up beside me. "You seem unsettled."

"There's a problem," I told him. "Cyra is afraid."

His eyes widened, and he looked stricken.

"The lady is in trouble?" he asked. "Is there anything I can do?"

"Yes, you can tell me there's someone else on board this ship who can breathe underwater," I snapped at him.

He took a step back from my wrath, and I felt bad for my outburst, but not enough to apologize at the moment.

"No, my lord. I'm sorry," he said tentatively, as if he wasn't sure I actually wanted him to confirm or deny that.

The sudden sense of exhaustion and despair that settled like lead in my stomach kept me from responding to him as I sunk to my knees.

"My lord?" Aramis asked.

Both he and the captain rushed forward to grab my arms.

"She's exhausted," I said, my voice breaking. "I can feel her strength and her power waning."

My eyes met Aramis's, and the horror in them mirrored my own.

"There must be something you can do," he whispered. "Please."

"There's nothing…," I said as I looked out over the water.

I fell forward onto my hands, and I sensed all activity cease as the sailors watched me, a Triumvirate lord, kneeling on all fours on the deck.

I didn't care that they saw me in this moment of weakness. I'd let them strap me to a mast and beat me bloody if I thought it would do anything to help Cyra. I tried to breathe, but I felt her growing weaker and weaker, and my throat constricted.

"She's dying," I whispered. "She's fucking dying."

*Bressen, I love you. I'm so sorry.*

Cyra's voice rose up into my head like bubbles from the depths of the ocean, and for a moment I was paralyzed by disbelief.

No, I couldn't have heard her right. But I felt the truth in my chest as something strangled my heart tightly and refused to let go.

I surged to my feet in blind terror and ran to the railing.

"Cyra! Don't give up! Please fight! Please!" I screamed over the water.

"My lord!" someone said from behind me, but I couldn't tell who from the ringing in my head.

"Cyra, hold on! I'm coming!" I yelled as I lifted a foot onto the railing and started to heave myself over into the water.

It didn't matter at all that I couldn't breathe underwater, didn't matter that I wasn't a merman or an elemental. I needed to get to her. Now.

Several pairs of hands grabbed me and pulled me back away from the railing, just as my mind connected with Cyra's.

"Cyra!" I screamed as I fought against the half dozen sailors trying to hold me back from jumping into the ocean.

*I'm sorry. I love you.*

Cyra's words again filled my mind, and terror like I'd never felt before surged through me at the defeat in them. Something in me snapped, and I let out a roar of pain that seemed to shake the ship. The sailors holding me were thrown backwards, and they sprawled across the deck in all directions as power erupted from me.

It wasn't unusual for my power to pulse when I felt strong emotions, but this time I directed it all at Cyra. She was weakening by the second, and I felt her struggling to stay alive.

I sent everything I had toward her. I had no idea how I was doing it or whether my power could actually reach her far below the water wherever she was, but I directed everything I had straight at her. My bellow of rage and pain rang across the water as power radiated out of me, and the ship pitched sharply beneath us. It sent me sprawling forward onto my knees again, and I felt something pop inside me.

My hand flew to my chest at the sensation, but it took me a minute to realize that what I felt was relief. I was breathing heavily as I knelt on the deck, but the tightening in my chest was gone all of a sudden.

Was she alright? Was Cyra still alive?

A seed of tentative hope blossomed inside me.

She had to be alive. If she was dead, there'd be a yawning void in my chest right now that I would've filled with death and destruction. If she was dead, I would've taken this ship and all the souls on board down to the bottom of the ocean to be with her.

I knew she couldn't be dead, or I'd be dead too.

## *Cyra, seconds ago*

I felt the jolt of Bressen's terror, and the pain of losing him turned my insides to acid. I couldn't hear him, but I sensed him begging me to fight, to not give up, and I almost screamed at the feeling of helplessness that overtook me. I wanted so desperately to make it back to him, but there was nothing more I could do. I had nothing left.

My head snapped back, and my eyes flew open as my entire body suddenly flooded with power, stronger than anything I'd ever felt before. Air filled my lungs nearly to bursting, and warm water enveloped me as all the powers I'd been using to keep myself alive surged at once.

I pressed my hands hard against the kraken's beak as it opened to snap down, and pure power flowed out from me. My phosphorescent light flared like a bright blue star, blinding me, and I blinked my eyes to banish the bright spots bursting in my vision. I felt something pop beneath my hands like a bubble, and the pressure around my waist from the kraken's tentacle was suddenly gone, as if it had let go of me.

As my vision returned, I almost gasped at what I saw…or didn't see.

The kraken was gone. I looked around wildly for the creature, but it had vanished.

Out of the corner of my eye, I saw Axenus below me on the sand. I didn't know where the kraken had gone, but I needed to take advantage of its absence to get Axenus out of here. I swam down quickly and shined the light in his face. Grief burned my insides until his eyes flickered open a second later, and I released a deep breath, letting a barrage of bubbles climb frantically toward the surface far above us.

*I thought you were dead! Come on. We need to get you out of here before the kraken returns*, I said into his mind.

The look Axenus gave me was one of deep shock and confusion, but I didn't wait for him to say anything. I pulled his arm over my shoulder, and we both winced as pain shot up his side. I pushed off the sand and began to swim upward, my power and energy somehow renewed. Axenus tried to beat his tail to help us, but he grunted as his cracked ribs objected to the movement, and I felt each sharp stab of pain in his mind.

*Stay still*, I told him. *I'll get us up.*

*Go slow*, he said. *You don't want to surface too fast.*

*Fast isn't really an option right now*, I assured him, and I felt the flicker of wry amusement in his mind.

My body was still bone-weary as I swam toward the surface, but at least my powers were stronger now. My phosphorescent light led the way up as I kept one arm around Axenus and used the other to swim.

I had no idea how long I'd been swimming, but it became brighter and brighter as we gradually made our way up, and soon we could see well enough that I extinguished the blue glow. Despite the burning in my muscles, I kicked harder and pulled upward with my one free arm as we came closer to the surface, to the air, to the sun.

Closer to Bressen.

Gods, I couldn't wait to see him. I'd been so certain I'd never see him again, that I'd never kiss him or hold him or make love to him again. It had been the worst I'd felt in my life, infinitely worse than seeing the fire-ravaged vineyard in Fernweh. I'd never again take for granted the feel of being folded in his arms or just being near him.

My muscles were on fire now with the effort of swimming, and my lungs were starting to burn as well. My power was fading again, and I was having trouble replenishing my air. I looked up and saw the light of the world above, but I couldn't tell how far down we still were. My body was screaming out for me to inhale, but I couldn't do it yet.

I kicked faster despite the burning in my limbs. Axenus seemed to sense my distress and beat his tail to move us faster. His pain clouded my mind at the effort, but I didn't have the energy to block him out. I only kicked harder, and the two of us rose ever closer to the surface.

I felt reborn when my head finally broke the water, and I sucked in that first gasping breath of fresh air with my lungs. I nearly sobbed with relief. Next to me, Axenus was expelling the water from his own lungs so he could once again breathe air, and I felt the stab of pain in his mind as his ribs throbbed with the effort.

Either we'd drifted while we were down or the ship had, because we surfaced a couple hundred yards or so from it. I'd merely been trying to get us up as soon as possible, and now the ship seemed so far off as I tried to haul Axenus's body toward it.

"Bressen!" I yelled, but my voice was hoarse from disuse and sounded soft and feeble in my ears. Then I remembered I didn't need it.

*Bressen! Help! Axenus is hurt!* I shouted into his mind, and I felt a swell of power as Bressen answered, calling my name in my head.

In the distance, someone dove off the ship into the water, and I was certain it must be Bressen. I pulled Axenus along, and he beat his tail again so we were propelled forward at the expense of his ribs.

"Stop that," I scolded him. "You're going to hurt yourself further."

"Are you alright?" he asked me.

"I'm fine," I said, still trying to catch my breath. "Exhausted but fine. It's going to be a very long time before I ever go swimming again."

Axenus chuckled and then grimaced as his ribs twinged.

"You saved my life," he said.

"Bressen is too busy to look for a new magic teacher," I said teasingly as I tried not to gulp in water.

Axenus's body was solid, and he wasn't at all buoyant in the water, so it was a struggle to keep him up as I kicked wildly to keep us afloat. I felt him flick the lower half of his tail every now and then to try and help, but I could still barely keep my chin above water.

"Cyra!" Bressen's voice carried to us from only a few yards away.

"Bressen!" I yelled, redoubling my efforts to pull me and Axenus toward him. Behind him the ship had turned and was sailing toward us.

Seconds later, Bressen was there, and his arms were around me as our legs knocked into each other while we both struggled to stay up.

"Gods above, are you okay?" Bressen said, taking my face in one of his hands as he looked over what little he could see of me.

"I'm just tired," I said. "Help me with Axenus. His ribs are broken."

Bressen's eyes fixed on the merman before he kicked away and pulled Axenus's other arm up over his shoulder.

"Let me take him," Bressen said as he shifted Axenus away from me. "You swim for the ship."

It was on the tip of my tongue to argue with him, but free of Axenus's weight now, every part of me rebelled at the idea of taking it back. I felt every ache and pain, so I just nodded and swam slowly toward the ship.

I reached it first, and two deckhands pulled me up, waterlogged and shivering, but alive. Someone dropped a heavy blanket onto my shoulders, and I pulled it around me before looking over the side to see how close Bressen and Axenus were. They were just approaching the ship, and four sailors hauled Axenus onto the deck still in his mer form. He grunted in pain, and I hurried to put my mental shield up now that I was on board so that I didn't feel his agony. My body and mind had reached their limits.

"Cyra! Thank the gods you're alive!"

A pair of arms encircled me, and I turned into Aramis's embrace.

"Are you hurt?" my father asked, and I shook my head against him.

"Axenus's ribs are broken," I said as I gently pulled away. "Help him."

Aramis nodded and was on his knees a second later next to Axenus using his power to check for injuries. I let my own power examine the merman and winced as it told me five of his ribs were cracked.

"Get back, Cyra," Aramis admonished me. "I've got him."

Strong hands pulled me away, and my legs gave out from under me. Bressen's arms encircled me, and I let him hold me up as every muscle in my body went slack at once. I felt completely numb.

"Please tell me you're alright." Bressen's voice was an urgent plea.

I nodded against him. "I'm okay."

He squeezed me hard and laid his forehead on mine.

"Thank the gods," he whispered. "I thought I'd lost you."

His voice cracked, and the sound lodged a knot in my throat. We both knew how close we'd come to losing each other, and I could do nothing but bury my face against his chest.

"Will Axenus be alright?" Bressen asked Aramis.

"He should be fine. I'm healing the last of the fractures now," my father said. His hands moved carefully over Axenus's torso as the merman lay quietly on the deck.

"You brought Cyra back safely to me," Bressen told Axenus. "I'm forever in your debt. If you want anything, you have only to name it."

Axenus looked at Bressen but shook his head. "As much as I'd love to have you in my debt, my lord, I can't take credit. It's Cyra who brought *me* home safely. I'd be kraken food if not for her."

Bressen's body jerked.

"A kraken!" he said.

"Just a small one," I said, waving a hand weakly as I continued to lean against him. I couldn't bite back the slightly hysterical laugh that followed. "Axenus exaggerates my role. We got lucky. The kraken must have been scared off by that flash of light."

Axenus looked at me as if I'd gone mad.

"Cyra, the kraken wasn't frightened off," he said. "You destroyed it."

# Chapter 39

*You destroyed it.*

The words rattled in my head as I just blinked at Axenus.

"What?" I asked, lifting my head from Bressen's chest.

"You destroyed the kraken," he repeated as Aramis helped him rise.

Axenus had shifted back into his human form and was naked, but the thought of looking down at him didn't even cross my mind.

I shook my head. "You must be mistaken."

"I'm not mistaken," he said. "I saw it very clearly."

"How?" I asked. "How could I have destroyed it?"

Bressen looked at Axenus, seeming very much interested in this answer himself. Axenus looked between us, and I had a feeling he was hesitant to admit in front of Bressen just how much danger I'd been in.

"The kraken nearly had you in its mouth," Axenus said finally as he eyed Bressen. "It looked to me like you'd given up. I was trying to urge you to keep fighting, but you were fading. I didn't know what to say to make you snap out of it."

I shook my head. "I didn't hear you. I was…"

I looked at Bressen. I'd been sending him a message at the time, telling him I loved him and that I was sorry. Telling him goodbye.

"I heard you," Bressen said softly to me. "I knew there was something very, very wrong. I could feel how weak you were. I did the only thing I could think of. I tried to give you my power."

My eyes widened. "That surge of power was yours?"

"I assume so?" Bressen said. "What did it do?"

"It restored me and then some," I said. "One minute I was so weak I couldn't keep replenishing the air in my lungs, and the next minute I felt as though the sun was shining through my chest. That must have been what destroyed the kraken."

"It wasn't the power alone that destroyed it," Axenus said, and I was relieved to see someone had given him a blanket to wrap around himself.

"What did you see?" Bressen asked him.

"I felt the power pass over me," Axenus said, speaking to me, "and I saw your phosphorescent light flare, but the kraken was still there for a second afterwards. You pressed your hand to it, and it…" His eyes grew vacant as he seemed to picture what had happened.

"It what?" Bressen prompted him.

"It turned to water," Axenus finished.

"What?" I said, my stomach coiling with unease as memories of turning the bear to earth months ago filled my mind. "That can't be right."

"I promise you, it is," Axenus said. "One second the kraken was there, and the next I was staring at nothing but water. I could still see the outline of it in the light of your phosphorescence. Its contours were there for a moment afterward until the current swirled them away."

I was shaking my head before he finished speaking. "I couldn't…"

"You did, Cyra. You did it to the bear that attacked you, and you did it to the kraken just a little while ago," Axenus insisted. "But more importantly, if you hadn't done it, we'd both be dead right now."

I stepped away from Bressen and tried to toe off the flipper shoes while keeping my balance against the rocking of the ship. I suddenly needed to get out of this suit and flippers. Bressen put a steadying hand around my waist as I finished freeing my feet.

"Cyra, let me check you for injuries," Aramis said, stepping forward.

"I'm not hurt," I insisted, but I let Aramis hover his hands over me as I felt his magic search for issues.

"Why are you upset about the kraken?" Bressen asked me.

"I'm not upset," I lied as I felt Aramis's healing magic work on me.

Both Bressen and Ursan had told me once that turning the bear to earth shouldn't have been possible. Aidan had said it was against the laws of magic to turn something alive into something inanimate and vice versa. I'd thought the bear was a fluke, but if Axenus was right, I'd just done it again. I didn't know why that made me uneasy, but it did.

"That should help," Aramis declared and stepped away from me. "Your body was straining from being under so long, but I fixed a few problems I found. Now you just need rest."

Bressen tilted my chin up so I was looking into his face.

"You were seconds away from dying. I'm glad you destroyed the kraken, however you did it," he said. "I have no plans to become a widower this soon in our marriage. Or ever," he added.

I opened my mouth to say something but closed it again. Bressen pressed a long, lingering kiss to my lips before he whispered in my ear.

"You're a Hand of the Gods," he said. "You were given powers like this for a reason. You need to get past your reluctance to use them. This time it saved your life and Axenus's."

"Do you still have the rings and collar?" Axenus asked.

Bressen pulled back in surprise, and his attention darted between me to Axenus. "You found them?"

"We found them," I said, pulling the satchel off over my shoulder, "but whether I was able to hold onto them during the battle with the kraken is another thing entirely."

I held the satchel in my hands, afraid to look inside. I was certain the collar was still in it, but one or both of the rings could easily have fallen out in the fight, and there was little chance that either me or Axenus would go back down to look for them if one was missing. I could try summoning them, but I wasn't sure what my range on that power was.

I took a deep breath, unclasped the satchel, and reached inside. The first thing I pulled out was the box that held the collar necklace. I handed it to Bressen, and he opened it. The collar gleamed within.

In the light of day, I could see it was pale gold with five large faceted oval gemstones of varying colors embedded in it. The center stone was an emerald, and it was the largest of the five. Next to the emerald was a slightly smaller clear stone I assumed was a diamond, and next to that was a ruby, again slightly smaller than the diamond. On the other side of the emerald was a brilliant blue sapphire the size of the diamond, and next to that was an amethyst the size of the ruby. The necklace gleamed in the sun, still perfect despite being underwater for four hundred years.

We all looked at the satchel again, and I reached into it to fish around. I found one ring immediately, but my heart dropped as my fingers closed fruitlessly around empty air in the rest of it. I opened the satchel wide to look inside but saw nothing.

"There's only one," I said numbly, laying the ring in the palm of Bressen's hand.

"It's alright," he said gently. "You did more than we could've hoped."

My hand fisted around the satchel in anger, and I was about to vent my frustration when I felt something small and hard against my palm. Confused, I lifted the satchel and touched the place where I'd felt the object. It felt like a ring.

I tore open the satchel again to look inside, and that's when I noticed the hole in the lining. I reached in and stuck my finger through it, feeling around in the space between the canvas and the lining. Relief washed over me as my finger looped through the second ring, and I pulled it out.

"Thank the gods," I said releasing a deep breath. I put the second ring in Bressen's palm, and we looked at the two identical bands.

"Should we try to see what they do?" I asked after the four of us had stood in silence for a few seconds.

"Not yet," Bressen said. "You and Axenus both need to rest before we do anything else."

"Agreed," Aramis chimed in. He gave Bressen a stern look. "You as well, my lord. Healer's orders. I'll be down in my cabin if you need me."

Aramis turned to head back belowdecks. Even with the tonic for nausea, he had a low threshold for being up on deck.

Bressen turned to Axenus. "Come to our cabin in three hours. We'll see if we can figure out why these things were worth almost dying for."

Axenus nodded and headed belowdecks. The ends of the blanket swayed around his thighs, and I couldn't help watching the muscles of his legs flex as he went. I blushed when I found Bressen watching me.

"I'm confused," he said. "When I catch you watching a half-naked man walk away, should I growl at him or at you?" His tone was amused.

"I'm sorry," I said. "I didn't mean to look. I'm just not used to seeing men walk around without any clothes on. Especially not men like…" I trailed off, realizing I should have stopped talking several words ago.

Bressen arched a brow. "Men like?" he prompted.

"Please don't make me finish that sentence," I said, and he chuckled.

"But I desperately want to hear the end of it," he teased as his hands grasped my hips and pulled me against him.

"It's not important," I said putting my arms around his neck. "It's not as though Axenus desires me anyway, so there's nothing for you to be jealous about."

Bressen cocked his head in question. "Why wouldn't he desire you?"

"I…thought Axenus likes to be with men," I said, a little confused.

Bressen frowned. "Why do you say that?"

I thought for a moment. What exactly had given me that impression?

"The last time you and I were together with Samhail," I said, "I teased Samhail that we asked Axenus to our bed first. You exchanged a look, and I assumed it was because you both knew Axenus took men to his bed."

"I see," Bressen said, furrowing his brows in mock contemplation. "So you've been under the impression since then that it was safe to stare at him naked because he couldn't want you?"

My mouth opened – to say what, I had no idea – and I knew I must be blushing furiously. Bressen just grinned at me.

"I wasn't staring at him on purpose," I said finally. "As I said, I'm just not used to men wandering around naked."

"Men like him," Bressen clarified, teasing me again.

"Fine. Men like him," I conceded. "Not many warriors came through Fernweh, so men with…bodies like yours were rare."

"Bodies like mine, or like Axenus's?" he pressed, too amused to let me off the hook.

"Like all of you," I tried to explain. "You, Axenus, Samhail, you're all…" I clamped my mouth shut, willing myself to stop talking.

Bressen continued to grin down at me.

"Warriors?" he suggested. "You do seem to enjoy a warrior's body."

I ran a hand over his chest. "I'm especially partial to angelus warriors."

His grin widened. "Are you?"

I was about to lean up and kiss him when I remembered what he'd implied. "Wait, so you're saying Axenus doesn't like to be with men?"

Bressen shrugged. "I don't know the full extent of Axenus's tastes. He may well take the occasional man to bed with him, but I do know he enjoys being with women. Does that matter?"

I exhaled deeply. In truth, part of me had been less self-conscious around Axenus because I'd assumed he didn't pursue women. I wasn't sure why knowing he took women to bed changed that, but it did.

"If Axenus enjoys women," I asked Bressen, ignoring his own

question, "then why did you and Samhail look at each other strangely when I joked that we'd invited him to our bed?"

The amusement left Bressen's face. "That's not something I can share," he said. "That's Axenus's story to tell if he so wishes, but I'd advise you not to ask him about it if he doesn't volunteer it."

I blinked at his sudden seriousness.

"It has something to do with why he owes you a debt," I said.

Both Bressen and Samhail had now warned me not to press Axenus about what had happened to him. While that only made me burn with curiosity, I knew the details must be horrible, so I didn't push the issue.

"I won't ask him," I promised.

Bressen nodded and shifted the rings and the box with the collar to one hand so he could take my own hand in his other.

"Let's get you rinsed off and warmed up," he said as he tugged me toward the door that led belowdecks.

I let him guide me down to our room, but the moment the door shut behind us and we were alone in the quiet of our cabin, whatever had allowed me to hold myself in check this whole time broke loose.

I threw myself into Bressen's arms and buried my face against his chest as my body heaved with sobs. He cocooned me against him, rocking me gently. I had no idea how long I cried against him, but it was a while before my tears finally waned.

"I thought I was going to die," I whispered to him, and I felt his body go rigid. "And the worst part wasn't even that I was going to die, but that I'd never see you again, that I'd never be able to tell you how sorry I was for causing you so much worry and pain."

Bressen stroked a hand down my salt-crusted hair. "You didn't die," he said, his voice heavy with restrained emotion. "That's all that matters."

He held me for a long time, neither of us wanting to let the other go. When he broke the silence again, his words made me shiver.

"I felt your fear long before I sent my power to you," he said. "I actually tried to jump in to…save you, I suppose. I'm not sure what I thought I'd be able to do, but I didn't care. If something happened to you, then I didn't want to live. I couldn't."

I inhaled sharply, and my eyes filled anew with tears.

"My darkness stirred," he said. "I was sure if I felt you die, I would've killed everyone on this ship. They all would have just fallen, not because I consciously willed it, but because my mind would just have taken them without me having to even think it. I wouldn't have been able to stop it."

I swallowed. He spoke as if his mind wasn't his own, but part of me understood. There'd been several seconds when I'd been close to being killed by the kraken that my mind had seemed to separate from my body.

"Thank the gods it didn't come to that," I said quietly, and he nodded.

Bressen pulled back from me. "Let's get you cleaned up and into bed. You can't survive a kraken only to die of pneumonia," he said.

"Thank you for sharing your power," I said. "It saved our lives."

"My power is yours, always. I'd give you every drop of it if I knew how, if it would somehow keep you safe. You must know by now I'd give you everything I have, including my life."

My chest clenched. "Don't say that," I whispered.

"My love, my power, my life. It's all yours," he said, kissing my head.

I swallowed. "How were you even able to give me your power? Is it because…because of this?" I touched my fingers to his shirt where the pale crescent moon circled his navel beneath the fabric.

He put his hand over mine. "I have no idea. We can ask Phaedrus when we get back. Maybe he'll know. I asked your father, but he'd never seen the mark before."

Bressen kissed me, then let go so he could put the collar and rings into a lockbox on a table at the side of the room. He came back to tug at the fastenings down the front of my suit.

"And for the record," he said, "I'm not letting you go swimming again anytime soon. If that makes me a tyrant, so be it."

I laughed softly. "Don't worry. After today, it will probably be a long while before I take so much as a bath again."

# Chapter 40

When Bressen told me he'd clean me up and put me to bed, I just assumed it meant he'd help me bathe and then throw me down and ravish me. But I'd only been right about the first part.

I'd rallied my power enough to fill the cabin's tub with hot water, and we'd bathed together despite my earlier vow not to step foot in a bathtub anytime soon. We'd rinsed away both the salt and our remaining anxiety, and then Bressen had dressed us both in clothes and steered me to the bed, but not to ravish me.

He laid me down, climbed into bed behind me, and then simply curled his body around mine so his warmth seeped into me to banish any further chill. It was only seconds before I drifted off to sleep.

I awoke sometime later to his arms still around me and his thumb lazily brushing my wrist.

"Have you been awake long?" I asked him.

"About twenty minutes," he said, pressing a kiss to my temple.

"You should have woken me."

"You needed your rest."

"I'm a little surprised. When you said you were putting me to bed, I actually expected-"

"Me to ravish you?" he finished for me, and I smiled, realizing my mind was open for him to read.

"Make no mistake," he said, "there will be ravishing later tonight. Lots of it, but you were exhausted, and to be honest, so was I. We both needed our rest. I also just needed to hold you for a while to convince myself you're really here and not lying on the bottom of the ocean somewhere."

Guilt surged inside me. "Are you convinced?" I asked.

"Not yet," he said, tightening his arms just a bit more.

I smiled and snuggled back against him further just as a knock sounded at the door.

"That will be Axenus," I said. "I should get up and let him in."

I tried to move but Bressen only locked his arms around me.

A knock sounded again, louder this time.

"I'm coming," I called to Axenus. "Bressen, I need to open the door."

"If you can get up, you can let him in," was all he said.

"Let me up," I said playfully as I squirmed against him.

"You're only bringing yourself closer to ravishment," he warned.

I squealed as he bit down gently on my earlobe, and I tried to launch myself off the bed.

All of a sudden, I was standing upright next to the bed, and I stumbled a few steps as the phantom feel of Bressen's arms around me lingered on my skin. Back on the bed, Bressen lay there for a half a second with his arms wrapped around nothing, and then he bolted up to a sitting position when he realized I was no longer there.

"Fucking hells! How did you do that?" he asked in astonishment.

"I don't know," I said, equally astonished. "What did I even do?"

"You ported," he said.

"I did what?"

"You ported. You moved instantaneously between two spots."

"Since when can I do that?"

"Presumably since you came in contact with another perimortal who can port," Bressen said, getting up off the bed.

"Who?" I asked.

"Your guess is as good as mine."

"Bressen? Cyra?" Axenus's voice sounded from outside the door. "It sounds like you're awake, but I can come back later if you're not ready."

I went to the door and opened it for him. "I'm sorry. Come in."

"Is everything alright?" he asked, eyeing us as he walked in.

"Cyra just discovered a new power," Bressen explained, and Axenus turned to look at me with interest.

"Apparently I can port now," I said.

Axenus raised his brows. "That's a rare skill. How far did you port?"

"Just from the bed to a few feet away."

"Do you know who you might have syphoned that ability from?" he asked, and I shook my head.

"Are there any perimortals on the ship?" I asked Bressen.

"No. It's one of the first things I checked when we came on board.

Everyone is mortal."

"Well, I suppose we can add this to the list of questions we need to answer," I said.

"Besides the collar and rings, what are the other questions on the list?" Axenus asked.

"We were curious how I sent my power to Cyra," Bressen said.

Axenus nodded. "I was wondering that myself."

"There's also this," Bressen said as he pulled his shirt up to show Axenus the moon on his stomach.

The merman's brows shot up again. "What is that?"

"That's what we're trying to find out," Bressen said before he filled Axenus in on what we knew about the marks so far, which wasn't much.

"Anything else?" Axenus asked when Bressen had finished, but his tone suggested that he thought we must have reached our threshold for strange phenomena.

I looked at Bressen, but he didn't meet my gaze before he answered.

"That's all for now."

He apparently wasn't ready to share what we'd learned from Phaedrus.

Axenus's expression suggested he knew there was more, but he let it drop for now.

"So where did you want to start?" he asked.

Both men turned to look at me, and I walked to the table where Bressen had put the collar and rings in the lockbox. I took them out and let my hands hover over them to see if I felt any particular pull, but nothing struck me. I was mostly drawn to the necklace for some reason, but part of me wanted to save that for later, so I picked up the rings instead. I tried one ring on the middle finger of my right hand. It fit, if a bit loosely, and I flexed my hand to see if I felt anything, but I didn't.

The other ring appeared to be the exact same size, so I slipped it onto the middle finger of my left hand. Almost immediately I felt something. I held my hands out, palms up and stared at them.

"What is it?" Bressen asked.

"There's some sort of energy pulsing between my hands," I said.

Bressen and Axenus both leaned in to look, but the energy wasn't visible. It felt like something between a faint heartbeat and a gentle breeze, but I had no idea what it meant.

"Try picking something up?" Axenus suggested.

Somehow I sensed this was the right thing to do, so I started to reach for the collar, but then thought better of it. Without knowing what the rings did, I didn't want to touch the collar. I saw Bressen's damp shirt hanging over a chair and picked it up. I could still feel the energy pulsing between my hands, but nothing seemed to happen. I shrugged and looked at Bressen and Axenus.

"Give me one of the rings," Bressen said, and I slipped the left one off to hand it to him. He tried it on his ring finger first, but it was tight, so he moved it to his pinky finger instead. It was loose there, but it fit enough that it stayed on without slipping off. As soon as he put it on, I felt the pulsing in my hand again, but this time it was only in the one with the ring on it.

"Do you feel that?" I asked.

"I do," Bressen said, sounding a bit awed.

"What in the name of the gods do these rings do?" I mused.

"I'm not sure, but be careful with my shirt while you're holding it with the ring," Bressen said teasingly. "I like that shirt."

And just like that, Bressen was holding his own shirt in his hand.

The three of us jolted as we realized what had happened.

"Nemesis take me," Axenus said. "The rings transferred the shirt."

"Let's see if I can take it back," I said.

No sooner had I spoken the words than the shirt reappeared in my hand, and we all exchanged looks.

"Well, I suppose that answers the question of what the rings do," Axenus said as he ran a hand through his garnet-colored hair.

"Give me the other ring back for a moment," I said to Bressen, and he handed it over.

I slipped the second ring onto my other hand again, and a moment later the shirt moved from my right hand to my left.

"I suppose it's good to know they work that way as well," Bressen said. "I assume that when worn by different people, the rings can probably transfer items over longer distances." He looked at Axenus, seeking confirmation.

"That would be my assumption," Axenus said. "I wouldn't advise experimenting here, but we should test them out when we get back."

"Agreed," Bressen said.

I nodded and laid Bressen's shirt back over a chair before taking the rings off and returning them to the box on the table.

Next, I picked up the collar. The gems seemed to flash even in the dim light of the cabin, and I turned the collar over in my hands, trying to sense anything about its power. It had shocked me when I first picked it up, but nothing happened now. I raised the collar toward my neck, but Bressen's voice stopped me.

"There's something I don't like about that collar," he said, eyeing it warily. "I'm not sure you should put it on."

I lowered the collar and examined it. I didn't sense anything amiss, although I noticed that three of the jewels did seem to have a slightly unnatural glow to them.

"I need to put it on," I said. Indeed, I felt a gentle pull to wear it, so I raised the collar again and slipped it around my neck.

The moment the cold metal touched my throat, a cacophony of voices invaded my head, and I staggered backward. I couldn't tell how many there were, but they seemed to be raised in alarm or pleading or anger. I couldn't tell which. Maybe all three.

The voices screaming in my head were crushing, and my vision started to blur as the uproar overran my senses.

I wrenched the collar off with a cry and flung it across the room as I grabbed for the chair in front of me. One hand found the back, but the other only grasped at empty air, and I pitched sideways, trying to catch myself from falling.

I felt two sets of hands as both Bressen and Axenus caught me before I toppled over. They steadied me as I breathed in heavily and tried to banish the echoes of the voices in my head.

"Cyra, what happened?" Bressen asked in alarm. "Are you hurt?"

"Voices. I heard voices yelling when I put the collar on."

"Voices?" Bressen asked, helping me down into the chair. "What kinds of voices?"

"It can't be," Axenus whispered next to me.

"What is it?" Bressen asked him.

Axenus didn't answer but went to retrieve the collar from where I'd thrown it. He stood looking at it for a long time, turning the necklace slightly in his hands as he examined it. He walked back to us, and I wasn't sure if it was more fear or awe I saw in his eyes.

"The legend," Axenus said. "The legend says Praya imprisoned the warriors who were sent to kill her in this necklace."

Next to me, Bressen went very still, and I inhaled sharply.

"You can't mean…," I said, letting the question trail off.

"I do," Axenus said. "If you heard voices when you put this on, it's possible the warriors are still trapped in the collar."

"Gods above," I breathed. "If that's true, they've been trapped in there for more than four hundred years on the bottom of the ocean."

"Fucking hells," Bressen breathed.

"Exactly," Axenus said.

I shook my head slowly. "A person would go mad."

"There's a good chance that's exactly what happened," Axenus said.

"Do we actually know for sure they're in there?" Bressen asked.

"Not definitely," Axenus said, "but look at the way the emerald, the sapphire, and the diamond seem to glow more brightly than the other two gems. Three warriors, three unnaturally bright gems."

"We have to figure out how to get them out!" I said, pulling the collar from Axenus. I started to put it back on my neck, but Bressen grabbed it out of my hands.

"By the Nemesis, Cyra! What are you doing?"

"I'm going to try to talk to them," I said, surprised at his vehemence.

"Absolutely not," he said. "If these really are the three warriors sent to kill Praya, you can't put this back on."

"Why not?" I asked, frowning. "They weren't sent to kill me."

"No, but they were sent to kill Praya because she was a syphon," he said. "If they sense you're a syphon as well, they could try to harm you."

"We can't leave them in there," I insisted.

"We can and we will, at least for now."

"I wonder what would happen if you put the collar on," Axenus suggested to Bressen.

Bressen furrowed his brows. "Why? What are you thinking?"

Axenus shrugged. "I have to wonder if Cyra can hear them because of her mind wraith powers, which in turn makes me wonder if you'll be able to hear them. If so, maybe we can get some information without risking Cyra's safety."

Bressen canted his head. "It's worth a try."

"So you get to risk *your* safety instead?" I asked him, crossing my arms.

"I'm not a syphon, and my mind powers are more developed than yours," he said. "I'm more likely to be able to shut them out if things get out of hand."

I wanted to argue with him on principle, but he had a point.

Bressen slowly placed the collar around his neck. I watched him carefully, expecting him to cringe back from the sound of the voices, but he didn't move.

"I don't hear anything," he said.

"Maybe you need to be a syphon to hear them," I suggested. "Let me try again."

"No," Bressen said as he removed the collar.

"It's not your choice," I snapped at him, and we stared each other down for a long moment, words unnecessary for me to convey my annoyance to him. Finally, he sighed and handed me the collar.

"Why don't you both try?" Axenus suggested. "Cyra will put the collar on, and you can connect to her. You can help reinforce her mind or help her fight back if they try to attack. At the very least, maybe you'll both be able to hear what the voices are saying."

Bressen and I looked at each other. He nodded and stepped closer, pulling me to him with a hand at my waist. His other hand came up to rest on my cheek. He could connect to my mind without touching me, but I knew he didn't want to take any chances. My powers tended to be stronger when I was touching the person from whom I drew them, and Bressen wanted to be sure our connection was as powerful as possible. He could also catch me again easily this way if I started to fall.

I put the collar back on my neck and jolted as the discord of voices once again screamed through my head. This time I felt Bressen's power trying to moderate them. The voices still reverberated in my mind, and it was difficult to make out what they were saying as they all spoke at once, but I could at least stand to listen to them now. I frowned in concentration as I tried to distinguish between the different voices and what they were saying, but I could only make out bits and pieces.

"That's enough. Take the collar off," Bressen said after a minute.

I obeyed only because I wasn't sure that listening any longer would yield anything beyond what I'd already been able to glean. My head went blissfully silent as the collar slipped from my neck, and I looked up to meet Bressen's turquoise eyes.

"One female, two males," he said, and I nodded.

"Is that consistent with what you know about the warriors sent to kill Praya?" I asked Axenus.

"I'm not sure," he said. "Not much was known about them, at least not that I've heard. They were three of the greatest warriors of the time, but in terms of who or what they were, I've never heard any details."

"Were you able to make out anything they said?" Bressen asked me.

I shook my head. "Only a word here or there. I'm pretty sure I heard one ask for help, and I heard the word 'alive.' What did you hear?"

"I heard the word 'destroy,'" Bressen said, "and one of them seemed to be mostly swearing, but that's about it. I wonder if maybe they couldn't hear each other. It would have made more sense for only one to speak at a time unless they didn't know the others were speaking. That would explain them talking over each other."

"So what do we do?" I asked.

"Nothing for now," Bressen said. "We bring the collar and rings back to Solandis and see what else we can find out about them."

"And the three warriors trapped in the necklace?" I asked.

Bressen sighed. "If we can find a way to get them out, and if we're certain they won't try to hurt you, we'll set them free."

I relaxed and nodded. That was a promise I'd hold him to.

"You realize that you want to set free three beings who not only agreed to assassinate a syphon, but who were thought to be capable of doing so, right?" Bressen pressed me.

Yes, I'd realized that on some level. Not only were the three people in the collar likely trained killers with unknown powers, but they were people who'd agreed to kill a woman like me just because of who she was.

Still, I couldn't help feeling horrified by the fact they'd been trapped in the collar and then lost at the bottom of the ocean for more than four hundred years. That certainly seemed like punishment enough for what they'd tried to do, and I hoped that if we were able to free them, they might be grateful enough not to kill me.

If one or more of them did attack, I was fairly confident that between me, Bressen, Samhail, and Axenus, we'd be able to defend ourselves. If we had to kill them, then at least they'd be free of their torture, because that's what I imagined them to be experiencing now.

"I do," I said, "but they deserve a chance to prove they're reformed."

Bressen gave me a look that said my naiveté was amusing, but I just raised my chin a notch, and he sighed.

"Fine," he said. "We'll try if we can, but first we need to figure out why Sandrian wants the collar and rings in the first place."

"Is it possible he knows the warriors are still in the collar, and it's them he wants?" Axenus asked.

"That's one possibility," Bressen conceded. "We should find out more about the warriors. If we can figure out who they are, that might guide us in the right direction."

Bressen picked up the collar and put it back in the box on the table.

"We're done with them?" I asked.

"We've learned a lot already, and we have enough information that we can start doing some research," he said. "I don't want to do too much with them until we get home. We went through too much to get them."

"Do you need me for anything else right now?" Axenus asked.

"You've done more than enough, Axe," Bressen said. "Go get some more rest."

Axenus inclined his head and slipped out of the room.

"Where were we?" Bressen asked huskily as the door clicked shut.

"I was practicing my new power," I said as I ported in front of him.

He immediately curled his arms around me and pulled me close.

"Are you sure that was it?" he asked, narrowing his eyes. "I could've sworn there was ravishment involved."

I ported out of his arms and onto the bed. "I don't see why it can't involve both," I said, deciding I liked this new power.

Bressen chuckled a little as he walked toward the bed. "I don't like how easy it is for you to get out of my arms now," he said.

I ported so I was right back in front of him again, and he captured me quickly, pulling me against him.

"Yes, but it's also easy for me to get back into your arms as well," I said as I leaned up to offer him my mouth. He accepted the invitation and closed his lips over mine for a hungry kiss. I wrapped my arms around his neck as I leaned into him, and a moment later we found ourselves on the bed with Bressen on top of me.

"Did I just port us both?" I asked in surprise.

"It looks that way," Bressen said. "I didn't even know that was possible. We need to figure out where you syphoned this power from."

I nodded my agreement. "Definitely. We'll do that as soon as we get home. In the meantime, can we get on with the ravishment?"

"I thought you'd never ask."

# Chapter 41

Bressen and I woke together as the violent lurching of the ship almost sent us both sprawling out of bed.

"What in the name of the Trinity is going on?" I cried as Bressen grabbed me just in time to keep me from toppling onto the floor.

"We must have sailed into a storm," Bressen said as he swung his legs out of bed and tried to get to a standing position.

The ship lurched again in the other direction, and Bressen was thrown toward the wall, but I was strangely relieved at the thought it was only a storm tossing us like this. I'd been dreaming about the kraken, and my first thought upon waking had been that the beast's sibling or mate had tracked us down and was now letting us feel its wrath.

Bressen and I struggled to dress as the ship continued to roll ferociously on the water, sending us staggering across the cabin every few seconds. We were almost clothed when a loud banging sounded on our door above the shrieking wind.

"Bressen! Cyra! Are you alright?" Axenus called from the hall.

Bressen managed to make it to the door and yank it open for the merman just as I finished pulling on a loose shirt.

"This weather is pushing the limits of my sea legs and my stomach, but we're not hurt," Bressen told Axenus. "You?"

"I'm fine," he said, then turned to me. "Cyra, are you up for trying to help me tame this storm so it doesn't tear the ship apart?"

"When you put it that way, do I have a choice?" I asked.

Axenus gave me a weak smile, and I followed him out of the cabin and up the stairs to the main deck with Bressen on our heels. The moment we were topside, we were blasted with rain that quickly soaked us through and felt like tiny needles on our skin. Flashes of lightning sparked behind ghostly clouds, and I jumped as a crack of thunder split the air so loudly that it vibrated in my chest.

"I'm going to try to calm the waves," Axenus shouted to me over the din. "See if you can blunt the wind around the ship." He turned to

Bressen. "You should stay belowdecks, my lord. I don't think there's anything you can do up here."

Bressen shook his head. "Wrong. I can be an anchor."

He wrapped an arm around my waist and pulled me toward some rigging on one of the masts. He wrapped his other arm around a rope and held on so that we weren't tossed as badly the next time the ship lurched. Axenus nodded and moved toward the prow of the ship.

The wind howled as it sent rain pelting sideways at us, but I had no idea what to do. I'd never been faced with trying to use my elemental powers on a force of this magnitude. I didn't even know where to start.

"Try an atmospheric bubble!" Bressen shouted to me, either reading my mind or sensing my uncertainty.

I closed my eyes and concentrated on trying to create a space of calm air around the ship, but I screamed a second later as the ship crested a huge wave and suddenly plunged downward so that the deck fell out from beneath our feet. Bressen held onto me, his strong hands keeping his grip on both me and the rigging as I tried to regain my footing.

"I've got you!" he said against my ear as he tucked me in closer.

I only hoped Axenus had found something to hang onto as well. He'd be fine if he went overboard since he could shift into his mer form and dive deep enough to escape the raging water, but finding him again when the storm passed might be an issue if he was swept too far from us.

I closed my eyes and tried again. I started with a small bubble just around Bressen and I, and my heart pounded faster as the wind calmed around us for a few feet.

"It's working," Bressen said with pride, kissing my cheek. "Try to make it bigger."

I nodded and slowly expanded the bubble of calmer air until it covered almost the entire deck. All around us, the rain stopped as the water met the pressure of the air inside the bubble and rolled away from it.

"A little more," Bressen said, and I heard the anticipation in his voice. "Push it just a little larger if you can."

I put everything I had into making the bubble ever larger so that it encompassed the entire ship. Below us, the deck had stopped bucking as fiercely, and I assumed Axenus had managed to tame the water beneath us or somehow push back the waves. I knew there was only so much he could do against the entire raging ocean, but whatever he was doing at least helped. All around us, the crew of the ship ran to secure the sails as the captain shouted for them to take advantage of the relative lull that Axenus and I were providing.

"We're taking on water!" one of the sailors shouted as he came up from belowdecks. "We need to stop it, or we'll sink."

Several sailors headed down the stairs after the man, although I wasn't sure what they'd be able to do. How would they be able to bail the water from inside the ship?

I was about to ask Bressen to send a message to Axenus about what to do, but he was ahead of me. I felt the prickle at my neck that told me Bressen was already communicating with the merman.

"Axenus says you should drop the atmospheric bubble and go below to get the water out of the hull," Bressen said a moment later into my ear.

"Alright. Are you ready to move?"

"Yes," he said. "Go now."

Bressen let go of the rigging, and we both made a break for the stairs down to the cargo hold. My air bubble broke as we descended belowdecks, and the ship pitched again as the renewed gales caught whatever loose sails the crew hadn't yet secured. The water was already ankle-deep and freezing cold as Bressen and I hit the bottom of the stairs into the cargo hold. Sailors were trying to lug buckets of it up the stairs, but that would be a losing battle.

I used my power to sense where the water was coming in from and felt the rush of it near the stern. I held my hands out and began to force the water back along the floor as I headed toward the leak. I needed to cut off the flow of water into the ship while forcing the water inside back out the way it came. Bressen hovered behind me as I walked, ready to catch me if the ship pitched again, but Axenus seemed to have the water outside under control.

It was several minutes before I was able to force all the water in the cargo hold back out of the leak, and I put all my strength into trying to hold it at bay.

"Get something to patch the leak!" Bressen ordered the sailors who stood around us, apparently in awe of what I was doing, and they jumped into action. The sailors returned a minute or two later with boards and buckets of tar that they began to slap against the leak.

The leak seemed to be contained for the moment, so I set my magic to keep the water back as well as I could while Bressen and I went topside once more to see if I could try to calm the wind again.

The storm was still raging when we got abovedeck, and I put my atmospheric bubble back in place while also trying to hold the water out of the hull. Bressen had given me some of his power today, and that was helping, but I hadn't rested much after diving to *The Stalwart*. I could feel my powers waning again, and I wasn't sure how long I'd be able to keep the bubble up if the storm didn't break soon.

Bressen wrapped his arm around the rigging again and pulled me against him as I tried to maintain the bubble, but my body was beginning to shake with the effort. A moment later, power flowed through me as Bressen's hand splayed across my stomach, and I knew he was once again buoying me with his own power. How he was doing it, I still didn't know, but fear gripped me at the idea of him draining himself.

Or maybe I was the one draining him. Maybe he wasn't giving me his power, but I was syphoning it. Fear turned to terror, and I tried to block his power out, but it continued to course through me, moving through my veins like molten gold.

"Take it," Bressen said against my ear. "I can spare it."

My mind and body relaxed as I stopped fighting his help, and I knew he was using his powers to ease my resistance. Part of me wanted to put up my mind shield and block him out, but the saner part of me knew that now wasn't the time to start using energy I couldn't spare. I'd take him to task later about his high-handedness, but for now I'd take his power, his protection, and his comfort, if only for the sake of the other souls on board the ship who didn't deserve to die for my stubbornness.

I had no idea how long we stood there as I held the bubble of air in place. My eyes were shut tightly as I focused on keeping the air around the ship as calm as I could. I wasn't even aware the rain had tapered off and the seas and winds were calming of their own accord until I heard the captain's shout.

"The worst is past!" he called down to us.

My bubble dissipated, and the wind blew the rain against our faces again, although much gentler than before. I allowed myself a moment of relief before my body let go, and I sagged against Bressen. Shouts sounded near the prow, and from what I could hear, Axenus had collapsed as well.

"Axenus," I said to Bressen as I tried to stand. "We have to help him."

"Don't worry, I'll take care of it," Bressen said as he scooped me up in his arms and carried me toward our room. "Have Axenus brought to my cabin," he ordered a sailor we passed.

"Yes, my lord," the man said and hurried off toward the prow.

Bressen brought me back downstairs to our cabin and quickly stripped off my wet clothes. He pulled one of his own black tunics out of a drawer and slipped it over my head before helping me under the covers. A minute later, several sailors struggled into the room with Axenus's unconscious body, and Bressen directed them to lay him down in the bed next to me.

"Axenus!" I cried, leaning across to see if he was alright.

Bressen's hand pressed me back down. "He's fine, just exhausted like you are. I'll keep an eye on you both while you rest."

I looked at Bressen and saw the weariness on his own face as well. He raised a hand to my cheek, but I gasped as I noticed the raw rope burns that curled around his wrist and forearm from when he'd held us in place.

I bolted upright in bed. "Your arm!"

"I'll live," he said, trying to press me down. "Rest."

I pushed myself back up and laid my hands on his forearm to heal the skin. The burns were warm under my cold fingers, but I felt them mend.

"Thank you," Bressen said as he flexed his hand. "Now go to sleep."

"What about you? You need your rest as well."

He smiled weakly. "I'll be fine."

"But-"

"Go to sleep," he said firmly, "or I'll make you go to sleep."

I frowned at him. "You were in my head before," I accused him. "You kept me from resisting your power."

"And I'd do it again, just like I'll put you to sleep right now if you don't lay down and rest," he said, completely unapologetic. "I let you have your way the last week or so, but I'm putting my foot down."

I frowned again, but he gave me a look of warning, and I sighed and closed my eyes. I must have fallen asleep almost instantly because there was sun streaming in the window of our cabin when I woke, and the ship didn't seem to be moving. I felt a warm body next to me and turned toward it, but I started when I realized it was Axenus and not Bressen. Then I remembered Bressen had ordered Axenus brought to our cabin. Thankfully the merman's chest rose and fell with even breathing.

I turned my head to the other side and saw Bressen curled up asleep on the couch against the wall. I was still beyond exhausted, but I wanted to know if the storm had blown us far off course or if the ship had sustained any other damage that we needed to know about. I sat up in bed, and Bressen was instantly awake on the couch.

"Cyra? Are you alright?" he asked quietly. He was trying not to wake Axenus, but the merman stirred next to me, and his eyes fluttered open.

"Cyra?" Axenus said, narrowing his eyes in confusion as he realized I was in bed next to him. He sat up quickly and looked around, obviously surprised to find himself not in his own room. "What am I doing in here?"

"I didn't want to leave you alone in your own room," Bressen explained, "so I had you brought to our cabin to recover a bit. You and Cyra expended a lot of power last night saving our asses."

"Thank you, my lord," Axenus said, sounding a little stunned.

"Are we safe?" I asked. "It doesn't feel like we're moving."

"Stay here," Bressen said, getting up off the couch. "I'll check with the captain to see what the situation is."

"Check on Aramis please?" I said, and Bressen nodded as he left.

I turned to find Axenus looking at me.

"That's twice we've cheated death in the last day or so," I told him.

He smiled. "You're really starting to use your powers well."

"I had a great teacher. You're the reason we didn't all get tossed overboard."

Axenus sighed and looked up at the ceiling. "I should have been able to control the waves better than I did. I was just too drained from earlier."

I put a gentle hand on his shoulder. "You saved us," I assured him.

"You did as well," he said. "I assume you were able to patch the leak in the hull?"

"I pushed the water back. The sailor's patched the hull."

Axenus and I both laid back down and waited in silence until the door to the cabin swung open again, and Bressen strode in.

"Aramis is fine, but I don't think he's coming topside anytime soon," Bressen said as Axenus and I sat up. "The captain is trying to determine how far off course we were blown. There are a few things that need to be repaired, including a more permanent patch to the hull, but the more interesting news is the island the look-out spotted not too far from us."

"An island?" I asked. "Way out here?"

Bressen nodded. "The captain doesn't see an island on any of his maps near where we found *The Stalwart*, so it's either uncharted, or we were blown much further off course than we originally thought."

I swung my legs out of bed and stood up. "I want to see it."

"You should rest some more," Bressen said.

"I've rested enough. Now I need some air."

"Nothing I say is going to make you listen to me, is it," he said.

I smiled at him as I pulled on a pair of pants. "Why would I start listening to you now?"

He sighed. "Why indeed."

"I'll come too," Axenus said as he got out of bed and followed us.

I shielded my eyes from the bright sunlight as we emerged from belowdecks. I blinked as my vision adjusted, then jumped in surprise a second later as a loud cheer rose up all around us. The sailors all looked at us as they whooped and hollered and waved their caps in the air.

"What's going on?" I asked.

"I believe they're showing their appreciation to you and Axenus for saving their lives in that storm last night," Bressen said.

Axenus and I glanced at each other a bit in disbelief before looking back out over the sailors who did indeed seem to be cheering for us. I smiled shyly at them and nodded as I passed.

The three of us joined the captain and the first mate at the railing to look out over the water as the cheering died down. Sure enough, a patch of green interrupted the endless blue expanse all around us. It wasn't a huge island by any means, but there was something about it that seemed to make my mind prickle. I stared at it, trying to make sense of why the island called to me, but the answer remained just out of reach, dissipating like Bressen's halo glamour when I tried to focus on it.

My mind must have wandered, because I snapped awake a moment later, as if I'd been pulled from a daydream. It took me a moment to recall where I was, and I looked around for Bressen. I'd thought he was right next to me, but he was several feet away, and he seemed dazed as well.

"Are we leaving already?" I asked as I noticed the sailors readying the ship for us to get underway. "I thought the hull needed to be fixed. And shouldn't we go explore the island?"

"The hull is fixed," the captain said from my other side. "It wasn't as bad as we thought. The island will have to wait. We really should get back to port, my lady."

I looked at Bressen, who was watching me closely.

"Are you alright?" he asked.

I blinked a few more times. "I think so. I just feel…strange."

"I do as well," he said. "Maybe it's best we head back. We don't want to risk running into any more issues."

I nodded, but the feeling of uneasiness remained. The sun seemed lower in the sky than I'd originally thought, and I wondered if we'd slept later than I realized.

"Let's get up on the helm so we're out of the way," Bressen said.

He slipped his hand into mine and tugged on it lightly, but I didn't move. I frowned as I watched two sailors secure one of the rowboats in preparation for our departure. Water dripped from the bottom of the boat, as if it had just been raised up out of the ocean.

I shook my head. It was probably still just wet from the storm. The rain had been torrential and soaked nearly everything on the ship.

I gave way to Bressen's gentle pull as he led me away from the side of the ship, but I spared a look back toward the island.

I had the oddest feeling there was something on it I needed.

# Chapter 42

We arrived back on the continent several days later than expected due to the storm, but we were alive and bearing the objects we'd sought. Something still nagged at me about the island we'd found, but all things considered, it had been a successful trip, and I was grateful to be back on dry land. Aramis and I were nearly out of the tonic he'd made for seasickness, and I'd started to fear we might both spend our last few days on the ship heaving the contents of our stomachs over the side.

Aramis had just barely managed to tolerate the ocean voyage and was even happier than me to be back on solid ground. I sent him home first before opening a portal for me, Bressen, and Axenus.

Samhail and Ferris met us in the foyer of Tide's End only a few seconds after we stepped through from the docks, and the five of us made our way up to the fourth floor to Bressen's study. Ferris and Samhail updated Bressen on territory business as we went, although Bressen would meet with both of them later to go over things more in-depth.

The steward peeled away from us as we approached the study, having received his orders from Bressen, and the four of us filed inside.

We all sat down at the meeting table and filled Samhail in on everything that had happened. The gargoyle shifted in his seat as Axenus and I recalled our battle with the kraken, and I sensed a tension in him that confused me. We were home safe, yet he seemed to radiate nervous energy at the thought of the danger we'd been in.

We ended by showing Samhail the items we'd recovered from *The Stalwart* and explaining what we'd learned about them. When we were done, Samhail sat quietly for a moment, seeming to digest it all. Finally, he turned to Axenus.

"So Cyra had to save you from a sea monster?" he asked, thoroughly amused. "Aren't you supposed to be this great oceanic warrior, Axe?"

Axenus narrowed his eyes in annoyance. "That's what you took away from this whole story?" he asked.

Samhail shrugged. "It's the part I'll remember most fondly."

I gave Samhail an exasperated look, but he just smirked at me before turning back to Bressen. "So what are the next steps?" he asked.

"We need to test out how far the rings will work, and Cyra wants to try to release whoever is trapped in the necklace," Bressen answered.

Samhail's eyes swung to me. "Are you sure that's a good idea? It sounds like they were trapped in there for good reason."

I raised a brow at him. "Are you afraid you can't handle them?"

Samhail glowered at me, but Axenus was now the one smirking. I knew I'd be running extra laps at my next training with Samhail for the comment, but the look on his face had been worth it.

"We'll see what Phaedrus has to say before making any decisions," Bressen cut in before Samhail could respond.

"That reminds me," Samhail said, "Phaedrus came by yesterday to speak with you. He said he had some more information that you've been waiting on from him."

Bressen and I locked eyes across the table before he turned back to Samhail. "Thank you for letting me know. Let's continue this discussion later so I can see what Phaedrus wants."

Samhail seemed a bit surprised that whatever Phaedrus might have to say could be more important than what we were discussing, but he nodded and rose, as did Axenus. The two men left the room, and Bressen went to pull a message leaf from his desk. He wrote on it and let the paper vanish between his two fingers.

"What if Phaedrus is busy?" I asked.

"He won't keep us waiting," Bressen said as he swung a painting away from the wall behind his desk to reveal a hidden safe behind it.

He laid a hand on the safe, and it clicked open. He put the collar and rings inside, relocked it, then swung the picture back into place.

Seconds later a portal flared open in the study, and Phaedrus stepped through carrying the ancient book he'd brought last time.

"What did you find?" Bressen asked Phaedrus as soon as he entered.

"Good morning, Phaedrus," I said, giving Bressen an admonitory look for his straight-to-business demeanor. "It's good to see you again."

Phaedrus smiled at me. "You as well, my lady. I'm glad to see you returned home safely."

"Thank you," I said. "We're both well and glad to be home." I looked pointedly at Bressen who stood with his arms crossed over his chest and the hint of an indulgent smile at the corners of his lips.

"My apologies, Phaedrus," Bressen said. "I seem to have left my manners in the middle of the Carkinos. I hope you're well."

"No apologies necessary, my lord," he said with a tip of his head. "I understand you're eager to learn what I found."

*Now can we get down to business, or should I call for some tea and cakes first?* Bressen asked into my mind.

I quirked a brow at him. *Tea and cakes would be lovely,* I shot back.

Bressen rolled his eyes. "Phaedrus, thank you for coming so quickly. Please tell us what you've learned."

Phaedrus set the ancient book on the table and carefully opened it as Bressen and I sat down around it.

"I found that the text goes further into the roles of the syphons as Hands of the Gods," he said. "In particular, it notes that each syphon is aligned with one of the Trinity. All three syphons serve the Trinity as a whole, but each god also grants specific powers and strengths to their chosen syphon so the syphon is better able to serve that particular god."

"So I'm bound to one of the Trinity?" I asked. "How do I know which one? And what does that mean exactly?"

"It will be related to your powers," Phaedrus said carefully, and I knew from his tone he had a theory about which god I served.

"You have an idea," I said, calling him on it. "Tell me which one."

He paused, then said, "My lady, your powers suggest you're aligned with the Nemesis."

I stared at him wide-eyed. Somewhere deep down I knew he was going to say that, but it was still jarring to hear it.

"How did you come to that conclusion?" I asked as calmly as I could, but I felt the blood racing through my veins.

My guess would have been that I was aligned with the Protector, given that my father was a healer, or maybe even the Creator since I grew grapes and made wine. The Nemesis actually would've been the last on my list.

"Well, to start, I think we can eliminate the Creator," Phaedrus said. "I'd expect the Hand of the Creator to actually be able to…well, create, and you've never shown any ability that has allowed you to create something from nothing. Correct?"

"Not from nothing, but I thought making wine might count," I said.

Even as the words left my mouth, I realized that growing grapes and making wine weren't the type of creation Phaedrus was talking about. He confirmed as much a second later.

"I'm sorry, my lady. While that's an ability I myself appreciate very much, it's not quite Creator-level power."

I nodded in acknowledgement, remembering now that Praya was said to have created a number of powerful magical items in her time, thus she'd likely been aligned with the Creator. I could draw the elements because of my elemental powers, but I'd never, as far as I knew, created something from nothing, and definitely not any kind of magical object.

"Fair enough," I told Phaedrus, "but how do you know I'm not aligned with the Protector?"

"I can't say with a hundred percent certainty you aren't," Phaedrus admitted, "but there are at least two things that make me think you're not aligned with the Protector."

"And those are?"

"First," he said, "I'd expect your healing abilities to be more potent if you were aligned with the Protector, but by your own admission, your abilities are rudimentary. Your father is a healer, yet you don't seem to have his level of skill in that area."

"Perhaps I just need more practice," I suggested stubbornly, but it was a valid point. I could heal minor to moderate wounds and maladies, but healing didn't seem to come naturally to me, and I certainly didn't have anywhere near Aramis's skill in this area. After Glenora and Jerram's coup, I'd seen him bring some of the wounded soldiers back nearly from the brink of death. My healing abilities were paltry by comparison.

Phaedrus shook his head. "If you were aligned with the Protector, that ability would be innate."

"And your second reason?" I asked.

Phaedrus swallowed before speaking. "The Nemesis is the god of death and equilibrium. In the end, the Nemesis takes everyone."

"And you think my powers are related to death?" I asked doubtfully.

"Yes. The bear proves that," he answered without hesitation.

I went very still as the truth of his words struck me. When I'd first come to Callanus and tried to explain away my powers before the Triumvirate, Ursan had insisted that what I'd done to the bear wasn't ordinary. His words came back to me now.

*The elements can be wielded as weapons to kill easily enough, but to kill another living thing by changing it into the element itself...well, that's something I don't think I've ever seen.*

Bressen had echoed as much to me the next day in the library.

*To change a living being into something inanimate, and to snuff out its life in the process, that's a power I've never seen. It's the opposite of giving life to something inanimate, which is a power only the Creator has.*

No, I couldn't give life to something, but I'd turned a living being into something inanimate. I'd killed that bear by turning it to earth.

I might almost have been able to dismiss the bear as an isolated incident, but my recent encounter with the kraken was only more proof that my power was something different.

Aidan had said it sounded like transfiguration, but it wasn't. It was my elemental power combined with the power of the Nemesis.

The power of death.

I turned to Bressen to see what he made of this, but I saw no sign of disagreement in his eyes. He and Phaedrus were of the same mind.

I'd always thought the Nemesis was the most misunderstood of the three gods. The Nemesis's power was in death, but I'd always viewed death as a simple inevitability, a necessary end. Granted that end came much sooner for some than for others, but I didn't believe death in itself had to be a bad thing. Just as light meant more to one who had experienced darkness, life had more meaning when one knew that death was inescapable. Things needed their opposites to give them value.

Nevertheless, faced with the idea that I was aligned with the god of death and reckoning, something in me balked, and I shook my head.

"No, that can't be right. How is that possible?" I asked.

"My lady," Phaedrus said gently, "I know this may be difficult to accept, but it's the explanation that makes the most sense. Even the fact that you and Lord Bressen were drawn to each other suggests as much."

I looked between the two. "What does Bressen have to do with this?"

It was Bressen who answered. "Surely you see the irony," he said, smiling at me wryly. "People call me the Nemesis Incarnate, but it's you who deserves that moniker far more."

I stood up from the table so fast that my chair fell back on the rug with a loud thud.

"That's not funny," I said as I willed my voice to stay calm.

Bressen was in front of me in a second, gathering me into his arms. I inhaled his scent, and my rising dread ebbed a bit as he pressed my head against his shoulder.

"I'm sorry," he said, "but it's true. You're the Nemesis's Hand in this world, more so than I ever was. That's no reason to be upset. It's nothing short of miraculous, and you should embrace it."

Bressen pressed a kiss to the top of my head and held me tighter as I tried to get myself under control.

"I told you once that you were simply the most remarkable woman I've ever met," he went on, "and this is unequivocal proof I was right."

"What does this mean, though?" I asked. "Do I need to start killing people? Because I don't think I can do that."

Bressen chuckled, and I felt the vibrations of his laugh against my ear. "I don't think that's how this works."

"Then how does it work?" I asked.

"That's something we're going to need to figure out," he said, "but for now, there's no need to start worrying. It's been thousands of years since the Hands of the Trinity ruled the continent, and if we never tell anyone else what we know, then all this is a moot point."

The room was quiet as Bressen held me. I felt ashamed falling to pieces like this in front of Phaedrus, although I'd probably been worse when he found me in the Priory on my wedding day. I seemed destined to have some of my most vulnerable moments play out in front of the priest, and he seemed to realize the same.

Phaedrus cleared his throat. "I should go," he said.

"Thank you, Phaedrus. Please keep us posted about anything else," Bressen told him.

"Of course, my lord."

"Wait!" Bressen said. He let go of me and turned to stop the priest.

"Yes, my lord?"

"There are a couple other things we need to ask you," Bressen said.

He untucked his shirt and lifted it to reveal his stomach, and I followed suit when I realized his intent. Phaedrus looked a little shocked to see us baring ourselves to him, but his eyes narrowed a moment later when he saw the crescent moon marks around our navels.

"What…What are those?" he asked.

"We were hoping you could tell us," Bressen said. "We noticed them the day after our wedding."

Phaedrus's head snapped up, and he looked between us.

"You told me a story about the Souls of the Moon," I said. "Could these marks be related? Have you seen others with such markings?"

Phaedrus shook his head. "No, I've never seen marks like that."

"Have you had occasion to see couples undressed before?" I asked carefully. "Maybe people have them, but you've just never seen them?"

Phaedrus gave me an apologetic look. "I often perform blessings for couples on the Harmilan who seek to conceive a child," he said. "I've seen my share of half-naked bodies, but I've never seen that before."

My stomach flipped over. Bressen had told me he'd asked Aramis about the marks as well, but if a healer and a priest had never seen them, then we were running out of options.

"There's one other thing," Bressen said, drawing Phaedrus's attention back. "Twice while we were out on the ocean, I was able to transfer some of my power to Cyra. Not my mind wraith abilities, which she's already syphoned, but my power in general. I was able to transfer my energy and strength to her. Have you ever heard of that?"

Again Phaedrus shook his head, eyes wide.

"No. Never," he said. "But I'll consult some of the ancient texts to see if there's mention of such things. Perhaps both are related to Cyra being a syphon."

"Please do," Bressen said as he tucked his shirt back in.

"Of course, my lord. I'll let you know right away if I find anything."

Phaedrus turned and opened a portal back to the Priory.

"I need to go rest," I told Bressen when the portal had closed. "I don't have the energy to think about this."

"Of course," he said, kissing me on the forehead. "You've had a very long few days. I have to meet with Ferris and Samhail, but I'll be back as soon as I can."

I kissed Bressen and headed for the door. Ferris was waiting outside, and the steward hurried into the study after I left.

Leeda was in our room when I entered.

"Welcome back, my lady," she said coming toward me. "How was your trip? Did you find what you were looking for?"

"It was tiring," I said, "but yes. We found what we went down for."

Leeda's face seemed to brighten. "Did you really?" she asked. "I was sure it would be impossible. Can I see what you brought up?"

I'd told Leeda before we left what we were doing. She'd been helping me practice my underwater breathing in the bathtub, so I'd had to explain some of our mission to her. She'd seemed excited about it, and I'd given her a few of the details as an offering of friendship.

After her hesitation early on, Leeda seemed to be coming around to the idea of us being friends, although she and I had yet to really click the way I had with Raina. It always felt to me like Leeda was holding back, and that barrier kept us from fully crossing into the realm of true friends. She'd opened up a little when I'd confided in her about my mission, and I was eager to keep her engaged.

I also suspected Leeda had more of an adventurous spirit than she let on. In addition to our trip, she was interested to hear about my training efforts and about both Samhail and Axenus. I was fairly certain that—like many of the female staff at Tide's End—she'd taken a fancy to the two handsome warriors, so I'd satisfied her curiosity a bit. Raina and I had bonded early on by sharing stories of our past sexual exploits, so I reasoned that perhaps that was the way to Leeda's friendship as well.

"Maybe later," I said to answer her question. "Bressen already locked up the rings and necklace in his study, and he's in with Ferris right now."

"What will you do with them now that you have them?" she asked.

"Find out more about how they work and just try to keep them safe, I suppose. The vision wasn't really clear on why they were important."

I'd told Leeda about the vision itself, but I hadn't mentioned seeing

Sandrian and Morland in it. Leeda was from Rowe, and I was afraid to ask about her thoughts on the war. She looked to be in her late twenties to early thirties, so there was a slim chance she was old enough to remember parts of it. If her sympathies leaned toward Rowe, then I didn't want her knowing too much about why we'd sought out the collar and rings.

I could've looked into her mind to see, but aside from that first incursion where I'd verified Leeda was who she said she was, I'd stayed out of her head. Bressen had read her mind as well and found nothing of concern, so I'd committed to not pushing any further. I remembered how violated I'd felt when I'd learned shortly after meeting Bressen that he'd seen into my mind, and I didn't want to make a habit of looking into people's private thoughts unless I felt it was truly warranted.

Bressen had a little less reluctance about using his gift than I did, but he tried to limit his mindreading to times when the good of the country was at stake. Sometimes he couldn't help it due to the strength of his power, but he really tried not to abuse his ability.

"I need a nap and a bath," I told Leeda wearily. I was exhausted, and, despite bathing on the ship, I'd never fully been able to get the fine film of salt off my skin while we were on board.

"Yes, my lady," she said. "Let's get you cleaned up and put to bed."

Bressen didn't make it down to dinner that evening but instead had food brought up to his study where he'd sequestered himself with Ferris. I was already in my nightgown reading a book in a chair by the fireplace when he finally came in. He walked straight over to me, picked me up from the chair, sat down in it, and then settled me in his lap. His arms snaked around me, and we both moaned a little as he nuzzled my neck.

"Long day?" I asked sympathetically.

"Time spent away from you is always an eternity," he said. "But yes, there was a lot to catch up on since I was away so long. There was only so much Ferris and Samhail could take care of themselves."

I frowned. "Samhail doesn't really strike me as someone who can play lord. Exactly what did you have him doing?"

Bressen chuckled. "No, Samhail doesn't have a lordly temperament, and he wouldn't want to be one anyway. He was mainly here to be a peacekeeper, much like in Derridan for the trials. That's where he excels."

I chuckled as well. "I imagine so. I doubt many people want to make trouble when he's around."

"How was your day? Did you make peace with being the Hand of the Nemesis?"

My stomach dropped at the reminder. I'd been trying my best not to think about it, but I'd only been partially successful. While we only practiced religion loosely out in Fernweh, every child nevertheless grew up learning a healthy fear of the Nemesis and then eventually a fear of the cruel and merciless Nemesis Incarnate.

I'd since discovered, of course, that the Nemesis Incarnate wasn't the soulless demon everyone believed him to be, but the fact remained that a significant part of my upbringing had been devoted to instilling a deep-seeded dread of the Nemesis and those who served the god. To learn that I'd been created to serve the Nemesis was unsettling at best, and one afternoon was not enough to allay that dread.

"That may take a while," I said.

Bressen ran his hand along my thigh as he exhaled. "I think we should go to the Priory," he said.

I lifted my face to look at him. "What? Now?"

"Now's as good a time as any. It should be quiet there."

"Why?"

"I want to show you something."

I got up off Bressen's lap, and he let me go reluctantly.

"Alright. Let's go," I said, turning to open a portal.

Bressen looked at the silky nightgown I was wearing.

"Do you want to get dressed?" he asked, getting up from the chair.

"No, I'm fine. Let's just do this," I said as I walked through the portal into the Priory. I didn't know what Bressen's plan here was, but I'd spent the day trying to pretend I was still just Cyra the winemaker from Fernweh, and it had done nothing but tighten the knot in my stomach.

Maybe it was time to face my fears head-on, to face not only my nemesis, but *the* Nemesis itself.

# Chapter 43

The cavernous space of the Priory's hall seemed to amplify the silence so that it almost pulsed in my ears when Bressen and I stepped through my portal. Something about the stillness reminded me of when Samhail and I had encountered the fog in the Soundless Woods, and I shivered at the memory.

Bressen took my hand and led me toward the dais at the front of the hall where we stopped before the hooded statue of the Nemesis as it held out a set of scales toward us. Behind us, the statue of the Creator extended its hands out in giving as it held a basin of oil that burned steadily to add its glow to the dimness of the space. The statue of the Protector stood sentinel to the other side of us, shield in one hand and sword in the other.

Just as Bressen ensured criminals faced justice for their misdeeds in this world, the Nemesis ensured that those who slipped through the cracks here received punishment in the next. But what people seemed to forget – what I myself often forgot – was that the Nemesis also made sure those who had lived good lives were rewarded. Somehow that part always got lost, and the Nemesis's role as an agent of retribution was all people remembered. The threat of punishment for wrongdoing seemed to be a stronger motivator than the promise of reward for living a good life.

"What are you thinking?" Bressen asked me as we stood in front of the Nemesis. His hands rested on my shoulders, and I knew his magic would keep anyone from entering the hall while we were here.

"I'm trying to remind myself how misunderstood the Nemesis always is," I said. "Too often people see the Nemesis as a god of vengeance rather than as one who maintains balance. The Creator's and Protector's gifts are given unevenly-"

"But the Nemesis comes for everyone eventually and rewards or punishes them as they deserve," he finished for me. "I've always thought that as well. The Nemesis isn't a force of darkness in the Trinity, as so many think. It's a force of balance. Surely that's not something to fear?"

"No, but who am I to judge what people deserve?" I asked.

I was uncomfortably aware I'd tried to do exactly that back in Fernweh a few weeks ago. I'd played judge with Eddin and the two other men, going so far as to sentence them to death. The inclination seemed to be more proof I was aligned with the Nemesis.

"You aren't the judge," Bressen said. "You're the Hand that helps the Nemesis. You only enact the Nemesis's will in the human realm, but it's not your command that reigns."

"But how do I know what the will of the Nemesis is?" I asked.

Bressen was silent a moment. "I don't know. Maybe that's more information that Phaedrus needs to find for us. Presumably the Nemesis will guide you in some way."

I pushed a deep breath out through my nose. The Nemesis had had twenty-two years to guide me, yet I'd never felt the slightest tug or suggestion in that sense, at least not that I was aware of.

Maybe it didn't matter anyway. Syphons no longer ruled the continent as they once had, so maybe my powers were only vestiges of an obsolete system that continued to exist only because the natural world couldn't be bothered to do away with it.

It made me curious about what had happened to that last triumvirate of syphons. Had they somehow been phased out over time, or had their end been more abrupt? Had they merely grown tired of the roles thrust upon them and renounced their service one by one? Or had their end been more immediate, more…violent?

I shook the thought away as Bressen's hands moved from my shoulders. One snaked around my waist while the other pushed the dark waves of my hair back from one shoulder. His lips pressed lightly against the crook of my neck before kissing a trail up toward my ear. My skin tingled where he touched as each brush of his lips and each exhale of his breath ignited other spots all over my body.

"I'm not sure why I get to call you mine," he whispered in my ear, "but I dread the price I'll pay in the next world to balance out this gift."

Something slipped in my stomach, like the sudden feeling of falling. Gods above, I hoped that wasn't how it worked. I knew we paid for our unpunished sins in the next world, but did we also have to answer for our happiness as well?

Because I too considered it nothing short of miraculous that Bressen was mine. There were days I woke before he did and simply stared at his sleeping face, wondering what I'd done to deserve him. I hoped to the gods I wasn't destined to feel an equal amount of pain or suffering for every minute of pure happiness I'd spent watching him sleep, or being in his arms, or making love to him.

Bressen's arm around my waist rose higher until his hand brushed over my breast. He raked his teeth across my neck as his tender touches turned rough and hungry. I shuddered in pleasure as his other hand crept to my hip to start pulling up the hem of my silk nightgown.

"I need to be inside you, Cyra," Bressen said, his voice a husky rasp at my ear. He pressed his face against mine, and I felt him struggling to keep himself under control. "Do you remember what I told you that day in the Great Chamber after we met Aidan?"

I furrowed my brows to think for a moment, but they shot back up when I recalled what he'd said. I turned in his arms to face him.

"You want to…," I glanced at the altar.

His lids were heavy with desire as he took my face in his hands. "I do. I want to make love to you on that altar."

My breath hitched in my throat, and I shook my head. "Isn't that blasphemy? I don't want to be struck down for desecrating the altar."

"We're not desecrating anything," Bressen said. "We celebrate joining on the Harmilan. Why shouldn't we celebrate it now? You and I are Souls of the Moon, aren't we? Meant to be together?" He pressed a hand gently to my stomach where the crescent moon mark was.

I opened my mouth, then closed it again, not wanting to remind him that – according to the myth – it was the gods that had split us in two to begin with because of our impudence.

One of Bressen's hands slipped into mine, and he pulled me toward the altar. "Let's see if we get a sign," he said as he led me up onto the dais.

"A sign?" I asked, a little confused.

We stopped in front of the altar, and I took in the smooth slab of milky white quartz. I'd never been this close to it before, and I noticed now there was a symbol etched into the top of it, three interlocking triangles. I felt like I'd seen the symbol in other places before, but this was the first time I'd really taken note of it.

Bressen took my hand and laid it on the altar with his. I brushed my fingers gently over the symbol, a little surprised at how warm the stone felt. I hadn't really expected anything to happen, but only a second after our hands touched the polished surface, the flames in the oil lamps around the hall all seemed to flare.

I turned quickly to Bressen. "Did you see that?"

His eyes were wide. "I did. I didn't actually expect a sign, but that seems like one."

"But what does it mean? Were the gods giving us their blessing or warning us off?"

Bressen paused a moment. "I don't know. I was really hoping for more of a tacit acceptance from them."

I stared at him. "So if they didn't strike us dead, you were going to assume they were giving us permission to have sex on the altar?"

Bressen smiled and shrugged. "Something like that."

We looked at each other for a long moment before I shook my head again. "I don't like not knowing. I don't want to anger the Trinity."

Bressen sighed but nodded. "Agreed. We should probably go."

We continued to look at each other for another moment, neither of us really wanting to leave. Now that he'd planted the idea in my head, part of me really wanted to do it, to make love to him on the altar, but it was just too risky without a clearer sign from the Trinity.

"I'll call a portal," I said.

I waited for Bressen to argue, but he only nodded his assent.

I turned and drew the circle to create a portal home, but when I came all the way around to the top again, nothing happened. I frowned and traced another circle in the air, concentrating on the idea of the portal back to Solandis, but again nothing happened. I turned to look at Bressen with apprehension.

"Perhaps it's another sign," he suggested. "What if the gods are telling us not to go?"

I looked at him as if he were mad.

"Try some of your other powers," he urged.

I held out my hand and a small flame ignited in my palm. I

extinguished it and looked around the room. I spotted a stack of candles someone had left on a side table and summoned one to my hand. Then I tried a third time to open a portal.

Nothing happened.

"It's only the portal that doesn't work," I said hesitantly.

Bressen arched a brow. "You wanted a sign," he said, "I'm not sure the gods can make it any clearer than that."

"You really think the gods are trying to tell us they approve of us having sex on the altar by not letting me call a portal back to Solandis?"

Bressen put a gentle hand to my cheek. "Cyra, if you aren't comfortable doing this, we can go."

I huffed a mirthless laugh. "No, we can't," I said wryly.

"Yes, we can," he insisted. "The gods may be blocking your power to call a portal, but we can still walk out those doors." He pointed to the heavy wooden doors at the other end of the hall. "I can fly us part of the way, or we can take horses. We aren't trapped here."

"What if it's no longer our choice?" I asked, panicking now. "What if the gods are telling us to do it?"

Bressen trapped my face between his hands so I had to look into his eyes. "Listen to me," he said seriously. "I'll make love to you on that altar if, and only if, you want me to. Will of the gods or no, we won't do anything you don't want to do."

I saw the flash of determination in his look.

"You'd really help me leave if I wanted to go, even if it meant going against the wishes of the Trinity?" I asked.

His expression turned almost pained, and I'd never heard his voice so intense as when he spoke next.

"Do you still doubt I'd do anything for you? Even defy the gods?"

Warmth spread through me at the conviction in his words. I knew Bressen wanted to take me on the altar, but he was willing to set aside that desire and potentially anger the gods to bring me home, if that's what I wanted. It meant more than I could say.

I tipped my face up so my lips met his, and I kissed him tenderly as one hand snaked around his neck to thread in his hair.

"Take me then," I said softly against his lips.

Bressen nodded and pulled back, dropping his hands from my face. He took my hand in his and turned to head toward the doors of the hall. When I didn't move, he looked back at me questioningly.

I shook my head. "Not take me home," I said. "Just…take me."

His eyes flicked to the altar and then back to mine. "You want…"

"I want you to make love to me on that altar," I said.

He swallowed. "You're sure?"

"I can think of nothing I want more than to make love on that altar to the man willing to defy the gods for me."

Heat flashed in Bressen's eyes before he pulled me to him, and his mouth devoured mine. I felt the urgency of his need in the kiss, and I met it with my own as I clutched his body to mine.

"If you change your mind…," he offered.

"I won't. Now stop talking and fuck me on that altar."

His mouth ground into mine again as if he meant to consume me, and I whimpered in pleasure at his intensity. His arms were like iron bands around me as I reveled in his strength. His body was packed with sinewy muscle, and I was always in awe of just how strong he was. Yet as tightly as he held me, he never hurt me. There was always a tenderness to his touch that made me feel both secure and cherished.

Bressen tugged at my nightgown, and I pulled back to raise my arms so he could pull it over my head. Then I was naked in the middle of the Priory, and my eyes drifted to the statues of the Trinity standing around the dais as he kissed my neck. I wondered if they were watching us.

If they were, I didn't care. Being here with Bressen was all I wanted.

He lifted me and laid me on the altar. The stone was hard against my back, but as before, there seemed to be an inherent warmth to it. I waited for Bressen to climb up with me, but he moved instead to the foot of the altar and pulled me toward him to press my knees open and hook my legs over his shoulders.

"What are you doing?" I asked, although I knew full well.

"Paying homage," he said huskily as he lowered his head between my thighs, and his mouth began to work.

I gasped and arched back against the altar as his tongue licked up the center of my sex, instantly driving me wild with desire. I tried to grab for something to give me purchase, but my fingers only slid across the polished surface of the quartz. I moaned and rocked my hips as Bressen sucked harder against the bud of nerves at my apex, and his hands wrapped around my thighs to hold me in place. A tempest built between my legs as I gasped softly under the attentions of his lips and tongue, and I finally managed to find the edges of the altar to grip the sides as Bressen continued to feast on me.

My climax crested over me quickly, and I screamed into the silence of the chamber, desperately hoping that Bressen's power was doing its job to keep people away.

Bressen didn't stop. His mouth continued to move on me, and I felt my pleasure rising again as his tongue circled my clit.

"Bressen, please! I need you now," I managed to rasp out, and I felt his mouth leave me finally.

I looked up between my knees and saw him removing his clothes. I pushed myself back along the altar so I was away from the edge, and Bressen climbed up to prowl over me. I opened my legs to him, and he settled between them, but he didn't enter me yet. Instead, he lowered his head to one breast and sucked the nipple deep into his mouth while his hand closed over the other one to knead it and pinch the tip.

I cried out and bucked under his touch, threading my fingers through his hair again, glad to finally have something easier to hold onto. He worshipped each breast before he moved up further, and his mouth finally captured mine again in a passionate kiss that curled my toes and made me throw my legs around his waist.

"Inside me, now," I gasped, and a wicked grin spread across his face.

His cock pressed at my entrance, and I arched my hips up to meet him, but he entered me so slowly I began to claw at his back. When he was fully inside, he only closed his eyes and held me there in his embrace for a long moment.

"Sweet gods above, Bressen," I said through gritted teeth, "if you don't start fucking me, you're going to find out what the wrath of the Nemesis feels like."

He opened his eyes and chuckled. "I was just taking a moment to say a prayer of thanks to the gods for bringing you to me."

The tension in my muscles eased a bit. "You were really praying?"

He nodded, and my frustration left me. I felt bad now for threatening him, but I didn't have time to apologize as he finally began to thrust.

Every nerve in my body came alive then, and I closed my own eyes before mouthing a quick prayer of thanks to the gods as well. I'd need to thank them more thoroughly later with some kind of offering, but this was the best I could manage for now as the fog of pleasure took hold of me. The only thing I was aware of was the feel of Bressen's body moving against mine.

I used my legs to pull Bressen into me, to urge him on, but he took his time, thrusting into me deeply but not hurriedly. The building tension was almost torturous as I moaned and writhed beneath him, trying whatever I could to increase the friction between us. Finally, even Bressen could no longer handle the unhurried pace he'd set, and he drove into me faster and harder so that what little composure I had left was hanging by a thread as I drew closer to plummeting over the thundering waterfall of bliss that waited ahead.

"I love you, Cyra," Bressen breathed, his words a benediction against my ear. "Gods above, I love you so fucking much."

"I love you, too," I whispered back.

I took his head in my hands and brought his lips to mine, letting out a soft whimper against his mouth as he drove into me. I was close to my second release, and I arched my hips up to meet his next thrust. I almost screamed in frustration as Bressen stopped moving suddenly, but his words cut the sound off in my throat.

"Cyra, you're glowing."

My eyes flew open to look down at myself. Bressen was braced above me on his hands so he could see me. Sure enough, the skin over my entire body seemed to be emitting a faint silvery glow.

"What's happening?" I asked, digging my fingers into the hard muscles of his arms.

"I don't know. Does it hurt?"

I took a moment to feel past my apprehension, but I didn't feel any pain beyond the ache of unspent desire between my legs. I shook my head.

"Does this make things better or worse?" Bressen asked as he thrust into me a few times.

My head arched back in pleasure, and the light from my body seemed to flare brighter.

"Both!" I gasped out.

Bressen smiled wickedly and lowered himself back down to renew his efforts. He slammed into me, trapping me between his hard body and the even harder stone, and all I could do was hold onto him as he drove us toward a release. All the while, the light seemed to grow between us so that it was nearly blinding.

Just when I didn't think I could bear it any longer, Bressen's next thrust pushed me over the edge, and I cried out, pulling him against me. The feel of my inner muscles clenching around his cock pulled Bressen over as well, and he roared his release against my shoulder.

As ecstasy flooded through our bodies, the light emanating from me suddenly burst forth in radiant glory, and we both shut our eyes tightly against its brilliance as we tried to contain it between us. Bressen closed his arms around me and pressed me against him like he was applying pressure to a wound, as if I was somehow leaking something important that he hoped to hold in. I wrapped my own arms around him and buried my face in his shoulder as both the flood of light from my body and the surge of pleasure from our near-simultaneous climaxes washed over us, dragging us along like a riptide.

A few moments later, Bressen lifted his head to look down at me. His gaze was thick and languid, but fear quickly overtook his features as he recognized my distress.

"Cyra, what's wrong? Are you alright?" he asked, lifting himself up.

I was breathing hard, chest heaving, as my body showed no sign of winding down. I felt like I was still in the middle of my climax, and each second that ticked by was a torment from the rapturous force lashing through my veins. Every nerve was raw as I lay on the altar trying to calm myself, power crackling through my body like lightning.

Bressen pressed a hand lightly to my face, but I whimpered and pulled away from his touch.

"Cyra!" There was real worry in his voice now. "What's wrong?"

"I can't…my body feels," I tried to explain, but even the heaving of my breaths seemed to make things worse.

Bressen waited anxiously for me to find the words, his hand hovering, not daring to touch me again.

"Too much," I gasped. "It's overwhelming. I can feel power roiling inside me, like it's trying to get out. My skin is on fire. I still feel like I need a release, but it's everywhere."

I'd felt something similar when I'd been underwater and Bressen had sent his own power to help me against the kraken. I'd gone from having almost nothing left to having a surfeit of power in seconds, and I'd instantly felt the need to release it. Luckily, I'd had an outlet at the time, and I'd used the power to turn the kraken to water, subsequently easing the pressure. This time there was nowhere for the power to go, and the excess energy surging through me was nearly unbearable.

Bressen withdrew from inside me and rolled off the altar.

"We need to get you somewhere to vent some of the power," he said as he grabbed my nightgown and helped me slip it on. I groaned as the soft silk slipped down my body. Light and delicate as the material was, it irritated my overly sensitive skin. Bressen yanked on his pants, grabbed his shirt and jacket, and held out a hand to help me slide off the altar.

"What if I can't call a portal?" I said with sudden panic.

"I have a feeling you'll be able to call one now," Bressen said.

I looped my arm in a circle in front of me and almost collapsed in relief when a large, brightly glowing portal opened in front of us. I felt a sliver of power drain off me, not enough to relieve me by far, but enough to confirm that venting the power was what I needed to do.

I was practically vibrating with energy as Bressen and I stepped through the portal onto the beach near Tide's End. The cold, salty air was usually soothing on my face, but tonight its brush was harsh against my overly sensitive skin, and I cringed into myself. Bressen was at my back, close but not touching me, yet his proximity made the hairs on my neck and arms stand on end. He seemed to have absorbed some of the power back at the Priory himself, and my body could sense it inside him.

I jumped when Bressen touched my shoulder, and I arched away from him, seeking relief from the way his nearness inflamed my senses.

"Release some of the power," Bressen said.

"How?" I asked, the question coming out in a sob.

"Use your magic. Do whatever you want. The bigger the better."

I stared out over the sea as gentle waves lapped lazily at the shore. The moon was full tonight, casting its pale blue aura over the dark water in a scene of serenity that was at complete odds with the energy rampaging through me.

I extended my hands in front of me and released a forcefield over the water, as big and powerful as I could make it. The sheer strength of it shocked me as the water rippled away from the shore, almost as if the very tide had been reversed, and I felt a moment of relief before the tension gripped me again.

"Good," Bressen said, "but you need to release more. Let your elemental powers loose."

I nodded and rallied them now, starting with air, which always seemed the easiest for me to wield. Wind kicked up on the beach, and I let the feel of it build within me as the power thrumming through my veins sensed an outlet and began to gather. Faster and faster the wind swirled around us, whipping the sand across our legs and stirring the water so that the waves grew larger and crested with whitecaps.

My hair lashed my face and my thin nightgown molded to my body as the wind continued to increase. The gales out over the water were soon like a hurricane, and I felt Bressen stagger against them behind me as he struggled to keep his footing. I stepped back against him then, and his arms circled around me, one at my waist and one across my shoulders. He was trying to hold me in place as he had on the ship, to keep me from blowing away as the wind surged in great, angry squalls. He was trying to anchor me, but he wasn't the anchor this time.

I was.

This was *my* power. *My* wind. I controlled it, not the other way around, and in the next instant I wrapped us in a protective cocoon of air as the tumult continued to rage around us. Out on the water, the ocean surged, not just from the hurricane-force winds I'd conjured, but because my water magic had now answered the call as well. Waves crashed against the shore as water stretched up closer and closer to where Bressen and I stood on the beach at the edge of the dunes. All around us raged a storm, yet there were no clouds in the sky, only the wind and water and the fury with which my power compelled them.

A massive wave gathered out on the water, one that would easily reach us as it headed for the beach. Bressen held me tighter as the wave broke, and water rushed up over the sand, finding the seagrass and beach roses on the dunes. The wave flattened some and ripped others from the ground to drag them back toward the water. The swell would have reached our waists if the water hadn't broken against my shield of air, like we were a rock standing against the surf, and Bressen's body twitched against mine as the water crashed into the shield.

The surf retreated, pulling shells and rocks with it, and I felt the sand winnow away beneath our feet despite my air shield. I remained affixed to the spot, keeping us from being swept out to sea.

Something about the ocean had always called to me, and I remembered the water lapping gently at the sand on sunny days from my youth as the shouts of my brothers roughhousing in the surf mingled with the calls of seabirds when we went to the shore. But if I was being honest with myself, I preferred the sea after a storm, where the churning and crashing water that beat against the beach reminded me of our relative insignificance in the world. There was so much more that lay below the depths of that water, and I never could have conceived of harnessing even a fraction of that power at the time.

Before I was called to Callanus months ago, I could fill tea pots and irrigate our vines, but the idea I might one day move the waves or draw the tides themselves had never crossed my mind. Out on *The Maidenhead*, Axenus and I had sought to buffer the storm.

Now, I *was* the storm.

I'd hoped the battering wind and water would level off my powers, but the tempest only seemed to stoke them. The ground began to shake as the sand slipped from beneath us, and Bressen's arms tightened again. This was the first time since the bear that the earth had obeyed my command, and I threw my arms out to the sides. Rolls of sand rippled down the beach as if fleeing before me, and I inhaled deeply in triumph to finally have that element under my control once more.

"Cyra!" Bressen shouted as the ground shifted, causing even my own footing to falter. He pressed his face into the crook of my neck, and his hand came up to brush my windblown hair back so his lips could find my ear. "Don't bring down the house, please," he said just loud enough to be heard over the din. "We need somewhere to sleep tonight."

He pressed a kiss near my ear, and his gentle caress did what the raging of my powers couldn't. Something eased in my chest as the ground suddenly stilled, the wind died down around us, and the waters calmed almost instantaneously, as if a candle had been snuffed.

My power had been building on itself, driving me to push myself to the limits of my abilities, but Bressen's sensuous voice and warm breath had somehow cut through that fury to break up the storm.

I'd been barely cognizant of what was happening as my mind and body were consumed by the excess of magic coursing through me, but awareness returned now. I still felt the magic just below the surface, but it was less urgent, less grating. I felt more stable, like I was no longer ready to claw at my own skin.

Bressen turned me in his arms, and his lips descended on mine as soon as I faced him. Something new began to build as his lips devoured me, and I wrapped my arms around his neck to pull him against me.

"Nemesis take me, that was incredible," Bressen breathed as his lips pulled back only enough to speak. "I need to fuck you again now."

I felt the hard ridge of his arousal between us and grunted my consent. Bressen's mouth plunged back down on mine, and a storm of a different kind began to rage between us.

We surrendered to its pull, too lost in each other to notice the two figures rushing toward us over the dunes with swords drawn.

# Chapter 44

"What in the name of the Trinity is going on?"

The voice jarred Bressen and I from our desire-soaked haze, and Bressen swore under his breath. We turned to find Samhail and Axenus standing on the beach a few yards behind us, both with swords in hand. They'd obviously witnessed my impromptu storm and earthquake and come to investigate.

As often as Samhail and Axenus seemed to squabble and compete with each other, they looked ready to have each other's backs when there was a threat of danger.

Samhail's eyes raked up and down me, and I remembered I was wearing my thin silk nightgown. Bressen was also bare-chested, having only donned his pants when we left the Priory. We should have been cold, but a thin film of warm air still circulated around us, a remnant of the shield I'd created that hadn't died when the storm did.

Samhail had originally spoken, but it was Axenus who followed up.

"Cyra, was that you?" he asked. "The hurricane and earthquake?"

I'd only been thinking about finding a safe place to vent some of my powers, but I hadn't considered who might see what I did. I probably should've taken care to find a more secluded place.

"It was me," I admitted.

Axenus looked thunderstruck. "How?"

Bressen and I looked at each other as understanding passed between us. Any simple answer we gave would only lead to more questions, and I could tell he'd reached the same conclusion I had.

"It's time to tell them," I said, and he nodded.

"Tell us what?" Axenus asked, canting his head.

"Not here," Bressen said. "Let's go back to the house." He turned to me. "Would you please?"

I nodded and opened a brightly glowing portal up to Bressen's study. Both Samhail and Axenus seemed to take note of the portal's unusual radiance as we all stepped through.

"Does anyone need a drink?" Bressen asked as we filed into the room.

"Yes," Samhail and Axenus both answered together, and it made me smile to once again see them so in sync.

Bressen poured himself, me, and Axenus each a glass of wine, then poured something amber-colored into a thicker glass for Samhail. Drinks in hand, we all moved to the chairs near the fireplace to sit down.

I held out a hand absently as I walked, and my fingers closed around my robe a moment later. I tied it around me and sat down in one of the chairs to find Samhail and Axenus staring at me. I looked down, certain too much of my skin must still be showing, but I was covered well enough.

"What?" I asked as they continued to stare.

"You summoned your robe so effortlessly," Samhail said.

"And used your wind to open a door," Axenus added.

As if to emphasize his words, the door to Bressen's study that I'd mindlessly opened to let my robe enter clicked shut.

"You should sit down," Bressen said to them. "There are some things you need to know."

Samhail and Axenus exchanged looks before taking their seats.

I waved a hand lazily in the air and the wood in the fireplace next to us burst into flames. Samhail and Axenus both glanced toward the hearth and then looked again at me, but I just shrugged.

"Phaedrus came to see Cyra and I several weeks ago when we were still in Callanus," Bressen began. "He's been studying an ancient text the Priory just took possession of, and he found something he thought we should know. He had more information when he came today."

He paused to glance at me, but I gave him a nod of assent.

"The text Phaedrus was examining pre-dates most other texts we have on the Trinity," Bressen said, "and he found a section in it that spoke of the Hands of the Gods, three women chosen directly by the Trinity to rule the continent in their name."

"The whole continent?" Axenus asked. "But the continent has been divided into individual countries for thousands of years now."

"Yes," Bressen said, "and now you understand how old the text is."

Axenus sat back in his chair to mull this over. His delicately iridescent skin flashed in the light from the fire.

"Phaedrus thinks this has something to do with Cyra," Samhail said, making the logical jump.

Bressen nodded.

"Why?" Samhail asked. "What makes him think she's involved?"

"Because, if Phaedrus translated the text correctly," Bressen said, "then the three Hands of the Gods are all syphons."

Both Samhail and Axenus lurched forward in their seats.

"What?" Axenus said, and I could see his knuckles had gone white from how hard he was gripping the arms of the chair.

"Bullshit," Samhail said, and Bressen raised an eyebrow at him.

"That would suggest-" Axenus started, but Bressen finished for him.

"It suggests there are always three syphons at any one time," he confirmed. "So yes. If Phaedrus is correct, then there are two more syphons somewhere on the continent right now."

Axenus fell back into his chair again looking a bit dazed. Samhail was still sitting forward in his chair, but his knee had begun to bounce.

"There's one more small thing," Bressen said, and the two men looked up at him. "Apparently each syphon is bonded specifically to one of the Trinity, imbued with gifts that help them carry out the will of that particular god."

Samhail and Axenus's attention swung to me.

"And do we know which god Cyra is bonded to?" Axenus asked.

Bressen smiled, and I knew he was enjoying this part.

"Let's just say that people should stop calling me the Nemesis Incarnate and start calling my wife that."

There was dead silence in the room that stretched on and on as Samhail and Axenus both stared at me. I finally looked away from them, unable to take the intensity of their gazes any longer. I knew they were just trying to process all this information, as Bressen and I had both been doing, but I still wasn't used to having such focused attention on me.

"And you didn't trust us with this information before now?" Samhail asked finally.

His voice was even, but I felt the anger and hurt coming off him, even with his mental shield up. I imagined my heightened powers were making me more sensitive to the thoughts and feelings of those around me despite any protections they might have in place.

"I don't trust anyone with this information just yet," Bressen said sharply as his eyes locked with Samhail's. "If I could wipe it from Phaedrus's mind I would, but we need him."

Samhail seemed a bit taken aback, but he nodded.

"It's not that we don't trust you," I said, trying to ease the sting of Bressen's words. "You know we do. It's just…there are implications we're still trying to wrap our heads around."

Samhail's eyes widened, and he launched himself out of his chair.

"Fuck me!" he swore, as he began to pace in front of us. "It all makes sense now."

"What is it?" Bressen prompted him.

Samhail glanced at Axenus, and I had a feeling he was reluctant to share what he realized in front of the merman, but he answered anyway.

"When I first met Cyra after Ursan and Jerram sent me to get her, I couldn't shake this strong feeling of protectiveness I felt toward her. It was my job to make sure she made it to the Citadel safely, but what I felt went beyond that. The need to protect her was so strong, almost overwhelming, and I didn't understand where it was coming from. For a while I thought…"

Samhail trailed off, glancing at Axenus again. I knew he didn't want to say what he was thinking, so I said it for him.

"You thought you might be…developing feelings for me?" I finished.

Samhail sighed deeply. "Yes," he confirmed reluctantly. "But that's not what it was. It was the divine imperative."

Bressen and Axenus made sounds of understanding, but I frowned.

"Divine imperative? What's that?" I asked.

Samhail sat down heavily in his chair again while Bressen answered.

"The gargoyles were supposedly created as guardians of the temples and the Trinity," he explained. "That was their purpose. Thousands of years ago, every temple would have had at least one gargoyle in its service. A temple like the Priory might have had a dozen or more. The gargoyles were divinely sworn to protect the Trinity and all those who served them."

"Protect the Trinity?" I asked.

"Not directly," Bressen amended. "They protected the temples and the priests and priestesses within them. They protected the Trinity's primacy among gods and enforced their doctrine."

I nodded, beginning to understand. "So as a Hand of the Gods…," I said, and Samhail picked up the explanation.

"As a Hand of the Gods, you would have fallen under my protection," he said. "I would have been…*I am* divinely obligated to protect you. Centuries ago, you might even have had your own personal cadre of gargoyle warriors guarding you."

My mouth dropped open. "That's…That's insane."

Phaedrus's information had been mind-altering enough, but to learn Samhail's connection to it added a whole other level of madness I'd need to sort through. Not to mention how it might or might not relate to what Samhail and I had done together in bed. Was this connection why we'd felt so drawn to each other in the first place?

I sat back in my own chair. So much had changed in my life in such a short time, and I was having trouble reconciling it all.

Then I remembered something Bressen had said once.

"The gargoyles that adorn the temples are based on your kind, aren't they?" I asked Samhail.

Bressen spoke up first, though. "That's not a subject you want to bring up. It's a bit of a sore spot for gargoyles."

I looked at Samhail, and his face did seem to have darkened a bit.

"I'm sorry," I said to him, but he shook his head to tell me it was fine.

"All this is incredible enough," Axenus said, "and it's going to take me a while to wrap my head around it, but what does this have to do with Cyra suddenly being able to conjure hurricanes and earthquakes? Her powers were never that strong."

I looked away, blushing. I'd hoped our other news might be enough to make Samhail and Axenus forget what drew them to us tonight in the first place. Apparently not.

"That part is a bit tangential," Bressen said. "Cyra was struggling a little with her status as the new Nemesis Incarnate…"

I threw him an exasperated look, but he ignored me.

"…so she and I went to the Priory earlier to, uh, commune with the Trinity," Bressen went on. "The gods, it seems, gave her their blessing.

Well, both of us really."

Samhail and Axenus exchanged confused looks for a moment until understanding dawned on Samhail's face.

"Gods above, Bressen," he said, half in awe, half in disbelief. "Did you do what I think you did?"

My eyes widened as I looked at Samhail. He couldn't possibly know what Bressen was talking about.

When Bressen didn't answer, Samhail's eyes darted to me, and one look at the blush I was failing to hide told him everything he needed to know. A wicked grin cracked his face.

"You did," Samhail said, turning back to Bressen knowingly. "Gods damn me, please tell me you fucked on the altar."

I let out a cry of indignation as Axenus made one of understanding.

Bressen opened his mouth to say something, but I cut in first.

"What we did or didn't do, and where we did or didn't do it, isn't important right now," I said, my cheeks heating worse than ever. "The point is, whatever we did, and I'm not admitting we did anything, the gods apparently approved. While we were there, I felt a huge surge of power."

"I'm sure you did," Samhail cut in with a grin, but I ignored him.

"In truth, it was overwhelming," I went on. "I felt like I was coming apart at the seams, and I needed to vent some of the power, so Bressen and I took a portal to the beach."

I sat back in my chair again and took a big gulp of the wine I hadn't yet touched. I set the glass down, crossed my arms over my chest, and looked into the fire blazing in the hearth.

When I was met with nothing but silence, I dared a quick glance at the three men sitting around me. Samhail and Bressen were both grinning, as I'd suspected, and Axenus looked bewildered.

"Nemesis take the three of you," I said, picking up my wine glass again to take another large swig.

"Just so I'm clear," Axenus said as I closed my eyes in embarrassment, "After you...did what you did, you experienced a surge of power?"

"Well, technically we began to experience the surge *during* what we did," Bressen said, and I groaned softly, "but I think Cyra took the brunt of it. I got a bit of it second-hand."

"Does that sound right, Cyra?" Axenus asked. His tone was gentle, an attempt to put me at ease, and I appreciated the kindness in his eyes.

"I don't know," I said. "Maybe. I started to glow at one point."

"Glow?" Axenus asked in surprise.

"There was a kind of silvery light coming from me just before…"

"Before?" Axenus prompted, but I only blushed and bit my lip, and he guessed the rest. "Before you climaxed," he finished.

If it was possible, I reddened even more, but I sighed and nodded. I looked at Samhail to see his reaction, but he seemed to be staring right through me, and I had a feeling he was trying to imagine everything. I let my power brush roughly against his mind shield, and he jolted as our eyes met. He tilted his head and gave me a wholly unapologetic grin.

"And when you were done," Axenus went on, "what did you feel?"

I really didn't want to keep talking about it, but Axenus knew about magic, so if he had insights about what had happened, it might be helpful.

"I felt overwhelmed," I said. "Like there was too much energy coursing through my body. Everything felt too bright, too loud, too…on the surface."

Axenus nodded. "So you came back here to expel the energy."

"I sent a giant forcefield over the water, but that did little to relieve the pressure, so Bressen suggested I let my elemental powers loose."

"It was an impressive display," Axenus said, giving me a smile, and I knew it was the teacher in him praising a student.

"Thank you," I said.

"Do you feel better?" he asked. "Do you feel as though you vented enough of the power to be comfortable again?"

I took a moment to assess. "I think so. I don't feel as charged as I did before. If I think about it, I can still feel the power humming beneath the surface, but it's not threatening to break through anymore."

He nodded. "Too much power can be as bad as not enough."

"What are you thinking, Axe?" Bressen asked. He'd been listening to our conversation carefully.

"I'm not sure of anything," Axenus said, "but I find it interesting the gods chose to give Cyra this surge of power, however it came about."

"Why?" Bressen asked.

"Being a syphon is one thing," Axenus said. "Syphons are powerful by nature, but to know that they are that way because they were chosen by the gods adds new meaning to their power. Yet Cyra often struggles with hers. She spent the first two decades of her life away from perimortals. If it is the intention of the gods that syphons are supposed to continuously accumulate power so they can serve as Hands, then Cyra is two decades behind. Her powers are underdeveloped. Cyra has been working hard to make up for lost time, but her powers are – or were – nowhere near where they should be by now."

Axenus looked at me apologetically, but I nodded my agreement.

"The only thing I can think of," Axenus went on, "is that the gods decided to give her a little boost to help her along, and Bressen just happened to get some of the ancillary benefits of that boost since the two of you were…connected at the time."

"I was feeling a little depleted after I sent my power to Cyra the other day on the ship," Bressen said, "but I'm back up to my usual strength now, if not more. Whatever happened, it was welcome. For me at least."

"I bet it was," Samhail said under his breath.

Bressen gave his brother in arms a grin, but I just glared at Samhail.

"So what does all this mean?" I asked. "Where do we go from here?"

"I suggest we stretch your powers a bit tomorrow during training," Axenus said. "We've been building them slowly thus far, but if the gods enhanced your powers tonight, it might be time to intensify your training."

I nodded.

"As for you being a Hand of the Gods," he went on, "I'd like to talk to Phaedrus. I have to wonder why the syphons went from ruling the continent to being hunted and killed."

"That's a good question," Bressen said, leaning back in his chair to consider. "It also doesn't feel like a coincidence that Cyra had a vision about items that used to belong to the last known syphon shortly after we learned all this. Axe, you thought Praya created the items herself? Does that suggest to you she was aligned with the Creator?"

Axenus shrugged. "We can't know for sure, but it makes sense."

"If our assumption is right and there are two other syphons on the continent, maybe we also need to look for them," Bressen said.

"How would we do that?" Samhail asked. "There hasn't been a whisper of a syphon for four hundred years until Cyra. If there are two more of them, they've managed to stay well-hidden for quite some time."

"Are we even sure they're on the continent?" I asked. "Maybe the reason we can't find them is because they left, like Praya tried to."

"What would we do if we found them?" Axenus asked. "Is there any reason to look for them? I could see doing so if we wanted to merge all the countries on the continent again and bring Arystria back under their rule, but we don't want to do that, right?"

"Probably not," Bressen said, "but I can't shake this feeling that Cyra's vision and the information that Phaedrus uncovered are connected somehow. If they are, I want to know why, sooner rather than later."

"Cyra's vision is also connected to Sandrian and Morland," Samhail reminded us. "That seems like the more immediate concern."

"Does Lord Aidan even know we have the collar and rings yet?" Axenus asked.

"No," Bressen admitted. "I haven't seen any dire need to tell him just yet, nor does he know anything about Cyra being a Hand of the Gods, so don't mention either of these things in his presence."

"I suppose we should feel honored you let us in on this before you told Aidan," Samhail grumbled, and Bressen narrowed his eyes.

I understood why Samhail was offended by us keeping this from him. He was used to being in the know about anything and everything important, and it seemed to have wounded his pride that Bressen hadn't let him in on this seemingly important piece of information sooner.

"Well, now that you do know," Bressen said, "you can help by finding out whatever you can about the collar, the rings, or about syphons. Do the gargoyles keep any kind of records that may be helpful?"

Samhail considered for a moment. "We aren't much for record-keeping, but my father is a bit of an amateur historian when it comes to our kind. I can set up a time to meet with him and pick his brain. The trick will be coming up with an excuse for why I want to know."

"I'm confident you'll think of something," Bressen said.

"And what do you want me to do?" Axenus asked.

"Talk to Phaedrus and compare notes about the collar, the rings, and syphons," Bressen said, "but that's your secondary job. Your primary duty is to make sure Cyra knows how to use her powers, especially now that the gods have augmented them. I'm inclined to think they know something we don't, and Cyra needs to be prepared."

Bressen turned to me. "Your focus needs to be on learning to use and control your powers," he said. "Axenus is right. Your powers are underdeveloped from living in Fernweh all those years. We need to work on catching you up."

"And what are *you* going to do?" I asked, quirking a brow at him.

"You mean besides running the country and the territory?" he asked, lifting a brow right back. *And keeping you satisfied in bed?* he added into my mind, making me blush.

"Yes, besides *all* that," I said, emphasizing the word 'all.'

Bressen shrugged. "I want to speak to Phaedrus again. The Priory has some of the oldest known religious texts on the continent, but there are others around. I want to see if he thinks it would be useful to study them. I might be able to use my influence to get him access to those texts. I also want to brush up on my history a bit more. I want to know what led the continent to be divided up in the first place. What led to the dissolution of the last triumvirate of syphons?"

The four of us were silent for a moment as we looked at each other.

"If there's nothing else," Bressen said, "I suggest everyone go to bed. You all have a lot of work to do in the near future."

Samhail and Axenus stood up and left, leaving me alone with Bressen.

"I believe it's your bedtime too, my lord," I said as I stood. "As I recall, you have quite a few items on your own to-do list."

Bressen's lids lowered so that his eyes gleamed up at me from under thick lashes.

"Indeed," he said. "What was on that list again? Rule the country, manage the territory, and…what else was it?"

I crossed my arms over my chest. "I'd think that a lord of your power and influence could remember a few simple items, especially ones of such importance."

Bressen rose from his seat to stand over me.

"How are you feeling?" he asked huskily. "Do you think you need help *releasing* anything else?"

I sucked in a breath and was rewarded with the wonderful scent of hot cinnamon and musk that wound its way up my nose and around my brain. I rose as well, and the belt of my robe came loose as Bressen pulled on one end of the tie.

"There might still be room for a little more…release," I said, his scent and nearness making it hard for me to think.

"I can help with that," Bressen said. "Do you think a long, slow release would be better, or do we need to relieve the pressure hard and fast?"

His arm snaked around my waist to draw me against him.

"Probably both," I said as he grazed his teeth along my neck.

"Both?" he said in mild surprise. "It sounds like I may need to have Ferris clear my calendar."

I nodded. "You have a lot of work to do."

He sighed. "A lord's work is never done, but I won't shirk my duties."

I shrieked as he tossed me over his shoulder and headed for the bedroom to prove just how hard he was willing to work.

# Chapter 45

I knew I must be dreaming when I realized I had no memory of how I'd come to be walking down a corridor behind a group of guards. The last thing I remembered was falling asleep after Bressen and I had spent another hour having sex until we could barely move, and now here I was.

The corridor was unfamiliar, darker and less elegant than the halls at either the Citadel or Tide's End, and the coarse stone of the narrow passage instantly gave me a sense of being trapped.

The red and blue uniforms of the guards ahead of me were nothing I'd seen before. There were four guards, two in front and two behind a man they led down the hall. I looked closer at the man now, then inhaled sharply at the sight of the familiar dark blue markings at his shoulders.

Oh gods.

I stopped walking as my heart leapt into my throat, but some unknown force propelled me forward as I was obliged to follow the procession down the hallway. The red and blue of the guards' uniforms had camouflaged the man between them, so I hadn't immediately noticed his long garnet hair or the dark blue whorls that rolled across the powerful muscles of bare shoulders that shimmered with a light iridescence.

Axenus.

I wasn't just dreaming. I was dream walking in Axenus's dream, and my gaze darted around as I tried to figure out how to get out of this before he realized I was here. There were a few doors in the hall, but I doubted I'd be able to open them. If my failed attempt to stop walking was any indication, I'd have to let the dream play out. I wasn't sure whether it was a dream based on memory or one of pure imagination.

Something tickled my brain then, and I looked back to Axenus. I hadn't fully registered that he was bare-chested, and my eyes drifted lower, expecting him to be fully naked, but he wore a tight pair of britches that molded to the thick muscles of his thighs. His feet were bare, and his hair looked damp, suggesting he'd been in his mer form recently.

The guards stopped at a door and knocked. Seconds later, a woman opened it. Her clothing was far too fine for a servant, and her bearing marked her as nothing short of nobility. She opened the door wide, but only Axenus stepped through as the guards turned to leave. I tried to step forward to make it inside before the woman closed me out, but I was too late, and the door shut in front of me.

It didn't matter. I materialized a second later inside an ornate bedchamber, smaller than the ones I shared with Bressen, and more cluttered with art and other décor.

A low growl sounded to my side, and I jumped a little when I saw a huge cat, something like a leopard, but larger, laying on a pillow in the corner of the room. The cat's fur was a pale cream color, not really white, and it had piercing blue eyes and ears tufted with shocks of black fur. It was unlike any large cat I'd ever seen, and it had a collar around its neck with a leather leash tethered to an iron ring in the wall.

My attention swung back to the center of the room, and I realized there were two women, not just one. The woman who'd opened the door stood near Axenus while another lounged comfortably on a chaise with one leg crossed over the other.

The woman who stood looked to be in her thirties perhaps. She was tall, with long, light brown hair that was pulled tightly behind her in a ponytail. Her makeup was heavy, with shadow applied thickly around her eyes so that the hazel pupils stood out more starkly, and her lips were a dark maroon that did nothing to help the pallor of her skin.

The woman in the chair was almost her opposite, small and blonde with pale blue eyes and lightly tanned skin that gleamed as if it might be covered in a fine sheen of oil. She looked older, somewhere around middle age. Unlike the taller woman, she wore no makeup, so her beauty was solely hers.

"We're so glad you could join us, Axenus," the taller woman said. "My friend, Lady Magdalene, is visiting this week, so I invited her to join us. She's been very curious about you."

Axenus's body tensed, and I narrowed my eyes, fighting the sickening feeling that I knew what was going on.

The blonde woman in the chair got up and came over to Axenus. She walked around him, examining him carefully as if inspecting a prize calf she meant to buy, and I was suddenly reminded of my first meeting with Bressen, when he'd done the same. I'd been more annoyed than anything at the time, and I'd even returned the favor later on the night we first slept together. This felt different, more sinister, and I swallowed down the bile I felt at the hungry look in the woman's eyes.

Magdalene ran a hand boldly down Axenus's chest, and he stiffened even more as cold fingers of disgust closed around my spine.

"He's magnificent, Clarice," Magdalene said, looking him over. "I'll have to get one of my own. Have you tried him in the water yet?"

I narrowed my eyes more. The woman spoke about Axenus as if he wasn't even human, as if he was a piece of artwork she wanted to acquire.

Clarice laughed. "I would if I didn't think he'd try to drown me," she said. "But trust me, he's just as much fun in this form."

"I can't wait to take him for a ride," Magdalene said, smiling.

My mouth fell open. She couldn't be serious. Some part of me had known where this was going, but I refused to believe it.

Axenus himself finally broke his silence.

"Are you whoring me out to your friends now, your majesty?" he asked the taller woman, and my mouth dropped at the title.

Magdalene looked a bit taken aback, but Clarice only smiled at Axenus, her dark lips making her expression seem all the more like a sneer.

"Whoring implies you're getting paid for your services," she said sweetly to him. "I'm letting a friend play with my favorite toy."

I gasped at her words as hot anger gathered in my chest. I had to remind myself this was a dream, and I couldn't just cut off this woman's air so she died clutching at her throat for breath. I hoped to the gods we were only in a nightmare of Axenus's own imagination and not one he'd actually had to live through, but in my gut, I knew the truth.

"He's rather mouthy," Magdalene observed, and I gave her a venomous stare that was completely lost on her since she couldn't see me.

"Unfortunately, yes," Clarice said resignedly. "Luckily, he's also very good at using his mouth for other things."

Axenus's hands curled into fists at his sides, and I wondered how in the name of the gods he'd come to be in this situation and why he hadn't been able to escape.

Part of my question was answered right away.

"And if he doesn't like what he's being asked to do," Clarice said, stepping close to Axenus so that she was right in front of him, "we can always move his accommodations to the dungeons."

Clarice reached up and grabbed a metal collar around Axenus's neck that I hadn't noticed before and yanked him forward by it. My eyes widened. The collar was made of caronium.

"Remind me again how long you can be out of water before your body will no longer transform?" Clarice asked against his ear.

She yanked on the collar again when he didn't answer. "How long?"

"About three days," he ground out.

"I heard it's painful as well, when your body loses its mer essence and becomes fully human," Clarice went on. "Is it true your skin dries out and begins to crack and peel back from your flesh?" She ran a finger over the swells of muscle on his chest, tracing one of the dark blue whorls that adorned his skin. "I like your skin the way it is, so it would be a shame to see you damaged in that way."

She tugged on the collar again when he didn't answer.

"Yes," Axenus said, and I felt the word stick in his throat.

I bristled. She talked about Axenus like he was a possession she was trying to keep in good condition.

Clarice let go of the collar and walked to a bedside table where she picked up a glass of golden liquid. She brought it back to Axenus and handed it to him. It looked somewhat like the liquor Samhail favored, but there was a slight greenish tint to it that made me think she was offering him more than just alcohol.

"I suggest you drink up and behave yourself for the rest of the night then," Clarice told him. "You're going to need your energy. Magdalene is expecting a lot from you, and you'll still need to please me after her."

Axenus looked at the glass in his hand for a moment before downing its contents.

"Good boy," Clarice purred as she ran her hand down his cheek.

He flinched away from her touch, and she turned to take the empty glass back to the bedside table.

Magdalene stepped into the spot Clarice had vacated and ran her hands over Axenus's shoulders and down his chest again before her fingers fastened on the front of his britches.

"Clarice promised I could have you first," she said, smiling up at him. "I wonder, is your cock iridescent like the rest of you? Let's find out."

"No!" I said out loud as Magdalene began to undo Axenus's pants. Nemesis take me, I couldn't watch this.

To my utter shock, Axenus's head whipped toward me, and our eyes met. His face showed every bit of surprise I was sure my own did before his expression turned to one of horror. Clarice and Magdalene seemed to freeze in place as he turned to face me.

"Cyra! What are you doing here?" Axenus asked, his voice girded with panic and disbelief. He stepped toward me, and I retreated back until I hit the wall and could go no further.

"I'm sorry," I hurried. "I didn't mean to. I don't know how I did it."

"You're dream walking," he said. His hands curled around my upper arms, firmly but not painfully. "You need to go."

"I can't. I tried already," I whispered, shaking my head.

He closed his eyes for several longs seconds before opening them again. "I wish you hadn't seen this of all things."

"I wish I hadn't either," I said softly, but then I couldn't help asking, "How long did this go on?"

I lifted a hand toward Axenus's face, needing to give him whatever comfort I could, but he jerked away from me, and I pulled my hand back.

"You need to go," he repeated.

I was about to ask him how, but instinctively I knew that waking myself up was the easiest way to break the connection. I wasn't going to leave him in this nightmare, though. If I was waking up, then so was he.

My hand shot up quickly, and I wrapped it around the back of his neck. He tried to pull back, but I held on.

*Wake up*, I said into his head, not through the dream per se, but in the way I'd communicated with him underwater, mind to mind. I sent the message through the house, down hallways and around corners until I felt it reach Axenus in his bedchamber.

The room in the dream started to fade and break up as I felt my eyes struggle to open. Axenus was still looking at me as his face gave way to the darkness of my own room.

I inhaled sharply and bolted up in bed, breathing heavily. The figure of a woman still stood in front of me, but she was gone a second later, and I blinked away the specter of the dream that must have followed me back into consciousness. Bressen's hand had been across my stomach, but my movement woke him, and he sat up in bed as well.

"Cyra? What is it? Are you alright?" he asked.

"I…I was in a nightmare, but not mine," I said, trying to calm myself. "Somehow I dream walked into Axenus's nightmare."

Bressen went still. "What kind of nightmare?"

My eyes met his in the dark. "Axenus was a bed slave, wasn't he."

Bressen loosed a deep breath. "That's what you saw in his dream?"

"The start of it, yes. He caught me there, and I tried to wake us both up. I don't know if I was able to wake him, but I couldn't leave him there."

"I'm sure he's fine," Bressen said soothingly as he stroked my hair.

I closed my eyes, still shaking off the memory of the dream and the fear and shame I'd seen in Axenus's face when he realized I was there.

"I don't know how I'm going to apologize to Axenus tomorrow for seeing what I did," I said.

Bressen brushed my cheek. "He'll understand."

"That's why you and Samhail exchanged strange looks when I teased him about asking Axenus to our bed. You both knew about his past."

Bressen nodded. "I don't know if you ever had hopes of inviting Axenus to our bed, but it can't happen."

"Because he was abused," I concluded.

"Because I'm afraid he wouldn't be comfortable enough saying no to an invitation," Bressen clarified. "Axenus was kept prisoner by a powerful queen who used him as a toy for her own pleasure and that of others. When she wasn't using him, she kept him on display in a tank, like some sort of pet or curiosity. He was powerless, utterly at her mercy. You and I hold positions of power in Thasia, and I'm not confident Axenus would feel free to decline our offer if we extended it, no matter how clear we made it that it was optional. You can invite others, but not him."

"Axenus said he owed you a debt. You freed him, didn't you," I said.

Bressen nodded. "Yes, and that's the other reason I'll never ask

Axenus to our bed. Between my position as lord and the debt he feels he owes me, he'd never feel free to say no." He paused. "I hope that doesn't disappoint you too much. I know you've been…admiring him."

It was on the tip of my tongue to deny it, but he'd caught me looking at Axenus too many times for me to contradict him.

"I told you before our wedding that I don't need anyone but you in my bed, and I meant that," I said. "I'll admit Axenus is very nice to look at, but I don't need to be with him."

I realized the truth of the words as I said them.

Bressen looked relieved. "Fair enough," he said. "Then I'll continue to growl at any man who comes too close to you if that's what you want me to do, but just know that you can change your mind."

I looked at him seriously. "Why doesn't the idea of me with other men make you jealous?"

He smiled wryly. "I never said it didn't. Part of me wants to rip out the throat of every man who comes near you, even Samhail sometimes. Samhail and I shared women before, but it's different with you. You have no idea how hard it was for me to watch you with him that last time."

"Then why are you still offering to let me bring other men to bed?"

"Other people, not just other men," he corrected me, and I blinked.

Bressen wrapped his arms around my shoulders and pulled me back against him so I was lying on his chest.

"Cyra, if you're truly happy with just me, that's wonderful. I love being buried inside you, and I'm happy to take you whenever and wherever you want me to. I offer to let you bring other people into our bed because I assume you didn't really have a chance to…explore your desires much before you met me."

"Explore my desires?"

"We may look about the same age," he said, "but I have to remind myself sometimes that I'm much older than you. I have almost a century of experience on you, and that includes sexual experience. I imagine you've had maybe…six years?"

"Four," I admitted sheepishly.

"Nemesis damn me. That's all?" he said in mock horror. "How many partners?"

"Are you really going to make me answer that?"

"Yes," he said, and I could hear the smile in his voice.

"Two before you."

"That's not bad."

"Don't patronize me," I said teasingly.

"I'm not," he insisted. "Fernweh is a small village. I was actually relieved you weren't a virgin when I first met you. Given that you started at eighteen, two is a perfectly respectable number."

"How many partners have you had?" I asked, not actually sure I wanted to know.

He was silent for a long moment. "To be honest, I'm not sure. I never really kept count."

I lifted my head off his chest. "You've had that many partners that you don't know the number?"

Something twisted in my stomach at the thought. Gods above. I didn't know if it would've been worse to know an actual number, or if it was worse that the number was so high, he didn't even know it.

Bressen exhaled deeply. "You have to understand that when we were younger, Samhail and I practically fucked our way across Thasia. I'm not proud of that now, but it is what it is."

"Were there women you…saw regularly?" I asked, and his body tensed beneath me.

"Very rarely," he said. "You have to understand that I spent most of my time with Samhail, and gargoyles are very promiscuous. It's difficult for them to form romantic attachments, so Samhail's sexual habits rubbed off on me." He shrugged. "Or maybe I spent my time with him because I liked having lots of partners too, and his habits just enabled my own."

I shifted so I was facing him. "So are there other people you want to bring to our bed? Do you need to do more…exploring?"

He took my face in one of his hands and ran his thumb over my lips. "I did plenty of exploring in my days. I haven't needed anyone but you since we met," he said.

I eyed him suspiciously. "Is that true?"

"You tell me. You're the truth seer."

"It's too dark to tell if you're glowing red."

"Then ask me again tomorrow."

I frowned at him in the dark.

"Cyra, I know what I want in bed because I spent decades exploring what I liked and didn't like. You've had two other partners. Can you honestly say sex felt the same between the three of us?"

I cocked a brow at him. "Are you trying to make me say that sex with you is better than it was with them?"

His grin was roguish. "You don't have to say it. I know it is."

I made a noise of indignation. "Your arrogance is truly astounding."

"But my arrogance doesn't make it any less true," he said, smirking.

I huffed in annoyance and tried to get up, but he held me fast.

"My point," he said, trying to regain control of the conversation, "is that sometimes, it's important to just do what feels good and not worry about how others will judge you. You've only had four years to experiment, and now you're married."

"You make it sound like a prison sentence," I grumbled, and his chuckle rumbled against my back.

"No, not a prison sentence, but I don't want you to feel like you missed out on anything by marrying me before you really had a chance to discover what you like."

"I like *you*," I said, aware I was in danger of inflating his ego more.

"That's good to hear." His voice was still full of humor. "Just know that if you decide you want to try something new, the option is there."

"Try something like what?"

"Just about anything you want. If you want to try a gods damned orgy, I'll arrange one for you."

I shifted so I could see his face again. "You're serious, aren't you."

"Yes." He cocked his head at me. "Why? Do I need to arrange one?"

I laid my head back on his chest. "I'll pass on the orgy for now."

"The offer stands," he said. "Personally I'd pay good money to watch you be with another woman, so just keep that in mind for the future."

I smacked his chest playfully. "What is it with men and a desire to watch women together?"

He shook his head. "I'm not entirely sure, but if you want to try it sometime, I'll gladly let you know as soon as the answer comes to me."

I chuckled. "It's not going to happen, but since you're so experienced, I'd like to hear about more of my options tomorrow."

"That can be arranged. For the record, not everything has to involve other people. Remind me to tell you all about the joys of restraints."

Something fluttered in my stomach as my imagination took hold, and Bressen rolled over so he was on top of me. One of his legs pressed between my knees, nudging them open.

"All this talk of sexual exploration has made me want to do a little exploring of my own," he growled as he pushed my legs wider so he could nestle between them, his cock nudging me open for him.

My breath caught as his mouth went to my neck to tease the soft flesh there, first with his lips, then his tongue, then his teeth. Bressen's hand closed over my breast, and I gasped as he slid inside me, all thoughts of what I'd seen in Axenus's dream dissipating as he began to thrust.

A while later when we were done, Bressen fell asleep easily with me tucked up next to him, but I lay awake for nearly an hour trying both to imagine and not to imagine what it had been like for Axenus to not have his body be his own. The thought of him having to let Clarice and her friends use him night after night or face the consequence of losing his mer essence sickened me, and I wondered where Clarice and Magdalene were now. I hoped they'd been punished for what they did to him.

Or perhaps I hoped they hadn't been punished so that I could find and punish them myself.

It was a long time before I finally fell back into a dreamless sleep in Bressen's arms, and thoughts of what I'd say to Axenus when I saw him in the morning once again dissolved into the darkness of my unconscious.

# Chapter 46

I was granted a reprieve from facing Axenus when he wasn't at breakfast the next morning, but I wasn't sure if I was still supposed to meet him for training as usual in the small yard behind the house. I was about to head there when one of the house guards pressed a note into my hand from Axenus that asked me to meet him down on the beach. I wasn't sure what to make of the request, but I went back up to my room for a heavier sweater and my cloak and then headed toward the beach.

I could see Axenus standing on the sand as I made my way down. His back was to me as he faced the water, and I got within ten feet of him before calling his name softly. His expression was unreadable when he turned to me, but I didn't hesitate.

"Axenus, I'm so-"

"It's chilly this morning. We could use a fire," he said, cutting me off.

I looked around, but I didn't see anywhere that we could get wood, or at least not enough wood to make a fire that would do us any good.

"I can summon some wood," I said, more to myself than him.

"You don't need to summon wood," Axenus said, exasperated. "You have elemental powers, and if last…if last evening was any indication, those powers are now very strong. You can create a fire without wood."

I knew why Axenus had stumbled over his words, and I tried to apologize again. "I'm s-"

"Stop wasting time and make a fire," he snapped at me.

I stiffened and just looked at him. For a brief second his expression faltered as he remembered he was talking to the Lady of Hiraeth. We'd never observed my status during our training sessions, but he'd also never spoken to me like that before.

Without a word, I held my hand out to my side and a huge fire roared to life on the sand. Its heat immediately warmed us, so much so that Axenus took a step back from it.

He looked at me, and I nodded once, my silent acknowledgment that if he didn't want to talk about last night, I wouldn't force the conversation.

"So what are we working on?" I asked, relieved to get a sentence out.

"Shifting."

My eyes widened.

"We know you syphoned Ursan's magic, and Ursan was a powerful shifter," he said. "I know you've been nervous to try shifting, but now is the time to do it."

"Do you know how shifter magic works?" I asked warily.

"I spoke with Raina at the wedding, and she laid out the basics."

"Well, that's comforting," I said a bit sarcastically.

"Are you going to try or not?" he asked, annoyance once again edging his voice. "Because if you're not going to let me train you, then there's no point in me being here."

I met his eyes, trying to decide if he wanted me to refuse so that he would have an out, an excuse to stop training me and leave.

I wasn't going to give it to him. I wanted him here. I needed him. If he no longer wanted to train me, he was damn well going to have to get rid of me another way.

"Tell me what I need to do," I said.

He nodded and asked, "What would you like to shift into?"

I paused. For as long as I'd known that I should be able to shift into any animal I wanted to, I'd never actually thought about what my preferred form might be. Something with wings, like Raina's peregrine falcon might be nice. I enjoyed flying with Bressen, and this way I could fly next to him instead of in his arms…although that wasn't necessarily preferable. My next choice was something with lots of claws and fangs, something I could change into if I needed to fight. Or run.

"A panther," I said. "I want to be a panther."

Axenus's expression didn't change, but I could've sworn I saw a flash of amusement in his eyes.

"Shifting isn't all that different from other magic," he said. "At its core, it requires you to concentrate on what you want to do, or in this case, be. Raina said that when she shifts, the most important thing for her is to simply believe it will happen. She said it took her a long time to be able to shift because she denied her relationship to Ursan and doubted that she'd inherited any of his power."

My face fell as Axenus spoke. I'd never known that about Raina. In the time we'd been friends, admittedly brief as it was, it had never occurred to me to ask about her shifting, so she'd never told me about the moments of doubt she'd had about herself and her relationship to Ursan. I vowed to ask her about it the next time I saw her. These were things I shouldn't hear second-hand from someone else.

"What's wrong?" Axenus asked, seeing the change in my expression.

I shook my head. "Nothing. You just reminded me I need to talk to Raina later."

Axenus eyed me closely. "I'm curious," he said after a moment, "does your own skin glow red when you lie like that?"

My chin went up a notch. Most of my answer was true enough – I did need to talk to Raina later – but when I glanced at my hands, I was shocked to see the faint glow of red on them. When I looked up at Axenus, he was smirking, as if he knew exactly what I'd seen.

"What else?" I asked, ignoring his smirk.

"That's basically it," he said, stowing his smile. "Visualize what you want to become and have confidence your magic will make it happen."

"Did Raina happen to say what it feels like to shift?"

"I didn't ask."

"Is there a risk I could get stuck as a panther?"

"There's always a chance you wouldn't be able to shift back," he said, "especially if you start to doubt yourself, but there are healers who specialize in undoing magical mishaps. I'm not sure if Aramis has experience, but there must be someone in Callanus at the very least who would be able to reverse the shift."

I pushed a breath out through my nose.

"What about my clothes?" I asked. "You and Samhail never seem to…keep your clothes when you shift. Should I have brought an extra pair of pants?"

I felt my face flush at the question. Raina and Ursan's clothing had shifted with them, but I wasn't sure what the rules were about that.

"For me and Samhail, our shifting is part of who we are as beings, merman and gargoyle," he said. "There's a kind of magic involved to a degree, but mostly our shifting is a result of the innate abilities our kinds possess. For some reason, that magic or ability does not extend to our clothing. For most traditional perimortal shifters, however, their magic treats anything they might be wearing as a part of them and changes it as well. You should, hopefully, remain fully clothed when you unshift."

My shoulders relaxed in relief. It would be only fair for Axenus to see me naked for once, but hopefully that wouldn't be today.

"Are you ready to try?" Axenus asked.

"As ready as I'm going to be," I said.

Axenus stepped toward me and took me by the shoulders, surprising me. I'd assumed he might not want to get close to me after last night.

"Cyra, you need to be ready," he said. "We don't have to do this if you don't want to, but there's no reason you shouldn't be able to shift. You're a powerful perimortal, whether you believe that or not. On top of everything, you're a Hand of the Gods who just received what appears to be a significant boost to your powers from the Trinity themselves. It's time for you to start believing in yourself."

My heart swelled, not at his words, but at the fact that he believed in me that much and was still willing to do whatever he could to help me, even after I'd violated his dream last night.

"Cyra!" he said, alarmed to see tears gathering in my eyes.

I wiped at them with the back of my hand. "I'm fine. That was just a nice speech."

He smiled. "So let me ask again then. Are you ready to try?"

"Yes," I said, clearing the rest of the tears.

"Then just picture what you want to be and let your magic do its job."

I nodded and concentrated on the idea of a panther.

The year after my parents died back in Fernweh, a traveling carnival had come through town, and Jaylan had taken Brix and I in the hopes of getting our minds off everything for a while. The carnival had several cages of wild animals on display, including some magical ones. My brothers had been drawn to the manticore and the harpy, both of which looked fearsome and deadly despite being locked behind bars. I'd been drawn to the pristine white unicorn at first, her beautiful horn glowing gently in the center of her forehead.

Then I'd seen the panther. Far fewer people gathered around the cages of the nonmagical beasts like the bear and the panther, but something about the sleek black cat with its green-gold eyes held me captivated, even more than the purity of the unicorn. There was power behind every padding step the cat took as it prowled behind the bars, and I had the overwhelming urge to break the lock and set it free.

It seemed I'd always had a preference for dark and dangerous things, I thought wryly as Bressen's face flashed in my mind.

Across from me, Axenus's brows furrowed for a brief second before he shook his head. He blinked as if he wasn't sure exactly what he'd seen.

I felt the shift then as I refocused on the idea of the panther. In front of me, my arms began to sprout short black fur as my fingers curled in, replaced by large paws that sported sharp, curved claws. My body thickened with muscle as I leaned forward toward the ground placing my hands, now paws, out in front of me. Behind me I felt the strange sensation below the base of my spine as a tail stretched out and swiped the air. In my mouth, huge fangs extended down as my teeth grew into flesh-tearing weapons, my jaw itself now powerful enough to crush bone.

It all happened in seconds, and I felt my ears flick where they now sat more on top of my head than to the side. All my senses seemed to be enhanced as well. I took in the smells drifting on the ocean breeze, like the fish someone had caught that morning down the beach, the faint tang of Axenus's sweat under his clothes, and Bressen's own scent on my body. My ears heard the call of gulls that I could barely see out over the water, and I tasted the salt of the air on my tongue.

I took a few tentative steps, trying out my new legs. The sand pressed between my toes, feeling grainy beneath the pads, and I stretched my neck as I opened my mouth and peeled back my lips to reveal the two sharp fangs extending from my top jaw.

I looked at Axenus to see he was pleased.

"Well done, Cyra," he said, nodding in approval. "You make a beautiful panther."

I tried to answer back, but only a snarl rumbled from my throat.

"You won't be able to speak while in animal form," he said, "nor do I think you'll be able to use the rest of your powers."

I looked at the woodless fire still blazing on the beach and tried to extinguish it, but nothing happened.

That was fine. I didn't need my magic for now, but I wanted to try out this body that felt so foreign, yet much freer than my own. I began to run, awkwardly at first as I adjusted to the feeling of having four legs, but I got the hang of it soon enough, and then I was racing down the beach, faster than I'd ever moved in my life. I leapt high into the air, landing and then sliding to a halt in the sand before I was off again, racing back down the beach toward Axenus.

I saw his smile start to fade as I didn't slow but continued to barrel toward him, my eyes fixed on him with a predator's focus.

"Cyra?" he said as I neared. "Cyra!"

I pivoted only a couple feet from him, leaping to the side and swiping at his leg playfully with a paw of sheathed claws. He tried to jump back, but my swat took his leg out from under him, and he stumbled backward before losing his balance and falling on his ass in the sand.

"Not amusing," he said as he stood up again, brushing the sand from his hands and clothes, but his faint smile said otherwise. "Try shifting back unless you need to take another run down the beach."

I thought of my own form, and I felt the shift once again take hold as black fur pulled back into my skin, and my tail and fangs receded. My own body was soon kneeling on all fours – mercifully clothed – and I picked myself up, brushing the sand from my knees and palms.

"Ursan somehow always managed to shift back into a standing position," I said. "I have to figure out how he did that."

"You'll get the hang of it," Axenus said. "That was a perfect first attempt. Do you want to try shifting into something else?"

"Yes!" I said, bolstered by my success. "I want to try flying."

Axenus looked a bit worried for a second, but he shrugged and waved a hand to indicate that I should go ahead and try.

By the end of our session, I'd shifted into an eagle, a horse, a newt, and – in remembrance of Ursan – a bear, although I was relieved to see my bear didn't have the white heart on its chest as Ursan's always had.

I asked Axenus about turning into something magical like a unicorn or a phoenix, but he advised me not to try it. He said he'd never seen or heard of a shifter who could take the form of such creatures, which had their own subtle magic, and he suspected it wasn't possible.

All in all, the session had been a rousing success with the one caveat that, while I'd been able to shift into an eagle, my body struggled with the movements that would allow me to fly. I'd have to get together with Raina for flying lessons sometime.

"Thank you," I said to Axenus as I extinguished the fire.

I'd been wanting to test my shifting powers for a while now but had always been too afraid to try it. Axenus always seemed to know just what to say to boost my confidence or push me further so I could develop my powers. I wanted to hug him, but I was wary of touching him. He'd never recoiled from me before, but that was before I'd seen his secret.

"I should go," I said. "I have to meet Samhail for combat training."

"Why are you still bothering with combat training?" Axenus asked. "You have plenty of weapons at your disposal with your magic."

I shrugged. "I want to be prepared for anything. Samhail's training kept me from being punched by Jerram months ago."

Axenus looked alarmed. "Lord Jerram tried to punch you?" he asked.

"Yes, and because Samhail taught me how to duck blows, he missed."

Axenus inclined his head to acknowledge the point, and I smiled at him before turning to head back to the house to meet Samhail.

That would be an awkward meeting as well. What Samhail had revealed about gargoyles being the guardians of the Trinity cast a different light on our friendship, one that I was still struggling to understand.

"Cyra," Axenus said, stopping me after I'd taken a couple steps.

I turned back to him, but he was quiet for a moment before he spoke.

"About what you saw…," he said.

"You don't have to tell me," I interrupted. "I'm just sorry I invaded your dream. I'll do my best to ensure it never happens again."

"Bressen probably told you he was the one who rescued me?"

"I already assumed as much," I told him. "Bressen confirmed it, but he didn't tell me much else."

"It was just at the start of the war," Axenus went on, seemingly unable to stop himself now that he'd started. "Clarice was the Queen of Sedonia at the time, and Bressen's father had sent him as an emissary to see if she'd support Thasia in the conflict against Rowe. I'd been with her for almost eight years by then. Clarice was a collector. She liked to possess unusual things, and we merpeople don't spend a lot of time on land as a rule. I like being on land more than most of my kind, and one of Clarice's lords found me napping on the beach one day. Hoping to gain some favor with her, he captured me and presented me to her."

His eyes met mine, but I didn't say anything, letting him decide for himself how much he wanted to tell me.

"She just kept me in a tank at first, one just barely big enough for me to turn around in. My body started to weaken and lose muscle because I didn't have room to move, so she began to let me out of the tank for periods of the day to get some exercise. That's when she realized she might have another use for me."

I swallowed but kept quiet.

"What you saw with that woman Magdalene was the first time she shared me with someone else. It wasn't the last time by far."

Tears formed in the corners of my eyes again, but I blinked them back. I didn't think Axenus wanted my tears or my pity.

"I don't know how Bressen found me," he went on. "He probably sensed me while he was walking around Clarice's palace. In any case, the door to the chamber that held my tank opened one evening, and there he was. He tried to talk to me, to ask me why I was there, but I didn't say anything to him. I'd tried to get others to help me before, but no one wanted to defy the queen. She'd punished me for trying, and I didn't want to risk it this time in case Clarice had sent him to test me."

He paused as if remembering.

"I hadn't used a mind shield in years, so Bressen must have read my thoughts," he went on. "He just turned and left, but he came back late that night and set me free. He'd invaded the minds of half of Clarice's guards to keep them away from the chamber that night, and he even brought me a towel and clothes. He helped me out of the tank and led me to where Samhail was waiting with Phaedrus and a portal. Samhail took me back to Solandis with him, and Bressen stayed to try and finish his diplomatic mission. Unfortunately, someone had seen him helping me and told Clarice. She waited until the next morning to confront him about it. She'd actually considered attacking him, but she had enough sense to realize how foolish it would be to attack the son of a Triumvirate lord, and one as powerful as Bressen. Instead, she refused to help Thasia against Rowe, and that was worse."

"Was Bressen's father angry with him for helping you?"

"His father wasn't thrilled, but he was a good man and understood why Bressen did what he did. Jerram and Ursan were less understanding, especially since the repercussions were disastrous. Sedonia threw its support behind Rowe, and Thasia was suddenly fighting on two fronts. The Triumvirate had hoped to secure Sedonia's armada to add to their own strength on the sea and cut off Rowe's coast, but when Sedonia joined with Rowe, Thasia had to split its own sea force to deal with attacks along the coast of Polaris. It nearly cost Thasia the war. At the very least, it dragged the conflict on for much longer than it should have lasted."

Axenus looked at me so seriously that I held my breath for a moment, and I heard the crack in his voice when he spoke again.

"Bressen saved me from being Clarice's slave, but it cost both him and Thasia dearly. It cost countless people their lives while the war dragged on. I will always owe Bressen," he said, and his voice was hard as granite. "I'll never be able to repay him. He asked me to train you as a favor, but doing this…it will never make me even with him. I just want you to know that while my debt to Bressen is what brought me here, it's not what keeps me here."

I went still.

"I enjoy working with you," he said. "It's my honor to help you learn your magic." He gave me a wry smile. "Although I wonder how much longer you'll need me now that the gods have enhanced your powers."

"You're not getting rid of me that easily," I said. "I need a good teacher now more than ever so I don't accidentally level a city."

He chuckled, and we looked at each other for a long moment.

"I should go now, or Samhail will make me run extra laps," I said.

"I can always write a note to explain that I kept you late," he teased.

"And you think a note from *you* will keep him from punishing me?"

Axenus chuckled again. "On second thought, you better run."

I turned to do just that, but then I stopped and turned back again.

"I just need to know one thing," I said.

"Yes?" he asked.

"Is Clarice still Queen of Sedonia?"

A muscle ticked in his jaw. "No."

"Is she still alive?"

I was starting to understand why I might have been chosen by the Nemesis. Whoever this woman was, I wanted to punish her.

"She's in Revenmyer," he said.

Part of me felt better hearing that, but another part was already thinking of what I'd do to the woman if I could somehow get access to her at the prison.

I wanted to ask Axenus what he thought about her being in Revenmyer, whether he felt that was a fitting punishment for what she'd done to him, but I was already going to be late for my training with Samhail no matter how much I hurried.

"Thank you for telling me," I said to Axenus, and he nodded.

I turned and broke into a run back toward the house, knowing that Samhail would only make me run even more if I tried to open a portal to the training yard.

I marveled that Axenus had managed to stay the kind, patient man he was after all he'd endured. I was grateful he had. I hadn't been kidding when I'd told him I needed him now more than ever. If Sandrian and Morland were back, I needed to know how to wield all my powers as well as I possibly could.

Perhaps he was now responsible for preparing me to be both a Hand of the Gods and the new Nemesis Incarnate, the latter a role I was becoming more and more eager to embrace.

# Chapter 47

Samhail was waiting for me in the small training yard behind the house when I arrived, his feet planted and arms crossed. I was breathless as I stopped in front of him, but I saw from his expression I wasn't likely to get any mercy. Not that I'd expected any.

"Thirty laps around the yard," he barked. "Your usual ten, plus ten for every minute you were late."

I was actually relieved. I'd thought I was more than two minutes late, and I assumed I'd be running laps the entire session. Luckily all the swim training I'd done with Axenus had built up my stamina, so I could manage thirty laps, even after my sprint from the beach.

I dared to take another two seconds to rest before I started my jog around the yard. Samhail remained in the center with his arms crossed, but I knew better than to take my eyes off him by now. Sure enough, on my fifth lap I saw his hand move, and my muscles tensed to take action.

A small forcefield resonated from his palm, and I dove forward to somersault under it before getting back to my feet and putting on a burst of speed in case he decided to follow up with another one. Instead, he moved toward the rack of practice weapons, and I groaned inwardly.

Samhail had only just started attacking me while I did my warmup laps a little while ago. The first time he'd stuck out a wooden practice sword to trip me, I'd only just barely managed to hurdle over it and avoid sprawling face-first in the dirt. I'd developed a healthy caution around him ever since, and I now expected him to attack at any time, which I knew was the point. It was his way of trying to sharpen my instincts and reflexes.

While Axenus's teaching strategy was heavy on instruction and support, Samhail's philosophy was more of a sink-or-swim mentality. He would act, and I could either react or end up bruised and on my ass.

As I ran, occasionally dodging forcefields or wooden practice swords, a dangerous idea crept into my mind. What if I dared to take the offensive?

Axenus had told me I needed to start thinking like a warrior, to start acting first or attacking when I thought there was danger. Well, with

Samhail there was always danger. Maybe I needed to start attacking him when I saw an opening.

The thought was ludicrous. Samhail was almost twice my size and a trained warrior with almost a hundred years of combat experience.

I shook the doubt away. If I ever needed to fight, I wouldn't have a choice who I faced. I couldn't request an opponent of equal size or strength. I might well need to defend myself against a large man – not as large as Samhail, of course – but someone still much larger than me.

I was on my last few laps now, and Samhail's back was to me. Even better, the weapons rack was between us. If I went for the rack, I might be able to grab a weapon and strike while he wasn't looking. That I'd be attacking him from behind didn't worry me in the least. By his own thinking, it would be his own fault for turning his back on an enemy.

How would I strike, though? In a real battle I'd aim for my opponent's head, but I wouldn't do that to Samhail, just in case I was lucky enough to hit him. A strike across his back then. Given how solid he was and the limits of my own strength, I didn't think I'd injure him too badly, and landing a hit – if I could manage it – would be a personal victory.

I didn't give myself time to second guess. I pivoted and broke into a sprint toward the rack, grabbing a sturdy wooden practice sword from it as I flew by. Feet from Samhail, I pulled it back and swung it with all my might at a spot between his shoulder blades. I imagined the sickening crack of the wood against his back, the vibrations I'd feel in my hands and up my arms as I made contact, but I willed myself not to pull back.

I needn't have worried since the blow landed only in my imagination.

Inches before the sword struck, Samhail was suddenly facing me, and the only sound was the thwack of the sword as it hit the palm that he held up to intercept it. For a moment I just stared at the large hand closed around the wooden sword, my eyes widening in surprise and then dread. I looked up into Samhail's face, and my legs turned to jelly to see the wicked amusement there as he looked back at me with one eyebrow arched in mild disbelief.

I tugged on the sword, but Samhail held it firmly, and I knew there was no way I was going to pry it from his grip. I saw his other hand move out of the corner of my eye, and I immediately surrendered my hold on the weapon to dodge under his arm. I threw an elbow into his side as I skirted past and was rewarded by his grunt as it found his ribs.

Buoyed by my success, I swung around to aim for one of his kidneys, as he'd taught me, but I should've taken the small victory and retreated when I had the chance.

The heel of Samhail's hand slammed into the center of my chest, and I went down hard on the ground, sprawled out flat on my back, coughing. Then he was on one knee beside me, his hand at my throat, not pressing hard enough to cut off my breath, but just hard enough to keep me down so I couldn't rise.

I grabbed at his wrist with both hands, but I had nowhere near enough strength to dislodge him. I tried to bring my leg up, either to get my knee into his chest or to hook it around his neck – also as he'd shown me – but he caught my thigh and pinned that too, turning me sideways so my hips were twisted and one leg was trapped under the other.

I was pinned and thoroughly out of options, but I continued to struggle as he simply knelt beside me waiting for me to tire myself out.

"Do you yield?" he asked calmly when I finally gave up and went still.

I refused to say the word. Instead I just nodded as best I could against his hold. Apparently it was good enough for him because he lifted his hands from my throat and leg and held one above my chest in invitation for me to take it so he could pull me up.

I had no pride left to save, so I took the hand, and he pulled me effortlessly back to my feet as he stood.

"That was bold of you," he said. "I wasn't expecting an attack."

"You could've fooled me," I said, rubbing the center of my chest.

I was sure I'd have a bruise there later to heal, but I was lucky he hadn't cracked my sternum.

"Your initiative was admirable, but your stealth leaves something to be desired. I heard you coming a mile away."

Dammit. I really thought I'd been quiet.

"What provoked you to take the offensive all of a sudden?" he asked.

I shrugged. "Axenus is always telling me I need to be aggressive."

Samhail raised a brow. "Is that what Axenus has been teaching you? To attack while someone's back is turned?"

"I just thought I'd have a chance with the element of surprise."

"So now I need to talk to Axenus both about keeping you late as well as teaching you to make foolhardy combat decisions?"

"It was my fault I was late, not Axenus's," I said. "I had something important I needed to talk to him about."

"So just about the foolhardy combat decisions then?"

I exhaled in frustration. "I'm tired of always being on the defensive with you," I snapped. "I figured I'd try something new. It didn't work."

Samhail shrugged. "I wouldn't necessarily say that. You did land one good elbow. Your mistake was letting it go to your head and trying for another hit."

"Yes, I realize that," I said in annoyance.

"In principle, I don't disagree with Axenus," he went on. "You do need to learn to take initiative. I'm just not sure doing it in physical combat is a good idea for you, and definitely not against me."

I raised a brow at that bit of arrogance, but he just smirked.

"So you agree with Axenus?" I asked teasingly. "I wasn't sure that was even possible."

"Breathe a word to him, and you'll be running laps until you drop."

I smiled sweetly. "Your secret is safe with me. For now."

He growled low in his throat, but I only crossed my arms.

"I thought you're supposed to be protecting me in any case," I said. "Since when does that include trying to hit me with forcefields or trip me with practice swords?"

"I'm teaching you to protect yourself, so I'm covered," Samhail said, crossing his own muscled arms over his massive chest.

"That's a rather convenient loophole."

He just smirked at me again.

I opened my mouth to say something else, but then closed it. Samhail looked at me in question, then rolled his eyes and groaned softly.

"You want to talk about it, don't you," he said knowingly.

I thought about letting it go but then decided against it. "Yes, I'd like to talk about this…divine imperative."

"What exactly do you want to know?"

I paused. "I need to know if it's the only reason you and I are friends, or if it's the reason that we…that we…"

"That we what?" he asked, but his look told me he knew exactly what I was trying to say. When I didn't go on, he narrowed his eyes at me.

"Is that what you think?" he asked. "That we're only friends or that I like being between your thighs because I'm divinely bound to you?"

I felt a flush of heat and looked away. "Something like that."

Samhail sighed heavily. "Cyra, I'm only going to say this once, so listen carefully. I told you before that gargoyles don't really do love or caring well. I've never been in love, and there's a very small group of people I actually care about. You're part of that group, and that has nothing to do with the divine imperative."

I opened my mouth again, but he held up a hand, and I closed it.

"When we first met, I didn't understand the protectiveness I felt toward you," he went on. "I'd never felt anything like it before, just like I'd never felt love before, so I mistakenly conflated the two. And yes, that initial protectiveness was the divine imperative taking hold, but I've since learned to feel a whole new protectiveness toward you that has nothing to do with the divine imperative and everything to do with the fact that I genuinely care about you and your well-being."

My eyes softened at his last admission. That couldn't have been easy for him to say, and I had the urge to throw my arms around him.

"Don't even think about it," Samhail said, recognizing the look in my eye. "As for what happens…or happened, between us in bed, I assure you the divine imperative doesn't work that way. I can only speak for myself, but I want you because you're a beautiful woman and because, as I told you before, gargoyles are a lusty bunch, and we'll rarely pass up a chance to have sex, especially if it's with a beautiful woman."

I caught his present tense use of the word "want," but I didn't comment on it, nor would I let myself think about it.

"Alright, fine," I said. "But what does this divine imperative mean for us moving forward?"

"It means I'll defend you with my life," Samhail said, "but that was as true a week ago before we knew about the imperative as it is now. In short, the divine imperative doesn't mean much unless Arystria abolishes the borders of all its countries, and the Hands of the Gods go back to ruling the entire continent in the Trinity's name. Or at the very least, the continent would have to acknowledge your divinely chosen status in some way, and the temples would need to go back to employing gargoyles for protection, neither of which is likely to happen."

"Are there a lot of gargoyles?" I asked. "You're the first and only one I've ever met. Would there even be enough for each temple to have one?"

"No, there aren't enough of us left."

I started to ask why, but Samhail stopped me again.

"Ten more laps," he said. "You need to warm up again now that you wasted time asking questions. And if you attack me, you'll regret it."

I gave him an innocent look. "Maybe you and I should train the way you and Bressen do," I suggested mischievously.

He frowned. "What's that supposed to mean?"

"It means I should try to break past your mind shield while we practice, and if I immobilize you, then…" My voice trailed off as Samhail's brows narrowed and his face darkened ominously.

Gods damn me. What was I thinking to bring that up? I'd learned a while ago that Bressen and Samhail engaged in a kind of mental combat when they trained, but I'd never told either of them I knew. I'd also promised the guards at the Citadel that I wouldn't tell anyone that they bet on the outcomes of those trainings.

"How do you know about that?" Samhail asked softly, but there was an underlying menace to his voice. "Did Bressen-"

"It wasn't Bressen," I said quickly. "I won't say how I know, but he didn't tell me, and I'm not the only one who knows you do it."

His face hardened. It was important to Samhail to maintain a strong mind shield since Morland had taken over his mind during the war, and it now seemed insensitive to have brought up how he trained with Bressen.

"I'm sorry. I shouldn't have suggested it. Forget I said anything."

His expression eased. "It's fine. We can train like that if you want."

I blinked at him. "Really?"

"Sure. I'd be a fool to pass up a chance to test my mind shield against a syphon who just got a power surge from the Trinity."

"I…suppose that's one way to look at it," I said.

"Besides, if your abysmal concentration is any indication, I have nothing to worry about. Now finish your laps."

I glared at Samhail and started running, a new surge of motivation putting a kick in my step.

I was going to shred his mind shield to ribbons.

Later that night as I lay stretched out across the bed waiting for Bressen to come in from working in his study, I was forced to admit to myself how right Samhail had been. I may have been a syphon with a power boost from the gods, but I apparently had a lot of trouble concentrating on more than one thing at a time.

Despite all the practice I'd done with Bressen on breaking past mind shields, I hadn't remotely managed to get past Samhail's shield even once. Time and again I'd been met with a wall of impenetrable stone in his mind, and all my attempts to get past it or around it had failed spectacularly. In hindsight, the fact that Bressen, the most powerful mind wraith currently in existence, could only get past Samhail's mind shield about half the time should have told me something.

Not only had I failed to break past his shield, but every time I'd tried, my mind had drifted away from whatever combat exercise Samhail was doing with me, and I'd immediately found myself knocked to the ground or being hit with one of the practice weapons. My attempt to attack him earlier was also still on his mind, because he didn't go easy on me, and I'd healed plenty of ugly bruises before bed to prove it.

Finally, the door to the bedroom opened and Bressen entered. I lifted my head from the bed and watched him head to the closet looking weary.

"I'm sorry," he said, not even glancing toward me. "There was something important I had to take care of before bed. I'll be right there."

He disappeared into the closet for a minute or so and emerged wearing the loose pants he normally donned before bed. My tongue licked out to see him in those pants that hung loosely off his hips. The oblique muscles at his waist made a tantalizing sight where they curved around his body to dip into the front of the pants, and I suddenly had the urge to run my teeth along them.

The lights in the room dimmed as Bressen headed toward the bed, fumbling with the drawstring of his pants. I wasn't sure why he bothered to tie them, or even put them on, for that matter. We rarely remained clothed at bedtime for more than a few minutes.

"How was your day?" Bressen asked as he looked up. "Did you-"

He stopped dead in his tracks as he took in what awaited him on the bed. He'd been busy today and only stopped in to have lunch and dinner quickly, so I hadn't gotten much chance to talk to him. As I'd waited for him to finish his work, I'd decided to give him a preview of my day.

The corner of Bressen's lips quirked up on one side. "Either you and Axenus worked on shapeshifting today," he said carefully, "or someone left a gate open somewhere."

My only response was to stretch two heavy black paws out in front of me and unsheathe my claws so they snagged lightly on the covers of the bed. For good measure, I yawned lazily to display the long, sharp fangs in my mouth. I licked my lips again, this time for Bressen's benefit.

He raised his eyebrows, and I felt his mind brush against mine. If I could have laughed in this form, I would've. He was double-checking to be sure it was actually me and not a real panther that had somehow wandered into our bedroom.

"I know we've never had occasion to discuss this," Bressen said teasingly, "but I generally don't allow animals on the bed."

I growled at him and ran my tongue up my paw. I wasn't sure why, but I enjoyed licking myself in this form.

"I'm…open to reconsidering that policy, though," Bressen said in answer to my growl.

He stepped closer to the bed, and I turned my green-gold eyes on him with predatory intent. He stopped, looking wary.

"I feel like that's the look I usually give you," he said moving forward once again. He put a knee tentatively on the bed then climbed on when I did nothing but watch him. He pushed closer to me and reached out to scratch behind my ears.

"Very impressive," he said. "I can't wait to hear all about your day."

It was a subtle suggestion to shift back, but I wanted to enjoy this game a little longer, so I just pressed my head into his hand.

Bressen sighed and laid out on the bed next to me, his shoulders propped against the pillows as he continued to scratch. I let myself enjoy it for a few more seconds before I lifted one large paw and laid it heavily on his stomach. I unsheathed my claws again and grazed them across the taut muscles there. Bressen's hand froze on my head as he watched my claws flex against his skin. One good swipe, and I could have opened his stomach. It was both a powerful feeling as well as a terrifying one.

"Is it wrong that I find that incredibly arousing?" he whispered.

The laugh I attempted came out as a growl, and I shifted quickly back to my human form before I accidentally cut Bressen's stomach to ribbons. He inhaled sharply at my sudden shift but then groaned as he realized I was already naked. He grabbed my arms and hauled me across him so I straddled one of his legs.

"Nemesis take me, that was making me hard," he breathed before he hooked his hand at the nape of my neck and pulled my mouth to his for a demanding kiss. I felt the truth of his words pressing against my thigh, and I moved up closer to him, meeting the drive of his tongue with equal fervor as he ran his other hand teasingly down my back. Gooseflesh rose on my body, and I repositioned myself so I was more fully straddling his leg. I pressed my breasts against his chest as my hand gripped his shoulder, and he groaned against my mouth.

"Was it your first time shifting?" Bressen asked between kisses.

I made a noise somewhere between an affirmation and a moan.

His mouth continued to ravage mine while one hand held my face captive. His other hand roamed over my back, and I rocked against his thigh as the tightening between my legs grew more urgent.

Bressen dragged his mouth from mine. "Oh no, if you're going to ride something, it's not going to be my leg."

Bressen yanked the drawstring of his pants loose, and I helped him pull them off. When they'd been discarded, he pulled me over him so I was straddling his hips. His long, hard cock twitched beneath me, and he guided himself to my entrance. The moment I felt him in place, I impaled myself down onto him. We both gasped in ecstasy as I closed around him, and then I was moving, pushing myself down as far as I could go while my nails dug into the muscles of his chest.

Bressen threw his head back against the pillows and let out a low groan as I flexed my nails. His hands came to my hips to help rock me, and I rode him faster, slamming myself down onto him as my breasts bounced between us.

"Fucking gods above, Cyra," he rasped. "That feels so damned good."

My release was building, and I leaned forward as I drove myself down onto him. I hooked one of my hands on the hard muscle of his shoulder for leverage and rocked faster, each second bringing me closer to shattering around him. His hips thrust up to meet me, once, twice, and then my release exploded through me as I cried out and pleasure rolled over me in waves. I felt his cock harden and throb as his hot seed spilled into me, and he wrapped his arms around me to pull me against him. He buried his own groan into my neck, and I sagged on top of him.

We both lay breathing hard for several long minutes before I finally lifted my head from his chest. He took my face in his hands, smoothing the sweat-dampened tendrils of my hair back with his fingers.

"I'll never get tired of that," he said as he pressed a kiss to my lips.

"Mmm," was all I managed to answer.

"Are…you aware you still have a tail?" Bressen asked.

"What?" My eyes widened, and I turned to look behind me. Sure enough, a sleek, black tail waved lazily in the air just above my backside.

"Sweet gods above!" I squeaked as the tail receded into my body.

"For every time you make me take my wings out during sex," Bressen teased, "you have to let me fuck you while you're wearing that tail."

My jaw dropped open and a sound of incredulity snuck out before Bressen pressed his mouth back to mine. When he pulled back again, I eased myself off him, although I didn't go far. I curled up against him and traced the nail marks denting the skin on his chest with my fingers.

"Did you shift into anything else today?" Bressen asked as his arm wrapped around me, pulling me even closer.

I gave him the list of animals I'd managed to shift into along with a brief rundown of how everything went.

"I couldn't fly yet as the eagle, though," I finished. "I'll have to get together with Raina and ask her how it's done."

Bressen's brow shot up.

"I'm sure flying as a bird must be different than as an angelus," I said in defense of why I hadn't asked him to teach me.

"I think the principles are the same," he said, "but you haven't seen Raina since the wedding. It's a good reason to make some plans with her." He paused before asking, "I take it you and Axenus patched things up?"

I nodded. "He wouldn't let me apologize at first, but we seemed to come to an understanding by the end of the session," I said. "He told me everything that happened, about how you and Samhail helped him escape, and what it cost you."

Bressen's arm squeezed me against him a little more, and he pressed a kiss to the top of my head.

"He told me she's in Revenmyer," I went on. "The woman who held him captive. Clarice?"

Bressen's body tensed next to me.

"I assume you oversee her punishment," I ventured.

"Yes, and you'll have to trust she's being punished fittingly," he said, sensing where I was going with this. I wanted to ask him if I could see her, but I knew he wouldn't let me. I also didn't think Axenus would appreciate me seeing her either, so I didn't ask.

"Talking to Axenus today, it…made me want to…" I trailed off.

Bressen remained quiet as he waited for me to go on. His chest rose and fell steadily under my hand.

"That time you told me about what you wanted to do to the men on the wharf who attacked me and Raina," I said, "I understand that now."

His breath hitched beneath my fingers.

"For the first time, I'm glad I serve the Nemesis," I said. "I don't know how to be the Hand of the Nemesis, but I want to learn."

Bressen opened his mouth to say something, but he was interrupted by a knock at the bedroom door.

"I'm not sure who thought it would be wise to interrupt my time in bed with my wife," he said loudly toward the door, "but if they know what's good for them, they'll go away."

Another louder knock sounded, and Ferris's urgent voice called out. "My lord, I'm sorry to bother you, but it's imperative I speak with you. Something's happened."

It was the panic in the man's tone that had Bressen swinging his legs quickly off the bed and striding for the door. I was about to remind him he was naked when he glamoured a pair of pants over his lower body.

I rolled out of bed as well and grabbed my robe off the chair to hurry across the room. I was at Bressen's side when he opened the door to reveal Ferris standing there.

Ferris's gaze flicked to me, and he seemed uncertain about whether or not to say what he needed to say in front of me.

"Speak," was all Bressen said, his tone brooking no questions.

"My lord, Lord Aidan just arrived by portal from Seatherny," Ferris said. "He said Lord Consort Jasper has been taken."

# Chapter 48

Aidan's face was ghostly pale as he stared with vacant, bloodshot eyes at the wall on the opposite side of Bressen's study. His hair, normally so kempt, looked as though he'd run his fingers through it repeatedly, and he didn't seem to be blinking at all. He was sitting at the meeting table when Bressen and I entered after we'd hastily dressed.

One look at Aidan, and I had to fight every instinct in me not to go comfort him. I knew Maziren wouldn't let me anywhere near him, so I fought down the urge to help and instead took a seat at the table as far from Aidan as I could get. Maziren stood behind him looking a bit shellshocked herself but still ready to cleave anyone in half who approached her lord. The tea Ferris had brought up sat steaming but untouched in front of Aidan, who sat perfectly still.

The door to Bressen's study swung open again only seconds later as Samhail and Axenus entered. Both also appeared to have hurriedly thrown on whatever clothes they had handy, pants and loose untucked tunics, and they headed straight to the table to sit down. The high-backed chairs were large and sturdy, but Samhail's still groaned a little under his solid weight.

Bressen took a seat across from Aidan and looked at Maziren. He inclined his head toward the sixth seat across from me, but Maziren shook her head and stood rigidly behind Aidan. Bressen shrugged and turned his attention to his fellow lord.

"What happened?" he asked.

Aidan just shook his head weakly. "I…I don't know," he said, and his voice sounded distant. I wasn't even sure he understood what Bressen had asked him.

Bressen looked to Maziren to fill in what Aidan couldn't.

"He struck while Jasper was out at the markets," Maziren said, her voice flat and hollow. "The Lord Consort only had two guards with him. Both were perimortal, fire elementals, but they didn't stand a chance."

That Jasper had even had perimortal guards with him at all was fairly uncommon. All the guards at the Citadel and the few at Tide's End were mortal, their primary roles largely limited to being the eyes and ears of those they served, or to handle mundane threats from other mortals.

Given how powerful lords like Bressen and Aidan were, the idea of having others defend them seemed rather ridiculous. Only exceptionally powerful perimortals like Maziren could usually attain high-level positions like Captain of the Guard for a Triumvirate Lord.

"He?" Bressen asked. "Who is 'he'? Who attacked Jasper?"

"Sandrian," Maziren said, and everyone else at the table shifted.

"Sandrian? You're sure?" Samhail asked.

Maziren reached into a pocket of her leather pants and pulled out a piece of paper that she handed to Bressen. "Sandrian left one of the guards alive to deliver this note," she said. "The other guard he hit with lightning until there was nothing left but a charred, smoking husk."

"Lightning?" I asked in horror.

Bressen nodded. "Sandrian's power is to call lightning to his will. He's the only one I've ever known to have such a power."

My dinner threatened to come back up as I imagined the guard being scorched to death by bolts of electricity coursing through his body. For his sake, I hoped he'd died within seconds of being struck.

Bressen opened the note Maziren gave him, and his face went ashen as he read it.

"What is it?" I asked.

"The note is addressed to me," Bressen said.

"And what does it say?"

Bressen read the note aloud. "Lord Aidan can have his husband back when you and the syphon bring me the collar and rings from the shipwreck of *The Stalwart*. Bring them to the temple ruins at the base of the Bullhorn Mountains tomorrow at noon, or the Lord of Derridan will get back the blackened remains of his consort."

Aidan's breath hitched in his chest, and he closed his eyes.

"How did he know we have the collar and rings?" I asked Bressen.

Aidan's head snapped up, and his gaze swung to me. "You have them?" he asked incredulously. "You actually have the collar and rings?"

I opened my mouth but didn't say anything. I'd forgotten Bressen hadn't told Aidan we'd found the items from the vision.

Aidan stood so fast that his heavy chair tipped back and almost crashed to the floor. Maziren caught it before it did and righted it.

"You found the items and you didn't tell me!" Aidan thundered at Bressen. "How long have you had them?"

Bressen looked calmly up at the other lord from his seat. "We found them a few days ago, and I didn't tell you because there was no readily apparent reason that you needed to know we had them."

Aidan grabbed the note from Bressen's hand and shook it in his face. "Is this a readily enough apparent reason for you?" he yelled.

He crushed the note in his own hand and threw it down onto the table so it bounced across the surface.

Both Samhail and Axenus started to rise when Aidan began shouting, but Bressen held out a hand to stay them. Behind Aidan, Maziren's hand stilled on the sword she'd been about to draw when Samhail and Axenus moved, and I couldn't help wondering once again how she'd fare in a fight against Samhail. Thankfully, we didn't yet need to learn the answer to that.

"I know you're afraid for Jasper," Bressen said to Aidan, his voice full of empathy, "but we're not going to let anything happen to him."

Aidan's anger left him as quickly as it came on.

"You and Cyra will go to the temple?" Aidan asked hopefully. "You'll give Sandrian the collar and rings?"

"*I* will bring him the collar and rings," Bressen clarified. "Cyra won't be going anywhere near there."

"I have to go," I said, standing up. "Sandrian specified that I needed to come as well."

"No!" Bressen said as his head whipped to me. He shot to his feet and slammed his palms down onto the table making the crumpled note bounce again, and I saw the furious flash of red in his eyes.

"This is absolutely non-negotiable this time," he told me. "If I need to lock you in chains in the basement, so be it. You can hate me for the rest of your life if you want, but you will not go anywhere near Sandrian."

He slammed a hand on the table again and glared at me.

I stood speechless, not at the shocking vehemence in Bressen's voice, but at the tears that threatened in the corners of his eyes. His voice had begun to break by the time he'd finished speaking, and I could do nothing but stare at him with my mouth hanging open.

"But if Sandrian says that she needs to be there-" Aidan began to argue, but Bressen whirled on him, his eyes now glowing steadily red.

"She doesn't go," Bressen said, his voice deadly calm. "I'll go myself with the collar and rings, and Sandrian will just have to be satisfied."

I looked at the note crumpled in a ball on the table. I could've sworn that Sandrian hadn't called me by name, only mentioned "the syphon," and I reached for the paper to check.

I picked up the note, and my body suddenly seized, arching like a bow. Pain raced through my veins like wildfire, but not physical pain. This was mental anguish and deep soul-rending agony like I'd never felt before as the last part of my vision from the wedding, the part that had been lost, suddenly burst into my brain. A scream tore from my lips, and I heard it from outside of my body, as if I'd somehow come apart from myself.

My hand clamped around the note. Its points dug into my palm, but I couldn't get my fingers to unclench from around it. The scream continued to well up from my throat before drawing off into a long, keening wail.

My vision had gone blank, but as the room rematerialized around me, I was aware that Bressen and Axenus had both grabbed for me and lowered me to the floor when my legs failed. I breathed in shuddering gasps as the memory of the vision squeezed my heart like a vice.

"Cyra! What's wrong?" Bressen's voice drifted to me through the haze, and my heart clenched even tighter.

"No!" I cried out, grabbing for Bressen. My fist found his shirt, and I yanked him down to me with a strength that neither of us expected me to possess. "No, no, no!" I said, sobbing the word.

"Cyra, what is it? Did you have another vision?" Bressen asked, trying gently to pry my fingers from his shirt so he could pull back.

I freed my other arm from Axenus's grip where he'd been trying to support me and locked it around Bressen's neck to drag him toward me even further. He let me do it this time, leaning over me as I continued to whisper the word no into his ear, my voice choked with sobs.

"Cyra." Bressen's soft whisper finally penetrated my anguish, and I was aware that his arms were wrapped tightly around me, cocooning me against his body.

"Cyra," he said again. "Tell me what's wrong. What did you see?"

But I couldn't. I couldn't say it for fear of making it real.

Bressen put his hand to the side of my face, and I knew he was trying to see into my mind, to see what I'd seen. I locked my mind down, and he jerked as he felt me close myself off.

"Cyra," he said, a light sternness in his voice, "if you won't let me see for myself, then you need to tell me what you saw. Please."

I closed my eyes at his plea, still not sure I could speak. Finally, the words rasped from my throat, hard and scratchy as if it had been years since I'd used my voice.

"Death," I said. "I saw death."

Bressen went still against me. "Whose?"

"Yours!" The word erupted from me as a hoarse cry, and I pulled him toward me again, burying my face in his chest.

The room had gone unnaturally quiet, and I felt the tension in Bressen's body as he held me. The utter silence was broken only by my jagged breathing as Bressen lifted me off the floor. He didn't try to set me down on my chair, rightly anticipating that he wouldn't be able to dislodge my grip from his shirt. Instead, he sat down on the chair himself and gathered me into his lap.

"What exactly did you see?" he asked me quietly.

My hands and voice shook as I answered him. "The part of the vision from the wedding I couldn't remember. It was as if my mind was blocking it out, but it all came back when I touched the note."

"And what did you see?" he prompted again.

The words were like razors in my throat and mouth. "You were lying on the ground in front of me, in my arms. Your eyes were closed, and I couldn't feel you anymore," I said with a shaking voice.

My entire body trembled, and Bressen wrapped his arms around me even tighter as if to hold me still.

"I felt death. It was so cold, so very, very cold," I said to Bressen, and my body shivered violently as the icy chill seeped through me. "If you meet Sandrian, you'll die."

The words settled on the room like a pall, and I heard a growl rumble in Samhail's throat.

Aidan's voice rose softly. "If he doesn't go, Jasper will die."

I closed my eyes. I couldn't think about that. I'd grown to like Jasper a lot, and I didn't want him to die, but I wasn't willing to sacrifice Bressen for him. I couldn't. I just couldn't.

"Foreseen is forewarned," Bressen said after a few seconds. "If I know what's supposed to happen, I can avoid it."

My head snapped up so my eyes locked with his.

"No!" I said. "That's not the way it works. You yourself were the one who taught me that. You were the one who convinced me that trying to subvert a vision all but ensures people walk headlong into it. You told me that when Jerram and Ursan brought me to Callanus, they guaranteed Jemma's vision would come to pass, and it did."

Bressen looked up at Axenus who was still standing close by. "What do you think? Do you have any knowledge of how visions work?"

"Visions aren't my area of expertise, but based on what I do know, it's already too late," he said apologetically. "We likely set the events of the vision in motion by retrieving the collar and rings. They were probably set in motion when Cyra had the vision to begin with."

"How can the latter be true?" Samhail asked. "If you hadn't gone to get the collar and rings, Sandrian wouldn't have taken Jasper to get them from us."

Axenus shook his head. "That's not necessarily right. We learned from the vision that Sandrian wanted the items. If he thought we had a better chance of getting them for him, he could have taken Jasper and made us find them in order to get the lord consort back. It's possible that Cyra couldn't remember the last part of the vision because whatever powers are at work knew we wouldn't go after the collar and rings if we thought retrieving them would cost Bressen's life. We went after them thinking we needed to find them before Sandrian did. We might have rethought that move if we'd known what...what the price of going after them would be."

I shook my head. "I wouldn't have gotten them if I'd known what could happen. I wish we'd never found them."

"Consider how much harder it would be to save Jasper if we hadn't yet retrieved the collar and rings," Axenus argued. "That we already have the items is almost a boon.”

“A boon?” I said incredulously, looking up at him. I launched myself off Bressen’s lap so I was inches from the merman, looking directly up into his face. “Nothing about this is a boon!” I yelled at him.

I slammed my fists against his chest. He didn’t move, nor did he try to stop me as I hit him again, another sob escaping my lips.

“I’m sorry, my lady,” Axenus said softly. “I misspoke badly.”

His use of my title rather than my name broke me, and I began to sob again. Bressen pulled me away from Axenus and back against him. I closed my eyes as I laid my head on his chest and tried to will the tears to stop. I’d weep until my eyes were as dry as the desert later, but I didn’t want to do it here in front of everyone.

“At the risk of being selfish,” Aidan said, drawing our attention back to him, “will you go or not? If you won’t go, then give me the collar and rings, and I’ll bring them to Sandrian myself.”

“I don’t think it’s that simple,” Bressen said. “There must be a reason he wants me and Cyra to bring them.”

“Sandrian specifically mentions ‘the syphon’ in his note,” Axenus said. “Either he doesn’t know Cyra’s name, or her name is incidental, and it’s something about her he wants, something he needs a syphon for.”

“Which is exactly why Cyra isn’t going,” Bressen said.

“You aren’t going either,” I said as I looked up at him.

“If I don’t go, Jasper dies,” Bressen said.

“If you do go, *you* die!” I countered, hitting my fist against his chest.

“Cyra,” Axenus said gently, “whether Bressen goes or doesn’t go may not matter at this point. The events of the vision have been set in motion. If he doesn’t go, it’s just as possible that Sandrian and Morland will come looking for you and…Bressen could die anyway. Unless you saw something more about what happens, there’s no way to determine which course of action would lead to his death. Perhaps they both do.”

I was shaking my head before he finished speaking. “No, I refuse to believe this is an inevitability.”

Bressen brought a hand up to cup my face. “I’ll be careful,” he said, “but I need to bring Sandrian the collar and rings. If I don’t go, we know Sandrian will kill Jasper. If I do go, there’s still a chance that both Jasper and I will make it out safe."

"No," I said. I was calmly resolute as I laid my hand over his. "You're not going. You told me I could hate you for the rest of my life for what you were prepared to do to keep me safe. Well, I'm prepared for you to hate me for this."

Bressen's eyes flew open as I broke the promise I'd made to never use my negation abilities on him. I felt his panic as his powers died, and with them no longer bolstering his mind shield, I broke past it easily and quickly seized his mind, holding it captive. I felt the betrayal course through him, saw it flash in his beautiful turquoise eyes, but I couldn't let myself think about it. This was the only way to keep him safe.

"Forgive me, my love," I whispered as I laid my hand over Bressen's heart and stood on tiptoe to kiss him gently on his silent, frozen lips.

# Chapter 49

Bressen didn't move as my lips parted from his, and I wiped away the tears that streamed down my face. There was silence around the room as it took the others a moment to realize what had happened.

Axenus was the first to understand.

"Cyra, what have you done?" he asked.

I whirled to face them. Axenus and Samhail had both taken a step toward me, but a forcefield from my palms sent them both flying back. Axenus hit the wall and fell forward to land hard on his knees with a groan. Samhail went sprawling across the floor on his back, but he was on his feet in a crouch a second later. He raised a palm toward me, and my second forcefield met his in the center of the room. The resounding crack of our powers meeting shook the entire house and sent everyone in the room staggering back a step.

Samhail fell back to the floor again, and I noted the look of shock on his face as he realized my forcefield was stronger than his.

"Stay down," I told Samhail and Axenus, "or I'll take your air next."

Both had started to rise, but they stilled at my threat, and I turned to Maziren and Aidan next. Maziren had drawn her sword and was staring me down, but I knew she wouldn't attack unless I made a move toward Aidan. Behind me, Bressen still stood frozen, but I wouldn't look at him.

I couldn't look. The betrayal in his eyes would kill me.

Aidan faced me, one hand held up in a placating gesture as his gaze locked with mine. He winced at whatever he saw there.

I scanned the room again, but neither Samhail nor Axenus had dared to move. Both had obviously decided I was serious about cutting off their air, and with Bressen stripped of his powers and immobilized, there was little anyone could do to stop me.

"Cyra, please," Aidan said, and I heard the desperation in his voice.

"I'm sorry, Aidan," I said, trying to keep my voice steady but failing miserably. "I can't let him…I can't lose…"

"I know," Aidan said, his own voice shaking badly. "I know what you're feeling. It's the same thing I'm feeling. The thought of losing…of losing your soulmate is unbearable."

He'd just barely managed to get the words out, and a lump rose in my throat, choking me. Aidan took a step toward me, and I readied to throw him back with a forcefield. I'd deal with Maziren if needed.

"If you feel like I do, you can barely breathe right now," Aidan said.

He looked steadily at me, and I tried to turn away, but something in his face held me captive, and I couldn't break his stare. I tried again, but I might as well have been as frozen as Bressen was now.

"Every inhale is a new dagger to your gut," Aidan went on. "Every fiber of your being is crying out in pain at the thought of losing him. I know. I feel it, too."

"Stop," I said to him, but the word was deep and guttural, as if it stuck in my throat.

Aidan took another step forward, and Maziren twitched behind him.

"You feel helpless right now, so gods damned helpless, that you just want to scream and scream and scream, but you don't have the breath for it," the lord went on.

"Aidan," I choked out, "you need to stop talking, or I'll make you stop." The last words were a sobbed whisper.

Aidan took another step toward me as he grabbed the fabric of his shirt and yanked it up to reveal his stomach.

"Do you know what this is?" he asked.

The ground seemed to fall out from under me as I took in the solid circle of pale white that surrounded his navel, stark against his tawny skin.

It couldn't be.

"Jasper and I found these marks shortly after we wed," Aidan said, and I knew every word pained him. "The priestess at our temple in Seatherny said she'd never seen such marks before, but she believed they were evidence that two people had found their soulmate."

I stared at the circle of lighter skin around Aidan's navel, remembering Phaedrus's story. The beings who looked like two men stuck together were Souls of the Sun, and that's what the circle must represent, the sun, just as the crescent shape Bressen and I bore represented the moon. Aidan and Jasper were Souls of the Sun.

I shook my head. "No, not their soulmate," I said, lifting the hem of my shirt to reveal my own crescent moon mark. "The other half of their soul itself." I was barely able to get the strangled words out.

Aidan's eyes had flown wide at the sight of the mark on my stomach.

"Then you know," he said, the words barely a rush of air. "You know why I'm begging you to help me."

"And you know," I returned, "why I have to say no. I can't risk my own soul to save yours."

The look of despair on Aidan's face was crushing, but he wasn't done. "Please," he whispered, and I felt him drop his mental shield.

My knees nearly gave out, and I grabbed for the back of the nearest chair as I suddenly felt everything he felt right then. The anguish radiated off him like heat from a fire. His pain melded with my own so I didn't know where mine ended and his began, and the force of our shared grief made stars burst behind my eyes. I had no idea how I was still on my feet right now other than sheer willpower.

The tears I'd been holding back rolled freely down my face as my efforts to blink them away proved futile. Aidan's eyes were red and wet with tears as well as he took another step toward me.

"I understand. You would do absolutely anything to keep him safe," he said. "You'd give anything, because without him, nothing you have really matters anyway."

Aidan closed the remaining distance between us, and I lurched backward away from him. I put my hand up to loose a forcefield, but he only grabbed it and fell to his knees before me instead.

"Please," he whispered as he grasped my hand with both of his and laid his forehead on the back of my wrist. "Please help me get my husband back. I'll do anything. I'll give you anything. If you want my power, take it. Take all of it. It's yours. Just help me get Jasper back."

And then he was sobbing openly. On his knees, on the floor, the Lord of Derridan was sobbing at my feet.

I stared down at my hand where Aidan's ungloved fingers held it, proof he was giving me his transfiguration power. I looked up at Maziren to find her standing frozen with her mouth wide open. It looked as though she couldn't decide whether to tackle me or Aidan, but it was too late.

Aidan's powers were now mine. Whether I could do anything with them that might save Jasper or Bressen was uncertain, but he'd given them to me nonetheless.

My anger flared briefly. Aidan had spent weeks avoiding my touch so I couldn't take this power from him, and the idea that he thought he could buy me this way – buy Bressen's life – with a power that I could've taken any time I wanted made my hackles rise.

I might have told him that it was too little, too late, that he would've done better to be more magnanimous early on in our acquaintance so that I'd feel more inclined to help him now. But all I could see right then was this lord on his knees at my feet making the only sacrifice he could think to make to beg for my help.

I broke then, and my legs gave out as I sunk to my own knees before him. I threw my free arm over Aidan's back and pressed my head against his shoulder as I began to cry too. Aidan pressed into me, accepting the comfort I offered, and the two of us wept in great heaving sobs against each other for what might have been either minutes or hours.

At some point I became aware of the strong hands resting lightly on my shoulders, and I raised my head. Aidan and I still knelt on the floor, and the lord lifted his face to meet mine, both his hands still clasped around one of mine. He held it firmly, and I saw the hope in his eyes.

My heart cracked because it was hope that I couldn't share. We'd likely get Jasper back, but I'd lose Bressen regardless.

"We'll help you get Jasper back," I said, and the tired, hoarse voice that left my throat was not my own. Every word was a slice of pain across my heart, and the gratitude and relief that spread across Aidan's face did nothing to ease it.

I pulled my hand from his and stood up.

The hands on my shoulders were Bressen's, and he turned me around to face him. My magic had released him when Aidan's words broke me, and now I had to face him after taking his powers and his mind.

There was no anger in his eyes as I looked at the man I'd met, fallen in love with, married, and would now lose in the span of mere months.

"We need to help Aidan get Jasper back. Both of us," I said to him.

Bressen only nodded and pulled me into his embrace. I broke again as I buried my face hard into his chest and wept silently while my body heaved against him for a long, long time.

Bressen and I were alone in the room when I finally lifted my head again. I hadn't heard him speak, so whether he'd sent Samhail and Axenus silent orders for tomorrow, or whether everyone had just known enough to leave quietly for now, I wasn't sure.

"I'm sorry," I said, my voice still ragged from crying. "I didn't know what else to do."

"I can't blame you," Bressen said, his arms still encompassing me. "I was prepared to use any and all of my powers to keep you here away from Sandrian. I can't fault you for doing the same."

"What are we going to do?" I asked.

He shrugged slightly. "I suppose we're going to go meet Sandrian tomorrow, bring him the collar and rings, and I'll try my best not to die."

Another sob escaped me. "Don't say things like that," I said, pressing my forehead back into his chest. "Don't make light of this."

"I'm sorry," he said, laying a hand gently over the back of my head. "I'm just trying to make sense of it all. I know I'm the one who told you that you can't fight fate, that you can't outrun or outmaneuver these visions, but…I just can't accept that I'll die tomorrow."

I couldn't bring myself to tell him that denial was a natural reaction to facing one's own imminent death. I was deep in denial right now myself only because I wouldn't be able to move at all if I let myself believe for one moment that I'd lose Bressen tomorrow. The only thing keeping me on the razor's edge of sanity was the shred of hope that the vision was wrong, that I'd mis-seen something, or that we could beat all of the odds and avoid what I'd seen altogether.

"We should go to bed," I said. "We can't stand here all night."

Bressen lifted me into his arms and carried me back to our room as I nestled my face against his shoulder and fisted my hand in his shirt again. We didn't undress as he laid me under the covers and then climbed in after me. Letting go of each other long enough to do something as mundane as undress was unthinkable right now, so we lay in bed, fully clothed, for a long while just wrapped in each other's arms.

Sleep was impossible as neither of us was willing to waste what might be our final moments together. Yet being awake was excruciating. Each second that ticked by was a cruel reminder of how our time together had suddenly gone from hundreds of years to only hours.

In the end, our clothes lasted only twenty minutes before we began to tear at them, the thought of anything coming between us on our last night together abhorrent. We practically clawed at each other in our efforts to get closer, to press ourselves so tightly together as to become one. Not in amusement as we'd done on our wedding night, but feverishly, desperately, heartbreakingly.

It wasn't enough for Bressen to be inside me. I needed to envelop him, to have him envelop me. Phaedrus's story of love became our unspoken purpose as we devoured each other, trying in all seriousness to shove our bodies back together and once again become whole.

We managed to undress without ever letting go of each other, our skin always touching at some point. Our mouths remained fused together, the rip of fabric keeping our lips from ever having to part. There was no playful experimenting with positions this time, only our bodies pressed navel to navel, his hips grinding into mine, as we molded ourselves together, every part of me fitting perfectly with every part of him.

I screamed as Bressen entered me, not from pleasure or pain, but from the sheer relief of having him inside me, of being as close to him as I could possibly get. I locked my legs around him and pulled him into me as hard as I could while my hand fisted in his hair, keeping his mouth smashed against mine.

Bressen snaked his arms under me, holding me against him so tightly I was barely able to breathe, let alone move. We crushed ourselves against each other at first, unwilling to part enough for Bressen to even thrust into me properly until the tension nearly made us go mad. Only then did we loosen our hold on each other just enough for him to drive into me with great pounding thrusts that vibrated through my entire body.

My climax was like nothing I'd ever felt before, more intense than anything at the Priory, and so blindingly powerful that my muscles nearly seized up. My pleasure was a song, its melody and lyrics so beautiful and true as to be almost painful. It wrapped itself around me like a fur cloak that's been warmed by a lover's body, and I trembled beneath Bressen as he roared his release seconds later.

Our lovemaking was frantic and frenzied as we nearly rubbed our skin raw from moving against each other. Each time we finished, we lay tangled in each other's limbs only until we'd rested long enough to do it all again.

When the pink light of dawn finally crept through the room, I lay awake staring up at the ceiling. Bressen slept beside me on his stomach, his long, muscled arm thrown over me and his face tucked against my shoulder. He'd dozed off half an hour ago, and I envied his ability to sleep. I'd managed to get only about an hour in total over the course of the night, yet I was still wide awake, albeit exhausted and disconsolate.

I summoned another small towel from the bathroom and caught it with my left hand since my right was currently pinned under Bressen. This was the seventh towel I'd summoned so far, and I held it out over the covers before it burst into a kaleidoscope of butterflies that scattered in all directions across the room.

The butterflies fluttered madly in a spray of colorful chaos before gradually losing vitality and drifting aimlessly to the floor. The bed was spotted with the paper bodies from the other towels that had already met the same fate, and I knew the magic of the house replenished each towel after I summoned it.

This was the power I'd gained in exchange for Bressen's life, the power to make lifeless butterflies that floated around the room for a few seconds before turning into nothing but litter that I'd eventually need to sweep up and throw away.

I summoned another towel and let it erupt into butterflies before it even touched my hand. I watched the butterflies flap above me, and I reached up to touch one of the closer ones. The moment my finger brushed it, the butterfly lost its energy and pirouetted onto the bed.

"What are you doing?" Bressen asked as he stirred beside me.

I turned my head to look at him, and he pulled his arm from around me to pick a butterfly off his cheek. I smiled and reached over to pluck a few others from his night-black hair. I saw behind him that one long finger of sunlight had started to reach for us from one of the windows.

"Playing with my new power," I said. "I figured I might as well enjoy it since it's going to cost me your-"

I'd been about to say "life," but I couldn't get the word past my lips.

Bressen surveyed the carpet of butterfly carcasses on the floor and the bed before he looked back at me and lifted a brow. "It looks like you've mastered Aidan's butterfly trick."

"Everything comes much easier to me now since the Priory," I said.

Bressen turned on his side so he was facing me, and I did the same, shifting closer to him so I was tucked into his chest.

"Is there any way I can convince you to stay here and not come today?" he asked. His breath was warm against my forehead, and I closed my eyes to try and embed the feel of it on my skin in my memory.

"No," I said. "I can't stay here and wonder what's happening to you. It will drive me mad. If you're going to die, I need absolutely every second I can get with you until then."

"I still don't accept it," Bressen said. "I don't believe I'll die today."

I whimpered and curled myself more tightly into him.

"We need to get up and get dressed at some point," Bressen said. "I told Samhail and Axenus I'd discuss strategy with them this morning, and I'm not sure they'd appreciate me showing up naked with you still wrapped around me. Although don't get me wrong, there's nothing I want more than to just wear you for the rest of the day."

The noise I made was somewhere between a laugh, a choke, and a sob. It was an ugly, unladylike noise, and Bressen chuckled at it.

"There's only one way that I'll let you get up," I said.

"And what's that?"

"Promise me that you'll come home with me today, alive and well, and that we'll be back right here together in this bed tonight. Promise me that, or I can't let you go."

Bressen pulled back a little from me and his expression was solemn. "I promise I'll come home with you today, alive and well, and that we'll be back right here together in this bed tonight."

I waited for his skin to glow red, confirming the lie we both knew it was, but his skin remained soft and golden in the morning light. It wasn't proof that he'd survive the day, only proof that he believed he would, and I knew he was determined to do so.

It was enough for now. It had to be, or we'd never leave this bed.

I nodded at him. "Go then. I'm holding you to that promise."

He smiled and his lips pressed against mine in a gentle kiss before we untangled ourselves from each other, and he threw off the covers to pad naked toward the closet. I needed another minute to collect myself before I rose, and then I too made my way to the closet.

Getting dressed was postponed for several minutes as our bodies crashed into each other again inside. I barely got through the door before Bressen was on me again. My back hit the wall so hard it drove the air from my lungs, but then he was inside me, thrusting hard as I dug my nails into his back and held on for dear life.

We climaxed within seconds of each other, and Bressen dropped to his knees as we caught our breath. I kept my legs wrapped around him as I sat on his lap, his length still inside me.

I felt his seed dripping between my legs when he finally withdrew, and I decided I wouldn't drink my turrow berry tea this morning. On the chance I lost Bressen, maybe…maybe I wouldn't lose all of him.

When we were finally dressed and ready to leave the room, Bressen took my hand in his, and I felt the prickle at the nape of my neck that told me he'd called Samhail and Axenus to meet us.

"I'll have breakfast brought up to my study," he said. "We can wait for Samhail and Axenus there."

I nodded and followed Bressen to the door that led to our sitting room. When he opened it, we found Samhail, Axenus, Aidan, and Maziren all sitting there waiting for us. Leeda stood there as well, looking a bit dumbfounded as to how she'd found herself in the middle of a room full of lords and warriors.

"I hope you haven't been waiting for us long," Bressen drawled, although his surprise was evident.

"Long enough to come up with a few ideas about how to handle our situation," Samhail said, standing up from the armchair he'd been sitting in. "Now, if you're done sleeping in, or whatever the two of you were doing in there, we'd like to discuss how to make sure you survive the day."

# Chapter 50

The temple that rose up before us through the portal I'd opened on the outskirts of Rowe was nothing like the Priory in Callanus. For one, it seemed to be in the middle of nowhere, likely an old pilgrimage site. For another, the stone that formed it was not polished and refined like the bright white marble of the Priory, but rather, it was a rustic-looking edifice made of rough-hewn sandstone. There were no towers or turrets on the building, which was set into the side of a mountain with about fifty stairs leading up to a landing where the main entrance was. The surrounding plants and trees had reclaimed much of the space, and vines grew up the stone, partially camouflaging the façade.

I'd opened the portal about a hundred yards or so from the temple itself just so we could survey the area before making a closer approach. Nothing seemed to be amiss, but Bressen stepped through to look around while the rest of us waited back in the house.

"I sense four people inside," he said as he stepped back through. "Two perimortals and two mortals."

"Jasper and Morland are the two mortals," I observed. "Sandrian is one of the perimortals, but who's the second one?"

"We'll learn soon enough," Bressen said.

"I assume your next portal can at least save us the trouble of walking up those stairs?" Aidan asked me. His tone was light, but he grimaced when I didn't respond.

I wasn't in a state of mind to joke. Aidan really wasn't either, I knew, but I couldn't find the energy to indulge his attempt to ease the strain we all felt. I did open the next portal at the top of the stairs, though.

"Is everyone through?" I asked, and the affirmations of four people under obfuscation glamours met my ears.

Bressen, Aidan, and myself were visible, but Samhail, Axenus, Maziren, and Aramis were all hidden by Bressen's glamour.

I'd suggested we bring Aramis because he was far more accomplished as a healer than I was, and if there was any chance his presence might make the difference in Bressen living or dying, I was willing to take it.

Aramis himself had readily agreed to come when I asked, even before I'd told him of the danger to Bressen's life. After learning of it, he'd insisted.

Aramis had spent twenty-two years as an innocent man in Revenmyer prison with Bressen as his warden, yet he'd never blamed Bressen for that. In fact, he was grateful to Bressen for eventually releasing him and helping him reunite with me, so if coming with us meant a chance to repay Bressen, Aramis was more than willing. I'd made it clear that he was to stay out of the way and hidden until needed, and he'd agreed.

"Everyone keep your eyes open and stay ready," Bressen said. "We have no idea what we're walking into."

Bressen started toward the temple door while Aidan and I followed a step behind. Samhail, Axenus, and Maziren would scatter themselves once inside and try to take up strategic positions if possible.

Aramis would stay outside until needed, but we'd given him a dagger just in case. He insisted he knew how to use the weapon, but just the way he held it made me doubt how well.

I blinked to let my eyes adjust as we entered the dimness of the ruins. Light filtered in through a few small windows and down from some holes in the ceiling, but it only did so much to illuminate the large space.

I heard Aidan's sharp intake of breath next to me and tried to focus my gaze ahead where I made out the shapes of several people.

The first person I noticed was Jasper. He stood on a wide wooden plank with his hands bound behind his back. The plank jutted out over what appeared to be a ten-foot chasm that separated the main part of the temple from the dais and altar. I couldn't tell what was holding the plank up to keep it from falling, so I assumed it must be some kind of magic.

The next thing I noticed was that there were a lot more than four people here. At least twenty guards stood behind a gaunt-looking blonde man that I recognized from my vision as Sandrian.

I let my powers reach out, but I could still only sense four people, and I caught Bressen's gaze as we exchanged a look of surprise and unease.

*Why can't we sense the guards?* I asked him.

*I'm not sure*, he answered back.

"Bressen, it's so nice to see you again," Sandrian drawled as we approached. "Your visits to me in Revenmyer were so infrequent. I'm glad we were able to arrange this little meeting so we could catch up."

"My apologies, Sandrian. I forgot you were there half the time," Bressen drawled right back. "I didn't really think about you much, you see, but it looks like you've thought about me a lot."

Sandrian smiled. "Maybe if you had thought about me a little more, you'd have noticed me missing sooner."

The barb hit home as I felt a wave of anger emanate from Bressen.

Sandrian eyed me and Aidan. "Such a small group you brought."

"We don't need any more than this to deal with you," Bressen said. "Shall we get on with this little exchange?"

Sandrian tsked. "You don't really expect me to believe you came all this way without Samhail, do you? I know he's here somewhere, probably under one of your glamours. Just have him show himself now before he does something foolish that gets the Lord Consort killed. We took a few precautions to be sure you can't attack us without risking dear Jasper's life. That plank he's standing on is cast with magic to let him fall into the chasm if you harm me or any of my people."

Bressen clenched his jaw, and I felt the prickle at my neck that meant he was likely warning Samhail he was about to remove the glamour.

Samhail had gotten closer to Sandrian and his people than they'd apparently expected. He materialized just across the chasm from them, swords drawn, and Sandrian's guards gasped as they took in the huge man suddenly before them. I felt a bit of satisfaction at the look of disquiet on Sandrian's own face as Samhail's hulking form loomed only feet from him.

Sandrian recovered quickly and held up a hand near Jasper's face as lightning crackled across his palm.

"Step back, gargoyle, or Lord Aidan's consort may start to sizzle a little," he warned.

Samhail didn't move at first, but I felt another prickle, and he stepped back, deferring to Bressen's order.

"I'm also willing to bet Lord Aidan's captain of the guard is here. Have Maziren show herself as well," Sandrian went on.

Bressen swore under his breath, and a moment later, Maziren

appeared on the same side of the chasm as Sandrian and his guards. The blade of her sword hovered just under the neck of one of the guards, and the man gasped and jumped backward at seeing her there. Maziren just smiled at him before lowering her sword.

"Oh, so close," Sandrian said with mock sympathy, "but I'm afraid I'll have to ask you to pull your people back now or I can't be responsible for what happens to Jasper." Sandrian moved his hand closer to Jasper's face as the lightning crackled across his palm again.

Aidan lurched forward. "No! Maziren, Samhail, pull back."

Maziren moved immediately to return to us, but Samhail didn't budge until I felt the prickle at my neck. He took another step backward, but before he could go any further, the guards parted, and a spear came hurtling out of the space between them. Samhail yelled out in pain as the spear lodged in his stomach below his armor and above his groin.

I screamed, and Bressen cried out as Samhail doubled over and sank to one knee, his hand gripped around the shaft of the spear. He roared in pain and tried to stand but sank back down a second later. I tried to rush forward, but Bressen grabbed my arm and pulled me back.

"Samhail!" I yelled, trying to shake Bressen off. "Let me go to him!"

A large man stepped out from behind the guards then. He was tall and burly with black-brown hair and a layer of rough stubble on his face. He held a second spear in his hand and wore a grin of satisfaction below a crooked nose that had likely been broken more than once.

"You missed his heart," Sandrian said to the man.

"I was aiming for his face," the man growled.

"Morland," Bressen said. It was between a question and a statement.

The burly man gave a small mock bow.

"I know I look a little different than the last time you saw me," Morland said, "but my hatred for you and this pile of stone over here hasn't changed a bit." He gestured to Samhail.

Samhail wrapped his other hand around the shaft of the spear, apparently intent on pulling it from his body, but Sandrian's next words stopped him.

"I wouldn't do that if I were you," he said. "The point of that spear is designed to do more damage on the way out than on the way in."

Morland held up the point of the second spear he held so we could see it. The tip was huge, and the barbs at the base of it curved backward so that they'd certainly rip flesh with them if the spear was pulled out.

"That tip is also made of caronium," Sandrian added, "so it looks like Samhail may not be of much use to you for a bit."

I stopped struggling against Bressen as Maziren reached Samhail's side. She grabbed the shaft of the spear and broke it off so only about a foot remained, then she pulled Samhail's arm over her shoulder and helped him stand. She was dwarfed next to him, but her strength let her hold him up as they backed toward us. They made it several feet when Samhail sank to his knee again and Maziren leaned him against a pillar.

I ran to Samhail and dropped to my knees next to him. I hovered my hands over him to assess his wound, and my stomach lurched to feel how much damage the spear had done going in. Blood soaked the front of his pants, and a smaller man might have been dead already.

"Let us heal him!" I begged, turning to Sandrian.

"Bressen, aren't you going to introduce us to your lovely wife?" Sandrian asked, ignoring me.

"I'll kill you if you so much as look at her wrong," Bressen spat back.

Sandrian only smirked and turned his attention to me.

"Since your husband has forgotten his manners, allow me to introduce myself. I'm Sandrian, the former but also future King of Rowe," he said to me. "I've been wanting to meet you for some time now, my dear."

"Let me help Samhail," I said again.

"I'm afraid I can't do that. At least not until we're done with our business here," he said. "It's safer for us, you understand, if Samhail is out of the way for the moment."

"Samhail isn't the one you need to worry about!" I growled as I shot to my feet and started toward him. Flames flared in my hands as hot anger burned in my veins. If Samhail died, I'd make sure that Sandrian and Morland's deaths were as slow and painful as possible.

Jasper cried out as the plank he was on suddenly wobbled, and I stopped moving just as Aidan and Bressen each grabbed one of my arms.

"None of that now," Sandrian said. "You don't want Jasper to lose his balance and fall, do you?"

I clenched my jaw as I glared at Sandrian, but I didn't move again.

"There's a table off to your right," he said. "I left you all a bit of jewelry to put on."

We all glanced at a small table to our right, and Bressen let out a growl when he saw what was on it.

"Forget it, Sandrian. You're insane if you think we're all putting on caronium cuffs."

My eyes met Bressen's for a brief second. Mine were wide with terror for him, but his were calm, and I knew he was remembering the cuffs wouldn't work on me.

"You'll put the cuffs on, or we're done here, and you can spend the rest of the day scraping the Lord Consort off the bottom of the pit here," Sandrian said, gesturing to the chasm. "I'm not actually sure it has a bottom, so it may take you awhile just to find his body."

Aidan moved immediately to the table and snapped a cuff onto his wrist, then he looked at Maziren, a silent order in his eyes. She moved more slowly to the table, and I followed her as I sent a quick mental message to everyone in our party, both visible and glamoured, to let them know the cuff – hopefully – wouldn't work on me.

I came up next to Maziren and reached for a cuff, but I was startled when her small hand slipped furtively around mine at my side. Maziren had removed one of her gloves and taken my hand in hers.

"I don't know if my power will help you," she whispered without looking at me, "but if you can use it to help me get Aidan and Jasper out of this, then take it."

I stood frozen in shock as Maziren slipped her hand out of mine again to take a caronium cuff off the table and snap it on. I wanted to say something to her, but I couldn't find the words as the magical cuff shrank down to adjust to her thin wrist, and she moved back to stand near Aidan.

I took a cuff of my own from the table and snapped it onto my wrist. The cuff didn't adjust as Maziren's had, and I took that as a good sign.

"Your turn, Bressen," Sandrian said with a sneer.

Reluctantly, Bressen moved to the table as I stepped back.

*I love you*, I said into Bressen's mind as he looked at me, and even in my head my voice seemed to break.

*I love you, too*, he said, *and I'm coming home. I promise you that.*

I managed to hold in the sob that threatened as Bressen clasped the cuff on his wrist. I felt his disquiet as the cuff took his power, and then my own panic rose as our mental connection seemed to sever.

My mind screamed at the sudden loss. My bond with Bressen had become a part of me, and I hadn't realized how easily our thoughts flowed between us now that there was silence in my head. I'd only experienced something similar once before in the Soundless Woods, an absence so profound that, paradoxically, it had a presence. I hadn't noticed it earlier when I'd taken Bressen's power, but the quiet yawned in my mind now.

My heart thundered in my chest as my power reached out desperately to reconnect my mind with Bressen's, and I closed my eyes in relief a moment later as I felt our link reform. I let out a deep breath. I hadn't realized Bressen had been maintaining our bond to such a degree, my own power letting his shoulder that weight.

*Axenus, where are you?* I asked.

I needed to get a sense of where he was and what, if anything, he could do to help our situation. His obfuscation glamour would have fallen off when Bressen put on the cuff, and he was likely hiding now. I could put the glamour back on him if I knew where he was.

*I'm behind a pillar near the chasm*, came his reply. *I'm trying to fill it with water, but it's too deep. I can't fill it fast enough to soften Jasper's fall if they throw him in.*

*I'm putting the glamour back on you*, I told him.

"Now that everyone is properly cuffed," Sandrian said, "let's get on with this. Did you bring the necklace and rings?"

I patted the satchel slung around my torso.

"They're in here," I said. "What do you want with them?"

"They're going to help us right a grave wrong, with a little help from you," Sandrian said. "You see, twenty-five years ago, Samhail tried to kill Morland. Fortunately, Morland was a mind wraith, and he was able to jump into the mind of another man before his body died. Less fortunately, that man was mortal and had no magic. You and those items are going to help us get Morland back into a perimortal body."

"That's impossible," Bressen said. "The mind can't jump bodies."

"I assure you it was very possible," Morland said. "Mind wraiths invade the minds of others by nature, although they always keep most of their consciousness back in their own bodies. It's only a small part that connects to the mind of another, but when you're seconds away from death, it's apparently very possible to detach your mind completely and pour it into someone else's head. Unfortunately, once your old body is dead, it becomes a one-way trip."

"Are we supposed to feel sorry for you?" Samhail growled from the floor where he lay, blood starting to pool under him.

I had to get control of this situation fast so Aramis could come in and heal him before it was too late.

"I don't care what you feel toward me," Morland snapped. "Your little syphon here is going to help put me back into the body of a perimortal."

Samhail huffed a laugh, then groaned in pain. "Fine. Let her make you perimortal again. I'll just kill that body as well."

A cold smirk curled onto Sandrian's face. "Oh, I don't think you will. You see, Morland doesn't want just any perimortal body. He wants one with mind wraith abilities."

There was a beat of silence while his words sunk in before both Samhail and I screamed, "No!" at the same time. Samhail's was followed by another grunt of pain.

"You're fucking insane if you think we're going to let that miserable piece of shit take over Bressen's body," Samhail spat at Sandrian.

"You don't really have a choice," Sandrian said. "You took Morland's body. You owe him a new one, and he's chosen the one he wants."

I jerked my gaze to Bressen. His expression was grim.

"It seems my new body also comes with a pretty little wife," Morland said as he leered at me. "I'm going to have so much fun fucking you, girl."

This time it was Bressen who launched himself toward the dais, and it took me, Aidan, and Maziren to all drag him back.

"If you even breathe on her, I'll take you apart piece by miserable piece," Bressen snarled to Morland.

I felt the fury radiating off him as I never had before, but I had no idea what to do.

Only Axenus and I had our powers, and Jasper was still at Sandrian's mercy. I'd already let my power reach out and brush against Sandrian's mind shield, but it was solid, and it would take me time to get through it without him noticing, if I even could. Morland didn't have a shield up, but I couldn't do anything to him without risking Jasper. I'd tried to connect with some of the guards Sandrian had brought with him as well, but I'd felt nothing from any of them. They didn't have mind shields that I could tell, but I couldn't sense a consciousness in any of them.

There was still one more person with Sandrian, but they must be standing behind the guards. I couldn't see them, but I sensed the impenetrability of their mind shield, and a shiver of unease shimmied up my spine. Why didn't the person show themselves?

"It's time," Sandrian said.

Morland walked to the side where another longer plank acted as a bridge over the chasm, and he traversed it to come toward us.

"I don't need my powers to break your neck, Morland," Samhail growled, but it was an empty threat given the spear still in him.

The sneer never left Morland's face as he approached us, especially as his eyes raked up and down my body.

"Bressen and Cyra come forward," Sandrian ordered. "Everyone else step back, or Aidan's consort becomes a stain at the bottom of this pit."

"No!" I yelled. I turned to Aidan, and his face fell as he saw the resolve in my eyes. "I'm sorry," I said softly to him. "I can't sacrifice Bressen to a fate like this, not even for Jasper."

"Cyra, please," Aidan begged, and I turned away from his desperation.

"Enough!" Sandrian yelled. He turned to his guards. "Take them!"

The guards didn't move at first, but my eyes rounded in horror a second later as something dark blue and liquid-like began to envelop their bodies. It seeped over their skin, covering them within seconds, and my stomach churned as I recognized the blue substance that swallowed their faces leaving only glowing yellow eyes.

Oh gods. All the guards were those creatures we'd faced at the gambling den. Bressen had said then that he couldn't connect to them. Perhaps that was because something else already had control of their minds, or maybe that strange blue substance was blocking the connection.

I threw my hands up and released the strongest forcefield I could muster. It did as I prayed it would and threw Sandrian and several of his guards backward while also pushing Jasper back off the plank and onto the relative safety of the dais.

Bressen launched himself toward Morland, and I swung around to hit the rest of the guards with another forcefield, but I never got the chance. Veins of lightning spider webbed through the space, and I screamed as the quick jolt of electricity shot through my body. I dropped to my knees as my heart raced faster than I thought possible. Next to me, Bressen was on the ground as well, and I glanced back to see Aidan and Maziren hadn't been spared the blast either. Only Morland seemed to have escaped it.

I could barely move as my entire body burned from the pain of it, and I tried to inhale gasps of air as my lungs refused to expand.

"Has everyone learned their lesson yet?" Sandrian asked, his voice booming across the room.

I shook my head. Now that I knew what Sandrian's endgame was, there was no way I was going to cooperate. Letting Morland take over Bressen's body was not an option, and I'd die before I let that happen.

I hadn't yet tried to use the sunfire I'd syphoned from Bressen's mother, but I needed a weapon. I let the fire build in my hands as Andromeda had done when she used it on me and then released it toward Sandrian. He screamed in pain as he seemed to burn from within, even though not a mark appeared on his skin. I stood, my hand outstretched as he fell to his knees, and my rage fueled the sunfire to burn even hotter.

I took a step toward him, but a second later, pain ripped through me as something icy gripped my chest. I found myself flat on my back, and I clawed at something that seemed to constrict around my heart. Frost caught under my nails as I raked my fingers down my neck and chest, and I looked down to see some kind of icy mass creeping over my torso.

"No! Stop!" Bressen's scream echoed off the walls of the temple as he dropped to his knees before me and pulled me across his lap. I looked up at him with wide, panicked eyes as I gasped for breath.

"Stop it now! I'll do what you want! Just stop! You're killing her!" he screamed. I shook my head at Bressen as he looked around wildly for whoever was making this happen.

Just as my vision started to fade, the icy hold on my chest eased, and

I gasped in a deep breath.

"No, please," I pleaded with Bressen. "You can't let them."

"The only thing I can't let them do is hurt you," he said.

"How very touching," Morland mocked. "Just don't expect such sentiments from me when I'm wearing that body."

Bressen raised his head, and I saw his eyes flash red. He got slowly to his feet, pulling me with him, and we scanned the dais for my attacker.

A small cloaked figure stepped from the shadows, and delicate hands lifted the hood to pull it back.

I gasped at the familiar face framed by blonde hair that lay beneath. Pale blue eyes looked at me with the same cruel amusement I'd seen so recently in a dream.

It couldn't be.

But there was no mistaking the face of Magdalene.

# Chapter 51

Somewhere across the room I felt Axenus's own maelstrom of emotions at Magdalene's appearance. I sent a mental message begging him to remain calm, even as I wanted to launch myself at the woman and rip her apart both mentally and physically. Axenus was my teacher, my mentor, and my friend, and every part of me was screaming to kill Magdalene, to take revenge on his behalf.

"Cyra, who is she?" Bressen asked, seeing my recognition.

Something snapped back into place in my head as I answered into his mind. *"Her name is Magdalene. I saw her in Axenus's dream. She's one of Queen Clarice's friends who raped him."*

Bressen's body jerked against me, and I felt his anger surge. "What? You're sure?" he hissed.

"I'll never forget her face, and Axenus hasn't forgotten it either."

Sandrian spoke before Bressen could offer any further response.

"Cyra, I'd like you to meet Lady Magdalene, the newest addition to my royal court. I have her to thank for getting me out of Revenmyer."

Few things would have gotten me to take my attention off Magdalene, but that was one of them. Both my head and Bressen's snapped to him.

"How?" Bressen asked in disbelief.

Magdalene smiled. "Let's just say I have an aptitude for raising and lowering wards."

Bressen shook his head. "Aptitude or not, those wards are supposed to be impenetrable. They were designed so the overseer and seneschals of Revenmyer are the only ones who can raise or lower them."

"That's mostly correct," Magdalene said. "Their creator can control them as well."

Bressen stared at her. "Are you saying you created the wards around Revenmyer?" he asked in disbelief.

Magdalene's answer was a self-satisfied smile.

Bressen shook his head again. "Impossible. Those wards were created thousands of years ago."

"Yes, they were created by one of my predecessors when the prison was first built," Magdalene said. "As her successor, their control and upkeep now falls to me."

I frowned. Successor to what?

Beside me, Bressen was vibrating with rage. "And you lowered the wards to let the likes of Sandrian out? Why?" he asked.

"According to the vision I had, King Sandrian plays an important role in a number of changes to come. In order for him to fulfill that role, I had to release him," she answered.

"He's no more a king than I am," Samhail spat out, then groaned as the effort cost him.

"What role? What changes?" Bressen asked.

But that wasn't the part that caught my attention the most.

"What vision?" I asked before she could speak.

Magdalene's pale blue gaze found me. "The vision I had that day you transformed the bear into earth," she answered, her smile growing in a way that only made it more disturbing. "The seer in Callanus wasn't the only one who sensed the shift in the world when you did that. I sensed it too, and that's when I was shown what I needed to do."

My mouth hung open as I tried to wrap my head around what Magdalene was saying. She'd broken Sandrian out of prison because she'd seem him in a vision that was sparked when I'd killed the bear back in Fernweh. Sandrian was free now because of me.

I looked at Bressen. His expression had gone from anger to fear, and I didn't blame him. We both now had a healthy respect for the power of visions, and if this woman had a vision that involved me and Sandrian, I needed to know the details of it.

"What exactly happened in this vision?" I asked Magdalene.

She only smiled. "You'll learn everything soon enough."

I hadn't really expected her to tell me. There was only one other way for me to find out what she'd seen, but I wasn't sure I'd be able to do it. Still, I had to try.

"Enough stalling," Sandrian cut in. "Morland has been waiting twenty-five years to return to a perimortal body. I don't want to keep him waiting any longer. Take him," Sandrian ordered the guards, and they moved toward Bressen.

"No!" I shouted, sending two of them flying backward with a forcefield. I whirled, intending to try my sunfire on Magdalene herself, but I felt the icy grip of her frost in my chest before I could, and I screamed as it squeezed my heart again. I barely felt it as my knees cracked against the stone floor, and I clawed at the frost creeping over my body.

"Stop!" Bressen yelled, pulling me against him again. "Let her go! I'll let you do it!"

My screams echoed off the walls of the hall for several more seconds until Magdalene released her frozen hold on me.

"The caronium cuff doesn't work on her," Sandrian observed as I took in great gasping breaths.

"No, it doesn't," Magdalene agreed, sounding intrigued.

Bressen's arms were around me again, helping me to my feet, and I curled my hands tightly in his jacket. "Please," I begged him, "You can't let them do this to you."

"They'll hurt you if I don't," he whispered to me.

"The worst thing they can do is take you away from me," I said desperately. "Please don't give in to them."

Before Bressen could answer, Magdalene let out a cry, and we all looked to the dais where Axenus stood behind her with a dagger pressed to her throat. His glamour had likely fallen away one of the times Magdalene froze me, but he'd managed to stay hidden until now.

"Tell the guards to step away from them, or I'll open her throat," Axenus snarled to Sandrian, and it sounded like he might do it regardless.

"Axenus? Is that you?" Magdalene purred, trying to turn her head enough to see him. She gasped as he pressed the dagger tip in harder, and a trickle of blood dripped down her neck.

"Don't speak," was all he said to her.

"It is you, isn't it," Magdalene said, delighted. "I'd recognize that sultry voice of yours and your ocean scent anywhere. It's been hard to forget you. I still feel your hands on me sometimes. You were so hard-"

"Tell the guards to step away!" Axenus yelled, cutting her off. He'd gone rigid, and he made no attempt to hide his look of disgust and rage.

Sandrian tsked at Bressen. "It looks like you brought one more with you after all." He turned to Axenus. "I suggest you lower your dagger, so I don't have to order my guard to kill Aidan's consort."

My eyes flew to the side of the dais where a guard held a sword against Jasper's neck. I'd forgotten to track what happened to him after I used my forcefield to push him back off the plank. He'd somehow freed his hands from behind his back, but he hadn't gotten away.

"You can't win this fight," Sandrian said. "Only two of you have any power, while I still have my special guards and Lord Aidan's husband at my mercy. If you try anything, at least one of you will die. Your only choice is to do as I say."

"And we're supposed to trust you won't kill us all anyway?" Samhail asked. His voice was hoarse with pain and blood loss, and I sent an order into his mind for him to conserve his strength.

"I never said any such thing," Sandrian said. "In fact, when Morland gets his new body, I promised him he could kill you himself."

"No!" I yelled as my gaze flew to Samhail.

"He can try," Samhail gritted out, ignoring my order.

Morland opened his mouth to speak, but his words were cut off as more of Sandrian's lightning suddenly lit up the temple. It jolted through me and Bressen just enough to send us sprawling back to the floor before my lungs could even consider a scream. I looked toward the dais and my heart sank as I saw the lightning had taken out Axenus as well. Somehow Sandrian had incapacitated him enough for Magdalene to escape his dagger, and he was now on his knees before her as Magdelene held his own dagger to his throat.

"My patience has reached its limit," Sandrian said as he strode across the plank that spanned the chasm and approached us. "The next person who attacks dies."

Sandrian extended a hand toward Samhail, and lightning shot from his palm, enveloping the gargoyle's huge form. The scream that tore from Samhail was unlike any sound I'd ever heard him make as his body jerked on the ground, the spear still lodged in his stomach.

"Stop!" I screamed as I tried to bolt forward, but Bressen grabbed me around the waist and pulled me back as I struggled against him.

Sandrian dropped his lightning, and I looked desperately at Samhail for any sign of movement. My legs gave out in relief when I heard him groan and shift slightly on the ground.

"Why did you do that? He wasn't attacking!" I shouted at Sandrian.

"I'm sure he was still thinking about it," Sandrian said calmly, "and that was a warning about what will happen if any of you move against me again. Now let's get started."

Sandrian came right up to where Bressen still held me against him.

"You'll have to let go now, Bressen. I need your wife."

Instead, Bressen's arms tightened around me, and Sandrian extended a hand toward Samhail again. "It's your choice. Let go of the lady or Samhail dies right now."

Bressen's hold didn't loosen, but I could read the turmoil in his mind. I tugged gently on his arms, urging him to let me go. I felt his mind balk at the idea, but with some effort he let me pull his arms from around me.

"If you hurt her, there's nowhere in this world you can hide that I won't find you and kill you," Bressen said to Sandrian with deadly calm.

"Your lady will be perfectly safe as long as you cooperate," Sandrian assured him.

I waited to see the red glow on his skin, but nothing happened.

*It's the truth*, I said into Bressen's mind. *He doesn't intend to hurt me.*

I felt his slight relief, but his fear didn't ebb.

"The necklace and rings, please," Sandrian said, and I reached hesitantly into my satchel for them. I held them out to him, but he didn't take them. "Put them on," he said.

I blinked at him. "What? Why?"

"Because you're going to use them to help Morland once again become perimortal."

The hell I was. I wasn't sure exactly how Sandrian thought this was going to work, but he was mad if he believed I was going to help him move Morland's mind into Bressen's body.

When I didn't move, Sandrian held out his hand again toward Samhail.

"Alright!" I said, holding up my own hand to stop him.

I slipped the rings onto the middle finger of each hand, then looked at the collar. I moved it toward my neck but stopped short of putting it on, wary of the cacophony of voices I knew would inundate my mind.

Sandrian raised an impatient eyebrow, and I thought about telling him why I didn't want to put it on, but something made me keep the information to myself. I took a deep breath and slipped the collar around my throat. I shut my eyes tightly as three voices roared into my head, and I gathered my strength to reinforce my mind shield against them. I breathed an inward sigh of relief at the merciful silence when they quieted.

"Now what?" I asked, opening my eyes again.

"Now you'll use the rings and collar to move Morland's mind into your lord's body," Sandrian said as Morland came up next to him.

"Exactly how am I supposed to do that?" I asked incredulously.

I had no intention of actually doing it, but I was curious how he thought this was going to work. Moreover, getting Sandrian to explain his plan might buy me time to think of how to get us out of this.

"I'm sure you've experimented with the collar and rings," Sandrian said, "so you must know the rings can transfer items between them."

"And you think they can transfer a consciousness?" I asked.

"We're going to find out," Sandrian said, smiling. "That collar is supposed to be able to trap others inside it. With you as a conduit, you can pull Bressen's mind out of his body and trap it in the collar while moving Morland's mind into Bressen's body."

I stared at him. "You can't possibly believe that will work."

"I can and I do," Sandrian said. "You're a syphon. You're a vessel in which various powers come together, so you should be able to harness and manipulate more than one power at a time to make this work."

"And if I can't?" I felt compelled to ask.

Sandrian shrugged. "Then I'll kill people until you can. Maybe I'll start with Lord Aidan as a demonstration that I'm serious. I'm sure the people of Derridan aren't that attached to him yet."

I heard a sharp intake of breath behind me but couldn't tell if it was Maziren or Aidan himself.

"I don't know how to do this," I insisted. "What if I kill them both?"

"That's the chance we'll have to take," Sandrian said, although the look on Morland's face said he didn't especially agree.

I looked at Bressen, and I knew he could read the helplessness in my eyes even before I spoke into his mind.

*I don't know what to do. I don't have a plan this time*, I told him.

*I don't either*, he said.

*I can't do this. I can't put that monster inside you.*

Bressen only looked at me with grim acceptance. *I won't take the chance Sandrian will hurt you if you refuse. Do what you need to do.*

We were jerked out of our mental conversation as lightning crackled and Aidan screamed behind us. I whirled around to find Aidan on the ground panting as faint tendrils of smoke curled up around him.

"That was a warning," Sandrian said. "No more private mental conversations, or Lord Aidan will feel my lightning for real next time."

I glared at Sandrian, but he only angled his head, daring me to do something. Oh, there were so many things I wanted to do...

Something clicked into place in my head, and suddenly I had a plan. There was little I could do to Sandrian with his mental shield up, but Morland was mortal. I'd already planted the idea that he might not survive the transfer of his mind. If I could kill him, perhaps I could convince Sandrian it was an accident, that the transfer had somehow gone wrong.

The bigger question was whether I could actually kill Morland with my mind. I'd tried once before and failed miserably, but that was before the Trinity had enhanced my power. Bressen's life also hadn't been on the line then, and I was fairly certain I could kill easily if it meant saving him.

I'd given Bressen my word I'd never try to kill anyone with my mind again, but I'd always known I was lying when I made that vow. I wouldn't feel guilty in the least for going back on it. Perhaps I could also convince Bressen that Morland's death was an accident. He'd never have to know I broke my word to him, and if there was ever a time to do so, it was now.

"I need a minute to say goodbye to Bressen," I told Sandrian.

It wasn't a lie. I had no idea if any of this would work, and if things went horribly wrong and I accidentally killed him instead of Morland, if the vision I'd seen came to pass...

Nemesis take me, I'd never considered for a second that I myself might be the one to kill Bressen. An icy grip, colder than anything Magdalene could produce spread through my body as I forgot how to breathe. Bile rose in my throat, and I swallowed it down hard to keep from vomiting at Sandrian's feet. Then I sent up a desperate prayer to the

Protector to keep Bressen safe while I tried to get us out of this.

"You've said enough," Sandrian snapped. "Make the transfer!"

Not without letting myself hold Bressen one more time. I said a silent apology to Aidan for any backlash he might feel before I turned to Bressen and wrapped my arms around his neck to pull him down to me. He surrendered, and I felt his desperation meet my own as our lips seared together, acknowledging that this might be our last kiss.

I sensed rather than saw Sandrian move, and I pulled back from Bressen to loose a small, concentrated forcefield at the hand Sandrian extended toward Aidan. My forcefield knocked his hand to the side just as a bolt of lightning that made my hair stand on end lit the room. Thankfully, I'd knocked Sandrian's hand out of the way just in time that the bolt shattered against the wall instead of hitting Aidan, although the look on the lord's face said it still hit too close for comfort.

"Don't!" I warned Sandrian before he tried again. "I'll do it. I just needed one last…"

I trailed off, unable to voice the idea.

Sandrian's eyes narrowed at me, but he lowered his hand.

I turned back to Bressen and reached up to place my hand on the back of his head. I had no idea if this was what I had to do, but if the rings could transfer a mind, this seemed like the logical way to do it.

I looked into Bressen's face and saw the same resignation I'd seen the last time I held his life in my hands. He'd been just as ignorant of my plan then as well, and I only hoped my luck would hold out a second time.

Instinctively my eyes sought Samhail's. His face was pained, and I knew he was hoping I had a plan, that I wasn't actually going to do what it looked like. I wanted to reassure him, but I didn't dare give even him a hint of what I was about to attempt. It was better all around if everyone assumed I'd simply killed Morland by accident.

I turned to Morland, who stepped closer so he was within my reach, but he wasn't looking at me. His eyes were locked with Bressen's, a triumphant sneer on his face.

"Don't worry, Bressen. I'll take good care of her," Morland said. "I'll even let her scream your name when I'm fucking her."

Bressen's body jerked, but I closed my fingers in his hair and sent a warning into his mind. I wanted to tell him I'd die before I let Morland touch me, but I settled for trying to calm him, promising him I'd be alright, even though I was far from certain about that.

My plan had to work. Bressen's mind powers surpassed my own, and if Morland inherited those powers, I wasn't sure I could stop him from turning me into a mindless husk he could use as he wanted.

For the first time, the enormity of what it meant to put Morland's mind into Bressen's body sunk in, and my knees nearly buckled.

Protector help me, this had to work.

I swallowed hard as I raised my hand to Morland's head. If there was ever a time to find enough darkness in myself to kill someone, it was now.

My breath came in a ragged exhale as my fingers slipped through the coarse hair at the back of Morland's head. My heart pounded in my ears so all I could hear was its desperate thudding.

I closed my eyes and let go of Bressen's hair as the word formed in my mind, and I directed my command at Morland.

*Di-*

The demand was cut off by the scuff of feet, a squelching noise, and the sound of grunting. My eyes flew open, and I searched frantically for the source of the commotion, hoping someone had come to help us or that one of my companions had found a way to get the upper hand.

What I saw when my eyes finally locked onto movement only filled my stomach with lead.

Aramis stood a few feet from where Samhail lay on the floor, the dagger we'd given him to defend himself partially stuck in the torso of one of the blue-skinned guards. He seemed to be struggling either to push the dagger in further, or pull it out of the creature's dense body, and my heart stopped altogether as the creature swiped its claws at my father.

Aramis's name rose in my throat, but it caught there as his silvery eyes locked with my own, and I saw the grim determination on his face.

A beat of silence passed as everyone absorbed what had happened, and then the three hells broke loose.

# Chapter 52

Sandrian's hand swung toward Aramis, and I acted on instinct. I hurtled between Bressen and Morland and grabbed his wrist to yank it up and point it anywhere but at my father. Sandrian screamed as several of his bones broke beneath my grip, which was now enhanced by Maziren's strength. I was so surprised to feel the bones snap that I let go, and Sandrian pulled his wrist back to cradle it against his chest.

A sudden swell in noise and movement brought my senses back. Bressen and Morland fought hand-to-hand while Aidan and Maziren had retrieved their weapons and were slashing at the guards. Across the room, Axenus was locked in some kind of magical battle with Magdalene, who was clutching at her chest. I imagined he was trying to drown her while she seemed to be countering his water magic somehow.

My eyes sought Aramis, and I sighed in relief to find him kneeling by Samhail. I cringed a moment later as Samhail ripped the spear from his stomach with a roar of pain, and then Aramis's hands were on him, trying to repair the damage.

I needed to give our people back their powers. I looked down at the useless caronium cuff on my wrist and wondered if Maziren's strength might do any good against it. It still hung loosely on me since it hadn't shrunk to fit me like the others, so I pulled it off and tried to snap it in half. I felt it start to crack, but before I could fully break it, I heard Sandrian yell to his guards.

"Throw him into the chasm!"

I whipped around to look for Jasper as I heard Aidan cry out from behind me. Two of the blue-skinned guards were wrestling Jasper toward the chasm.

I put out a hand to loose a forcefield, but I was knocked sideways as someone in the melee crashed into me, and I looked up from the ground just as the two guards shoved Jasper over the edge.

Jasper had been pushing back against the guards, but at the last minute, he tried to leap forward toward the far edge of the chasm. His hands caught the ledge, but he had no grip, and he slipped free as Aidan screamed behind me.

I screamed too and gathered every ounce of my power to rally my elemental magic as Jasper's fingers disappeared from the ledge.

The ground shook as I fought my way back to my feet and willed the earth to rise up with me. I'd only recently reconnected with that particular element, but it heeded my call now, and seconds later, dirt and rock spilled up from the chasm to fill the void and dump Jasper onto the stone floor.

Axenus had been right. The chasm was nearly bottomless, and weeks ago Jasper's fate might have been sealed, but the response from my magic now was instantaneous and intense, thanks to the Trinity. The earth had obeyed my command to catch Jasper before he'd fallen too far, and he shot me a grateful look as he lay on the floor panting.

"Send in the rest!" Sandrian screamed – to whom I had no idea – but the question became moot a second later as more blue-skinned creatures poured from somewhere behind the altar, the now-filled chasm giving them a clear path as they rushed toward us.

"Bressen!" I yelled, and I saw his eyes widen as he took in the dozens upon dozens of new enemies streaming toward us.

I ran to him and grabbed hold of his caronium cuff to break it.

It snapped in half with some effort, and a second later, his eyes blazed with fire as black smoke began to curl around his ankles. His wings flew out from his back, but he didn't beat them as he rose into the air, arms outstretched. Then I heard the clambering I'd heard only once before months ago when I'd freed Bressen from Jerram's control, and he'd let his darkness loose. It was the sound of hundreds of tiny monsters climbing over each other in a mad rush to get to their prey.

Demoni.

Bressen had called The Wrath.

My eyes flared wide as a horde of not even knee-high scaley gray creatures burst forth from the thick smoke now billowing around Bressen's legs. I knew from experience that the smoke was cold enough to burn, and my heart skipped as I remembered pushing through it months ago to pull Bressen back from the brink of madness.

The demoni poured out of the smoke, all snapping teeth and swiping claws, and they hit the oncoming guards like a wave crashing against the shore, swarming them, engulfing them. Their screeches fused with the screams of the guards in a near-deafening din that was joined a second later by the roar of something large.

I gasped as Samhail, now in his huge stone gargoyle form, met the oncoming blue creatures and began to tear them apart. His stone wings were tucked in behind him, but his tail swiped out, throwing guards and demoni alike against the walls. The bright blue glow of his eyes lit the sharp fangs that flashed from his mouth, and the demoni retreated from him at once, giving him space to fight his own battle while they sought opponents farther away.

The guards scratched and clawed at Samhail, attempting to tear flesh so they could turn him as they had the people at the gambling den, but their claws only grazed off his stone-hard skin without leaving so much as a mark. For their trouble, Samhail grabbed them and tore heads and limbs from their bodies until the ground pooled with swirls of crimson and dark blue. His own body was quickly splattered with it as well.

I tore my attention from the battle and turned to find Sandrian, who seemed momentarily stunned by the turn of events. He raised his uninjured hand to attack, but I threw my magic at him and created a hollow sphere of water around him. The lightning he tried to fire at Bressen hit the inner surface of the sphere and dispersed around it, and I heard Sandrian's scream of rage from inside.

He burst through the sphere a moment later, and I kicked myself mentally for not just making it solid water so he electrocuted himself.

No matter. I seized his air, and he gasped and clawed at his throat while I pulled it from his lungs. I'd missed my chance to kill Morland with my mind earlier, but suffocating Sandrian to death worked just fine by me.

Sandrian's hand shot toward me, and I screamed as a jolt of lightning shot through my body making my teeth clench and my pulse jump.

He wasn't trying to kill me, I realized, just stop me.

I sent another forcefield at him that knocked him over and pushed him across the floor where he disappeared into the writhing throng of guards and demoni.

My eyes sought Bressen, and I found him at the edge of the horde, still hovering just above the ground, the smoke billowing from beneath him as he controlled the demoni. A pang of unease crept over me as I wondered if I'd have to pull him back from the darkness again.

I caught movement in my periphery, and a scream lodged in my throat as the clawed hand of one of the guards slashed toward my chest.

A sword slammed into the creature inches before it reached me, and I turned to see Maziren at my side. She might not have her strength, but she still knew how to fight.

She pulled her sword from the creature and thrust the wrist with the caronium cuff toward me.

"Get this thing off me!" she yelled.

I immediately grabbed the cuff with both hands and pulled as hard as I could. It cracked beneath my hands a few seconds later, and Maziren and I looked at each other in triumph.

It was only a fleeting glance, a shared understanding that maybe we were no longer opponents, but allies against a much bigger and deadlier enemy. It was enough.

Maziren smiled and whipped around to send her fist flying into one of the guards so hard that its spine severed completely. The creature's face looked out over its back before it fell in a heap and the blue substance that covered it leaked into a puddle on the floor.

Then Maziren ran for Aidan.

I turned to look for Bressen again but ran into something solid. I shrieked as I was jerked around, and a meaty arm circled my neck. The point of a dagger jabbed against my throat, and I nearly gagged as the smell of sour breath and sweat shoved its way up my nose. I could easily guess it was Morland who had hold of me.

I didn't move as the dagger bit into my skin, but a second later, the realization struck me that I was no longer the nearly powerless elemental I'd been a few months ago. All the ways I could easily get myself out of this situation flashed through my head at once, and I smiled as I chose the power closest to my heart.

Morland's body froze as I seized his unshielded mind, and his arm fell down so I could walk away from him.

I was about to decide what to do with him when lightning crackled through the chamber to my side. I turned to see Bressen caught in Sandrian's lightning, and I cried out as his body jerked and spasmed while the electricity jolted through him.

My scream was cut off by the sensation of freezing in my chest, and I stumbled backward as I tried to draw in breath that wouldn't come. Panic like I'd never known before gripped me as the vision of Bressen's death rose in my mind, and I struggled to make my body obey me as I tried to get to him, but I couldn't move.

The cold crept over me, and my heart slowed as my vision grew fuzzy. In desperation, I called a ball of sunfire to my palm and smashed it down against my own chest. I screamed as the burn of fire mixed with the burn of ice, nearly making me black out, but a moment later something ruptured within me as the clash of sunfire and hoar frost sent power rippling through the space, and the two magics canceled each other out.

Air filled my lungs again, and I whirled toward Sandrian to send more sunfire toward him at the exact moment I felt a part of my mind go blank. A new kind of chill shot through my bones as I saw Bressen's body crumple to the ground.

For a moment, my limbs no longer worked as the tether that held me to Bressen seemed to sever, like it had been snipped in two by a pair of scissors. My mind reached out toward his but found nothing but empty darkness, and terror gripped me as I ran to him and dropped to my knees.

I felt as if I was being ripped in half as I grabbed his limp form and shook him as hard as I could. My shaking hand rested on his chest as my healer magic searched frantically for a pulsing beat that wasn't there.

No.

No. It couldn't be. He couldn't be dead.

I held out my hands as Aramis had taught me, hovering them desperately above Bressen's body as I searched for injuries, something I could heal, something I could fix, but I felt nothing but cold emptiness.

No, no, no! Bressen was not dead.

I clutched at his body and pulled him against me, realizing a second later that I was doing exactly what I'd seen myself do in the vision.

And then I screamed.

The noise that tore from me was barely human. It seemed to claw its way up from my chest as a soul-wrenching anguish I'd never felt before slashed me from the inside.

I'd felt pain when my parents in Fernweh died of the Great Flu, but it hadn't been like this. My brothers and I had known for days their deaths were coming. The pain of their loss had been worse than anything I'd felt until that point, but it had been almost a relief when they'd finally passed because we'd known they were out of pain and at peace.

That relief hadn't been enough to dispel the soul-deep ache I'd felt for months afterwards, nor had it kept me from crying myself to sleep on most nights only to wake a couple hours later with a clenching in my chest and a knot in my throat that I couldn't swallow down, but it had made their deaths slightly easier to accept.

What I felt now was different. This was a pain so deep and binding I was certain I'd die right along with Bressen because it was not possible to live without him. He was the air I breathed, and without him, there was nothing to fill my lungs.

I heard Samhail's own roar of anguish somewhere close by, and something seized inside me so tightly that I doubled over across Bressen's body. Through the pain, rage sparked in my gut, and white-hot flames of fury burned through my body as I snapped upright. Another scream ripped from my throat, and I threw my hands out wide.

Power rushed into me, as if I was drawing it in from everyone and everything around me. It built inside until I was sure I couldn't take anymore, but I didn't stop pulling it.

It was more power than I'd felt in the Priory, more than what had torn out of me on the beach the night I'd become the eye of a storm while Bressen tried to anchor me. The power speared through me as it masked the agony, overwhelming it, and I welcomed the way it numbed me.

Lightning crackled in my palms, and I released it, this time with a scream of wrath. Electricity filled the temple, so bright I was blinded by it as I let my rage and misery flow out of me, a torrent of sound and fury.

The rings on my fingers and the collar around my neck turned burning hot as the lightning flowed through them and seared my skin. I wrenched the collar from my throat to fling it across the room, barely aware of the clang it made as it hit the stone wall and clattered to the floor. And still my lightning cracked through the room, filling the air and sizzling along the stone. Where everyone else was, whether I'd killed them all, I didn't know and didn't care.

I screamed and screamed and let the lightning I'd taken from Sandrian give form to my anguish until I thought my body itself might break apart.

Finally, I hunched over as the tumult began to ebb, my body no longer able to sustain the power and emotion emanating from me. I laid a hand on Bressen's chest, needing to touch him, and his body stiffened as the lightning still crackling from my palm jolted through him.

I pulled my hand back as something sparked inside me, and I clutched at my chest, trying to understand the sudden surge I felt. It was as if the emptiness there a moment ago was no longer quite so empty, and I struggled to gasp in air as my lungs finally remembered how to work.

Then it was there, that thread, that strand, that mental connection I shared with Bressen. It twined faintly between us again connecting our minds, and I cried out in shock as Bressen seemed to stir.

"Bressen!" I shouted as my voice broke.

I didn't dare to believe he was alive, and the world stopped as his eyes fluttered open so his gaze met mine. I couldn't breathe again, but for an entirely different reason. I touched his face with a hand that shook so badly it stuttered against his cheek, and Bressen's own hand pressed against mine. A ragged cry escaped me as tears rolled down my face.

"Please tell me…this isn't a dream," I managed to say between heaving sobs. "Please tell me…you're really alive."

Bressen struggled to sit up, and whatever control I had left broke. Tears streamed down my cheeks as I threw my arms around his neck and buried my head in his shoulder to sob. My body heaved against his as he laid a weak hand on my back and let me cry against him on the floor.

I didn't know how long I knelt there crying in Bressen's arms, but I suddenly remembered we'd been in the middle of a battle, and I looked around, waiting for the attack I was sure was coming.

But everything was quiet.

Movement against the wall caught my eye, and I saw Samhail's hulking gargoyle form rise from where he'd been crouched on the floor. His stone wings were flared, like he'd thrown them out as a shield the way he'd done when I'd collapsed Bressen's library on top of us at the Citadel months ago. He tucked the wings back in as he rose to reveal Aidan, Maziren, and Jasper on the floor against the wall where his stone body had been protecting them from my lightning.

My gaze swept the temple. The bodies of Sandrian's guards lay scattered on the floor in pools of blood and thick blue liquid, but there was no sign of Bressen's demoni. No little gray bodies lay among the guards, and I wondered if the creatures could even be killed.

Bressen tried to stand, and I pulled his arm around my shoulder to help him up. I placed a hand against his chest and let my healing magic look for any lingering injuries. His body was weak from being nearly dead, and I healed some burns and internal injuries as I also tried to give him some of my own strength and power as he'd done twice now for me.

"Where are Sandrian, Morland, and Magdalene?" I asked as we rose.

"Sandrian fled when he saw the lightning storm you were about to release," Samhail said to me.

He'd shrunk back down to his human form, but he was still covered in blood and gore. I glamoured a pair of pants on him, and he gave me a nod of thanks.

"Magdalene as well," Axenus said as he came up next to us.

I gasped and threw my arms around him.

"Thank the gods you're alright!" I said. "I was afraid my lightning…"

Axenus returned my hug before releasing me.

"I managed to throw myself behind a pillar and put up a wall of water when I saw the first sparks," he explained.

"And what of Morland?" Bressen asked.

Samhail gestured to the side where Morland's large form lay on its side, his eyes wide and lifeless.

"Dead," he said. "Likely a victim of the lightning."

I couldn't help the relief that washed through me. I'd been prepared to kill Morland before, so I wouldn't feel guilty if it was indeed my lightning that killed him. There was no part of me that regretted he was dead and that the danger to Bressen was now passed.

"Aidan!"

We all turned as Jasper's panicked voice reached us from where he and Maziren knelt next to an unconscious Aidan propped against the wall.

"Is he alive?" Bressen asked as we all hurried over.

Jasper didn't look up as he shook Aidan's body.

"He's breathing, but he won't wake up," he said. "Samhail tried to shield us from the lightning, but I don't think Aidan was fully protected. I felt his body jerk."

I was about to bend over Aidan and check him for injuries when the lord suddenly inhaled sharply and looked around.

"My lord, are you alright?" Maziren asked, genuine relief in her voice.

"Thank the gods!" Jasper exclaimed as he pulled Aidan against him. "I was afraid I'd lost you."

Aidan was wild-eyed as his gaze darted around to each of us.

"What the fuck is going on?" he asked as he pressed himself further against the wall.

I blinked. I didn't think I'd ever heard Aidan curse like that.

Jasper only pulled back and took Aidan's face in his hands as he searched his husband for any signs of injury.

"Aidan, do you know where you are?" he asked. He paled as a more concerning thought occurred to him. "Do you know *who* you are?"

"I'm…Lord Aidan of Derridan," he said. There almost seemed to be a question in his voice, but it was enough for Jasper, who crushed his mouth against Aidan's in a relieved kiss.

Aidan jolted a little, and Jasper pulled back again.

"I'm sorry," Jasper said. "Did I hurt you? I'm just glad you're alright."

Aidan was dazed as he looked at Jasper, but he shook his head. "I'm…I'm fine. What happened?"

"I think you caught some of Cyra's lightning," Jasper said.

There was no accusation in his voice, but I felt a stab of guilt anyway. I'd been so seized by my own grief and rage at Bressen's apparent death that I'd almost killed everyone in the room. It was only by some miracle everyone was alright. Axenus had managed to put up his water wall, and Samhail had been able to shield Aidan, Jasper, and Maziren from the brunt of the lightning. Aramis had healed him just in time.

The sigh of relief I'd been about to breathe stuck in my throat like a bone as I realized who was missing.

"Where's Aramis?" I asked as my eyes darted around the temple.

There was a collective pause as we all stopped to look at each other.

"Aramis!" I yelled as I swung around to look for him. "Aramis!"

"Cyra." Bressen's voice was gentle as his hand closed around my arm.

"Do you see him? Where is he?" I asked. I tried to look around Bressen, but he shifted, and I realized he was trying to block my view.

My stomach turned over as my knees threatened to buckle.

"Move aside," I told him, my voice shaking.

Bressen gripped my shoulders gently. "Cyra, I don't think-"

I shook off his hold and pushed past him. Off to the side, not far from where Aramis had first stabbed one of the guards, I saw a body slumped on the floor.

"Aramis," I whispered.

Bressen tried to grab my wrist as I started toward the prone figure, but I shook him off again.

Samhail stepped in front of me next, but I held out a hand, and he grunted as my forcefield pushed him back a couple steps.

It was Aramis – I knew it – and my steps quickened as I realized he might be injured and in need of my help. I prayed his wound wasn't bad, since I wasn't nearly as good a healer as he was.

I tamped down violently on the twinge of my power that told me I could no longer feel his mind.

No, he was just injured. I had to help him.

I dropped to my knees and pulled Aramis over onto his back, but I cried out as bitter cold bit at my fingertips. I looked down at the frost covering my father's torso and a violent wave of nausea choked me.

Aramis's eyes were open, and the already silvery pupils shimmered even brighter under a thin layer of ice.

"Aramis!" I screamed as I shook him. "Aramis!"

I hovered my hands over him, searching for his heartbeat, the feel of his blood flowing, anything to tell me he was still alive, but there was nothing. Terror surged inside me as I put my hand on his chest and charged his body with a small bolt of lightning as I had with Bressen.

It had worked once, and it could work again. But Aramis's body didn't so much as twitch as the lightning traveled through him.

"Aramis!" I screamed again and sent another bolt into him. "Please!"

I put both hands on him and let a sustained stream of lightning flow through him, but he didn't move. His eyes remained open but unseeing.

I screamed into the silence of the temple once more as I crumpled over him. The frost on his body burned my skin where I laid my cheek on his chest, but I didn't care as tears once again streamed down my cheeks, freezing into little beads of ice as they touched his form.

"No, please…Papa," I sobbed against him.

Strong hands closed around my shoulders, and this time I didn't resist them. I turned and threw myself into Bressen's arms as my tears flowed in a torrent down my face. His arms enveloped me as he laid his chin on top of my head and let me pour out my anguish against him.

My throat hurt, and I could barely see through the puffiness of my eyes when my sobs finally subsided. I was completely drained when I lifted my head, so I didn't fight when Bressen lifted me into his arms and turned to carry me away from Aramis. Samhail moved forward, and I knew he was going to pick up the body.

Bressen had only taken a step or two when he stiffened, and I registered the alarm in his mind.

"Samhail!" he yelled as he set me down quickly and stepped in front of me. Samhail was beside us a second later, his swords in hand. Maziren, Aidan, Jasper, and Axenus were in front of us, but they whirled to see what had caught Bressen and Samhail's attention. Maziren snapped into action first, drawing her sword and shunting Aidan and Jasper behind her.

I peered around Bressen and gasped as I saw the three people standing in a row watching us. If the abundance of leather they wore didn't mark them as warriors, then the array of weaponry they carried certainly did.

The first was a tall, muscular woman with pale skin, long night-black hair, and deep brown eyes. A scar cut across the side of one eye so there was a break in her eyebrow, and part of her head was shaved on the side like Axenus's. A small metal ring pierced her bottom lip near one corner of her mouth. There was a giant broadsword across her back, and her hands rested on two more short swords sheathed at her waist. The touch appeared casual enough, but something told me she could draw the swords in a heartbeat if she sensed we were a threat.

The second was a man of about Axenus's size and build. He wore a leather vest over his white shirt that had sheaths for close to a dozen small knives. Two short swords also crisscrossed his back. He had short flaxen blonde hair, fair skin, and chiseled features that made him nearly as beautiful as Bressen was. His lilac-colored eyes were stunning, but they held a wild look that made me think he might be slightly insane.

The final warrior was nearly as big as Samhail, with mahogany brown skin and close-cropped black hair. His eyes looked milky, and I wondered if he might be blind. Like the woman, he wore a huge broadsword across his back, but instead of short swords at his hips, he had four axes on his belt, two on each side. Markings on his forearms above his vambraces caught my eye, and I did a double take. I'd almost missed them since they were nearly camouflaged against his dark skin, but I was almost certain I knew what they were.

*Look at the markings on the big one*, I said into both Bressen and Samhail's minds. *He's gargoyle, isn't he.*

Both of them stiffened the slightest bit.

"Yes, he is," Samhail said softly.

Like the woman, the other two warriors seemed deceptively at ease, yet they too rested their hands within quick reach of their weapons. All three seemed to be waiting patiently, despite that half the people on our side of the temple now held out weapons toward them.

"Who are you?" Bressen asked, stepping forward as Samhail moved in to shield me with his own body.

In answer, the woman stepped forward and held up two objects. I inhaled sharply as I realized they were pieces of the collar, which had fractured in half. The three jewels that had once emitted faint glowing light now looked dull, and cracks spiderwebbed through them.

I moved around Samhail and Bressen. They both hissed my name in warning, but I stepped forward as the eyes of the warriors swung to me.

"My lady," the woman said, "you released us from four centuries of imprisonment. We are, to put it mildly, in your debt."

With that, they all sunk to a knee before me in deep bows.

# Chapter 53

I sat numbly in my chair only half-listening to the conversation going on around me. I barely remembered portaling us back to the meeting room across the hall from the Great Chamber in the Citadel where we were now gathered.

The warriors from the necklace were seated at the table across from me, Aidan, and Jasper. Samhail and Axenus stood near the door with their arms crossed over their broad chests, while Maziren was stationed as usual behind Aidan. Bressen had claimed the seat at the head of the table, to no one's objection.

The warriors had readily agreed to come back to the Citadel with us to tell their story once introductions had been made. They were perimortal, but we'd been surprised to learn they didn't have shields up, and Bressen had asked permission to look into their minds to confirm they meant us no harm.

They didn't. Rather, they were overwhelmingly grateful to me for freeing them from the collar, to the point that I'd had to shut out their thoughts. I couldn't stand their gratitude right now.

My father was dead.

A persistent ache gnawed inside my chest as I tried to wrap my mind around losing yet another parent, one that I'd just been coming to see as family. When we first met, Aramis had rejoiced in finding the daughter he'd lost, but I'd felt little for the man who shared both my blood and my eyes but not much else. The father who'd raised me had died a decade earlier, and Aramis was just a stranger to me. It had taken me a while to open up to him, but we'd finally been getting somewhere recently.

I shut my eyes tightly as a wave of grief hit me.

The discovery of Aramis's death had been a sucker punch straight to my gut. After the elation of finding Bressen still alive, I'd had the hubris to think we'd somehow eluded the vision. I'd been so very, very mistaken.

I had indeed seen Bressen lying seemingly lifeless in my arms in the vision, but it hadn't been his death I'd felt. No, the cold, icy death I'd felt was Aramis's, and a chill shuddered through me at the memory.

Bressen's hand slipped into mine under the table, and he squeezed my fingers lightly. I didn't have the energy or the will to squeeze them back.

*Cyra?* he asked into my mind, his voice full of concern.

I hadn't had a chance to say goodbye to Aramis before Magdalene stole him from me. I'd never told him I loved him.

And I did love him, I realized only now. I loved him as any daughter could love her father. He'd told me at the wedding he loved me, but I'd stopped myself from saying it back, and he'd died not hearing it from me.

Pain and regret nearly doubled me over in my chair, and Bressen paused in what he'd been saying to the group.

I just shook my head the faintest amount, and he went on.

I looked at Aidan. He'd been quiet since he awoke in the temple after my lightning had rendered him unconscious. I wasn't sure how close I'd come to accidentally killing him, but it was possible I'd addled something in his brain because he didn't seem quite like himself. It was a worry I'd seen in Jasper's face as well.

I shuddered at how much danger I'd put my companions in when I'd released my rage at the temple. Even if Magdalene hadn't frozen Aramis to death, there was a good chance I would've killed him myself if he hadn't been able to get to shelter in time.

It wasn't completely clear when she'd killed him. It was possible she'd struck him down right after he'd healed Samhail, or perhaps it had been her parting shot before she fled from my lightning.

"What can you tell us about how you were trapped in the collar?" Bressen asked the three warriors as I dragged my attention back.

The woman, Diora, was the first to speak up. She seemed to have taken on the role of their representative.

"We were hired to find and bring back a woman by the name of Praya," she said.

Bressen cocked his head. "Bring her back? Back where? I was told the rulers of Arystria had hired assassins to kill Praya."

He looked to Axenus, and the merman nodded with a shrug.

Diora shook her head. "The job was never to kill Praya. Our employer needed her for something, and Praya fled."

"Who was your employer?" Bressen asked.

"We knew her only as Magdalene," Diora said.

"What!" Axenus and I both exclaimed together, causing Diora to jolt back in surprise.

The new gargoyle, Ajax, sat forward in his seat. "You know her."

"If it's the same woman, she was there at the temple tonight," I said, glancing quickly at Axenus. His face had hardened again.

"I can show you what she looks like," Bressen said.

Diora nodded and then winced a little as Bressen sent the image of Magdalene into her head.

"Yes, that's the woman who hired us, although she looks older now of course."

"So Magdalene is more than four hundred years old," I said.

"Do you know why she wanted Praya?" Bressen asked.

"She never told us," Diora said. "We were just supposed to bring her back, alive, and by whatever means necessary."

"Did you know Praya was a syphon?" I asked.

Flynt, the warrior with lilac eyes, huffed a bitter laugh. "We knew, for all the good it did us." He glanced at Ajax, who shifted in his seat.

There was something about the blonde man that seemed slightly off, as if maybe he hadn't handled his four hundred years of confinement quite as well as the other two warriors.

To be sure, all of them bore signs of their ordeal. They flinched at the slightest motion, and their own movements were sometimes odd or shaky, as if they needed to readjust to once again having bodies.

Nevertheless, they'd fared far better than I would've expected. I'd have gone mad long before now if I'd spent four hundred years on the bottom of the ocean.

"What went wrong?" Bressen asked.

Diora started to speak, but Ajax answered first.

"It was my fault," he said. "We had a plan in place to subdue Praya, but when it was time for me to do my part, my powers wouldn't work right. I felt a stabbing pain in my head when I tried to attack her, so rather than taking Praya by surprise, she was alerted to our presence, and she turned the tables on us." He looked to Diora and Flynt. "I failed you."

Samhail spoke up from the door. "As a gargoyle, you wouldn't have been able to attack Praya. The divine imperative prevented it."

Ajax's brows furrowed as a look passed between the two gargoyles. An unspoken respect had settled between them when they'd recognized each other for what they were.

"What does the divine imperative have to do with it?" Ajax asked.

"Divine imperative?" Diora questioned.

Samhail and Bressen exchanged looks, and I saw that Bressen wasn't necessarily pleased Samhail had shared this information. He nodded for Samhail to go on, though.

"It's a constraint that prevents gargoyles from harming anyone who works on behalf of the Trinity," Samhail explained. "We're the guardians of the Trinity and all those who serve them directly, so we're forbidden from doing their servants any harm."

"And how does that apply to Praya?" Diora asked.

"We discovered only recently ourselves that syphons are the Hands of the Trinity," Bressen answered. "Praya would have been considered a servant of the gods, so, as a gargoyle, Ajax would have been incapable of doing her harm."

"Fuck me!" Ajax growled, slamming a huge fist on the table. He looked to Samhail for confirmation, and Samhail nodded.

"Did Magdalene know that?" Flynt asked, sitting forward in his seat. "Did that bitch lead us into a trap?"

"She probably had no idea," Bressen said. "We only learned it when one of our priests who specializes in ancient manuscripts deciphered a passage from a several thousand-year-old text that was discovered in an abandoned temple."

I looked at Aidan, wondering if he was angry we'd kept this information from him, but he just listened quietly. There was no shock or fury in his expression when his eyes met mine. Instead, there was something strange in his look, and I resisted the urge to slip past his mind shield and figure out what he was thinking.

"Even if Magdalene knew about syphons," Samhail added, "the existence of the divine imperative isn't widely known by anyone who isn't a gargoyle. Not anymore, anyway. There was a time most people would have known about it, but that knowledge has faded more and more the further we get from a time when actual gargoyles guarded the temples."

Something about this conversation nagged at me, and I furrowed my brows, trying to put my finger on exactly what it was.

"Cyra? What is it?" Bressen asked.

"I don't know," I said. "There's something odd about this whole situation that doesn't make sense."

I turned to the warriors.

"We originally thought you were sent to kill Praya because the rulers around the continent were afraid of her power, and that reasoning makes sense. It doesn't make sense that Magdalene, who isn't a queen or any other kind of ruler that I know of, would want you to capture Praya and bring her back. To what end? What could Magdalene possibly want with her, and how does this relate to whatever Magdalene is doing now with Sandrian? She broke him out of prison for some re-"

I stopped as I felt a possible connection click into place. Something important was on the edge of my consciousness, but I couldn't quite wrap my mind around it yet.

"Do you have something, Cyra?" Bressen asked.

I looked up, trying to will the puzzle pieces into place. My eyes met Axenus's, and then widened as another piece fell into place.

"How many powers do regular perimortals normally have?" I asked.

"Most only have one dominant power," Bressen said. "A few more powerful ones might have two, but rarely more than that. Why?"

I looked at Samhail. "Don't you have three? Your forcefields, summoning, and shapeshifting?"

He shook his head. "Not exactly. My power enables my shift to a gargoyle, but I'm not considered a shapeshifter. I'm a demi-human. My gargoyle form is part of who I am. As for my forcefields and summoning, they're two sides of the same power. I can propel things away from me, or I can pull them toward me, but it's the same base power, in the same way Bressen's glamours are an extension of his mind powers."

"What are you thinking?" Bressen asked me.

"I'm thinking Magdalene has too many powers for a normal perimortal," I said. "I remember either seeing her use or having her tell us about at least four. There was her freezing power, to start. Then she told us how she lowered the wards at Revenmyer and that she had a vision about me that morning I killed the bear." I turned to Axenus. "At one point it looked like you were trying to drown her?"

Axenus's eyes were already wide. "Yes, I was trying to fill her lungs with water, but she was fighting my water magic, which suggests she has elemental powers. You can't think…"

"That she's a syphon?" I said. "That's exactly what I'm thinking."

"She called a portal for us once as well," Diora offered. She shook her head. "For some reason it never occurred to me to question who she was or why she wanted us to hunt down a syphon for her. Her coin was good, and she had enough of it to hire the three of us to work together."

"And that's a lot of coin, mind you," Flynt chimed in. "I don't know what these two charged, but my services didn't come cheap at the time."

"All this can't be a coincidence, right?" Jasper asked. "It's not a coincidence that Magdalene sounds like she's a syphon, she was having them hunt down another syphon, and now, four hundred years later, she and Sandrian are going after Cyra?" His eyes darted around the room looking at each of us in turn.

"What do you think about all this, Aidan?" Bressen asked the lord. "You've been uncharacteristically quiet."

When my eyes swung to Aidan, I found he'd been watching me, but he seemed startled out of his gaze as he turned to Bressen.

"You'll have to excuse me," Aidan said. "I'm still a bit out of sorts after what happened. I'm not sure what to make of everything just yet."

Guilt nagged me again, and I gave Aidan what I hoped was an apologetic smile.

"Do you think Praya knew why Magdalene sent the three of you after her?" I asked the warriors, and they glanced searchingly among each other.

"If she knew, she never gave us any hint why," Diora said, and the two men nodded their agreement. "Not that Praya did much talking to us before she trapped us in that collar."

"Do you know where she got the collar?" Bressen asked. "Magical objects that powerful aren't easy to come by."

Diora shrugged. "I'm fairly certain she made the collar herself. I felt her essence the entire time we were trapped in it. She wanted us to feel it, to remind us she had ultimate power over us."

"Was she ever planning to release you?" I asked, appalled by that.

"No, she definitely wasn't," Flynt spat out, "and if I ever find her, I plan to make her pay for every day she kept me locked in that thing."

"I don't think you'll get that chance," I said. "I don't know if you knew where you were all this time, but we found the collar at the bottom of the ocean in a shipwreck. According to what we've heard, Praya's ship was caught in a storm, and she died when it went down."

Flynt's pale lilac eyes met mine, and the hint of a cold smile turned up the corners of his lips.

"Oh, we knew where we were," he sneered. "And Praya isn't dead. She survived that shipwreck."

"Why do you think that?" I asked in surprise.

"I don't think. I know," he said, the harsh tenor of his voice seeming so at odds with his gentle coloring and beautiful face. "She'd taunt us occasionally when she wore the collar, telling us we'd only be released when she died and that she planned to live a very long life. When that ship went down, she purposely left the collar on board because she knew when she eventually did die, we'd be released from it at the bottom of the ocean. We'd be freed only to drown to death."

The entire room was dead silent as we all stared at Flynt in horror. I looked at Diora, hoping she might contradict his story, but she only nodded solemnly.

"It's part of why we're so grateful to you for freeing us," she said. "Even if you hadn't broken the collar and set us free, just bringing it up from the bottom of the ocean saved us from a horrific fate."

I swallowed back the bile in my throat as I considered what kind of person Praya had to be to leave anyone to that kind of fate. Granted, these mercenaries had been hired to kidnap her, but there was a difference between killing in self-defense and delighting in someone's torture.

Perhaps it was because Praya was a syphon like me that I couldn't believe she'd do something like that. Somehow I felt as though I…knew her, and I found it hard to believe her so cold-blooded.

"How could Praya have done that to you?" I asked. "You said you weren't trying to kill her, just bring her to Magdalene. Leaving you to die at the bottom of the ocean for that seems…overly cruel."

In truth, it seemed outright sadistic.

"Do you have any idea where Praya is now?" Bressen asked.

"If I did, I wouldn't still be sitting here," Flynt bit out as he leaned back in his chair.

"You'll have to forgive my colleague," Diora said to Bressen. "He's always been a little hot-headed, and four centuries in that collar with only Ajax and I for company did nothing to improve his temperament."

Flynt snorted.

"So you could hear each other in the collar?" I asked.

"We could," Diora confirmed, "but…"

She glanced at the other two.

"Well, let's just say there were times when I think we all felt we would've been better off not being able to speak to each other."

"I'm not sure what awaits those who go to one of the three hells," Flynt said, "but I've done my time. Hell is the company of these two."

"May I ask what you plan to do with us?" Diora asked, ignoring him.

She glanced at Aidan and me, but the question was directed at Bressen, as she'd likely gathered he was the one here with the most power.

"Do with you?" Bressen said, arching a brow. "I have no plans to do anything with you. You aren't prisoners anymore. I'll ask you to stay here at the Citadel another day or two in case we think of any additional questions for you, but then you're free to go where you wish."

Diora raised her own brow and glanced in question to where Samhail and Axenus stood guarding the door.

"Just a precaution until we got to know you," Bressen said, answering the unvoiced question. "You won't be under guard while you're here."

I suspected that's because the three warriors still hadn't bothered to put up mind shields and, like me, Bressen hadn't read any hostile intentions in them.

Not toward us at least. Praya would be in trouble if any of them ever found her, especially Flynt.

"I imagine you want to get some rest," Bressen said to the warriors. "I'll have someone escort you to your guest quarters. We can talk more tomorrow if you think of anything else important we should know."

"I should get Aidan back to our wing to rest as well," Jasper said, smiling at his husband. "It's been a long day for both of us."

Aidan looked as though he might protest for a moment, but he smoothed his features and nodded at Jasper.

"Yes, I am exhausted," he said.

Aidan and Jasper bid us goodbye and made their way toward the door, followed by Maziren. Gilbert was just outside ready to knock when they opened it, and he entered after they left.

"Gilbert, please escort our three guests to their quarters and let them know where and when they can join us for meals," Bressen told the Captain of the Guard.

Gilbert gave a quick bow. "Of course, my lord."

Diora, Flynt, and Ajax all rose to follow Gilbert, but Diora turned to address me before they left.

"We were serious when we said we owed you a debt, my lady. A life debt. Before we leave, we'll give you the means to summon us if you ever find yourself in need of our services."

"I appreciate that very much," I said. "I'm not sure how much credit I can take since most of what I did was by accident, but I'm glad I was able to help you avoid the fate Praya had planned for you."

All three warriors bowed deeply at the waist to me and followed Gilbert out the door. Once they'd left and the door was closed behind them, Axenus and Samhail took seats at the table.

Axenus laid his hand gently over mine. "I'm so sorry about Aramis."

I blinked back the tears that rose instantly at his words, then swallowed and smiled weakly at him. My eyes met Samhail's, and he opened his mouth to express his condolences as well, but I nodded at him to let him know I understood, and he simply inclined his head back.

"We need to figure out what Magdalene and Sandrian are up to," Axenus said, turning to Bressen.

"You recognized that woman Magdalene, didn't you," Samhail said to him. "Who is she?"

Axenus stiffened, and both Bressen and I opened our mouths to deflect the question, but he held up a hand to stop us.

"I'm not sure who she is or where she came from," Axenus said, "but I know her because she was a friend of Queen Clarice of Sedonia."

Samhail looked confused for a moment, but I saw the moment he put everything together by the look of distress that crossed his face.

"You mean she…never mind," Samhail said, cutting off the thought. "Forget I asked."

Axenus nodded and a look of understanding passed between them before they both turned back to me and Bressen.

"So what do we do?" Axenus asked.

"I saw some of the vision Magdalene mentioned," I said, and three heads snapped toward me.

"How?" Bressen asked.

"Once we had on the caronium cuffs, I don't think Magdalene was trying very hard to reinforce her mind shield," I said, "so I slipped past it when she wasn't paying attention." I looked at Bressen and smiled weakly. "All those lessons finally paid off."

Bressen's answering smile was brilliant with a mixture of surprise and pride. "You're amazing. What did you see?"

"I didn't see everything clearly, but I can piece together a few images at least," I said. I closed my eyes and tried to recall the fragments of the vision I'd been able to pull from Magdalene's unguarded mind.

"It started much like Jemma's vision with me killing the bear, but then I saw what I think was Revenmyer as Magdalene freed Sandrian."

I shuddered as I recalled the image of the imposing obsidian edifice that sat at the end of a jetty at the northernmost tip of Hiraeth. I'd only gotten a brief glimpse inside the prison, but it had been more than enough to see why people feared the place.

"They were able to find Morland because she saw him in the vision," I went on. "She knew what he looked like in his mortal form and where he was. She also saw the collar and the rings and knew they might be used to restore him to a perimortal body."

"That didn't work out so well for him," Samhail growled. He looked at me. "I'm glad Morland's dead, but you should have let me pull his head off like I did with Jerram."

I raised a brow. "Have you considered you might have an unhealthy obsession with pulling people's heads off?" I asked him.

Samhail shrugged. "The popping sound relaxes me."

Axenus rolled his eyes, but I shuddered again. That same popping sound had haunted my dreams for weeks after the coup. I didn't find it nearly as soothing as Samhail did.

"What else did you see?" Bressen asked. "Was there anything about those things that Sandrian calls guards?"

"They're some kind of symbiont, a creature that forms a mutual relationship with its human host," I said. "They can't keep a solid shape on their own, so they use humans to give them form, and in return they make the host less vulnerable. Once they bond to their host, though, neither can live without the other."

"Where did they come from?" he asked. "How many do they have?"

I closed my eyes, remembering the living nightmare I'd seen.

"I didn't see where they came from, but they have…or will have an entire army of them."

I sent the image I'd seen of the thousands of symbionts stretched out across a battlefield into Bressen, Axenus, and Samhail's minds. The sea of blue bodies rippled over the land like water, and I felt the shock and horror of the three men.

"Gods above," Bressen breathed. "Tell me you saw how to kill them."

I shook my head. "No, but we shouldn't be trying to kill them anyway," I said. "We need to find a way to safely separate the creatures from their human hosts. I got the sense that most of those people are innocent."

Bressen's face was grim as he exhaled heavily through his nose. The warrior in him saw a battlefield of enemies that needed to be defeated, not a mass of people who needed saving. I couldn't forget the face of the man I'd killed at the gambling den or the look of terror Heren had worn as the symbiont had taken over his body, though. The vision had suggested there was no safe way to separate the creature from its human host while they lived, but I had to try to find a way.

"Is that everything?" Bressen asked.

"There was one more thing," I said. "I saw the three chairs again, and this time all three had figures seated in them."

Bressen frowned. "That doesn't make any sense. Sandrian wants to destroy the Triumvirate, not join it."

"What if," I said carefully, "it's not the Triumvirate I'm seeing. Or at least not Thasia's Triumvirate. I've seen those chairs three times now, and they never look like the chairs in the Great Chamber."

Bressen's eyes widened a little. "Are you thinking the three figures are the syphons?" he asked. "The three Hands of the Gods?"

I nodded.

"It would make sense," Axenus said. "We think Magdalene is a syphon, and she was trying to capture Praya four hundred years ago. We know that Praya is still alive, and we know that Sandrian and Magdalene wanted Cyra to come today. What if they wanted her for more than just trying to put Morland into a perimortal body? After all, if they just needed a syphon to use the collar and rings, Magdalene could have done it herself. They specifically asked for 'the syphon' to come."

I felt a tremor pass through Bressen.

"What is it?" I asked. "You just thought of something."

He was quiet for several seconds, and I felt the indecision in his mind.

"It's not the first time Sandrian has tried to take you," he said finally.

"What?" I asked. "When else has he tried?"

Bressen's eyes flicked to Samhail before they met mine again.

"The day you and Ursan were attacked outside Callanus. The second attack, not Ursan's farce of a first one," he amended. "The men were from Rowe. When I read their minds, I learned that they'd been given a description of you and were told to bring you back to Sandrian."

There was silence as I stared at Bressen. "How did they know we'd be out there? I wasn't allowed to leave the Citadel. How could they have known Ursan would be riding with me?"

Bressen's face grew dark. "I didn't know at the time how they knew, but in hindsight, I assume Glenora told them. She knew you'd be out riding with Ursan that day. It's possible she hoped they'd kill him as well."

I instantly knew that to be the case as another fragment of Magdalene's vision clicked into place, and I saw Glenora's face swim by.

"I'm not sure how or when Sandrian and Glenora would have met and decided to work together, but it's the only thing that makes sense,"

Bressen said. "When Ursan offered to take you riding, Glenora likely saw her chance and sent him a message. He in turn, could have sent men he had in the area. That's around when the attacks on towns started."

I narrowed my eyes at him. "And you're just telling me this now?"

He sighed. "I…didn't want to frighten you."

I glared at him. *This conversation isn't over. We'll discuss this more later,* I said into his mind, and he nodded the barest amount.

"What happens if the three syphons are reunited?" Samhail asked, breaking through the sudden tension in the room. "Is Magdalene trying to restore the rule of the syphons over the continent?"

"If she is, does Sandrian know that?" Bressen asked. "I got the impression he was planning to do the ruling himself. He introduced Magdalene as a member of his court."

"Maybe she's using him," Axenus suggested. "She has no qualms about using others."

There was a bitterness in his last words that twisted my heart, and I felt his pang of regret at having said them as he looked away from us.

"There's clearly a lot more we need to know about what's going on," Bressen said. "If even half of what we now suspect is true, we have a far bigger problem than just Sandrian trying to restart his war against Thasia."

I leaned back in my chair, wondering exactly how Magdalene thought this would work. If she was trying to gather the syphons to reform the continental triumvirate, she'd need both my cooperation and that of Praya, and I, for one, had no plans to comply with her. She'd already tried once to take Praya by force, and that had failed spectacularly. How she planned to make us work with her, even if she managed to get us together, seemed like a serious challenge.

I shook my head in bewilderment. A few weeks ago I'd been the first syphon in four hundred years. Now there were three of us, and Magdalene apparently had big plans to unite us for some reason.

I didn't know where Praya was now or if she knew what Magdalene planned, but I only hoped that – wherever she was – she stayed hidden.

# Chapter 54

The breeze off the ocean whipped my dress and cloak around my legs as I stood with the small group on the beach the next morning, a torch in my hand. Bressen pressed close behind me with his hand on my hip, his touch not possessive as it normally was, but gentle and supportive. In front of us, Aramis's body lay wrapped in a shroud on the small funeral pyre on the sand. Behind us stood Samhail, Axenus, Aidan, Jasper, Maziren, Calanthe, my brothers, and the three warriors.

The warriors had insisted on coming to Tide's End for the funeral, more out of respect for me than for Aramis. I'd debated telling Raina about my father's death, but Bressen had gently advised against it, since he didn't want the High Council to know yet what had happened.

That was fine with me. I'd decided on a private gathering rather than opening it to the people of Solandis. Aramis had found regard as a healer in the city quickly, and plenty of his patients would've been eager to attend his funeral if allowed, but I didn't want to share my father with a crowd today. Part of me would've been happy to mourn him by myself, but I wouldn't begrudge those behind me the opportunity to pay their respects.

"Do you want to say anything?" Bressen asked quietly.

It was a few seconds before I nodded and turned to address the people gathered. A lump rose in my throat as my gaze drifted down the row, but I swallowed it down as best I could.

"My father spent the last twenty-two years of his life protecting me," I said, my voice breaking horribly before I'd made it halfway through the sentence. I swallowed again and pushed on. "He already made sacrifices no person should ever have to make for his family, yet his final act was to make the ultimate sacrifice to save not only me, but half of you as well."

My eyes met Calanthe's, and my stomach caved at the look of anguish on her face. Tears rolled freely down her cheeks, and I knew she felt a gut-wrenching guilt over the part she'd played in the sacrifices I'd noted. I'd hated her for what she'd done to Aramis when she first dared to seek me out, but her regret over her actions was genuine. It was tragic she and

Aramis hadn't had time to make their peace before his death.

I'd already forgiven Calanthe for the role she'd played in the course of my own life. She was one of the few blood relatives I had remaining, and I wouldn't take that for granted, especially now that Aramis was gone. I was fortunate to have her, Jaylan, and Brix, and I'd embrace my patchwork family to the fullest, particularly since Andromeda was disinclined to welcome me into her own.

"Aramis was a healer," I went on, willing my voice to be strong. "He spent his life taking away people's pain, fixing what was broken, mending what was torn, and putting people back together in a world that too often tried to take them apart. He gave me life, and while I only got to call him father for a time far too short, he'll be with me from now on, looking back at me in the mirror, and acting through me when I use his gift."

I paused, not sure what else to say. Words seemed so inadequate to capture who Aramis was and the sacrifices he'd made. I wished I could be more eloquent, that I could find something to say to do him justice, but I'd never been able to find the right things to say in the face of death. My inability to express myself now only made my grief more acute.

I turned and made my way to the pyre with the torch. I lit the wood on all four corners and then lodged the torch in the middle of it.

The flames started slowly, but I coaxed them with my wind, and they flared higher as the wood caught. I stepped back away from the heat until Bressen's hand landed on my shoulder. I watched the flames steal closer to the shrouded form, blackening the white fabric where they licked at it.

I wanted to do more to honor Aramis, and as the flames engulfed the body, it came to me.

I waited until I was sure some of Aramis's ashes would mingle with those of the wood and return to the earth, and then I held out my hand. At my command, Aramis's body burst into thousands of butterflies that rose into the air, and I heard the crowd behind me on the beach murmur. Aidan had learned how to simulate life from something lifeless, and I hoped he appreciated the use to which I'd put his gift.

The flames caught most of the butterflies as they scattered, setting them alight while more of my wind blew them out over the ocean where they burned quickly and fluttered down into the water as ash. Only a few butterflies escaped the blaze, and my breeze brought one right to my hand where my fingers closed carefully around it to shelter it in my palm.

The elements were my original powers, and now my father's body would be borne to his final rest by all four, burned by fire, returned to the earth as ash, carried on the air by wind, and pulled out to sea by the tides.

The pyre was hardly needed anymore, but I wouldn't put it out, and no one moved as we all stood on the beach to watch it burn. It was several minutes before Bressen shifted slightly, and I knew he'd nodded to the others to return to the house as he remained with me.

It was a long while before I finally turned and looked up at him. He wrapped me in his arms and pressed a kiss to the top of my head.

"I think Aidan has to touch something to transfigure it," he observed.

I shrugged and slipped the butterfly into the pocket of my cloak. Ever since the Priory, my powers were coming easier and easier to me. I barely needed to think about something to make it happen, and I'd noticed that my abilities in particular areas had started to surpass those of my sources.

"How are you?" Bressen asked.

"I intend to kill Magdalene," I said, and Bressen's body tensed. He pulled back to look at me, but I went on before he could say anything.

"Before Aramis attacked, I was going to kill Morland using my mind. I know I promised you I wouldn't, but it was the only way I could think to save you."

Bressen took in a deep breath and released it before nodding.

"I wish Aramis hadn't tried to help," I said, tears rolling down my cheeks. "I could've killed Morland with my mind. I know it. And when I find Magdalene again, I'll kill her for what she did to both Axenus and Aramis." My voice had taken on a hard edge, and I felt the turmoil in Bressen as he looked down at me.

"Will that make you feel better?" he asked, and I knew from his tone he didn't think it would. "You almost killed the men who burned your vineyard in Fernweh, and it bothered you afterward. Would taking their lives have filled the void you felt? Will killing Magdalene give you peace?"

"Yes," I said stubbornly.

"You're angry and you need somewhere to channel that hurt, but you and I both know you're not a vengeful person, Cyra."

"But I am," I said, pulling away from him. "Don't you see that? I'm the Hand of the Nemesis. The Nemesis Incarnate, as you're so fond of telling me. Doesn't that mean I'm vengeance incarnate as well?"

"Too often people see the Nemesis as a god of vengeance rather than as a god who maintains balance," Bressen said, and my chin went up a notch as I recognized the words I'd said to him in the Priory.

"That sounds like the rantings of a naïve fool to me," I said.

He shrugged. "It sounds to me more like the musings of a wise woman who was chosen to serve the gods."

I scoffed.

"Do you think Aramis would want you to seek vengeance?" he asked. "You just made a beautiful speech about how he spent his life taking people's pain away, fixing what was broken, mending what was-"

His words were cut off as I seized the air in his lungs, and his eyes widened in shock.

"Stop throwing my words back at me!" I screamed and stepped back from him as tears streaked down my face once again.

I released his air, and he inhaled deeply, but he didn't try to speak again. Not out loud anyway.

*Be angry at me if you want*, he said into my mind. *Hit me if you need to. I can take it. I'd rather have you hurt me than do something you'll regret.*

I tried to throw up my mind shield, but he anticipated the move and stopped me from blocking him. It was as if he'd stuck his foot in the mental door I'd been attempting to slam in his face.

"Get out of my mind!" I yelled, but he just shook his head.

"No."

I tried to propel him out, but even my enhanced syphon abilities were no match for him. His mental powers had always been stronger than mine, and he wrapped my mind in a coil of smoke that disoriented me.

I screamed in rage and launched myself at him, but he again anticipated my move. He caught my wrists and spun me around so my back was trapped against his chest while he held my hands crossed in front of me. I struggled against him, trying to call on the strength I'd syphoned from Maziren, but it didn't come.

The only time I'd been able to use Maziren's gift was back at the temple. I'd been prepared when we returned home to have to be careful not to break things I touched, but I found I didn't need to worry. My access to Maziren's strength seemed to have been temporary, because I hadn't been able to call on it since.

I jerked and bucked against Bressen as hard as I could, trying to wrench free from his grasp, but he was nearly as strong as Samhail, and I couldn't dislodge him. I could've used my powers to free myself, but I wanted the physical confrontation. I needed to lash out with my body.

Bressen only held me against him, absorbing the few blows I was able to land with my feet or elbows, and I silently cursed myself for not being able to get free despite all the training Samhail had given me. I tried to throw my head back against him, but he was too tall for me to hit his face. He grunted as my skull hit his collar bone, but his hold didn't loosen.

Finally, I screamed again as tears of frustration ran down my cheeks. He turned me around and wrapped me in his embrace. He was still in my head, and he knew the fight had left me. I buried my face in his chest to sob against him, and he didn't move other than to stroke my hair.

My breath came in hitching gasps as my sobs subsided a while later, and my eyes were so puffy I could barely see. I was so tired of crying.

"I'm sorry," I said.

Bressen kissed my forehead and stroked a thumb along my cheek.

"There's…something I need to show you," he said.

He took my hand and led me back up toward the house. I could've called a portal to get us there quicker, but I needed the walk to get myself under control before I got near anyone else again.

When we reached the house, Bressen surprised me by leading me toward the door to the basement. The only things down there were the pantry, the armory, and…the wine cellar.

I pulled up short. "Bressen, I'm not-"

"We're not going to the wine cellar," he assured me, reading my thoughts. "I've been trying to find the right time to show you this."

I frowned but followed him as he continued down the stone stairs. At the bottom, the hall split one way toward the pantry and wine cellar while the other path went toward the armory and other storage rooms. Bressen took the hall toward the armory, and at the end of it was the door to the holding cells where he'd imprisoned his mother.

I'd never gone through it since it was always locked. It didn't even have a space to put a key, so I had no idea how it opened.

My question was answered a second later as Bressen touched his palm to the door, and it swung open.

"It's warded to admit only me, Samhail, or Ferris," he said.

Another set of stairs led down a level even deeper below the house, and we began to descend. At the bottom, we stepped into a small room that led to another hall, and I saw the rows of metal bars for the cells.

"The dungeon?" I asked uneasily. "Should I have brought my toothbrush?"

"We just call them holding cells," Bressen said as he smiled and pressed a hand to the small of my back to steer me down the hall. "Don't step too close. The bars have caronium in them, and it's under the floor inside as well, so it will neutralize your..." He trailed off as he remembered caronium had no effect on me. "Never mind."

"Who's down here?" I asked warily, not sure I wanted to know. My first thought was that maybe he'd brought his mother back.

He led me to the first cell. Unlike what I might have pictured a dungeon...um, holding cell to look like, the space was well-lit, and very clean. A lone figure sat on the cot inside with his arm in a sling.

The man looked up, and my eyes locked with those of the last person I'd expected to see.

# Chapter 55

"Eddin," I breathed in disbelief. I turned to Bressen. "How? I thought he was in jail in Gendris."

"I may no longer be the Nemesis Incarnate, but I still have some pull left," he said wryly.

I just stared at him before asking, "How long has he been here? How long has he been living right under my nose?" My temper rose. "Why didn't you tell me?"

Bressen sighed. "He's been here since we returned to Solandis. To be honest, I'm not sure why I had him brought here. I suppose I was hoping you'd be able to make peace with what happened if you could confront him, but I never found the right time to tell you he was down here."

I raised a brow. "And you thought a good time would be after I told you how much I want to kill Magdalene?"

Eddin had been down here for our wedding. Bressen's mother had been with him. It was why Samhail hadn't let me come down to get her.

"Wait here," Bressen said as he went back into the small room and returned with a set of keys. He unlocked the door to Eddin's cell and opened it so I could enter.

"Aren't you afraid I'm going to kill him?" I asked.

I saw Eddin flinch on the cot out of the corner of my eye.

"Don't let her in here!" he said to Bressen.

Bressen shook his head to me, ignoring Eddin. "No, I'm not."

He was much more confident about that than I was. All my hurt and rage from that day on the vineyard had ignited again the moment I'd seen Eddin, and it was bolstered now by the fresh pain of my father's loss. I really had no idea what Bressen could possibly be thinking by bringing me down here, but I stepped into the cell, intending to disprove whatever point he was trying to make.

"Stay away from me you perimortal bitch!" Eddin yelled, scrambling back against the wall of his cell as I approached. There was a mixture of disgust and fear on his face.

I hadn't seen him since that day in Fernweh, and everything suddenly came rushing back to me. I smelled the acrid reek of smoke in the air, felt it cling to my skin and burn my lungs. I saw the burned husks of the grape vines and the skeleton of the collapsed barn as a stream of wine ran down the path away from it. I hadn't seen the bodies of our horses, but I could imagine them. I could practically hear their screams as they tried frantically to get out of the stable, and I closed my eyes as rage welled up inside me.

Eddin had used me for sex for months while he'd been fucking Pryn as well, and when I'd dared to break things off with him, he'd had the nerve to be angry. He'd been willing to spread vile rumors about me, and when he'd found out what I really was, he'd taken it out on my brothers. He'd burned the vineyard my parents had built and destroyed everything my brothers and I had worked so hard for.

I opened my eyes, and Eddin screamed as my gaze bore into him. I wasn't sure what he saw in my face, but it terrified him. Perhaps my eyes were burning like infernos right now, as Bressen's sometimes did. Brix had told me he'd seen as much.

I held out a hand as I closed the space between me and Eddin, and my forcefield pinned him against the wall. I was on him a second later, and I placed my hand on his chest. Eddin's eyes flew open wide as his lungs began to fill with water. His hands clutched at his chest and his body heaved as he coughed up the liquid. It gushed from his mouth as he tried and failed to gasp in air.

Behind me I heard Bressen call my name, but I ignored him. Fire flared to life in my other hand, and I brought it up toward Eddin's face, ready to sear his flesh.

Eddin's expression was a portrait of terror, and I opened my mind so I could feel his fear. Bressen shouted my name again, but still I ignored him. I brought my hand so close to Eddin's face that I knew his skin must be singed. He would've been screaming if there was any air in his lungs to do so, but water continued to burble from his lips as they turned blue.

Eddin's eyes were so wide that the irises were surrounded on all sides by white, but still I held the hand to his cheek. His pain and fear swam through my head like liquor, intoxicating me, and I didn't need to read his mind to know he realized he was going to die.

My flame was nearly touching his face when my magic pulsed in my chest, and I stopped. My mind swam with his fear, but an awareness lingered in my periphery.

I glanced over my shoulder to see Bressen still standing in the door of the cell looking worried. He hadn't entered, and he'd also stopped calling my name.

He wasn't trying to stop me.

The realization hit me like walking into a stone wall. The last time I'd tried to kill Eddin, Bressen had broken into my mind to stop me, to make sure I didn't become a cold-blooded killer. But not this time. I saw the agony on his face, the pleading in his look, but also the determination that this time it was my choice what happened to Eddin. He wouldn't stop me. He wouldn't break into my mind again.

My power pulsed inside me, and I recognized it then as Aramis's healing magic flaring up to tell me where Eddin's pain was, urging me to help ease it. I was so shocked to feel it that I stepped back and pulled my hand from Eddin's chest. He fell forward onto the floor, coughing and choking as he spit up the water in his lungs.

The healing magic ebbed away as Eddin took in deep gasping breaths now that he'd dispelled the water. The magic didn't ease fully, though.

Eddin was still hurt.

"What happened to his arm?" I asked, turning to Bressen finally.

Wary relief painted his face as his throat bobbed in a swallow. "Samhail visited Eddin the day I brought him here," he said.

I looked down at Eddin. "Samhail broke your arm?"

"Fuck you!" Eddin shouted from his knees as he struggled to breathe. He braced himself with one hand on the floor, the other still in its sling.

"If you don't want to start drowning again, I suggest you answer my questions," I said coldly.

Eddin glared up at me but said, "If you mean that giant perimortal freak, then yeah, he broke it. You're all just fucking aberrations, so if you're going to kill me, then just go ahead and do it!"

Eddin pushed himself back into a sitting position against the wall as I looked down at him. There was so much hatred in him, not just for me, but for all perimortals, and not for any reason that I could tell. I didn't know what might have happened to him before he came to Fernweh, but he'd never hinted at any kind of past wrongs, no reason he might have to hate us so much other than simply because we were different than him.

Of course, I'd given him a reason to hate me since then.

"Why do you hate us so much?" I asked Eddin, suddenly curious to know. "Did a perimortal do something to you or your family?"

Eddin narrowed his eyes at me. "Why do I hate you? You mean other than the fact that you all look down your noses at us mortals? That you've all been given huge advantages that you've done nothing to earn? That you have everything so easy because you have magic and practically live forever?" Eddin scoffed. "Why do I hate your kind indeed."

I was taken aback by the ferocity of his resentment. He assumed I had everything easy because I had magic, but so far my magic seemed to cause almost as many problems as it solved. Yet I couldn't deny that magic and long life were significant advantages for most perimortals and that we hadn't done anything to earn those advantages other than be born that way. Despite everything I'd been through in the last few months, I'd still choose to be perimortal over mortal.

But perhaps the gifts I'd received from the Creator weren't free. Perhaps they came with some sort of obligation, a responsibility to use them to make the lives of others who were not so fortunate easier.

Raina's suggestion that I do something good to balance out the harm I'd done surfaced in my mind again.

I was suddenly very aware of just how much better I had it than Eddin in so many ways. There were a few drawbacks to being perimortal, of course, such as knowing I was destined to lose those mortals I was close to, like my brothers, but I couldn't deny my powers were a significant boon. For that matter, my syphon powers gave me an advantage even over regular perimortals since I had access to so many more abilities.

None of that excused what Eddin had done, but he was in jail for his actions while I'd faced no real consequences for setting his tavern on fire and nearly killing him and those two other men. What right did I really have to be his judge and executioner?

I looked at the sling on Eddin's arm and reached into his mind to find the memory of the day Samhail had broken it. I knew it was a violation, but I needed to see it, to indulge in just this one small taste of retribution.

The memory came readily to me, and I felt Eddin's fear weeks ago when he'd heard the door of his cell open and looked up to see the giant, imposing figure of Samhail filling the doorway. He'd nearly wet himself again but had managed to hold his bladder.

The expression Samhail wore might appear neutral to someone who didn't know him, but I recognized the carefully controlled signs of his fury beneath the surface. It was evident in the way his eyes narrowed ever-so-slightly more than normal and in the barest thinning of his lips as he pressed them together.

Samhail strode into the cell, his eyes fixed on Eddin. The caronium would have taken his power, but Samhail gave no outward sign of any discomfort. For that matter, he had no need of his power to handle Eddin. Eddin was a little taller than an average man, and he was strong from years of lifting crates of liquor, but he wasn't close to a match for Samhail.

Samhail crossed his arms as he stood before Eddin, and the exasperation in his voice masked the anger I knew lurked just beneath.

"Perhaps I should've been clearer the last time we spoke in Fernweh," Samhail said. "I assumed you'd read between the lines of my warning and not fuck with Cyra and her family at all, but apparently I should've spelled everything out for you."

I felt the urge in Eddin's mind to tell Samhail what he thought of him and his warnings, but Eddin wisely kept his mouth shut on that count. Instead, he said, "Maybe you should have. My misunderstanding."

Samhail arched a brow but didn't say anything as the silence stretched for nearly a minute before Eddin finally spoke again.

"Are you just going to stand there staring at me? What in the three hells do you want, you perimortal freak?"

Samhail's eyebrow arched higher, but he only smiled. It was a smile I recognized, one that told whoever he was looking at to start running.

"I'm just trying to figure out what Cyra ever saw in a bullying coward like you," Samhail said with a shrug.

I was wondering the same thing myself now, but Eddin just snorted.

"You'd have to ask her, but if I had to take a guess, I'd say she loved the way I fucked her."

Samhail's face darkened, and Eddin felt a surge of satisfaction at Samhail's reaction. He may have been behind bars, but Eddin felt a degree of confidence that no one would hurt him.

"Take care how you speak about Cyra," Samhail warned, and Eddin shivered at the menace in his tone.

Eddin recovered quickly and shrugged. "You asked what she saw in me. I gave you an honest answer. She liked to bounce on my dick. It's not my fault she doesn't want yours."

Samhail's mouth twitched, but he didn't say anything, didn't admit that he'd in fact fucked me several times and driven me so mad with desire that I'd screamed his name on more than one occasion.

Yet Samhail's silence seemed telling to Eddin.

"Or is that why you're here?" Eddin asked, realization dawning. "The little whore let you between her legs and-"

Panic surged through Eddin as Samhail charged forward and grabbed his arm to pull Eddin off the cot. Samhail's grip was painful, and I felt Eddin's wince.

"You seem to think you have immunity to say whatever you want," Samhail snarled. "I could care less what you have to say about me, but I told you to watch your tongue with regard to Cyra. You're speaking about the Lady of Hiraeth, who also happens to be a friend, and I won't allow your unworthy mouth to speak ill of her."

Samhail's defense of me sent warmth through my heart, but I could see now where this conversation was going, and my stomach coiled in anticipation of its inevitable end. In my own mind I willed Eddin not to say anything back, but I knew he would.

"And what the fuck are you going to do about it if I do?" Eddin asked.

The smile on Samhail's lips was predatory as his hand clamped around Eddin's arm near his elbow while his other hand wrapped around Eddin's wrist. I felt the second Eddin realized what Samhail intended to do as panic rampaged through him. Eddin shook his head violently, trying to force a plea for mercy out of his mouth, but the crack of bones lodged the words in his throat as his scream of pain pushed past instead.

Stars flared behind my own eyes as Eddin's agony lanced through me from his mind, and I fought down the bile that rose in my own throat.

The break had been so quick and effortless that Samhail might have been snapping sticks to throw on a fire.

I disconnected my mind from Eddin's and closed my eyes as I fought down nausea. I'd thought seeing Samhail break Eddin's arm would give me a degree of satisfaction after what he'd done to me and my family, but I'd mostly found it disturbing.

I didn't fault Samhail for what he'd done. I knew he'd done far worse to the men who'd attacked me and Raina on the wharf in Callanus, but I no longer had the stomach to watch it, let alone revel in it.

I opened my eyes and stepped toward Eddin. I reached out, but he flinched back, the memory of Samhail's assault now fresh in his mind.

"Stay away from me!" Eddin screamed again as he tried to push himself as far back against the wall as he could.

"I'm not going to hurt you," I told him. "Let me help you."

"I don't want your help! Don't touch me!"

I sighed and considered honoring his wish to leave him alone. I knew he wouldn't thank me for what I wanted to do, but I wasn't doing it for him anyway. I was doing it for me and for my father.

"I'm sorry," I said as I seized Eddin's mind so he couldn't move. I knelt on the floor as I took his arm out of the sling and unwound the bandages holding the splint in place. I saw the dread in Eddin's frozen eyes as he waited for me to hurt him again, but I only laid my hands over his arm where I'd sensed the broken bones and let my father's healing magic flow through me.

The bones had been set by a mortal healer and were already mending, but I hurried them along now, and a minute later my magic told me the task was done. My hand hovered over Eddin's arm as I let my magic check my work, and it confirmed Eddin's bones were fully mended.

I stood up and released his mind.

Eddin blinked at me. He flexed his hand and examined the arm before looking up at me. "What the fuck did you do?"

I sighed, not really expecting him to thank me, especially after I'd just tried to drown him.

"I healed your bones. Samhail shouldn't have hurt you. *I* shouldn't have hurt you," I told him.

"I didn't ask you to do that," Eddin spat out. "I didn't want your filthy perimortal hands on me."

"I know. I didn't do it for you."

I turned to go but then looked back at him with a smile.

"And just in case you forgot," I said, "your dick has been between my filthy perimortal legs. You should pray to the Protector it doesn't fall off."

Eddin's eyes widened, and I left the cell, more satisfied to see the look of horror on his face than I'd been to feel his bones break.

Bressen was fighting a smile himself as he closed the door of the cell behind me. He pulled me into his arms and kissed my forehead.

"You really have a way of using your sexual exploits to wound the men who've hurt you," he said in amusement. "First Jerram, now Eddin. Remind me never to piss you off."

I smiled wanly as I recalled how I'd used my mind powers a few months ago to show Jerram every erotic detail of my first threesome with Samhail and Bressen. Jerram had considered Samhail beneath him, and seeing both Samhail and Bressen fuck me – as he'd hoped to do himself – had thoroughly enraged him.

"You didn't kill him," Bressen said.

I was confused for a moment until I realized he meant Eddin and not Jerram, then I huffed a laugh. "Something tells me you knew I wouldn't."

He kissed my forehead again. "I didn't doubt you for a second."

I gave him a dubious look as he slipped his hand into mine and led me back toward the stairs.

"Sparing Eddin doesn't mean I won't kill Magdalene if I get the chance," I said.

Bressen nodded his acknowledgement. "I assume Axenus didn't tell you about the time I let him see Clarice in Revenmyer?"

I frowned at him. "No. What happened?"

"Axenus was angry, like you were. I knew he wanted to kill her for what she'd done to him, so I took him to see her. I told him I wouldn't stop him if he wanted to take his revenge."

"He decided not to kill her," I concluded as we ascended the stairs.

"Not immediately. He filled her lungs with water, just as you did with Eddin, and stood there watching her drown for several very long seconds.

I started to think I'd made a huge mistake bringing him there, but he seemed to have a change of heart and pulled the water back. I can't tell you how relieved I was, both then and today."

I sighed. "I don't understand. You and Samhail have killed plenty of times before. I saw Samhail cut down almost twenty men when he was bringing me from Fernweh to Callanus. Axenus was trying to kill Magdalene when we were at the temple. I've even killed someone before myself. How is any of that different?"

"There's a big difference," he insisted. "Taking a life is never easy, and that's true even in battle or for self-defense. When you stand over someone who can't fight back and willfully take their life, there's a qualitative difference to that action. That's wrath, not justice. Back at the gambling house, you killed in self-defense. I'm sure Axenus wanted to kill Magdalene in the temple, but he was also battling her to save his own life. Samhail killed to protect you and himself when you were attacked."

"Samhail also ripped Jerram's head off when he was paralyzed under your magic," I reminded him.

Bressen canted his head to acknowledge the point. "That's true, and I know Samhail well enough that I'm sure he doesn't regret that at all, but that's between him and the Nemesis. He may well have to answer for Jerram's death when the Nemesis takes him. But regardless of what Samhail does, or what I do for that matter, it doesn't mean it's something you should aspire to."

We reached the top of the stairs and were back in the hallway to the storage rooms.

"So you'd be fine if I killed Magdalene in self-defense?" I ventured.

Bressen gave me a look that told me I was missing his larger point, but he just said, "If she or Sandrian attack you, I sincerely hope you fight back, and if that results in their deaths, then so be it. I just don't want you to go looking for vengeance."

I reached into the pocket of my cloak and felt the paper butterfly there. Grief seized me, and I swallowed down the lump in my throat.

"There's something I need to tell you," I said as we walked.

He looked at me with concern. "This sounds serious."

"It may be. I'm not sure what to think of it just yet."

He waited for me to go on, and I took a deep breath before speaking. "Brix told me that he saw my eyes flash red back in Fernweh," I said. Several seconds faded into the shadows as Bressen frowned at me.

"I…don't understand," he said as he paused on the first step to the next level. "What do you mean he saw your eyes flash red?"

"Like yours do when you're angry. He'd said something that upset me, and he saw my eyes glow red. I think it happened again just now."

He was shaking his head before I'd finished speaking.

"That's impossible," he said. "That's an angelus trait. I don't know of any other beings who do it."

I shrugged. "Maybe I can syphon more than just your magical power," I suggested. "Maybe I can syphon your angelus abilities as well. When I was underwater with Axenus, I could create phosphorescent light like he could. He wasn't sure if that was part of his magic or if it was a mer ability, but maybe it was the latter."

Bressen considered this as he started up the stairs again.

"We'll need to explore this more," he said. "If you can manifest my angelus abilities, that may mean…"

He trailed off, but I thought I knew what he was thinking.

"It may mean you can fly," he continued suddenly, and I blinked.

That hadn't been what I was thinking, but it was certainly something to consider. Gods above, was it possible I might be able to grow wings?

I stopped Bressen as we reached the top of the stairs and took his face in my hands. I smiled as I ran my thumb over the dimple in his chin that had so fascinated me when I first met him. I still loved it, and I wondered if any children we had would inherit that trait.

"It might also mean I can have angelus children," I said to him.

Bressen's body went preternaturally still, and I wasn't sure he was breathing anymore.

I jumped a little as he finally inhaled sharply, as if he'd just learned to breathe. He took my hands in his and brought them to his chest.

"That would be wonderful," he said, "but it's the least of our concerns right now. We'll consider that possibility later, but right now we're a long way from thinking about children." He paused. "Do you agree?"

I nodded. I did agree. As much as I'd love to give Bressen angelus children, I wasn't ready to be a mother yet. Not for a few years at least, and definitely not with the threat of Sandrian and Magdalene looming.

"I also don't want you to get your hopes up or put pressure on yourself," he said. "I don't want you to be upset if it turns out you can't. I don't need angelus children. I just need you."

I swallowed as emotion swelled inside me, then nodded.

"Can you send Eddin back to Gendris?" I asked. "I don't want him here anymore."

Eddin was a reminder of my past, and I wanted to move on. I was ready to embrace my future with Bressen, and I didn't want Eddin anywhere near that future.

Bressen brought my hands up to kiss my knuckles. "Of course," he said. "I'll make the arrangements, and he'll be gone by tomorrow."

My heart felt lighter than it had in a while as we left the basement and continued up to the fourth floor. We turned into the hall that led to our suite and saw that two large figures waited for us outside the door.

Samhail and Axenus both pushed off from where they'd been leaning against the wall and waited for us to join them. My eyes met Samhail's, and an understanding seemed to pass between us, as if he knew where I'd just been and seen what he'd done. I gave him the barest nod to tell him I understood and didn't blame him, and he nodded back.

My eyes met Axenus's next, and a different kind of understanding passed between us, a kind of kinship that said he knew exactly what I was feeling and wouldn't judge me for it.

"What's our next step?" Axenus asked, turning to Bressen.

"We prepare for war," Samhail answered for him.

Bressen looked from Samhail to Axenus. "To be clear, I don't expect either of you to do anything if you're not up for this," he said. "Samhail, you helped fight Sandrian twenty-five years ago, but that doesn't mean you need to fight him now. Axe, I brought you here to train Cyra, and while I'd appreciate your continued help with that, you're under no obligation to stay at this point."

Both Samhail and Axenus narrowed their gazes and crossed their arms over their chests almost simultaneously. I bit my lip to hide my smile at the twin gestures, knowing neither man would appreciate my amusement at how in sync the two of them now were.

"You don't really expect us to leave you to handle this by yourself, do you?" Axenus said, surprising me at how genuinely offended he sounded.

"And if you ever suggest as much again," Samhail added, "I'll kick your ass so hard it will take Cyra a week to heal you."

Bressen smiled at Samhail despite the threat. "Duly noted. In that case, I'll need a general if you're up for it."

Samhail nodded solemnly and held his hand out to Bressen. The two men grasped forearms, and a look of brotherhood pass between them.

Bressen turned to Axenus.

"I could also use someone to act as my advisor and occasional emissary," he told the merman. "We may need to seek allies soon if this turns out to be as big a problem as I'm afraid it is."

Something flashed across Axenus's face as his gaze locked with Bressen's, and they shook hands as he also accepted the role offered.

"Very well then. Welcome to my cabinet," Bressen said.

"And what's *my* role in your cabinet?" I asked him.

Bressen grinned at me. "Flag bearer?" he suggested.

I crossed my arms over my chest. "Try again."

"I could use a squire," Samhail mused.

"You both remember that I can bury you alive without half a thought, right?" I said as I glared at the two of them.

I looked at Axenus, but he held his hands up in surrender.

"Don't look at me," he said. "I've learned not to fuck with you."

"Smart man," I said.

Bressen sighed and clasped my shoulders. I looked up defiantly at him.

"Weeks ago when we first discovered you were a syphon," he said, "I warned you that if someone ever learned how to control you, they could turn you into their own personal weapon."

I gave him a dubious look. "And you think you can control me?"

He rolled his eyes. "Clearly I can't. But more importantly, I don't want to think of you as a weapon. Because you *are* a weapon, Cyra. A powerful one, but one I don't want to use. I'm afraid of what will happen if I try to use you and someone else gets their hands on you."

I smiled up at him and put a hand on his cheek. "You're the only one

I'll let wield me," I said.

Bressen opened his mouth to speak but then snapped it shut so hard his teeth clicked together. Next to us, Samhail cleared his throat.

"I could use a drink," Axenus said. "Does anyone else need a drink?"

Bressen chuckled and turned to head down the hall to his study as the three of us followed.

Once inside, Bressen opened the doors to the liquor cabinet behind his desk and pulled out an ornate box to reveal a bottle of wine nestled into a black velvet cushion.

"My father was given this bottle of wine from the king of one of the eastern countries as a congratulations when he became a Triumvirate Lord," he said.

"Perfect," Samhail said. He reached for the bottle, but Bressen snapped the lid of the box shut before he could touch it.

"This is not the kind of bottle you drink at the start of the war," Bressen said. "It's the one you open when all the battles are won and you drink to celebrate your victory, but also to mourn your dead."

He looked at me, and I stared back at him.

"We've had our first casualty," he said, "and tonight we'll drink a toast to Aramis, but we won't drink from this bottle until we've brought the people responsible for his death to justice. We'll save *this* bottle until we've earned it."

Bressen looked at the three of us, and we all nodded back solemnly.

"So then what bottle do we drink to toast Aramis?" Samhail asked.

Bressen put the box back in his cabinet and rummaged inside. When he turned back, he had four bottles clutched in his hands, two in each. He set them all down on the table with a clunk.

"These are the bottles we'll drink to Aramis," he said as he grabbed a corkscrew and began to open one. "These are the bottles you drink at the start of the war, before the blood is spilled, before it's too late to go back. These are the bottles of optimism, the ones of hope, and the ones you drink to forget the terrible things you'll need to do tomorrow and the day after that and the day after that."

We were all somber now, and Bressen turned to look at me seriously.

"The three of us have seen war," he said, indicating him, Samhail, and

Axenus. "You're too young to have been in the last one, and Glenora's attempt at a coup was too short-lived to have been much of a conflict."

I nodded in understanding.

"I know you want to fight, and I won't stop you from doing so," he said to me, "but you need to understand the risk you're taking."

I nodded again, and Bressen pulled the cork out of the bottle with a pop. He took four glasses out of the cabinet, poured a little in each, and handed them out to us.

"To Aramis," Bressen said.

"To Aramis," we echoed and drained our glasses.

Bressen poured another round.

"To a short war that sees the four of us back here at the end of it to drink my father's bottle," he said.

"To a short war," Samhail and Axenus echoed, but the words caught halfway up my throat.

The war had barely started, and I'd already lost my father and nearly lost both Bressen and Samhail. I did want to fight, but it was just now sinking in that we might not all survive the coming conflict.

Bressen, Samhail, and Axenus were all watching me as I held my glass.

"To a short war and all being back here together at the end," I whispered before draining my wine.

Bressen gave us each another pour. "To the calm before the storm."

"To good wine and good friends," Axenus added.

"To a full liquor cabinet and hours of night still ahead," Samhail said.

"To watching a woman half your size drink you all under the table," I said and threw back my wine.

I set my glass on the table and looked up to see them all staring at me, each wearing half a smile.

"Well, the gauntlet has been thrown down, gentleman," Axenus said with an answering smile as he drained his glass. He looked at me. "Still making promises you can't back up?"

"I was a winemaker, remember?" I said. "Besides, I think the gods increased my tolerance for alcohol when they enhanced my powers."

Samhail and Bressen both drank and Bressen poured the next round.

"I'm going to enjoy watching you stumble through training tomorrow with a hangover," Samhail told me. "You'll run extra laps every time you have to throw up."

"We'll see if you're even conscious by then," I fired back.

We all clinked glasses and drank, and I looked around at the three men who'd given me so much. Love, friendship, mentorship, confidence, comfort, and trust.

Bressen, Samhail, and Axenus would survive this war. I'd make sure of that if it was the last thing I did.

Magdalene would not. I didn't know what she was up to yet, but I'd make her regret dragging me and my family and friends into it. I was a being of wrath and storms, and I'd make her pay.

That was the promise I made to myself as I sipped my wine, and one I suddenly knew I could keep as I stared into the dark liquid and saw the red flashes from my eyes reflected back at me.

I smiled. Magdalene should run far and run fast.

The Nemesis came for everyone, and I was coming for her.

# Epilogue, Part I

Despite spending the better part of his day trying to navigate the palace at Seatherny, he was lost again. The place was bigger than he'd expected, and he was having a hard time remembering how to get around.

Actually, it wasn't even the size that made it difficult, but its endless monotony. Why bother building a palace this big if one hallway looked like every other hallway, if one floor had the same color scheme and décor as every other? He was hardly an aficionado of style and design, but would adding a little nuance have killed the architects?

He passed a guard but came up short on how to ask for directions in a way that wouldn't rouse suspicion. Then he noticed the guard was female and fought the urge to shake his head. Women were as pointless as guards as they were on a battlefield. Cooking, cleaning, and fucking were the only good uses he'd ever found for them.

"Aidan? What are you doing?"

The voice was both a relief and an annoyance as he turned to see the Lord Consort striding toward him. Another voice immediately rose up from deep in his mind, pleading with him, screaming at him, trying to reach out, even though the one called Jasper would never be able to hear.

Morland crushed Aidan's voice back down in his mind and put up a shield to block out the lord's cries. Much to his chagrin, he hadn't been able to kill Aidan's consciousness when he'd entered the lord's body.

Whether that was because Aidan was perimortal or because he hadn't been as weak as the soldier whose body he'd originally taken, Morland wasn't sure. He'd find a way to destroy Aidan so he could take full control soon, but for now the lord was a nuisance he'd just have to live with.

All things considered, it was a small price to pay for being back in a perimortal body again, for having some power back. He would've preferred to have Bressen's body with its mind wraith abilities, but he had to admit that Aidan's transfiguration power wasn't a bad consolation prize. Once he got the hang of it, he was certain he'd be able to put it to good use. At least he hadn't jumped into the mortal's body.

The mortal in question, Jasper, reached him and slipped an arm around his waist. Morland tried to stop his body from stiffening at the touch but only partially succeeded. Concern showed in Jasper's face, and Morland tried to force himself to relax.

Bressen's powers wouldn't have been the only advantage of taking the Lord of Hiraeth's body. Having Bressen's wife would have been a huge benefit as well, but instead he was stuck with this man.

Disappointment swelled in Morland as he thought of the dark-haired beauty Bressen got to fuck every night. The man really did lead a charmed life. The thought of pinning the woman down and driving into her had been making him hard while he'd waited for her to perform the magic that would transfer his mind into her husband's body, and he hardened again now at the memory.

Unfortunately, Jasper felt him harden against his hip and smiled.

"I was starting to worry about you," Jasper said, sounding relieved. He took Morland's hand to lead him back down the way he'd come.

Morland followed only because he'd have to find his way to their bedroom eventually, and this time he'd pay more attention to where it was. Once there, he'd make some excuse or another to put Jasper off.

Or maybe he'd just go ahead and fuck the mortal. He didn't know what their dynamic was in the bedroom, but as long as he was the one doing the penetrating, he could make this work for the time being. He doubted this man would like the way he fucked anyway, so perhaps the problem would take care of itself in time.

Sex aside, it would've been ideal to take over Bressen's body for what he and Sandrian had planned, but Aidan's was almost as good. Aidan had access to the Citadel, and as a Triumvirate lord, Bressen would share information with him, *had* already shared information with him in fact.

Sandrian had a spy in Bressen's household who was also poised to kill the lord and lady if needed, but being in Aidan's body would put Morland close enough to pick up the slack if the spy failed.

Maybe now that their plan to put him into Bressen's body hadn't worked, they could just go ahead and kill Bressen. Morland knew Magdalene had plans for Cyra, but he didn't know what they were.

The information he'd learned from the conversation with the warriors who'd escaped the collar had been enlightening, but it didn't bring him any closer to understanding what Magdalene's goal was. She'd been vague about what she wanted out of all this, and it made Morland uneasy. He knew Sandrian felt indebted to her for releasing him from Revenmyer, but he trusted her too much. He gave her too much leeway.

Morland wondered if Sandrian knew Magdalene was a syphon, as Bressen and his group now suspected. He hadn't seen it himself, and it had been right under his nose. Perhaps he'd missed the signs because the thought of one syphon had seemed impossible enough. The idea there might be two – or even three – was downright inconceivable.

He'd been so pleased when Sandrian found him that night months ago and had taken him back into his service. Morland was less pleased when he'd found he now answered to two people, one a haughty woman. Magdalene was the female version of Bressen, and he itched to put her in her place, preferably on her knees with his cock in her mouth. Then it would be harder for her to spew her bullshit or whisper in Sandrian's ear.

He needed to get a message to Sandrian tomorrow to let him know what had happened and that he was still alive. There hadn't been time today when he and Jasper had returned from Callanus.

Morland realized they'd stopped outside a door, and Jasper was looking at him with concern.

"What?" he asked the man.

"Are you alright?" Jasper asked. "You've seemed out of sorts since the temple. Should I call for the healer?"

"No healer," he said quickly. "I'm just still dazed from when that bitch shocked me."

Jasper looked taken aback, and Morland wasn't sure for a moment what he'd said to distress the mortal so much.

"Aidan," Jasper said gently, "I realize Cyra got out of control, but…"

Morland grimaced. Right. The stupid mortal didn't like the name he'd called Bressen's little whore. He had to remember to watch what he said around these people.

"I'm sorry," Morland said, feigning his best contrition. "I'm not myself right now. I just need to rest."

Jasper's expression softened. "Of course. Let's get you a bath and put you to bed."

Morland jerked back as Jasper leaned in to kiss him and then kicked himself mentally at the devastation that strained the man's face. If he was going to play this part, he had to convince this man he was his husband. The thought disgusted him, but he'd do it for Sandrian, for their plans.

"I'm sorry," he said again, hating the taste of the words on his tongue. "Just give me another day or two and I'll be fine. I promise."

Jasper's face eased the slightest bit.

Morland forced a smile onto his face and reached out to take the other man's hand. He pushed on the handle of the door, hoping to the gods they'd stopped in front of the bedroom.

"Let's go," he said, tugging on Jasper's hand. "You can wash me."

A tentative smile crept onto Jasper's face, and Morland breathed an inward sigh of relief. He'd let the man help him bathe if it made him happy, and maybe he could tease out the details of their relationship so he knew how to act around this man that was supposed to be his husband. Gods above, he hoped Sandrian appreciated the lengths to which he was willing to go for their plan.

Morland leaned forward then and let his lips touch Jasper's. He closed his eyes, doing his best to picture Bressen's wife as he wrapped his hand around the back of the man's neck, thinking how easy it would be to just snap his spine. Jasper moaned, and somewhere deep in the back of Morland's mind, muffled behind his shield, Aidan screamed.

Morland pulled back slowly from the kiss, and a smile curled his lips as he tugged the mortal into the bedroom.

He'd been going about this all wrong. The trick wasn't to suppress Aidan's consciousness or kill it – not yet – but to use it. Aidan would tell him anything in order to keep his husband safe, and he'd use the lord's knowledge to get close enough to kill Bressen and bring Cyra to Sandrian.

*Listen carefully, Lord Aidan,* Morland said, opening a channel between him and the trespasser at the back of his mind. *If you want your husband to stay alive, here's what you're going to do…*

# Epilogue, Part II



*A week or so earlier*

Praya stood on the beach with her toes dug into the sand and sent up a silent prayer to the Trinity as she watched the rowboat make its way back to the ship anchored a few hundred yards from the shore.

Neither she nor Ariel had noticed the ship that morning until the landing party nearly made it to their small island, and by that time it was too late to throw up glamours to hide any evidence that someone lived there. Truth be told, it had been so long since they'd seen another human besides each other that they'd been admittedly eager to have guests. They'd expected a merchant crew blown off course by one of the many storms that battered the area regularly, but that's not what they'd gotten.

Nothing could have prepared them for what they'd actually gotten.

"Do you think they'll come back?" Ariel asked as she slipped an arm around Praya's waist.

"I'm almost certain they will," Praya answered her wife. "I doubt my wipe of their memories will last long once it takes hold. Not on the lord and lady at least."

"Why do you say that?" Ariel asked.

"The lord is a mind wraith, the most powerful one I've ever met."

Ariel came around to face Praya, frowning. "But you're a syphon. Surely your powers are stronger than his."

Praya shook her head. "My powers are blunted out here, especially after so long away. My power in general may still be greater than his, but his mind abilities far surpass my own. We're lucky he wasn't inclined to force his way into our thoughts because I couldn't have stopped him."

Ariel looked shocked. "He didn't notice you in his mind?"

"I couldn't get into his mind directly," Praya said. "I had to go in through hers. Their connection is strong. Her own mind powers are fairly prodigious, but they both seemed fatigued, and I was finally able to slip past her shield and plant the memory wipe. From there I used her own connection with the lord to get into his mind and do the same."

Or so Praya hoped. Planting the command to erase their memories of landing on the island had been tricky, and the effort had taxed her. Unlike the lord's mental powers, the lady's were unpracticed, but it had been centuries since Praya needed to perform such complex mind magic. She'd sensed that they were both weakened at the moment, though, and that might have been her only saving grace. If the erasure did take hold, she had no idea how long it would last, but she was optimistic. Crissail, her mentor and friend, had taught her well.

"It took though, right?" Ariel asked.

"I can't be sure. Once I was in the lord's head, I buried the command as far down in his consciousness as I could. I can only hope he doesn't find it before they get back to the ship and it triggers. Even then, I'm not sure how long it will last. We can only hope that they won't be able to find their way back here if it fails."

"And the woman? Cyra?" Ariel asked. "She's a healer?"

Praya finally looked away from the small boat bobbing offshore and met her wife's gaze. "Cyra is a syphon," she told Ariel gravely.

Ariel blanched as her eyes widened. "What? Did Magdalene send her?" she asked, her voice brimming with unease.

Praya shook her head and turned to walk back up the beach toward the small house. Ariel fell into step beside her.

"I don't think so," Praya said. "She's young and inexperienced. Her powers are underdeveloped. I can feel them in her, dormant and waiting. When she finally comes into her own, she'll be…devastating, but right now, the lord is the bigger threat."

"Maybe we should've killed them and been done with it," Ariel suggested, but Praya heard the half-heartedness in her voice.

"You know that would have cost me," Praya said. "I belong to the Creator. My power to destroy is limited. That one, though…Cyra belongs to the Nemesis. She could tear the world in half if she wanted, and that lord of hers would help. He's a dark angelus."

Ariel's head snapped up. "Fucking hells! That's a dangerous pairing."

Praya nodded. "Even with Cyra's powers being underdeveloped, it's likely she and the lord could've killed us before we could have done them any harm. It's better that we just hope the memory command works and they forget they were ever here. It should take hold when they get back to the ship. It will tell them there's no time to explore the island and they should just get back to the continent. Luckily the mortals on the ship were easy enough to reach."

Ariel nodded. "Do you think they suspect who you really are?"

"Possibly," Praya said. "I saw a look in Cyra's eyes when I said my name was Miranda. I suspect she has truth seer abilities."

"Will the memory command hold on her?"

"She doesn't have as much mastery of her mind wraith abilities as the lord, but being a syphon herself, that may not matter. Her powers may break through the command anyway."

"And the others?" Ariel asked.

Praya shrugged. "They won't be able to break the memory command themselves, but if the lord breaks his, he'll be able to break theirs as well."

"And you're sure Magdalene didn't send them? They could be heading back to her as we speak," Ariel said.

They'd reached the house, and Ariel went straight for one of the closets to pull out a long sword with an ornately carved hilt and a large obsidian cabochon in the pommel. She grabbed the whetting stone that sat next to it and unsheathed the sword to begin sharpening it.

"Be careful with that," Praya said, not bothering to hide the nervous edge in her voice. "Didn't you learn your lesson the last time?"

Ariel's eyes flicked to the bandage that had been a permanent fixture on her arm the last several hundred years. "I wasn't sure what to do when Cyra offered to heal the wound for me," she said with a chuckle.

Praya eyed the bandage and shuddered as she remembered the day Ariel had come to her, blood welling up from between the fingers she'd clamped over the wound. They'd both been frantic that day, trying everything they could to stop the bleeding.

A sword that left unhealable wounds had sounded like such a good idea, such a powerful weapon. That is, until Ariel had been too careless sharpening it and cut herself. Then Praya had wondered what she'd been thinking to create it. She'd wanted to destroy the thing later, but Ariel had talked her out of it. Once they'd gotten the bleeding under control.

Even Praya's own healing magic hadn't been able to close Ariel's wound, but the cut had been shallow enough that Praya could stitch it up and staunch the blood so Ariel wasn't in danger of bleeding to death. More than four hundred years later, the wound was still there and needed to be tended regularly. They replaced the stitches every couple weeks, and the bandage was changed daily. They'd done it so often by now that it was as routine as getting dressed in the morning.

"You did the only thing you could do, decline politely," Praya said, still eyeing the sword. "Are you planning to use that if they come back?"

"If they come back with Magdalene, yes."

"If they come back with Magdalene, I doubt that sword will help," Praya said darkly.

"Do you believe their story about why they were out here?" Ariel asked. "Treasure hunting? They knew about *The Stalwart*. Maybe they were really looking for you."

"I don't think so. Cyra must suspect I'm not who I claim to be, but I don't think she knew who I actually am. Hopefully everyone back on the continent thinks I died in a shipwreck centuries ago."

Ariel opened her mouth to say something, then closed it again.

"What?" Praya asked.

"Should we consider going back? Maybe it's time to stop hiding and face Magdelene. If Cyra is as powerful as you say, she could help us."

Praya was quiet for a moment before she shook her head. "No. We can't take that chance. We have to hope Magdalene thinks I'm dead and that she's spending her time searching for my replacement."

Ariel paused in her sharpening of the sword. "Would it really be that bad if she managed to bring the three of you together?"

Praya watched the whet stone scrape over the blade as Ariel resumed.

"It would, quite simply," Praya said softly, "be the end of the mortal realm as we know it."

*A preview of book 3…*

# Prologue

Talyn of Avril – or "The Raptor" to those who paid her to end their enemies – stood over the sleeping couple and wondered if she should just kill them now and be done with it.

They slept soundly enough that she could easily slit their throats. The only complication was the size of the bed. It was huge, and the couple slept in the middle of it, so she wouldn't be able to reach them without either climbing onto it or porting into the middle. She was still confident she could strike quickly enough that both would be dead before they knew what was happening, but that wasn't her assignment…Yet.

Talyn studied the man. He was one of the most exceptional-looking males she'd ever seen, more beautiful than handsome. His night-black hair stood out starkly against the pillow, and she knew from glimpses of his bright turquoise eyes that they were mesmerizing under lids heavy with long lashes. It would almost be a travesty to kill someone as stunning as him, but she'd do it if asked.

Actually, she was looking forward to killing him. She hadn't seen much of him while she'd been here, but when she did see him, he'd oozed arrogance, and that alone made her want to stab him.

She turned her gaze to the woman sleeping beside him whose rich brown hair spilled across the pillow behind her as if being blown in a strong wind. The woman was beautiful as well, with haunting silver eyes that were so light they almost seemed to glow when she was awake. Together, Talyn had to admit, they made a devastating couple.

While Talyn was certain she wanted to kill the man, her feelings about the woman were less clear. The woman was the reason she was here in the first place, but nothing Talyn had seen of her said she deserved to die.

If anything, Talyn felt like she needed to help the woman. Just a week or so ago, she'd heard a scream come from this bedroom, and she'd rushed in to see what the matter was. Never mind that she was supposed to be just a servant and probably shouldn't be rushing toward danger quite so eagerly. She'd flung open the door without knocking, and called to the woman to see if she was alright.

She'd stopped short when she found Cyra, the Lady of Hiraeth, sprawled on the bed with her husband's dark head between her legs. Talyn realized immediately she'd grossly misinterpreted Cyra's scream, and she'd been about to leave when she noticed that the man, Lord Bressen, had pinned Cyra's wrists to the bed.

Talyn had stopped, suddenly not sure everything was as innocent-looking as it seemed. Some men believed they owned their wives and could have them anytime they wanted, regardless of the woman's wishes, and she'd questioned then just how willing Cyra was in this.

"Are you sure you're alright, my lady," Talyn had asked.

Lord Bressen had looked over his shoulder at her. He'd seemed amused that she was daring to question his intent, but she hadn't backed down. She'd kept her eyes locked on Cyra's, watching closely for any hint whatsoever that the lady was under duress. Talyn had a dagger at each hip hidden under her dress, and it would've taken only seconds for her to draw them and port to the bed to plunge them into the lord's neck.

Whether seconds would have been fast enough was the question. Lord Bressen was a mind wraith, and if the stories of him were true, he was probably the most powerful mind wraith to ever exist.

Mind wraiths weren't common in general, but a wraith of his abilities was almost unheard of. Most minor-level mind wraiths could read people's thoughts, which was dangerous enough by itself, but more powerful ones could compel a person to do things.

According to what she'd learned, Lord Bressen could not only read minds, he could glamour people into seeing things that weren't there. He could control the minds of hundreds of people at once, and it was rumored that his ability to dominate a person's will was so strong he could literally compel them to drop dead with one thought. As if that wasn't enough, he was also an angelus, a winged being that came with its own innate set of terrifying powers.

What this amounted to was that, if Talyn had needed to strike at the lord to save Cyra, it was by no means certain she would've succeeded before he killed her himself. Fast as she was, Talyn wasn't faster than someone's mind. She always kept a mental shield up as a precaution, but the shield would only slow the lord down, not stop him entirely.

She'd been relieved when Cyra assured her she was fine, and the lord had released his wife's wrists. Still, there'd been a kind of wild look in Cyra's eyes that had haunted Talyn ever since, and she still wondered if she'd made the right decision.

Talyn looked down at the sleeping couple again and had to admit they looked perfectly happy and peaceful at that moment. Cyra's body was free of the bruises she supposedly got while training, and the two were curled around each other, their heads tipped together as if they'd fallen asleep whispering. Cyra's hand rested lightly on the lord's chest while his arm lay across her waist.

Talyn shook her head in bewilderment. After a decade of sneaking into people's bedrooms to kill them, she'd seen a lot of people sleep, but she'd never actually seen anyone sleep this way before, pressed together as if love drew them toward each other, even while unconscious.

In Talyn's experience, most couples liked their own space. It was rare she encountered a couple sleeping in each other's arms, and never anything like this. If Cyra was afraid of her husband, her unconscious body language didn't show it.

Talyn took her hands off the hilts of the daggers sheathed to her thighs and resigned herself to waiting. She wasn't sure what had made her port into the lord and lady's bedchamber tonight to begin with, other than curiosity and perhaps the need to do something daring so she didn't go mad from the monotony. She'd been working as Cyra's lady's maid, Leeda, for several weeks now, trying to gather information where she could, but spying wasn't her usual role.

She was an assassin. She killed people for a living, and she liked doing it because there was a certain rush that came with it, a surge that — ironically — made her feel alive even as she took the life of another.

Spying was different. There was danger involved to a degree, but it didn't come close to the same feeling.

This job was actually more dangerous than most, considering that both the lord and lady could read minds. Talyn was actually surprised they hadn't already seen through her disguise, but apparently her masquing power had done its job and hid who she really was from them. The power allowed her to not only shift physically into someone else, but to mask her mind so her thoughts reinforced who she was supposed to be.

Still, Talyn didn't want to be here any longer than she had to be. She was just waiting to hear from Sandrian. She'd sent a message to him this morning to let him know that the lord and lady had returned from their ocean voyage with the collar and rings he wanted, but she'd been unable to get them for him. He'd sent a message back telling her he'd take care of it, and that, if all went well, her job might be over soon.

She hadn't heard from him since.

Talyn was just about to leave when the lady stirred, and she froze. She may have been angling for some action, but she wasn't stupid. Being caught in here at one in the morning would be catastrophic, and she'd been careless to come.

Talyn took a step back, but a second later, Cyra gasped and bolted upright in bed.

Talyn ported immediately, throwing herself across the room and around the corner where the door to the bathing chamber was. She thought Cyra might have seen her for a brief second before she was able to port, but perhaps the lady had still been too muddled with sleep to understand what she'd seen. Her heart hammered in her chest as she waited for Cyra to scream or sound the alarm, but she did neither.

Instead, Bressen's voice rose around the corner. "Cyra? What is it? Are you alright?"

"I…I was in a nightmare, but not mine," Cyra said. "Somehow I dream walked into Axenus's nightmare."

Axenus. It took a moment for the image of the merman to come to Talyn, but his garnet-colored hair, cerulean eyes, and iridescent skin finally swam to the surface of her mind. Axenus was the second after Bressen of the three devastatingly good-looking men that currently lived in the house.

And the third of those men…Gods above.

Talyn had thought she was immune to fits of thigh-clenching arousal, but when she'd seen *him* for the first time, Protector save her.

She sometimes wondered how any of the female servants got anything done with those three men around. She'd seen most of the women, and even a few men, blatantly staring at them on occasion.

The rest of Cyra's words hit her then, and Talyn snapped back to attention. *"Somehow I dream walked into Axenus's nightmare."*

Fuck. The woman could dream walk. As if Talyn didn't have enough to worry about with the lord and lady's mind reading abilities, now she also had to make sure she didn't dream anything that might give her away.

She reinforced her mental shield. If either the lord or lady suddenly sensed her consciousness in the room with them, things would go from bad to worse very quickly.

Sandrian wasn't paying her nearly enough to do this job.

*To be continued...*

# Acknowledgements

First let me acknowledge that I blatantly stole the concept of the Souls (aka Children) of the Sun, Moon, and Earth from Plato. This story can be found in his book *The Republic* and is also beautifully told in the song "The Origin of Love" from the musical *Hedwig and the Angry Inch*.

Many, many thanks as always to my alpha reader Karen Pasquale who has a true gift for helping me tease out the themes and story elements that are already (sometimes accidentally) built into the book. Her insights were beyond invaluable and got better with each bottle of wine we shared.

Thanks to my husband Pat for his unwavering support of my writing and his continued acceptance of my dalliances with Bressen and Samhail. And a huge thank you to him for dropping everything to write a software program at the last minute to find all the orphan quote marks in this book.

Thanks to my beta readers – Liza Boritz, Mindy Petruck, Emily Rice, Heather Lee, Erin Estabrook, and Lana Zadrosny – for their keen eyes and great feedback. A special thanks to Heather for the stream of unhinged and highly entertaining reactions I woke up to every morning while she was reading, and extra thanks to Liza who promised to call me on my BS and then did.

Thanks to my cover designer Mick Estabrook for his endless patience and understanding, even when he disagreed with me about the design. By now he's used to getting messages from me that say, "I love it. Here are the ten small changes I need you to make…"

Thanks to my omega readers, Pam Bedore and Joshua Hamel for scouring the final draft for typos and other mistakes. And special thanks to Josh for continuing to let me have my way with Samhail.

Thanks to everyone who read the first book, raved about it, and gave me the courage to publish the second one.

**Author's Note**: I did my best to make the physics of Cyra surviving underwater work, but I'm sure there's still a certain amount of 'willing suspension of disbelief' in which I'll need to ask readers to indulge. Just do me a favor and don't overthink it.